PERFECT FIT SERIES

BOOKS 1, 2, 2.5, & 3

KB ALAN

Copyright © 2018 by KB Alan

Second Shift Publishing

All rights reserved.

No part of this book may be reproduced in any form or by any electronic or mechanical means, including information storage and retrieval systems, without written permission from the author, except for the use of brief quotations in a book review.

❀ Created with Vellum

CONTENTS

PERFECT FORMATION

Chapter 1	3
Chapter 2	15
Chapter 3	23
Chapter 4	35
Chapter 5	53
Chapter 6	63
Chapter 7	75
Chapter 8	91
Chapter 9	101
Chapter 10	111
Chapter 11	119
Chapter 12	129
Chapter 13	139
Chapter 14	147
Chapter 15	159
Chapter 16	171
Chapter 17	183

PERFECT ALIGNMENT

Chapter 1	197
Chapter 2	211
Chapter 3	223
Chapter 4	237
Chapter 5	251
Chapter 6	267
Chapter 7	281
Chapter 8	295

Chapter 9	309
Chapter 10	323
Chapter 11	337
Chapter 12	349
Chapter 13	363
Chapter 14	377
Chapter 15	395
Chapter 16	411
Chapter 17	425
Chapter 18	437
Chapter 19	451

PERFECT STRANGER

Perfect Stranger	469

PERFECT ADDITION

Chapter 1	507
Chapter 2	521
Chapter 3	533
Chapter 4	551
Chapter 5	569
Chapter 6	587
Chapter 7	601
Chapter 8	621
Chapter 9	641
Chapter 10	649
Chapter 11	661
Chapter 12	675
Chapter 13	691
Chapter 14	709
Chapter 15	735
Chapter 16	751
Chapter 17	769

Excerpt	779
Also by KB Alan	791
About the Author	793

PERFECT FORMATION

PERFECT FIT BOOK 1

CHAPTER ONE

Caleb Black checked his watch as he exited his SUV. It was almost one o'clock in the morning. His destination was a lively Irish bar on the main street of town, owned by his brother Sean. He had been working later than expected but Sean and his wife Lisa were closing tonight, so the late hour shouldn't be a problem.

Up ahead, the door of the bar, *Roisin Dubh* , swung open, emitting a man and a woman clinging to each other, clearly drunk. The woman's laugh captured Caleb's attention. Her long, thick hair was rich brown and his fingers itched to run through it. The man's hand on her ass showed off her sexy curves to great appeal. For that matter, there wasn't anything wrong with the man's ass, either.

They stopped under a streetlight at the curb in front of the bar, hanging on to each other. Caleb chuckled as a wayward curl defied the man's clumsy attempt to push it back and it flopped onto his forehead, the muted light picking up golden highlights in the light brown locks. His eyes tracked down over strong features to full lips that invited a nibble or two.

Caleb suppressed a slight groan as the woman brought one hand up to the man's neck and rested her head on his shoulder. He wanted to feel that slight weight on his own shoulder. Well, on his chest anyway, she wouldn't have been able to reach his shoulder. Something about the two of them together hit all of his buttons just right. He tried to determine which he found more attractive as he began walking again, heading toward the pub door.

The man started to fall, obviously trying to let go of the woman so as not to drag her down with him. She was just as obviously trying to hold him up, and not about to let go. Caleb hurried to reach them and held the man steady while he got his feet back under him.

Bracing one hand on Caleb's shoulder, the man closed his eyes in an obvious attempt to gain his equilibrium.

"Thanks."

Caleb looked at the woman who was eyeing him like a box of chocolates.

"Yummmmm," she murmured under her breath, though Caleb heard it clearly. She put one hand out and laid it on his chest, her eyes glassy, her expression dreamy. She gave a tiny whimper and her fingers gripped tightly into him. Caleb worked hard not to smile. He checked her companion for a reaction, but the man's eyes were still closed.

"Taryn," the man said, then went quiet.

"Richard," Taryn answered.

"Taryn," Richard tried again. "Are we still moving?"

Taryn seemed to think this over for a minute, but then lost track of the question.

"Ricky, he's so frickin' *hot*," she said, somehow under the illusion that Caleb couldn't hear her. Her eyes hadn't left his chest, but now they began to make their way south.

Richard blinked his eyes open, looked at Taryn, then followed her gaze straight to Caleb's crotch. He licked his lips. His hand clenched where it rested on Caleb's shoulder as he swayed.

"Taryn."

"Richard."

"Taryn, you are really drunk."

"Okay."

"No, I mean really. Are you aware that you're staring at this nice man's crotch?"

Taryn considered this. "Yes, but I don't think it's real."

Caleb gave an astonished gasp, while Richard blinked some more. "It looks real to me. It looks real big. It looks real..." He licked his lips again, swallowed hard.

Taryn's brows crinkled in confusion. "No, I mean, I don't think the man is real. This is a dream, or maybe an hallucination. He's like, our dream man or something, don't you think? What're the chances a perfect man would be standing right here, right now, while we're really drunk?" she asked.

Richard started to nod his head and then started to fall over. Caleb stepped in closer to prop him up, bringing the three of them into a tight formation. He couldn't remember the last time he had been so entertained by such nonsense. Drunk people tended to strike him as very stupid, but he liked these two. And not because they were attractive, but because they seemed like nice people. He snorted his disbelief at himself. His movement closer to the girl had gotten her hand moving and it began to roam his chest.

"Well," Richard said. "Is it your dream, or my dream?"

This stumped Taryn for a good minute.

"Maybe it's my dream," Caleb threw in.

Taryn's hand on his chest tightened and Richard's moved down from his shoulder to his biceps.

"Huh," they both said, then looked at each other.

"Do you know this hot man, and you've been holding out on me? Is he gay?" Taryn asked Richard.

"No. Do you know him and you've been holding out on me, worried he'd turn gay if he met me?" Richard asked in return.

"No," Taryn said, then turned back to Caleb. "It can't be your dream, you don't know us."

"I'm Caleb," he said.

"Oh," Taryn said.

"Huh," Richard said.

"This must be your dream," said Taryn. "If it was my dream I'd be naked by now."

"You don't think we'd be naked by now if this was my dream?"

"Oh. Maybe it is my dream, 'cause if it was your dream, I don't think I'd be here right now. You don't dream about me with other men, do you?"

"I never have before, but it seems like a fine time to start."

"Do you dream about Richard with other men?" Caleb asked Taryn.

"Well, I had that weird dream where he was being stalked by that creepy doctor guy on that show *Doctor England, MD*. Remember that, Richard?"

"No," Richard said. "I don't think I was there for that dream."

"And then there was the dream with that hunky action hero, from that movie this summer, remember, Ricky?" Taryn went on, not listening. Her eyes got wide and dreamy. "That was an *excellent* dream. You were still seeing Bruce then, so I might not have told you about that one. I was getting horny, because we hadn't had sex in like, six months. I had to go buy a new vibrator after that dream." She closed her eyes, smiling as she remembered.

"Huh," Richard said. "I can't believe you didn't tell me about that one. Taryn."

"Ricky."

"I don't think we're dreaming."

There was silence for a few minutes.

"I don't ever remember dreaming that I was going to throw up before."

"Maybe you guys should walk down to the diner on the corner. Get some food into you," Caleb suggested.

"How long have we been out here?" Taryn asked. "The taxi still hasn't shown up." She looked up and down the street in irritation.

"About fifteen minutes," Caleb told her. "You should get some food into your systems, soak up some of the alcohol."

Taryn looked at him some more, blinked a few times. Then the color washed out of her face. "Oh shit. I'm not dreaming, am I?"

"Nope. Neither am I. Neither is Richard."

She blushed. "I'm sorry, I don't usually drink this much. I'm sorry we're acting like idiots. You don't have to stand here. We can wait for the taxi." Her eyes were fixed on his chest, but not quite in the awe-inspired way as before.

"Don't worry about it."

Richard spoke up. "I think the food thing is a good idea, Tare. We should have thought of it. We'll go down to the diner. By the time we sober up a bit, maybe we'll have managed to forget that we're idiots."

"You guys don't do this kind of thing much, do you?" Caleb asked.

"Proposition studly strangers?" Richard asked.

"Caress strange men in public?" Taryn asked.

"Drink," Caleb answered.

"Caleb?"

"Yes?"

"I just wanted to say, before I get sober enough to care that I'm a fool, that I'm pretty sure I've soaked through my panties as well as my jeans, 'cause you guys are so fucking sexy. Thank you. Bye." With obvious care, she took her hands from both men, turned around and began walking toward the diner with only a slight wobble to her gait.

"Damn," Richard said.

"Damn," Caleb agreed.

Richard began to follow Taryn, and Caleb began to follow Richard. He pulled out his cell phone and sent a quick text message to his brother to let him know he wouldn't be in tonight.

TARYN FEARED she was sobering up. She was not completely sure, as she wasn't used to being drunk in the first place, but she was pretty certain that an hour ago she would have hardly remembered she'd said those words to Richard and a stranger, let alone be freaking out about them.

She walked into the diner and straight to a booth, sitting down with her back to the door, not wanting to see who might follow her inside. She managed a weak smile at the waitress who materialized and asked for a cherry Coke and a chocolate milkshake. Taryn put her elbows on the table and her head in her hands and stared down at the table.

She heard the two men slide into the seat across from her and managed, just barely, not to whimper. She was sure her face was still as red as the table, though. She heaved a huge sigh and sat back, her gaze straight ahead, right between the two men's faces. Richard ordered a strawberry shake and an iced tea, Caleb ordered black coffee, and the waitress left.

"Taryn."

A beat. Then two.

"Caleb."

"You're not allowed to say things like that then walk away."

"I'm not?" Her brow crinkled. "Says who?"

"Me."

"Huh." Taryn looked at Richard, raised her eyebrow at him.

Richard just shrugged his shoulders and mouthed, "Oh my *God*." Or maybe it was "He's so *hot*."

Either way, Taryn had to agree, so she nodded her head, looked at Caleb and said, "Sorry."

Caleb nodded in return.

"Caleb."

"Richard."

"What are you...I mean, why are you...I mean, who..." Richard stopped.

Caleb looked at Taryn for an interpretation.

"I'm just as confused as he is. We don't usually do strangers."

Caleb's eyebrows went up, Richard began to choke and Taryn's eyes went wide.

"That's not what I meant," she squeaked.

"So you do," Caleb purred at her, "do strangers?"

She whimpered.

"What she meant was, we're kind of shy and besides, we think most people are irritating, so we don't do so well at the whole 'meeting new people' thing."

Taryn nodded emphatically, giving Richard a grateful look.

The waitress brought their drinks. Caleb looked at them sternly and said, "Food."

They both ordered burgers and Caleb ordered a piece of cherry pie. The waitress left. Taryn tried to think of something to say that had nothing to do with sex or strangers. She tried to remember if she had *ever* been so instantly attracted to a man before. Maybe it was being drunk. Maybe she should try that more often. Of course, with her luck, not to mention family history, she would be an alcoholic before the year was out. Probably not worth it. She sucked on her milkshake, eyes staring down into the glass, while she considered what had happened since leaving the bar.

"Taryn."

She looked up at her best friend.

"He's still here."

Taryn glanced at Caleb then looked at Richard, confused. "Huh?"

"He hasn't called the funny farm to come take us away. Or the prude police to come lock us up."

Taryn considered this then looked back at Caleb. Almond-brown eyes watched her. The man was gorgeous—short, dark brown hair, his skin tan, different from Richard's natural olive, as if he spent a lot of time outside. Muscular, but not overly so. She couldn't get the phrase "tall, dark and handsome" out of her head. Her eyes began to glaze and she forgot what she'd been thinking about. The corner of his mouth quirked up as if he knew that.

"Ricky."

"Taryn."

She swallowed, caught in Caleb's gaze. "I love you." She couldn't decide what to make of the flicker in Caleb's face at that.

"I love you too. But?"

"But I'm about to melt into a puddle of goo, and he's just looking at me."

"I wish he'd look at m—" Richard's voice jerked into a squeak. Taryn looked at him and his eyes had gone wide. He flicked his eyes down to his leg, next to Caleb.

"I mean, yeah, me too."

Taryn nodded her head and decided she was done talking for a while. The waitress brought their burgers and Caleb's pie. Nobody spoke, they just ate.

Caleb pushed his pie plate away and wiped his lips with his napkin. Taryn's eyes remained riveted to his lips. He licked them then smiled just a bit when she gulped.

"Taryn. Richard."

"Caleb," they said at the same time.

"What's your story? You two are...?" He waved his hand between them. "A couple? Fuck buddies?"

Taryn looked at Richard and he nodded at her.

"We've been friends for a long time. After a few years, when we were both single, we started sleeping with each other. Sometimes one of us will meet someone we want to date, so we stop sleeping with each other. We've been doing that for about three years."

Caleb looked at Richard. "You usually sleep with women?"

"No, only one woman other than Taryn, and it didn't last very long."

Caleb looked at Taryn. "You usually sleep with men?"

"I've never slept with a woman."

"What about you?" Richard asked Caleb.

"I usually sleep with women," Caleb answered, looking Richard up and down. "But I've had my share of men."

"Together?" Taryn's voice cracked so she cleared her throat. "Do you ever sleep with them at the same time?"

"A couple of times," Caleb answered, "with two women. A couple of times with one woman, one other man."

"And how did you find that?" Richard asked.

"Each situation was different. There can be...some confusion about who's in charge."

Taryn's eyes went wide at this. She thought she might be bug-eyed at the end of this night. "In charge?"

Caleb's eyes pierced her. "That's right. What about you two—who's in charge when you're fucking?"

Taryn looked at Richard, who cleared his throat.

"I guess you could say we switch off." He flushed. Taryn wondered if he was flushing in manly embarrassment at not being in charge all of the time, or at the idea that Caleb would want to be. It was not something they had ever discussed, and she realized he was right. Sometimes she was more aggressive, sometimes more nurturing, while other times he took charge, or was especially sweet and caring of her. They had a good, complementary relationship and suddenly she wondered if they were endangering that right now. If something happened with this man, even if it were only for one night, would it change them?

She finished her burger and soda and moved back to her milkshake.

Caleb's long right leg stretched out, coming to rest between her legs. Taryn was pretty sure the action was deliberate, but was becoming more and more sober, and less and less able to admit to how badly she wanted something to happen.

"Taryn."

"Caleb."

"Have you ever slept with a stranger?"

"No."

"Richard?"

"Not since college."

"Have you both been tested?"

Taryn's heart rate doubled. "Rick's a doctor, so he tests us every year, for everything, no matter what. I'm clean," she managed to get out.

"Ditto," Richard said, his voice thick. "And we made a promise not to have unprotected sex until we were married to someone else and knew we wouldn't be sleeping together anymore."

Caleb waited, then looked at them both sternly, until Richard said, "And you?"

"I haven't slept with a stranger in the last twelve years, and I get tested every year. I'm clean. I do not have unprotected sex, ever."

There was silence for a few minutes.

"Caleb." Taryn's voice was small.

"Taryn." Caleb's voice was gentle, soothing and in control.

"We're not...we don't...earlier we..." She gave up, took a long drink from her soda.

Caleb looked at Richard for an interpretation this time.

"She means that earlier, when we were so...um...outspoken, that's not what we're really like. If that's what you liked..." He stuttered to a stop, licked his lips.

"Why don't you guys worry about whether or not you want to see me again, and let me worry about what I want?"

They were silent again for a time. "Caleb," Richard said.

"Yes?"

"Who are you?"

He seemed to think about the best way to answer that.

"You guys go to that pub much?"

"Sometimes we meet there after work, have a burger and a drink, listen to the music. We've never stayed that late before," Richard answered, pushing his plate away. The waitress came to take their plates and refill Caleb's coffee.

"Have you ever met the owner?"

"We met one of them, what was her name, Richard? Linda? No, Lisa. You were attracted to her, even before she got up and joined the band for a song."

Caleb nodded. "Lisa. She and her husband are the owners, and he's my brother, Sean." He looked at Richard. "You have excellent taste in women."

Taryn blushed.

"I grew up in the city, went into the military, retired, started a security firm, Precision Security, in Boston, with a partner. Moved here to North Fork last year when we decided a second, smaller office might be useful and I was getting tired of the city."

The waitress asked if they needed anything else and left the check when they declined. Caleb asked her for a pen.

Taryn was losing steam, fast, and could tell that Richard was as well. He'd had a long, tough day, which had led to her encouraging him to let loose tonight. She had a feeling Caleb had realized this before either of them.

He took a napkin from the dispenser and handed it and a pen to Taryn. She looked at him for a few seconds, then at Richard, then down at the napkin. She drew in a deep breath and wrote down her name and cell phone number. She slid it across the table to Caleb, not meeting his eyes. Caleb handed it to Richard. Richard wrote on it and gave it back to Caleb.

He looked down at the napkin. "Taryn Moss. Richard Daniels." He looked back up at them. "I'm Caleb Black. It's been my pleasure to meet you both tonight. I hope you'll have dinner with me sometime this week. I'll call you, see if we can set something up." He stood up, pulling out his wallet. He glared at them when they made to do the same. "Let's walk back to the pub. There will probably be taxis out now." He waited for them to exit the booth then followed them out.

They walked back toward the pub where they could see people getting into taxis.

"I'm going to tell you guys one thing, right now. I will not tolerate anything except honesty. If you like something, or don't like something, if you want to have dinner with me or don't want to have dinner with me, if you think I'm a controlling bastard or can't wait for me to tell you to suck my cock, whatever. Just be honest." He stopped two buildings down from the pub, put one hand on each of their waists, leaned in and kissed Richard, long and hard.

Taryn thought she might pass out, she was so turned on. She had seen men kiss before, and it had been pleasant to watch, but this, this was so clearly foreplay and not just for the guys. Despite the fact that they were the ones kissing, she didn't feel left out. Caleb's hand inched its way higher, his thumb coming to rest just under her breast. Her breathing deepened, as if her breast was trying to coax his hand higher.

Then Caleb's mouth fastened on hers. She tasted him, warm and hard, with a hint of Richard underneath. He fucked her mouth, plunging his tongue in and out and around. Normally she hated that in a first kiss, but the last hour had been working her up to this and she was *so* ready. He broke off and she couldn't suppress a whimper. He chuckled warmly, his hands going up to cup each of their necks. Then his look grew stern.

"You two can sleep together, but no sex until you talk to me, or you decide you're not going to have dinner with me. I'm not going to be the only one not getting any, clear?" He quirked one brow until they both gave small nods.

"Be safe going home. I hope you answer my call." Then he was gone. Taryn grabbed Richard's hand and they walked to a waiting cab.

CHAPTER TWO

Richard and Taryn woke up in Richard's bed early the next morning. Or rather, Taryn woke up and made sure Richard soon followed. He moaned. Taryn fetched him a glass of water and a couple Tylenol.

"I love you. Thank you. But this is all your fault, don't forget." He swallowed the Tylenol and finished the glass of water.

"True, but look what happened. Isn't that worth a bit of a headache?"

"Asked the brat who doesn't get hangovers."

She leaned down and kissed him. "I'll go make you a BLT."

Richard sighed and rolled over. He was so lucky to have her in his life. They had talked once, maybe a year ago, about the fact that they were both still looking for Mister Perfect, but that they were losing hope such a man existed for each of them. They decided if they reached a certain age, they would just go ahead and marry each other and have kids. They'd never chosen what an appropriate age might be.

He pushed out of bed and jumped into the shower. He made it quick, threw on sweats and a t-shirt, and arrived at the kitchen just as she put a plate down on the table.

"Thanks, sweetie, I really appreciate it."

She sat down with her own sandwich and they ate.

"Ricky, do you think...I mean, could we be...er...do you think Caleb thought we were..." She paused. "I liked him, a lot, but he was awfully...bossy."

"You mean domineering. Or rather, *dominating*."

"Yeah, I guess so. That's what he was implying, right? That he likes to dominate in bed? That he wants his partners to be submissive."

They both mulled that over.

"Do you think we could be submissives? Wouldn't we already know that about ourselves if we were?"

He thought about it for a minute. "I think it's just never been much of an issue for us before. You've never met a man who has wanted to...dominate." He watched her face for a reaction but she was carefully keeping impassive. "So it hasn't really made a difference. But then again, you haven't stopped looking for 'something more'. For me, gay guys tend to be a bit more conscious of the whole label thing. Like the fact that it really bugs some of them that I like sleeping with you."

He reached over and held her hand, plying his fingers through hers. "Plus, they tend to be a bit more literal with the whole top and bottom thing, which I don't really get. I mean, I like to do both, I can't imagine limiting myself to just one."

"So you've had lovers who expected you to always be in charge? How did that go?"

"Fine for a while, but then it got kind of tiring." He thought it through, did some calculations. "I've never lasted in that role more than a couple of months."

"And you've had lovers who expected you to be submissive. How did *that* go?"

He grinned. "*That* depended on the guy. Some were too controlling, especially outside the bedroom. Some were just not very good at it, at least in my opinion. It didn't feel, I don't know, natural, I guess."

"It just seems like, at our ages, we should know something like that about ourselves. But maybe we're not, maybe we're just reacting to Caleb that way, 'cause it sure as hell made me hot."

"Maybe so, but what's bad about that? We, of all people, know that getting wrapped up in labels is ridiculous. We can consider the labels guidelines, but that doesn't mean we always have to color inside of those lines. Just remember, we're always talking about how we're looking for something different, some *one* different, we just didn't know what."

"So, it seems that while we've been perfectly happy without it, that doesn't mean we couldn't give it a try."

"Well, not perfectly happy. Mostly happy. Maybe this is what we need to try in order to find perfectly happy."

"Huh."

"Yeah."

They washed the dishes and went into the living room, curling up together on the couch. Taryn opened her book and Richard started to read the newspaper.

"Taryn."

"Ricky."

"Do you think he'll call?"

"Do we want him to call?" Her voice was barely a whisper. She looked at him. "Are we asking for trouble here? Risking our relationship for the sake of a stranger, just because he's so damn sexy?"

"Have you ever reacted that way to someone you've just met? Because I haven't, and I'd like to explore what that might mean. Maybe it will crash and burn, but then again, maybe it won't. If it does, we'll still have each other, just as we always have."

She nodded. "Well, I hate to bring it up, but it certainly seems like it helped take your mind off work. How are you feeling about that?"

Richard put the newspaper down, rested his head back on the couch and closed his eyes. "Damn, Taryn, that sweet little boy. His body was so broken. They said the driver was drunk. I wasn't even any help. The ER staff was working on him, I just sat there with his mom, and she's beside herself with guilt, which is ridiculous. They worked on him for two hours, and then he was gone."

Taryn put her arms around him and Richard let himself cry. It had been so hard sitting with Elsie Jones at the ER, trying to keep her hopeful but also prepared for the worst. The poor woman had finally collapsed and been sedated, just after her ex-husband had arrived. Her mother and father were there to help her and to start the arrangements, so Richard had called Taryn and she had talked him into meeting her at the bar.

He had resolutely put all thoughts of little Matt Jones out of his head once they started drinking. He had concentrated on the music, the food, the drink and the lady. Then they had met Caleb, and it was that much easier to focus on the moment, on the lust rushing through him, the excitement, the nervousness. Hell, not so much nervousness as downright fear. He had never been so strongly attracted to someone so quickly before. At first he had to fight off a feeling of jealousy as the man's eyes had devoured Taryn's delicious curves, but then that gaze had focused on him.

He had never thought about having a threesome with Taryn, but he was sure thinking about it now. They had such a good thing together, sometimes he wished they could just get married and start getting on with the rest of their lives. Maybe have kids. But while they loved each other, they had each always wanted something more, had never stopped looking for it.

Richard sat back, wiping his eyes. Taryn kissed his cheek, then laid her head on his shoulder. She was so important to him and he could always count on her to be there for him. "Let's take a walk."

The early September heat was stuffy, so they walked slowly to a park in the neighborhood, watching the kids playing soccer for a while. Thoughts of Matt and Elsie Jones had him watching the parents, hoping they understood and appreciated this gift of watching their children run and play.

"Do you think he'll call?" Taryn asked him, her voice uncharacteristically small.

Richard drew in a deep breath, letting it out slowly. "I think he will. He seems like the kind of guy who knows what he wants. I just don't know if he wants a quick, one-time thing, or something longer lasting. Hell, I don't even know which of those I want."

Taryn nodded. "It's too early to say if there's enough there for long term. We just have to be willing to risk that one or more of us will want long term, but not all of us."

"Or that sex with a guy is something he likes to try once in a while, but he really wants a relationship with you, and I'll be the guy standing by the side watching it all happen, after I've gotten a dose of how good it could be."

"That could go the same way with me." She sighed. "I guess we just have to see what happens. At the very least, I trust you to do your best not to hurt me."

Richard put his arm around her shoulders. "Yeah, me too. Holy hell, though, I want him so badly."

"Yeah, me too. I'm already way more attracted to him than the last guy I dated. Other than you, I mean," she added with a smile. "And I don't just mean physically, either, although he's sexy as hell."

"The last guy you dated. Let's see, that's the one you broke up with because he called his mom every day."

"Well, yeah. But seriously, *every* day. Sometimes more often."

"Uh-huh. And the guy before that lasted what? A week?"

"He was always telling me what to do. You know how much I hate that. For crying out loud, he told me to go to the bathroom before the movie started so I wouldn't have to get up while it was playing."

Richard laughed, remembering. "I can't decide if you're too picky or if you just have lousy taste in men. With notable exceptions, of course."

"Of course," she agreed wryly.

They walked back to the house and Taryn gathered her things to go home. She showed him how to work the three-way calling feature on his telephone, just in case, then kissed him goodbye.

Richard cleaned the house a bit then decided on a nap.

The phone woke him an hour later, not the ring he had designated as being from the office answering service.

"Hello," he got out then cleared his throat, rubbing his eyes with his hands.

"Richard." Caleb's voice was strong and sure and sexy as hell.

"Caleb."

"Were you sleeping?"

"Mmm. Yeah. Sorry, just taking a nap. Taryn doesn't do sleeping in no matter how late she gets to bed."

"Is she there?"

"No, she went home a few hours ago."

"Did you guys talk about me?"

"A little bit. Do you want me to call her? She showed me how to do the three-way calling thing."

Caleb laughed. "No, I've got it. Hold on." He went away for a minute then clicked back over. Richard could hear the phone ringing, as well as Caleb's breathing.

"Hello?"

"Taryn."

"Caleb. Hi, how are you?" She sounded nervous, talking faster than normal.

"I'm...anxious. I want to see you both again. I've had a hard-on since last night and it doesn't seem to want to go away."

Richard cleared his throat again. "Maybe we could help you with that."

"I had hoped maybe you could. Are you available for dinner tonight?"

They both agreed they were.

"I could make something here," Richard offered.

"No, we're going to go somewhere nice. I'll wine you and dine you and we can learn a bit more about each other. In public. So I'm not too tempted to tear all your clothes off and attack you both."

"Uh," Richard said.

"Aah," Taryn said.

"How does Indigo's at seven sound?"

Taryn's "Okay" was a whisper and Richard had to force away the image of her looking breathy and nervous and ready to be ravished.

"Sounds perfect," he managed.

They all hung up and he lay back down, his hand going to his cock. He pictured Taryn on her knees sucking Caleb's cock. Richard groaned, shocked at how arousing he found the scene. He put himself behind Taryn, snuggling his cock into the crack of her ass, leaning over her so that his face was close to her mouth, breathing in Caleb's scent.

He could reach his hands around and gently work her breasts, then surprise her with a quick pinch on the nipples. She would groan and that would vibrate up Caleb's dick, maybe push him into orgasm. As she was milking him clean, he would put his fingers into Taryn's pussy, sure that it would be sopping wet. He would only need to pump her once or twice, caress her clit, and she would go off.

Richard erupted, spilling his seed onto his stomach. He sighed, hoping his imagination was not better than reality.

CHAPTER THREE

Caleb looked around as he entered Indigo's. It was a restaurant he did not indulge in often, but one he liked very much and treated himself to when he was in a good mood.

"Caleb, it's nice to see you again," the hostess said with a sultry smile when he walked in.

"Melody, always a pleasure." He waited while she used the phone to call Andrew, one of the restaurant's co-owners.

She hung up as a couple opened the door behind him. "If you don't mind waiting a minute, Andrew said he would show you to your table himself."

Nodding, he stepped out of the way to wait for his client and friend. He'd worked closely with Andrew while modernizing the restaurant's security system

The small, middle-aged man didn't keep Caleb waiting but appeared quickly to escort him to the back of the restaurant.

"Business looks good," Caleb commented with a look around.

"It is, excellent in fact. I'm guessing you're here for a date, since you requested this table?" he asked with a raised eyebrow.

"First date," Caleb confirmed with a grin, "so make me look good."

"As if you need any help," Andrew scoffed. "Is your date bringing a chaperone?" He indicated the three place settings.

"Sort of," was all the answer he wanted to give right now. "Everything working out all right with Tom?"

After the initial setup of the security system Caleb had handed the account off to one of his best employees.

"Of course, my friend. You would have heard from me by now if there was a problem. But we can talk business some other night, I'll leave you to your date for now. I'm glad you chose us for your special night."

Caleb shook his hand and turned to the table. He chose the chair in the back, wanting Taryn and Richard to be seated on either side of him. As much as he liked the bond they shared, he didn't want them falling back on it when they became nervous. He chuckled to himself, because he had plans to make them both nervous tonight. When was the last time he'd looked forward to a date so much?

By the time he got home last night, Caleb had stopped examining his surprising feelings. During the drive he had vacillated between cursing himself for not pushing them for more that night, and plans for drawing this out, letting it build until they were all crazy with the need to be together. He had finally decided that he would ask them to dinner, make the whole evening foreplay.

This morning, he had only allowed himself a moment to wonder if they would be receptive to his calls, but he was not a man who doubted himself often. For many years in the military his safety and those of his teammates had depended on his ability to read people, as well as situations, to reach a conclusion and come to a decision. Still, he'd been unprepared for the punch to his gut at hearing their voices on the phone. Hearing the combination of anticipation and apprehension in both of them.

Caleb had taken a long shower, letting the various shower heads pound into him as he imagined Richard on his hands and knees, taking everything Caleb had to give him, while Richard noisily slurped and sucked at Taryn's sweet pussy, her eyes glued to Caleb's.

His orgasm had seemed to be never-ending and his knees had been weak by the time he was finished.

Adjusting himself under the table, Caleb took a drink of his water. He looked to the entrance and saw Richard walking toward the table, alone. Where last night he had looked like a professional after work cutting loose, tonight he looked like a man dressed to impress. His charcoal suit set off his brown hair and eyes, his boyish good looks now more sophisticated.

Caleb rose, his eyes steady on the younger man's, resisting the urge to smile as Richard blushed and dropped his gaze. Caleb reached his hand out and Richard took it, flicking his eyes back up to Caleb's. He smiled and caught his breath as Caleb's other hand rested on his hip for just a moment, before moving to his back and guiding him to a chair.

They heard the sound of heels clicking on the wood floor and Caleb looked up to see Taryn approaching. Her dress was sophisticated but undeniably sexy, nearly reaching her knees but faithfully showcasing her hourglass figure. Her hair was swept up, leaving tendrils that his fingers ached to wrap around. Her eyes bounced briefly between them before settling on Caleb's. Her lips parted on a sharp inhale when he stepped toward her. He leaned in slowly, brushing her cheek with a kiss then putting his nose to the sweet spot just below her ear and inhaling deeply.

"Mmmm," he murmured, again having to hide his smile as she gave a small gasp. He settled her in the chair across from Richard and took his own seat. The waiter asked if they were ready to make their drink orders.

Richard grimaced, reassuring Caleb that last night's heavy drinking was not a usual occurrence.

Taryn laughed at him then switched her attention to the waiter who was watching her with interest, though she didn't appear to notice. Caleb restrained his impulse to redirect her attention.

"I'll have a Manhattan please."

Caleb resisted the urge to narrow his eyes as the waiter's interest lingered on her.

"Richard?" Caleb prompted.

"I'll take a light beer." He smiled when he said it and this time it was Caleb who had to force his attention back to the waiter.

"Guinness, thanks."

"I'll give you time to look at the menus," the waiter suggested and left.

"Richard. Taryn."

They smiled back. "Caleb," they answered in unison.

"I'm glad you came."

Taryn pulled her lips between her teeth then blushed when Caleb's gaze narrowed on them. "We were glad you called."

"You didn't really think I would be able to stay away, did you?" he asked. She ducked her head shyly.

"We weren't sure how much of last night was real and how much was wishful thinking," Richard said.

Caleb's lips quirked. "You were pretty drunk."

Richard's face went sad and he looked down at the table. "I lost a patient yesterday. Seven-year-old boy." He swallowed hard.

Caleb and Taryn both reached out to lay their hands on his. "It's not the first time...it's just hard." He gave a bitter laugh. "I thought family practice would be easier, after I did my ER rotation. But in the ER, you don't really get to know them. This kid, he's been mine for four years. I saw him through the measles, a broken arm—" He broke off. "I'm sorry." He shook his head.

Caleb brought his free hand up to Richard's neck, giving a gentle squeeze.

"Don't apologize. It's to your credit that you care about your patients. It's hard for you, I'm sure, but I have no doubt it makes you a better doctor."

Taryn smiled proudly. "Richard is a fantastic doctor. His patients love him. The mother called him when she got to the hospital, even though the ER was taking care of her boy. He stayed there for hours, making sure she had all the updates he could get, making sure they were doing everything they could. It was a difficult day."

"I'm okay," Richard said, picking up his menu, obviously wanting to drop the subject.

"This is a nice restaurant," Taryn commented as she looked at the menu.

"It's one of my favorites." Caleb put his menu down. "I'm sure you'll find something you like."

"I think it's going to be more of a case of too many choices," Richard said.

The waiter arrived with their drinks but left when he saw that they weren't ready to order. Caleb waited until Taryn put her menu down.

"What work do you do, Taryn?"

"I have a coffee shop, near the college. It's called Grounded." She glanced at him. "I don't actually like coffee, so I figured I wouldn't get into too much trouble sampling my wares that way."

Caleb laughed. "Good thinking. Have you been there long?"

"I bought a coffee shop that had been around a while and was a bit stale about eight years ago. The owners had been putting off retiring for a long time before they finally gave in. I updated the look, modernized the equipment and the menu, put in wi-fi and a couple of rental computers, tried to make it more college friendly."

Richard looked up from his menu. "It's a great shop. I spent a huge portion of medical school in there. When our practice was looking for a new building last year I managed to maneuver them into one across the street. Our coffee habit has skyrocketed but we aren't complaining." He smiled at Taryn with pride.

Caleb raised his eyebrow. "Considering you described yourselves as 'kind of shy' and 'think most people are irritating', you both seem to be in jobs that work with the public," he pointed out.

Taryn frowned. "Well, it's different when you can kick them out if they annoy you."

Caleb laughed and Taryn blushed.

The waiter came to take their orders. When he left, Caleb decided it was time to redirect the conversation for a while.

"Richard." Caleb's voice was hard and strong and Richard's eyes went a little bit wide.

"Caleb."

"I know you didn't have sex with Taryn after you left last night. Did you masturbate?"

Richard nodded his head but Caleb just kept looking at him until he answered. "Yes."

"What did you think about?"

Richard shifted and glanced around the area.

"Richard." Caleb added a bite to his words, bringing Richard's focus back to his face, which he kept stern. The other man swallowed hard.

"I, uh..." He cleared his throat. "I imagined Taryn sucking you off."

Caleb's face softened in approval, his voice less harsh. "And what were you doing while she did that?"

Caleb could hear Taryn's breathing picking up, matching Richard's.

"I played with her breasts and her pussy. I pinched her nipples and her moaning made you come. I brought her to orgasm by playing with her clit. I licked you, next to her mouth, so that I could taste your cum."

Caleb nodded without smiling and turned to look at Taryn. Her eyes had gone a bit glazed and she was biting her lower lip, sucking it into her mouth.

"Taryn."

She blinked, moved her gaze from Richard's to his.

"Taryn," he said again when she didn't answer.

She blushed again, snapping back to the conversation.

"Caleb."

"Did you masturbate after you left last night?"

"Yes, Caleb."

He smiled, liking very much the way she said that.

"Tell us what you imagined."

She opened her mouth, shut it, opened it again. She looked down at the table, watched his hands instead of his face.

"You were both holding me, between you, my legs around Richard's waist, your hands on my hips. He was fucking me, using his hands to hold my..." she broke off, took a drink.

"He held me open for you and you filled me up." She stopped again.

"Go on," he ordered.

"Ricky was kissing me and you were nibbling on my shoulder, my ear. Then you guys kissed, over my shoulder, and I came."

The waiter chose that perfect moment to bring the appetizers to the table. When he left, Caleb asked them how they had met. They were taken off guard again by the switch in conversation, but told him about meeting in college. He let them relax into the more casual discussion, telling them about the security firm that he and his partner ran, about the challenges of opening a second office there, dealing with new clients, hiring new employees. They had a lot to talk about, no awkward silences as they ate their delicious meals. He was impressed by them, would be happy to be their friend if it were not for the incredible sexual tension gripping them all. No way would he be happy being anything less than their lover, for now.

When they ordered dessert and the waiter had left again, Caleb sat back and looked at them both. They were relaxed and smiling again, comfortable with each other, comfortable with him. He asked them about their homes and was pleased they all lived relatively close to the restaurant. One of the benefits of living in a smallish college town. While they ate dessert, Taryn talked about her apartment above the coffee shop that she had fixed up once the shop was put together to her satisfaction.

"Decorating has been slow and interesting, because I have no sense of style whatsoever." She laughed at herself then blushed when Caleb leaned over to look at her very stylish dress and raised an eyebrow at her.

She gave her best haughty look and said, "Richard bought this for me for my birthday." She managed to hold the look for two whole seconds before giggling.

"True, and her place has great style, mostly because she listened to me on pretty much everything."

"What about your place then?"

Richard grimaced. "Well now, that's different. I have my grandmother's house. I keep meaning to renovate it but it's going to be a big project. Actually, I'm thinking of selling it to my cousin Mark and letting him deal with it."

Caleb nodded his understanding. "Family and real estate can be tricky. I'm renting because my brother is trying to guilt me into moving into our parents' house. Right now we have renters in there, since my parents gave it to us and moved into a retirement community in Florida. It's too much house for one person, though I like it and the neighborhood. It needs work, too."

Taryn rested her chin on her hand. "So why doesn't your brother and his wife live there? Don't they have kids?"

"One and hoping for more, which wouldn't fill up the house but comes a lot closer than me on my own. But Lisa's father built their house for them as a wedding present. He's a contractor."

"Yeah, I suppose that would be hard to give up. Where is your parents' house?"

"Ridgewood Heights."

"Oh, that's a great neighborhood. It's behind the coffee shop."

"Well, much as I like it, I'm not in any hurry to try to update its style. Although since we have a confirmed decorator in our midst, maybe I could gather some advice."

"I trusted him on everything but the bed sheets," Taryn laughed. "I drew the line at black satin."

"But you don't mind enjoying the ones at my house," Richard pointed out.

They all laughed until Caleb, keeping his voice even, slid in with, "Why don't you show me?"

Richard and Taryn both stopped laughing and looked at each other, then at him.

"Okay," Richard answered, his expression nervous but determined.

"Did you guys drive here?"

Taryn shook her head and Richard said, "I took a taxi."

"Me too."

Caleb smiled, pleased. He stood and they followed. He began to lead Taryn out but she glanced back at the table.

"Caleb, we haven't gotten the bill."

He smiled at her. "Don't worry."

She frowned at him. "Caleb, we don't expect..."

He interrupted her with a light kiss. "Don't worry," he said again, when he had pulled back. He ushered them outside to where his SUV sat waiting at the curb.

When they arrived at Richard's house, Caleb complimented it. It was small but charming and obviously well maintained, despite his earlier comments. Caleb grabbed a small bag from the SUV.

As Richard unlocked the door and motioned them inside, Caleb took Taryn's hand and gave it a reassuring squeeze. She held on to him tightly while they walked in. He let her go with a gentle push to the couch and indicated that Richard should join her. He sat in the matching chair next to it, turned so that he was facing them.

"I told you that I believe very strongly that we need to be completely honest with each other. That doesn't just mean not lying, but in communicating fully. It's pretty obvious I very much want to fuck you both tonight. I think I can assume you're both on the same page, as far as that goes."

He waited for them to nod, noticed they were holding hands, gripping each other tightly .

"I need you to tell me if you have any specific expectations from this, and if you have any limits. You know that I am a Dominant, I like to be in charge in the bedroom. Not necessarily every night, but a good portion of the time. I am not into pain, although I can be persuaded to indulge some if you're into that." They both winced a little and he figured he was safe on that score. Hurting people, even when they wanted him to, was not how he got off. He much preferred torturing them with pleasure.

"I'm just not sure how I'm going to feel about that. I've never tried it and I for sure don't like people telling me what to do in my everyday life. But nothing you've done has turned me off so far, so I'm willing to give it a try." Taryn looked nervous but relaxed somewhat when he smiled.

"Fair enough."

Richard cleared his throat. "I'm definitely not into whips and collars, but I don't mind, um," he glanced at Taryn, "being tied up occasionally."

Caleb nodded his agreement, happy that they were opening up. He kept his tone light, wanting them to be comfortable talking about these things. "It's important to understand that there is no black and white. There are levels to everything. When I say I don't like to give pain, that means I don't do whips, but doesn't mean that a nip here or there, or a good nipple twist, doesn't have its place, as does a nice spanking when someone earns it. If at any time you're uncomfortable with something, if I've misjudged what you want or are capable of handling, you have to feel like you can tell me that."

"Like a safe word?" Richard asked.

"That's the idea, yes, but I don't plan on doing anything intense enough where that would be necessary. If you tell me to stop, I'll stop. If you want to slow down, or pause to talk about something, that's okay, too. I expect to earn your trust." He waited, made sure they were with him. "Now, what else? Anything you particularly want to try, or want to avoid?"

Taryn seemed to be debating something with herself so Caleb looked at Richard, who glanced back at Taryn.

"I've never done anal with Taryn, and I don't imagine she has with anyone else, either."

Caleb looked at her, could see that this was what she had been debating in her head. "Your fantasy was just that, a fantasy."

She nodded, squared her shoulders. "I think I would like to try it, to have two men, at once, but not tonight. I think it would be better as a gradual thing, don't you think?" She looked at Caleb, as if worried he might be mad.

"That's not a problem. There are plenty of things we can do besides that, and plenty of ways we can introduce it gradually to make the journey as enjoyable as the end result."

Taryn relaxed a little, then nudged Richard's arm, gesturing to Caleb.

Richard mumbled, "I have a strong gag reflex." But Caleb heard him. He nodded at the man, encouraging him to continue, careful not to laugh at how cute Richard was.

Richard just shrugged. "It's always been a problem."

Caleb made no reply and waited for more.

"Do you have any, uh, fetishes, or something, that we should know about?" Taryn asked him.

He gave her a pleased smile. "Good question. Obviously, being in charge is a big turn-on for me. I like to see my lover bound at my mercy sometimes. I'm a big fan of using toys. For the most part though, there is nothing that I think you would consider weird or a fetish."

When they had all remained quiet for another moment, Caleb stood up.

"We're all going to take a potty break and meet back here. Rick, you get us some water from the kitchen. I've got condoms. Anything else?" They both shook their heads and headed out in different directions, Caleb using the master bath so he could check it and the bedroom out. They met back up a few minutes later, in the living room.

"Excellent," Caleb said. "Let's take this to the bedroom."

CHAPTER FOUR

Taryn couldn't remember being this excited or nervous entering into a new sexual relationship. This afternoon she'd been worried Caleb was only interested in a one- night stand, but now she couldn't imagine any of them getting this out of their systems any time soon. The trick was going to be making sure that when the time came, they all parted amicably.

The conversation in the living room had made her a little uncomfortable. She'd never had such a discussion with a lover, let alone a potential lover, even Ricky. They'd just bumbled along, learning each other's likes and dislikes through trial and error. Now that she thought about it, it was stupid. If you were willing to share body fluids, surely you should be capable of discussing your wants and limits with that person, rather than risk misunderstanding. It hadn't been easy, but now that it was over she felt less nervous and more anxious. Her estimation of Caleb rose even higher.

She led the way into Richard's master bedroom, then stood to the side so that the men could enter behind her. They stepped inside and Caleb closed the bedroom door. For some reason that struck Taryn as very important, like he was saying from now on they were in his territory and they better be prepared to do what he said. She shivered.

"Richard. Taryn. You're mine now. You understand?"

They both nodded.

"Say it."

"Yes, Caleb," they answered simultaneously. Though his expression didn't change, Taryn could tell he was pleased by the response.

"Taryn, undress Rick." She didn't hesitate. She turned to Richard and started to work on his tie. Their eyes met and she saw excitement with an edge of nervousness, and gave him a tiny smile, knowing he probably saw the same in her. Her fingers shook and she jerked, nearly choking Richard when Caleb came up behind her and rested his hands on her shoulders. He squeezed gently and she realized she'd stopped moving. She resumed her task, pulled the tie loose and began unbuttoning Richard's shirt.

Caleb's hands moved to the zipper at the back of her dress and she had to concentrate very hard to get the last of the buttons open. She used her hands to push the shirt off Richard's shoulders, sliding them down his arms, taking strength from the familiar feel of him. The sleeves caught at the wrists because she hadn't unbuttoned the cuffs, and she growled in frustration. Her breathing was heavy, and so was Richard's. She glanced at him and saw that he was looking over her shoulder at Caleb with heat in his eyes. It was a little strange to see that heat directed at someone else, especially when she was standing between them, but a shiver of excitement raced through her.

Taryn felt cool air at her back and realized that Caleb had brought her zipper down without actually touching her. She fumbled with Richard's cuffs and finally freed his shirt just as Caleb slid his hands into her dress at her waist. His skin was warm with small calluses, which raised goose bumps on her arms. She realized he wasn't moving, probably because she had stopped as well. She forced her hands to Richard's belt and Caleb resumed his upward path, his fingers curled to her sides, his thumbs tracing her spine.

She ripped the belt off in record time and attacked the button and zipper, while Caleb remained unhurried. Looking up, she saw a bead of sweat roll down Richard's temple and she was impressed by his restraint at standing still while she and Caleb were able to touch. She would have liked to touch more but it surprised her that she had no desire to ignore Caleb's directions and hurry things along. Apparently Richard felt the same because his hands remained at his sides.

Taryn eased a hand into Richard's slacks to cup his enormous erection so that she could pull the zipper down safely. Richard's dick practically leapt into her hand and she definitely was tempted to say hello, but Caleb had paused again. When she removed her hand as soon as the zipper was down, he moved on to her bra. She held her breath as he traced the band with his thumbs, then continued on his journey, his fingers curling in so that his knuckles brushed the sides of her breasts.

She pushed Richard's pants down, making sure his boxers went too. They dropped to his feet and she stood still, quivering, while Caleb's hands curved over her shoulders and sent her dress down to puddle at her feet.

"Kick them away, Rick," Caleb said, his voice only slightly betraying his arousal.

Richard did as he was told, toeing off his shoes, then kicking them, his slacks and his boxers away, so that he was left only in his socks, which he quickly removed.

Caleb tapped Taryn's right thigh with his fingers and she lifted her leg. She could feel him gently maneuvering her dress away from her foot. He tapped her other ankle and she switched legs. Her dress now gone, she was left in her bra, panties, garter, hose and heels. Richard glanced down at her and smiled. He started to reach his hand to her, then stopped, his eyes widening. He looked over her shoulder again and dropped his hand.

Caleb came around from behind Taryn, looking Richard up and down very slowly. He came in close so that he was touching both of their thighs with his, laying one hand on Taryn's bra strap, idly caressing the flesh underneath. He leaned in and kissed Richard, resting his other hand on the curve of Richard's lower back. Taryn's heart felt as if it was going to beat right out of her chest. She licked her lips and whimpered as Caleb feasted. She could tell the moment that Richard came to his senses enough to kiss back. The heat ratcheted up a notch and Richard's hand came up to rest on Caleb's chest.

Caleb backed off from the kiss, giving little mini kisses until Richard's eyes opened again and he was steady on his feet.

"I've been wanting to do that since you walked into the restaurant," Caleb said.

Richard licked his lips. "I've been wanting you to do that since you did it last night."

Caleb smiled then turned to look at Taryn.

She'd dressed in the fancy lingerie, not sure if it was making her look sexy or just fat, but Caleb's eyes said that she had managed sexy just fine. That, coupled with Richard's reaction a minute ago, gave her the courage she needed to keep her hands where they were, even though she wanted to hug them to herself. She fisted them to keep them still. Caleb apparently recognized this victory, running his hands down her arms in approval. He wrapped his long fingers around her wrists and brought her arms up away from her body. She relaxed in his grip, no longer having to concentrate on keeping herself still.

"Richard, we're going to have to reward Taryn for dressing so nicely for us."

Nodding, Richard reached a finger out to trace the lacy bra cup. "Seems your style doesn't need all that much help after all, sweetie."

Taryn studied Richard's face, worried that he might be jealous that she had never worn such a thing for him before, but his eyes were glued to her body and he seemed perfectly happy with what he was seeing now.

Caleb transferred one of her wrists to Richard then led her to the bed. He backed her into it so that she was standing with her thighs pressed against the mattress.

"Rick, get up on the bed behind her and hold her hands for me."

Richard complied, holding her wrists so that they were behind her, her elbows bent. The position thrust her breasts toward Caleb and her nipples hardened in expectation. Caleb hooked his finger into the cup of her bra, drawing it down until it was below her hard peak, which he promptly took into his mouth, sucking gently. She jerked, then jerked again as she felt Richard's firm hold. Her heart was going to burst from her chest, it was beating so fast.

"Breathe," Caleb reminded her, releasing one nipple before moving to the other. He wet that one thoroughly as well, then stepped back to view his handiwork. He smiled, then leaned down again and blew a cool stream on both breasts. Taryn gasped. Caleb drew in close, chafing her with his hard chest, reaching behind her to work the bra clasp. He stepped away, pushing the fabric down her arms as far as it would go while Richard still held her.

Hard hands cupped her breasts and his thumbs flicked her nipples, causing electric sparks to shoot through her body. Taryn moaned, leaning forward, only to be brought up short by Richard's hands on her wrists and the bra pulled tight across her stomach. Caleb reached a hand over her shoulder and brought Richard forward for another kiss, rewarding him for his hard work and restraint. Squeezed between them, she didn't think she'd ever felt so alive, so hot, so ready. Her skin was so sensitized she felt every point of contact from both men and ached for more.

The kiss almost distracted her from the feel of Caleb's hands sliding back down her body, his fingers untying the tiny bows at the sides of her panties, which were surely soaked through. Caleb pulled back from the kiss, leaving Richard panting in Taryn's ear. Richard leaned forward, warming her back as he looked over her shoulder and down her body. His warm breath caressed her chest and she tilted her head to rest against his. They both watched as Caleb squatted down to the floor, eased the panties to her feet, and helped her step out of them. He looked directly at her crotch and smiled, then blew gently on her curls, which were soaking wet. He stood up abruptly and Taryn moaned in denial.

"Rick, you can let go of her now. I want you to sit up against the pillows at the headboard, legs wide, so Taryn can sit between them."

As soon as Richard let go of her hands Taryn brought them forward, letting the bra fall off. Not to cover herself, but to touch Caleb. She wanted that damn shirt off, so she could see him.

Caleb immediately caught them up again.

"Naughty girl, that's not going to do at all. Go sit on the bed, make sure your ass is hugged in nice and tight to Rick's balls." She turned to get on the bed, wiggling her ass in his direction as she crawled to Richard. Richard's eyes were fastened on her breasts as they swayed toward him.

Caleb's hand smacked her behind. It didn't hurt but it startled the hell out of her. She looked back over her shoulder at him, but he just quirked his brow. She rolled her eyes. She had to admit, she had pretty much asked for that. Richard's amused smile in no way diminished the heat in his eyes. She stuck her tongue out at him and he bit his lips to keep from laughing out loud. She turned around and sat in front of Richard, scooting back until she was tight against him. He was a hard heat at her back and she had no questions about how excited he was. She looked back at Caleb.

He had taken off his tie and was climbing onto the bed. He nudged one knee between hers, the other next to Richard's, so that he was kneeling over both of them.

"I want to see you naked," she said to Caleb, trying not to pout.

"I second that," Richard added, his hands coming to rest on her thighs, thumbs moving restlessly over her skin.

"Well then, you should probably stop interrupting me." His tone was hard as he stood watching them, but Taryn was sure she saw a twinkle in his eye. She gave him a warning glare but kept her mouth shut.

"Taryn, put your hands behind Rick's neck," Caleb continued after a heartbeat.

She did as he said, then closed her eyes as he leaned into her, reaching behind Richard to tie her wrists with his tie. He smelled delicious and she missed his heat when he pulled back. She opened her eyes and watched him survey his work. He ran his hand down Richard's side, along his hip, all the way to the ankle. He lifted the ankle then placed it on the inside of Taryn's leg, pulling it out so that her legs went wider. He repeated the action with Richard's other leg. Then he put a hand on each ankle and pulled, sliding Richard down a couple of inches, taking Taryn with him. Taryn could feel Richard's heartbeat under hers, going a hundred miles a minute. She was lying more firmly against him now, his cock trapped beneath her lower back. They were both totally at Caleb's mercy, and he was still fully clothed.

"Ricky, you can use your hands however you want, but keep your legs where they are."

Richard's hands immediately went to her breasts, caressing them. She could feel his lips in her hair, his breath on her ear.

She was spread wide open to Caleb's gaze, still wearing her garter belt, stockings and heels.

"Caleb, please."

"Please what, baby?" he asked softly.

"I want to see you, touch you."

"Shhhh." He leaned in, pressing his lips to hers, but not opening them.

He retreated and she laid her head back against Richard's chest.

Caleb got off the bed and kicked off his shoes. He unbuttoned his cuffs, then his shirt. His eyes were on them, on Richard's hands playing with Taryn's breasts.

Her eyes were glued to the chest he revealed as he finally removed the damn shirt. "Mmmm," she hummed her approval.

"Oh yeah," Richard agreed.

Caleb's lips twitched into a grin before he smoothed it out.

"You have marvelous tits," he said. "Squeeze her nipples for me, Ricky." Richard complied and Taryn's back arched, pressing her more firmly into Richard's cock. They moaned in unison.

Caleb took off his belt and unbuttoned his pants, but didn't pull the zipper down. He climbed back onto the bed, lying between their legs, his hands caressing Richard's hips, his breath hot on Taryn's pussy.

"Mmm, you smell delicious."

"She is," Richard said. He took his hands from Taryn's breasts and slid them down her body to her pussy. He used his fingers to open her folds for Caleb. Caleb murmured his approval, leaned in and ran his tongue from bottom to top.

Taryn moaned, tilting her pelvis to get more, feeling Richard's hard cock jerking under her. Richard put his finger into her hole while Caleb watched, swirled it around in her juices, then brought it out, offering it to Caleb, who sucked it into his mouth. Taryn had never been turned on with so little actual touching in her life. She felt like she might explode at any moment. Caleb lowered his head and thrust his tongue into her channel while Richard used his wet finger to caress her clit.

Taryn's head thrashed from side to side. Caleb fluttered his tongue and she came with a long moan.

Caleb raised his head and looked at them. He smiled. "Okay, we're almost ready to get started."

"Fuck," Taryn breathed.

"Eventually," Caleb answered.

He attacked her with his tongue then moved up to her clit, sucking it into his teeth. Richard's hands moved back up to her breasts, pulling gently at first, then more firmly.

Caleb slid one hand under Richard's ass, pressing him harder into Taryn's back. He brought his other hand around and slid one finger into her, followed quickly by another. Taryn would have thought it would take awhile after her orgasm to be ready again, but she felt like she was already on the edge. Caleb pumped the fingers in and out of her, in and out, then curled them up to find her G-spot. She creamed around him and he moaned his approval, which vibrated her clit.

Those now wet fingers brushed up her side and into the space between her and Richard's bodies. He gripped Richard's cock, his fingers warm and wet against the small of her back as they moved up and down in the tiny movements allowed by the limited space. Caleb's tongue went back to her passage, fucking into her in a steady rhythm. Richard's hands jerked against her breasts as he lost his own tempo and tried to work his hips beneath her.

"Rick."

"Ye-yes, Caleb?" Richard gasped.

"Taryn."

"Yes, C-Caleb," Taryn moaned. They were all breathing hard.

"I want you to come now," he said, then lowered his mouth to her clit.

Richard and Taryn cried out in unison, her orgasm going on and on, Caleb not letting up until the end, Richard's seed scalding her back.

They lay there, unmoving, exhausted, eyes closed.

Finally Taryn opened her eyes a slit.

"Caleb. What about..." She gestured vaguely in his direction.

"Don't worry," he said. "We haven't really started yet. That was just to thank you for wearing the pretty underwear."

"Holy hell."

"Yeah," said Richard. "What she said."

Caleb moved Richard's legs from hers and took off her shoes. He unhooked the garters and rolled down her stockings then held a hand out to her. Raising her bound hands over Richard's head, she offered them to him. He untied her and pulled her up and off the bed. He slid her garter belt down and she stepped out of it. Then he kissed her long and hard, wrapping his strong arms around her to support her, his chest hair brushing her sensitive nipples.

"Go start the shower."

She walked to the bathroom, looking over her shoulder to see Caleb offering a hand to Richard.

Richard could hardly believe he'd experienced such a powerful orgasm from Caleb's hand barely able to massage his dick between the press of the sexy, squirming Taryn on top of him. He got off the bed with a hand from Caleb. He put his other hand on the man's chest, admiring the flex and play of muscles, and the contrast of his own olive skin against Caleb's lighter complexion. Licking his lips, he smoothed his hand over to Caleb's nipple.

Caleb grabbed his wrist and held it away.

"Ah, ah, ah. I've got other plans for those fingers right now. I assume you have some lube handy?" he asked. Richard opened a drawer of the nightstand and pulled out a bottle. Caleb added the condoms from his pocket and set them on top of the nightstand.

Taking Richard's hand, he pulled him into the bathroom, where Taryn had the water running nice and hot. Caleb pulled his pants off and stepped to Richard and Taryn. Putting one arm around each of their waists, he leaned in, letting his very erect cock tickle their stomachs while Taryn's nipples tried to play with each of their chests. Richard rested one hand on the top of Caleb's ass, the other on Taryn's hip. He watched Caleb's face, wanting so badly to kiss the man, but waiting for Caleb's next move.

Caleb moved his hands up to cup each of their necks, and pulled them together so that they were all kissing. It was sloppy but oh-so glorious. Richard closed his eyes, amazed at the difference in feeling Taryn's tongue versus Caleb's as they all danced together. He and Caleb both chased Taryn into her mouth, then Caleb changed direction and he and Taryn came at Richard. After a minute they all broke away, breathing hard.

"Let's clean you two up a bit."

They stepped into the shower and Taryn grabbed the bottle of shower gel. She lathered it up then placed her hands on Richard's shoulders and began running them down and around, making sure to pay particular attention to his nipples. He groaned when she gave them an extra sharp tug, then groaned again as Caleb's hands began massaging his shoulders with deep, powerful strokes.

As with the kiss, it was amazing how good it felt to experience both of their different touches on him at the same time. Taryn's sweet, feminine hands smoothing down his chest, heading for his cock, which was valiantly trying to rise to the occasion. Caleb's hard, calloused hands, kneading his muscles, then moving lower, firmly gripping the globes of his ass.

Richard reached for the shower gel and worked up some lather. He massaged Taryn's shoulders as Caleb had done his, then moved them down her back, trying not to jerk as her hands worked his penis back to life and Caleb's hands smoothed over his back hole. Richard gave Taryn the same treatment and she squeaked and nearly slipped.

Caleb laughed. "I think we're clean enough. Let's dry off." They each took a towel and tried to dry each other off, not accomplishing a whole lot but laughing hard. They stumbled back into the bedroom at last, mostly dry. Caleb took two of the condoms and handed one to Richard. They covered themselves quickly. Caleb picked up the lube.

"Richard, hands and knees, on the bed."

Richard heard Taryn gasp and angled his head as he climbed onto the bed to see her face. Anticipation gleamed from her eyes and she was pulling her lower lip into her mouth. She was watching him and the heat in her eyes made his blood burn.

"Taryn, give him your pussy."

Taryn levered herself onto the bed and maneuvered so that he could reach her comfortably.

Caleb put his hand on Richard's back. "Don't let her come." His hand moved to Richard's cock. "And don't you come." He began pumping, slow and sure. Richard thought his eyes would roll up into his head, but then Caleb stopped. He slapped Richard's ass, making him jump.

"You going to leave Taryn out of this?"

Richard realized he had been concentrating on what Caleb was doing and abandoned Taryn. He immediately put his face down and gave her a long lick in apology. She whimpered, then moaned as he found her clit and fluttered it with the tip of his tongue. He moved to her pussy and thrust his tongue in as far as he could just as Caleb put one lubed finger up his ass.

Richard moaned, which caused Taryn to shriek. Caleb laughed. Richard was so focused on pleasuring Taryn and enjoying what Caleb was doing to him that he almost let Taryn come. He jerked back just as Caleb thrust another finger home.

"Caleb!" he shouted.

"Richard!" Taryn wailed.

Caleb scissored his fingers inside Richard's ass for a minute, then backed out. "Come here."

Richard turned around and found Caleb sitting back against the pillows at the headboard. He spread his legs and fisted his cock, which was red and glistening with pre-cum.

"Bring me that ass," Caleb growled, and Richard hurried to comply. He turned around and offered himself to Caleb, who used his hands to guide Richard home. Wishing he could watch the other man's face, he closed his eyes and concentrated on the hand caressing his hip, the strong thighs quivering just slightly beneath him. As he seated himself fully, Caleb brought his arms around to hug him closer, deeper, and kissed his way up Richard's neck.

"You're so tight, so perfect," Caleb murmured into his ear.

Ah fuck, it felt soooo good. Caleb's cock was thick, stretching him oh-so nicely. Had he ever been filled so completely? He looked up to see Taryn watching them, her mouth open and panting, her fingers stealing down to her pussy. Caleb must have seen her too, because he barked at her.

"Taryn!"

She jerked, her eyes flying to Caleb's face.

"My pussy," Caleb growled. Richard saw cream run down her leg. "My ass," Caleb continued, tightening his hold on Richard to force him down onto that amazing cock. He clenched his muscles and was rewarded with Caleb's groan.

"Aargh," was all Richard could say. They sat that way for a minute, without moving. Caleb's breath was loud in Richard's ear.

"Don't move, Richard. Taryn, come fill my pussy with my cock." He reached around and grabbed Richard's cock, holding it steady for Taryn who wasted no time in moving to join them. Carefully, she lowered herself down, Richard holding her steady while she worked her legs around to where they needed to be.

Her warm, snug heat surrounding his flaming cock was nearly more than he could bear when coupled with the steel that was filling him. He ground his head into Caleb's shoulder, moaning with desperation while he held the rest of himself still.

Taryn softened around him, dropping down that last little bit, then Caleb bit his ear. Richard's hips arched in surprise, sending him surging into Taryn, then he bounced back down onto Caleb. He bellowed, trying to keep from coming. Taryn leaned over and kissed Caleb, while Caleb's fingers snaked around and pinched Richard's nipple. Richard managed to arch up again, pulling a groan from Caleb as he tightened his muscles and dropped back down.

"Now."

That was all it took. Taryn came first as Caleb's other hand worked her nipple, her rippling orgasm setting Richard off. Richard's clenching brought Caleb, who had not yet come that night. They rolled onto their sides in a sweaty tangle. They rested for a minute, then Caleb went into the bathroom. He came back with a couple of washcloths and used them to clean everyone up and disposed of the condoms. He shoved at Richard until he could pull down the covers, then they all climbed underneath.

Caleb lay in the middle, with Taryn pulled snugly to his right side, her head resting on his shoulder. Richard lay on Caleb's left side, on his stomach, his head on the same pillow, his arm across Caleb's chest to rest over his heart. They were asleep within seconds.

"Ricky."

Caleb vaguely heard Taryn's voice, her breath tickling across his neck. "Caleb."

He grunted and she shoved at his shoulder. "I have to pee."

"Okay."

"I can't move."

"Okay."

"Caleb!"

Caleb cracked open an eye and found Taryn looking at him with exasperation. She'd spent half the night draped across him, a position he heartily approved of. Somehow she'd ended up between Richard and him, with Richard wrapped around her back, the man's arm coming around to rest on Caleb's hip. All of their legs were entwined. There was no way for Taryn to move without one of them giving her some room. He grinned.

"How badly do you have to go?"

She narrowed her eyes at him, reached forward and nipped his jaw. He kissed her hard, then rolled away, freeing her to get off the bed. Richard grunted in his sleep, reaching out until he felt Caleb, then snuggling in to fill the space Taryn had left. Caleb bent his elbow and propped his head on his hand, looking down at the younger man. It turned him on, knowing this very smart man, this doctor, had been his to command last night. The combination of Richard and Taryn had been more than he had ever dreamed of. He couldn't ever remember such a perfect evening, let alone such a perfect fantasy.

His cock stirred just from the thought. He heard the toilet flush and the shower turn on. Moving carefully so as not to disturb Richard, Caleb reached over to the nightstand and picked up a condom and the lube. He stroked himself while replaying the night's events in his mind and watching the sleeping man's chest rise and fall. After a couple of strokes, he sheathed himself with the condom, lubed it liberally while rehearsing his moves, then attacked. One hand grabbed Richard's wrist, yanking him so that he was fully on his stomach while Caleb's body moved to straddle him with his superior weight and strength. As Richard came awake, Caleb grabbed his other wrist, manacling both of them with his right hand, over Richard's head, Caleb's arm angling down across Richard's upper back to hold his head down on the bed.

Richard gasped but Caleb was still moving. With his free hand he reached under Richard's hip and pulled his waist up, into the cradle of Caleb's thighs. Caleb's legs moved to hold Richard's so that they were bent at the knees, spread wide and anchored at the shins to the bed. One more silent move brought Caleb's dick to Richard's hole. Caleb leaned down, draping his body over Richard's. He bit down on Richard's shoulder just as he slid home.

"Oh fuck, Caleb!" Richard shouted.

Caleb brought his left hand around to find Richard's shaft hard and leaking.

"Ricky," Caleb panted, holding still despite every nerve in his body screaming for more. He waited until Richard began pushing back into him, then thrust in and out, hard and fast. He could feel his balls tightening. He pumped the cock in his hand, pumped his dick in and out of the tight hole and came the second that Richard groaned and spurted his release. They collapsed on the bed, laughing when Taryn shook water at them.

Caleb gave Richard a light smack on the butt and got out of bed. He took a quick shower and pulled on jeans from his bag, brushed his hair and teeth. As he passed the bed he nudged the sleeping man, who ignored him. He went into the kitchen to find Taryn pouring a cup of coffee, which she held out to him. He quirked a brow at the cup but accepted it gratefully. He took a sip and moaned in pleasure.

"I'm going to have to try out your shop."

She laughed then sat at the kitchen table. "I made the coffee. I think that means you have to make the breakfast."

She looked so good sitting there, her hair still wet from the shower, her face scrubbed clean, loose pajama bottoms tied at her waist and a tiny tank top that was doing nothing to hide the nipples poking into it. He licked his lips. "I can do that." He took another large swallow of the coffee then set the mug down on the counter. "After."

He stalked to the chair and knelt between her legs, pushing her thighs apart to give him room.

"After?" she gasped as his hands spanned her waist.

"Definitely after."

He lifted her tank top and stabbed his tongue into her bellybutton. She squeaked and fisted her hands in his hair.

"Caleb."

"Taryn."

She didn't say anything further as he pushed the tank top over her head. "Hold them for me."

Taryn blinked at him. Caleb took her hands and moved them to her breasts. She bit her lip and cupped her breasts for him. Leaning in, he used just the tip of his tongue to torture her nipples while his hands found the waistband of her pajamas and pulled them down. He bit, gently, on one puckered offering as his hands cupped her sweet ass and pulled the pants down.

"Ahrgh."

"Mmm-hmmm." Caleb moved to the other nipple and breathed on it, then watched as it, too, puckered for him.

"Squeeze."

Taryn's hands jerked in surprise then began massaging her breasts. Caleb nuzzled between the mounds, licking between her fingers. His hands moved between her thighs and he used his thumbs to part her.

"Caleb. Please." Taryn's breath was coming out in pants now, music to Caleb's ears. He gave one last swipe of his tongue.

"Move your hands down here. Show me how wet you are." He stood up and took a step back, his hands going to the button of his jeans. He paused, waiting for Taryn's brain to catch up with his orders. She had that adorable look of glazed incomprehension that he was coming to love putting on her face.

"Are you wet, baby?"

"Y-yes."

"Show me."

Her tongue darted out to wet her lips and her eyes went to his hands, which were holding still on the button of his jeans. Slowly her hands moved to her wetness. Using one to hold herself open, she used the other to circle her passage, then pulled it free. Reaching her wet fingers up to him, she offered him a taste.

Bending over to reach her fingers, Caleb kept his eyes on hers as he sucked the fingers in hard and fast, then used his tongue to explore and clean every inch of them. She tasted like woman, his woman. He pulled back, letting them go with a pop, then shucked his jeans, grabbing a condom from the pocket before moving back to her.

"Stand up."

Taryn stood, shakily, holding on to the edge of the table for support. Caleb turned her around and bent her over the table, his hand on her back positioning her how he wanted her.

"Don't move."

He brought his hands to her hips and plowed into her in one thrust. Taryn gasped and tensed, getting leverage to thrust back. Caleb put his hand on her back again and she settled. He waited until she made whimpering sounds he guessed she didn't even know she was making. Her inner walls clutched at him, and when he could stand it no longer, he held her tight and pounded into her. Lifting her hips a little higher, Caleb knew the moment he hit her sweet spot. Taryn screamed and came around his cock, and there was no holding back his own release.

Careful not to crush her into the table, Caleb kissed Taryn's neck, then got up to dispose of the condom. When he came back, she hadn't moved. He picked her up and carried her back to the bed, laying her next to Richard. She rolled over and snuggled into the sleeping man's side with a sigh. Caleb smiled and went to make breakfast.

CHAPTER FIVE

Taryn practically floated her way into Grounded Wednesday morning with a satisfied grin as she took a look around. When she'd spoken to Caleb on the phone that morning, he'd thought he might have a chance to drop by the shop today. She hoped so, looked forward to showing off her pride and joy. Besides, she just couldn't wait to see him again. They hadn't managed to mesh schedules since their amazing date Friday night and she missed him. She'd missed Richard too, having only seen him a couple of times while working.

Talking on the phone with them, separately and together, was good, but not nearly good enough. She greeted a couple of regulars and slid seamlessly into a conversation one of her employees was having with their mail carrier at the front counter. It never ceased to amaze her how comfortable she felt here. In college she had been shy and insecure for the most part. She had made a few good friends but had not been comfortable speaking up in class or attending most of the parties.

When she met Richard her junior year they had bonded instantly over a tragic server crash in the computer lab. She had been impressed by his dedication to becoming a doctor and loved to hear his stories about the town he had grown up in, his family's Italian restaurant and the mischief he and his twin had gotten into as teenagers.

As soon as Tony, their mail carrier, left, Emma narrowed her gaze on Taryn. Emma was a student at Kennington College and one of Taryn's best employees.

"What?"

"That's what I want to know. What is up with you lately? You're so...you've been so...happy."

Taryn laughed. "I wasn't happy before?"

"Not like this you weren't. What's the story? Did you win the lottery? Did you fall in love with someone, and does that mean Richard's available?"

Taryn gave her a measuring look, judging how much to tell. It was hard to keep secrets in her shop and besides, she didn't want her happiness to be a secret.

"Well, it's too soon to say if it's love, but I did meet someone and it's making me very happy. But no, that doesn't mean Richard is available. He's been very happy too, if you haven't noticed."

Emma's eyes narrowed as she ran the possibilities through. "Actually, I did notice he was in a very good mood yesterday when he stopped by. It's probably best if I don't guess. Why don't you just tell me? Start with who it is you've met."

A young couple walked in, which gave Taryn the perfect opportunity to make Emma wait, just to drag the suspense out. "You do your job well and maybe I'll reward you with the details. Do it really well and you might get to see for yourself, in a little while." She laughed and walked to the back to work in her office, ignoring the pout she knew Emma was directing at her.

Putting in two solid hours on the computer had Taryn groaning when she stood up. She stretched then answered the phone as it rang.

"Hey, sweetie, how's the grind?"

Taryn rolled her eyes at Richard's oft-used joke. "I've been stuck to the computer for a couple of hours. I'm just about to go out front and remind myself that there are people here I can boss around and that my job isn't all invoices and emails."

"I don't suppose there's anyone there I could bribe to run some mochas over here?" He almost, but not quite, succeeded in keeping the whine from his voice.

"Busy day?"

"Very. Brad got called to the hospital and Petra's on a tear about something." Brad was Richard's partner and Petra, their office manager, had become her good friend.

"Put Petra on the phone. I'll convince her to have girl's night tonight. She probably just needs a night away from Bob and the kids."

He sighed pathetically into the phone. "I will and I'm sure that will help, but it won't do much for right now."

"Yeah, yeah, stop your crying. Derek should be here by now. I'll send him over when there's a lull. He loves the tips you guys give."

"You're a lifesaver and I love you to death."

"Sure, that's what they all say." She laughed when he gave noisy kisses into the phone before transferring her to Petra.

Taryn hardly voiced her idea for girl's night before Petra jumped on the bandwagon and had it all planned out. Smiling, Taryn hung up and went to make the coffees.

Out front, Derek was helping an older gentleman on one of the computer stations and most of the couches were filled by college students. A group of ladies had pushed two of the tables together and were deep in conversation. Emma was ringing up a woman's order and Taryn gave her a second look, trying to place her. She prided herself on recognizing her repeat customers but she was pretty sure that wasn't how she knew this woman.

Her cell phone rang with the ringtone she had assigned to Caleb's number and that prompted her memory. This was Lisa, Caleb's sister-in-law. She answered the phone with a smile that she knew he would hear in her voice.

"Hey."

"Hey yourself. I'm on my way over. I just spoke to Richard and heard about his desperate need for a caffeine infusion. I told him I'd play delivery man if his tips were good enough."

"Hmm, I have a feeling your definition of what makes a good tip from Richard, and Derek's definition, are not quite the same."

She loved the sound of his laugh, loved bringing it out of him.

"I should certainly hope not or our boy is going to be in trouble." A sexy shiver shot down her spine.

"I'll get the coffees ready, but you might prefer to have Derek do the deliveries after all, if you want to talk to your sister-in-law."

"Really? Lisa's there?" He sounded surprised.

"I'm pretty sure it's her, but I only met her once, a few months ago."

"Well, I'll be there in a couple of minutes."

"I'm glad."

"Me too."

Making the coffees for Richard and his coworker was too routine to keep her mind busy. Taryn found herself wondering how she should behave with Caleb when his sister-in-law was present. She wasn't used to dealing with families, had not gotten that far with any of her last four boyfriends. She finally felt comfortable with Richard's family, but she didn't consider them typical.

When the bell over the door tinkled, she knew without looking that Caleb had arrived. She felt more than saw Emma perk up next to her. Putting the coffees into a to-go carton, she turned around. She felt her smile stretch into a silly grin but couldn't stop it, even if she had wanted to. He was just so damn...*yummy*. She gave Emma a saucy wink as she passed through the counter and headed over to the table Lisa had chosen. Caleb stood next to his sister-in-law, saying something to her though his focus was clearly on Taryn as she approached.

"Ah, my unpaid delivery boy, you're just in time." She handed him the drinks, determined to follow his lead on how he wanted to act in Lisa's presence. She wasn't worried about what her employees or customers would think of her dating two men but she certainly could not assume the same would be true of Caleb and his family, let alone friends and coworkers.

Caleb took the carton and leaned in, kissing her on the lips. It was clearly meant to be a public kiss but her breathing picked up and it took a great deal of willpower not to grab onto him with both hands and sink into the kiss.

"Hi," he whispered against her lips before pulling back.

"Hi." She hoped she didn't sound like an idiot.

"Lisa, this is Taryn. You may have met her. She's been to the bar a few times. Taryn, my sister-in-law Lisa."

Lisa stood to shake hands. "It's nice to see you again. I do remember speaking to you and your...friend about the music one night."

"Yes, Richard and I have enjoyed your place many times but the band was really good that night, your song especially so. I briefly considered doing some live music events here but decided it wasn't the direction I wanted to go."

"Oh, I didn't realize this was your place. It's wonderful. I've just started my daughter Katherine in a school down the street. I got here early for pick-up so thought I'd get a quiet cup of coffee."

"If you ladies don't mind, I've promised to get these coffees across the street while they're still hot. If you're gone before I get back, Lisa, I'll see you for dinner on Sunday. I want to hear all about Katherine's first week at school." He gave Lisa a brief kiss on the cheek then Taryn a not-so-brief kiss on the mouth. She resisted the urge to lick her lips as she watched him walk out the door.

Turning back, she found Lisa watching her. Her stomach churned in nervousness but she fought it down and did her best to keep her smile. "Let me know if there's anything else we can get for you." Knowing she was running away did not stop her from going back behind the counter to ring up the next customer.

She told herself she wasn't paying any more attention than she would to any other customer, but knew that for a lie when her shoulders relaxed as Lisa picked up her purse and headed for the door. Managing a smile when the other woman turned and met her eyes, she gave a cheerful wave goodbye then breathed a sigh of relief.

Checking her watch, she turned to Emma. "Petra and I are having a girl's night tonight. Would you like to come?"

"I would love to, thanks," Emma said with real pleasure in her voice.

Taryn was glad she'd issued the invitation. "Are you good for today, or would you like a couple more hours?"

"I would like lots more hours—I'm saving up for Spring Break—but I have my three o'clock class today. If you can give me until two, though, that would be awesome."

"Perfect. I'm going to see if Caleb has time for lunch, but I can be back by two."

"Caleb, huh?"

"Yes, Caleb Black. Richard and I met him the other night."

"He's frickin' hot."

"Yes. Yes, he is." They giggled together as they watched Caleb come back into the shop. He quirked an eyebrow at their laughter but didn't seem intimidated.

"Do you have time for lunch?" Taryn asked as he approached the counter. "Or would you like a coffee?"

"I would love lunch, if you have time."

Walking to the Mexican restaurant down the street, Taryn smiled and ducked her head when he took her hand in his, swinging their arms like a little kid.

"You make me feel young and alive," he said.

Surprise washed through her, along with a spurt of fear. "That's..." She didn't know how to finish.

Pulling her to a stop, he ran his free hand over her cheek. "That was supposed to make you smile."

She still couldn't smile as she studied his face. "I'm a little bit scared about how...right this is."

"I think you're brave." His voice was low as he studied her face.

She wondered what he saw that made his mouth curve up into a smile, made his eyes warm as she watched, made one hand squeeze hers tight while the other caressed her cheek so gently. "Being scared is easy. Doing what needs to be done despite that, that's brave. Everything I learn about you makes me want to learn more." Leaning down, he brushed the barest of kisses across her lips. Pulling in a deep breath, she finally gave him his smile.

"It may be scary, but you're not alone. We're all in this together." Nudging her back into motion, he resumed swinging her hand, smiling when she laughed.

When they were settled, orders placed and guacamole on the table, Taryn felt Caleb's scrutiny like an examination. She darted her eyes to his then blushed at the heat focused on her. She looked away quickly.

"You are so beautiful."

Unable to stop the involuntary jerk of her head, she wasn't the least surprised when he cupped her chin in his hand and forced her to look at him.

His face was hard but compassionate, knowing but implacable.

"Do you think I'm lying to you?"

She blinked, wanting to look away but unable to. "No, I think you're...exaggerating. You haven't known me long enough to think I'm beautiful."

She saw that her answer had surprised him and he released her but she knew he would not let her look away—hide—again.

"You think our perception of beauty changes as we get to know a person?"

"Yes, sometimes. There are plenty of people we simply find attractive, their features somehow coming together in a way that works for many people." He was one such person but she didn't feel the need to point that out.

"Then there are the people we know. Who they are becomes entwined with how we see them, and they're beautiful. Like parents and their children."

"Uh-huh. So you think you're beautiful only to people who know what a good person you are."

"Well...yeah. Basically. Like Richard. He tells me I'm beautiful sometimes, and I believe he sees me that way. But he didn't, not for a long time. Only after he came to love me."

"I can sort of see your logic, so I'm not going to get mad. But let me be real clear here. I'm not in love with you, I've only known you for six days. I think you're beautiful and sexy and I want to get to know you better. Not the other way around, not I've gotten to know you and therefore think you're beautiful. So get used to the idea and don't you dare convince yourself that I'm lying to myself, or you, when I tell you how you look to me. Got it?"

She knew her eyes had grown big as saucers and she couldn't quite speak around the frog in her throat, so she had to swallow a couple of times before she could answer him. "Yes, Caleb."

He leaned in and gave her a quick kiss of approval before returning to the chips and guacamole.

"Taryn."

"Caleb."

"Will you tell me about your family?"

"There's not much to tell. My parents died when I was thirteen. I lived with my grandmother until I was seventeen, but she had to go into a home. I lived with my aunt until I was eighteen. My parents were good parents, they loved me and I miss them still. They left plenty of money so I didn't have to worry about college and I knew that as long as I was careful I'd have enough to buy my own business."

He watched her while she spoke and she had the unnerving sensation that he could see inside her head.

"That's a tough age to lose your parents. How did they die?" He took her hand and brought it to rest on his thigh, his fingers playing with hers.

"They were killed in a train wreck. Their commuter train hit a car that was left on the tracks. Eight people died."

"I'm so sorry. What a tragedy." His warm hand held hers firmly, his thumb rubbing small circles on her wrist.

"It was...horrible. The police and a social worker came to my school to tell me. They took me to my grandmother, but I didn't know her very well. She lived in Arizona."

"So you had to go to a new house, a new school, a new state. You said your parents left money, they didn't leave a guardian?"

"Apparently they had asked a friend, years before, who agreed to be guardian. But when the time came she had moved on, had a husband and kids, a whole different life. When the social workers told her I had a grandmother and an aunt, she figured she was off the hook."

"It never occurred to any of them that if your parents had wanted you to live with your grandmother or your aunt they would have listed them as guardians?"

His voice was eerily calm and she forced a smile to reassure him. "It was fine, we just didn't know each other very well. We pretty much stayed out of each other's way until she became too sick and needed to go into the home. Then I went to Colorado with Aunt Peggy. By then I was seventeen, so we were more like roommates. We didn't bother each other, much."

The food arrived and Taryn was relieved. She didn't like to talk about her teenage years. They sucked, they were over, she had moved on. Caleb was quiet and she was worried what he might be thinking, but when he looked at her she could see only approval and desire on his face.

When they finished, he looked at his watch. "I need to get to an appointment. I have some work to do after but I'm hoping my night will be free. Richard said he would be free tonight, what do you think?"

"I'm having drinks and dinner with my friends Petra and Emma." She watched him, prepared to be pissed if he considered time with her friends less important than time with him. "I wouldn't get there until almost midnight."

"I'd rather have you there sooner, but if later is what I can get, I'll take it." He walked her back to the shop, stopping at the door. He kissed her then, not like earlier, but like that first night. A kiss that went soul deep and left her breathless and hungry for more.

"Tonight," he promised, and walked away.

CHAPTER SIX

Richard hummed as he prepared dinner. He had been so thrilled to see Caleb that afternoon, even if only for a couple of minutes. They had talked on the phone a number of times but it was shocking how much difference it had made to see him, talk to him, stand next to him. He'd wanted to drag the sexy-as-hell man into his office and attack him.

Grimacing to himself while he chopped the garlic, Richard tried to remember his resolve not to get in too deep. The chances of things working out with both Caleb and Taryn were pretty slim. Probably the two of them would become serious, maybe even marry, leaving Richard on the sidelines. The funny part was, he would be equally jealous of both of them. Where before he had no problem with the idea of Taryn falling in love with someone else and getting married, would have been thrilled for her in fact, now...now things were different. It felt so right, so perfect, when the three of them were together.

He missed Taryn, too. While she rarely spent more than one night at a time with him, they usually got together at least every other day and she generally spent those nights at his place. They hadn't spoken of it but it hadn't felt right for the two of them to get together without Caleb. He was glad that the two had been able to have lunch together and though he wished she was able to make it to dinner, he was pleased at the idea of cooking for Caleb.

Cooking was a valued tradition in his family and he could hold his own with those who made their living at it. It was a skill he was proud of and he liked to show it off. It was a completely different feeling than being a doctor. That was hard work and dedication, not something he was proud of, but something that he felt he had to do.

He moved from the garlic to an onion, chopping while humming to the blues coming from the radio. He wondered what kind of music Caleb liked, what his family was like, what his time in the military had been like. There was so much he wanted to know. Other than Taryn, it had been too long since he was actually interested in a person separate from the sex. He missed that connection, which was probably a big reason why he continued to go back to Taryn. Was he going to be able to handle it if they broke up with him? Would he lose not only the new friend but his best friend as well?

The knock on the door caused his heart to skip a beat. Not wanting to smell of onion, he washed his hands quickly and grabbed a towel to dry them off as he walked to the door. Unlike this afternoon when he had been forced to look at Caleb without touching, the minute he opened the door he grabbed Caleb's hand and pulled him inside, slamming the door shut behind them.

Caleb pushed him against the wall, threading his hands through Richard's hair. Richard felt them clench, pulling his hair tight as Caleb angled him just so and lowered his mouth. Richard was expecting an attack, a harsh reacquainting of lips and tongue. Instead Caleb barely brushed his lips, avoiding Richard's searching advances. The hands in his hair tightened even further and Richard made himself relax, gave himself into the situation. Caleb murmured his appreciation and bit gently at the corner of Richard's mouth then soothed the spot with his tongue.

Somehow Richard found himself relaxed, yet anxious for more. Wanting yet waiting. Breathing deeply but unmoving. Caleb loosened one hand from his hair and moved it down to his neck, his fingers curved around the nape, his thumb on the pulse point in front.

"Caleb." It was a greeting, a plea and a sigh, all at once.

"Richard." It was a promise, a demand and an acknowledgment.

Richard opened his eyes, having no idea when they had closed. Caleb watched him, his thumb moving idly, his eyes fierce. Richard felt his body soften even further, except for that one very hard part of himself. As if that was what he'd been waiting for, Caleb moved in.

Lips met lips, tongue met tongue. Caleb gave and Richard took and they both sighed with pleasure. Then Caleb growled and pushed away, leaving Richard feeling cold and empty.

"We're going to wait. Right, Ricky?"

The tiny hesitation in that last word was enough to remind Richard of where they were and what they were doing. Yes, they should wait. He would feed Caleb dinner, they would talk and then Taryn would come home. He pushed himself off the wall.

"Beer or wine? Something else?" he offered as they walked into the kitchen. He turned at Caleb's growl to find the man staring at his ass. "No," he insisted. "You aren't allowed to be all growly and sexy and expect me to be the stronger person here." He laughed and pushed Caleb to a chair at the table. "Now sit down and behave while I make dinner."

"Yes, Richard."

Richard had to bite his lips to keep from laughing out loud at the strangled resignation in Caleb's voice. He certainly had no doubts about this man wanting him, at least sexually.

He went to the fridge and got them both beers, then returned to the cutting board.

"So, you're in security?" Richard asked.

"That's right. Mostly corporate, but I do some home security as well."

"My sister Laura is a police officer here." He moved to the stove and began to sauté.

"Officer Daniels, of course. I should have noticed the resemblance when I saw your name."

"Well," Richard laughed, "I like to think you were otherwise distracted at the time."

"I certainly was. I've met Laura a few times, I like her. You must be pretty close in age."

"Twins, actually."

"Do you have other siblings? Someone must have gone into the family business— your cooking smells too good for it not to continue on after your parents."

"One brother and one other sister. My sister Michelle is in Italy studying cooking and my brother Brian is finishing his MBA this year. He and my mother get positively giddy discussing the management of the restaurant. I think they want to expand the bar area, give your brother a run for his money."

"I can't believe I've never eaten at Mama's. I tend to find a couple of good restaurants I like and stick with them."

"We'll all go for dinner soon. I'd like you to meet everyone." Richard's eyes widened as he realized what he'd just said. Caleb didn't comment, just watched as Richard plated up the food and brought it to the table.

"It looks delicious. I can't wait."

Richard told Caleb stories about his family, his childhood. There had been plenty of fun and mischief in the Daniels household. He had worked in the restaurant off and on, both in the kitchen and out, until graduating college.

"Why did you decide to become a doctor?" Caleb was pushing his plate away, every bite gone. "That was fantastic."

Richard rose and took their dishes to the kitchen. Caleb followed with more items and began helping to put the food away and the dishes in the dishwasher, both of them taking frequent opportunities to brush against each other.

"When I was seven I was at the restaurant, sitting at a table with my brother and sisters, entertaining ourselves. A man at the table next to us had a heart attack. Luckily there was a doctor eating dinner, too, and she saved the man's life, doing CPR until the ambulance arrived. We were all just stunned, sitting there watching, while this woman, this unassuming woman, was saving a man's life. It stuck with me. I knew I didn't want to go into the restaurant business, I enjoyed it too much as a hobby to risk hating it as a job."

"How did you end up going to college in California?" Caleb asked while they picked out a DVD and settled on the couch.

"I wanted to leave the state. I love my family, but being one of four, and a twin no less, I thought I needed a chance to settle my identity by myself. At least for a while. My dad's sister and her family lived in southern California, so my parents were more comfortable with me going there than anywhere else out of state. They knew I wanted to come back here for medical school, that it was only four years."

"And then you met Taryn."

Richard smiled. "And then I met Taryn."

"Part of me is amazed that you didn't just snatch her up right then and there."

Cocking his head, Richard thought about that while trying to ignore the thigh pressed hard against his, the fingers idly brushing over his knee. "I think that mostly had to do with the fact that while I was comfortably gay while living here, there weren't a lot of options open to me at the time. So when I got to college and there were gay groups on campus, gay bars nearby, I went into a bit of overload. Plus, I was so gung-ho about being gay, determined to be myself and not hide, it took me awhile to realize I was still attracted to women occasionally. It wasn't until I got a crush on my biology teacher that I realized there was no good reason to limit myself just because I found guys attractive more often."

"What about you, Caleb? How come you joined the military?" Richard put his arm on the back of the couch, letting his hand fall to rest on Caleb's shoulder, trying not to let the feel of solid muscles distract him from what the man was saying.

"When I was in college one of my instructors was ex-Navy SEAL. I don't know, I was just so impressed by how intelligent he was, how...steady. I had this vision of military guys as being either dumb grunts or adrenaline junkies. I had a lot of energy and no direction. My parents had money but I wanted to make my own way. I wanted to go new places, see new things and he showed me how."

"You enjoyed it."

"Yes, for the most part. It's a weird thing, the military. It's obviously not just a job, but I didn't want it to be my whole life, either. I didn't want a military family, someone at home waiting for me, wondering if I was going to make it back this time, kids who hated me for dragging them around. Some of my teammates were getting married and getting out and the opportunity came up to start something new with one of them, my partner, Michael. It was something I could be proud of but could also share with my wife and children when the time came, seemed too good to pass up."

"Have you regretted leaving?"

"No. Sometimes I miss the action—that adrenaline rush is addictive for a reason. But I've enjoyed the challenge of building our business and I like knowing that when the time comes I'll be able to have a family without worrying about leaving them behind."

"You're a good guy, Caleb Black." The hand on his knee squeezed briefly.

"You're not so bad yourself, Dr. Daniels."

"Have you, uh..." Richard didn't know what had possessed him to start the sentence, but he was determined to finish it. "Have you done the sex clubs and stuff?"

"And stuff?"

Richard scoffed. "You know what I mean."

"I do, and I'm sorry, I don't mean to make fun. I want you to be able to ask me this kind of thing. To answer your question, yes, I did go through a club phase, learning to what extent I wanted to take the whole Dominance and submission thing."

"And?" Richard hoped he managed to keep his voice even, because he thought the answer to this question was going to be very important to him.

"And I found that while the clubs were fascinating and I enjoyed my time there, I wasn't interested in playing with strangers, or in having a slave."

"So the other night was fairly typical?"

"No, the other night was...special. But if you mean did I hold back what I wanted, then no. I got what I wanted. I imagine, if things continue on like I hope they will, that sometimes we'll do more than we did the other night, and sometimes less. I don't need a scene every time I have sex, but I will push for certain things when I want them and feel you're both ready and willing."

"But you're not going to try to talk us into going to a club or sharing us with strangers."

"Hell no." Caleb's voice was steel and left no doubt.

"Okay, cool. Just checking."

"Good. Now turn on the movie before I forget we're waiting for Taryn to get here."

Richard smiled and turned on the movie.

CALEB LOOKED up at Taryn when she walked into the living room. He'd heard her at the door and would have gone to let her in but hadn't wanted to disturb Richard. Sprawled on the wide, comfortable couch, with Richard's head on his chest, he was watching the end of the movie, waiting for her. His fingers were tangled in Richard's hair, stroking the sleeping man. He watched Taryn's reaction, not surprised to see her licking her lips. He wanted to see if he could get her to bite her lower lip, even though it wasn't much of a challenge.

"I told him to take a nap since we had plans to keep him up half the night," he said quietly. And yep, there it went, plump lip being nibbled on by small, white teeth. *Tasty.* "Come here."

She walked to him slowly, kneeling down beside the couch.

"Closer."

She leaned in, stopping just short of his lips. He growled and watched the pleased smile stretch across her face.

"Oh, it's like that is it?"

Her smile blossomed into a full grin.

"Too bad you can't reach me, isn't it?"

"Taryn."

"Caleb."

"Put your lips on mine."

She gave him a saucy grin then did as she was told. He drank her in, only her lips touching him while his arms were full of Richard. Not bad. For a start. He drew back. "Maybe you should wake Sleeping Beauty."

Sighing happily, she complied. Caleb watched her lay her lips lightly on his lover's. She knew those lips better than he did. She knew his body, his heart. But he would learn. He had to, because he wasn't letting them go, either of them.

Richard's body stirred, his lips parting under Taryn's delicate touch. She took full advantage and surged in, wringing a groan from Richard who started to bring his hands up to hold her to him. Caleb used his arm to hold Richard's in place and felt Richard shiver in response. He saw Taryn's hands move toward Richard, saw the moment she realized that would change the game and rested them on the couch instead. He smiled. They were perfect, so perfect. He didn't know what he'd done to deserve them, but he was thankful for it.

While Richard and Taryn touched only at the mouth, Caleb began to use his hands. He pressed firmly on Richard's arm, signaling that it stay in place. He moved one hand up to Taryn's nape and the other began a slow slide under the hem of Richard's t-shirt and along the waistband of his shorts. At Taryn's neck, his thumb brushed over her jawline and up to their joined lips. They broke apart and Richard bit Caleb's thumb.

"Let's go into the bedroom," he growled.

They stumbled to the bed, legs and arms entwined. Caleb briefly considered stepping back, regaining control and slowing things down, but it had been so long, too long. There was no way he could take the time to torment them with foreplay, it would be too much torture for him. They tried to tear each other's clothes off but got tangled up. It didn't even slow them down. Richard and Caleb kissed, Taryn wrapped a hand around both cocks. Caleb still wore his shirt, Richard's pants were caught at his knees and Taryn's bra dangled from one arm. They twisted and turned until they managed to get on the bed.

Caleb barely remembered to grab a condom and put one on while Taryn shoved Richard down and covered his cock with her mouth. Richard clenched his fists in the spread, whipping his head from side to side. Caleb reached for Taryn, testing her, so thankful to find her soaked. He was going too fast, showing no finesse, but they were right there with him, desperate to be inside each other. Too long, it had been too long.

Taryn hummed and Richard groaned. Caleb grabbed her hips and eased himself slowly inside her, determined not to rush this one thing. She squeezed so tight around him that he had to pause and wait for her to open to him. Heaven, pure heaven.

"Baby, you feel so good." He leaned down to kiss her shoulder, inhaling the combined scents of Taryn and Richard.

"Oh yeah, you feel soooo good," Richard agreed.

Taryn took her mouth from Richard.

"Caleb," she begged, spurring him to action. Richard erupted and Caleb watched Taryn drink him down. He felt her flutter then spasm as she collapsed on top of

Richard, spent. He reached down and picked her up so that she was on her knees, back to his chest. His eyes were on Richard who took the hint, scooting forward so that he could play with her clit.

He saw Taryn look down just as Richard's tongue touched both her slit and Caleb's cock, heard her breath catch. Richard helped him support Taryn so that he could move in and out of her. His strokes became shorter, more desperate, and he reached around to brush her nipples before clamping down on them with his fingers. She screamed and came again. He let himself go, holding her up as she nearly collapsed. Richard helped ease them down and they somehow managed to get under the covers.

Caleb woke sometime later to find himself spooned around Richard who was in turn spooned around Taryn. He supposed that made the most sense, height wise. He couldn't resist, even knowing poor Richard had to go to work in a couple of hours. He began nibbling an earlobe while his hand crept between Taryn's legs. He played with her curls and wondered if she would like being shaved. They might have to try it sometime.

Sucking Richard's earlobe between his teeth, he gave it a sharp nip. The other man's rear pressed more fully into his cock, which was already hard. Taryn was still motionless though becoming wet, so he whispered in Richard's ear.

"Let's show her what two mouths can do."

"Mmmm."

Caleb got out of bed and walked around to the other side, getting two condoms out and handing one to Richard. They put them on then arranged themselves next to the still-sleeping Taryn. Eyes on each other, they synchronized their movements. Each cupped a breast, shaped it, tested it, then lowered a mouth to the tip.

Taryn made a noise that was half moan, half squeak. Caleb's eyes were glued to Richard who followed his every movement. They pulled her nipples up, letting them loose with a plop, then turned to look at her. There were tears falling from her eyes and Caleb's heart stuttered in alarm.

"Baby, what's wrong?" He sounded desperate, even to his own ears.

"Sweetie, what—?" Richard asked, adding to Caleb's certainty that Taryn wasn't usually a crier.

She shook her head. "Nothing, you're just so beautiful, the two of you. You make me feel so good."

Without even looking at each other, both men rose to nuzzle the wet tracks from her face.

"No more of that now. You're going to scare me and I'm supposed to be fearless."

She gave him a tremulous smile and leaned up to kiss him. He gave in readily, soothing her and himself with her sweetness. He felt, more than saw, Richard move down between her legs. He used his hands to please her abandoned breasts, all the while keeping their kiss going. They stayed that way for what seemed like forever before Taryn could no longer contain her need.

"Please, Caleb. Please."

Caleb moved down to give each nipple a farewell kiss then scooted back. Richard had risen to kneel between her legs, his lips shiny from her cream. Caleb reached over to guide him to her entrance, letting just the head slide in before he squeezed the shaft.

"Don't move." His command was whispered but Richard grunted his anguished acknowledgment.

Caleb knelt behind Richard and lubed his ass until he saw Richard's arms shaking with strain and need. Then he pushed into him, slowly, as he'd done with Taryn earlier.

"Caleb...I can't...please."

"Give it to her, Ricky, take her." And as Richard surged into Taryn, Caleb seated himself fully inside Richard. Richard waited until Caleb began to move, then matched his strokes. They moved as if choreographed, drawing it out, until they could no longer be slow. Caleb began pounding into Richard who let his movements fuck Taryn as well. Caleb wasn't sure who came first, only that they all screamed in completion before once again collapsing to the bed.

CALEB AND TARYN had to bribe Richard with coffee to get him out of bed the next morning. Neither of them had to be anywhere for hours but Richard had appointments starting at nine. They dragged him to the kitchen table and left him to drink coffee while they made breakfast.

They were comfortable together, anticipating each other's moves and needs. Things were moving fast but Caleb already felt like he was a part of their lives, and they were part of his. Walking into the coffee shop yesterday, knowing that Lisa was inside, had been slightly unnerving. High-school prom was the last time he had brought a date home and it had been strange introducing Taryn to his sister-in-law. Not bad, just strange. On the one hand, he wanted Taryn to like his family. On the other hand, he didn't have any plans to stop seeing her, or Richard, if his family didn't like or approve of them.

That was what felt so strange, he realized. The idea that he was seeking anyone's approval to make a place for these two people in his life. Because he didn't want them to be a small part, kept away from the rest of his life. It was already clear to him that they needed to be integral and that meant making them comfortable with his friends and family.

When Richard left the table to go take his shower, Caleb had to restrain himself from joining in and making the poor man late for work. He eyed Taryn, then the kitchen table they'd broken in last week. She saw him looking and smirked at him.

"You don't work office hours?" she asked.

"Sometimes. I make a lot of the onsite visits. Meeting clients at their offices to do the initial consult, following up on problem incidents. I'm not fond of staying in one seat all day ."

"Neither am I. If I have to be at my computer for more than an hour, I get jittery. Even at home, I hardly use it."

Richard came out shortly, dressed for work. He gave them both a quick kiss, then strode out the door. Caleb had a vision of them like this, ten years in the future. It wasn't quite the future he would have guessed at two weeks ago, but suddenly it was the one he wanted more than anything he could remember in a very long time.

The look on Taryn's face suggested she might be thinking something very similar, but the crinkle between her brows warned him he needed to stay on his toes. Everything was falling into place so easily, it was only a matter of time before reality hit. He hoped he was ready for it. He hoped *they* were ready for it because no matter the difficulties, he had every intention of seeing his vision come true.

CHAPTER SEVEN

Three weeks later, Taryn turned the "Closed" sign on the door of Grounded then leaned her forehead against it. It had been a long day. Early in the morning a man had come in who had, for some reason, made her uncomfortable. Something about the way he sat watching everything going on around him unnerved her. He sipped one coffee after another for long enough that Taryn seriously considered calling Caleb and asking him to stop by and tell her she was being paranoid. She hadn't wanted to leave the shop while the man was there and so had skipped lunch, settling for a pastry. He finally left shortly after the lunch crowd thinned out.

Later, one of her employees, Stan, had spilled hot coffee on himself and she had taken him across the street to the medical building. By the time she got back to the shop her two remaining employees were in over their heads. She had grabbed Caleb the minute he walked in the door a short while later, barely giving him a kiss before she shoved him behind the counter to help.

Turning around, still leaning against the door, she gave him a weary smile. "Sorry about that."

Taking off the apron he'd worn to protect his suit, he came to her. Cupping her face in his hands, he leaned in and kissed her gently on her mouth, her eyes, her nose. "You've had a tough day. I'm glad I could help a little. The tips were nice, but I think I'll keep my day job."

She smiled. "That's okay, I'm pretty sure I couldn't afford you. In fact, I just don't know how I'm going to be able to pay you for your help today." She pushed her hips forward, meeting the length of him. Moisture pooled between her legs at the hard contact.

His grin was feral. "I'm sure we can work something out."

He kissed her, long and slow, until she was melting against his body. When he pulled away, she whimpered. Opening her eyes, she found him watching her, his look at once hungry and possessive, but also soft and slightly awed. Her heart stuttered.

Steadying her with his large hands on her shoulders, Caleb took a step back, narrowing his eyes at her when she moved her lips into a pout.

"I spoke to Richard a few minutes ago. He's making us a very late dinner at my house, since we all have tomorrow off. And you've got two employees still here, trying to close up."

Taryn's stomach growled at the thought of an actual meal. The two pastries she had scarfed down were not cutting it. She began running through the final closing steps for the shop. She and her employees had done as much of the cleanup as possible in the last half hour as things had finally slowed down. Now Derek was cleaning up the coffee machines while Sara worked in the kitchen.

"Did you stop by for anything in particular?" she asked as she mopped the floor. He moved ahead of her, putting the chairs up on the tables.

"I had a late meeting with my brother so I thought I'd stop by for coffee and a kiss." He grinned at her. "I didn't know you'd put me to work."

They finished up quickly and she locked the door and said goodbye to her employees.

Getting into his SUV and closing her eyes, Taryn let the stresses of the day fall away. The trip to Caleb's house took only ten minutes, but she fell asleep, waking when Caleb opened her door and reached over her to unlock the seatbelt. When they walked into the house, the delicious aromas of dinner greeted them, along with a kiss for each from Richard.

"I put the pasta in when I heard you pull up. It will be ready in a second."

Taryn's stomach rumbled as she went to wash her hands. When she came back out she saw that the table was set, and Caleb was lighting the candles while Richard put the food out.

Her heart gave a quick squeeze of love at the sight of her two men. She had loved Richard for a long time, but had known something was lacking in their relationship. They had been better off as friends, lovers even, but not truly a couple. Until they met Caleb. Where they hadn't been a couple, only two individuals who cared deeply for each other, with Caleb they were more, the three of them were a unit.

Remembering how she had worried that starting something with Caleb would threaten the relationship she had with Richard, she marveled that instead it had been strengthened. He added so much more, she couldn't imagine not having him with them anymore.

They ate the delicious meal, then worked together to clean it up.

"I'm so ready for a day off tomorrow," Taryn said as they moved into the living room. "I sincerely hope nobody calls in with any coffee emergencies." She flopped onto the couch and leaned her head back, closing her eyes.

"Not only do I not have to go in, I'm not even on call." Richard joined her on the couch then laid his head on her lap. She ran her fingers through his hair.

Caleb sat on the coffee table and looked at them. Taryn's breathing picked up when she saw the look on his face, and she heard Richard's do the same. Taryn had learned over the past three weeks that while Caleb liked to be in charge in the bedroom, he didn't find it necessary to make every sexual encounter a game of dominance. Many nights she was happy to have sweet sex with her men. It never failed, however, when Caleb gave that certain look, used that certain voice, or took her with just that kiss, that her body became eager for his mastery.

"Do you trust me?"

Neither Taryn nor Richard hesitated even a moment.

"Yes, Caleb," they answered in unison.

He stood and they did as well. "I've been shopping. Get ready and I'll meet you in the bedroom."

Taryn went to the guest bathroom, wondering what Caleb had bought. All this time he had made use of whatever was handy to pleasure them, or what toys they already had. He had restrained her with silk ties once, bathrobe ties another time. Her favorite was when he had Richard do the restraining for him. She shivered in anticipation. Sometimes he preferred making them obey him without benefit of restraints. He had used the few toys she owned— her silicone vibrator, the little finger vibrator she'd bought for the bathtub, and the vibrating egg. Before, she had only ever used her toys when alone. He added them into their group play with amazing results.

Excited, she went into the master bedroom and sat on the side of the bed next to Richard, waiting. She heard the sink in the bathroom shut off, then Caleb came in. He looked so sexy. He had changed into a pair of worn jeans and wore nothing else. He was well aware that both she and Richard found this to be his most appealing look. As hot as he looked naked, or in a suit, to them nothing compared to the worn-out jeans with nothing else.

"I want you both naked."

Taryn stood up slowly, as did Richard. She pulled her shirt over her head then reached down to remove her socks. Unbuttoning her jeans, she slid them down, her eyes glued to Caleb's, which were hot as he watched them both. When they were naked, they stood waiting.

"I am a lucky bastard."

Taryn blushed when he said it, then moaned when he kissed her. He dominated the kiss, giving her a taste of what was to come. Sliding one hand up to cup the back of her neck, he broke the kiss then used the hand that he had similarly on Richard's nape to bring the other man to him for a kiss. All three were breathing hard when he pulled back.

Caleb reached down into a drawer and pulled out a handful of leather cuffs. Holding four in each hand, he extended one set to each of them. "Do you trust me?" he asked again.

They answered by immediately reaching out and accepting his offerings. Taryn had learned in the past weeks that if she did what Caleb told her to do, the pleasure would be exquisite. He had never done anything to give her the slightest pause or doubt. He had taught her things about her body, as well as his and Richard's. She trusted him completely.

"Do your ankles first, then you can help each other with the wrists." They did as they were told then stood still while Caleb checked each cuff to make sure that they weren't too tight. Satisfied, he returned to the drawer. Taryn shivered. He had restrained them before, but there was something different about wearing a cuff meant solely for this purpose. She flexed her fingers, amazed at how different it was to put them on like this, rather than have Caleb restrain her when she was already mindless with lust.

Caleb went to Richard and kissed him. As his tongue plundered Richard's mouth, his hands ran down the man's shoulders to his wrists and brought them gently behind his back. Richard's heavy breathing hitched as Caleb used a metal clasp to attach the two wrist cuffs together. Taryn sucked her lower lip between her teeth. She watched as Richard's cock grew harder, a small drop beading at the head.

Her eyes moved to Caleb as he came to her. Leaning down, he took first one breast, then the other, into his mouth, as much as he could. Pulling back, he moved to kiss her neck, then the curve of her shoulder as his hands tenderly drew her arms behind her and attached the cuffs together.

"Go stand at the foot of the bed, one on each post." He turned his back to rifle through the drawer again as they followed his instructions.

The bed was a giant four poster with sturdy wood posts. Taking more cuffs from the drawer, Caleb wrapped them around the bed posts then attached them to the clips holding their wrists together. The contours of the posts were such that the cuff would not be able to move up or down more than half an inch.

Though she had been expecting it and had experienced similar, the actuality of being cuffed by him, bound to an immovable object, had her eyes wide, her breath fast and cream dripping down her thighs. He had positioned them so that they were facing in toward each other as much as possible. Taryn looked at Richard, saw the same trepidation and arousal on his face and wished that she could touch him.

Caleb knelt at Richard's feet and pulled a bar from beneath the bed. He attached it to the ankle cuffs, spreading Richard's legs so that he couldn't move them. Then he quickly did the same with Taryn. When he was finished he stood in front of them, the apex of the triangle they formed together. He looked at them carefully, reached one hand to cup Taryn's sopping pussy, and used his thumb to move the moisture Richard had produced around the head of his penis.

Stepping back, he looked at them. She absorbed the hot look in his eyes like a shot of whiskey. The fact that seeing them like this, standing at the ready for him, gave him such pleasure, satisfied her like no alcohol could.

He returned to the drawer and came back with something small enough to fit in his fist. Taryn looked down into the hand he held in front of her and gasped. Nipple clamps. She had never tried them, associated them with painful bondage. She said nothing but took a deep breath and consciously relaxed her shoulders.

Caleb stepped in close to her. He dropped the clamps onto the bed and cupped her breasts in his hands. He had bound her wrists just above the small of her back, so her breasts were lifted out as offerings to him. He took them, caressed them lightly at first, then, in tandem, pinched the nipples hard. She gasped again, this time in total pleasure, no fear, feeling the answering tug in her vagina.

She moaned when he took one nipple into his mouth, sucking hard on it then flicking at it with his tongue. She whimpered when he pulled back then watched wide- eyed as he took up a clamp and brought it to her wet nipple. The clamp went easily on her hardened peak. There was a little pain but Taryn felt more cream slide down her leg at the sensation.

"Caleb!"

"One more. You can do it, baby, I know you'll like it." He picked up the other clamp as he worshiped her free breast with his mouth. He pulled the nipple between his teeth and tugged hard then released it. He put the other clamp on then blew air on both dark red nipples. Taryn gasped again. He kissed her then moved away.

Taryn was bereft until she opened her eyes and saw him sucking on Richard's nipple. Richard had thrown his head back and didn't see when Caleb brought the clamp up to the first nipple and attached it. He gave a small bellow and his eyes popped open wide. He was breathing so hard, Caleb had to time the second clamp just so. When he had it placed, he gripped Richard's cock tightly, his thumb brushing over the head until Richard strained against his bonds.

Again, Caleb stepped back to survey his lovers. Clearly pleased with what he saw, he nodded his approval. Going back to the drawer, he pulled out a butt plug and bottle of lube. He stood behind Richard and prepared the plug with a generous amount of lube.

"Are you ready for me?" he murmured.

"Always," Richard gasped as Caleb pressed on his shoulder, forcing him to bend, despite the awkwardness on his bound arms. Taryn couldn't see Caleb's hands but knew the instant he thrust the plug home by Richard's grunt and the sweat dotting his brow. Caleb's hand on Richard's shoulder pulled him back, while the other hand snaked around his hip to play with his hard cock.

Taryn saw Caleb bite Richard's shoulder before he pulled away and returned to the drawer. She swallowed hard when she saw another, smaller plug. Caleb had used his finger in her, as had

Richard, but they hadn't put anything else into her yet. She wanted to reach the point where they could both fill her up, but wasn't sure she was ready. If Caleb thought she was ready for this, though, she would trust him. He stepped forward and laid the lube and the plug on the bed, along with a small dildo she hadn't seen him take out. As he did so he thumbed a remote he was holding and she heard Richard give a surprised start.

Caleb moved to kneel in front of Richard and buckled a cock strap around him. Rising, he used his hands to come all the way up Richard's body then gently tweaked the nipple clamps.

"Ah fuck!"

"Eventually."

Taryn was not so distracted by the sight of Richard's straining that she didn't see Caleb pick up the bottle of lube, open it and tuck it into his pocket. He picked up the small plug and the dildo before coming to straddle her leg. He looked hard at both of them.

"Do not come unless I say you can."

He slid the silicone cock into her wetness in one smooth thrust. She worked hard not to move while Caleb slid it in and out of her. Keeping her eyes glued to the sexy vision in front of her, Taryn concentrated on watching the sweat roll down Richard's chest. She saw him jerk forward as he watched Caleb work the dildo in and out. Fighting to stay still, knowing she wasn't supposed to rock forward into his hand, was supremely difficult but she managed it. She was rewarded with a kiss to her shoulder. With his free hand he brought a very slick finger to her rear hole and rubbed it back and forth.

Taryn's butt clenched, holding his finger immobile before she relaxed. He tickled her and she couldn't keep from moving forward, then back. As she moved back he pushed the finger all the way in. Taryn moaned. Caleb added a second finger, scissoring them apart, stretching her. She looked at Richard again and saw that he was straining forward, against his bonds. Caleb saw as well.

"Richard," he barked.

PERFECT FORMATION

Richard's glazed eyes met his, then he blinked. He relaxed back, his shoulders quivering.

Caleb picked up the plug and lubed it liberally. He laid it against her hole and gently pushed. She took a deep breath and bore down on it. The tip slipped inside and Caleb paused, letting her adjust. The feeling was very different from his fingers, as she tightened around it. Her muscles clenched, squeezing both objects inside her.

"Caleb, please." He went back to working the fake cock in and out of her pussy with one hand and when she breathed in, urged the plug the rest of the way inside her with the other. Stepping in front of her now that the plug was seated, Caleb worked the dildo in and out, twisting it around. Her passage was tight, filled as she was. He seated it fully then reached up and took off the nipple clamps.

Taryn wailed as sensation rushed back into her nipples. Caleb moved the toy in and out of her. Her fingers were clenching, unable to grasp anything, unable to move, do anything but stand there and take what he gave her.

"Caleb, I need...please...Caleb."

"Come now." He leaned in and took a nipple into his mouth and she erupted. The spasms went on and on. Her knees went weak and Caleb supported her with his arm. He waited until she was almost done then dropped to his knees, removed the dildo and plunged his tongue into her.

It took both of his hands to hold her up now. She went over again, fast and hard, her vision graying, her breath rasping. She didn't have enough energy to scream this time. Caleb licked her clean, then, supporting her with his body, released her from the spreader bar, then the bedpost. He settled her onto the floor and reattached the cuff to the bed at a comfortable spot. Taryn was surprised—he had never kept them bound for very long in one night, but she was too worn out to care. She rolled her head to look at Richard.

Richard's cock was dark and wet, his breathing fast. Caleb placed a kiss on Taryn's forehead then went to Richard. Taryn watched him attack Richard's mouth with his own, then watched his hands sneak up to the clamped nipples. He removed the clips simultaneously then dropped to his knees and enveloped the straining erection in his mouth. He reached to the bed and took the remote in one hand while the other came around to release the cock strap.

Richard tensed visibly when it was removed, clearly fighting his release. Caleb took his mouth off him, turned up the dial on the remote and said, "Now." He covered the shaft with his mouth as Richard bellowed with his eruption. Caleb released his ankles while licking Richard's dick clean. He came up to release him from the bedpost, then lowered him to the floor, reattaching him at a comfortable level, as he had done with Taryn.

Caleb returned from the bathroom with a couple of warm washcloths. Richard watched him use one on Taryn's backside. His cock jerked at the thought of Caleb and him taking her at the same time, and he wished he could stroke it. Probably it was for the best that his hands were otherwise occupied. He might not have been able to resist the need otherwise.

These last few weeks had been amazing. He had never felt such a strong connection to a man so quickly as he did with Caleb, and it was amazing how much it had deepened his relationship with Taryn. The group they formed together was so much more than he could imagine with either alone. He had always loved Taryn, but now was *in love* with her. And Caleb. At the same time. He was afraid to tell either of them, not sure what exactly the future was for them. He only knew that he was happier with the two of them than he had ever been in a relationship.

Caleb used the other cloth on Taryn's front then went back to the bathroom. When he came back he used fresh cloths on Richard. Richard arched his back to push farther into Caleb's grip, the washcloth on his still-sensitive cock almost too much. It had been an incredible climax. He loved it when Caleb took him into his mouth —there was no other feeling like it. Not to say that he didn't love it when Taryn took him also. It was different. They just felt totally different.

Caleb dropped the washcloth and retrieved two pillows from the bed. He placed one in front of Richard.

"On your knees now." Caleb leaned over Richard to once again adjust the strap holding him to the bedpost. Richard had to swallow hard to keep in a groan. He could hardly wait to see what else Caleb had planned. He rose to his knees and licked the hip bone that was conveniently in front of his face, while pulling the pillow under him. Caleb leaned his body into him further while he made the adjustments.

"Okay?" Caleb asked softly, running his hand over Richard's chest and up his neck.

"Very okay." He looked into Caleb's eyes, hoping to show him his love, even though he wasn't ready to give him the words. Caleb blinked then leaned in slowly, never losing eye contact, to give him a soft kiss.

"Good."

Richard tried to ignore his slowly swelling cock while he watched Caleb help Taryn into the same position. She looked so beautiful. Flushed and sated, but starting to get aroused again. Her nipples were still red from the clamps, still peaked. She leaned her head against Caleb's thigh as he made the adjustments behind her then helped her get the pillow under her knees.

When he was finished, Caleb stood in front of them and removed his jeans. His cock sprang free, hard and ready, and Richard licked his lips. Caleb came to Richard and fed him just the tip. Richard knew that Caleb would remember his gag reflex, so he didn't worry about Caleb giving him too much. His throat spasmed at the idea of feeling that thick cock as far as it could go. He sucked hard on the head then licked all around it, playing with the slit. Caleb groaned then backed away.

He moved to Taryn who eagerly opened her mouth and slid down, nearly to the root. Richard was amazed she could take so much, though she had practiced on him often enough. He watched as Caleb held steady, letting Taryn decide how far she could go, her head setting the pace. Licking his lips, Richard hoped Caleb would come back for more on his side. It had been a while since he'd experimented, and with Caleb he wanted to try, see how much of him he could take in.

When Caleb backed away from Taryn, he bent down to give her a kiss before turning back to Richard. Richard opened his mouth readily. Too enthusiastic in his excitement, he dropped his head too far over Caleb's erection and immediately gagged. Caleb pulled back and put his hand on Richard's head, stroking his hair while Richard fought to relax his throat.

"Easy now," Caleb said, softly. "Take it easy."

Richard's shoulders slumped and he refused to look up at Caleb.

Caleb dropped to his knees, the hand in his hair lifting Richard's face to meet his straight on.

Lust still burned in Caleb's eyes, but it was tempered by compassion.

He smashed their lips together, a fierce taking leaving Richard with no questions as to how much the man desired him. Abruptly Caleb pulled back, gave him a stern look and stood back up, bringing his cock right back to Richard's eye level.

"Lick it."

Richard wet his lips and did as he was told. He licked from the root to the head, then back down again. He swirled his tongue around then took the head in his mouth again and sucked hard, before licking down the side. Caleb's hands tightened in his hair as he let out a groan, spurring Richard on. He wanted to make this man come down his throat. He used his teeth to nibble a bit and Caleb's shaft jerked.

Caleb stepped back and Richard lunged forward, caught by his wrists. Caleb gently pushed him back then leaned down and kissed him, before going back to Taryn. Richard was breathing hard again, his cock straining for contact. He wished he could join them, wished he could use his tongue on Taryn's pussy while she sucked Caleb. She moaned and Caleb's back arched as he came. Taryn swallowed but it overwhelmed her mouth. Caleb staggered back to

Richard and presented him with his cream-coated cock. Richard leaned in and cleaned him up, the salty taste just what he needed.

Caleb unlatched all of the cuffs and they staggered onto the bed. Caleb sat against the headboard and pulled Taryn into his lap. She rested her head against his shoulder but her eyes were glued to Richard's growing erection.

"Taryn."

"Yes, Caleb."

"Are you wet?"

"Y-yes."

"Show Richard. Let me taste."

Taryn used her hands to open her lips to Richard's view. He sat cross-legged a foot in front of her and could easily see the moisture gathered there.

"She's gorgeous and juicy."

Taryn used two fingers to wipe up some of her cream then offered them over her shoulder to Caleb. He took the fingers in his mouth and sucked them clean. Richard had to keep his hands fisted on his thighs so he wouldn't touch anything without permission.

"Richard, touch yourself, but don't come."

Richard did as he was told and watched Caleb's fingers come around to Taryn's glistening folds and start playing with her. Richard began by matching his strokes with Caleb's, but it became too much. He had to slow down or he was going to come, and he was really hoping Caleb would let him come inside Taryn. Caleb moved his wet fingers to Taryn's clit and squeezed. She jerked and moaned, her hands resting on his knees beside her.

"Taryn, lie down." When she got up, Richard was amazed to see Caleb was already hard again. Taryn lay down between them, the cuffs on her wrists and ankles dark against her pale skin, a turn-on Richard had never expected.

Caleb reached over and got two condoms. He handed one to Richard and put one on himself. He gestured to the lube on the bed behind Richard. Richard grabbed the bottle and opened it, preparing to squeeze it over Caleb's cock. Caleb took the bottle from him though, and used it on Richard's straining penis.

Richard's eyes went wide as he glanced from Caleb to Taryn. Caleb's hands felt amazing on him, squeezing him firmly, but not as amazing as pushing himself into someone's tight hole was going to feel. He didn't think Taryn was ready though.

Caleb handed him back the bottle then moved up over Taryn, entering her in one smooth thrust.

"Caleb!"

Caleb leaned down and kissed her, then flattened himself on her, resting his forearms on either side to make sure he didn't give her too much weight. Her arms came around him, trying to get him closer.

"Richard."

"Y-yes, Caleb."

"Start with your fingers."

Spurred into action, Richard put lube on his fingers. He carefully tickled one wet finger over the larger man's hole, watching it flutter. Caleb moved his mouth to Taryn's and Richard pushed one finger in. Caleb's asshole seemed to suck him in eagerly so he added another finger.

Caleb groaned and Taryn whimpered. Richard moved the fingers in and out until they were sliding smoothly, then added another.

"Hurry, please," Taryn begged.

Making sure his cock was slick, Richard brought it to the waiting pucker. He braced his hands on Caleb's hips and moved in gently. Caleb thrust his ass back, impaling himself on Richard. Then he moved forward, pounding back into Taryn. Richard picked up his rhythm and they fucked in tandem. Taryn reached her legs up, sliding them behind Richard's ass. Her hands were in Caleb's hair, pulling him in closer.

"Hell, oh hell. Caleb..." Richard panted, wishing he could last longer. But there was no way, not the first time he got to fill this tight hole.

Caleb reached one hand to Taryn's clit and sucked her still sensitive nipples. She bucked and screamed.

"You're both so fucking perfect. I love you. Now, come now."

They all erupted together, collapsing in a messy pile. Richard carefully pulled out and removed his condom. Caleb was still lying with his eyes closed, so Richard removed his condom, too, and went to the bathroom to dispose of them and get a couple of washcloths. Now he knew why the man had so many of the things.

Caleb grunted his thanks and used one cloth on Taryn while she and Richard used one on Caleb. They threw the cloths back toward the bathroom and got under the covers. Richard rested his head on Caleb's shoulder, his arm wrapped halfway around Taryn who was lying partly on Caleb.

Richard looked into Taryn's face and they both opened their mouths.

"Love you, too," they said in unison, and both smiled when they felt the arms holding them squeeze tighter.

CHAPTER EIGHT

Caleb was very much not used to being unsure and it pissed him off that he was very unsure right now. Last night had been everything he had hoped it would be times ten. He had been unable, at the end, to keep from telling them he loved them. That they had responded in kind still made his chest hurt, in a good way.

But...

"Fuck." He dipped his head under the spray of the shower and let the water wash over him. He wanted more. He wanted to come home and know that one or both of them would be there. He wanted to feel free to walk through the door because it was his door, too. He wanted a home. With them. This was new, not something he had ever wanted with anyone before and it left him...unsure.

Disgusted with himself, he pulled his head out of the water and reached for the shampoo. He believed that they loved him. How could that be the easy part? It was everything else that was complicated. Believing Richard loved him did not keep him from being aware that the other man was holding back. Not in bed, not in trust, but despite the love there was something there that Richard was not giving and it was time to find out what that was.

And Taryn. Again, he fully believed she loved him and that she liked him as well, liked spending time with him, with and without Richard, but she was very careful to not spend every night with them. He hadn't really noticed at first, because they all had such different schedules. If she had a late closing it was easier for her just to go home upstairs than to come to his or Richard's house. Or she might be having a girls' night with her friends or babysitting for Petra, her friend from Richard's office. Whatever it was, somehow it ended up that she wasn't with them at least two nights a week.

It wasn't that he minded, exactly. He enjoyed the time spent with Richard, just as he enjoyed the times he was alone with Taryn. Suspecting she was keeping her distance intentionally, however, was another matter. This relationship shit was very annoying. Usually he was in a relationship until it became annoying and then he wasn't. This was annoying but there was no way he wasn't going to do whatever was necessary to fix it. It was...annoying. He sighed and resisted the temptation to bang his head against the shower wall.

Toweling himself off, he checked on Richard. The good doctor was lying diagonally across the bed, head pillowed on one arm while the other was tucked under his cheek. His fabulously naked ass was only half concealed by the sheet. Caleb smiled in satisfaction. Tossing the towel onto the counter, he moved to the bed. Sitting down carefully so as not to jog the bed, he reached one hand out and brushed it lightly across Richard's back, causing a shiver. Caleb moved his hand down to the tempting ass and used a finger to trace the contours, which clenched and unclenched in response.

Richard opened his eyes and rolled over, Caleb letting his finger trail across his lover's butt and over hip as the body moved under him. Caleb studied his face, hoping to find the answers he needed. "I love you, Ricky."

Richard's face, relaxed from sleep, went blank. He closed his eyes. "I love you, too."

"Open your eyes."

Richard shook his head. Caleb's stomach clenched in unfamiliar fear. He forced himself to watch, to observe. Bringing his hand up to settle on Richard's throat in gentle but unmistakable warning, he growled, "Don't lie to me."

Richard forced his eyes open and Caleb saw that they were wet and sad. Part of him wanted to pull the man to him, hug him close and tell him that everything would be all right. Another part of him wanted to pull him over his knee and spank his ass until Richard acknowledged what they had.

Richard kept his eyes on Caleb's. "I love you, too."

Caleb saw the truth, heard it, felt it. But there was still a wariness. Caleb waited.

Richard sighed, letting his eyes fall closed again. "It's going to hurt like hell when you leave."

There was real pain on his face and in his voice, which was the only thing that kept Caleb from erupting in anger. He very carefully took his hands from Richard and rose from the bed.

He pulled on running clothes and shoes mechanically, all while listening to Richard sit up and pull the sheet and blanket around himself in defense. Caleb refused to look back, just tied his shoes and left before he said something that couldn't be taken back.

Passing the living room, he waved vaguely at Taryn who was curled up on the couch with a book and a bowl of cereal. He opened the door and paused at the idea that he didn't need a key, didn't need to lock up behind him so that he could come back to an empty house. How had he not even been aware that he needed that until he saw it within his grasp? Frustrated with himself, he stretched on the porch then jogged down the front walk.

Abruptly he stopped, stilling as his whole body tuned in to the surroundings, seeking danger. When he sensed nothing, he made his way to Richard's car and what had caught his attention. The car was parked on the street in front of his house and both tires that he could see had been slashed. Hacked, actually. Circling the car, he confirmed that the other two tires had received the same treatment. After taking a look around he headed back into the house, his previous concerns pushed to the back of his mind.

Taryn looked up in surprise when he came back in so quickly. "Did Richard come out yet?" he asked her.

"He just went into the kitchen." She stood, concern written on her face. He held a hand out to her and she took it, letting him lead her into the kitchen. Richard was leaning against the counter drinking from a coffee mug, both hands wrapped around the heat.

Caleb pulled a chair out for Taryn then sat down. "Richard, someone vandalized your car last night."

Surprise had Richard putting the mug down. "What?"

"Someone slashed your tires last night."

They stared at him for a moment then Richard pushed away from the counter and headed out of the kitchen, Taryn hot on his heels.

Richard led the way outside then stood on the walkway and stared at the car before looking at Caleb in confusion. Caleb took his hand and pulled him back inside the house. "You have AAA? It would be easiest to get a flatbed to take it to a tire shop."

"Yeah. You think I should call the police? My sister is on duty, I think."

"There's not much the police can do except take a report. I'm sorry, Rick, we don't often get vandalism in this neighborhood."

"Just one of those things, I guess. I'm going to take a shower, then I'll call."

"We'll call while you're in the shower, honey. And make breakfast." Taryn gave him a quick kiss and went to her purse. She pulled out the Automobile Association card and picked up the phone while Caleb started breakfast. They were just sitting down to eat, the tow truck promised within the hour, when the doorbell rang.

Caleb motioned the others to continue with their meals and went to answer the door. He raised his eyebrows in surprised inquiry to find Officer Laura Daniels and her partner Kevin on his porch, but the rest of him stilled as if bracing for impact. Clearly something was wrong.

"Caleb, long time no see."

"Laura, Kevin. Would you like to come in?"

"Richard's here?" she asked, stepping inside.

"In the kitchen."

He led the way back, going straight to the coffee to pour two mugs. Richard and Taryn stood up to greet the pair before they all took seats.

"Rick, have you been outside?"

"The tow truck is on its way."

Laura nodded then looked at him sympathetically. "I'm afraid there's more. Your house was vandalized last night. Since you weren't there, they called me and I thought you might be here, so we came over. When we saw the car, we realized it was more of a problem than we initially thought."

Richard's brow creased in confusion. "Vandalized how?"

Laura cleared her throat. "Spray paint on the house and a dead cat on the porch. It looks like it was road kill, not killed at your house."

"What the hell?" Richard shook his head in denial.

"What did the paint say?" Caleb asked, knowing there had to be more.

"It's not pretty."

Richard narrowed his eyes at his sister. "What did it say?"

"God will punish you."

Taryn's hand went to her mouth to stifle a cry of shock. Richard's fists clenched on the table. Caleb put his hand on Richard's shoulder and felt the muscles, tight and stiff.

"Officers are at the house, taking pictures. I called home and Brian's in town for the weekend. He and Dad are going to get some paint. They'll meet us at your house when we're done here."

Kevin cleared his throat. "Have you had any run-ins lately? With a patient? With anyone?"

"No."

Laura looked to Caleb and Taryn. "You guys experience anything weird? Have trouble with anyone?"

Caleb shook his head and Taryn answered negatively.

"No fights, nobody looking at you funny, nothing?"

All three indicated that there had been nothing. Laura focused her attention on Caleb. "The fact that they hit two different locations is not a good sign."

Caleb nodded, determined to maintain control despite the fury running through him. "They've either been following him or done a fair amount of research."

Richard was looking more and more upset. "You don't think it was random?"

"Either might have been random. Both is not." Laura nodded along with Caleb's assessment.

"I think you have a problem, Rick."

"Oh God." Richard stood up so fast his chair would have fallen over had Caleb not caught it. "The office!"

"I sent a car over. There was no sign of trouble," Laura reassured him.

Taryn and Caleb stood up, both putting a comforting hand on Richard. "We'll need to call and cancel the tow truck, I assume?" Caleb asked Laura.

"Yes, I'll send the guys at the house over here to take photos when they're done."

"Fine. We'll make some calls and head over to the house. Unless you'd rather wait here, Rick? We can get this done without you having to see it."

"No, I want to see."

They took Caleb's SUV to Richard's house. He asked Taryn to drive so that he could make phone calls from the back. Richard sat up front looking shell-shocked.

Keeping his voice low, Caleb called his employees. He sent one person to his house to set up video surveillance of the street with instructions to do the same at Richard's then go to the medical office and check the security set up there. He sent another to Taryn's apartment to check that nothing had happened and to maintain a personal watch. He had helped Richard upgrade his security system weeks ago and Taryn already had a top-of-the-line system that included both the shop and her apartment. When he was finished he took a minute to calm himself. He had been in many situations that had felt personal at the time, but nothing compared to this. This felt like an attack on his home, on his family.

"Richard, you go in and pack some things while we help get the painting done. As soon as it's finished we'll go to Taryn's so she can pack and we can check on the shop." Taryn pulled up to the curb at Richard's house. "We can pick up her car while we're there."

He opened the car door before realizing that they were both staring at him, Richard with irritation and Taryn with something more like anger.

"What?"

"What response are you expecting, Caleb?" Taryn asked, her tone biting. "Sir, yes sir?"

"Well, that would be nice, but a simple okay would work as well."

"Exactly what aspect of my personality has led you to believe that I am happy to follow orders willy-nilly?" Her glare was enough to warn him that he better be careful of his response.

"For fuck's sake, Taryn, this has nothing to do with the bedroom. I suggested the most obvious next move. I have the best security and the most space, so you should move in with me, at least until we figure out what the hell is going on here."

"Wow, what a charming offer, but I'm afraid I have a policy against roommates, let alone allowing other people's actions to make my decisions for me."

Caleb knew he was handling this badly but couldn't seem to stop himself. "Don't be a martyr, Tare. You need to be safe. I can provide that."

"My apartment and the shop are safe, they have excellent security, you said so yourself."

"Security, yes," he ground out through gritted teeth before making himself take a deep breath. "But considering anyone can walk in during business hours, that's hardly safe if someone is trying to hurt you."

"We have no reason to believe that anyone is trying to hurt me. And the only solution to that problem would be me not going to work at all." She sounded as frustrated as he did. "I'm not moving in with you because someone is vandalizing some of our property."

"How about moving in with me because you said you love me?"

"This isn't about you, Caleb, this is about Richard. He needs our help now, in case you hadn't noticed, not you being an overbearing ass." She didn't wait for a response, just slammed her way out of the car.

"That was," Richard paused, looking back at Caleb, "a very interesting way to ask the woman that you love to move in with you."

"Well I'm so sorry if my desire to keep you both safe is overbearing. And I asked you both, the two people I love, to move in with me." It was an effort to keep from yelling and Richard's relatively calm voice only pushed his anger higher.

"Well, it sounded more like you were offering your protective services, at least to me."

"Maybe because this morning you didn't fucking believe me when I told you I loved you."

"Fuck you, Caleb. Now is not the time for this." Richard got out and closed the door with a quiet snick.

"Son of a bitch." The words were barely whispered as Caleb tried to figure out what the hell had happened. He was a trained soldier for fuck's sake. He knew how to handle himself under pressure. He knew how to lead his team through a mission successfully and safely. What he had suggested was the most obvious next step. Period.

His phone rang and he answered it while finally getting out of the car. He looked around and saw that Richard was talking to a small army of people who were probably his family. Caleb had not yet met any of Richard's family or Taryn's friends other than at the shop, something he had been hoping to discuss with both of them today. Maybe he had been vastly overrating their commitment to him and this relationship. The very idea pissed him off further. He was *not* used to second guessing himself, damn it. Taryn, he noticed, was standing next to the group, but to the side, staring at the ugly words painted on the house.

Kevin approached him when he hung up the phone, as his partner was in the middle of explaining something to the group. "They're a good family, very close. This is going to piss them off."

"I wouldn't know, I haven't met them."

"Oh, sorry. I guess I thought you guys were pretty tight, but I know it hasn't been long."

"Yeah. Well. Have they found anything helpful?" He gestured toward the black and white that was now leaving, hopefully having collected some evidence.

"Not really."

"Great."

"This is probably nothing. Just some jackass kids."

"Yeah, jackass kids love to invoke God in their Friday night spray painting parties," Caleb answered, his voice tight.

"We had a car drive by the coffee shop but everything looked normal."

"I sent someone out there."

Kevin nodded and headed back over to his partner. Caleb followed along, getting there in time to hear the man he assumed was Richard's father. "Why don't you stay with us for a couple of days while your sister looks into this? Taryn, you could stay as well, you know we'd love to have you."

"I'll stay where I was last night, it's plenty safe, Dad." He looked around, gesturing as he spotted Caleb's arrival. "This is Caleb. It happens he's in the security business, so his house is very secure. Mom, Dad, everyone, this is Caleb. Caleb, this is my mother Sylvia, my father Don, my brother Brian, his girlfriend Callie, my cousin Clara and her husband Steve."

Caleb shook the hands closest to him and attempted a smile. "It's nice to meet you all."

"It's so nice of you to *ask*, Don." Taryn gave a significant look to Caleb. "But this is very minor, there's no reason to believe that anyone is in danger and Caleb has already vetted my security system, so there's no reason to put you out."

"Don't be silly," Sylvia chided, coming to put her arm around

Taryn. "You know we love to have you at the house. We miss having you kids around. We can have a good dinner at the restaurant then go home and pop popcorn and watch movies like we used to do when you came home from college."

Caleb had never seen Taryn so...reserved. He wondered if that was due to her being pissed off at him, or if she didn't particularly care for Richard's family. She had never said anything bad about them but that didn't mean she liked them.

Taryn announced she was going inside for a drink and asked if anyone else wanted something. Caleb's phone rang again and he moved off to answer it.

CHAPTER NINE

Taryn needed to calm down. Caleb had likely not meant for his words to be taken as an order. Probably, if she had actually voiced another suggestion he would have listened. She would never know, because she hadn't really had another suggestion. What she had was a knee-jerk reaction to people telling her what to do. Well, outside of the bedroom anyway. This was why she owned her own business, rather than working for someone else.

But she was uncomfortable, as she always was around Richard's family, which made it harder to let her mad go. They were good people. They'd worked hard to help her feel welcome since the day they met her and had tried to make her feel like family since the day they realized she and Richard were more than friends. She just...wasn't comfortable with families. Didn't really know what to do with them.

At first she had tried to keep her distance because what was the point of getting to know people who lived in another state? When she moved here she was focused on getting her shop open and settled, not making friends. At least, that's what she told Richard the first dozen times he asked her to join him at family functions. She joined him occasionally and liked them well enough, she just didn't feel like one of them. Didn't want to feel like one of them.

She had her friends and her employees and her customers. She had Richard. She didn't need his family, too. Now she had Caleb. Crap. How had they gone from saying "I love you" last night to this? She knew he was probably pissed at how she had overreacted in the car but she was damned if she was going to move in with the guy because he decided it would keep her safe. Although, to be perfectly fair, she wouldn't have moved in with him for any other reason, either. What was the point? They saw enough of each other now, they had plenty of sex. And if he liked someone in his bed every damn night, then wasn't it lucky that he had Richard, too? Aargh! She was making herself crazy.

Richard's dad was getting the painting organized and he handed her a brush. "You okay, sweetie?"

"I'm good, Don, thanks. It was nice of you all to come out here like this."

"Of course, that's what family is for." He paused, ducked his head. "You know, uh... You know that if you all want to stay at the house, Sylvia and I, we won't be real particular on who, you know, stays in what room." He blushed but managed to look her in the eye.

Taryn felt her heart go soft. Richard was lucky to have such caring parents who put their son's happiness in such high regard. "You're a good guy, Don. Thank you. But I don't see any reason that's necessary. We'll be just fine. I know Sylvia wishes otherwise, but I'm afraid we're just not kids anymore." She gave him a wry smile and he laughed.

"Well, she'd probably forgive you for that if at least one of you would get around to having some kids of your own so she can start the spoiling all over again."

Taryn opened her eyes wide and gave him her best over-the-top horrified look, getting another laugh out of him. She took the paintbrush and went to the wall. It had been determined that the paint they had was close enough in color to the house that they could just paint the one side, for now. The whole house could use a new paint job, but Richard didn't want to decide on a new color scheme now. With the number of people involved it would take no time at all to do just the one side.

She looked over and found Caleb and Richard coming to paint on either side of her. She waited to see if it would make her feel claustrophobic but she felt fine. Losing herself in the easy rhythms, she thought back to her dinner with Petra last night.

Petra had quizzed her on her relationship with Caleb and Richard. She had always pushed for a stronger relationship between Taryn and Richard, despite fixing him up with her gay friends when Taryn was dating other men. She had been a little hesitant at first, unsure about Caleb's addition but Taryn had told her how happy he made both her and Richard. By the time they finished with drinks and moved on to dinner Petra was happy for them and pushing for sexy details, with Emma egging her on. Taryn managed to get away with only a few teasing comments. Why had she been so happy and in love last night and then so pissed off this morning?

The painting was finished quickly and Richard handed their brushes to Caleb and pulled Taryn to the SUV. She was suddenly very tired and rested her forehead against his shoulder as he leaned against the truck and brushed the hair back from her face.

"You got up awfully early this morning, sweetie, considering we were up so late."

Taryn sighed. "You think I'm doing it again, but I'm not. Hell, I told him I loved him last night. And I meant it. I can't help it if I like my alone time."

"You do have a tendency to pull away from a guy just as things start to get serious," he reminded her. "Sweetie, you know I don't think there's anything wrong with liking your own space now and then. But you're not being fair if you're implying we've done anything to restrict that." He frowned. "Look, I don't know what's going to happen here but I feel like I want to milk it for everything I can. This is something special and I want to enjoy it for as long as possible. Don't you want that?"

"I am enjoying it. I love you. I love him. It's all good. So what's the problem?"

"The problem," Caleb growled from behind her, "is that you're holding back. You both are."

Taryn felt Richard stiffen in surprise and realized they had both missed his approach. She kept her head where it was, her eyes closed. "Yes, well. What, exactly, is wrong with that? It's only natural. It's been an amazing few weeks, but it has been only weeks."

"You said you loved me. And that you trusted me. I thought that meant something." She felt him step closer so that they were in a tight group, like that very first night.

"It does. It means I love you. And that I trust you. It doesn't mean I give my life to you. It doesn't mean you can just order me around because I love you."

"It wasn't an order."

"It sounded like one."

"Fine, then I apologize for that. But it has nothing to do with the fact that you're both holding back." She opened her eyes, unhappy to hear the weary frustration in his voice. He ran a hand through his hair and glanced over at the crowd. "Can we go inside to talk about this?"

Taryn looked up at Richard. "Would you rather stay here or go somewhere else?"

"I don't want to smell paint right now. Let's go back to Caleb's house."

Taryn climbed into the driver's seat while Richard thanked everyone. Caleb got into the front passenger seat and looked at her. "I am sorry."

"Fine. I appreciate that." He continued to watch and she sighed and turned to face him. "I'm sorry I overreacted. It's a pet peeve of mine."

"How come I haven't heard about it until now?"

Taryn looked at him closely to see if he was being a smart ass but she couldn't tell. "Because it hasn't come up. Because you haven't pushed that button."

He just nodded his head and looked forward as Richard climbed into the backseat. She started the car and pulled out as the last of Richard's family drove away.

Caleb spoke up as they neared the main street. "Does anyone feel like cooking or should we get some lunch to take ho...back to the house?"

"I definitely do not feel like cooking." Taryn slowed and pulled over to the curb.

"Me neither. Why don't I run into the deli real quick?" Richard suggested, pointing to the small shop across the street from where she had stopped.

Caleb and Taryn agreed then watched him as he crossed the street. Caleb waited until he had entered the deli before speaking.

"You don't like Richard's family?"

Taryn frowned. "They're nice people. Very loving and supportive of Richard. Of each other."

"So why don't you like them?"

"I like them just fine. They're Richard's family, not my friends." She watched him out of the corner of her eye, refusing to give him her full attention.

"Why does it make you uncomfortable?"

"I don't know, why don't you tell me?" She was mad again. Damn it, what was his problem today?

"So there's nothing I should be concerned about? On his behalf?"

"What do you mean?" She looked at him now, confused.

He shrugged his shoulders, his expression even. "I mean, I love him. If they treat him badly or put unusual stress on him for some reason, I want to know about it."

She turned back, facing forward. "No," she said softly. "They're very good to him. Like I said, they're a good family. He's lucky to have them."

"Okay. Thanks."

She just nodded, having no idea why she was choked up.

Richard's car was gone from the street when they got back to Caleb's house. They went inside and sat down to eat without saying much. Taryn was barely able to force down half her sandwich. She wrapped the rest up and put it in the fridge. She stared inside, seeing her favorite drinks, the cheese she preferred that Caleb hated. In her mind, she saw the load of her clothes in the washer that she had started that morning, reminding herself she needed to transfer it to the dryer. She saw the extra bottle of shampoo and conditioner she'd bought rather than continue to bring them from her house or Richard's where an identical set remained.

She felt drained, defeated somehow. Last night had been so wonderful. Nothing had changed really and yet she felt so afraid. She was thirty-one years old and she was afraid of...what? Love? How pathetic was she?

Warm hands drew her back from the open refrigerator. She kept her head down as she realized that tears were threatening to fall. Richard's hand lifted her chin, brushing her hair back so he could see her face. Caleb's hands rubbed up and down her arms, warming her chilled skin.

"I love you." Richard's quiet statement broke her control. At her first sob, Caleb scooped her up and walked her into the living room. He and Richard sat on the couch together, draping her across their laps. They held her tight while she cried.

"Oh sweetie. You're killing me here." Richard's voice was full of soft concern while Caleb's hands held her to him, her head on his chest.

"I don't..." she hiccupped. "I don't cry," she managed before full racking sobs overtook her. Richard scooted even closer, practically sitting on Caleb's lap with her.

"Tell us what's wrong." Caleb's voice was soothing while his grip was almost painful.

"I don't know."

"Yes you do."

"I'm scared."

"Of the vandal?" Richard sounded surprised. Taryn didn't answer.

"Taryn."

"Caleb."

"Tell us."

"You're telling me what to do again." She tried not to sound petulant.

"This is different. Don't pretend otherwise."

"I'm scared."

"I know," Caleb said patiently.

"Taryn."

"Richard."

"You must know we won't let anyone hurt you."

"What if you hurt me?"

"You can't mean that." He sounded shocked and hurt.

"You told me you love me. Caleb told me he loved me."

"I've told you I loved you before. Lots of times."

"This is different," she insisted.

"Yes, it is. But it's supposed to be good different, not scary different."

"You got scared," Caleb pointed out to Richard. This got Taryn's attention and she looked up at Richard.

"Yes, well, that's different too."

Taryn wrinkled her brow. "Why did you get scared? This is everything you've wanted."

"Isn't it everything you've wanted?"

"I guess...I guess it's everything I said I wanted. Maybe even what I thought I wanted."

Richard pulled back. "You're telling me now that you don't want it, even though it's pretty fucking perfect, and you don't expect me to get scared? Of course I'm scared, I'm fucking terrified you guys have made me fall in love with you and you're going to take it away."

"That's what I'm saying! Shit happens, you can't expect perfect to last. It doesn't last, it never does!"

"It's one thing for it not to last, for whatever reason," Richard yelled, getting to his feet, nearly dislodging Taryn. "It's totally different when perfect moves down the road, sets up housekeeping and leaves you behind."

"What the hell does that mean?" Taryn struggled out of Caleb's arms and they both stood up to face Richard.

"It means how do you think I'm going to be able to stand it if you guys get married and move into the perfect house, in the perfect neighborhood and start the perfect family?"

"There's no such thing as perfect! That's why this is so scary, because it can't last. Something will fuck it up. But I figured it would be something else, some outside thing screwing with us, not you insulting me! How could you think that I would ditch you for him? I've loved you for years. You're my best friend, the only person who has loved me for a long time and you think I'm just going to throw that away!"

"Yes, you love me like a friend, you always have. But look at him!" Richard gestured to Caleb who was standing very still. "No such thing as perfect, my ass! We've never met anyone who's so perfect for us—of course you're going to want to have it all with him. I said we would remain friends but how hard do you think that's going to be for me, to sit back and watch you create a family with him?"

"For fuck's sake, Richard, I don't want a family! If I wanted a family I would have joined yours, years ago. And if I did want one with him, why wouldn't you be there with us? You keep saying that like I'm going to choose him over you. Where would you get an idea like that? You're insulting both of us. Besides, where would you get the idea that he would choose me over you?"

They were both fairly close to screaming now. Taryn's tears were falling unchecked but now they were tears of anger. "This..." she pointed at Richard. "This is why I don't want a family. If the person I love and trust most in the world doesn't trust me, why would I choose to give myself to anyone else?"

Caleb stepped forward. "Enough." He pulled them both in close and Taryn thought about struggling but her anger drained from her suddenly and it was all she could do to remain standing. "Enough," Caleb whispered again, tightening his grip on them both. Taryn's arms went around him and Richard's went around both of them. They stood that way until their breathing had evened out.

Finally Caleb took them each by the hand and began pulling them toward the bedroom.

"Caleb." Taryn knew she sounded unsure.

"Taryn."

She gestured toward the bedroom with her free hand, then let it drop.

"Shh, it's going to be fine. We're all tired, we need a nap."

"You're telling us what to do again." She wasn't angry and knew she didn't sound it so she wasn't surprised when he just smiled back at her.

"I know. I think I know the difference now, but you be sure and point out to me if I get it wrong, okay?"

She rolled her eyes at his back. When they got to the bed he left them standing at the foot while he closed all the drapes and turned on the ceiling fan. He pulled the covers back on the bed then undressed Richard. Kissing him lightly on the lips, Caleb ushered him under the covers then turned to her. He undressed her with a minimum of fuss, as he had done Richard, then gave her a light kiss too before urging her into bed. Richard opened his arms to her and she snuggled in, laying her head on his chest. The bed sagged behind her as Caleb joined them, spooning her back, draping his leg over both hers and Richard's, his arm coming over her to rest on Richard's chest.

"Sleep," was his last command, or at least the last she was awake for.

CHAPTER TEN

Richard woke from their nap feeling better. How could he not feel good with Taryn draped over him and Caleb snuggled in close? They were probably both still pissed at him but here they were, wrapping him up in their heat. Taryn shifted a bit and he paid close attention to what her knee was doing until she stilled again. It wouldn't be the first time she kneed him in her sleep.

Running a hand down her back, he let it rest at her waist. He needed to talk to her about what she had been yelling about. It wasn't rare for them to squabble, but it was rare for them to fight like they had that afternoon. He'd been stunned to hear her talk as if she didn't expect her relationship with Caleb to last. He had honestly thought she was imagining getting married, though they hadn't discussed it. Hell, this was what she had always wanted, what *they* had always wanted. Now she was saying she didn't want a family? Color him confused.

Richard rolled his head to look up at Caleb who was sharing the same pillow. Caleb's eyes were open and steady on him. Richard gulped at his lover's expression. He looked...disappointed. And sad. Feeling ashamed but not exactly sure why, Richard looked away and closed his eyes. His arms tightened accidentally on Taryn and she stirred. Lifting her head, she saw that they were both awake and moved off Richard to sit cross-legged. Seeing Caleb's expression, she flushed and looked down at her knees.

"Richard, you want to tell me where you got the idea that we were going to dump you and get married?"

"Uh. Well. Logic, I guess."

"Not good enough."

"What do you want me to say? Of course you didn't say or do anything, but that doesn't mean it's not what's going to happen." Knowing he sounded belligerent only made him more defensive.

"Taryn's right, I find that very insulting."

Richard sat up, leaning against the headboard, pulling his knees in close.

"Taryn."

Taryn's heavy sigh spoke volumes.

"Caleb."

"I love you."

Taryn's shoulders slumped and her sullen expression vanished as tears threatened to fall, unnerving Richard.

"Damn it." She shook her head.

"I'm sorry, it may not be easy for you to hear, baby, but I do. So does Richard, and whether you like it or not, so does his entire family. I'm willing to bet you can add Emma and Petra to the list too, and those are just the people I can think of off the top of my head. I have no doubt there are more."

"Stop it."

"No."

"Of course my family loves you. Why would you think they didn't?" Richard asked, confused. "And what's this about not wanting a family? Isn't that what you've always wanted?"

"I thought I did, I was wrong. Your family is super nice and polite to me because they love you, that's all."

"Your parents dying had nothing to do with how much they loved you," Caleb said quietly.

"Oh please, what? Are you a fucking psychologist now?"

"It doesn't take a psychologist to figure it out when you were shouting it to us an hour ago."

"I didn't say anything about my parents. And their dying had nothing to do with me. It had to do with the piece of shit who left his car on the tracks and killed them."

Richard felt like he was playing catch-up. "Then you went to live with your grandmother, which wasn't the greatest."

"Not everyone get's greatest, but it wasn't bad. I'm not complaining about 'wasn't bad'."

"She was a drunk."

"Lots of people are."

"And so was your aunt."

"Again, lots of people are. Look, I don't know what you guys are trying to imply. I wasn't beaten or starved."

"You weren't loved," Richard said with understanding.

"My parents loved me."

"Until they died." Caleb said it straight out and Richard watched Taryn's face tighten even further.

"Whatever." She unfolded her legs and made to get up but Caleb reached out and grabbed one ankle and Richard grabbed the other.

"We love you."

"It's not that simple."

"Why not?"

"I don't know, Richard, why not? Why don't you tell me? An hour ago you were telling me my love for you wasn't good enough."

Richard blushed. "That's not what I said."

"It sounded a whole lot like that. You didn't believe that my love for you was as strong as my love for Caleb, which is only weeks old. What does that say about me and my ability to love and be loved?"

"All right, let's not start screaming again." Caleb interrupted, earning glares from both of them. "This is obviously all my fault."

Taryn narrowed her eyes at him and Richard wondered what was coming next.

"Neither of you trusts me. That's a little...hard for me to take. I thought we'd gotten way beyond that. I forgot that trusting me with your bodies, even your hearts, is not the same as trusting me with your futures. I'm sorry I pushed. I shouldn't have said that last night I guess. It wasn't meant to be a burden."

Caleb got up off the bed and left the room. Richard looked at Taryn. "Everything seemed so easy," he said.

"Until it wasn't," she agreed.

"Yeah. I'm going to take a shower."

Letting the water wash over him didn't seem to help. Logically, he knew that neither Caleb nor Taryn had said or done anything to give him the impression that they wanted to be a couple without him. He knew it was his own assumptions and insecurities, but that didn't make them any harder to put away. Replacing Caleb's shampoo on the little ledge next to Taryn's, it occurred to him that he hadn't brought over many personal items to this house. Taryn had, and she frequently left extras at his house as well.

And yet she was the one who refused to spend more than a couple of nights away from home. She was the one who didn't invite them to her apartment, preferring to come to their houses. Her excuse that they had a lot more room than her apartment suddenly struck him as just that, an excuse. Why had he never noticed that about her? He was supposed to be her closest friend yet he hadn't even realized she was keeping herself apart.

Shit, maybe they did need therapy. Couples therapy. His laugh did not exactly sound amused as he turned off the water. Stepping into the room while toweling off, he met Caleb coming in.

"I'm going to take my run now. You want to come?"

They had jogged together a couple of times and Richard had enjoyed it. Caleb clearly held his pace back but they'd had some good conversations.

"Sure."

They started out at the pace they had found comfortable the last time they'd run together. Richard found the combination of exertion and peaceful surroundings compelling. He found himself thinking about how he hadn't invited Caleb to his family's restaurant, nor introduced Caleb to his parents. They had only gone on a few actual dates, preferring to spend their time together at Caleb or Richard's house.

Knowing, vaguely, that he was holding part of himself back had seemed smart. Now it seemed unfair. Like he was cheating. Cheating the very people he was claiming to love.

It wasn't until they neared the house that Richard realized he had increased his pace, as if running away from the hard truths. He was gasping for breath and tried to be impressed, rather than irritated, that Caleb was barely breathing heavily. Whatever, at least he got to enjoy that body. He'd just have to think of other ways to make the man pant. They walked the last half block, cooling down, Caleb shooting glances at him now and then. When they reached the yard Richard braced his hands on his knees until he was breathing normally.

Finally he stood up and looked Caleb in the eye. It wasn't easy, but he said it. "I'm sorry."

Caleb blinked, his face clearing of all expression. "For what?"

"For not trusting you. For telling you I loved you but not being willing to give you all of myself in return."

Caleb's eyes closed for a minute then opened again. Their heat seared him straight to the soul. "And now?"

"I feel like I'm jumping off a cliff. It's scary as hell, no safety net."

"It's also a rush."

"Yeah. Yeah, it is that." Reaching out, he grabbed Caleb's waist and drew him in. Eyes locked, they met each other halfway. Richard moaned at the feel of Caleb's warm lips and wet tongue. The smell of sweaty man made him even hotter.

"Do I need to turn on the sprinklers?" Taryn's voice reached them from the front door and they pulled away, laughing.

Caleb caught his arm before he could head up to the house. "Thank you."

"For apologizing?"

"For trying."

Richard nodded. "I need to apologize to Taryn too. Not just for my thing, but for not even realizing she was having a problem."

"I think she's pretty good at hiding it, even from herself."

"Then it's a good thing she has two of us to keep an eye on her."

Caleb laughed and shoved him toward the door. "I don't think I'd mention that to her, if I were you."

"Duh."

When they reached the door Taryn was standing behind, she said, "Ugh, you boys need another shower." She pushed the door shut behind them, revealing her naked self. "I think I'll join you. Save water, you know."

"Social responsibility is so sexy," Caleb said, snatching her up and throwing her over his shoulder as she shrieked at him.

After they showered and managed to get dressed again, Richard ushered them into the living room. He kneeled in front of Taryn, sitting on the couch. "Sweetie, I'm so sorry that I was holding back on this new relationship. I can't promise that I'll have it all figured out now, but I promise I will try to open my whole heart to it. I was afraid of loving you guys too much, afraid of how it was going to hurt if it didn't work out. But I'm done with that. I love you. I love him." Trying not to be upset at the panicked look on Taryn's face, Richard looked to Caleb.

Caleb quirked an eyebrow. "Gee, all I got was an, 'I'm sorry, Caleb.'" They all laughed and Richard figured now was not the time to tackle Taryn's issues. At least not verbally. He had another plan entirely for that. Standing, he yanked her to her feet as well.

"Let's go to dinner, I'm starved and we haven't been to Mama's in ages." Turning to Caleb, he said, "Will you come meet my family properly?"

Caleb nodded. "I'd love to." They didn't give the sputtering Taryn much notice as they dragged her outside.

"Maybe I don't feel like Italian."

"You know Pop will make you whatever you want." He shoved her into the SUV and closed the door on whatever protest she was forming. By the time he climbed in, intentionally taking the long way around to the other side, she was silent.

When Caleb pulled into the parking lot he glanced back at

Richard. Sitting forward on his seat, Richard leaned against hers until he could see her face.

"You've never had a problem coming here before."

"I know."

"If you really don't want to go inside, that's fine, we can go somewhere else. But I think we need to talk about what the problem is."

She gave him her most irritated look and he had to bite his tongue not to laugh. She was just too damn cute. "I'm hungry," she said, opening her door. By the time Richard got out and made it around to their side of the truck, Caleb had Taryn frozen with a kiss. Richard moved up, covering her back, showing her with what he had that he was there for her, that they were both there for her. He put his arms around her stomach, holding her close. Caleb's hands were cupping her face and Richard moved in to nuzzle the other man's hands on her cheek. Caleb moved one hand to thread his fingers through Richard's hair and Richard turned in to join the kiss. It was an awkward angle and they broke apart, laughing.

"Fine, whatever. Let's eat." Taryn pushed through them and headed for the door.

CHAPTER ELEVEN

Caleb had to admit that he was a bit nervous coming to eat at Mama's. Luckily he could concentrate on Taryn's issues and pretend he was totally fine. Mentally kicking his ass for feeling hurt that Richard hadn't invited him here before when he hadn't exactly gone out of his way to introduce them to his family either, he straightened his shoulders and prepared to do the family thing. The truth was he didn't actually have much experience in this regard. He had never taken a date "home" and had never allowed anyone he was seeing to take him home, either.

Watching Richard hug his cousin Clara who stood at the hostess stand, Caleb leaned into Taryn. "Maybe Chinese would have been good, now that I think this through."

Glad to see that she was straining to keep from laughing at him, he gave her a comically nervous look.

"I tried to warn you, meeting the parents is scary stuff." She slung her arm as far up to his shoulders as she could reach and gave an exaggerated sigh. "It's okay, baby, I'm here for you."

Caleb couldn't resist bending down to kiss her. Which was, of course, the perfect time for Richard's parents to show up.

"Welcome, welcome." Sylvia Daniels gave him a motherly hug

before turning him over to her husband for similar treatment. So at least they were welcoming, not suspicious or judgmental. He could deal with this. Right? He would just stick close to Taryn, make sure she was doing okay.

As they all took their seats at a large table in a semi-private room, it occurred to Caleb that the only reason he hadn't been nervous about this, like Taryn, was because he was an idiot. He seriously had not given the reality of being on the receiving end of this much curiosity and protective instinct the attention it deserved. Reminding himself to do some major apologizing to her at the earliest possible chance, he tried to draw on his training to at least ensure that his fear was not actually showing.

Despite his brief pessimism—well, okay, fear—the Danielses put a great deal of effort into making him feel comfortable at their table. They told stories about Richard as a kid and even about Richard and Taryn's visits home during college. It was quickly clear to him that the whole family made a project out of convincing Taryn that she was one of them. Now that he thought about it, he was somewhat surprised they didn't see him as a threat to that goal. Laughing at a story Richard was telling about Laura's first day on the police force, he finally relaxed.

When dessert was brought to the table, Caleb stared at it, trying to convince himself his body could somehow hold another couple of bites. Richard brought up the vandalism, asking his sister if there had been any updates.

"Nothing yet, it's too early for any lab results, and I'm not really optimistic about those anyway." Frowning, she shook her head. "I don't know, brother, it seems personal, like you should know what it's about and who it might be."

Richard glanced at Caleb, his frown matching his sister's.

Richard's father spoke up. "Do you think it might be..." He paused, gesturing to the three of them. He looked embarrassed but was obviously not willing to ignore the elephant at the table if it meant danger to his son. "I don't know, some idiot concerned about your love life?"

"I don't know, Dad. I can't imagine."

"What are you going to do?" Sylvia asked.

Caleb cleared his throat. "I've set up some surveillance in case they come back. In the meantime we'll all just be very aware of our surroundings and anybody who strikes us as odd. I have a lot of resources in that area so we can check out anyone we're concerned about, no matter how unlikely. You should all do the same, actually. It can't hurt for everyone here to be extra aware. You can send any information about suspicious people to me and I'll have my people check them out." He nodded at Laura. "Unlike the police, I don't have to worry about stepping on anyone's toes."

Everyone nodded their agreement to that as they finished their desserts.

As they made ready to leave, every single one of the Daniels clan made a point of saying goodbye and showing their acceptance of both Caleb and Taryn. He was damn near choked up by the time they exited the restaurant and made it to the car.

The ride home was quiet, each caught up in their own thoughts.

"I need to do a little work on the computer before I turn in," Richard said, and headed to the office.

"I'm tired, I'm going to bed." Taryn yawned and headed to the master bedroom.

Caleb took the leftovers into the kitchen and set up the coffee pot to turn on in the morning, since they all had early starts for the next day. He double-checked the house to make sure everything was locked up, even though he knew it already was. He stopped at the door to the office. Richard had made himself at home at the desk, he was pleased to see.

He walked in and Richard looked up.

"Caleb."

"Ricky, you look tired," Caleb said.

Richard's smile was wry. "I am, believe me, I'll be done in a minute."

"Good." He leaned down and kissed Richard's cheek then left him to it.

When he got to the bedroom he could see that despite their nap, Taryn was sleepy. She usually propped up against the headboard to read but now she was already lying down, her eyes half closed as she read her paperback.

"Richard said he wouldn't be long," he told her as he stripped down to his boxers. Putting her book away, she waited until he had climbed in and was resting against the headboard so that she could snuggle against him.

"You were right," he told her. "That was scary." She sighed, melting into him, resting her head against his chest so that he could feel her warm breath against his skin.

"But being brave is about doing it even when it's scary." He felt the smile that curved her lips, even though he couldn't see it, as she echoed his earlier words.

"Brat. Well then, we were brave tonight. Or you were, since I wasn't smart enough to be scared until it was too late."

She burrowed in closer. "But you were scared in an immediate, 'they could really hate me and make my life miserable' way. I've got this whole rest of my life thing going on. I guess I need to figure that out."

"You think?"

Without looking, she reached up and bopped him on the head.

"Hey, violence is not the answer."

"Whatever."

Richard came back in, rubbing his eyes in fatigue. He watched them as he shucked his jeans. "Thanks for tonight. I hope it wasn't excruciating."

"You know it wasn't. Your family is too awesome to leave anyone uncomfortable in their presence for long," Taryn chided him.

"Well, you've proved a unique challenge to them for a long time."

"I wasn't uncomfortable with them. I just didn't want to be absorbed by them."

"And now?"

Groaning, she rose from her position on Caleb's chest so that she could see them both. "And now I see that they are a very important part of who you are, and since you are a very important part of who I am, I need to make peace with the fact that they are stuck with me and I am stuck with them."

Richard grimaced. "Is it that bad?"

"No, honey, you know it's not. I was just being neurotic. You have an awesome family and I'm lucky that you come as a package deal. I'm sorry I haven't realized that before now, I didn't mean to make things difficult for you."

"You didn't." He kissed her as he joined them on the bed. "I guess now, looking back on it, it's just one of the things that kept us as friends and lovers, but not partners. One out of many. We weren't ready. Obviously we needed an overbearing asshole to really pull the whole thing together."

Caleb growled and launched himself at Richard. Laughing, Richard dodged at the last second, ending up on his side instead of his back. Caleb still would have had the advantage had Taryn not joined Richard in pushing him to his back. He debated toppling them both versus letting them have their way but lost his train of thought as two hands, one small, one large, reached inside his boxers at the same time, clearly intent on the same goal.

Remaining still, he waited to see what they would do. Richard shoved his shoulder, encouraging him to lie back all the way.

"You're ours," Taryn said, her free hand pulling his shorts down.

"And we want to play," Richard added, giving him a squeeze.

He collapsed back and lifted his hips, deciding to let them have their way. At least for now.

Releasing Caleb's dick to Taryn's mercy, Richard moved up to kiss him, hard and demanding. Caleb's heart raced as the other man fisted his fingers through his hair while he attacked his mouth, in direct opposition to the sweet, tender torture Taryn was performing down below. Her hands were like silk on his rock-hard shaft as she peppered tiny kisses up his thighs, coming ever closer to his balls.

He tried to shout when hard fingers tweaked and pulled his nipples at the exact moment wet heat enveloped his aching balls, but the fierce kiss left little room for breathing let alone speaking.

When Taryn's sweet mouth moved up his shaft to the head, he couldn't hold back. Using his hands to tear Richard's mouth from his, he looked the other man in the eye. "I want to taste you." Richard's breath hitched and he scrambled up, knees to either side of Caleb's head.

Caleb braced one hand on Richard's hip and used the other to feed himself warm cock. He had to be careful not to bite down when Taryn's tongue teased his slit. Using his own tongue, he thoroughly wetted the cock he held captive, his hand at the base squeezing tightly. Richard's groan seemed to egg Taryn on and she began to fuck him with her mouth. He hummed his own appreciation and Richard couldn't keep from pumping himself into Caleb. Caleb let him, his hand on the man's hip keeping his pace in check as his own hips began to thrust.

Taryn used one hand to tease the skin behind his balls. Caleb groaned, the vibration proving too much for Richard who came with a shout. Caleb swallowed him down until he was empty then gently pushed him away and let his own orgasm wash through him with a shout. He heard Taryn's cry of release and rolled his head to watch her, eyes closed in pleasure as her hand dropped away from between her legs.

He very nearly didn't have the energy to sit up, but reminded himself that he was a tough guy, in excellent shape. He shoved Richard over and kissed him, loving the taste of Richard, double. Then he pushed the man up toward the pillows and turned toward his woman. She was almost asleep already, cracking her eyes open when he leaned over her. Pulling her fingers into his mouth, he cleaned her juices off before giving her a kiss.

"Good girl." He pushed her toward Richard then collapsed beside her, one arm over her head, playing with Richard's hair, the other over her waist, resting on Richard's hip.

THE NEXT MORNING, Taryn was already out of bed when Caleb woke up. He left Richard to sleep a little bit longer and took a shower.

When the door opened, he accepted a sleepy kiss and helped her shampoo her hair, but refrained from any activity that might make her late.

While Richard took his turn in the shower and Taryn worked in the other bathroom to dry her hair, Caleb made breakfast. It was nice to open the refrigerator and find so many choices. He didn't mind cooking but grocery shopping was another story. Taryn, however, seemed to prefer to do the shopping, load the fridge and stand back while others produced meals from the food she'd selected.

The system was working well for all of them, he decided as he sautéed some onions and mushrooms for omelets. When the others joined him at the table, he squelched the brief impulse to bring up topics heavier than breakfast and morning schedules. It was time for him to do what he had accused them of not doing, treat this relationship as if it were permanent. Until he could honestly say he was doing that, he had no room to call them on their own hesitant behaviors.

They finished breakfast and headed out the door. Caleb dropped Richard and Taryn off in front of the coffee shop then drove to work. He checked with all his people as well as the surveillance tapes and found nothing helpful. He was carefully observant of his people, alert to any looks of distaste or even irritation, but saw nothing. He put in some hours on one project then drove out to an office building on the edge of town for another. By the time he was finished it was late afternoon and he had skipped lunch. He squared his shoulders and entered *Roisin Dubh*, reminding himself that he was a badass, and while his brother's approval would be nice, it certainly wasn't necessary.

A quick look around found Sean behind the bar and no sign of Lisa. By the time he got to the bar his brother had a glass of soda waiting for him.

"Want some lunch? I have some of mom's meatloaf."

"That would be perfect, thanks." Taking the soda, he moved to a table and sat down. Sean joined him quickly with two plates of meatloaf. They ate in silence, rolling their eyes at the antics of some college students nearby playing with the juke box.

Finally pushing the plate away, Caleb eyed his brother. They hadn't talked sex in a very long time, not since his older brother had shoved a handful of condoms at him when he was thirteen and told him to always be smart.

"I'm thinking of moving into the house. The renters' lease is up next month."

"You said you had some guys at work who might want to rent it."

"They'll find another place."

Sean got up and came back with a glass of water.

"Like you've said all along, it's too much house for one person."

"Probably even too much house for two people, especially if they're sharing a bedroom."

Sean's lips quirked. "Yeah? How 'bout three people?"

"Probably they would need more space, whether they're sharing a room or not," Caleb answered carefully.

Nodding his head, Sean only said, "Probably." Then he lost his cool and gave his brother a pained look. "So, guys, huh?"

Caleb just shrugged. "In general, very rarely. Specifically, and with her, yeah. It works. It's right." Taking a long drink, he watched for a reaction but got only a small nod. "You knew?"

It was Sean's turn to shrug. "You weren't exactly hiding it."

"No. But I'd understand if you were...uncomfortable."

"Look, I won't lie and say I get it. Mostly I'd rather just not think about it in too much detail. But I hardly see what other people get up to in the bedroom as having anything to do with me."

Caleb nodded. "And if it goes beyond the bedroom?" He laughed at Sean's confused expression. "These people are important to me. Like family, I hope."

"Oh. Right. Well, I don't see why that would be a problem. I mean, if you like them that much, chances are we will, too." He cleared his throat. "Why don't you, you know, bring them to the pub for drinks and dinner. We can work our way up to dinner at the house."

"Actually, we met here."

Sean looked at him, goggle-eyed. Caleb barely kept from laughing. "Well, outside. They were a little bit too full of your spirits and needed a hand."

"Well, okay then. Shows they have good taste."

Caleb stood and picked up his plate and glass, leading the way back to the kitchen. He put the dishes in the sink and turned to his brother, pulling him in for a hug. "I'll call you, figure out a date. I have to warn you though, Richard's got a little bit of a crush on Lisa."

"Oh, well, see. Like I said, good taste."

"That's what I told him." He slapped his brother on the back and headed outside. Putting on his sunglasses, he took a careful look around. Nothing unusual caught his eye, nobody appeared to be focusing their attention on him. He drove to Richard's medical office on full alert. Parking on the street, he watched the busy afternoon traffic, both cars and pedestrians.

About to get out and go into the coffee shop, he paused when his phone rang. When he saw that it was Taryn he couldn't hold back his grin.

"Taryn."

"Caleb, hey. I was just, well, ummm..." She sighed and he could picture her rolling her eyes. "There's this guy in here, he was here before. He's not doing anything weird, but I can't help thinking he is. Weird, I mean. I'm sure it's nothing..."

"I was about to come in," he interrupted. "No worries, I'll just take a look, see if he hits my weird meter too."

"Okay. I just...feel strange, making snap judgments about people like this."

"You make snap judgments about people all the time, it's natural. The question is whether or not you do anything based on those judgments. I'll be right there."

After ending the call, he pressed the speed dial for Richard's office and got voice mail, as expected. He climbed out of the car and crossed the street.

"Hey, just checking to see if you've seen anything or anyone strange today. Call me when you have a chance."

He hung up the phone and put it in his pocket as he opened the door to Grounded. He breathed in the delicious aroma and enjoyed the warm, inviting atmosphere. He spotted Taryn behind the counter immediately and made his way to her without appearing to look around.

"Guy in the blue sweater, northeast corner?" he asked her after giving her a kiss.

She glared at him. "How in the hell am I supposed to know which direction is north? He's by the hallway to the restrooms. How did you know it was him just from walking in here?"

"Because he's weird."

He had to bite his cheek to keep from laughing out loud as she actually gaped at him. He kissed her again and dragged her to her office.

CHAPTER TWELVE

Taryn was bouncing between curious and irritated and validated. Obviously she had been at least a little bit right to think there was something strange about the man in her shop, or Caleb wouldn't have known exactly who she was talking about. *Right?*

She had debated calling him for an hour before finally deciding there was no downside to making the call, other than slight embarrassment. He had told them to tell him about anything that was strange or just gave them a weird feeling and there was no question that this guy did that. So she called. And here he was.

He pulled her into her office, closing the door behind them, then paused. "Is this okay? Do you have a few minutes?"

She rolled her eyes at his tardiness in asking but smiled in pleasure that he had asked at all. He assumed correctly that meant an approval and brought her with him until he was leaning his butt against her desk and she was standing between his legs.

"Hi. Miss me?" he asked.

"Desperately," she laughed, and kissed him. She had known she couldn't keep it light so she didn't even bother trying. She practically attacked him and giggled at his surprised "oomph". She ran her hands through his hair, easily one of her favorite pastimes these days, then smacked his arm when he tried to do the same.

Pulling away from her, he narrowed his eyes. She tried to keep from laughing at him but couldn't quite manage it. His arms fell away in disgust and he just stared at her incredulously as she continued to laugh.

"Baby," she tried, but had to stop as another round of laughter hit her, more from his expression than from the original moment.

He crossed his arms over his chest. Sucking in a huge breath to calm herself, Taryn attempted her most conciliatory expression.

"Caleb, if I run my fingers through your hair it looks like you finger-combed it. If you run your fingers through my hair it looks like we just fucked on the desk."

He considered this for a moment, then relented. "It's just a theory. Maybe we should put it to a test."

"Fine. But tonight, not now. Not at work."

"You're staying with us tonight?" he asked carefully.

Sighing, Taryn turned around and leaned back against him, smiling when his arms automatically came around to hold her tight. She leaned her head against his shoulder and closed her eyes.

"Yes, I'll stay tonight. Are we still at your house? Or Richard's?"

"We have all those leftovers from Mama's in my fridge. We need to eat those."

"Okay, your house it is." He squeezed her tight then let her go, spinning her around in his arms.

"Taryn."

"Caleb."

"I like you."

She searched his face and understood. Sometimes, liking was even harder than loving. She nodded. "I like you too, a whole lot."

He gave her a quick kiss then set her away from him. "No ravishing you in your office, I assume?"

"Well, not during work hours, anyway."

He gave her a put-upon sigh. "Well then, let's talk about the guy in the blue sweater, by the bathrooms. He's been in here before?"

"The only time I've seen him was on Monday. I can ask the others if they remember seeing him before."

"Hmm. Not yet. Let's go sit at a table, see what we see."

"Okay. If we get busy though, I won't be able to stay."

"No problem."

They went out and Caleb sat at a table while Taryn made him a drink and got herself a soda. When she joined him she sat next to him, rather than across from him, so that she could see the guy too. They had only been sitting for a minute when Richard walked in.

He dropped kisses on both of their cheeks then went to the counter to order drinks for himself and his coworkers. Taryn was pretty sure the weird guy's lips pursed in disapproval, but she was afraid to stare and get a good look. She and Caleb made light chatter until Richard came and sat down while the drinks were being made up.

"How did you get stuck with delivery-boy duty today?" she asked him with a smile.

"Petra cheated. When we were giving arguments why each of us couldn't be the one to leave for a few minutes, she mentioned that she was pretty sure she'd seen Caleb walk in a little while ago, and how often did I get to see both of you in the middle of a work day?"

"So the question is, did she really see me? Or was she just lucky?" Caleb asked.

Taryn and Richard both laughed.

"Oh, she saw you, no question," said Taryn. "That woman has eyes in the back of her head. She sees all and knows all. She should have been a spy. Nobody would suspect her of a thing."

Richard nodded along with Taryn's assessment of their friend. "It's a fantastic trait in an office manager, but a little bit intimidating and occasionally frightening, too."

"Interesting," Caleb mused. "Does she have a pretty good memory for faces?"

"The best," Richard confirmed. "And names. I make her go with me every year to the big charity ball so that she can tell me who everyone is that I'm supposed to know."

Taryn was beginning to catch on. "I'll call her and ask her to come over. If Richard goes back and asks her in person she'll assume he's getting back at her for making him do the coffee run. It's sort of an ongoing battle at the office."

Richard looked confused and Caleb began to explain while Taryn used her cell phone to call Petra.

"Hey, it's Taryn. I have a huge favor. I know it's a pain, but do you think you could come over here? I swear, it's nothing to do with the coffee run and I only need you for about two minutes."

"It's important?" Petra asked.

"It is, or I swear I wouldn't call like this in the middle of the day. And seriously, I doubt it will even take the full two minutes."

"I'll be right there, but you have to send Richard back, ASAP. Mrs. Morgenstern is here and she says she's having a heart attack. You know she only listens to Richard or me."

"Will do, thanks."

"She's on her way, but you have to get back to the office. Mrs. Morgenstern is having a heart attack."

When Caleb's whole body went on alert she put her hand on his arm to reassure him. "She does this every couple of weeks, it's not a problem. She just wants to be looked at and hooked up to the machines. But Richard is always thorough, just in case."

Richard had retrieved the finished coffees while she explained to Caleb and he again kissed their cheeks before heading for the door, which Petra was holding open for him. She took her drink from the tray he was holding and joined Caleb and Taryn at their table. Caleb stood and pulled a chair out for her so that she would not have her back to the guy they were checking out. Petra gave him a startled but pleased look and took the seat.

"Hey, kids, what's up?"

Taryn leaned in and kept her voice low.

"We need to know if you recognize someone in here, but we don't want it to be obvious that you're looking."

Petra immediately became serious. "This has something to do with the vandalism?"

"Possibly. We don't really have anything to go on, we just wondered if you had any idea who the guy in the blue sweater by the bathrooms is," Caleb explained.

Leaning in even closer, Taryn whispered, "Northeast corner." She only smiled when Caleb burst out laughing. Petra at least looked like she was trying not to laugh. Taryn's abysmal sense of direction was well known.

Petra stood. "I'll just use the restroom and be right back."

Caleb waited until she had disappeared down the hallway before leaning in to kiss Taryn on the nose. She just smiled at him.

Petra reappeared quickly and they knew immediately that she had recognized the man. Her expression managed to convey both worry and sympathy. Caleb stood and Taryn realized he thought they shouldn't have this conversation in the shop. She stood too and they all walked out and headed across the street.

"I've only seen him once, at Matt Jones' funeral, a few weeks ago. That's Paul Jones, his father." Petra blurted this out in one breath, clearly concerned.

"Uh-oh," Taryn said.

"Shit," Caleb agreed. "I'm going to have one of my guys come down and keep an eye on him while I go back to the office and do some checking. If this pans out to anything, I might be pretty late tonight. This is going to seriously suck for Ricky."

"I know. I'll switch closing so I can go home with him. Call when you have an update and don't stay too late." She gave him a kiss goodbye then went with Petra to tell Richard the bad news."

Driving home after work, both she and Richard were on edge, as if the man was going to ram them in the car, despite their knowing Caleb had someone watching the guy.

Richard looked miserable and Taryn cursed to herself. It had been hard enough on him when Matt had been killed. She was certainly sympathetic to the boy's parents but none of what had happened had anything to do with Richard. He dragged his feet from the car to the house, looking morose. She pushed him into the living room and onto the couch.

Sitting next to him, she brushed his hair from his forehead and ran her other hand over his chest soothingly. "Baby, you know this has nothing to do with you. If Paul Jones is the guy who vandalized your car and house, he's obviously gone off the deep end. It's sad, yes, but not your fault. Just like what happened to Matt wasn't your fault."

"Jeez, Tare, I didn't even recognize the poor guy."

"Richard, you didn't even meet him! You saw the back of his head at the funeral service—that's about it."

He sighed and leaned his head back against the couch. Taryn had been planning on raiding the fridge for Mama's leftovers but decided that drastic cooking measures were called for to get Richard's mind off deranged fathers. She hopped up off the couch.

"Come on, let's make dinner."

"I think Caleb wanted us to eat up the leftovers."

"Too bad. Let's make him something extra yummy for having to work late." She grabbed his hand and pulled with all her weight so that he was forced not only to stand but catch her when the action nearly sent her to the ground. He didn't smile but he did follow her instructions to go change clothes. Taryn went into the kitchen and made her own special preparation.

The look on Richard's face when he walked in made being a bit uncomfortable totally worth it. She had taken off her jeans and t-shirt and was wearing only her bra, panties and an oversized apron that hung very low on her chest.

He came to her and squeezed her tight. "I'm so glad you're a part of my life."

"Yeah, whatever. What are you going to make me for dinner? I think it should involve dessert. Preferably, something with chocolate."

He swatted her on the butt. "Let's see what we have."

They opted to make chicken picatta for dinner and strawberry shortcake with chocolate sauce for dessert, since Caleb actually had fresh strawberries in the fridge.

"Do you ever wonder if Caleb appreciates the fact that he now has a well-stocked kitchen?" Richard mused, pulling out the cutting board.

"Well, if he's anything like me, mostly he appreciates that he has a well-stuffed chef." Taryn started doing what she always did when cooking with Richard. Put together the salad then sat on the counter to entertain him. She had turned the radio on, deciding it was a rock kind of night, and stopped on a station known for its eclectic mix. Aerosmith was playing and she turned it up.

"I can't believe you just said that. You want to pound the chicken breasts?"

Abandoning the tomato she was chopping, Taryn bopped her way over to where Richard had put a chicken breast into a large Ziploc bag for her. She took the offered mallet and enjoyed pounding the breast until Richard made her stop and switch to the next piece.

"I'm sorry that as your best friend I never realized that you had a problem with the whole family thing. I hope I never made you feel too uncomfortable with mine."

She paused mid-swing to look at him. "It wasn't like that, I swear. They're great, I didn't mind being near them. I just didn't want to be...well, part of them, I guess. I don't know, it's not like I was thinking, 'hey, I really like Richard but I don't want to be part of a family'. It was more unconscious, you know?"

"I still should have noticed."

Resuming her strikes, Taryn shook her head. "Hell, Rick, I barely noticed. I should be apologizing to you, not the other way around."

"Mmm-hmm, because it's all about you."

She stuck her tongue out at him.

They worked in silence for a few minutes. Richard was shuffling around, doing things with flour that she didn't pay much attention to. She switched to the last chicken breast then moved back to the tomatoes, humming along with Weezer on the radio.

The sizzling sounds of meat hitting the pan brought her to him. He angled so that she could lean in and smell the delicious scents, knowing that was one of her favorite parts of "helping" him cook. She moved back a bit so he had room to do his thing, but rested against his side.

"A lot has changed in four weeks. For both of us. For all of us, actually," he said, using the tongs to peek at the underside of the chicken.

"I wonder what he was like, as a single guy."

Richard cocked his head in thought. "That's a good question. I don't get the feeling he went out a lot, partying at least. Probably he spent a little more time at his brother's house. It's kind of weird that we never met him at the bar. I mean, we didn't go all the time, but we must have been three or four times this year."

"Maybe we weren't ready for him."

"Maybe not. I'm not sure we were ready for him four weeks ago." Richard turned the meat.

"Good point," she answered as he casually put his free arm around her before letting that hand roam her mostly naked backside. She let him play for a moment before spinning away, dancing to the Rolling Stones.

"Can't let dinner burn," she teased him.

She returned to the salad, putting the avocado pieces she had been cutting into the large bowl then tossing everything together. When she turned back he had put the chicken on a plate and was once again working with the pan. She went to set the table and called Caleb to make sure he would be home soon. He assured her that he was on his way.

Taryn hopped up on the counter to watch Richard finish the meal. He was so sexy in the kitchen, masterful but relaxed, always enjoying himself. She had seen him in doctor mode a couple of times, and while that had a high hotness factor as well, it was different. In that situation he was supremely focused on the patient, his whole being centered on what he was seeing, hearing, learning. When he cooked, it was more instinctual and much more relaxed.

"Caleb said he would be here soon, you can go ahead and plate his up, too," she told him as he turned the flame off.

"I'm glad. I hate the idea of him working late to deal with this."

"I think he enjoys it. Just like you enjoy cooking for us."

"Yeah, yeah."

CHAPTER THIRTEEN

They worked together to get everything on the table. When it was ready, Richard reached over and switched the stereo from FM to CD. Ella Fitzgerald came on and he pulled Taryn into his arms.

Neither of them were really dancers but they could sway with the best of them. Besides, it was hard to focus on what moves to make when his arms were full of nearly naked woman. His woman. When he had walked into the kitchen and seen her like that, his heart had skipped a beat. Not only at the sexy package she presented, but knowing that she was doing it to distract him and to lift his spirits. It had certainly worked.

He let one hand drift to her ass and the other played with the hair at the nape of her neck. She leaned into him, so trusting, and he vowed not to let his insecurities damage what he had. Because they were right, he had both of them, damn it, and he wasn't going to let either one of them go.

He heard the front door open and waited until he was sure Caleb could see them before spinning around so that he was facing the hallway and Taryn's backside was presented to the other man.

Taryn burrowed her face into his shoulder but he could feel her smile.

"Well. That's a lovely sight. Delicious dinner waiting on the table for a man when he gets home from a hard day at work."

They all laughed and Taryn turned in his arms. Caleb came to them and kissed first Richard, then Taryn. They stayed that way, not moving, for a whole minute before Caleb cleared his throat.

"Let's eat. Fast."

Smiling, Richard pushed Taryn toward the table.

Richard waited until they had enjoyed at least a few bites. "So?"

Caleb frowned. "So, it looks...interesting. Paul and Elsie divorced five years ago. I didn't contact her, I'd rather not until we're more sure of what's going on. She's got enough to deal with right now. I called his office and they haven't heard from him since he called and said his son was in the hospital."

"They told you that?" Taryn asked in surprise.

"Well. It's not like I just called up and asked for him. I said I was from the funeral parlor."

"Oh, right. Okay."

"My guy, Tom, followed him to a motel on the edge of town. He'll keep an eye out for any nocturnal activities. If he's our guy, I doubt it will take long for him to try to make another move, which means we'll have him. The only thing we need to do is watch him."

"It's so sad," Taryn sighed. "But I don't understand what his problem with Richard could be. Do you think it's us? Doesn't he have enough on his plate to deal with right now than to spend time worrying about what we're up to?"

Caleb nodded. "It is sad, but this kind of stress can do crazy things to a person. Maybe he's had some sort of mental meltdown. I mean, let's face it, both of us thought he was putting out a strange vibe, and really, he was just sitting there. It's entirely possible that he's not our guy and he's just coming across as so strange because of what he's going through. I'm sure there's some guilt given the fact that he doesn't live here. It sounded like he didn't spend a lot of time visiting his son."

Richard stood and began to clear the plates. "I have sympathy for the guy, but Taryn's right. I don't understand how he could fixate on me. I wasn't even working on Matt at the ER. I guess it would be different if Matt had been sick and his father thought I didn't catch it early enough, or do a proper job of treatment or something. But he was hit by a drunk driver! Why isn't he stalking that man?"

Caleb stilled, his eyes hard on Richard's. "I never actually asked what had happened. A car accident? They know who the driver was?"

Richard nodded. "Yes, it was some account exec from an advertising firm. Three DUI's on his record and he had a suspended license."

"Okay, I read about that in the paper but didn't put it together. I need to make some phone calls." Caleb stood up.

"Wait," Taryn rushed. "There's dessert."

Caleb eyed her up and down, causing Taryn to blush and Richard's heart rate to speed up.

"No! I mean, there's really dessert. Strawberry shortcake, with chocolate sauce." She rolled her eyes at both of them.

"Sounds almost perfect. Let me make one phone call, I'll be right back."

Richard let Taryn grab more dishes from the table before following her into the kitchen, so that he could watch her mostly naked body. He about ran into her when she stopped to look back at him. She quirked an eyebrow and he just grinned. Shaking her head, she began loading the dishwasher. After pulling out the dessert items, he whipped the cream and heated the chocolate sauce.

They hadn't even finished setting out the strawberries and sauce when Caleb returned. He dipped the spoon into the chocolate, letting the sweet sauce dribble back into the bowl. "Hmm. This looks...promising."

Richard cut portions of the cake for each of them and added strawberries. They worked around each other until they all had the amount of cream and sauce they wanted. Somehow, though none of them spoke or touched, eating became foreplay. Richard alternated between watching Taryn's tiny tongue dart out to catch licks of cream to Caleb's licking his fingers clean of the chocolate sauce. He might have had trouble remembering to eat his own if it hadn't been so tasty.

They were nearly done when Caleb's cell phone rang.

"I'm sorry, I have to get this." He rose from the table and left the room.

Sighing, Richard made to gather the plates but Taryn stopped him.

"I'll get these, why don't you go into the living room, he probably won't be long. I'm sure we won't have any trouble getting him back on track."

He kissed her fingers. "Thanks, sweetie."

In the living room, he collapsed on the overstuffed couch he never would have picked for its style, though he couldn't deny its comfort. Closing his eyes, he imagined what a living room decorated for the three of them would be like. While he was very style conscious, he was also a believer in making a room fit its inhabitants. That could be a challenge sometimes, depending on current styles, which only made things more fun.

Smiling to himself as he imagined Taryn's reaction to the idea that decorating was fun, he populated a large but imaginary room in a way that would suit their three distinct personalities. It had to be a made-up room, he mused, as none of their current houses would work for all three of them. Best if they all started somewhere new together.

As if it were already decided. Hell, just yesterday he had been convinced they were going to dump him and get married, and now he was ready to make a home with them.

Caleb came in holding his car keys, with Taryn just behind him. He sat down on the edge of the coffee table, his look very serious. "The call was the answer I was waiting for, but also an emergency with one of my clients. I have to go deal with that." He shook his head. "The timing sucks, because the answer to my question wasn't good." Taking a deep breath, he reached a hand out to Richard.

"The bastard who hit Matt Jones, Louis Arnold, is dead. He was knifed in the county lockup last week."

Richard wasn't sure if he should feel happy or sad, pity or relief. Mostly he just felt numb. "You think Mr. Jones arranged it somehow."

"It's a possibility I think we should raise with your sister. Laura can get the info to the right people. They may even be looking for him, to ask him some questions. He would be an obvious suspect, but they might not know where he is."

"He wasn't exactly hiding at my shop," Taryn pointed out.

"True, but I doubt he guessed anybody would recognize him. At any rate, it can't hurt to give the cops a heads-up. I've sent a second operative to stay with him, make sure we don't lose him. I should be back in a few hours. I'm hoping you guys will stay inside."

Richard laughed at Caleb's obvious attempt to not tell them what to do and piss Taryn off again. "I seriously doubt we'll have any desire to leave the house before morning, but if we do, we'll call you."

Caleb stood and so did Richard and Taryn.

"What you're doing tonight, it's not dangerous is it?" Taryn asked.

"Not at all. Just corporate hand holding." He kissed them both goodbye and Richard set the alarm behind him.

They returned to the living room and he flopped down onto the large chair, pulling Taryn down onto his lap. She snuggled in close, resting one hand above his shirt collar, her thumb tracing his collarbone. The sweet smell of her warm skin surrounded him and he drew in a deep lungful.

"Sweetie, this apron's not quite soft enough for your skin. It's probably irritating. Why don't I help you take it off?"

A smirk was her first response. Turning to present the tie at the back of her neck was her second. The ties were quickly undone and he unclasped her bra while it was handy. His hands caressed her shoulders as lightly as he could manage, pushing the bra straps down and causing goose bumps to pebble on her skin.

She was a vision, wearing only her panties while seated on his jeans-covered lap. He reached a hand out and used one finger to trace her cheekbones, her chin, her nose. She narrowed her eyes at him but he ignored that and let his eyes show her what he was feeling. Her teasing expression fell away and she closed her eyes, just long enough for him to get nervous. When they opened, they were shiny with unshed tears and his heart skipped a beat. Already beautiful, the love and vulnerability so clear on her face transformed her into extraordinary.

"Sometimes, when we're walking down the street together, you'll catch a man's eye. You're completely oblivious but I'll watch him turn to take a second look, watch his eyes rake you up and down, watch his pants bulge. Watch his irritation as he realizes you're with me. I think it's the only time I ever feel arrogant. That this beautiful woman is with me, and they're just out of luck."

She blinked and one of the tears fell. He leaned in and traced its path with his tongue, ending at the corner of her mouth. She opened her mouth to respond but he stopped her with a kiss. He explored her in a way he hadn't done in months, maybe even longer. He explored her like he didn't already know how wonderful she tasted, the fascinating textures that she was made of. After a time he pulled back and rested his forehead against hers.

At some point his hands had found her breasts and they squeezed gently, caressing the round globes but neglecting the tight points until she whispered, so softly, "Please."

He took both nipples between thumbs and forefingers and pulled, giving a sharp pinch. She cried out and launched into her own action. Her hands tore at his t-shirt, trying to get it over his head despite the fact that he was now lowering his head to one nipple and sucking it in, hard. She gave up on his t-shirt with a cry, her fingers going to work on his belt instead. She froze when he switched to her other peak, then resumed with a frantic groan.

"Ricky." Her desperation made him soar.

"Taryn." He whispered it, a benediction.

When she jerked his fly open and reached inside he was so thankful he had chosen to go commando tonight. He'd had a vague thought about checking out Caleb's reaction but now all he could think was *thankyouthankyouthankyou.*

He barely had the presence of mind to let her go long enough to reach into the drawer in the table between the chair and the sofa and hand her a condom, before returning his hands to their treasures. He pushed her breasts together and tongued the peaks simultaneously. Her delicate hands fumbled to pull him out of his jeans and put the condom on. He helped her rise up and position her legs to either side of his, then stared into her eyes as she lowered, sliding home.

Aaaahhhh. He couldn't think, couldn't plan, could only revel in the glorious sensation of hot, wet Taryn gripping him so tightly. Bracing his elbows against the chair arms, he held her waist and pulled her up while easing back. They watched each other's eyes as he slowly brought her back down, hips rising to meet her.

"Taryn." He tried to tell her everything, tell her how much she meant to him, how much he loved her, but all that he could manage was her name.

"Richard." It started out a whisper but ended on a gasp as he thrust into her again.

Losing the ability to pace himself, Richard urged her to ride him hard, and she did. He took one hand from her hip and sifted through her curls to find her clit. She jerked and leaned over to brace her hands against his shoulders. He wanted to see her come, wanted to watch the pleasure overtake her while he could still pay attention. He pinched the small bundle of nerves then massaged it.

Her head fell back, her mouth open on a silent scream as her hips stilled, her inner muscles clenching and unclenching him in climax. It was almost impossible but he held back, determined to watch her to the end. Her eyes were closed, her breathing harsh and she had never looked more beautiful. Finally she opened her eyes and looked at him, her smile supremely satisfied before it turned wicked. She clenched her muscles tightly, everywhere, thighs, arms, pussy, and ground herself against him. The surge overtook him in a heartbeat, his balls emptying out in a rush that seemed to last forever.

Sighing, she draped herself over him and went boneless. He clutched her close and fell asleep.

CHAPTER FOURTEEN

Caleb saw that the lights were still on when he got home, so he wasn't particularly quiet coming into the house. He assumed they were still talking in the living room or watching television. Despite the noise he had made, they were fast asleep when he spotted them on the large chair in the living room. Richard appeared to still be dressed but Taryn had lost her apron and underwear. She was draped over him, his arms tight around her.

He watched them for a few minutes. They were part of his life now and he had never been happier, despite the craziness of the last couple days. He wanted to ask them to move in with him, to his parents' old house, but he wasn't sure they were ready and didn't want to scare them. Used to being confident, his uncertainty was maddening. They were obviously tired and he debated waking them up only long enough to shuffle them off to bed versus taking the time and pleasure to remind them that they belonged to him now, just as much as he belonged to them.

"Taryn. Ricky."

Taryn stirred, stretching her naked body against Richard as she yawned and blinked up at Caleb. Oh yeah, there was no need to struggle with the decision, it was clearly time to remind them that in one thing, at least, he was in charge.

"Taryn. Stand up." His voice was even and firm. She responded to it instantly, her breath picking up, her nipples beading. She carefully got out of Richard's lap and stood next to the chair, her eyes glued to him.

"Richard." He scanned the other man's face, relieved to see that much of the exhaustion he'd seen at dinner was gone. Now Richard looked sleepy but ready. "Stand up."

Complying, Richard stood next to Taryn. He was fully dressed except for his dick hanging out of his pants. Caleb saw a used condom in a Kleenex on the table by the chair. He ran through a nearly endless list of possibilities on what he wanted to do next. He considered using the cuffs but decided that for tonight he wanted them following directions without the benefit of restraints.

"Ricky, take off your clothes." Taryn jerked as if she was going to help him but her hands stayed at her sides as Richard hurriedly undressed. Caleb took his time undressing, not matching the other man's pace. They waited, silently, while he finished.

"Richard, will you get the down comforter from the linen closet? It's on the top shelf, and get one of the blankets, too. Taryn, help me slide the couch back a bit."

When he had the comforter, Caleb spread it over the wide coffee table, doubling the comforter up, then covering it with the soft blanket. It was a wood coffee table, with drawers underneath, very solid, about knee high. With the couch pushed back he could easily walk around it.

"Taryn, get on the table, on your knees." Her eyes darted to his, then Richard's, as she made her way to the table and slowly climbed on. She knelt back on her heels but he shook his head at her and she rose up to her full kneeling height.

"Richard, on your knees, too, behind her. I want your legs bracketing hers." Richard did as he was told, holding Taryn's shoulders carefully while he balanced himself as Caleb wanted him. "Get in tight, I want you almost touching her back." His voice was getting rough but he fought to keep it even. Taryn and Richard were both breathing harder, unsure of what he was going to do.

"Now, don't move unless I tell you to," he reminded them.

Centered as they were, there were only a couple of inches of table left on either side of them. Caleb was able to stand next to them, and touch them easily. He brought his left hand up Richard's thigh, over his buttock, the dip of his waist. He spread his hand wide to fully appreciate the muscles of the back, smoothing his hand up the shoulder blade, sliding in slightly until he could cup the nape of his neck. He squeezed gently and Richard's eyes closed.

He used his right hand to follow a similar path, up Taryn's thigh, tickling through the crease where thigh meets hip, over the slightly rounded stomach, hand spreading wide to cup the breast for only a second before sliding over the begging nipple and farther up to curve along her shoulder and in, until he was cupping her neck, his thumb caressing her jaw, his fingers loosely about her throat.

Both of them trembled under his hold, ever so slightly, but they remained still. "Mine." Taryn swallowed hard under his hand. He ran his fingers through her hair, twisting the mass into a rope he draped over her shoulder so that he could see both of their faces.

Nipping Taryn's shoulder blade, he nibbled his way up to her earlobe. She started to turn her head, to meet him, but he stopped her with a hand on her chin and she resumed her position. He let the hand fall away as he kissed and licked and nipped his way around her chin to the corner of her mouth. "Don't move," he reminded her, the barest of whispers just above her lips. She made a tiny sound of distress, probably without even noticing it. He licked her lips, already parted for her panting breaths, but she stayed still. He breathed her in, nuzzled her nose with his own while he brought his right hand to the juncture of her thighs.

He knew she could feel the heat of his hand, so close but not actually touching. He swore he could feel her own heat and moisture, begging for him to touch her. With his mouth, he worked his way back to ear and sucked the earlobe in hard while he tested her readiness. She was wet and getting wetter. He cupped her gently at first, then firmly, pleased when she resisted rocking into his hold.

"Mine," he whispered again, directly into her ear. "Tell me."

"Yes, Caleb. Yours."

He removed his hand slowly and turned to Richard. "You're being so good, both of you. Is it hard, Rick? What would you do now, if you could?"

"Sli-slide into her."

"Is that right?" Caleb asked, licking Richard's shoulder. "But you're not going to, are you?"

Richard swallowed. "No, Caleb."

Caleb gave him a small bite then soothed the spot with kisses. He worked his way down to Richard's nipple and took it between his fingers, tweaking it while he sucked gently on the hollow of Richard's throat, then teased his lips as he had done Taryn's. He pulled the full lower lip between his teeth, letting it go with a pop.

Resting his forehead against Richard's temple, he eased his hand down between their bodies to find the hard arousal waiting for him. The cock pulsed hot in his hand, jerking slightly at his touch. He rubbed the tip against Taryn's backside, the pre-cum sliding along where their skin made contact. Richard gasped and he squeezed in warning.

"Mine," he whispered again. Richard shuddered but said nothing. Caleb leaned in so that Richard could feel the smile against his cheek, feel the words against his jaw. "Tell me."

"Yes, Caleb, yours."

Letting go, Caleb walked around the table, using just one finger to trail along their bodies. He traced nipples and biceps, ears and elbows, using only the one finger as he circled them. They were beautiful. They were his. Stopping at their side, he once again captured Richard's cock and cupped Taryn's pussy.

"You'll move when I tell you to move."

"Yes, Caleb," they both answered.

"You'll stop when I tell you to stop."

"Yes, Caleb."

He stepped away and pulled a condom from the small table drawer. He held it out to Richard. "Put it on." While Richard did so he moved to the overstuffed chair and sat down. It was perfectly positioned so that he could see them both, see where they came together, or would, in a minute. When Richard had returned his hands to his side, Caleb spoke.

"Taryn, I want your face flat on your hands, looking at me." She lowered herself down, elbows bent to the side, hips high in the air.

"Richard, she's ready for you. Fill her up." Richard glanced at him in slight panic. "You can use your hands."

With one hand on her hip, he used the other to guide himself in, one long, slow movement. Taryn sighed and Richard let out the breath he had been holding.

"Now stop." Though they hadn't actually been moving at that point, they both somehow stilled further, frozen. "Look at me, Richard."

Chocolate-brown eyes turned to him, burning with need. Caleb let them both see his desire for them, his appreciation for what he was seeing. He slowly stroked his own shaft while his eyes roamed the pair. They clearly strained to remain still, melded from knee to groin, Richard's olive hands steady on Taryn's pale hips.

He increased his pressure, then his pace, imagining Taryn's wet pussy holding him tight, imagining Richard's tongue working him like a popsicle.

"From the moment I saw you, I wanted you both. Give him a squeeze, Taryn, one good one. I wanted you both because you looked so good together, and then I talked to you." Sweat dripped down Richard's temple, his hand slippery on Taryn's slick hip. They were both breathing faster, eyes becoming desperate the more he spoke.

"The more I got to know you, the more sure I was that you were mine. The more time we spent together, the harder it was to imagine my future without you both." His hand picked up speed once more and his speech became a little rougher.

"I know that if you tell me that you can't be with me, I'll have to let you go, but you would take a part of me with you. I don't think I told you before, but I've never said 'I love you' to any other lover. Ever." He paused for a couple of beats. "Richard, in and out, just once, nice and slow."

Groaning, Richard did as he was told. Taryn's eyes squeezed shut, but only for a second, opening again before he could tell her.

"I want to go to sleep to the sound of your breathing every night and wake up in the tangle of your arms and legs every morning." He squeezed just under the head tightly before continuing. He pumped hard now, their eyes locked to his hand on his dick, his hips meeting his own thrusts. He could see Taryn's juices running down both of their thighs.

He came, hard and fast, splashing his release onto his stomach. "Don't move, either of you." He could see the desperation on their faces, knew it was time, knew they were barely holding on. "Come, now."

Without any further movement, they both shouted as they came. Richard fell over Taryn, elbows locked to hold himself off her. Caleb stood and knelt beside them. He kissed Richard, then Taryn. "Thank you. That was beautiful."

He helped Richard up off the table while Taryn let her legs fold underneath her. Richard hobbled a bit but managed most of his weight as Caleb led him to the bathroom, then the bed. Returning to the living room, he scooped Taryn up and brought her to Richard's side. He left them only long enough to turn off all the lights and double-check the security alarm, then he climbed onto the bed and snuggled in tight before falling asleep.

THE PHONE RANG much too early and Caleb knew it couldn't be good news. Richard was immediately awake, and being closest to the phone, he answered before the second ring. Despite his foreboding, Caleb nearly laughed when, after barking hello, Richard suddenly realized it wasn't his own phone he was holding. He grimaced a sheepish apology to Caleb and cleared his throat. "Yeah, he's right here." He handed the phone over and Caleb smiled his reassurance.

"Yes."

"It's Diana. The subject left his motel room a few minutes ago. I think he's headed to your house. At least that's the direction he's going right now."

Caleb stood up and motioned to the others to get up as well. "How far away are you?"

"If he goes straight to your house, about seven to ten minutes."

With the phone tucked between his shoulder and his ear, he pulled on his jeans. "I'm going to call the police, ask them to send a patrol this way." He hung up and pulled on a t-shirt. The worried expression on Richard's face reminded him to keep his cool.

"Paul Jones left the motel a few minutes ago and my operatives think he might be headed this way. I just want us dressed and prepared, that's all. I think it's better if the police handle it. That way, even if he doesn't start anything, they can just ask him to move on." He paused to dial the phone. "If he does try something, then they can witness it and deal with it rather then get into a he said/she said situation. Even with witnesses, you shouldn't have to defend your actions. We'll stay inside, see what happens."

Richard picked up his cell phone. "I'll call Laura, too, see if she's on duty."

They made their respective calls, then hung up.

"They're sending a car," Caleb said.

"Laura's off duty, but is going to come by anyway." Richard studied Caleb's face. "You're staying inside with us because you know we won't stay if you don't. But you'd rather go out there yourself."

"Shit yeah. But it's not the smart plan for me either. Maybe in my younger days, I would have anyway, but this is your reputation at stake here, I'll take smart over action, no matter how fun it might be."

Nodding his head, Richard finished getting dressed. Taryn gave him a kiss on the cheek and headed down the hall. Knowing her, she was probably putting on coffee. That worked out well, since he had already determined the kitchen was the safest place to put them until he knew what was happening.

Richard paced while Taryn pulled out mugs, sugar and cream.

Caleb tried to reassure him. "It's going to be fine. This is why we had a team on him, so there wouldn't be any surprises."

Richard just nodded and Taryn sat down, then jumped when the phone rang.

"Yes," Caleb answered.

"It's Diana, he's still headed your way. I would say there's little doubt."

"Fine, hang back, I don't want him getting nervous. There will be a patrol car here in a couple of minutes. They know you're following so they shouldn't bother you." He hung up and turned off the light in the kitchen. He'd left a light on in the bedroom so they had enough spilling down the hall to see, but wouldn't themselves be visible through the windows.

"He's almost here. Stay in the kitchen and I'll take a look, see what's going on."

Taryn actually laughed at him and Richard just shook his head.

They started out of the kitchen but he stepped in front of them. "Richard. Taryn. Let me do this. Please." He wished he could just order them but that didn't seem to be working so well. "This is what I do."

"Caleb, he spray painted my house, but there's no reason to think we're in danger watching out a window."

"He also knifed your tires and might be responsible for the death of his son's killer." Aggravated, he ran his hand through his hair and sighed. "How about if you stand just inside the living room. You can still see out when I open the curtain a bit, but you can be back in the kitchen in one step."

"Sure," Taryn agreed, "if you stay with us. Or give us a good reason why it's more dangerous for us than it is for you."

"Because I know when to duck." He raised his hands against further protests. "Fine, I'll stay back here with you." Clearly it was the only way he was going to be able to make sure they stayed out of trouble.

They both nodded and he went to the curtain, peeking out to make sure there was no activity on the street, then opening it just enough that they could see from the back of the room.

They stood in silence for a couple of minutes before a pair of headlights turned the corner at the far end of the street. The car slowed then stopped in front of the house. The headlights turned off and nothing else happened. The nearest street light was close enough that they could just barely make out someone sitting in the driver's seat, but nothing more.

The phone rang and this time it was Richard who jumped. He laughed ruefully at himself while Caleb answered.

"Yes."

"We're just around the corner, but we have a good visual. The patrol car is just about to pass us."

"Thanks." Hanging up, he relayed the information to the others as they all watched another set of headlights turn the corner. The patrol car approached the parked car and stopped just behind it. Two uniformed officers got out and made their way up either side of the car. The patrolman on the driver's side directed his flashlight at the driver.

In an instant both officers pulled their guns. Caleb opened his mouth to order Taryn and Richard back into the kitchen then shut it. They would never listen to him if he kept telling them to do things that weren't yet necessary. He had to bite his tongue but he kept silent.

"Put your hands on the wheel." They could just make out the words from the street. "On the wheel!" The officer on the driver's side shouted while the other cop tried the passenger side door and opened it. He reached in and came out holding a gun.

The first officer opened the driver's door. "Out of the car and on the ground, now!"

The man stumbled out of the car and fell to the pavement, sobbing. The officers quickly had him handcuffed and in the backseat of their car. One of them stayed with the car while the other approached the house. Taryn and Richard both looked shaken but they all moved toward the door. As he opened it, Caleb saw Laura drive up.

"We might as well wait for Officer Daniels. She'll want to hear this, too," Caleb said, shaking hands with the man who introduced himself as Officer Morales.

"There's coffee if you'd like to come in," Taryn offered, her voice unsteady.

She had a cup ready for Laura as the woman walked in, taking it with a grateful sigh.

"So what happened?" she asked, directing her question to Officer Morales.

"We approached the subject sitting in his car. When we got close enough, we saw he was holding a revolver. He didn't seem to be aware of our approach until I called out to him. He was fixated on this house. Officer Tucker was able to secure the gun and the subject was handcuffed. We searched the subject and he had no other weapons and no identification, let alone a gun permit. He was unresponsive when questioned, other than incoherent babbling. Officer Tucker is searching the car."

"I'd like to see if these guys recognize him." Laura gestured to the group and Officer Morales nodded, grabbing a fresh cup of coffee for his partner then leading the way outside.

Officer Tucker took the offered mug. "There was a vandalism incident? With spray paint?" he asked.

"That's right, at my house," Richard confirmed.

"Well, there is spray paint in the trunk. Red."

They moved closer to the squad car. Caleb nodded. "That's the man we saw at Taryn's coffee shop yesterday, who was identified to us as Paul Jones."

"So, that's it then, right? He's the guy?" Richard asked. "I just don't get it. I didn't do anything to him."

"Probably he's the guy," Laura said. "Definitely, he's going to jail. They'll take him down to the station, see if they can get anything out of him." She turned to Officer Morales. "You'll want to let Detective O'Reilly know. He's looking for Paul Jones for questioning about a murder case."

Morales nodded and moved off, pulling out his radio.

"Well," Taryn pointed out. "That was briefly frightening but mostly anticlimactic."

"That's the way we like it." Caleb gestured them back into the house. He watched them closely. Richard seemed sad and Taryn a little shaky. She really had underestimated the danger and he was glad to see she was finally realizing how serious the situation had been.

CHAPTER FIFTEEN

"I'm going to take a shower," Taryn announced as soon as they walked back into the house. "I might as well go into the shop early."

She didn't wait for a response. She showered and dressed in record time, refusing to slow down enough to let her brain work. She didn't want to think about what had just happened. Or what could have just happened.

Moving quickly, she gathered her purse from the living room and stuck her head into the kitchen where Caleb and Richard were offering more coffee to the officers.

"Off to work, see you later." She was out the door before they had a chance to respond, as long as she didn't take Caleb's eyes narrowing dangerously at her or Richard's look of surprise as a response.

She had to enter the code on the alarm twice to get it right. Finally, she was able to open the door to the coffee shop. She shut it behind her and went straight to her office, moving quickly. The door closed with a soft click and she leaned against it. Space, her space. She had been spending too many nights at Caleb's house, she needed some time to herself.

Dropping her purse on her desk, she sat heavily in the chair, angrily pushing the power button on her computer monitor. Remembering the looks on Caleb and Richard's faces as she'd left, she scowled. They had to understand that she wasn't used to spending 24/7 with other people, even people she loved. It was perfectly normal to want some space and time to herself, right?

They should respect her right to privacy, damn it. The phone rang and her irritation intensified, knowing it was one of them. She snatched it up.

"What?" she asked, barely managing to keep from shouting.

"Taryn? This is Claudia, are you okay?"

"Oh." Oh shit. Her paper products distributer was in a different time zone and frequently left her messages early in the morning. "I'm so sorry, Claudia, can I call you back in a little while?"

"Of course, I never expected you to answer in the first place. I'll talk to you later."

"Thanks, Claudia."

The phone hit the cradle with a loud click. Taryn's head hit the desk with a dull thud. What was wrong with her? Why couldn't she just be happy? She finally had everything she'd ever wanted—the perfect guy *and* Richard, who had become even more important to her than before. She had...she had family. Groaning, she thunked her head again. Family. She had to give Caleb credit, he was pretty smart to have hit on that little issue as quickly as he had. She'd never even admitted to herself how much the idea terrified her.

I mean, really. Was it worth the risk? Look how close they had come to disaster this morning. If Paul Jones hadn't been stopped before Richard walked out the door this morning... If he had pulled out his gun...

She shuddered and her head swam as all the blood drained from her face. Richard could have been shot, or even Caleb. Caleb probably would have tried to race in front of the bullet to save Richard. They would both get shot but Caleb would stop the asshole before he shot Taryn. And then where would she be? Standing there, with both of them shot. Both of them dead. And her alone. Again.

She picked up her stapler and threw it against the wall. It made a satisfying crack so she tried the tape dispenser. Suddenly the door burst open and she screamed, grabbing the phone to throw next.

Caleb and Richard stood there, eyes darting around the office.

"What? For fuck's sake, what?" She was nearly shouting but couldn't seem to stop herself. "Can't I spend just a few minutes by myself without you breaking into my shop and busting down my damn door?"

Richard's eyes were wide in astonishment and Caleb's soft with pity. The blood returned to her face in a boiling rage. Pity? What the hell did he have to pity her for? She had a fantastic business, an adorable apartment, and regular sex with two sexy men. She did not need his pity.

Forcing her voice to a normal level, she didn't wait for them to respond. "I'm trying to run a business here, if you two don't mind."

"You have cockroaches?" Caleb asked evenly.

"What!? Of course not, how could you say that? I do not have cockroaches!" Damn it, now she was yelling again.

"I figured that's what you were throwing the office equipment at." He used his foot to nudge the stapler lying on its side.

"That is not funny."

"Neither is you running away," Richard said quietly.

"I am not running away. I am working."

"You don't open for another two hours," Caleb reminded her.

"I don't tell you how to run your business, you stay out of mine."

Caleb nodded, took a step forward. "I can do that, but this has nothing to do with business."

Her throat was getting tight and it was getting harder to breathe. Shit, what was wrong with her? She needed them to leave so she could think.

Richard took two steps forward and Caleb another. She didn't want them here, didn't want them to touch her.

"Go away." She barely managed a whisper around the lump in her throat.

They separated, one coming around each side of the desk. She eyed the desk to see if she could cross over without killing her computer. Before she had a chance to decide, they were too close.

"Go away," she tried again, but this time she actually croaked. Shit, shit, shit. She was not going to cry. There was nothing to cry about, damn it. Everyone was safe. Nobody was shot. Nobody was dead. They were still here. She just needed them to go away.

Caleb pulled her in tight, her back to his chest, and Richard moved in to hug her from the front. She remained stiff. They would take the hint, not to mention the outright orders, and leave, as long as she didn't respond.

"I don't want you here," she tried again.

"Here, at the shop? Or here, hugging you? Or here, in your life?" Richard asked. He lifted her chin, tilting her head back until it rested against Caleb's chest and he could see her face clearly.

"We don't have to be together every minute. Or every day."

"No?" Caleb asked. "So how much time do we need to spend together to be just friends with benefits? When does it edge into lovers? Are we lovers, Taryn? Or are we in a relationship? How many hours equals a relationship? Is that the edge we're drawing too near? Or are we past that and heading at warp speed toward family? How many hours a week do we have to spend together to be a family?"

His breath caressed her ear as he spoke softly. She could hear the steel in his voice but his hands were gentle on her arms.

"Are we a family now, Taryn?" Richard picked up. "Is that what you're running from? Because some stupid piece of shit threatened us, you're going to give this up?"

"I didn't say...I don't...It's not..." She couldn't breathe, couldn't think, couldn't speak. She pushed at Richard but that just brought her closer to Caleb. She tried to pull back but Richard stepped impossibly closer.

"Please, please leave me alone. I want to be alone." Horrified, she felt a tear escape. She hated to cry, never did. At least, not before she'd met Caleb. Somehow this was all his fault.

"You're not alone, not anymore." Caleb's voice broke and she was so surprised she tried to look back at him but he wouldn't let her move. "You have us now, whether you want to admit it or not. We're not going anywhere. We love you."

"That's stalking," she hiccuped. "I'll call the cops."

She heard him sigh as his chin dropped to rest on her head. She brought her eyes up to Richard's and her heart broke at the pain she saw there. A tiny whimper escaped. She hadn't done that, had she? She didn't want to hurt him, them. She just needed some time to herself, was that too much to ask? She tried to explain, tried to make them understand, but the words wouldn't come. The tears were flowing freely now so it took her a minute to realize that Richard was crying, too.

"No," she sobbed. "Don't cry. Please, Richard." Her voice was rough, cracked. He just shook his head at her.

"Don't you understand how much we hate to see you in pain? How much we hate that our love hurts you?" he asked.

"It doesn't!" she cried. "I love..." She tried to take a breath. "I love you both, so much."

"Then don't you see?" Caleb asked, his voice sounding desperate. "It's already too late. It will already hurt if we die. So why not take what you can get. If we both died tomorrow, wouldn't you rather have loved us today than run from us?"

Whatever tiny shred was holding her together to that point dissolved and she would have collapsed if they weren't propping her up. Caleb scooped her into his arms, following Richard out of her office and to the door leading to her apartment. Richard had a key and he used it now while she tried to gather herself back together, tried to stop crying, to figure out what she needed to do to get them to leave. She needed to regroup, figure out how to make them...how to keep them from being so important...how to love them a little less.

Fuck. *Fuckfuckfuckfuck.* "I can't...I ca-can't..." She was gasping so hard she could feel Caleb struggling to hold onto her as he climbed the stairs to her apartment, but she couldn't stop.

"Shhh, baby, don't try to talk, you need to calm down, just a little bit, just so you can breathe."

"But...I can't..."

Richard unlocked the door and led the way to her bedroom. He sat on the bed and Caleb deposited her into his arms.

"Shush, sweetie, breathe. You're going to make yourself sick."

Caleb came back with a wet washcloth and tried to wipe her face. She batted him away but was breathing a little better.

"I can't love you this much. Please, Caleb, please, not this much. It hurts too much to be alone."

"I know, baby, you don't want to be alone."

"Right. No. No, I don't want to love you. Not this much."

"Because then it will hurt when you're alone. So you'd rather be alone now."

"No, no, that's not what I'm saying!"

"Okay," Richard soothed. "Okay, we can talk about this later. Why don't you close your eyes, get a little more sleep."

"I have to work."

"I thought you said Emma was opening for you today?"

"You have to work."

"What's that got to do with your getting some sleep?"

She wrinkled her brow, confused. "But..."

Caleb leaned in, kissed her forehead. "Shh, baby, just close your eyes."

She huffed, sure he was being unreasonably demanding, but unable to figure out how or why just now. Her eyes hurt anyway, since the jerks had made her cry, so she closed them. Richard scooted down a bit so they were lying more fully on the bed and the cool washcloth settled over her eyelids, feeling heavenly.

She had no idea how much time had passed when she woke. All three of them were in her bed and she was wearing just her t-shirt and underpants. She took a minute to wonder if they had taken off her shirt, then her bra, then put the shirt back on, or if they had managed to remove the bra without taking the shirt off.

She must have moved because Caleb propped his head up on his arm so that he could look at her.

"Hi," was all he said.

She couldn't meet his eyes or stop the blush from creeping up her neck.

"Hi. I'm sorry."

"Are you?" she heard Richard ask from behind her.

"Yes." She rolled over so that she was on her back, staring at the ceiling.

"But do you still feel the same way?" Caleb asked.

"Yes. I don't know. Maybe."

"Oh well. Okay then." Richard's wry response wrung a small smile from her before she sighed and closed her eyes.

"Everything changed when they died. My whole world...changed."

She kept her eyes closed, listened to them breathing, waiting.

"I know it's ridiculous that something that happened so long ago is still screwing me—" She stopped when a finger crossed her lips.

Startled, she opened her eyes and found Caleb above her, frowning.

"I want you to tell us without putting yourself down." He quirked an eyebrow. "Think you can manage that?"

She rolled her eyes at him to keep the sheepish expression off her face. "Fine. They died. Were killed, actually. Did I tell you it was a train accident?" She tried to remember but gave up. "I used to use that word—accident—but mostly now I say they were killed. It sure as hell wasn't an accident."

She sat up and rearranged herself more comfortably against the headboard.

"This...man parked his car on the tracks when he knew the commuter train was coming. He wanted to die. Nobody knows what thought he gave to the people on the train. If he was just an ignorant asshole or if he wanted to take as many people with him as he could. His wife had just left him, you see. She was tired of his cheating on her and spending all of their money. So she left him and took their daughter with her."

"Did you know all of this at the time?" Caleb asked.

"Oh sure. It was on all the news and everyone at school was talking about it. Everyone knew. I always wondered what it was like for his daughter. She was seven." Richard moved so that he was facing her and took her hand in his. She stared at that, at their hands clasped together, before forcing herself to go on.

"The funeral was awful. The guardian my parents had chosen didn't want me. My grandmother was a drunk. She didn't want me either, but they basically bribed her to take me, so she did. I spent the next few years pretty much trying to hide the fact that she was a drunk because I figured living with her was better than some sort of facility or unknown foster care home." She stopped, shook her head. "I need something to drink."

They trooped off to her tiny kitchen and she got a bottle of water. Turning to ask the guys if they wanted anything, she caught their looks of surprise. "You thought I meant alcohol? I'm not averse to it, as you know, but it's for when I want to have a good time with friends, not drown my sorrows."

They went to the couch and Caleb pulled her onto his lap, resting his chin on her head, as he liked to do. She felt so safe and comfortable, she couldn't exactly remember why she had run from this.

"One day my grandmother went grocery shopping while I was at school. I have no idea why, since I always did the shopping, but she was drunk. She made a scene at the store and then hit a car in the parking lot. My aunt came over from Colorado and put her in a nursing facility and took me back with her. She was mostly fine as long as I didn't bother her and stayed in the spare room whenever her friends came over."

"Male friends?" Richard asked.

"Yes, but also her regular friends. She liked to party. I bet most of them never even knew I was there. The day I turned eighteen I left.

Stayed with a couple of friends until graduation then went back to California for college. You know the rest."

"Why did you go back to California? It would have been cheaper to do college in Colorado, where you had residency, right?"

"I had enough money and there was no reason to stay."

"You had that little apartment, and were never frivolous with your money, but you would have saved more if you'd taken a dorm or shared an apartment. But you never had roommates," Richard commented.

"I needed my own space."

"Yes, you did. Do you still?"

She swallowed hard and Caleb's arms tightened around her. "I don't know. I thought I did. This morning, I needed it."

"But not because we were crowding you," Caleb pointed out. "So why this morning? Why so soon after they took him away? You didn't even wait until all of the cops were gone."

She tried to sit up but he held her close. "Tell us."

"He could have killed you." She spat the words out like they tasted nasty on her tongue.

"He could have killed you, too. But he didn't. We stayed safe and smart and no one was hurt."

"He had a gun and he could have killed you. Either one of you. Both of you."

"And then you would have lost us. What difference does it make, though, to have us if you don't want to be with us?" Richard asked.

"I never said I didn't want to be with you!"

"You told us to go away and leave you alone."

"Not forever!" She was verging on the very edge of mad again but couldn't quite summon the energy.

"No, just when you needed us."

Her shoulders slumped in defeat. She couldn't exactly argue. What the hell was wrong with her?

"I went to their house—once." She didn't know she was going to say the words until they were already said.

"Whose house, baby?" Caleb's rational voice from a minute ago was replaced by one of compassion.

"The meant-to-be guardian's. Her name was Megan, but I always think of her as The Guardian."

"What did you find?" Richard asked.

"Two happy people with two happy children. And a dog. Nice cars, little league."

"Did you talk to them?"

"No. I just watched. One whole day, from the park across the street. Can you believe it? A park, right across the street."

"I'm sorry," Caleb said. "She should have cared. They both should have."

"I'm sure she thought she did. I'm sure they convinced themselves they were doing the best thing for their family. They were right to make their own kids their priority."

"What they did was wrong, plain and simple," Richard disagreed. "Did they ever even check on you, to see how things were going?"

"Not that I know of."

"What was their last name again?" Caleb asked, his voice playfully menacing. At least, she hoped it was playful.

Richard looked down at the bed, then back up, looking almost...shy. She reached out, took his hand.

"Do you think..." He shook his head, opened his mouth again, then closed it, before giving a forced chuckle. "Never mind.

"Richard." She couldn't stand to see him like this, wanted to smack herself for causing this when he'd already had a shitty day.

Caleb reached out too, resting his hand on Richard's arm. "Tell us."

"It's stupid, I was just...well, I was just wondering if this is why you stayed with me for so long." He ducked his head again and she tried to pull him closer but he was already there.

"What do you mean?"

"You know, because I wasn't any threat to being permanent. I was just, you know, a lover. Not a boyfriend. Not potential family."

Pulling her hand back, she glared at him. "I loved you. Not like I do now, sure, but you didn't think of me like that, either."

"I know, you're right." He shook his head, grimacing. "It's stupid, to look back on how things were, when as great as it was, it didn't come close to what we have now."

Caleb nuzzled her hair as he brought his hand down Richard's arm to entwine their fingers. "I think you asked it in a...well, not brilliant way, but you're partially right. She wasn't ready for that, for home and family, but then neither were you. At least, not with her. But you were able to give each other so much love and happiness while you waited and grew and..." He paused as if unsure how to finish.

"Waited for you?" Taryn asked with a smile.

"Well, yeah. I'm hard to resist."

She gave him as much of a laugh as she could. She didn't want to be sad anymore, or angry. Or alone. "I have no idea what time it is, or if I should be at work. I'm pretty sure you both should be, though."

"I called Sara, you're covered. Richard called Brad, he's covered. I called Peter, I'm covered. I think it's time for the wild monkey sex."

"Oh. Okay."

This time they all laughed, and it actually sounded genuine.

CHAPTER SIXTEEN

Richard didn't know for sure if the next couple of hours qualified exactly as wild monkey sex, but neither could he bring himself to care. They made love and not to be too much of a dork, but he was pretty sure that they'd made a family. Of course, he hadn't exactly proved to be the most aware of what Caleb and Taryn were thinking when it came to the permanence of their relationship. Hell, he hadn't even been completely honest with himself in the beginning. But today had definitely felt right and good and real. And permanent.

Caleb led credence to his suspicions that they had all felt the same by suggesting they get dressed and go to *Roisin Dubh* to see who was playing and have dinner and drinks with his brother and sister-in-law. It was the first time he'd invited them there, the first time that he and Taryn would be going to the bar since meeting Caleb.

Caleb dropped him off at home with a promise to bring his things by. The freedom to move between their houses that he had enjoyed until today was suddenly irritating. It felt like more of a nuisance than a wealth of choices. He didn't want to figure out whose house had the leftovers, or the food that needed to be cooked, or the most laundry piled up or whatever. He didn't want to worry about overstepping his bounds at Caleb's or annoying himself by forgetting something he wanted at the wrong house. He wanted...simple. A home. A place they could make theirs, all of theirs.

The sound of the door opening nudged him from his musings and he stepped into the hallway, adjusting his belt. Hard, familiar hands grabbed him and pulled him in for a kiss, which he melted into. When Caleb stepped back he was breathing hard.

"You look hot," Caleb told him, presumably as explanation for the attack.

Richard frowned. He hadn't done anything special, just put on the jeans he knew Caleb liked and the shirt he knew Taryn liked.

He looked up to respond but it got stuck in his throat when he saw Caleb. The black jeans were tight in all the right places. The t-shirt was practically molded to his chest and the motorcycle boots lent an air of danger that had Richard wondering if Caleb knew how to ride one. Maybe they could...

Caleb snapped his fingers in front of his face and Richard blinked at him. Chuckling, Caleb just took his arm and dragged him out of the house, pausing while he activated the alarm. They arrived at Taryn's house about an hour after they'd left her. When she opened the door, however, it was a completely different Taryn.

She was wearing jeans, of course. She hardly ever wore anything other than jeans. But these must have been new, because he was sure he would remember her looking...like that. The tank top was one he had seen before but only managed to convince her to wear once. The muted green brought out the gold in her brown eyes, the top was cut low for her, enough to show the most enticing hint of her cleavage. It crossed over her breasts and wrapped around her middle, tying off on one side. The hem just met her jeans, so hints of skin peeked through as she moved, her reason for not wearing the top often.

"Amazing," was all that he could manage to say. His eyes made it up to her face, finally, and he saw that she was chewing on her lip just as Caleb reached over and tugged it out from beneath her teeth. She gave him a wry smile and closed the door behind her.

It was almost dinnertime when they got to the bar. Caleb led them to a table already occupied by a woman Richard recognized as Lisa.

"Lisa, you remember Taryn and Richard? This is my sister-in-law Lisa and here comes my brother Sean." They all shook hands and Lisa invited them to join her.

"We're expecting a big crowd tonight, I hope you're planning on staying awhile."

"I guess that depends on how well you feed us," Caleb answered with a smile as they all took seats.

"I heard there was some trouble out at your house this morning," Sean said, motioning a waiter over.

"Word travels fast," was Caleb's wry response. They all ordered drinks and Sean asked the waiter to bring menus. "It wasn't a big deal, the cops handled it. Hopefully that should be the end of the drama." He quickly sketched the situation.

"That's awful." Lisa's turned compassionate eyes on Richard. "For you to have to deal with this nonsense on top of the pain of losing your patient like that, I'm so sorry."

"I'm worried about the boy's mother, Elsie. This is not going to be easy for her." The waiter reappeared with drinks and menus. The Blacks waited while Richard and Taryn scanned the menu. It offered a standard collection of bar foods and Richard decided on one of his rarely permitted indulgences. He put the menu down and found Taryn watching him.

"Grilled cheese sandwich?" she asked.

"You know me too well." He grinned at her and watched while she made her own order. He'd hated seeing her so hurt this morning, hated that he was the cause, no matter how indirectly. He knew it was too much to hope that her issue was totally resolved now, but he felt confident that she had made some strong headway. Already she looked more comfortable around Caleb's family than he would have guessed she would be. He could tell it was partly forced, but once they began eating and drinking, he was sure she would relax.

A glance at Caleb found the other man watching him, not Taryn as he would have expected. He quirked an eyebrow in question.

"Grilled cheese?"

"What? I like cheese."

"Grilled cheese is for people who can't cook, and you can definitely cook."

"No, it's for people who like ooey, gooey yumminess."

Sean laughed and Lisa smacked Caleb on the shoulder. "Leave him alone, he can eat whatever he wants in our bar." She turned to Richard. "Have you guys noticed that a lot of your lives revolve around food and drink? Your family's restaurant, which I like very much, by the way, Grounded and here?"

Richard opened his mouth to make an automatic response, then realized that she was right. "Wow, no. I hadn't realized that before."

"Maybe we should start going to a gym," Taryn suggested.

"Hell," Caleb agreed, "we should probably invest in one."

"Or start buying some equipment, at the very least. We need a place with a basement so we can make our own gym. Then we can work out naked." As soon as the words left his mouth Richard remembered that there were other people at the table.

Sean and Lisa just laughed. "We got a treadmill after Katherine was born and we both had a fair amount of baby weight to work off," Sean told them. "Eventually we added a weight bench. I definitely preferred that to Lisa hanging out in a gym full of guys panting after her."

"I didn't mind that part. It was the bimbos who kept asking you to spot for them that annoyed me," Lisa reminded him archly.

Their food arrived just as a band started tuning up on the small stage. "These guys are good," Lisa assured them. "We've had them before and they always get people dancing."

Richard bit into his grilled cheese sandwich and managed to keep from moaning. He saw Caleb laughing at him silently, so he grinned and offered it up. Caleb met his eyes as he leaned in and took a big bite, licking his lips clean of cheese while he chewed.

Taryn cleared her throat and took a large sip of her beer, smiling behind the glass. Sean was studying his plate and Lisa was watching them, fascinated. Richard remembered that Caleb's family had rarely seen him with a girlfriend, and never with a boyfriend. He felt the heat crawling up his face.

"Katherine still enjoying school?" Caleb asked, breaking the quiet.

Lisa launched into a long narrative about her five-year-old's first month at school. Her pride was unmistakable and her pleasure very attractive. After a few minutes she wound down and flushed. "Sorry, I didn't mean to go on like that."

"You weren't," Taryn reassured her. "It must be tough for you, your baby out of the house most of the day now."

"Wellll..." Lisa drawled, glancing at her husband. She rested her hand on her flat stomach. "That won't be the case for too much longer."

They all congratulated Sean and Lisa until the couple rose. "It's time to call Katie and wish her a good night. We'll be right back," Sean told them. "You guys will stay awhile longer?"

"I think we're ready for another round of drinks, actually." Caleb stood and helped Sean take their plates to the kitchen, stopping at the bar on his way back to order fresh drinks for them.

Richard took Taryn's hand. "How're you doing, sweetie?"

"They're good people. I was a little worried, but I like them. I think Sean's a little weirded out, but as long as you don't start kissing each other in front of him, at least for a little while, he'll probably mellow."

Richard nodded, agreeing. Caleb returned with their drinks and a soda for himself. "Katherine spends Thursday dinners with Lisa's parents so that they can watch over the bar together. They split up the other nights between them and a manager. The baby is good news. They've actually been trying for a couple of years and were starting to get worried."

"That is good news," Taryn said. She cocked her head and eyed them both. "We should talk about that, you know."

"If we're all ready to acknowledge that there's a future for us. All of us," Caleb agreed. "We should talk about that, and a lot more."

Sean and Lisa returned to the table and they turned the conversation to the college football team's chances for the season. The band began to pick things up a bit as more people finished their meals. When Taryn started fidgeting in her chair, Richard asked her to dance. She hopped up immediately, earning a laugh from both Richard and Caleb.

Leading her to the dance area, Richard felt like the eyes of everyone at their table were on them. He spun Taryn around and used the opportunity to look back, but Sean and Lisa were talking to a waiter, leaving only Caleb watching them. The heat and promise in his smile nearly made Richard falter in his steps.

"Hey," Taryn laughed, punching him lightly in the shoulder. "You're supposed to be watching me, not Studly."

Snickering at that, Richard focused his attention appropriately. "I dare you to call him that to his face."

Her haughty look took up the challenge. "You think I won't?"

With a laugh, he swept her into his arms and swung her around.

"I love you," he told her, placing her gently on her feet.

"I know," she sighed, tossing her hair back dramatically. "I'm irresistible."

"At least to some," he agreed, twirling her again.

"So long as it's the right 'some', I'm good with it."

The band changed to a slow song and he brought her in close.

"We should drive up to the city one of these nights, go to a gay bar so we can all dance together," Taryn murmured, her head a sweet weight on his shoulder, her hands lightly caressing his back.

"That would be nice. We could do a long weekend, take a mini-vacation."

"Yeah. Ricky, do you think this is all too fast? Talking love and vacations, houses and babies?"

"I do think it's fast, but I don't think it's too fast. I think it's one

PERFECT FORMATION

of those 'you'll know it when you find it' things. This is so far and away different than what I've experienced before that I have almost no doubts."

"Almost?"

Richard paused, hoping he could find the right words. "The thing with Paul Jones, even though it was annoying and scary, it didn't really affect us, you know? But what if we all move in together and people freak? My patients, your customers, Caleb's clients? They have a direct impact on our lives. I guess I just wonder how we'll handle that."

The song ended and Taryn pulled back, looking at him.

"We should talk about that, too. Like Caleb said, there's a lot we should talk about." She took his hand and led him back to the table.

By the time they left, Richard was pleased to see that Taryn seemed to be enjoying Caleb's family as much as he was. They were both a little bit buzzed, which reminded them all of that first night as they exited the bar.

"We could have taken a taxi home again, Caleb. You didn't have to stop at one drink." Taryn took Caleb's hand and twirled herself around.

"I was keeping Lisa company. Did you put your hand on Sean's ass when you two were dancing?"

"Well, sure and I did, Studly," she answered with an affected Irish accent. "And a fine ass it 'tis."

"Richard managed to keep his hands off Lisa's ass," Caleb pointed out, giving her a quizzical look at the nickname.

"Well," she answered, thankfully dropping the brogue, "in my ever-so-humble opinion, Lisa's ass has nothing on Sean's. And Sean's has nothing on either of yours. Either. Too. Whatever."

They loaded into the car and drove to Richard's house. He took the time now that he hadn't during his brief stop earlier, to water the plants and open some windows. It was amazing what a few days away could do to an empty house.

By the time he made it to the bedroom, Caleb was propped up

against the headboard with Taryn draped across his lap, sound asleep. Caleb was stroking her hair but his eyes were on Richard.

Richard unbuttoned his shirt. "She had a long day."

"We all did. Did you talk to Laura earlier?" His voice was even but his eyes were on Richard's hands as they unzipped his pants.

"Yes, he was spouting something about being God's tool, so they're sure now he's the one who painted the house and knifed the tires. They're still working on the murder charge. They're going to do a psych evaluation on the guy."

Caleb nodded. "I expected as much from the way he was behaving. Do you think it was an act?"

"No, it felt genuine to me. I think I'll call Mrs. Jones tomorrow, see how she's doing. I haven't spoken to her since the funeral." He shucked his underwear and headed into the bathroom. When he came back into the room Caleb was gently moving Taryn to the side so that he could move down on the bed. Richard turned out the light and slid in next to Caleb.

"Tired?" Caleb asked him.

"Not too tired. Kiss me."

"Getting kind of demanding, aren't you?" Caleb asked, his voice low and gravelly.

"I have my days."

Caleb swooped in and halted further conversation with a hard kiss. He tasted of a hint of beer and he felt like heaven. Richard relaxed as Caleb's weight pressed into him, the hard length of cock pressing into his leg.

The kisses changed, going from hard to soft, fast to slow, until Richard was chasing Caleb, trying to bring him back. Caleb held himself just out of reach and Richard moaned in denial.

"Tell me what you want." Caleb's whisper was so quiet Richard almost didn't hear him over the blood rushing through his head.

"You." He reached up, intending to pull Caleb's head back down, but the other man took his wrists firmly in hand and held them above his head.

"Are you done fighting this then?" His voice was serious and Richard fought to understand.

"What?"

"This. Us. Are you ours? Are you done hiding?"

"Yes, Caleb. No more hiding. All yours." He was panting and working hard not to struggle in Caleb's grasp. Didn't he know? Didn't they both know that he was theirs and he wasn't letting them go either?

"I want you, I want you both. I want a home, for all of us."

"That's good, because I'm not letting you go. Now tell me, what do you want me to do?" Caleb sat up a bit so that his knees pressed against Richard's sides, holding him still.

Richard couldn't quite get his brain to function. "I want you." He lifted his head again, trying to reach those firm lips, but Caleb brought one hand down to bracket his throat, keeping Richard's head still while he rained kisses along his cheek, suckled his earlobe. Richard could only face forward, trying to concentrate on what Caleb had asked him.

"I want you inside of me. I want you to kiss me again."

"Hold onto the headboard. Don't let go." Caleb released his wrists and his throat and retrieved a condom and lube from the bedside drawer.

Kneeling up over him, Caleb looked dark and dangerous and oh-so sexy. Richard couldn't believe that this man belonged to him. In hardly more than a month, he knew that to be true. Caleb was his, and Taryn's. Taryn was his, and Caleb's. And he. He belonged to both of them, and nothing had ever made him feel so wonderful.

He wanted to let go so that he could help Caleb with the condom, but he tightened his grip on the headboard. Caleb took his time rolling the condom on, then rubbed himself absently while watching Richard.

"Please, Caleb."

As he moved down Richard's body, Caleb leaned in and left a wet trail of kisses in his wake. Finally Caleb squirted lube onto his fingers but instead of putting them inside he used his hand to squeeze Richard's cock, making it even harder. He rubbed his thumb over the head then brought his other hand up to lift and tug on his balls.

Richard gasped in pleasure. Sweat coated his whole body and he ached to feel Caleb's weight on him again. "Caleb."

The hand on his shaft tightened further but the other hand returned to the lube. Richard nearly rejoiced when slick fingers tickled his hole. He bucked his hips as much as he could into the hand holding him, then came down on the fingers seeking entrance. Two fingers impaled him and he bit off a moan. Twisting and turning, the fingers opened him up, but he needed more. "Caleb," he whispered again, begging.

Caleb released his cock and surged up his body, mouth landing on mouth, chest hard against chest. Richard opened for him, tongue and cock filling him in one swift surge. He cried out, though it was mostly muffled as he eagerly matched Caleb's dueling tongue. He bent his legs, fighting for leverage, meeting Caleb's thrusts. The angle made the friction of Caleb's hard abdomen against his straining dick send him over the edge. He clamped his muscles hard and Caleb came, collapsing fully against him.

Richard was just starting to think he should clean up when he heard Taryn stretch next to them. He and Caleb both turned to look at her. Taryn's eyes were half closed, the sheet kicked away, her hand between her legs, her smile somehow both sweet and naughty. "Pretty," she whispered, then let her eyes close fully.

Caleb got up to fetch washcloths. Richard took the opportunity to pull Taryn into him. She came willingly, pillowing her head on his shoulder. When Caleb lay down at his side, he wrapped his long arm around both of them. Richard was almost asleep when Taryn shifted.

"I've been thinking." Her voice was a drowsy murmur. Richard wasn't convinced she was entirely awake.

"Hmmm?" Caleb asked.

"I don't want to get married." She said it offhand, but Richard opened his eyes and saw Caleb prop up on his elbow.

"Now?" Richard asked.

"Ever. I mean, it's silly, don't you think?"

"Well—" Caleb's response was cut off as sleeping Taryn apparently wasn't finished.

"It's not like any of us go to church, so I don't really care about the whole saying I love you in front of a priest thing. And I don't need the government to tell me we're family."

"How ab—" This time it was Richard who tried to speak, unsuccessfully.

"Seriously, whose business is it that we're in love and want to be together forever? Our families will certainly get the point when we move in together and make a life together and have babies and stuff."

There was silence as both Richard and Caleb waited to see if more was coming. More came in the form of a small snore.

"Taryn?" Caleb's voice was much more tentative than Richard had ever heard before.

No response.

"I think she's still asleep," Richard murmured.

"I think you're right. Do you suppose she'll remember any of this in the morning?"

"No clue. Do you agree with what she said?"

"I couldn't care less who she wants to formalize the commitment with as long as she makes the commitment." Caleb was starting to sound sleepy.

"I think the big test will be giving up her apartment."

"You're right. What about you? You want the church wedding and all the trappings?"

"Whatever. As long as I have you both." Richard yawned and closed his eyes.

"Good answer."

CHAPTER SEVENTEEN

Two months later

Caleb paused in the act of climbing into the back of the moving truck to watch Taryn and Richard negotiate the walkway while sharing the load of a coffee table. They were arguing good-naturedly about the hassles of moving.

"We would have been moved in by now if you hadn't insisted on completely remodeling the kitchen," Taryn grumbled.

"I wouldn't have insisted on that if you didn't insist on eating," Richard responded. "Besides, we still would have had to do all this."

A nudge on his shoulder had Caleb glancing away from Taryn's ass to see his brother watching him. "I knew there were downsides to having two lovers. Do they squabble like that a lot?"

Caleb managed to keep a straight face. "Only out of bed. But don't get me wrong, it's a lot of work keeping two people satisfied. One likes coffee, one likes Coke. One likes showers, one likes baths. One wants a new stove, one wants a pool."

"Uh-huh. And the upsides?"

"Oh brother. The upsides are nearly limitless. There's always someone to enjoy a meal with, to bathe with, to cook with, to swim naked with. To sit on the couch and watch a movie with or to jog with. Plus, a whole extra set of hands." He glanced back at the couple. "You know, to help on moving day."

"Riiiight," Sean drawled.

"And of course, when you just want to be alone, there's someone else around they can go bug."

"One of the reasons," Sean agreed, pulling a dining room chair out of the truck, "that we wanted a second kid."

Caleb laughed and followed him into the house with a second chair. They found Richard and Taryn sprawled on the sofa, feet on the coffee table they had just been carrying. Caleb thought he might join them but then Mama came in from the kitchen and gave them the evil eye before spotting Caleb and Sean. She gave them a huge grin and went back to the kitchen. Somehow, and he really didn't know how but wasn't going to complain, Mama had become his biggest fan.

Taryn hopped up and went to help Emma with the large armful of clothes that she was trying to negotiate down the hall. Richard's brother gave him a hand up and they went back to the truck for another load.

Four hours later everything was moved in and all of their friends and family had left. They were in the Jacuzzi, exhausted.

"Please tell me we never have to do that again," Taryn said. She moved so that a jet was pulsing at her back and groaned.

"We never have to do that again," Caleb confirmed, pulling her into his lap so that he could massage her shoulders.

"Unless we have so many kids we need a bigger house," Richard added.

"I think we were all clear that three kids would be plenty, and that's perfect for this house," Taryn reminded him. "Besides, I like an equal parent-to-kid ratio. Means we have a fighting chance."

"Well, now that we have the house, think we should work on filling it up?" Richard asked.

"Not until it's perfect, which for you may mean never. I can't believe how many stores we had to go to just to pick out a couch."

Taryn laid her head back against Caleb's shoulder so he stopped massaging and wrapped his hands around her.

"True, but it looks great in that room. And it's comfy as hell," Caleb said.

"Yeah."

"That reminds me of something I wanted to ask you guys," Richard said.

"Does it involve furniture shopping?" Taryn asked.

"No, jewelry shopping."

That peaked Taryn's interest and she turned her head to study Richard. "Jewelry is good."

"I understand," Richard said slowly, "your position on marriage, the ceremony and everything. But I thought it might be nice if we went and got some rings. All three of us."

Caleb's arms tightened around Taryn.

"Oh," she said. "Yeah, that sounds good. I like that plan."

They stayed silent for a time, enjoying the hot, bubbly water in the cool night air.

"Richard. Caleb."

"Taryn."

"I'm glad we're here."

Caleb stood up, holding Taryn until she set her feet down. "Let's go inside."

After drying off, they made their way to the master bedroom, turning off lights and closing windows. The house that had belonged to his parents was now theirs, all of theirs. They each owned a third and had spent the last three weeks co-managing the renovations and choosing the furniture and appliances. Lisa's family's construction company had done the work, quickly and cheaply. This complete acceptance by not only his and Richard's families but Lisa's as well had meant a great deal to all three of them.

They made it into the bedroom and Taryn took their wet towels to the bathroom while Richard went to adjust the heater. Caleb checked around and found the box labeled M. Bedroom 3. Unlike some of the boxes, this one had been taped shut so he looked around until he found something he could slice through the tape with. Finally spotting scissors on top of another unopened box, he made quick work of it and found the condoms and lube right where they should be. He pulled them out and turned around.

Candles were set out on the surfaces that were not yet too cluttered and Richard was lighting them. Caleb realized Taryn must have arranged them after her shower, while he and Richard were getting dinner ready. Deciding the candles were a good start, Caleb went to the stereo that Laura had helped her brother set up and checked the CD. It was one of Richard's favorite jazz discs, so he left it in and turned it on low.

From the different parts of the room, they came together slowly. Arms slid around waists and shoulders, mouths touched, bodies swayed. It was all so...right.

"Taryn," Caleb murmured, just loud enough to get her attention. He knew that she would hear not just the words but the soft command. She turned her eyes to him, waiting, always ready.

"Yes, Caleb."

"Kiss Richard."

Her smile was soft and sweet and she wasted no time following his order. Richard stayed still, letting her reach up for him, letting her pull him to her, willingly following her lead and Caleb's instructions. He watched them kiss, watched Richard's arms twitch as they automatically moved to encircle his lover, but stayed at his side because he had not yet been told he could move.

Stepping behind him, Caleb rested his hands on Richard's shoulders and leaned in to lick the smooth skin between his shoulder blades. Clean but sweaty in a very good way. Caleb moved his hands down muscled arms until they covered Richard's. Lacing their fingers together, he guided Richard's hands to Taryn's waist, up the curve to her rib cage and in to her breasts. They explored there, together, until Taryn was panting, her nipples hard points jabbing at Richard's palms, begging to be suckled.

"Taryn, get on the bed." Caleb heard the roughness in his voice, felt Richard shiver against him, saw Taryn squeeze her legs closed in reaction.

Backing away from them, Taryn reached behind her to find the bed then slowly scooted onto it, never looking away. When she was in the center, knees bent and splayed wide so they could see her wetness calling to them, she propped herself on her elbows and waited.

Arms wrapped around Richard, Caleb leaned close into his ear and whispered so that Taryn couldn't hear. "Breasts, then pussy. Tongue only." Richard nodded and they advanced.

Climbing up on either side of her, they went straight to her straining nipples, sucking them in hard and fast. Taryn cried out and Caleb heard Richard release his prize with a pop before returning for more. Caleb lashed the nub with his tongue then nibbled all around it. He ran into Richard in the valley between her breasts and paused to kiss the man he loved so much. When they separated he jerked his head south and they moved down her body as one, kissing and licking a path to where she wanted them most.

Caleb got off the bed and knelt at the edge, using Taryn's ankles to drag her closer. Richard lay down next to her, one arm draped over her abdomen as he bent to kiss her waiting clit, Caleb holding her folds open to give him easy access. Taryn bucked when Richard sucked the bundle of nerves into his mouth. Caleb left Richard to his task and moved down, breathing heavily on her curls to remind her that there was more to come.

Delicately, Caleb swirled his tongue through the folds, circled her opening but didn't go in. He pulled back and watched as her interior muscles squeezed her opening, begging to be penetrated. He couldn't resist such an invitation and filled her as much as he could with his tongue. Jerking, she caused him to bump heads with Richard, which made him chuckle. She gasped at the sensation this caused and he could tell she was close.

Again, he drew back, blowing on her wet folds, watching Richard suck her clit. He waited until she was clearly struggling to hold back her release.

"Mmm, so good, baby, I love the way you taste."

Richard stopped, licking his lips and looking longingly at her pussy. Caleb laughed and kissed him, giving him her taste that way. Richard groaned and fed freely, while they listened to Taryn's breathing even out. Pulling back, Caleb led Richard on a kissing journey back up her body, until he reached her neck. Her breathing had picked up again by the time he found the sweet spot behind her ear. Satisfied, he sat up, Richard following his lead, smiling when Taryn whimpered.

Offering Taryn a hand, Caleb pulled her to her feet, then sat on the edge of the bed. He rested one foot on the frame of the bed, leaving plenty of room in front of himself.

"Taryn, kneel here." He pointed to the space in front of him, slightly to the left of center. She dropped to her knees, her eyes glued to his cock.

"Richard, kneel behind her, and to the side here," he pointed. There was just enough space that Richard could kneel partly behind and partly to the side of Taryn, his face over her shoulder.

"Suck me, Taryn. Richard, you can use your hands and mouth, but don't let her come."

Taryn's hot mouth engulfed the head of his cock, and he had to clench his teeth not to shout. He brushed the drying hair back from her face so he could see himself filling her small mouth. She used her hands to caress his shaft, startling when Richard's tongue found her ear as his fingers found her wet folds.

Caleb watched, entranced, as one of Richard's hands worked her pussy and the other made its way down her arm to join her smaller hand wrapped around his dick. This time he did groan as the larger hand squeezed the smaller hand tight around his hard length. Richard kissed down her jaw, which was opened wide around its burden.

Caleb groaned again as Taryn pulled free to kiss Richard, then offered Richard his dick like it was an ice-cream cone.

Richard must have done something to Taryn that Caleb couldn't see because she squeezed her eyes shut, breathing deeply to stave off her release. Richard took the opportunity to lick Caleb around Taryn's fingers before sucking the head in.

"Up." Caleb had to clear his throat and try again to get the word to come out as more than a croak. "Up."

They both gave him one last lick before helping each other to their feet. Caleb grabbed a condom and handed it to Richard. Once it was on he grabbed the man by the back of the neck and kissed him, hard. Not releasing his mouth or his neck, he backed Richard up until he had him where he wanted him. Finally, he pulled back.

"Taryn, get the plugs from the box and lube one up." He went back to kissing while Taryn rummaged through the box. He heard her giggling and knew without a doubt that she was remembering the morning she'd opened the dishwasher and screamed at finding the two silicone toys inside, freshly cleaned. Still kissing, he turned Richard around and presented his backside to Taryn.

To help, he palmed the taut ass cheeks and pulled them apart. Richard moaned as Taryn pushed the plug inside. Caleb turned him around again and presented his own backside to Taryn. "I'll take the other one." Richard broke the kiss to glance at Taryn but Caleb bit him on the chin and pulled him in for more.

He felt Taryn's tentative touch, then Richard's hands as they gave her the same help he had. The plug went in easily and he clenched his muscles when it was seated fully. Taryn took the opportunity to nip his buttock then lick the spot, sending electricity through his whole body. His dick jerked against Richard's and they both moaned. Pulling back, he let Richard go.

Taking Taryn's hand, he pulled her up beside him and gestured that she should follow him. While his hand went down to find Richard's cock, his mouth went to the man's nipple. Together they gave him the same treatment Taryn had received.

Caleb pulled back and put his hands at Taryn's hips. He lifted her up and she wrapped her legs around Richard's waist. Richard's hands came up to hold her to him and Caleb let go. He kissed Taryn's shoulder and palmed Richard's cock, bringing it to her entrance. She moaned and slid down, Richard helping her control the descent. When she was seated, they paused, waiting for his instructions. He could see the excitement in both of their faces.

The truth was, they could have done this weeks ago, but it had come to mean more than a physical act to Taryn, and Caleb knew that. It had become more than fantasy, something of a symbol of their relationship, the three of them together. Now, in their new house, it was time.

He got another condom, put it on, then lubed his fingers liberally. Richard leaned back against the wall for support and used his hands to open her wide. Caleb brought one finger to her puckered hole and eased it in. She remained perfectly still, resting her head on Richard's shoulder. He added another finger and she squirmed against him. With his other hand he reached around and plucked at Richard's balls then moved to Taryn's clit.

Shit, they were so hot. How could he ever get enough of them? After Taryn's sleepy talk about marriage, he and Richard had privately agreed to wait until she brought it up again on her own. When she'd finally broached the subject of the three of them moving in together, he and Richard practically had her signing mortgage papers before the sentence was all the way out of her mouth.

He looked at them, watched them while he lubed his cock, stroking himself, knowing he had never been as happy as he would be in the morning, waking up in their bed, in their house, with the knowledge that it was only the first of many mornings.

Ready, he brought his cock to her hole and eased in slowly. She stiffened at first at the unaccustomed width, then bore down on him. He could feel Richard through her sheath, as he moved slowly inside.

"Caleb," Richard groaned as he slid past.

"Caleb," Taryn moaned as he seated himself fully.

They were still as the perfection of the moment hit them. Finally, Caleb could stand it no more.

"Move as you want," he whispered, pulling out. "Come when you want," he added as Richard pulled out. He thrust in, then withdrew,

Richard working in counterpoint. Every time he was inside her, Taryn clenched around him and he squeezed his own muscles around the plug, adding to the exquisite pleasure.

They didn't last long. Taryn came first, loud and long as they continued to move within her. Caleb held back, determined to send Richard over. He reached around but didn't have time to do anything before Richard climaxed with a shout. Caleb could hold back no longer and spilled himself into Taryn.

Pressing them both against the wall, he leaned over Taryn's shoulder and kissed Richard softly, gently, before helping Taryn down. He turned her around and kissed her just as gently. Perfect, they were both so perfect.

"I love you," Caleb told them both, again, always.

They responded in unison, in a way that he hoped would never fail to make his heart squeeze, as it did now.

"Yes, Caleb.

PERFECT ALIGNMENT

PERFECT FIT BOOK 2

For Leslie, a storyteller and a reader to the very end, we miss you.

Thanks go to Thomas, for giving me the apple blossoms; To Vivienne Westlake, Zoe Archer and Nico Rosso for helping to push me when I was ready to be pushed, but not so hard I'd topple; and to my vacation crew, Jennifer, Sara and Charlyn, who gave me the relaxing boost of time and amazing Caribbean inspiration to get to the end.

CHAPTER ONE

"Nice Necklace."

Emma's head whipped around and a blush heated her cheeks. Oh god, that really had been the voice of her boss's husband. She raised her eyes to his slowly, hope flaring that he was just being polite. One look at his sharp-eyed gaze killed that hope. How had she never pegged the man as a Dom? Alpha, sure, but it had never occurred to her that the tall, dark and scrumptious ex-military man would recognize the BDSM symbol she'd talked herself into wearing. Clearly she was an idiot. Her blush went supernova.

His grin softened into a more gentle smile. "Hey, don't worry. I'm sure most people here won't know what it means."

Gamely she cleared her throat. "Yeah, well, that's sort of what I figured. But here you are, only a few hours after I put it on."

He laughed and reached out to take the coffee she'd been making for him, adding the lid to the to-go cup himself. "I'm sure anyone around here who knows what it means will be respectful of it." He frowned. "And if they're not, you let me know."

She fiddled with the silver pendant and took a deep breath, forcing the remainder of her embarrassment away. Wasn't this what she'd wanted? To be free to be herself? Soon she'd be starting her senior year in college, her last year of freedom. Once she went back home... Well, she didn't want to think about that too much right now. Not when she had a full year left to live the life she wanted to live. "Thanks, Caleb."

Another cocky wink and he turned to find his wife, interrupting the chat she was having with one of their usual customers to kiss her soundly before walking out of the coffee shop. Emma sighed as she started working on another coffee order. That was what she wanted. Not Caleb himself, exactly, though the man was pure sin. But what her friend and boss, Taryn, had found with the hottie. Love.

She'd been surprised when Taryn had hooked up with Caleb, who was so unlike her previous boyfriends. But that surprise had been nothing compared to the shock of discovering that Taryn and Caleb weren't a couple. They were a threesome with Taryn's best friend Richard. Emma had known the handsome and sweet doctor was gay. She hadn't known that when Richard and Taryn weren't involved with other people, they kept each other company in bed. All that had changed when the three had come together.

They were exclusive and though Taryn refused to do a civil or religious ceremony, Emma knew they'd done something private and they all wore rings. She thought their relationship was the healthiest one she knew of, outside of her parents. And now Emma had to wonder if the fact the three shared a bed was the most interesting thing going on in their bedroom. *No!* She would not imagine her boss in bed with all those hands gliding over her... *No!* Absolutely not going there.

She forced her mind back to her work, handing off the drinks she'd made and starting another round. Her shift wouldn't be over for another hour. She'd been filling in for a coworker between her vacations. Junior year had come to an end and she'd immediately headed home to California to spend time with her parents. She'd loved seeing them, being there, working the family store, but she'd also been excited to come back to take a private vacation. One that would keep her mind on her own sexual needs, not those of her friends.

Being with her parents had shown her how different her life would be once she graduated college and returned full time. Not that she didn't love it there, she did, but she just couldn't be the free-spirited person there that she'd started to become here. Especially when it came to sex. Which was why she'd put the necklace on that morning. If this was the last year she'd be able to express her sexuality in the way that felt so natural to her, then she was going to live it to the limit.

A not-too-sharp slap on her butt startled her. "Hey, that's sexual harassment," she complained.

"Yeah, yeah, take it up with human resources." Taryn grinned at her, unrepentant.

"You are human resources. And payroll, corporate and whatever else you want to be."

"I know. I love being boss. Which reminds me." She pulled a key ring from her back pocket and handed it to Emma. "This is your birthday present and bonus combined. It's rented for the week, all paid up. As long as you don't get in any accidents or anything," she added with a grin.

Emma frowned. "I have a car. It's not the greatest or anything, but it gets me around."

"It's not the greatest, and you know I hate when you take it into the city. I know you plan on going out there while you're off, and I thought you might like to do it with your top down."

It took a second for the meaning of that to work its way through Emma's brain. Finally she got it and squealed. "A convertible? You got me a convertible?" She launched herself at Taryn, wrapping her up in a bear hug.

Taryn laughed. "Rented. Not got, rented. For one week, that baby's yours."

Emma followed the pointed finger and looked out the window to a black Mustang, top down, gleaming in the parking lot. She turned back to Taryn as the woman pressed the car key into her hand.

"Go ahead, get going. Derek just got here, I'm sending you home early. Have a great vacation."

"Thanks, Tare. You're the best boss I've ever had."

Laughing, Taryn pulled back and shoved her toward the door. "If we don't count relatives, I'm the only boss you've ever had."

LATE THE NEXT MORNING, Emma was on her way. She'd tossed and turned all night, like a kid who couldn't sleep before going to Disneyland. She laughed as she put her suitcase in the trunk. She wouldn't mind a visit to that park, but she was much more excited to be going where she was. Not just to Boston, but to the club she'd found, filled with people like her. And sex.

Stupid sex. Wonderful, glorious sex. Damn annoying, complicated sex. Because she couldn't be simple. No, not Emma Lee. She had to go and get herself caught up in something fringe. Something alternative. It had taken her a long time to figure out that there was a name for the thing she wanted. Submission. She swallowed hard just thinking the word. Claiming it for herself.

She'd stumbled around, finding some books, some sites on the internet. Finally, two years ago, she'd made it to a club she liked in Boston—Apex. And she'd found home. Well, not completely, but it had been so much closer to what she wanted, what she needed, than she'd ever found before, that it had taken her a while to realize it wasn't quite everything she dreamed of.

The club scene was fun. It was entertaining and it was hot. It was empowering. But she found it nearly impossible to actually form a relationship with anyone. There were lots of reasons, but one of the biggest was distance. The three-hour drive didn't work well with her busy school, homework and work schedule. Normally she stayed with her friend Stephanie, but this time she'd found an online hotel deal and had treated herself. In the last year, she'd made the trip only twice, which was why she was heading there as the first part of her vacation. She was horny as hell.

Laughing at herself, she turned up the radio. The sun was shining, but not terribly bright, and the wind from the open top kept things cool. She'd chosen to take a back road rather than the highway, and had hit a long, solitary stretch. There was no one else in sight, only the occasional small side streets and driveways shooting off to either side of the road. Her foot pressed down harder on the pedal and she yanked the ponytail holder out of her hair. The wind whipped the fine strands in a massaging caress, the sun warmed her cheeks and she sang along to the music at the top of her lungs.

At the bleep of a siren, her foot eased off the gas before her brain caught up to the situation. *Shit.* She looked down at the speedometer and groaned when she saw it was at fifty, despite the fact she'd already slowed down some. Easing off even more, she flipped the blinker on and looked in the rearview mirror. The cop car was exactly what she'd expected to see. Sighing, she eased onto the side of the road and came to a stop. Well, she wasn't going to let this ruin her vacation. She'd been having fun, and if she had to pay a little bit more for the privilege, so be it.

When the officer approached her door, she smiled up at him. "Sorry, I guess I got a little carried away."

"Yes, ma'am. License, insurance and registration, please."

She pulled the rental car paperwork from the center console and handed it to him, then grabbed her wallet out of her purse and gave him the insurance card and her driver's license. He didn't say anything else as he walked back to his car, so she just leaned her head against the headrest and watched his ass in the side mirror. It was a mighty fine ass.

Fifteen minutes passed quickly, spent daydreaming about men in uniforms. The cop returned, handing her back everything and giving her a ticket to sign. She did as he asked and returned it to him with a bright smile. "Thanks."

His lips twitched a bit, but he didn't say anything.

Returning her cards to her wallet, she was surprised when he didn't leave. She zipped her purse closed and looked back at him. His expression, which had been casually stern before, was now hard. And…heated? Surely she was mistaken.

"Ma'am, I'd like you to step out of the car."

She blinked as he pulled on the handle, opening her door wide. "Um. Okay." She unbuckled the seat belt and eased out of the convertible, carefully ensuring the long skirt of her dress covered everything it should. He gestured for her to walk to the shoulder of the road. Nerves began to dance through her stomach as he led her to the back door of his cruiser. She noted the car read "Jackson", so she'd only gone about forty miles from home before getting into trouble.

"Turn around."

Her stomach was a hard knot as she obeyed, turning back to face him.

"Lace your fingers behind your neck."

What the fuck? Slowly, she did as he'd ordered. She waited, but he didn't say anything else, just stared at her. It took her a minute to realize that he'd told her to put her hands behind her neck, rather than on her head, like the TV cops did. The position was so familiar to her she hadn't given it any thought. She blinked and looked at him again. He'd taken his sunglasses off and his eyes were steady on hers. And they were hot. *Ohhhh.*

He must have seen the moment she began to get it, because he moved. Smoothly he put one hand on his gun holster, unclipped it from his belt, reached through his open window and put it into his glove box. She could hear the key turn, locking, then the clink of the keys as they dropped down onto the car seat. Other than a few quick glances at what he was doing, he kept his eyes on her. Once that was done, he released her gaze and made a visual inspection of her body. She watched his eyes lower to her neck, where they studied her necklace for a beat, then lower. Her nipples tightened under his scrutiny and she was glad she was wearing a bra. Or, maybe not.

Finally he returned his look to her face and took two steps

closer. His body heat enveloped her and she had to fight not to lean forward the fraction it would take to touch his chest with her breasts. He was only a little taller than her, just enough that she was staring at his mouth until she lifted her chin a bit.

"Are your arms tired?" he asked, his voice soft but no less commanding than before.

"Yes, Sir."

"But you'll leave them there for me, won't you? For a little while longer?"

"Yes, Sir."

He stepped back again, three full paces, and she had to fight not to whimper.

"This is a bad idea."

She blinked. Whatever she'd expected him to say or do next, that wasn't it. But he was right.

"For both of us," she agreed. The sexual tension didn't go away, but her mind cleared a bit and she focused on the reality of the situation, rather than the fantasy-like haze she'd let herself fall into. This wasn't the club, wasn't a pre-established scene. She didn't know this man, wasn't in a safe place, surrounded by people she trusted. And surely it was the kind of thing he could get fired for. He was trusting her not to cry foul to the authorities.

"You'd be a fool to do this."

"So would you." She gave him the safe words from the club. "I know when to say red and yellow." Forcing herself to meet his eyes, to show him she was sure, she begged him with a whisper. "Please."

He cursed and stepped forward. His large hands came up to bracket her wrists and ease her arms down to the small of her back. One hand held her wrists steady while the other came up to her cheek. His thumb brushed along her jaw line, teased her lower lip, then he dropped his hand down to finger her necklace.

"And green?" he asked, his gaze intent.

She nodded and gave him the word that would let him know it was okay to proceed. "Yes. Green."

"Follow me," he snapped. Drew took her hand in his and practically towed the lovely siren to her car, gently pushed her into the driver's seat and stalked back to his cruiser. He shouldn't let her drive, but they were only going a mile down a back county road, and taking her away from her car wasn't safe for her. He couldn't seem to stop himself, couldn't seem to let logic overcome his desires. And fuck, he desired. He'd just come home from a long shift and stopped at the end of his driveway to get the mail when a car had blown past him, going too fast. Reversing quickly he'd been shocked to find himself smiling at the sight of the black hair streaming in the wind, the face turned up to the sun, and the pouty lips he glimpsed in the rearview mirror, singing enthusiastically.

When he'd gotten to her door, he'd been expecting attitude. Or nerves. Those were the normal reactions to being pulled over. But no, not this one. She'd smiled up at him, bright with a touch of apology, and not a single hint of complaint. He'd thought maybe she was about to turn on the charm, try to flirt her way out of the ticket. The brief consideration he'd given the idea had pissed him off, but no. She hadn't flirted, hadn't teased. Hadn't done anything but wait patiently for him to return. And the whole time he was running her on the car computer, he was seeing that necklace of hers in his mind. He knew what it meant. And his cock was telling him it had been far, far too long since he'd gone into the city to satisfy his needs. Needs he found too dark to attempt to meet in the small town he lived and worked in. Needs she would know all about.

Still, he hadn't planned his next move. He'd meant only to caution her to drive more carefully and send her on her way. Her surprise at his words mirrored his own, but he didn't let her see that. Didn't let her see anything other than calm confidence and command. And she'd responded. A touch of fear tempered by the fact that she knew she hadn't done anything wrong. He'd led her to the other side of the cars for a little bit of cover, though he didn't think anyone would come along the road anytime soon. But better safe than sorry.

He snorted to himself as he eased the car back onto the road and moved ahead, waiting for her to fall in after him. Safe? None of this was safe. It was about the stupidest thing he could ever remember doing. Not only did he risk his job if she turned out to be crazy, but he never mixed his work life with his play life. Hell, he really didn't mix his home life with it either. Playing was for the clubs, for the city. Not for home, where it would be too easy for his coworkers to discover his less than typical sexual proclivities.

But he held his breath until she moved in behind him and followed as he made a wide U-turn and headed back to his driveway. Within three minutes they were bumping along the dirt drive and he wished he'd thought to warn her to put the top up. She slowed down, letting him get farther ahead so the dust didn't completely swamp her. But she kept moving forward.

Parking next to the old barn, he rolled up his windows and waited patiently for her to catch up. When she turned off the Mustang, he got out of the cruiser and hurried over to open her door. The surprised pleasure on her face almost made him grin, but he held it back, felt himself falling back into Dom mode. A quick glimpse of a tattoo on her ankle made him itch to get a closer look at her. All of her. He took her hand and led her into the barn.

It was a clean space that hadn't been used for its intended purpose since long before he'd bought the house. He occasionally brought furniture in here to strip and refinish, stored some of his brother's belongings in the hayloft, and had some gym equipment set up in one corner for when the weather was too nasty to jog. Flipping on the lights, he pointed to a spot in the center of a large, clear area. She walked to it and sank down to her knees gracefully, resting her butt on her heels, her hands on her thighs, legs parted. Then she betrayed herself by glancing up to check his reaction. Again, he had to hide a smile. She was freaking adorable.

Twenty-four, according to her license, which had told him her full name, as well as her address in North Fork, the college town a few miles away. It had listed her height at five foot nine and her weight at one hundred and twenty pounds, though he suspected she should add some to that now. Not that he was complaining. He was quite happy with every pound he'd seen, every inch, everything. Her black hair and brown skin spoke of some sort of heritage, though he couldn't quite figure out what. Emma Lee was young and beautiful and his. At least for the next little while.

He wondered what she was thinking. *He* was thinking that if she were a friend of his he'd paddle her bottom black and blue for doing such a stupid thing with a complete stranger. It was totally irresponsible to be contemplating something like this without knowing who he was, let alone talking first and setting up parameters. *He* knew he wouldn't do anything dangerous, wouldn't skirt any lines that might be troublesome areas for her. But she couldn't know that.

He took the handcuffs out of their case on his belt and watched her eyes narrow. She took in a breath and opened her mouth, then shut it as he tossed the cuffs off to the side. Good. It would have been idiotic to allow a perfect stranger to restrain her that way, and he was glad to know she would have objected. The rest of the items on his belt followed the cuffs, then he reached for the buckle. She nibbled on her lip as he slid the leather free and added it to the pile. He didn't want all that creaking bulk for the next little while.

"What's your name?" he asked, wanting to hear her say it.

Her pink tongue darted out to moisten her lips. "Emma." She started to say more, stopped herself, clearly unsure whether she was allowed to talk or not.

He nodded. "It's not so easy when you don't know what protocol to follow. Not so smart, either."

She didn't deny it. "I thought we'd already established that."

A snort escaped him. "So we did."

"What's your name?"

"Andrew Robinson. Drew."

Her lips formed his name, testing it, but she didn't give it any sound. He wanted that, to hear his name on her lips. Luckily, in these situations, what he wanted, he got.

"Say it."

"Officer Robinson."

He shook his head. No, despite the stupid situation he was

currently pursuing, and despite the increasingly demanding desire to use his handcuffs on her, work was separate from play. "Drew."

"Drew," she repeated. "Sir."

His heart gave an annoying little thud. He liked the way those words sounded on her lips.

"I'm going to need to search you." He gestured to the wall behind her. "Hands against the wall, feet spread wide."

She rose slowly and swiveled around, putting a little extra sashay in her hips that the low sandals she wore didn't account for. Little tease. No, that wasn't right. She wasn't teasing him because he was pretty sure she had every intention of following through. Only his damn honor would dictate how far he'd let it go. Leaning forward, she braced herself against the wall and spread her legs wide, tilting her hips so her pert ass pointed right at him.

Adjusting his cock behind his uniform pants, he moved forward, past the inviting ass, until he was next to her face. He speared his fingers through her silky hair, grazing her scalp with a little massage before fisting what hair he'd caught and using it to turn her head up to him.

"Do you have anything dangerous on your person? Any weapons or needles?"

Her breath came out in tiny little puffs that he felt against his arm. Her eyes were dilated and heavy with need.

"No, Sir."

He let her hair go and slid his hand down the back of her neck, squeezing gently. He brought up his other hand and moved them along her bare arms to her wrists, gave another squeeze. Since she'd dropped her head back down, he didn't hold back the little smile that her answering moan brought to his lips. Sliding his hands back down the insides of her arms, he gave a quick tickle at her armpits. She jerked slightly, but held her position.

He cupped her breasts. She sawed in a much deeper breath, pushing herself into his grip. A perfect handful, deliciously heavy. His quick swipe of her nipples brought a nearly soundless gasp. Spreading his hands wide, he moved lower, tracing along her ribs, molding the dress to her body as he stepped around and between her legs. It took more effort than it should to keep from pressing up against her ass. Continuing the journey, he brought his hands down her hips and the outsides of her legs until he reached her ankles.

He rubbed his thumb along the small clutch of flowers inked into her skin. Stretched out as she was, it forced him to crouch down, putting his face against the fabric of her dress, pulled tight between her legs. A quick squeeze of her ankles and he curled his hands in, beginning the return journey. Her calves flexed under his palms, his skin encountered fabric as he reached her knees, and from that point on, the dress rose with his arms.

When his hands came back together at her center, he gave only the barest brush against her underwear before letting go and standing up. He moved so that his legs where on either side of her right leg and placed his left hand on the back of her neck, feeling the slight shiver just as he moved his right hand to cup her pussy. She lifted to her toes for just a second before settling back down into his touch. Silky panties did little to keep him from the wet heat. He pressed in close, tucked his face into the crook of her neck and inhaled deeply. Little goose bumps raced up her arms and the fabric under his fingers got wetter.

"Hmm," he murmured into her neck. "Nothing in your clothes, no weapons strapped to your body."

"No, Sir, nothing hidden, I swear. Please, Sir, let me go, I won't trouble you any further." She'd pitched her voice into that of a helpless maiden, and he had to smile at her role-playing. Somehow, though, he didn't think the breathless quality of the words was feigned.

"I don't know, missy. Seems there are still a few places you could be hiding things."

She turned her face up to his, her eyes over-wide. "Sir! I don't know what you mean!"

"Mmm, hmm." He lowered his head the scant distance to mate his mouth with hers. She responded instantly, boldly, tangling her tongue with his until he nipped her, reminding her of her role. She obediently pulled back, letting him explore her mouth at his leisure. Her ass, however, began a slow movement, her hips swinging just a bit, just enough to brush her against his already achingly hard cock.

He pulled back from the kiss and swatted her pussy at the same time. She gave a startled squeak and stilled her movements.

"Nothing hidden in your mouth," he commented.

She stuck her tongue out at him, but he chose to ignore it, moving behind her so she wouldn't see his grin. He had a feeling role-playing wasn't her usual game. It wasn't his, either, but the situation fairly demanded it. The fingers he held against her panties slid carefully up to tease at the elastic edge.

"What about here?" he asked. "Are you sure you don't want to admit to anything hidden here? Anything dangerous?" He punctuated the question with a sharp nibble on her neck.

She gasped but remained quiet.

"I guess I'll just have to check for myself." He slid one finger through her cream and then into her. Her muscles clasped him tightly, his dick swelling further in envy.

"Well, well, what have we here?" he asked. "You seem to be all wet, missy."

She choked, then coughed what he was sure had started out as a laugh.

"I don't know, Sir. It's never done that before."

The laughter in her voice faded as he added a second finger. He lifted up, bringing her to her toes, his palm smashing her clit, his fingers pulsing against her squeezing pussy.

"Ahhh." Her head dropped back, her hair brushing his cheek.

He scissored his fingers and circled his palm, listening to her gasps and pants pitch higher and higher. She started to bounce on her toes, her body instinctively trying to catch his rhythm. He placed a gentle kiss on her damp throat and lowered her before removing his fingers.

"Nooo," she moaned.

He pinched her stomach with his wet fingers to still her seeking hips. She dropped her head between her arms and went motionless.

"That cavity seems to be empty, as well. But I believe there's still one left to check."

Her head swiveled just enough for her to peek at him from behind her arm. Her expression was not particularly compliant. He narrowed his eyes at her and she blinked, seeming to recall herself to the situation. To the man. Her tongue darted out to wet her lips and she faced forward again.

"Please, Sir. I haven't done anything wrong."

"Mmm, hmm. We'll see about that."

Switching hands, he swiped up more of her cream and raised her skirt again, teasing his wet finger against her puckered hole. She took a deep breath, then pushed out, giving his finger entry. Clearly she'd played here before, but he had to fight against her muscles to go all the way in, so he guessed it wasn't a frequent thing for her. He'd given her plenty of time to stop him with her safe word. If she'd been the least bit hesitant, he wouldn't have pressed in. Too many people had issues and since they hadn't discussed her limits, he made sure he had her unspoken agreement before continuing. When she'd relaxed completely around him, he began to move the finger in and out.

"Sir, please. Drew." Her muscles quivered against his leg as she fought to remain still this time, fought to do as he'd instructed. "It seems I was mistaken." He slid his free hand back under her panties and fit two fingers into her grasping sheath. "There's nothing inside you but me. I'll just have to fill you up myself." His long fingers stroked her everywhere and he was sure she was near her peak. "Give me your mouth," he commanded.

CHAPTER TWO

Emma didn't hesitate, but turned her face to his and opened for him, accepting him in as he thrust with his tongue in rhythm with his hands, filling her in a way she'd never been filled before. With no toys, no props, and only their silly game, he'd taken full possession of her. And they were both still dressed. Her vague thoughts shattered as he twisted his fingers just so, sending her over the edge she'd been riding. She cried out his name, forcing her knees to lock so she didn't fall out of position. She moaned as he pulled free of the kiss, her arms sagging. But he was there, pulling out of her, bringing her into his body and holding her tightly. He lowered them both to the ground, settling her into his lap as she leaned against him and practiced breathing.

Wow. That hadn't been the biggest orgasm she'd ever had, but it certainly had been the most clothed. "That was easy," she said, waving a hand over her still fully clothed body as explanation. She grinned.

He snorted, which she felt, more than heard, since she was leaning against him. "Easy for you."

"Well, yeah. That's what I meant."

He slapped her thigh. "Brat. Is that your thing? Do you like to misbehave and drive your Doms crazy?"

"Hasn't been my thing before, but I'm giving it new consideration," she teased. She squeezed her thigh muscle against his hardness. "Don't you, um, want to do something about that?" she asked, irritated that it sounded more shy than sultry.

"Who's in charge here?" She might become addicted to that stern but teasing voice if she wasn't careful.

"Sorry, just trying to be a good and helpful sub," she answered primly.

"Mmm, hmm." His fingers had started inching her dress up. "I don't exactly carry condoms in my uniform, or leave a store of them in my barn."

"Ah. That's good to know." His fingers played along the inside of her thigh, just above the knees. He took his hands away and she tensed her muscles not to move, not to chase him down.

"Feel okay to drive now?" he asked, tearing her attention from his clever fingers.

She forced a smile and nodded, hoping her uncertainty wasn't showing. Surely he meant drive to his house, not get back on the road. *Please, please, please.*

He held out his hand and she took it gratefully, still a bit wobbly as he led her out of the barn and to the Mustang's door. His thumb brushed over her lips and she was convinced he was going to kiss her goodbye and send her on her way. She pulled her shoulders back and met his eyes.

"It's only about half a mile." He pointed past the barn, farther up the way they'd been driving. "Go first so you're not eating my dust."

She nodded, afraid to open her mouth and babble out something ridiculous in her relief.

The dirt road curved gently until she could see an old ranch house. It looked freshly painted and well maintained. Not much of a garden but what was there was neat and tended.

Pulling to a stop, she parked the car and put the top up, latching it into place. She grabbed her purse and got out, breathing deeply to keep her nerves from ratcheting up to fear. The rational part of her knew that she was being unsafe, but that the chances of running into a homicidal Dom cop was much, much less likely than running into a Dom cop who was simply enjoying the unusual opportunity, as she was. If he'd wanted to harm her, he'd already had plenty of opportunity.

He took her arm and led her up the steps, quickly unlocking the door and motioning for her to enter. "Welcome to my house."

"Thanks, it's lovely." It was. Masculine but not bachelor, comfortable but not rustic. He led her to the kitchen and pointed to a seat at the table. By the time she'd sat and placed her purse on the chair next to her, he'd returned with a portable phone, which he held out to her.

"Am I calling someone?" she asked.

"Don't you think you should?" He didn't sound bossy exactly. Just...firm. She wasn't sure how he managed the difference, but gave him credit for it. And he was probably right. If she was going to stay with him any longer, she needed to let someone know where she was and who she was with. Which put her independent streak up, but she was adult enough to do what was smart, despite being annoyed by it. The real question was how long she might be staying.

"Fine. Thanks." She waited, but he didn't leave. Rolling her eyes, she turned her attention to the phone. Which was useless to her. *Who remembered numbers anymore?* Besides, she didn't want to have an actual conversation. She put the handset on the table, fished her cell phone out of her purse and started typing.

"What's your address?" she asked without looking up. She punched in what he told her, adding his phone number when he supplied that as well. "There," she announced with a flourish, snapping the phone closed and setting it on the table.

He narrowed his eyes at her. "When did you say you'd check in?"

She opened her mouth but was interrupted by her ringing phone. When she saw Taryn's name on the screen, she frowned. Didn't her friend realize she'd texted instead of calling for a reason?

"Hi, Taryn."

"Hey, girl. Caleb wants to talk to you."

"I don't—" She stopped talking when it became obvious Taryn hadn't stuck around long enough to hear a response.

"Emma."

She darted a quick look at Drew who was leaning against the counter, legs crossed, arms crossed, face impassive.

"Hi, Caleb."

Drew narrowed his eyes at her.

"Where did you meet this guy?"

"Caleb. You're not my father, or my brother. You've never interrogated me about my dates before."

"You've never called to set up a safety check."

"How do you know?"

"I asked. Who is this guy?"

"He's a police officer. We got to talking. I'm at his house. Like I texted, I'll call Taryn in the morning, let her know I'm safely at the hotel."

"Three hours," Caleb said.

"Two hours," Drew said loudly at the same time.

"Fine!" She pushed the off button and slammed the phone down on the table, glaring at it rather than the man in front of her. Then she bit her lip. Crap, she hoped Caleb wasn't pissed at her. Of course, she had another man to worry about at the moment. She turned to face Drew, trying to look stern.

"Look, bossing me around in the bedroom, or the barn as the case may be, is one thing. Telling me—"

She broke off when he dropped to his knees in front of her chair, pushing between her legs. He grabbed her hair in his hand and pulled her head down for a kiss. He teased and tasted, nipped and sucked, never letting her get a handle on the kiss, never letting go of the control. His fingers tightened and the tug against her scalp made her shiver. She wasn't into pain, but this she liked. This physical manifestation of his control of her.

Relaxing, she stopped trying to chase him with her tongue, stopped trying to do anything but take, receive. He changed the kiss again, softening, the hand in her hair easing into a caress. Oh, she liked that too. She liked it all.

When he moaned and pulled back, she could only sigh. She seemed to do that a lot around Drew.

He rose, pulling her up with him, moving back only half a step. Crowding her.

"More?" he asked quietly.

She wondered if he was unsure of the answer or just being a good Dom.

"Green."

He didn't smile, but she would swear his eyes got hotter.

"Strip."

She wasn't particularly fond of being the only naked person in a room, but she wasn't altogether unused to it, either. It was a common enough order, so she swallowed her nervousness and reached behind her to pull down the zipper of her dress. Stalling, she kicked off her sandals, then inched the skirt up until she could grasp the hem. And then she stopped. For the life of her, she couldn't remember which underwear she'd put on that morning. Was it an old, raggedy pair, or something cute?

He raised his eyebrow at her and she bit her lip, pulling the dress up and over her head in one quick move. As soon as she was clear of the fabric, she looked down. Oh, yeah. She'd put on her peach panties and matching bra, wanting to feel pretty under the dress that she rarely wore. Normally she was in jeans or shorts, and a t-shirt or sweater. Unless she was dressed to go clubbing. But a flirty dress had seemed like the perfect thing to wear on her top-down trip to the city.

Realizing she'd taken a bit longer than she should have, she reached behind her and unhooked her bra. She quickly shucked it and dropped it to join her dress, then did the same with her panties. It was awkward, reaching down to free the underwear from her feet with the limited amount of space Drew had given her, but she managed it, bumping his chest only once.

Finally she stood before him, naked and hugely thankful that part of her pre-drive prettification had included a session with her razor. He inspected her casually, motioning with a twirl of his finger for her to turn. She did so slowly, knowing it was what he wanted.

"Any medical issues I should know about?" he asked.

"No, Sir."

When she'd completed the turn, he motioned for her to resume her seat.

"Do you belong to a club?" he asked.

Surprised, she nodded.

"Did they do a worksheet with you? The yes, no, maybe kind of thing?"

"Yes, Sir." She told him the club's name when he just looked at her inquiringly.

He checked his watch. "They should be open. We'll give them a call, see if they can fax it over. And we'll eat lunch."

She blinked at him. It was a good plan, certainly she preferred it to doing full negotiations verbally. And it was smart. She just wasn't quite sure why she had to be naked for it. He was watching her process with a knowing smirk. Oh, right. He was the reason she had to be naked for it.

"Yes, Sir."

He smiled and held his hand out to her, leading her to an office. Opening a laptop, he soon found the club's phone number and once again placed the house phone in her hand.

The call to Apex took only a minute, someone in the office promising to fax the paperwork once she'd answered some security questions to prove her identity. The employee wished her a cheery "Have fun!" and hung up.

Drew herded her back to the kitchen. He patted the table when she would have resumed her seat on the chair. She blinked at him, but he just gave her that "I'm in charge here" look that made her wet. Which was sort of the problem.

She grimaced. "Er. Yellow. No, red. Yes, definitely red."

He looked at her in surprise, then at the table, then back at her, clearly confused.

"Sitting naked in front of me is a problem?"

His tone was that of someone trying not to sound judgmental while he was in fact being exactly that.

"It's the table! People eat there. I can't—" She bit her lip, shook her head. "No. I really can't do that. I'm sorry." She couldn't seem to tear her gaze away from his knees, even though she wanted to check his reaction. Finally, when he hadn't said anything for more than a minute, she gritted her teeth and forced herself to look up.

The contorted shape of his lips suggested he was trying very hard not to laugh, which she supposed was better than anger or annoyance.

"I do have cleaning supplies," he said.

She wrinkled her nose and shook her head. "People eat there," she said again. Really, it couldn't be said enough. "I might eat there."

"I see."

"Maybe I can do it if you don't get me horny." She turned back to look at the table. "No. Never mind, not even then."

"What if I put a tablecloth down?" he asked, still sounding amused.

She just shook her head.

"I was going to use a plate, not put the food directly on the tabletop."

She shook her head again, beginning to feel like an idiot.

"So, you don't eat breakfast in bed? No popcorn while you're watching a movie?" he asked.

This time she just frowned at him. "It's not the same."

He took her face in his hands and kissed her lips. She didn't open for him, pouting, but he didn't press the issue. Just kissed her lips, her nose and her forehead. "Sit on the chair, hook your ankles around the legs, put your hands behind the back and hold on to the lowest rung."

The last thing she was feeling now was sexy, but at least she could follow this order without making a bigger production out of the whole mess. She sat down and did as he'd directed, fighting the instinct to grab her clothes and make a run for it.

He gave her an approving look, which she could only guess was for her speed in following his new instructions, then began pulling items together to make sandwiches. Slowly she relaxed again. She still didn't feel sexy anymore, but neither did she feel the need to hide her head or run for the car.

Watching him make their lunch shouldn't have been particularly arousing. He was still fully clothed, his uniform looking slightly incomplete with the gun missing. His dirty-blond hair wasn't even mussed and she suddenly worried about how she looked after he'd run his hands through hers. She hoped she looked sexily tousled instead of demented. It took a great deal of self-control to keep from reaching up and fussing with it, her fingers tightening on the chair rail.

She blinked back to awareness to find him watching her. She gave him a questioning look, but he just quirked his lips slightly and went back to building the sandwiches.

They remained silent except for when she asked him to leave the mustard off her sandwich, and he was soon carrying a plate with two sandwiches to the table.

"Hungry?" he asked, setting the plate down on the sex-free table.

"Yes, Sir."

Instead of telling her that she could let go of the chair, he held the sandwich out to her for a bite. She hesitated, then leaned in.

"College student?" he asked when she'd finished, before taking a big bite of his own sandwich.

"Yes. One more year to go at Kennington. I started late. Can I have something to drink, please?"

"Sure. Water or soda?"

"Water's fine, thanks." She stayed still while he retrieved a bottle from the refrigerator. It wasn't as awkward as she feared when he carefully held the bottle to her lips, giving her a couple of swallows. He fed her another bite then resumed the conversation, asking her questions while she chewed, eating while she answered.

"What did you do between high school and college?"

"I spent a year in the Philippines with my father's family, then a year in Mexico with my mother's family."

"Wow. Did you enjoy both?"

"Sure. I'd spent time in both places while growing up. I'm glad I did it. Not that I was against the idea, exactly, but I probably wouldn't have done it if my parents hadn't pushed. I was able to travel around with my relatives, see a lot of Asia and Central America. A bit of South America."

"I'm impressed. I made it to Canada once, that's about it."

She laughed. "You should travel. It's good for you."

"You're right, I should. My best friend and his wife used to visit different states during the summers. I haven't even managed to get out of New England much."

She told him a few of her favorite traveling stories. He finished before she did, since she was doing most of the talking. Though she felt he was listening attentively the whole time, he began to stroke her between bites. Running a finger along her collarbone, sliding a lock of her hair between two fingers, making a zigzag along her thigh with his fingernail. It was distracting, but not enough to make her fumble the stories.

"What kind of work do you do?" he asked.

"I work at a coffee shop, part-time. My parents cover the tuition, and they pay for my books, but I share an apartment with two other girls and I pay for my rent and food and stuff."

"You're not from around here, though." He cocked his head and looked at her. "West Coast?"

"Bingo. California. North of San Francisco."

"Is it hard, being away from your family?"

"Sometimes. But it's been good for me too. I have a tendency to be The Good Girl at home. I love my parents but it's been good to focus on who I am and who I want to be, rather than always trying to be the person that I think they want me to be."

"They push you to be perfect?" he asked.

"Not really. I had a brother. He was the good kid. I wasn't a bad kid, but I was more into having fun with my friends than making good grades or helping out in the family store. I thought my family was restrictive because I had a couple of friends whose parents let them get away with anything. Of course, looking back I can tell that those parents just didn't really care and the kids weren't as happy as I thought they were."

She took a long drink of the water he offered and was silent for a minute. She'd never really told the story to anyone, put it into words, even for herself.

"So, even though he was the good kid, he died. He and his friends decided to get acquainted with a bottle of tequila. The parents were out of town." She swallowed hard. "My brother never did anything by halves. Between the three of them they finished the bottle off. When his buddies woke up, he didn't."

He'd stopped the teasing touches and rested his palms on her thighs. She looked down, focused on the warmth of his hands, the strength of his fingers resting lightly on her legs. Even after all these years, it hurt.

"It was...huge. My world just changed, in an instant. I loved him so much, had always looked up to him and been jealous of him. He wasn't bad, but he wasn't perfect, either. I saw how much it devastated my parents, and it just became so important to me to never disappoint them."

"How old were you?"

"Twelve." She gave a wry smile. "I had therapy, and understood on one level that they didn't need or expect me to be perfect. My therapist helped me decide to go to college away from home. It was hard for my parents. They were much more okay with me staying with my family when I was out of the country than they were with me being all the way across the country by myself. But they supported my decision. And they trust me."

She ate the last bite of sandwich. "Sorry, that got a bit heavy, didn't it? Is it my turn to ask questions?"

He used his fingers to wipe crumbs from the corner of her mouth, then licked them clean. Then her lips. She fought to keep still, to keep her hands where they were and her lips closed, her mouth compliant. Oh, who was she kidding, her mouth rarely managed compliant. She opened her mouth and he retaliated by moving to her jaw.

A frustrated moan escaped her and she felt his lips smile against her cheek. Then he was at her ear, teasing the lobe, pulling it between his lips. She tried to turn toward him, but he bit her and stood. She watched in dumb fascination as he took the plate into the kitchen, cleaned up, winked at her and walked out of the room.

CHAPTER THREE

Emma couldn't decide if it was annoying that he didn't give her any directions or reminders not to move when he left, or if she was pleased. Did it mean he trusted her to know that she shouldn't move until told otherwise, or that he hoped she'd make a mistake so he'd have a reason to punish her? She'd known Doms who made a habit of goading their partners into misbehaving for that reason, which she always thought was silly. If they wanted to "punish" the sub, they didn't really need a reason, right? But she'd also seen many subs who responded well to that, so what did she know?

It was hard not to shift around, harder than she normally found it to stay in position. Not because she was nervous, exactly, but because she felt out of her element. In the club, even when she wasn't sure what was in store for her, she felt ready and eager for whatever it might be. Once she started dressing in her club wear, she found herself entering what she thought of as her sub headspace. Which was so not where she was right now.

Thinking about it, she realized that it had been effortless to slip into that mode when he'd pulled her over. The slight nervousness of being ordered out of the car by a cop, the command in his voice and actions, followed by his making it clear to her what sort of situation she'd stumbled upon, had all helped her slip into that place enough that even driving to the barn hadn't broken her out. But apparently eating lunch, talking about school and work and family, even if she was stark naked and being fed by hand, did the trick. Kept her from submitting.

She blinked. She was submitting, though, wasn't she? Doing everything he'd told her to, without question. Other than the bit about the table, but really, that was just gross. So why did this feel different? Because she wasn't enjoying it? She wasn't hating it, she just wasn't getting off on it. Well, except for the kissing part. She just wasn't so fond of the leaving part.

Taking a deep breath, she forced her shoulders to relax and her fingers to unclench. Submission wasn't supposed to be just about sex. Not just about getting off in the most spectacular way possible. Doing what he asked, pleasing him, that's what she was supposed to be doing right now. *Right?* Right.

Focusing, she imagined what she looked like, how she would appear when he returned. She pulled her shoulders back slightly, lifted her chin but directed her gaze to the floor about three feet in front of her. She licked her lips and consciously reset her facial muscles, imagining she looked ready and waiting as opposed to bored or irritated.

Kind of surprised when it all worked, she felt calm and relaxed, but with a delicious thread of anticipation. That he would see her and be pleased. She'd never meditated before but thought her slow, even breaths and focused thoughts might be very close to what it was supposed to be like.

She was certain she knew the second he came into the room, though he made no sound. Her breathing came a little faster, but she no longer found it difficult to hold her position. In that moment, doing nothing but sitting still, she couldn't help but think she was being more true to her submissive nature than ever before. More honest than all the times she'd allowed men to bind her, spank her, do whatever they wanted to her. She felt beautiful.

When long fingers wrapped around her neck, she wasn't surprised, didn't move, though she felt goose bumps spark to life all over her body. He was pleased. She could tell from just the soft caress of his thumb along the column of her neck. It made her happy.

He leaned in, his lips nearly touching her ear, and whispered, "You impress me." He nuzzled behind her ear, then licked a path to her shoulder. "I've read the fax. We have an hour and a half before you need to check in with your friend." He nibbled her shoulder then moved around her to kneel between her knees. "Give me your hands."

It took her a second to get the message from her brain to the hands she'd been so careful not to move and bring her arms in front of her. He took her wrists in his hands and rested them on her thighs.

"Look at me."

She met his hot gaze, and her breathing picked up another notch. Excitement brought awareness back into her limbs and she felt the small ache in her shoulders from the change in position.

"Do you trust me?" he asked. "We have your safety check set up and I've read your limits sheet. Do you trust me to go farther than we did earlier?"

She didn't answer right away, but looked into his eyes. He could be crazy, mean, or even just foolish. But he'd already demonstrated more than once that her safety and welfare were his main concerns. And he'd been amused when she'd refused to sit on the table, not annoyed. Maybe those weren't foolproof reasons to trust him, but they were more than she often had when playing with someone new at the club.

"I trust you." It came out strong and confident, and she smiled.

He answered with a quick grin. It slowly morphed into stern watchfulness, and her body prepared for what he was about to do. Her nipples hardened and cream slid from her sex.

Letting go of her hands, he sat back on his heels. "Put your hands back where they were."

This time she didn't hesitate even a second before complying.

He watched her closely as he reached into his back pocket and pulled out his handcuffs. She admired the gleaming silver, wanting desperately to feel the cold snap of metal around her wrists. She'd wanted it before, in the barn, but known it would be beyond stupid to give that kind of control to a complete stranger. But now…

"I should tell you that Caleb works in security. He has armed men at his beck and call."

He smiled. "That's good to know."

He didn't move behind her but knelt back up so his body was between her knees and reached around to slip the cuffs onto her wrists. He watched her face and must have been satisfied with what he saw as he snapped the circles closed with a sharp *click*.

DREW HAD NEVER USED his police issue cuffs for play before. Never even been tempted. Putting them on Emma stirred something inside him. He leaned in and sucked her nipple into his mouth, surprising a cry from her. She didn't move, arch into him or pull away. Following his instructions so nicely. He'd been surprised when he'd returned after retrieving the fax from the office. Expecting to find her pouting or bored, he'd been mildly turned on by the idea of correcting her. Instead, he'd gone from partly hard to raring and ready to go at seeing the expression of patient waiting on her face. Unlike when they'd been eating and talking, her whole body had been relaxed and yet expectant.

Switching to give her other nipple the same treatment, he tugged slightly on the cuffs to make sure they were secure but comfortable. Her tiny moan sounded musical to him.

"You have the right to remain silent," he whispered, leaning in close to abrade her puffy nipples with his shirt and bring his lips closer to hers. "Or to scream my name at the top of your lungs."

A smile curved her lips and he kissed the corners.

"You have the right to do as I say." He ran his hands up her thighs, teasing the inner legs with his thumbs. "Or be punished if you don't." He bit her lip, almost gently. She opened for him, but he didn't move, his lips just barely brushing hers. He felt her breath in tiny gasps, but she stayed still. He fought with himself, debating between instant gratification and his plans. Finally, with an internal sigh, he pulled back, away from temptation, and rose to his feet.

She blinked up at him, her eyes heavy with need. Perfect. She was just perfect.

"Stand up, Emma."

He gripped her upper arm, helping to support her as she unwrapped her legs and rose awkwardly until her arms were free from the chair back. He kept hold of her in a classic cop move, giving her a little more encouragement than was strictly necessary to walk forward. The slight hesitation in her step when they approached the front door satisfied him. It had occurred to him that she was used to playing only in the club scene, and resuming their scenario outside might keep her off balance. Besides, imagining her pretty ass bent over his official vehicle had been one of the images that had started this whole thing. He saw no reason to deny either of them. There was very little chance of anyone driving close enough to see them, and if they did, he'd hear them with more than enough time to get her inside.

Marching her up to the cruiser, he pushed her down over the hood, his leg automatically going between hers to spread hers wide. She didn't need much encouragement.

"Please, Sir! I haven't done anything wrong."

He could hear the smile in her voice, the excitement at picking up where they'd left off.

"I'll be the judge of that, missy. Don't you move."

He let go of her arm and ran his hands down her sides to rest on her hips.

"But, Sir, you've already searched me. I'm not hiding anything."

"Nothing physical. But that doesn't mean you're not hiding something. Like information. Tell me what you know, or I'll have to force it out of you."

"I-I don't know what you mean." She managed to get a little

quaver in her voice, but couldn't stop her ass from giving an inviting shimmy.

"Are you sure about that?" he asked, making the rasp of his belt as he unbuckled it as loud as possible.

"I swear it! Please don't hurt me, I don't know anything about those guys."

He folded the belt in half, gave it a snap. She gasped and wriggled again and he realized she was pressing her clit into the car. He pulled back and gave her a good solid lash with the belt.

Her cry was mostly shock and a little bit of pain. He grabbed her hips and tilted her up away from the car. "Don't. Move." The steel in his voice froze her minor squirming and she sucked in a breath. "Now. Tell me about these guys." He pressed the ridge of his dick between her legs, his fingers firm on her hips to make sure she followed his order.

"Wh-what guys?"

"The guys you just told me you know nothing about." He pressed harder, then pulled back and gave her two lashes. Watching her—her face, her hands, the slashes of red developing across her ass, he was tempted to end the game and haul her up to his bed. Instead he cupped her from behind, the heat of her pussy convincing him the game was worth it.

"I swear, I don't know where they're hiding!"

He stepped back, tossing the belt to the car's roof. "Stand up. Turn around."

She struggled to rise and turned to face him, her chin down near her chest, posture totally subdued. Except for the nipples reaching out for him and the fact that she kept her legs spread apart.

Moving in close again, he made sure the fabric of his pants chafed over her clit, the buttons on his shirt flirted with her nipples as he grabbed a handful of her hair and yanked her head up and back.

When her eyes met his, fierce with need, he almost smiled. "You need to tell me. They're dangerous men, they could hurt you."

She blinked and he thought she might have lost the train of their conversation. "They'll hurt me if I tell," she whispered.

"I'll protect you."

She gave him a shy look and licked her lips. He loosened his grip on her hair, making it more of a caress. Brought his other hand to her breast, cupped it gently. "Give me what I want. Tell me what I need to know. And I'll protect you. I'll help you."

"Why? Why would you?"

He pressed his thigh harder between her legs, tweaked her nipple, stared her down. "They're bad men and I want to take them down. You can help me, I can help you. Trust me." He made the last part a croon, rubbed his cheek along hers. "Trust me."

Her body went soft under his and he smiled into her ear, moved his hands to her shoulders and pressed down. She resisted only for a moment before sinking to her knees. When his hands went to the button of his pants, she licked her lips. He was pretty sure she was forgetting her character, but that was fine with him. She struggled against the cuffs for a second, trying to bring her arms forward, before subsiding. She didn't look up at him, didn't move her gaze as he lowered the zipper and dropped his pants, then slid his boxers down. He was absurdly pleased when she started to lean forward but then stopped herself and finally glanced up at him.

"Please, Sir, I'm not that kind of girl." She batted her eyelashes at him, in direct contradiction to her words.

"I thought you were the kind of girl that wanted my protection." He fisted his hand in her hair again and pulled her face into his cock. She needed no more encouragement than that, licking him from bottom to top, then sucking the head into her mouth. Her cheeks hollowed out and he closed his eyes in ecstasy. She moved on him, taking more of him in, and he opened his eyes to watch.

There was no more lipstick left on her, just her bare lips pressed around his dick. Her eyes were closed in concentration, and she relied on his hold of her hair to keep her balance, throwing herself forward to engulf him. He couldn't keep the grunt from escaping and wasn't surprised to see her smile around his shaft. Tightening his grip to remind her where her focus should be, he pulled her back and held her still, pushing himself into her, taking the little bit of control she'd managed.

She made no noise of complaint, just kept still and used her tongue to caress him as he moved in and out, slowly working his length in farther each time. When she'd taken all of him, he paused. She raised her eyes to meet his and for the first time it occurred to him that he might not get enough of this, of her, in one day. She waited patiently, and he took it for the gift it was. His free hand caressed her cheek once, then he slowly drew back before pulling all the way free.

One more soft caress of appreciation, and he returned to the game at hand.

"Tell me where they're hiding."

She lowered her eyes, unable to drop her head with his firm grasp, and whispered, "In the old Miller house." Then she bit her lip, and he was positive it was to keep from smiling.

"There, that wasn't so hard now, was it, missy?"

"No, Sir. Thank you, Sir."

"Stand up."

He helped her stand, then turned her around again, folding her back over the hood of the car. He fished the handcuff key out of his shirt pocket, as well as the condom he'd stashed there. Setting the package on the car roof, he unlocked the cuffs and tossed them aside. "You're going to be good now, aren't you? Do what you're told?" he asked.

"Yes, Sir."

He pulled her back up and turned her to face him. "Take off my shirt."

She responded eagerly, attacking the buttons with relish. Her eyes went a little wide and a lot greedy when she bared the Celtic tattoo that swirled over his shoulder and down his arm, ending just above his elbow. She started to lean in, licked her lips, and froze, before straightening and finishing the job he'd given her.

"Get the condom," he told her, gesturing to where he'd set it.

She moved quickly, tearing the wrapper open and waiting for his nod before rolling the rubber down his length. If she spent a little more time and effort smoothing it down than was strictly necessary, he wasn't about to complain.

He moved them over to the driver's side door and pushed her against the car. His hands under her ass, he lifted her until she wrapped her legs around his hips, and he drove into her. Her short cry rang out, her arms wrapping around his shoulders, her pussy gripping him tightly. He rested his forehead against hers, fighting to keep from spilling his release like a damn teenager.

"Drew." She moaned, her fingers flexing against his shoulders the only movement she allowed herself.

"Fuck." He forgot all about the game, all about anything except finally being inside her, the feel of her, the look on her face as he began to move.

"Christ, Emma. You feel so good."

Her heels dug into his ass as she did her best to meet him thrust for thrust. The car rocked slightly under her, her breaths coming out in panting gasps.

"Please, Sir. Please. I can't—"

"You can come when I come," he told her forcefully. And made himself slow down. Concentrated on slowly sliding in and out. Her legs trembled against his hips, her breathing was almost a sob, but she held on, held back, until he no longer could. He dropped his head back and shouted. Her short nails bit into his shoulders and she screamed.

Gravity helped him support her against the car while he regained his sense of the world. She'd rested her head against his shoulder and was giving tiny little licks to his neck. He pulled back so she could drop her legs and gave her a slow, leisurely kiss. When he was pretty sure they could both walk, he pulled off the condom, stepped back and gathered up his things. Silently, she followed him back into the house and to the couch where they both dropped down. He pulled the blanket from the back of the cushions down around them and she snuggled into him.

"Missy?" she asked him after a few minutes, her finger lightly tracing over his tattoo.

He frowned at her. "What?"

"Why did you call me missy?"

He smiled. "I try to be a polite cop. I usually call women ma'am, but that didn't seem quite right."

She laughed. "No, I suppose not. Drew?"

"Yeah?"

"Thanks. That was fun. All of it, I mean. Today."

He kissed the top of her head. "My pleasure, believe me."

They rested for a while before he nudged her up. "You need to go make your phone call."

"Seriously? You want me to call another man right now?" she teased.

"Better than having him show up here. I might have to shoot him then."

She laughed. "Yeah, that wouldn't be quite the right ending to the day."

He helped her roll off him and get to her feet, then followed, enjoying the view. She plodded unself-consciously to the kitchen to retrieve her phone, and didn't seem to mind when he leaned against the wall instead of offering her privacy.

"Richard! What are you doing answering Taryn's phone? I figured Caleb would want to grill me." She paused, listening. "Ah, you're so sweet. Yes, I'm still alive and very, very well. You go help Taryn entertain Caleb and tell her I'll call her later."

She slapped the phone back onto the table and looked at him. "Okay, you're safe for another day."

"Are you going to stay a while?" *Smooth, Drew. Real smooth.*

"Are you inviting me to?" she asked.

"It seemed like a better idea than ordering you to."

She laughed, stood and walked to him, wrapping her arms around his waist, laying her head against his shoulder. Only two inches shorter than him, he realized. He liked the fit.

"Yeah, that's definitely better. Good call."

He cupped her ass and lifted her even closer into him. She lifted her face, offering her sweet lips to him. He took what she offered, enjoying that despite the fact that earlier he'd insisted her kiss be submissive, now she wasn't shy in giving as well as taking. He massaged her ass in encouragement, sucked her tongue hard into his mouth, then let her loose to play as she pleased. When her leg began to climb up his, he gripped her hips and pushed her back a step. "Let's take this to a bed."

THAT SOUNDED like a brilliant idea to Emma. She turned toward the stairs, giving what she hoped was a saucy shake to her ass. She was excited to see his intimate space. The downstairs had been fairly neat, only moderately cluttered for someone who hadn't been expecting company. Pushing open the door he directed her to, the first thing she noticed was that while the bed hadn't exactly been made, the blue comforter had been pulled up to the pillows, leaving a cozy, casual and totally inviting scene.

Drew took her arm and led her to the closet, which had a full-length mirror on one door. Ugh. She wasn't fond of mirrors mixed with sex.

"Kneel."

She assumed the position, watching his reflection as he pulled the bedding down. She hadn't had much of a chance to ogle him when she'd been wrapped around his body. Not a huge fan of gym rats, she appreciated that he had just the right amount of muscles to show he took his workouts seriously, without enough to bulge unattractively. And she figured a cop had more need than most to stay fight ready. He bent over to reach the far side of the bed, and the flex of his butt muscles was a visceral reminder of the strength he'd used to hold her against the car and thrust into her.

"Yum."

He winked at her as he came over and dropped down behind her, his thighs bracketing hers. He put an arm around her stomach and eased her back to rest against him.

"Excuse me?" he asked in that tone that meant *did you really just say that out loud*.

Had she? "Er. Yum, Sir!"

His lips twitched, and she was glad for the mirror after all.

"Put your hands under your thighs."

Not sure exactly what he wanted, she lifted her body up slightly and slipped her hands under her thighs, then lowered her weight back down. Immediately she realized that her own weight would trap her as surely as most restraints, unless she moved out of position. She checked the mirror for his approval and found it in his steady gaze, then blushed as his focus lowered, the mirror hiding nothing. He swirled a finger lightly through the hair between her legs, pulling on the short strands that had gone super curly with the wetness he'd caused. His warm hands moved up to her stomach, toyed with her belly button, then moved on to her breasts. He cupped them gently, weighing them in his palms, then closed his hands in a firm grip that had her struggling to stay still.

"Eyes open," he told her firmly. She hadn't even realized they'd drifted shut, was surprised they had when she was now mesmerized by the view of his large, tanned skin gripping her darker flesh, her nipples jutting out in need. He slid his grip forward, slowly, squeezing tighter as there was less flesh to fill his hands until he gripped only her nipples in his strong fingers, pulling them out against the weight of her breasts. It was almost too much, but when he let go, she cried out, already missing the sensation.

His chest was hard against her back, slick from their combined sweat, the hairs moving against her sensitive skin as they both breathed hard. His cock was pressed against her ass, already hard again, and she suddenly felt empty, wanting him inside. She squeezed the muscles of her channel, which only made the emptiness worse.

"Tell me what you want," he whispered into her ear before pulling the lobe between his teeth, his gaze steady on hers in the mirror.

"You!"

He suckled for a minute before letting go and nipping her shoulder. "Be more specific."

"Fill me up, please. I need you inside me."

He bit her, then sucked hard in the same spot. He'd leave a mark, she knew, but couldn't seem to care.

"That's not very specific," he admonished.

"Fuck me, please. I want to watch your cock fill me."

He smiled and she knew she'd given him the right words. He banded his arm around her stomach and knelt up, taking her with him. "Put your hands behind my head."

She linked her fingers behind his neck and they both looked down, watched as he sheathed his cock then fucked into her with one quick thrust. He gripped her hips, tilted her just right, and slid back out. She'd seen people having sex at the clubs, but never really watched the actual joining so closely before. Now she couldn't look away from the sight of his hard length being revealed inch by inch as it left her body, slick with her juices, before making the return journey, slowly disappearing inside her.

She squeezed hard and he grunted, driving himself through her clenching muscles. She forced herself to look away from where their bodies met, watched his face as he, too, looked up, meeting her gaze with a fierce expression she couldn't quite interpret. He brought one hand up to squeeze her nipples, one after the other, still tender from his earlier attentions. When his other hand dropped down to her pussy, they returned their attention to watch as he smoothed her curls to better open her up to view.

"Drew, please! Sir!"

"You look so pretty, taking me in. All puffed up and wet, letting me slide in…" he matched actions to words, and slowly inched back in, "…and out." She tried to hold him in, but could only beg.

"Please, Sir." It was almost a sob, and it had no effect. His rhythm stayed steady, though his hand on her breasts picked up speed, squeezing the globes, plucking at her nipples.

"Put your hands on the mirror. Brace yourself." Whether he'd noticed her arms had begun to tremble as she'd fought not to pull her weight against his neck, or he'd just decided enough was enough, she didn't know or care. She braced her body, praying her sweaty hands wouldn't fail her as he finally, finally began to fuck her in earnest. He moved his hand from her breast and threaded his fingers through her hair, met her gaze in the mirror.

"Come for me," he growled. "I want to watch you come for me." He pinched her clit and she couldn't do anything but obey. His fingers tightened their hold, keeping her still as he watched her reflection. She came hard and fast, an explosion that overtook her whole body. When her arms shook and her hands began to slide, he pushed her forward until her forearms rested against the glass. He gripped her hips and resumed his furious pace until he, too, came with a small shout. He pulled out, dropped to the ground, and pulled her to his side.

"Didn't you say something about a bed?" she asked, teasing her fingers over his chest.

"I decided on the view instead." He pinched her butt and she squeaked. "Why, are you complaining?"

She pinched her fingers around his nipple, shaking it without any actual force. "Nope, no complaints."

CHAPTER FOUR

"And then we watched a movie," Emma said, reaching a toe out to turn off the tub's jets. Maybe recounting the story while in a bubble bath hadn't been the best plan for relaxing, after all. It wasn't just the hot water making her steam up. Not that she'd given too many details, but she'd certainly been thinking of them while telling her friend the edited version.

"You watched a movie?" Taryn asked over the cell phone, sounding incredulous.

"Well, what else were we supposed to do? We'd already had three amazing encounters in just a few hours. I think if we'd tried again we might have broken something."

"Hmm, I suppose so, but a movie only lasts two hours. What did you do after that?"

"He grilled steaks while I made a salad and then I left."

"I can't believe he didn't ask you to stay the night. You did give him your number, didn't you? Don't tell me you're going to leave this as a one-afternoon stand. I don't think I'll be able to live with it if you do."

"Well, you're safe for now. I gave him my number, and he gave me his. But he has to be at work at seven tomorrow morning and I needed to check into my hotel. You know I got this awesome deal from that website and it's nonrefundable. Besides, I do have things I planned on doing here in Boston, you know." She was beginning to think the scheduled trip to her club would be anticlimactic and unnecessary. She'd already gotten what she'd wanted.

"Tell me you made some firm plans, though."

"We made tentative plans. He said he'd call me tomorrow."

"Call you? That's it?"

"Did you just harrumph?" Emma asked with a laugh.

Taryn made the noise again. "Maybe."

"Look, Taryn, maybe it's not the kind of thing you want to hear about, but hooking up with a hot guy for a hot encounter does not necessarily mean an automatic relationship. We'll see how things progress. I'm not really looking for a serious boyfriend, not when I'm going to leave the state in a year."

"But—"

"Taryn, let's let it be for now, okay? I promise I'll stop by your house on my way back into town. We'll see where we're at then."

"Well, all right." Taryn paused and Emma narrowed her eyes at the charged silence. "I should probably tell you that Caleb checked him out."

She shot up, sloshing water over the side of the tub. "He *what*?"

"Calm down, it's not really a bad thing. He just spoke to someone he knows at the police department, asked her about him professionally."

"Damn it, Taryn, what if it gets back to Drew? What if his bosses think he's trying to get a job with Caleb or something?"

"Emma. Seriously. Don't you trust Caleb to know how to handle it without messing up?"

That calmed her down. She did trust Caleb and was certain that part of his job in the security business included getting delicate information. "Fine, but tell him I'm mad at him. Doesn't *he* trust *me* to go on a date without picking a homicidal maniac?"

"He just did it because he cares about you."

"Yeah, well." She lay back down. The fabulous tub was one of the reason's she'd chosen this hotel. "By the way, I forgot to say thanks for distracting him from the phone when I called to check in. I appreciate you and Richard taking one for the team."

"Two."

"What?"

"Well, we took two for the team."

They both laughed and then said their goodbyes. Emma tossed the phone lightly to land on a towel where it would be safe, then closed her eyes. Sighing, she swirled the hot water up over her breasts then toyed with her necklace. When she'd bought it, she'd never imagined it leading to an encounter like what had happened that day. Her thoughts had been more along the lines of her need to embrace her alternative side as fully as possible this last year before heading back home.

It wasn't that she planned on giving up the lifestyle completely. She didn't think she'd do well in a vanilla relationship. But visits to BDSM clubs would have to be few and very far between. Maybe a once yearly vacation to San Francisco. It was just too risky, playing any closer to home.

Though she fully understood that her need to please her parents wasn't entirely healthy, she also knew that she could never risk hurting them by having them discover this side of her. She wasn't ashamed, but she couldn't expect them to understand, and didn't want them to have to struggle with the shame that they would automatically feel for her.

As much as being a submissive was a part of who she was, so was keeping her family happy. Maybe it wasn't the healthiest attitude in the world, but it worked for her. So she'd decided to have a little fling with her sexuality, and really make this year count. Then, when she graduated, she'd settle down into "real life" and figure out a balance between the two aspects that were so important to her.

Of course, she'd expected to have all her fun at the club. But maybe meeting Drew would give her a chance to figure out how to play with someone discreetly, outside the club scene. She leaned her head back and decided to stop worrying about the future for the rest of the night.

Instead, she could concentrate on the more mundane worry of whether Drew would actually call. She thought he would. There was just a tiny part of her that doubted. A totally and completely ridiculous worry, which was why she hadn't mentioned it to Taryn.

Drew wasn't some fraternity stud trying to rack notches on his belt. He was an adult, one who'd enjoyed his time with her as far as she could tell. She'd had her share of dates with losers who never called, she should be able to tell the difference between them and a stand-up guy by now. And she could. She was positive he would call. Positive she would see him.

Ugh, she was annoying herself. And being such a girl. Did guys have these ridiculous insecurities and tendencies to overthink every freaking thing? She suspected not. The bastards.

Laughing at herself, she bent her knees and submerged herself under the hot water for as long as her breath lasted. When she came up, she wiped hair and water from her face and pulled the plug on the tub. Careful not to fling water around, she dried her hands on the towel before moving her cell phone to the safety of the counter, then toweled herself dry.

The bathroom had a large mirror and when she dropped the towel and grabbed the plush robe, she stopped and stared at her reflection. She wasn't an unattractive person, she knew that. She had what she considered a relatively appealing nature, and had never had too much trouble finding dates. But it had still been uncomfortable being in front of the mirror with Drew that afternoon, being more than bare to him. At least that's how it had felt. And again, it wasn't as if it was anything new. She'd been naked in front of complete strangers at the club. Somehow that was easier. The guys she hooked up with at the club were looking, but they weren't looking at *her*. They were looking at the sub they'd selected for the night, trying to decide how they wanted to use her.

She wasn't sure, exactly, how it had been different with Drew. Just like usual, he'd picked her because he'd known what she was, known what he could do with her, what she wanted from him. The fact that he'd picked her from a selection of one, rather than a room full of available subs should make her feel less chosen, not more. *Right?*

"Ugh!" Yanking the robe on, she turned from the mirror and left the bathroom. She was going to drive herself bonkers. The bed bounced as she flopped onto it, trying to decide what to do next. Her original plan had been to hit the club, but there was no way she was going tonight. For one thing, she felt plenty satiated. Plus, it just didn't feel right. She sent a quick text to her friend Stephanie. Steph had been a member for ages and went on her own all the time, she wouldn't feel abandoned that Emma was canceling.

Of course, Stephanie immediately responded back, thinking Emma needed encouragement or a pep-talk. Emma told her she had a hot date with a guy and would explain later. They made plans to meet at the nail salon the next day. And she was back to deciding what to do for now.

She could pull out her vibrator. She'd brought one along to get her revved up for her planned evening out, but that sure hadn't turned out the way she'd expected. It was nearly ten, but she'd had a fairly exhausting day, all things considered. She left the vibrator in her bag, shucked the robe and climbed under the covers. Flipping through the channels netted her a romantic comedy about to start, and she settled in. Maybe watching someone else go through the paces would help keep her mind off her own situation.

SHE DREAMT of him and woke up wet and aching. Without thinking about it too much, she grabbed her vibrator and brought herself to completion. It was satisfying, but not very. Not when she had the memory of his hands on her so fresh in her mind. It left her own attempts feeling sort of feeble. She came with a soft sigh and turned the toy off. She dozed some more until her cell phone rang. She checked the clock and saw that it wasn't even eight. Nobody who knew her well would expect her to be up and about on a non-work day. The screen showed her that it was Drew. Someone who barely knew her, and yet knew her better than most.

"Hey." She sounded soft and sleepy and cleared her throat, pulling herself up and stuffing pillows behind her back.

"Hey. Did I wake you up?" he asked, not sounding particularly sorry.

"Yes, but that was a little while ago."

It took him a minute to figure out she meant her dreams, but then he chuckled. "Well, turnabout is fair play. I had a hell of a time getting to sleep last night."

She smiled, but tried to keep it out of her voice. "Shouldn't you be at work?"

"I am. Got clocked in and now I'm parked at a speed trap, enjoying my coffee and a donut."

She laughed. "Mmm, does it have chocolate?"

"Nah, I prefer my coffee black."

"That's just boring. Didn't I tell you I work at a coffee shop? I'll whip you up something fantastic one of these days, and you'll never go back to plain old black coffee."

He waited a beat. "I'm sorry, I got stuck on whip and started visualizing you naked and in need of punishment. What did you say after that?"

She shivered. She wasn't much into pain but couldn't deny that occasionally being flogged by someone with skill was a nice treat. She inched her palm under the sheet so it lay flat on her stomach, and pretended the hand was his. "Nothing important," she murmured.

He cleared his throat. "Right. Working here. And trying not to spill my clichéd meal."

"And keeping Jackson safe from unruly speeders. You be careful how you treat them, you hear me?"

"Yes, ma'am. You about to get bossy on me?"

"I have my moments."

"You sure do." It sounded like a purr and she easily imagined the grin on his face.

"Should you be calling me while you're working?" she asked.

"No. But sometimes you just have to be a rebel," he said dryly.

She laughed. "Yeah, and sometimes being a rebel gets a girl ticketed."

"Yes, but you took it like a trooper."

She snorted, then tried to cover it up with a cough.

"Hey, you have a dangerous job. Don't get distracted." She tried to sound teasing but was pretty sure she failed.

"I'm careful, I promise. What about you? Out there in the big city today, you better be careful yourself. No hooking up with strange men and letting them take you into their homes, you hear me?"

"Yes, Officer, I hear you. I'll only let normal men take me into their homes, no strange ones."

"Ha. Ha."

She giggled. "I'm careful, Drew. Hey, you know what happened yesterday was unique, right? I don't normally let unknown guys have sex with me. Well, outside of the clubs, I mean." It suddenly seemed important to her that he know what had happened between them was out of the ordinary. In more ways than one.

"I know. I still want you to be careful, though, all right?"

"Yes, I will."

"I get off work at seven tonight. Are you interested in company? It would take me a while to get up there, but I have tomorrow off, so I could stay as late as we'd like."

The flutter in her stomach turned to a leap in her heart that she tried to repress.

"That would be nice, as long as you don't mind the long drive after a full day at work."

"I think I can handle it after a day of sitting here waiting for cars to drive by too quickly."

"Do you have a club you go to up here? Would you like to go to the one I told you about? Or…"

"Why don't we play it by ear?" he suggested. "I'll bring my bag of toys and something appropriate to wear. But I might just like to keep you to myself, if you're okay with that."

She smiled. "I think I could make do with that. I'm glad you're coming up. And I'm glad you called."

"My pleasure. What are your plans for the day?"

"Shopping and lunch with a friend."

"That sounds nice. I should go. I need to keep the streets safe for sexy speeders who might be coming back this way."

"How hard was it for you not to warn me to be safe again?" she asked.

"My tongue might be bleeding a little."

She laughed. "You take care of that tongue. I'm rather fond of it. I'll see you tonight."

The ridiculous grin she was sure she was wearing faded away slightly as she hung up the phone. *Damn.*

Tempted to order up a big room-service breakfast because she was in such a good mood, she took one look at the prices and laughed her ass off. Her mood would be better spent taking a walk outside and enjoying the summer day anyway.

THE TRIP into Boston seemed especially long and Drew had to set the speed control to keep himself from getting pulled over. He couldn't spend too much time thinking about how he wanted the night to progress because it just made him more impatient to get to Emma's hotel. Unless she was dead set on going to her club, he was pretty sure they wouldn't make it out of her room.

He'd considered waiting until the next day, when he was off. Going up early enough to take her out to dinner. And couldn't believe the thought had crossed his mind. He didn't date submissives. Didn't date within the lifestyle. Not that he dated much outside the scene, but definitely not within.

With his job, it was just too dangerous. He wasn't willing to risk his livelihood over someone he'd just met. And yes, he realized the complete ridiculousness of that idea when he'd already risked everything by taking Emma to his house. Hell, just by taking Emma at all. The moment he'd asked her to step out of the car, he'd done the one thing he'd sworn never to do—let his lifestyle choices put his career in jeopardy.

The smart thing to do would be to quit while he was ahead, while she presumably had no reason to go crazy on him and rat him out to his superiors. But then again, if he hadn't called, that might have pissed her off enough to do exactly that.

He really didn't think Emma would act out that way, but what the hell did he know? Not her, not really. What he did know was that he hadn't been able to convince himself not to call. But he had managed to keep from offering a *date*-date, instead keeping things on the play-date level. There was still a risk, of course. Usually when he played with someone at the club, he kept his personal details to a minimum. Unless he'd known the person long term, they were unlikely to be able to track down his job and cause trouble.

Emma would have no difficulty in doing so, but he had a hard time imagining that she would. *Damn.* His mind was just going in circles as he tried to justify the actions he'd already taken. At this point, it didn't really matter. What was done was done, and what would happen would happen. Because there was no way he was turning around, no way he wasn't going to meet with Emma at least one more time.

As he'd expected, traffic snarled up even more coming into the city. He switched the radio from music to talk, hoping to find a lively discussion to distract him. When that didn't work, he called his best friend. He'd gone to college in New York with Toby and they'd both begun exploring BDSM around the same time. Toby had stayed in New York but they still managed to see each other once or twice a year. When his best friend's wife had been killed in a bad car accident two years before, Drew had taken a week off to be with his friend, support him through the funeral and nurse him through a much deserved drinking spree.

"Hey, buddy," Toby answered.

"Hey. Entertain me so I don't go road rage on these poor, unsuspecting fools I'm surrounded by."

"Where are you? You can't be at home. Podunk doesn't have traffic."

"Tell that to the thirteen people I wrote citations for in the last few days."

"Oh, poor baby, are those mean citizens you're supposed to be protecting actually making you work?"

"Bite me."

"Yes, Sir. Just tell me when and where."

Drew laughed.

"Sorry, I'm on my way into Boston, not New York. And the subbie I'm looking to hook up with has much better equipment than you do."

"Ah, you wound me. But if you tell me more, I may forgive you. Details, man, details."

"I pulled her over for speeding."

"And got her number? Nice."

"Eventually I got her number." He let that hang for a minute of silence.

"No. No way mister straight arrow banged a hottie on shift."

His lips quirked. Toby, a high school teacher, had a tendency to sound like his kids, and Drew knew him well enough to know he hadn't meant to be disrespectful.

"Well, it was after shift, and no, I'm not going to give you details. I'll just say that after the ticket was given and the official transaction complete, we took things to a different level."

"Nice. And now you're driving into the city to see her?"

"Yeah. She goes to college near me, actually, but is spending a few days in Boston."

"Mmm, young and experimental?"

"Twenty-three and been experimenting for a little while. She was wearing a necklace with that BDSM emblem, so not a newbie." He changed lanes to get around idiots who seemed to have no clue what they were doing. "And…we had a good time and I'm driving up to meet her rather than waiting until she goes back home."

"Ah, come on! You have to give me more than that."

"I used my police issue handcuffs on her."

"That's more like it, give me more."

"I'm not giving you details, you perv."

"Even if I beg?"

"Even if."

"Fine, let's talk about me then. Are you still up for a visitor?"

Vacations were hard for Toby. His wife had also been a teacher and they'd taken a trip every summer, something they planned together. The first summer after she'd died, Toby had spent the whole vacation at Drew's house. The second year he'd stayed home, and Drew had gone up to visit for a long weekend. This year Toby had decided to do a summer trip on his own, but he was starting off with a short stay at Drew's.

"Of course. I took a couple of days off work. Looks like the weather will probably hold for a nice sail."

"I think you're right. You going to invite your new friend along?"

"We're not dating. We'll be playing tonight, and hopefully she'll be up for doing that again. But don't get the wrong idea. We're not starting a relationship."

There was a long pause. "Well, you're definitely starting a relationship, but not the kind you mean. I get that. Well, actually no, I don't get that. Why are you determined to limit the type of relationship you might have?"

"Okay, it's a relationship. A club relationship."

"Without the club."

"The actual setting isn't really the point, it's the attitude and expectations."

"Exactly."

Neither spoke for a minute and Drew tried to expel the irritation that was building. "I like club relationships. I like keeping things within those boundaries. I don't see any reason to change that."

"Like meeting the right woman?"

"Emma is a great person, we had a lot of fun. I'd like to continue having fun with her. But no, I'm not interested in introducing her to my parents, or my coworkers, or whatever it is that people expect when they're in the kind of relationship you're talking about."

"The kind of relationship where you share your lives together?"

"Yeah, that kind."

"Does she know that?" Toby's voice was sharp, surprising Drew. They'd had similar conversations, once before Caroline had died, and once after.

Drew sighed. "I'll make sure we're both clear on what we want before we set anything else up."

"So, how about introducing her to me? Are you going to use my visit as an excuse to not see her?"

"How about you let me have this, our second encounter, before you get too far ahead of yourself?"

Toby sighed again. "Fine."

Drew changed the subject before his friend could go off on another tangent. "Have you mapped out the rest of your trip yet?"

Toby only hesitated a moment before describing the Civil War sites he planned on visiting. This first real trip alone was going to be tough and Drew wished he could make it better for his friend.

"Toby, are you sure you don't want some company for all that?"

"You know you would hate this kind of trip. I'll be fine. I'm not ready to think about a relationship myself, but unlike someone I know and love, I'm aware that I need to live my life and not get hung up on only thinking about the worst that can happen."

"Toby. That doesn't even make sense."

"Yeah, yeah, I'll shut up. For now. I'll see you in three weeks."

When he'd hung up, Drew jerked the Bluetooth out of his ear and dropped it on the passenger seat. When Caroline had been alive, he'd begun thinking it would be nice to find someone like her in his life. Someone permanent, someone to share the good times and the bad. Since he'd long before determined he couldn't risk inviting someone in the lifestyle into his professional life, he figured he should give vanilla dating a try.

It hadn't taken long to discover that a vanilla relationship wasn't going to cut it for him, either. And then bad weather mixed with a truck driver who'd maybe not had enough rest had resulted in a car accident that had taken his friend's wife. Drew had discovered that the good times weren't worth having if losing her was the ultimate bad time. Toby still hadn't dragged himself back to the life he'd had before. Probably never would. The hole Caroline had left was just too great.

Trying to shake off the black mood, Drew turned the radio back on to a music station and followed the map he'd memorized to the hotel Emma had chosen. He pulled up to the front and grabbed his bag, taking a ticket from the valet. A quick glance at his watch showed he was fifteen minutes early.

A small bar area off to the right was mostly empty. He was able to get a glass of ice water quickly, and took a seat. The drive should have given him plenty of time to get himself ready, but being annoyed with the other drivers, talking to Toby...thinking about Caroline. No, he needed to get his head in the game, bring his control to the forefront, and give Emma a fantastic evening. Dwelling on the pain that Toby had endured, the might-have-beens and the maybes, was useless.

When the glass was empty, he took a deep breath and rose. He made his way to the room number Emma had given him and checked his watch. Exactly on time. He knocked, unsurprised when she answered almost immediately.

CHAPTER FIVE

She looked stunning. The strappy dress hugged her breasts and ribs before cupping her perfectly rounded ass. It didn't go much farther before ending, leaving a lot of leg for him to admire. The muted purple somehow set off her fabulous skin and her legs looked ten-feet long, ending in sharp heels that gave him a new appreciation for the whole foot fetish thing.

He raised his eyes back up to hers and smiled. That was all it took to bring a soft flush to her skin. Stepping in, he encouraged her to move back. He pulled a long-stemmed single red rose into view and handed it to her while dropping the bag to the floor. She smiled and brought the flower to her nose. Just because it wasn't a date, didn't mean he couldn't show his appreciation for their time together. He shoved away the thought that her smile made him want to do whatever he could to be able to keep seeing it.

He let the door close behind him and leaned back against it, watching her. She lowered the flower and met his gaze.

"You're gorgeous," he said.

She blushed again, but smiled. "Thank you."

"Come here."

He didn't move, waited for her to take the step and a half until she was only a couple of inches from him. Then he reached out, grabbed her hips, and pulled her in tight. With the heels higher than the sandals she'd worn the other day, her lips were perfectly matched to his. He kissed her hard, taking, giving. Her breasts pushed against his chest, her thigh notched neatly between his legs, and her forearms braced against the door next to his head as her body easily surrendered to him.

He didn't know how long they stayed like that, but he wasn't really ready to quit when the knock sounded loudly on the door. Breaking free, he cursed softly. She blinked up at him in confusion.

"It's okay. Go into the bathroom for a few minutes. I'll let you know when you can come out."

She didn't like it. Her eyes narrowed and he could see her think up an argument. He reached his hand up and brushed her cheek softly, his thumb caressing her slightly swollen lips. "Go on. It'll just be a few minutes."

Turning on her heel, she did as she was told. When the bathroom door clicked shut, Drew turned and let the room service waiter in. It only took a minute to have the items set up on the little coffee table, the waiter tipped and on his way.

"Emma. You can come out now."

He enjoyed watching her expression change from irritation to another smile. He gestured for her to take a seat on the sofa and sat next to her, as close as he could without quite touching.

"I hope you like strawberries and champagne."

"When the strawberries are dipped in chocolate, I certainly do. This is lovely."

She started to reach for one, then stopped and looked at him, dropped her hand. "Are we starting?"

"Would you like to be starting?"

"I guess since you ordered me into my own bathroom, we already have."

She said it wryly enough that he chuckled. "I guess we have. Would you like to have a snack here, then go out? Or stay in and start now, snack included?"

She watched him as if he were going to give her a clue to his preference, then drew a deep breath. "I'd rather stay here."

"Is there anything you need to tell me? Any negotiations? Anything different for you since last time we were together?"

Keeping her gaze steady with his, she shook her head no.

"You're sure? Because I won't be relying on handcuffs to hold you down this time." Her responding shiver kicked his pulse into a higher gear, but he forced it down. He wanted to take things slow and steady tonight.

He reached out, caressed his fingers down her cheek. "All right then." Picking up a strawberry, he swiped it through the whipped cream, painted her lips with it.

"How's that taste?" he asked.

She ran her tongue through the cream, swallowed.

"Very good."

He raised a brow.

She blushed a little and looked down. "Very good, Sir."

He added more cream and nudged the strawberry between her lips.

"Bite."

She did, licking her lips when she'd finished chewing to clean up the mess he'd left behind. Her eyes had closed in appreciation of the dessert and his cock jerked. He leaned forward and kissed her, tasting sugar and chocolate and Emma. His hands were threading through her hair, holding tight, before he knew it. Another reminder to himself to slow down had him pulling back.

"You had lunch with your friend?"

She blinked a couple of times before answering.

"I did, yes. It was good to see her and we had a great talk."

"Does she know the other reason you came up here?"

"No." She frowned. "I thought about telling her, but it never felt right for the conversation. Do you find it annoying, having to hide things like that? Or is it stupid to even assume that you hide too?"

"Not stupid, no. And yes, sometimes I find it annoying, but not as annoying as trying to live a totally vanilla lifestyle."

"Which you've tried."

"Honestly, I haven't had much luck in long-term relationships, vanilla or not. I think—" He drank some champagne, knowing it was a stall tactic. He didn't want to sound like a cynical bastard, but he didn't want to lie, either. "I won't say it's the same for everyone in the lifestyle, but for myself, I've come to the conclusion that permanent, long-term relationships aren't really possible. I don't think it's compatible with the life I've chosen to live."

He watched her carefully, waiting for anger or even doubt. For some reason her nod as she swallowed her food was…surprising instead of a relief.

"That's kind of what I've been thinking. When I move back to California, I'm going to have to figure out a way to balance living with my family, being the person that I want to be around them, and yet not denying this part of myself. I'm not quite sure how it's going to work. I want to be true to myself but then again, a lot of what I do isn't really other people's business."

"That is a very true statement." He handed her the other glass of champagne while he bit into a strawberry. "Do you think you'd try a vanilla relationship?"

She shook her head. "No, I don't really see how that would work. I mean, maybe if I met the right guy I could introduce him into the lifestyle, but that would be too risky. And he'd have to be pretty amazing for me to want to…well, train isn't the right word. But I do prefer a Dom who already knows what he wants."

"And if you met a Dom that you wanted to take home to your parents?"

"I guess that's what I'm hoping for. But it's kind of hard to picture. All the guys I've played with in the clubs have been just play. I can't really imagine any of them turning into real relationships. And I guess it would partly depend on what kind of life he lived outside the clubs."

He nodded. "My best friend and his wife were in the lifestyle, and they had a fantastic marriage. So I've seen it, respect it, but I was always afraid it would become public somehow and ruin their lives. They were both high school teachers. I just can't risk my job like that. The best compromise I could come up with was keeping the play to the clubs, which doesn't leave much room for an out-of-club relationship."

He fed her another strawberry, then set their empty glasses aside, deciding one glass each of champagne was enough.

She rested one arm along the back of the sofa, her fingers drumming a soft beat. "So it can be done, but you live your life in fear of being found out. That sucks."

He reached out, touched her naked neck. "You're not wearing your necklace."

"No. I got it because I wanted to give myself this one year of really living that life, making the most of it, I guess. Not that I'm going to give it up, but that it will be different. More subtle. I guess I thought having a year of not having to be subtle would make it easier, later. Kind of like spending all that time out of the country made it easier to stay here and go to school. I'll still travel, but never like that again." She licked the cream off the strawberry he held out for her. "Does that make sense?"

"Sure." And brought him the relief he'd been looking for earlier. "Makes sense to me."

"This is weird, but nice." She waved her hand between the two of them. "It's like a club relationship, but without the noise and people of a club."

He smiled. "That's exactly what I was thinking." Now that he was sure they were on the same page, he was eager to get his hands on her. He fed her another strawberry, trying to keep his focus on what she was saying and not on the shape of her lips as she pulled the fruit in, licked the cream up.

She must have seen a change in his expression because her breathing picked up speed and her nipples beaded under her thin dress, making him wonder if she was wearing a bra. Luckily he didn't need to keep wondering.

"Emma. Come here." He took the accent pillow from behind his back and dropped it to the floor at his feet.

She rose, moved so she was next to his right knee, and knelt. Beautiful, absolutely beautiful. He cupped her cheek, rubbing his thumb along her lips. He was becoming addicted to touching her.

"Stand up. Leave your shoes on, but take your clothes off. Slowly."

Her lips curled up slightly on his last word. She rose gracefully to her feet and turned, offering him her back. Obligingly, he inched the zipper down, one finger trailing behind to run down her increasingly bared back, bumping over the strap of her bra. So she was wearing one. He wanted to see what thin confection she'd chosen that had done nothing to hide her desire from him. He was pretty sure he'd approve. When the zipper was all the way lowered, he ran his palms up her back, parting the fabric until it barely clung to her shoulders.

When he withdrew his hands, she turned carefully until she faced him. One deep breath dislodged the dress and it pooled at her feet. She wore a stark red, lacy bra that cupped her breasts lovingly and didn't cover her nipples. It matched the equally lacy underpants that did very little to hide her assets. He most definitely approved.

"Beautiful. Take it off."

Her smile was full this time as she reached back to release the flimsy excuse for a bra. It, too, dropped to her feet, followed by the panties. He loved that while she was clearly not an exhibitionist, neither was she terribly shy about her body. She'd been embarrassed to be in front of the mirror at his house, but she stood in front of him now and she smiled. Oh yeah. He liked that a lot.

He directed her to remove her shoes and hang up the dress, then rose to stand in front of her.

"Now you can undress me."

She didn't hesitate, but reached for the knot of his tie. It occurred to him he'd never worn a suit and tie to a club, though it had seemed like a natural choice for picking her up at a nice hotel. He'd never had feminine hands loosen the knot at his throat and release the silk from around his neck. It was sexy, but somehow sweet. She slipped it over his head, bringing her mouth so very close to his, letting her breasts tease his chest.

He narrowed his eyes at her when she leaned in even closer, but she just smiled serenely and laid his tie over the back of the couch. It took more effort than it should to hold back the smile he wanted to let escape. She stepped back, though only a very small step, and brought her hands between them to work on his shirt buttons.

It was torture, one he nearly ended a number of times by pulling back and taking care of the job himself, but he maintained control and forced himself to savor the feel of her warm hands making their way down his front. When she'd released the last button, she followed his example and ran her hands up his chest to separate the shirt panels. He took in a deep breath and her fingers responded by digging into the muscles of his chest. Ten small points of contact that made him ache.

When she seemed inclined to linger, he forced his brain to clear.

"Emma."

"Hmmm."

"You're supposed to be doing a job."

She blinked up at him and stopped her explorations of his chest through his undershirt. The blush she'd held back while he'd examined her naked sprang to her face and he had to bite his cheek to keep from laughing.

"Sorry, Sir."

She yanked her hands from him and moved them to the hem of his shirt, sliding it up his chest with a bit more speed. He raised his arms until she had the shirt clear of his head before he took over the job and dropped the shirt to the chair behind him. Her attention had already refocused on his belt.

EMMA WANTED to rip the belt from Drew's pants and get down to business, but she was pretty sure he'd see that as disobeying his orders. Instead, she forced herself to remove the belt slowly and add it to the growing pile of his things. She resisted the temptation to curl her fingers into his waistband while unbuttoning his pants, and instead held them as far away from his skin as was possible while sliding the zipper down. She let the pants fall to his ankles while she dealt with shoes she'd forgotten. She untied the laces and held the shoes steady while he stepped clear.

"Hang the clothes up," he directed.

She did as she was told and turned to find him sitting at the foot of the bed, the throw pillow again on the floor at his feet. Licking her lips, she didn't need his pointed finger to know what her next task was. Sinking to her knees, she waited for his instructions though her mouth watered in anticipation.

"Tell me what you want," he said.

She blinked. Okay, not the order she'd been expecting. "I want to take you in my mouth."

"Be more specific."

"I want to lick your cock and wrap my lips around you. I want to hold it in my hands and play with your balls. I want to smell you and taste you and swallow you down."

He gripped her hair in his hand, wound the length around his fist and pulled until she was forced to look up at him. The heat in his eyes matched the fire racing through her system. Without rushing, he lowered his face and kissed her. It was slow and easy, when she expected hard and fast. She wanted to run her hands through his hair, over his body, pull him closer and coax him to matching his kiss to the need building between her thighs. She sighed.

His lips curled against hers in answer and he backed away, holding her head still when she tried to reach higher.

"Go to it, then," he said.

It took her a second to understand that he was giving her permission to do the things she'd said she wanted. Less than a second later, her hands were on him. Last time she hadn't been allowed to touch. Now she'd make up for that. She wrapped both hands around him, gently at first to feel the softness, then tighter to feel the underlying hardness. When he didn't react, she squeezed just a tad bit harder and hid her smile when the thighs that bracketed her tensed. She loosened her grip and slid her hands up and down, one thumb exploring the tip while her other hand moved down to cup his balls.

Lowering her head, she stiffened her tongue into a point and drew it up the underside of his cock. His legs jerked in against her, holding her tight. Without pausing, she flattened her tongue and followed the same path, then opened her mouth wide and took him in. She worked his length up and down until she'd taken as much as she could, one hand braced on his thigh, the other continuing to work his balls. His grip on her hair tightened when she sucked in her cheeks and wiggled her tongue.

"Christ," he gasped.

"Mmm," she hummed.

She continued for long minutes before releasing him to use her stiffened tongue to tease at the sensitive spot under the head. When he shifted in his seat, she darted back in, engulfing him in one smooth thrust, able to take him farther now. She would have moved but he used his hold on her hair to keep her still and thrust in and out, in and out, then erupted into her in one long stream. She swallowed quickly and held still, letting him use her as he wanted.

When he pulled her back she carefully withdrew, giving one thorough lick to clean him up as best she could. He released her and she sat back on her heels, eyes down, waiting for more.

"That was very nice." His voice was rough and she curled her lips in to keep from smiling.

"Thank you, Sir."

He ran his thumb over her lower lip, something he seemed to do a lot. She liked it. She liked him. A lot.

"Can you get my bag for me?" he asked, pointing to the duffel bag still sitting by the door. She rose, glad to be off her knees for a minute, and fetched the bag. She could hardly wait to find out what was inside.

"Stand here," he said, indicating the spot she'd just vacated.

She set the bag down on the bed next to him and took her spot. He opened it carefully so that she couldn't see in and she tried not to pout. Damn know-it-all Doms. He pulled out nylon wrist cuffs and she held out her wrists, one at a time, while he fastened them. They were the typical black and she was pleased to see that they looked brand new. Either that or he kept them in superb condition.

Instead of ankle restraints, she was surprised when he pulled out thigh cuffs. She remained motionless when he attached them. Next came similar straps that she wasn't sure what he was going to do with until he wrapped them around her lower leg. *Okaaaay.* Usually she had a pretty good idea, going into a scene, what was going to be happening. Now she was clueless, although fairly certain there would be sex. Glorious, explosive sex, if history was anything to go by. So she took a deep breath and tried to stop overthinking and trying to guess his plans.

She didn't realize she'd closed her eyes with her little bit of meditation until she opened them and found her gaze snared by his. He ran his palms up her hips, waist and ribs without breaking eye contact. Though his face was mostly expressionless, she got the feeling he was pleased.

He pushed her back slightly and rose. Wordlessly, he took her hand and led her into the bathroom, carrying the duffel bag. Of course, as soon as she entered the room, she felt the need to use it for its intended purpose. How embarrassing. She had little hope that he'd allow her any privacy and the more she tried to ignore the sensation, the more urgent it became.

He'd set the bag down on the counter and was leaning over to turn on the tub faucet. Crap, there went her carefully styled hair. She'd used hot rollers and everything. She took the opportunity to admire his ass, but when he straightened, she cleared her throat.

Turning, he gave her a questioning look.

"Sir, I, um, could use the toilet." She looked down at the floor.

"Go ahead." He didn't move.

Sure her face was flaming, she glanced up to see if there was any hope of a different outcome, and met his implacable expression. *Fine.*

She did her business as quickly as possible, refusing to look at the man leaning against the counter, watching her. When she was done, she washed her hands and dried them before turning to face him. He didn't bother to hide his smile.

"Get in the tub."

She started to climb in, only then realizing he hadn't used the stopper, so the tub wasn't filling up. *Hmm.* Sitting in the center of the tub, she crossed her legs and waited.

"Down on your back."

It wasn't easy sliding down the mostly dry porcelain until her back was flat. She had to lift her legs up onto the large ledge surrounding the tub to get all the way down. Once she was settled, he motioned for her to lift her head and slid a rolled-up towel underneath for a pillow. It was bulky and forced her chin almost to her chest.

He reached over her body and took her left ankle, folding her leg back until he had her knee bent all the way in. Then he attached the thigh cuff to the strap around her shin. *Oh.* He repeated the action on her right leg, then attached her wrist cuffs together and pulled them above her head. His hands came back to caress her ankle, his finger tracing the tattoo.

"Pretty. Does it mean anything in particular?"

She shrugged as best as she was able.

"They're apple blossoms. I liked them."

His sharp gaze suggested he'd noticed her evasion.

"Mmm, hmm. I like it too. I didn't realize they were apple blossoms, though. Apples. Are you trying to tempt me?" he asked.

Damn the man. He was the first person to figure it out. Even her roommate who she'd gotten inked with had simply believed her when she'd said she just thought the design was pretty. Her blush gave her away.

"Something like that. I liked the idea of a design that was pretty, girly, but also secretly naughty."

"I like the idea too. A lot." He teased his finger around the design some more, than sat back on his heels.

The tub was wider than the one she had in her apartment, so

when her spread legs rested against the sides, she was wide open. He looked satisfied with her positioning and reached his hand to test the water streaming from the tap at the end of the tub. When he placed his wrist in the stream, she figured she had a pretty good idea what was coming. He adjusted the taps a bit, tested the water once more, then met her eyes.

"Hold on to your pillow," he suggested, and grabbed her hips, pulling her down the tub until the water was falling on her pubic bone. It was warm, not hot, and the stream wasn't very heavy. She readjusted the towel under her head and waited.

Cupping one hand under the water, he angled it away from her as he used his other hand to push down on her knee, tilting her pelvis higher. Then he redirected the stream. Even knowing it was coming, she gasped at the sensation. Warm water ran from his fingers and landed directly on her clit. The need already spiraling through her ratcheted up a number of notches.

"Oh god," she moaned, knowing this was only the beginning.

The evil guy at the controls just smiled. He played with his fingers, letting the stream hit her full force, then easing it away so that part of the stream hit her clit while part heated her sex. It didn't take long before she was edging toward orgasm, and he knew it. Her channel clenched and unclenched, empty and waiting. When he let the full force of it stay on her clit for a whole minute, she had to beg through gritted teeth.

"Please, Sir, may I come?"

"No."

"Ah, fuck. Please, Sir, I can't—" She wailed as he twisted the cold water tap and aimed a much heavier stream of water to hit her channel. Her hips tried to buck but the straps and his hand held her down.

"Oh, please, oh please."

He moved his hand again and now the water returned to her clit, shockingly cold, though he didn't give her the whole stream.

"I want to you to remain perfectly still now. Don't even clench your muscles." He circled her opening. "At least not these ones. Understand? Can you do that for me?"

She swallowed hard, took a deep breath. "Yes, Sir." She forced her thigh muscles to loosen, her hands to unfist.

He released her knee and dipped his finger in the water, then allowed the cold drops to fall on first her nipples, then her navel. He repeated the move, then leaned in and blew on her breasts. Her breath caught and she fought her muscles to keep from contracting.

His smile rewarded her. "Very good, Emma. Keep it up. I'll tell you when you can come."

"Y-yes, Sir."

She was relieved when he readjusted the taps and warmer, softer water began to flow. He cupped his hand just so and once again the lighter stream landed directly on her clit. Breathing faster, she turned her eyes, watched his face instead of the water.

"Now. No moving, of course, but you can tense whichever muscles you like, except for that grasping cunt. It stays passive until I tell you to squeeze. You understand?"

What, like doing Kegels? "Yes, Sir."

"Good."

Nothing changed. He didn't move, didn't change the flow of water, didn't do anything. She just watched his face, while he watched her pussy. And suddenly, more than anything in the world, she needed to do those damn Kegels. She wanted to squeeze those muscles tight, though there was nothing but a teasing trickle of water to hold on to. Her clit damn near throbbed, she wanted to shift her hips, get more, get less, get something.

Begging hadn't worked before, but it was all she had. "Please, Sir." It was nothing more than a whisper this time, and sounded much more like an entreaty than the badly couched demand from before.

He smiled. "Soon, Emma. Soon."

She closed her eyes tightly, then forced them open as that only seemed to intensify the sensations. Her abs contracted and she honestly wasn't sure how much longer she could go without clenching—

"Squeeze," he said softly.

She was so lost she didn't understand at first, but then she complied. It was at once a relief and a torture as the motion shot sensation to her already burdened clit.

"Release."

Still watching his face, she realized he wasn't as unaffected as he sounded. His breathing had picked up and his eyes blazed. Knowing that what they did excited him didn't exactly help her to relax.

"Squeeze."

Before the word was fully out of his mouth, she was complying. He retaliated by giving the next order immediately.

"Release."

It felt like a million bubbles were rising up through her pelvis, trying to escape through her clit. She couldn't remember the last time she'd had to work so hard to avoid coming before she was allowed to.

"Pleeeeeease," she moaned.

His free hand reached to wipe the hair from her brow. "I'm going to count to four. You can give a quick squeeze on each number, and hold it for a second. You can come on four."

I can do this, I can do this, I can do this. Torturous bastard. For a second she worried she'd let the thought slip free of her lips, but he began to count.

"One."

She gave a quick squeeze.

"Two."

Another. She gritted her teeth and forced a deep breath through her nose.

"Three."

Oh god, oh god, oh god.

"Four." She clenched again and let the tidal wave wash over her. Her vision blacked out and she didn't realize she was screaming until the sound died out. The water became painful half a second before it turned off, leaving her pussy twitching in the sudden silence.

She only realized Drew had unhooked the cuffs when he lowered her feet to the bottom of the tub, her leg muscles shaking. Like a rag doll, she let him pull her arms down, free her wrists, without any help from her. He didn't seem to mind. Hooking his arms under hers, he pulled her to a sitting position, then climbed in behind her. He reached forward and turned the water back on, making it nice and hot. Cupping his hand over her pussy, he swiped a finger through her cream and brought it up to his lips.

"Mmmm, more dessert."

She couldn't summon more than a small smile.

The tub filled quickly and he turned the taps off, turned on the jets, and leaned back, tucking her carefully between his legs and urging her head back to lie against his shoulder. His hard cock pressed into her but she figured it was his fault she was too limp to do anything about it, and closed her eyes, drifting.

He was the most comfortable bath cushion ever. She wondered what kind of tub he had in his house, because in addition to the annoyance of roommates, she had a small, apartment style tub which would so not work for this type of thing. If he didn't have a nice one, maybe they'd have to make a point to visit hotels occasionally.

She blinked, realizing she'd put "future them" in an ongoing situation without thought. Well, she couldn't really deny it anymore. She wanted something with him despite knowing she wasn't going to be around much longer. But he'd also said he wasn't looking for anything permanent. So maybe he'd be happy to keep things going for a while. He seemed to be enjoying himself as much as she was.

CHAPTER SIX

When Emma stirred, stretched slightly with a satisfied hum that could truthfully be called a purr, Drew began moving his hands. Lazily, he played with her fingers, explored her arms, caressed her thighs. When a light tension seeped into her body, he moved to her breasts, plumping them gently, scraping her nipples with his thumbs. Her skin was damp from the steam and his hands felt rough and hard. He dipped them into the bath water and poured a stream down her center and over her breasts. He did it again, then massaged the water into her before pulling on her nipples.

She angled her hips down, rubbing against his dick, which had fully recovered from the blow job and was ready to sit up and beg.

He sat up himself, taking her with him, turned off the jets and flipped the drain switch. As the water began to lower, he made sure she was steady and carefully levered himself out from behind her. The towels were large and fluffy, and he handed one to her then lifted her to her feet. Helping her step clear of the tub, he brought her in for a quick kiss. Just one taste before he got back to business. When she shivered against him, probably from excitement as the bathroom was still steamy, he finally pulled back and toweled her dry, paying careful attention to those bits he liked best. He didn't let her reciprocate, but sent her to wait for him on the bed while he dried himself briskly.

Picking up the restraints he'd tossed aside earlier, he laid them out on the counter to finish drying. They hadn't gotten too wet and should be fine by morning. Good thing he'd had the foresight to bring more than one set. He grabbed his bag as he made his way back to her, setting it within easy reach.

She blinked when he set the additional nylon cuffs and straps on the bed, but made no comment as he went about restraining her as she'd been before the bath.

"On your knees, butt in the air, head on the bed," he instructed.

She rolled over and assumed the position. He connected the thigh and calf straps, as well as a short strap between her legs. "Give me your hands." She rested her weight more firmly on her shoulders and moved her arms back to rest along her legs. He clipped them to the thigh straps and stepped back, then moved a pillow from the head of the bed, and arranged it under her cheek.

"Comfortable?"

"Yes, Sir."

"Good."

Her ass was round and inviting, her pussy puffy and slick. He slid one finger straight into her, moving easily through the wetness. When he pulled free, he was nicely lubricated, and moved his finger directly to her asshole. She tensed when he pressed against the pucker, but only for an instant. Then she pushed back, accepting him into her body. He worked the finger in and out for a few minutes while he pulled the next items from his bag.

When he removed his finger, she arched back, searching for more. He took his time, lubing the plug he'd brought, letting her see him prepare it. When he brought it to her hole, she pushed back, accepting the first part easily. As it widened, she squished her eyes closed. He slowed, pulled the plug out a little, worked it back in farther. While he worked the toy, he caressed her butt with his free hand, then moved it around to her front. She moaned when he explored her wetness, jerked back against him when he teased her clit.

The plug settled into position, the flared base flush against her bottom. "Okay?"

"Mmm."

He smacked her ass.

"Yes, Sir!" she said smartly.

He turned away, hiding his smile. A quick trip to the bathroom to wash his hands had him back in control. Returning to the bed, he studied her. The languor from the bath had vanished. While technically remaining still, she made needy little movements that she was probably unaware of. Her thighs clenched and unclenched, her hips shifted slightly, and her head moved restlessly. He was very pleased. The bright red base of the plug looked downright festive next to her skin. It had been fun, choosing things from the online shop just for her. He hadn't even blinked at the overnight shipping costs, just been satisfied he'd had the option of getting what he needed before he saw her.

Walking to her slowly, he enjoyed the way her eyes settled on him, though they were somewhat hazy with her need and submission. She watched him, and she licked her lips. His cock jerked, as though it hadn't been fully satisfied between those soft lips just a short while ago.

He reached out a hand, sliding it over her ass, across her hip, down her stomach and to her pussy. She mewled like a kitten unable to voice its needs. "Are you ready for me, Emma? Tell me what you want." He petted her curls, caressed her stomach, teased her belly button.

"You. Please, Sir, I just need you."

"I'm right here."

"I need you inside me. Filling me up. Please, Sir, please."

"So pretty. So ready. The plug was a little hard to take. Are you sure you want more? I'm not taking it out." He was such a bastard for teasing her.

She sobbed. "Yes, Sir, please, Sir. I need you."

He reached down to her grasping hand, let her take his fingers, squeeze tight. Bending down, he nibbled that perfect ass cheek, then sucked hard. She clenched around the plug, but didn't move. When he pulled back, he examined the hickey and decided to make a matching set. He repeated the action on the other side, then admired his work.

"Please, please, please." It was a whisper he barely heard, but it was enough. He couldn't hold back any longer, and donned a condom. She moaned in anticipation when he knelt up on the bed, his legs bracketing hers. He guided himself to her pussy and lodged just the head into her opening.

"Oh god!" she wailed.

"More?" he asked through clenched teeth. He was torturing himself as much as her.

"More, more, more!"

"You can come when you're ready." He gripped her hips and plunged deep. Her pussy quivered around him as she came. He closed his eyes, willed himself to hold on, waited her out. When the quivering stopped, he counted to thirty. Then he began to move. With her legs strapped so they were only inches apart, and the plug filling her ass, she was even tighter than before. He watched her face closely as he slid in and out. She opened her eyes, stared right at him and smiled. Christ. Satisfied she wasn't in any pain, he lost himself in the sensations, the tight, grasping heat. His fingers dug deep, probably bruising, but he needed to hold on to her. Needed her.

His balls drew up tight and his eyes rolled up in his head as the orgasm seemed to blow through him, over him and around him. It took all of his concentration to roll to the side so he didn't squish his captive sub. He scooted so they were face to face, her sleepy eyes watching him, her grin lazy and wide.

"Hey there," he managed.

"Hey."

"Having a nice night?"

"I've had worse."

Apparently his brain wasn't ready for conversation beyond clichés, so he decided to go with it. "Come here often?"

She giggled. "It's my first time."

"Ready for another round?"

Her eyes got adorably huge and the laughter gave him enough energy to sit up. He got her free of her bonds and they cleaned up before collapsing onto the bed. He wasn't so tired that the pleasure of wrapping his arms around her and holding her close against him went unnoticed. It had been quite a while since he'd actually slept with a woman. It was so much easier to go to the club, satisfy his needs and go home. Alone.

Despite what Toby thought, this situation was about as perfect as any he could imagine. They were both on the same page, wanting to keep their sex lives separate from their everyday lives, neither looking for a relationship that would lead to anything permanent. Emma would be in Massachusetts for a year.

They could have the next little while to play with each other, please each other, but they would both keep it light. They'd have to. He drifted off to sleep, satisfied with the shape of his near future.

Emma wasn't sure if going out to breakfast after checking out of the hotel would count as a real-world date or an ending to their very nice play date and she didn't want to risk having the morning end too soon, so despite the ridiculous room-service prices, she grabbed the menu, bounced onto the bed next to Drew and asked him what he wanted.

At his insistence, she stayed naked, moving to the bathroom while he accepted the delivery. He'd pulled on his boxers and a bathrobe, but thankfully discarded the bathrobe as she walked back into the room. They sat on the couch, using the coffee table, and he let her eat her waffles without his assistance. But he did settle his left hand on her pussy, his fingers giving random little taps and wiggles.

She almost spit out her bite the first time, but managed to maintain her decorum.

After a healthy swig of orange juice, he eyed her and she braced herself for whatever was coming next.

"You seemed to enjoy having both holes stuffed last night. Have you ever had a threesome? Done double penetration?"

She swallowed her food carefully and took a drink of her coffee. "No."

"But you've thought about it."

"I've considered it once or twice over the years, but never met the right combination of guys at the club." She cleared her throat. "My friend recently married two guys. I'm not going to lie, it gave rise to some fantasies."

"Two guys, not two girls." He sounded only slightly curious.

"Hmm. I never really thought about it. I suppose if it worked out to be a scene like that, I'd be willing. Probably, depending on the people, of course. But I've never fantasized about it."

She eyed him over her cup. "What about you?"

"A few, here and there. Mostly with two women. But my best friend, he's a sub, he lost his wife, who was his Domme. He hasn't been ready to sub to another woman yet, but he's not really into guys. I've topped him a couple of times in the last two years, but the focus was really on them."

"Oh, wow, that's so sad. You mentioned them before." She set her hand on his shoulder. "You knew her well, too?"

"Yeah, she was a wonderful woman. I honestly wasn't sure how Toby would get better. But he has been."

He picked up her hand, nibbled on her fingers. "Actually, he's coming to visit me in a few weeks. If you're interested, you could meet him, see how you'd feel about us all doing a scene together. Maybe we could fulfill some of your fantasies."

Her stomach gave a little lurch at the idea and apparently so did other parts of her body. He laughed and wiggled his fingers at the edge of her sex. "I think you like that idea. My dick in your pussy, his up your ass. Two tongues to drive you crazy."

She grinned. "Yeah, I'd be okay with exploring that option." She also hadn't missed the fact that he was making plans for weeks in advance. But she needed to be clear about what they were doing.

"I'm definitely glad you checked with me first, though. I should ask, are we going to be exclusive while we're playing?"

"Is that what you want?"

"I'd want you to tell me if you're playing with anyone else. Dating or having sex with anyone that's not playing too."

"Fine. No sex or dating without informing each other."

She let out a little whoosh of breath, relieved that he wasn't annoyed. Taking the last bite of waffle, she checked her watch and squeaked. "Shit, checkout is in thirty minutes. I need to get my things packed."

Leaving at checkout would give her just enough time to get to her salon date with Stephanie. Jumping up, she rushed around getting her things together, fixing her hair and getting dressed. Drew took much less time, then read the newspaper while she finished. Part of her was relieved that they didn't have time for any weirdness. As much as they both wanted to keep things club-like, they weren't in a club. This felt a lot more like the morning after of a very successful date than it did the end of a long night at the club.

As they walked out the hotel's front door, the valet drove up in her rental car. She turned to Drew, but he grabbed her suitcase and wheeled it to the trunk, watching as the driver jumped out and loaded it. Drew paid the valet and held her door open, standing in front of it, letting her come to him. She walked right into him, laying her lips against his. He opened, pushed her open, took possession. She immediately got wet for him. His hands gripped her arms, pulling her closer before finally setting her back.

He cleared his throat. "I'll call you." Squeezing past her, he gently nudged her into the car, closed the door, watched while she lowered the top. Then he leaned on the door and lowered his sunglasses, meeting her gaze.

"You be careful driving home."

She smiled. He just couldn't help himself. "Yes, Officer."

When she walked into the nail salon, she spotted Stephanie immediately. The bright streaks in her hair might be magenta today, cobalt tomorrow, but they were ever present, whatever the color. The natural blonde had decided to both embrace her given color and defy it. She spotted Emma's approach and rose to greet her with a huge hug.

"Hey, girl," Emma said, once she could safely breath again.

"Emma! I can't believe you came all the way up here, finally, and you didn't come play!"

"Oh, I played." She couldn't keep the satisfied smirk from her face. Didn't even try, actually. "Just not at the club."

"So he's in the scene, then? I thought maybe you were trying out something vanilla."

They paused to choose polish colors than moved to the spa chairs that they were directed to, picking the conversation right back up. That was one of the things Emma liked best about Steph. They could go months without seeing each other, but fell easily back into step.

She groaned as she placed her feet into the hot water. All her walking the day before had been in cute sandals instead of sturdy shoes. *Oops.*

"He's in the life. It just…I don't know…didn't seem necessary to go to the club. He can get me in that space with just a couple of items and his imagination. We don't need all the equipment. Hell, we don't really even need the toys, they just make it more fun."

"I get that, but don't you miss the activity, the people, the *energy*? I hope you're not turning into a fuddy-duddy on me."

"Eh. I was never as much into exhibitionism as you. The only reason I didn't go more toward the private rooms was I never developed enough of a relationship with any of the guys to trust them in private."

Steph shrugged. "I guess. It just makes it so much more exciting, knowing other people are watching, getting off on what I'm doing. Being able to scope the whole club, see who's doing what and who I want to try out next."

"Believe me, any more exciting than what we've been doing and I'd probably have a heart attack."

Stephanie perked up. "Ooh, do tell!"

They both picked up their remotes, turning the massage settings on. "Sorry, girl, I'm not telling you everything."

But she did sketch out the main parts, related the basic story of how she and Drew had met. The other woman's eyes glittered in appreciation and she tried to pry for more, but Emma laughed her off.

"Well, maybe once things settle in with you guys, you'll come to Apex."

"Maybe."

Stephanie cocked her head.

"That didn't sound like a very definite maybe."

"It's weird. I don't know what it would be like to do a scene with him with other people around. I guess it would feel normal pretty quickly. But it was fun being at his house and at the hotel."

"As long as you feel safe, I guess the location doesn't really matter. But the equipment! All the things you're missing out on playing with."

"I'll repeat, if things got any hotter than they already are, I'd have a problem."

They high-fived.

"So tell me, what's the new gossip. Anything good?"

"Well, I didn't mention it since I know you won't be up here next weekend, but they're doing another one of those charity auctions. This time it's the Doms being auctioned but there's a twist. Someone bet someone else something about sports that I don't care about at all." She waved her hand to brush that part of the story aside. "But what it comes down to is that the Doms lost and they have to wear cuffs and collars in the auction."

Emma's mouth dropped open. "No! Who are the Doms?"

"Drake, Eric, and Daniel are the ones that you would know for sure. There's seven in all."

"Holy shit, I wish you could take pictures. Eric and Daniel in collars?"

"Yep, full sub gear."

She sat back into her chair, trying to picture the men she knew dressed like that. Then she tried to picture Drew dressed like that. Then she burst into laughter so strong she had to wipe away a tear.

EMMA THOUGHT about her conversation with Stephanie on the drive home. With the top down and her hair once again up in a ponytail, she enjoyed the ride but kept a careful watch on her speedometer. Just before she hit town, she called Taryn, which netted her an invite to dinner. It was her policy to never, ever turn down Richard's cooking, so it was a no brainer to accept the invitation, even though she knew her friend would try grilling her for more details.

When Caleb opened the door, he studied her. She wasn't sure what he was looking for, but he seemed to approve. He gave a quick grin, a hug, then turned and tugged her into the house. "I'm helping Richard cook. Taryn's in the backyard. Go keep her company."

"Aye, aye, Sir!"

He swatted her on the butt as she strode past him and out into the backyard. A week ago that would have shot fire through her body, but now, it only brought a smile. She had her own hot guy to play with. Besides, a week ago, he wouldn't have done it. Interesting that he had now.

Taryn was kneeling next to a patch of dirt.

Emma frowned. "Are you gardening?"

Taryn sighed. "Yes. Supposedly. I have no idea what I'm doing, but yeah. That's the idea."

Sitting down in the grass, Emma laughed. "Then why are you doing it?"

"I don't know, it just seemed like the thing to do. I have a house now. And husbands who mow the lawn and take out the garbage. I thought I'd, you know…" She gestured vaguely over the disturbed earth.

"Ah, I see." Trying not to laugh, Emma leaned back on her hands. "Are you planting flowers or vegetables?"

"I hadn't gotten that far. I was getting the dirt ready. I read a thing on the internet that said how you should prepare the spot. But I was thinking vegetables. And herbs. I thought Richard might like to have some fresh stuff." She reached in and pulled out a few weeds and added them to her small pile.

"Sounds like a plan," Emma said.

"It's kind of annoying, though."

"What."

"This. It's like…work."

Their eyes met and they both lost it, laughing until they were lying back on the grass, holding their sides.

Emma managed to stop long enough to gasp, "But at least there are no people to deal with." Which only set them off again.

Finally, Taryn wiped her hands together and stood. "Come on, I need to get cleaned up, and you need to tell me how your trip was."

They trooped into the house. Music came from the kitchen and she saw the boys standing over the stove, Caleb's arm around Richard's waist as he did something with a pot. Their affection was so easy, like with her parents. She had to stifle a laugh at the idea of sharing that comparison with her boss.

Taryn jumped into the shower while Emma brought her up to speed. Again, Taryn demanded more details and Emma teased, but didn't follow through. She offered to blow-dry her friend's hair for her, and Taryn accepted. They bantered back and forth until Emma had told her everything. Mostly.

She'd never been very specific with her friend about the goings on at the club she went to, although now that she'd begun to see Caleb in a more commanding light, she wondered if that was a conversation they should have. But she was tired of analyzing her sex life and desires for now, let alone those of her friend.

"So, let me make sure I have this right," Taryn shouted just as

Emma turned off the blow-dryer. She rolled her eyes and continued at a normal volume. "You don't want to start a serious relationship. He doesn't want to start a serious relationship. But you want to keep seeing each other, exclusively, for the foreseeable future."

Emma thought about it for a moment, then nodded. "Yeah, I guess that sums it up pretty nicely."

Taryn nodded. "Awesome." She took a deep breath. "Come on, let's go see what those wonderful smells are all about."

Not hearing any sarcasm in the other woman's tone, Emma decided her best bet was to take the comment at face value, and followed her down the hall.

AFTER SHIFT, Drew took his third shower of the day. He'd had one before shift, and one in the middle, after chasing an idiot burglar through the alleys and into the trash bin the dumbass had decided to hide in. Hell, he still wasn't sure he didn't stink. He hoped not, because Emma had called and he'd invited her over. He put on a little more speed than usual to get home, wanting to get there before she did so she wouldn't have to sit around and wait.

He reached the house and was both relieved and disappointed to see that she wasn't there. Fine, it would give him time to take another shower. Somehow he felt his own shower would get him more clean than the one at work. But he'd just unlocked the door and set his keys on the side table when he heard the engine. Leaning against the jamb, he watched the Mustang approach. He wondered what she normally drove, instead of the rental. Shit, maybe she didn't even have a car. And then he just stopped thinking as she got out, came toward him. Her jeans were tight, her t-shirt snug and her toes bare but for the bright-pink paint she hadn't sported last time he'd seen her.

He wanted to eat her up.

When she reached the top step, she paused.

He stared at her. The nearly black hair was thick and straight, just past her shoulders, with a little bit of bang that focused his attentions on her eyes. Those eyes. How could her brown be so much more compelling than those he saw in the mirror every single day? He didn't know, but it was very true. He wanted to drown in the liquid heat of her brand of brown eyes.

He grasped her hips, pulled her forward. Pulled her into him. His lips met hers and she opened for him easily, eagerly. After what could have been a minute or thirty, he came up for breath. "Would you like to come in?" he asked.

She laughed. "Yeah, thanks, I'd like that."

He pulled her up the stairs and to the bedroom, but she laughed again. "How was your day?"

"Smelly. Yours?" He gripped the hem of her t-shirt and pulled it up. She raised her arms but made no other move to undress. Fine, he could handle it all on his own.

"No speeding tickets on the trip home?" he asked.

"It was tempting, but no. I decided to wait for the cop who I know could give me what I wanted."

CHAPTER SEVEN

Emma's wide smile undid him. He took her mouth again, abandoning her pants to spear his fingers through her silky hair. She met his kiss boldly, and when her arms came up around him to grip his shoulders, he was done thinking. Without leaving her lips, he finished the job with her jeans. Now she helped, shrugging out of the pants, moving in synch with him to bare his body as well. When they were both naked, he tumbled them to the bed.

He left her mouth only to move down to her breasts. Fuck, her glorious breasts. He sucked one nipple into his mouth, hard, while teasing the other with his fingers, softly.

"Drew, oh god, Drew."

He worked her nipple with his teeth, then suckled, before switching to the other. Her own fingers came up to soothe the abandoned breast, so he moved his free hand down to her core. Found her wet and grasping. She was always so eager, so ready for him. He knelt up so he could reach the bedside table. Her hand grasped his cock while he fumbled for a condom. He handed it to her, knelt up over her waist so she could reach him easily. Watched her face as her hands smoothed the rubber down his shaft. She looked hungry. And pleased. When she'd finished the task, she met his eyes. Smiled and reached her hands out for him. He slid his legs down, dropped into her embrace and met her lips for the kiss she offered. So good, every inch of her felt so damn good.

Her hips arched into his and he broke the kiss, braced his forearms beside her head, his hands finding their way into her hair again.

"Guide me in," he said, his lips barely above hers.

She reached down and grasped him, gave a little squeeze.

He groaned. Her answering smile wasn't teasing so much as happy. She lined him up and he inched forward, through her clutching palm and into her. The contrast was amazing, moving through her delicate fingers into her wet heat. He pushed forward until she had to move her hand. She took his balls instead and he groaned again, dropped his forehead to hers.

"I'm glad you came by." The words slipped out and were too close to *I missed you* for comfort. She gave a little chuckle, but her hands came up to frame his face. Slowly, he eased out of her, back in, bringing his lips to hers and matching the rhythm with his tongue. When her hands grasped his hair, tried to urge him on, he took her fingers with his so they clasped hands, and he continued his slow assault. Her heels dug into the mattress and she lifted to meet him, but he maintained his pace.

When her gasps became frantic, her fingers gripping his tight, and the blood in his veins boiled, he broke the kiss, threw back his head and gasped his release. She bucked under him, gripped him tight as the orgasm washed through her. He rolled off, disposed of the condom and was pulling her into his side before she'd managed to blink her eyes open.

"Mmm." She smiled into his chest, traced her finger along the tattoo on his opposite arm. "You haven't told me about this. Does it mean anything in particular?"

"Not really. It's Celtic, which is my ancestry. Mostly I guess I just thought it was manly. It was my college graduation present to myself. Just before I joined the academy."

She laughed. "It is certainly manly. And hot."

"I'm glad you think so."

They drifted for a bit, not quite sleeping. He just enjoyed having her in his arms. Eventually he roused enough to ask her about her drive home. She told him about dinner and he told her about having to drag his suspect out of a dumpster.

"Eww. Your job is disgusting sometimes. But I guess that's better than dangerous."

He hugged her close and kissed her temple. "My job is rarely dangerous. I've never even had to pull my gun."

"Good. I hope it stays that way."

He squeezed her ass and tried not to think about the fact that assholes with guns weren't his biggest job concern. Not when he had to worry about being outed for his sexual lifestyle and losing his job. That was a much more likely life ender than getting killed on the job. Which made his actions when ticketing Emma all the crazier. But holding her in his arms, he couldn't bring himself to regret it.

He nuzzled her neck until she giggled, then launched into round two. He'd had plenty of time between showers to think up plans for their scene. The fact that he'd launched them into straight sex rather than starting the scene was something he decided not to think about, and hoped she hadn't really noticed.

Emma returned the rental car, the official end to her little vacation. Her first summer class began and her hours at the coffee shop picked up as she covered the shifts of others who were on vacation, as planned. It didn't leave a lot of time to go to Drew's, but they managed a couple of times a week. Which was still a lot more than she was used to playing, so she figured it was all good.

Since they weren't really dating, she'd been a little worried that he'd kick her out in the middle of the night or be weird about the next morning, but that hadn't happened. There was no awkwardness. Sometimes he stayed in Dom mode while they ate, but not always. Like that first time at his house, they would curl up on the couch and watch a movie or sports if they ended up with more time than they could possibly spend having sex.

One thing that was confusing was their phone calls. What had started out as calls to set up their get-togethers had gotten longer and longer. They'd actually had phone sex once, a first for her, but mostly the conversations were more mundane. And yet enjoyable. They talked on the phone more than they did in each other's presence, actually, since when they were together they were usually having sex or watching TV. Unless they were eating. He still liked to interrogate her while she ate.

He'd told her about his family, the brother he hardly ever saw, the parents he saw only out of a sense of duty that he couldn't quite shake. There was no particular love there, something she had a very hard time getting. She could only assume the feelings, or rather, the lack thereof, were reciprocated, even though she just couldn't understand parents not loving their children. She knew it was possible, it just didn't make sense to her.

She'd told him about her own family after he'd insisted. Afraid she'd hurt him with her tales of love, she'd had to be drawn out, but eventually he'd gotten her to spill. What could she do? She loved her family, missed her brother. While there was the huge part of her that was focusing on her last year on her own, there was always, without question, her intention to be home. Eventually. Just not quite right now.

For now, she was going to meet his friend, Toby. Technically, it was their first non-play date, even though they weren't dating. She knew that the only reason he was introducing her to his friend was because he wanted them to play together. What she wasn't sure was if he wanted the threesome because she'd expressed an interest in one, because his friend needed some play time, or some other reason. And she supposed it didn't really matter, as long as they were all fully on board with the plan.

She checked the clock as she turned off the highway. They were going sailing and Drew had promised that nothing needed to happen that day. They both had two days off, and Toby was going to be in town for a week. Drew was giving them this chance to get to know each other a little bit and decide if they wanted to try something.

She was nervous and had almost broken down and talked to Taryn about what she was thinking of doing. It wasn't that she'd never contemplated a threesome before. It was that she'd never considered one with people she actually knew. In the past it had always been theoretical and she'd never found anyone she thought it would work with.

Part of her nervousness was wondering if she would be attracted to Toby enough to make it work. Or that he would be attracted to her enough to want to go through with it. Then of course there was the worry about the encounter itself. If there was an encounter.

She wasn't really concerned about the sex. She trusted herself and Drew well enough to figure they could make the most of any situation, no matter what it was. It was the emotions she was worried about. Toby was still in a somewhat delicate emotional state, according to Drew. And who could blame him? Not her. She was just worried she'd do something to mess him up more, or somehow mess with his relationship with Drew. Or her relationship with Drew.

There was no denying they had a relationship, even if it wasn't what she'd typically use that word for. They were exclusive, planned their time together and had lots of sex. They just acknowledged that there was no long-term future in store for them. Which made it all the more important that the time they did have together go well. She didn't want to risk that, so she was going to be very careful, very certain, before moving forward with the idea of a threesome.

The good thing was that she trusted Drew to be on the same wavelength, as well as trusting in his experience with ménages to know what they should and should not get themselves into. As well as his knowledge of his friend and what would be best for Toby.

She figured, at the very least, it would be fun to get to know one of Drew's friends and have a nice sail. Not having spent much time on boats, she couldn't quite imagine how the day might go, but she supposed fresh ocean air, warm summer sun and two men who would hopefully take their shirts off, she was all good.

Pulling up to the house, she parked in her usual spot next to the SUV that was Drew's personal vehicle, and grabbed her bag. Drew was there immediately, taking her bag and walking her to the house. Within a minute and without her exactly knowing how, he had her laid out on the couch, shoes off, shorts on their way past her knees when the phone rang.

She blinked at him, glanced around. Her bag was on the floor, the door was half open. He growled and went to the kitchen to get the phone. Putting her clothes back to rights, she followed him into the other room, but he was already hanging up.

"That was Toby. He said he's about half an hour away." He gave her a stern look. "Why aren't you waiting for me on the couch?"

She stuck her tongue out at him and grabbed a pop from the fridge. "You got me so distracted I didn't even notice I was on my way to being naked in the front room with the door still open. Not nice, especially when you have a visitor on the way."

He only harrumphed at that, took the can from her for a quick drink, then handed it back with a smirk. "Maybe I did that on purpose and you're now defying orders just by standing here."

Without looking away from him, she reached for the chip clip magnet on the side of his refrigerator and threw it at him. He caught it with a laugh, sauntered over to return the magnet, pressed his body into hers. "Are you looking to be punished?" he asked.

"No more than you're looking to have me make you a special batch of brownies laced with laxatives."

He cocked his head. "Does that actually work?"

"I have no idea, but I'm willing to do some research to find out." The indignation in her voice gave way to an embarrassing breathiness as he cupped her breasts. Her nipples tightened. He brushed them with his thumbs. "Did you bring a jacket? Might get cold out on the water."

She swallowed hard, nodded. "A jacket and some long pants, just in case."

He slid his hands around to cup her butt, pulled her closer into his body. She braced her hands against his shoulders. "We don't have time," she reminded him.

"No?" He gave a squeeze.

"Not unless you want us to be in the middle of something when Toby gets here." She met his eyes. "Is that what you want?" She'd been sure he was teasing before, but maybe she was misreading him.

He leaned in the last bit necessary to give her a kiss. When she'd just about forgotten the question, he pulled back. "No. That's not what I want. I'm just having a hard time keeping my hands off you."

"Oh. Well. Okay." She tried to kiss him, but he backed away.

"No, you're right. We don't have time."

She smirked, then had to jump out of the way to avoid his hand connecting with her butt.

They packed a cooler and Emma tried on some of Drew's baseball hats until she found one she liked and added it to her bag, which already had sunscreen, a hairbrush, and ponytail holder, along with her jacket and pair of pants. By the time they were all set, they heard the sound of a car coming down the lane. Emma wiped her suddenly damp palms on her shorts and followed Drew out to meet the best friend who was more family than his relatives.

The man who emerged from the car seemed younger than Drew, but maybe that was his infectious energy. Somehow she'd been expecting a sad-eyed man who wore his grief as extra years on his face. Instead, Toby could have answered a Hollywood casting call for a California surfer boy. His light brown hair was longer in front, brushing over his twinkling eyes. His jaw was narrow and he had a dimple in his chin. She couldn't help but be affected by his warm smile and that damn adorable dimple.

He met her eyes then glanced away, and it suddenly occurred to her that he was as nervous about meeting her as she was him. Her heart melted a little and she gave him a hug. "I'm really glad to meet you, Toby."

They took his bags inside but were soon loaded up into Drew's car for the two-hour drive to the marina. Drew and Toby had a college friend who'd loaned them the use of his sailboat.

Emma had told Drew she'd never been sailing when he'd suggested the idea, but he hadn't seemed concerned, just told her she'd love it. She'd focused her nerves on meeting Toby and didn't have any left for the boat. Besides, she trusted Drew to know what he was doing, if he said he did.

She'd insisted, over strenuous objections, that Toby take the front seat with Drew. It pleased her to hear the two catch up, and they made an effort to keep her included in the conversation. At a couple of points she had no idea what they were talking about, but that was okay too. It was an easy drive and they pulled off the freeway faster than she'd expected. In the distance, she could see the tops of the sail poles—masts?— bobbing in the water. It was charming and inviting.

They unloaded the car and made their way down the docks to a white sailboat with little blue stairs next to it. Drew went first, unhooking part of the line that ran along the side of the boat so that he could step on. He took the bag she carried and helped her climb on board. She expected the movement her boarding caused, and braced herself against Drew as she stepped onto a benchlike seat, then down to the floor. Toby hopped on easily behind her.

She watched carefully as the guys went about opening the bench seat, removing the panels that made up the doorway to inside the boat and putting them neatly away. Toby began to uncoil various ropes but Drew led her down the short stairs where she found a tiny kitchen, a table with more bench seating, a very tiny bathroom with a showerhead over the toilet, and two berths, as Drew called them. Little rooms that were basically crawlspaces with mattresses.

She was impressed that there were also a microwave, little stove, and television. Did people often watch TV while sailing? She put her bag where Drew pointed and slathered on sunscreen before fixing the baseball cap on around her ponytail. By the time she made her way back up into the fresh air, sunglasses clutched in hand, Toby was turning a key to make an engine rumble to life. She was relieved to realize that they weren't totally at the mercy of the wind, and glad she hadn't voiced that concern to Drew.

He held his hand out to her and helped her maneuver to a seat at the back of the boat that sort of hung out over the water. It was padded and had a cup-holder next to it. Perfect. Toby backed the boat out of its space and rumbled out to join its fellows.

Once they were heading away from the marina and out to sea, Drew looked back at her.

"Okay so far?"

She thought about it. Her stomach seemed fine, so she nodded.

"Want to help?"

She blinked at that, but figured what the hell. "Sure."

He told her to lift levers and pull ropes until she realized that above her head, a sail was going up. The wind pulled the sail out almost faster than she could with the rope. At least until she hit a certain point. Drew gestured for her to keep pulling, so she focused on the rope instead of the sail and gave it several firm tugs.

"Okay, that's good," Drew said.

She blew out a breath, then followed his instructions to lock the line in place and tuck it out of the way. Drew braced one hand against the overhanging bridge and pulled her against his body. She relaxed into him and looked forward. The boat was about to hit open water and she could see the waves. When the first one hit, she let Drew keep her steady, but then she set her feet, bent her knees slightly and rolled with the next one. He planted a kiss on her temple, then showed her what to do next. With his help, she pulled another sail out from hiding. Toby's arm brushed past her butt when he leaned over and fiddled with a key, and the engine noises halted.

Drew positioned her back in her little seat and fetched them all drinks. She drank some water and tilted her head back to enjoy the warm sun and cool breeze. The boat moved steadily forward, not too fast, but fast enough that she felt like they could get somewhere. Toby steered them parallel to the coast, which made her feel better.

She wasn't sure how much she'd like being out in the middle of the ocean without being able to see the land.

"I think she likes it," Toby said.

"I'd say so."

She opened her eyes to find both men watching her. Which alarmed her. Shouldn't the driver be looking forward? "I do like it. But, shouldn't you be watching for waves and boats and sharks and things?"

"Relax, we've been doing this a long time." Drew didn't exactly try to hide the laughter in his voice.

Toby smiled at her, but faced forward. She wasn't sure if it was because he thought he should or to make her feel better, but she relaxed. "How did you guys get into sailing?"

"My dad always sailed," Toby said, turning slightly toward her but keeping most of his attention facing forward. "I dragged Drew out the first time. He got sick as a dog." His big grin was infectious and Emma knew she mirrored it.

"Hey, don't tell lies. I got a little sick, that's it. Once I started helping with stuff, I was fine."

"Hmm, not exactly how I remember it."

"Emma knows who to believe, I'm sure."

"Mmm hmm," was all she said.

"Anyway," Toby continued, "we went out enough that first summer that this guy got the hang of it. After that my dad let us take his boat out whenever we wanted." He gave her a wicked grin. "It was great for impressing the girls."

"Where's your dad and his boat now?"

"They sold the boat and retired to Arizona." He glanced up over toward the coast, which they seemed to have angled away from. "Let's tack." It sounded like a suggestion, but Drew hopped up and got to work. She liked watching him move, liked the way the guys worked as a team without needing to say much. The boat picked up speed and gained an alarming tilt, but neither man seemed the least bit nervous so she settled back.

Another boat made its way toward them and the guys raised

their hands in greeting as it passed. A man was standing at the wheel, a young boy and girl on either side of him, the kids waving madly at them, and she had to smile.

"After that, we had to find someone else's boat to borrow. Luckily our college friend has this beauty and trusts us enough to take her out on our own."

"Do you do this often?"

Drew glanced over at Toby and his smile faded. "Not for a couple years."

Oh. She glanced at Drew but he didn't seem alarmed. "I'm sorry about your wife, Toby."

Toby looked over at her and the sadness was so clear on his face that her throat clutched. "Thanks. I haven't been out since she died, that's why I asked Drew if you guys might be up for it." He flipped a lever and sat back on the seat behind him, letting go of the wheel. She wasn't sure what expression crossed her face but he laughed, which made her feel better. "Don't worry, it's on autopilot. We just have to keep an eye out." He gestured to the wide-open view. "I wish she could have met you. Caroline, I mean. She was really looking forward to the day someone put that look on his face." He nodded to Drew.

She thought the look on Drew's face was all about love and sympathy for his best friend, but she didn't say that.

"She liked to come on the boat, as long as she could just sit and watch," Drew said. "She said she liked watching us work up a sweat to get her where she wanted to go."

"It was a good thing she didn't know how to sail. I'm not sure what would have happened if she'd tried giving orders to Drew."

Drew scowled. "I have an idea what would have happened."

They laughed, then Toby blushed and stood up to take the wheel again.

"Oh, no! What was that for?" she asked.

He looked back at her, then quickly glanced away, the blush climbing higher.

"I've a feeling Toby's remembering when Caroline and I accused him of mutiny."

"Did you make him walk the plank?" she asked with a laugh. Then the full implications of the kind of games they all might have played together hit her. She looked around the boat, seeing it in a whole new light. "Or…tie him to the mast?"

Drew leaned back so he could face her better, though he kept his eyes on his friend. "We went out to the open sea, dropped anchor for the night. I got to be lookout and voyeur while Caroline lashed Toby to the main and, er, interrogated him about his loyalties."

Toby ducked his head, made some minute changes with the wheel. She didn't want to embarrass him if he wasn't up to talking about such games publicly, but she trusted Drew to know his friend. "Sounds delicious." She pictured the scene. It surprised her that rather than imagining herself tied to the large pole, Drew standing over her menacingly, she imagined Toby up there, hair disheveled, eyes wide with innocence, body tight with need. With his hands tied behind his back, his feet fixed to the pole, he'd be at her mercy. Would the pole have been pressing between his ass cheeks? She licked her lips, then blinked when Drew's laughter startled her back to reality.

She gave him a grin and held the water bottle to her forehead. "Sorry, it's a little warm out here."

They tacked again and Drew showed her how to lift little tables up from the center console so that they had somewhere to eat. She took the items he handed up to her from the little kitchen and set up their spread. When it was all laid out, Toby reactivated the autopilot and joined them, getting up every so often to make changes to their course.

After they finished and put the table back down, she stretched out along the bench seat, her back resting against the cabin, her feet tucked up against Toby's leg, while Drew took the wheel. Without thinking about it too much, she kicked off her shoes and set her feet in Toby's lap. He didn't even hesitate to take one foot in his strong hands and begin massaging it. She groaned in heartfelt appreciation, and met Drew's eyes. She could tell that he was pleased. Closing her eyes, she let the heat, the massage and the sway of the boat relax her into near sleep while the guys continued to chat. And she debated.

When she'd imagined being part of a threesome, she'd pictured herself between two hard bodies, being helpless to the whims of all those hands. And mouths. She'd known Toby was submissive, of course. But she'd never really played with another sub, so she hadn't fully considered that. In her mind, there were two Drews. Which was ridiculous, now that she thought about it, because she had a hard time imagining Drew sharing. How did he think this would go? It was confusing, even more so because she wasn't reacting to Toby the way she'd expected. Not only did she not see herself subbing to him, she was sort of having a hard time seeing herself subbing *with* him. He made a particularly deep push with his thumb along her arch and she sighed with pleasure. No, what was weirding her out was this sudden desire to top him.

The very idea made her a little nervous, and she must have tensed, because Toby lightened his touch, soothed his hands along her foot and up her calf. She took a breath and relaxed again. She was a submissive, there was no question about that. When she pictured Toby tied to the pole, what she saw clearly was her hands running down his chest, but Drew's hands solidly on her shoulders. Supporting her. Guiding her. Topping her.

Confused, she was relieved when Toby got up to do the switching directions thing again. She tried not to think about the fact that she could no longer see land. Clearly the guys knew what they were doing. Rising to her feet, she went to join Drew at the wheel. He raised one arm and guided her to stand in front of him, then replaced his hand. Safe between his arms, she leaned back against him. The boys' conversation had turned to sports and she joined in for a while, teasing with her preference for California-based teams. Drew nuzzled her ear, then nipped it.

"Want to steer?" he asked, raising his hands from the wheel without waiting for an answer. Her stomach lurched and she grabbed the wheel.

"Um, is this really a good idea?"

"Sure it is. Try to get a feel for the wind, how it hits the sail and pushes us forward.

"Uh huh."

He laughed. "Go ahead, turn the wheel a few inches to starboard, see what happens."

She translated in her head, based on their earlier conversations. *Starboard equals right, port equals left.* Turning the wheel, she thought at first nothing was going to happen, but then the boat started to change direction. And the sail started to flap.

"See, now the wind isn't filling the sail the way it was before. Turn it back, see if you can find the sweet spot."

They continued like that for a time, Toby working the sails when Drew decided she should tack. Sometimes she thought he was making stuff up when he talked about the wind, but sometimes she could totally see what he was saying, so she gave him the benefit of the doubt and figured it would come to her with more practice.

Toby disappeared for a while and came back with glasses of a sweet white wine that she didn't bother asking him to identify, and she decided that sailing was an excellent way to spend a sunny afternoon.

CHAPTER EIGHT

His friend was unusually antsy. Was it because he didn't like Emma? Something about her put him off? Drew knew Toby well, and didn't think it was that. The relaxed conversation in the car had been genuine. He'd been fine as long as he was working the boat or while they were eating. He'd even been relaxed massaging Emma's feet, so it probably wasn't about her. So what was it?

He studied the man who fidgeted with one of the lines, retied the drawstring on his swim trunks, settled and resettled himself. Emma probably hadn't even noticed, but Drew was used to seeing Toby calm. He hadn't seen him like this in ages. And then it hit him. The only time he'd seen Toby acting somewhat like this was when Caroline had been out of town for a couple of weeks, Toby unable to join her. The man had gotten more and more twitchy as the days had gone by, to the point that Drew had been forced to stifle his laughter and pull forth every bit of sympathy he could to not make fun of the head-over-heels sub so desperately missing his Mistress.

So…what did that mean now? Drew would know if Toby had begun seeing someone, he had no question about that. He and Toby had gone to the club a couple of times since Caroline had died, though Toby's heart hadn't really been into it. They'd both been convinced it was a good idea, though, so they'd pushed through the experiences. Toby had seemed appreciative at the time, a little more relaxed after each visit, but he hadn't really been ready to move forward, to experience a true scene.

Maybe that had changed. Drew pressed a kiss into Emma's temple, checked around them for any other boats, judged the wind. But when Toby jumped to his feet again to adjust something that didn't need adjusting, Drew made his move.

"Toby." His voice wasn't any louder than it had been since they'd started. But he used that tone that worked so well for both his cop side and his Dom side. Emma, still resting against his front, stiffened a little. Toby stopped in his tracks and turned to Drew, his eyes a little wide.

"Go down and get us some more wine and the sunscreen."

He didn't ask, didn't say please. No one on the boat mistook the statement for anything less than what it was. An order from a Dom to a sub. Toby stared at him for one second longer than he strictly needed to, dipped his head, gathered their empty cups and went below.

Emma took a deep breath, one he felt through his whole body.

"He's so…lonely." She shivered.

Drew took his hands off the console and rubbed them up and down her arms gently, not disrupting her hold on the wheel. "Yes. But maybe he's ready to start changing that. Soon."

"I hope so. Do you think we can help? Would this help? Or make it worse."

"Do you trust me?"

The tension in her shoulders dropped free and she laid her head back against his shoulder. "Yes. If you think it's good for him, I'm ready."

He ran a finger up her neck, turned her chin until he could arch around and kiss her lips.

"If we do this now, we take it slowly. But it would be okay to wait. It doesn't have to be right now. I think he'll be okay with some warm-up orders that don't have anything to do with sex."

She abandoned the wheel and turned in his arms. He put one hand on the wheel, brought one up to her cheek, surprised by the blush that was climbing there.

"You okay?"

"Yes. It's just…not how I thought it might be. Any of the ways I thought it might be."

"It never is."

"I guess not."

"You like him. I'm glad about that. It's completely fine if we just leave it like that."

"I want to hug him and hold him. Take care of him. And—"

"And?"

She took a deep breath. "And…I kind of want to spank him."

"Hmm. Not what I was expecting."

"See?"

He brushed his thumb along her lower lip. "It's not bad, though."

"No, not bad. Just weird. Even if it's something we can figure out, are you sure he's ready?"

"No. But I'm sure he's ready to face the question. Ready to have the option and decide if it's something he wants or not."

She nodded. "Okay."

He spotted Toby's head coming up the steps and raised a hand to hold him back.

Speaking softly, he watched her carefully.

"Do you know what you're doing?"

She swallowed hard. "I think so. I'll move slowly, so we can both see how he reacts. Nothing sexual without some direction from you. You…this is a lot of responsibility on you, isn't it?"

He smiled. "It always is. It would have been the other way too."

She nodded. He was pleased to see she understood the dangers. Trusted him to watch out for all of them.

"Can you kiss me?" she asked softly.

A direct sign of submission before moving forward. He rewarded her with a long kiss, pleased that she'd forgotten to be worried about where the driver's attention was. When he finally pulled back, she was flushed in a different way than before.

She took a deep breath. "I'm going to use the restroom."

"Head."

She rolled her eyes at him so he smacked her butt as she shimmied out from between him and the console. Toby made room for her to go below, then dropped the cups of wine into their cup holders. He shook the sunscreen bottle, tapped it against the bench seat.

"Toby."

The man took a sharp breath...and settled. He met Drew's eyes. "Are we going to play?"

"Do you want to?"

"I...I think I'm ready."

That wasn't exactly the response Drew wanted, but since he was going to see to it that they took things slowly, for both Emma's and Toby's sakes, he figured it was enough. Almost.

He raised an eyebrow in a look that no sub would misunderstand.

"Sir. I think I'm ready, Sir."

They both understood that Drew was assuming responsibility for what was about to happen, and would do what was necessary to make sure that they all got what they needed, what they wanted, what they could handle.

"Very good."

With those words, his friend's forehead smoothed out, his shoulders dropped and a hint of a smile found its way back to his lips. The twitches were gone as Toby waited to be told what to do next. Emma stepped through the hatch and set her hand on Toby's shoulder, leaned into him a bit.

"Let's make sure Drew's protected, shall we?"

Toby looked at the bottle of sunscreen, then over to Drew. He inclined his head in permission. Though he was surprised this was the direction that Emma wanted to start with, he wasn't going to question her very first move.

The two of them took the couple of steps necessary to bracket him and Toby squeezed lotion onto both of their hands.

"Sir. Will you please take off your shirt?" Emma asked.

He set the autopilot back on then did as she'd requested. Four hands immediately found his skin and began to slide their way across his body. Emma's fingers toyed and lingered while Toby's were more simply efficient. It didn't take long for Toby to have covered his arms and legs with sunscreen while Emma worked on his back and torso. Finally she smoothed her hands along his neck, face and ears.

WHEN EMMA WAS SATISFIED that Drew was covered in sunscreen, she offered her lips up for a kiss. An offer he immediately accepted. She may have been imagining it, but it felt like he was managing to convey trust and encouragement in the gesture. Yeah, she was probably imagining it. But she was sure he felt both of those things, anyway. She smiled at him and turned to Toby.

He had picked up his cup and taken a sip of wine while she and Drew kissed. She hadn't thought he'd been tense before, but he seemed more relaxed now. Which was weird, because she most definitely wasn't relaxed. She felt revved.

"Your turn, shirt off."

He glanced at Drew, then put his cup back in the holder and quickly removed his shirt. When she gestured for him to lie down on the seat, he blinked, but didn't hesitate, lying down on his back. She filled her hands with lotion and ran them over his pecs. A quick glance at his face showed his eyes closed, his expression easy.

He remained relaxed under her touch, but she couldn't help noticing a difference between doing the same with Drew. Somehow, and she really couldn't even define how, Toby's stillness was more...passive.

It was interesting how intent could change one's actions. If this had been just a friend of Drew's, if they'd really only been out for a fun sail, she would have been happy to rub lotion onto him in a purely platonic way. But that wasn't what this was, and she allowed herself to feel pleasure in her touch, in the feel of Toby's warm muscles, his skin slightly slick with sweat. She pressed her fingers in more tightly than she needed, smiled when his breath stuttered just a bit.

Another check of his face found his eyes open and intent on her. She smiled at him and knew it was a wicked smile. His eyes widened and she couldn't believe the satisfaction she felt. And the power. For this moment, he was hers.

When she'd gotten his chest, stomach, arms and legs, she murmured, "up." Toby's abs bunched and he sat up. She rose to sit behind him, one leg in front of her, tucked up against his ass. She resisted the urge to linger, but neither did she hurry.

When she was done, she whipped her t-shirt off, then her shorts. "Trade places," she told Toby. He stood and she stretched out so that she was on her stomach, her face turned toward Drew's face.

THE SMILE EMMA gave was pure wickedness and Drew delighted in seeing this new side of her. She'd always been confident sexually, something he found highly attractive. But she'd also been nothing but submissive with him, and this touch of dominance, as long as it wasn't directed at him, was hot to watch.

"I think now's my best chance ever of no tan lines, don't you think, Drew?"

"Not many other places you can soak up the rays without something on," he agreed, failing to mention the privacy of his own land and his perfect willingness to see her lying around it without clothes on.

"Toby, untie my bikini."

Toby's hands didn't hesitate, and a grin flirted around his lips. The command had hovered somewhere between that of a top and a bottom. But it was a good start and Toby seemed inclined to let her take the lead.

The strings on her top came loose easily, but Emma didn't move, so nothing was actually revealed. Toby reached for the lotion bottle he'd set down but paused as Emma addressed him sharply.

"Toby."

She'd achieved a much more commanding tone already, and paused to wait for a response. Drew approved of her methods and remained silent, completely entertained. He adjusted his cock as discreetly as possible, not wanting to draw attention to himself just yet.

"Yes, Ma'am?"

"I said untie my bikini."

Toby blinked, blinked again. Stared at Emma's butt, covered in the emerald green material that was joined at the sides with little string bows. He drew in a careful breath and moved his hands to the bow on the far side of her body.

"I'm sorry, Emma."

She remained silent as he tugged the string loose, then repeated the action on the other side. He started to peel the suit down, but hesitated just in time. She hadn't told him to take her suit off, only to untie it.

Toby's hands fell to rest on his thighs.

"Now the lotion. You can move the material when you need to."

Drew liked that she continued to watch him while she spoke to Toby. He was easily able to spread his attention between the water, the sails, and Emma and Toby. He took a drink of his wine, letting his expression show her his approval of her actions. Nobody spoke as Toby worked the lotion into her skin. He massaged her shoulders and she gave an appreciative moan that Drew was sure Toby found as encouraging as he did. She was letting them know that this was working for her. It sure as hell was working for him.

Watching Toby ease the fabric over her ass, it worried Drew that the idea of anyone else's hands on her besides Toby's would make his blood boil. Yes, they had an agreement to be exclusive, but his emotions were *not* supposed to be this involved. *Shit.* Now was most definitely not the time to think about it. He needed to be paying full attention to what was going on. It was his responsibility to see that everything went well for all of them.

When Emma had deemed all of her reachable skin protected, she sat up. The bikini top stayed behind, of course. Without looking away from Drew, she patted the space behind her, indicating that Toby should take a seat as she had with him. Only she'd been working his back at the time, and Toby needed to lotion her front.

Drew smiled in appreciation of her plan. He could watch both of their faces as Toby's hands slid over and around her breasts and belly, slicking the sunscreen on everywhere. Toby leaned over her shoulder so he could see what he was doing, his hair brushing against her cheek. Emma's eyes closed and she pulled in a deep breath before resuming her eye contact with Drew.

Finally Toby had rubbed her whole body except for between her legs. Emma leaned back into Toby and lowered one foot to the deck, and the other to the side of the boat. She lifted one arm to curl behind Toby's neck as he carefully spread the lotion on her most tender skin.

When he was done, she kissed his chin. "Thank you, Toby. You should probably go help Drew now." She sat up until he was out of her way, then lay down and closed her eyes.

Drew and Toby just stared at the gorgeous view for a full minute until Emma cracked an eyelid. "Don't you boys think we should be working our way back to land about now?"

Toby cleared his throat and moved to the jib line. Drew turned the big wheel and started them back toward the marina. Who was he to argue when she had an excellent point?

EVEN WITH THE sunscreen freshly applied, Emma only risked the direct sun for about twenty minutes before heading down the stairs to re-dress. When she returned, Drew pulled her to the wheel, standing behind her but letting her steer. The wind was heavier and the boat sailed tipped at more of an angle, which made her nervous. But she got used to it quickly and played with the wheel a bit at

Drew's direction, getting a feel for the wind in the sails and the boat's responsiveness. If sailing meant steering the boat while leaning back against the warm, naked chest of her man, she was going to become a regular.

Toby took the wheel as they neared the marina and Drew talked her through bringing down the sails.

"That was easy," she declared. "And fun."

"Well, this boat is easier than some." Drew laughed and kissed her. "But it was fun." They put the boat back to rights and hosed it off. Drew dropped them off at a decent chain restaurant to wait for a table while he ran an errand he refused to explain. She had no difficulty talking to Toby while they were alone, their conversation spanning a wide variety of topics. She found him funny, smart and endearing. They ate dinner without lingering, then headed home. Again, she insisted Toby take shotgun. She sat in the middle of the backseat and leaned forward, resting an elbow on each front seat. The feeling of being closed in, surrounded by darkness, after spending the afternoon on the open sea, gave her a sense of intimacy. Keeping her voice low, she took a chance.

"Toby, you don't have to talk about it if you don't want to, but I was just wondering if you were thinking about dating, yet."

Drew's eyes met hers in the review mirror, then he glanced at his friend before looking forward again.

Toby remained silent for a minute, then he leaned back against the headrest and rolled his head so he could see her. "I'm at the point where I'm thinking that it is a possibility for the future. I'm not ready right now. I'm just...not." He looked away from her. "But, I did go to the club. For the first time since Drew and I went together."

"How was that?" Drew asked.

"Fine. It was good to see friends. Mistress Donna let her Rose suck me off." He shrugged and Emma thought he was embarrassed, though she wasn't sure if it was for the act or for talking about it in front of her. She let her hand drop down to his shoulder and gave it a squeeze.

"I was thinking it might be a good idea to date outside the lifestyle, when I'm ready. Just until I get my feet under me."

"Why?" Drew asked.

"Partly I'm nervous about trying to find someone now that I'm a teacher. I met Caroline just before I started my first position. I have to be more careful now."

Drew nodded. "It's a serious concern. The last thing you need is to get fired. It would be very difficult for you to find another job in that situation."

"That sucks that you even have to worry about that," Emma said.

"But he does," Drew snapped.

She pulled back. "I know he does. And it sucks."

"Anyway," Toby said softly, "it's not really a problem yet. Just something I'm starting to think about. For later."

They stayed quiet for a while, Emma leaning back against her own seat, trying not to stew. She told herself Drew hadn't meant to be pissy with her, he just hated the situation. And so did she. Closing her eyes, she drifted for the rest of the drive home. It was late when they pulled up to the house.

They unpacked the car and got Toby situated in the guest room without bringing up what had happened on the boat. It seemed by unspoken agreement, they would let it rest for the night, decide what more would be done, if anything, the next day. Emma had no doubt at this point that it would be something. She just wasn't sure what.

She took a quick shower, then flopped onto Drew's bed while he did the same. When he joined her, she waited for him to get comfortable, then draped herself over him.

"That was a really nice day," she said, then yawned hugely.

He ran a hand over her hair, settled his palm at the nape of her neck. "I'm glad you enjoyed it. I'm glad you like Toby."

"Maybe I was pretending, putting on a good face since he's your best friend."

"Mmm hmm. I'm sure you rub lotion all over the bodies of men you merely tolerate to keep the peace."

"Oh, sure, all the time."

He smacked her butt.

"You're right, of course, oh great and wonderful Master. I liked him. A lot. I hate that he's so sad."

"I hate it too. I wish there was something I could do."

"You do what you can, by being his friend. Being there for him. Tell me about when you took him to the club. If it's not private."

"I told you we never interacted together, sexually, until he was with Caroline. She wanted to explore his bisexuality a bit, something he hadn't ever done before. Neither of us had. I don't really think I am, in the truest sense, but sometimes a good sub is a good sub, regardless of gender, you know?"

"I think so. I've been attracted to a couple of Dommes just because of how they scene, how they treat their subs. Who they are. I might have been willing to do something with them, given the opportunity."

He nodded. "Caroline was attracted to the idea of two men together, but she knew she could never actually share Toby with someone in a relationship. Neither of them would have been okay with that. But as long as she was controlling the situation, she wanted to have some interactions. She asked me if I'd be willing to let him serve me, under her direction."

He shrugged, adjusted the pillow under his head. "I'd seriously never considered him sexually before. But I'd found their interactions compelling. And attractive. And I'd never had a guy blow me before, so I thought, what the hell?"

She snorted. "What, a mouth is a mouth, right?"

This time he pinched her backside. "You asked me to tell you the story."

"Yes, Sir. Sorry, Sir."

"She discussed the whole thing with him. We considered doing it somewhere else, but decided the club would be more appropriate. To make it completely clear it was a scene, not something more… intimate, I guess you could say. Toby knew it would be me, knew he would be expected to obey everything Caroline ordered immediately and completely unless he said his safe word or gave his signal. She got him into the club, had him kneel at her feet for an hour while she petted him and talked to him about what they could see."

"She was making sure he was as fully in sub mode as possible without actually starting a scene," she said, imagining it from Caroline's perspective.

He smiled at her understanding. "She blindfolded him and put on nipple clamps and a cock ring, locked his hands behind his back. Then I came over from where I'd been staying out of sight." He paused and gave her a look. Though he'd been talking about sex and clubs, he'd been relaxed. Now, with one small change in attitude, he was in Dom mode. Before he even spoke, she knew his next words would be an order. Her pussy clenched.

"Sit up."

His hand stayed on her neck as she rose slowly to her knees. He sat up, plumped the pillow behind him and leaned against the headboard. Then he pulled her into his lap. She snuggled against him, back against his chest, her legs on the outsides of his so that she was wide open. He rested one hand possessively over her center while the other began to tease over her breasts.

"Caroline gave me her chair and she stood on a little platform over Toby so that his face was level with her pussy." Drew's low murmur in her ear, his words, his tone, all had her sex getting wet. She fought not to move, not to buck up into his hand.

"She freed one of his hands and moved it to her pussy. She pushed his fingers into her." Drew slid two fingers into her, timing it with his words. She dropped her head to his shoulder and forced herself to stay still.

"When his fingers were good and wet, which didn't take long, she guided his hand to my dick." He trailed his fingers up her stomach, leaving a line of wetness.

"She wrapped his hand around me, wiping her cream onto my skin while she moved to stand over him so that the heat of her pussy was against his neck." His questing fingers found her nipple, circled it slowly. She bit her lip to keep from crying out or begging.

"Caroline relocked his wrists behind his back and held my dick steady for Toby. She brushed me against his lips and when he tried to take me in, she pulled his head back hard, reminded him that she was in charge and he wouldn't do anything without her direct permission." He squeezed her nipple sharply, as if in reprimand for the actions of another sub years before. A small gasp escaped her.

"She made Toby stick his tongue out, swore she'd punish him if he so much as moved a muscle, including his tongue, then ran that tongue up my cock by moving his head for him."

Emma swallowed hard, as affected by his words, by the visual he painted as she was by the return of his fingers to her core. He dipped inside, gathered more cream, brought it to her clit, circled.

"When she'd decided he was being obedient enough, she ordered him to open his mouth and she directed him to cover me. Then she told him to do as they'd practiced. Apparently she'd had him blowing her strap-on for lessons."

"How—" Emma had to swallow a couple of times before she could continue. His fingers never stopped moving gently, slowly, around and around her clit. "How did that feel?"

"Amazing. I don't know how much of it was watching the two of them together. They had an incredible connection. Of course, some of it was just that he had a hot mouth and was eager to put it to use. He worshiped my cock, with Caroline standing over him, probably dripping all over his back, until I came." He moved his fingers back down, slid inside her and began to pump. His other hand squeezed her breasts and flicked her nipples until she moaned.

"When I had come, and Toby had cleaned me up like a good sub, Caroline took another seat and made him sit with his chin resting on the chair, between her legs, ordering him to lick her every few minutes, but only one or two licks at a time, while she and I discussed his cock-sucking technique."

He caught her chin in his hand, angled her head so that he could kiss her cheek. He thumbed her clit while speeding up his thrusting motion. "Come for me, Emma. Come, now."

She did, with a low cry she could only hope didn't carry down the hall. He lifted her limp body, fit her over him and pulled her down until he was buried deep within. He pushed her forward until she was on shaky hands and knees, thrust in and out of her in a frenzy that should have hurt but felt oh so good. He came with a groan, rolling them to their sides.

"Caroline finally let Toby bring her to climax, then she took him home," Drew mumbled.

"Mmm."

He pushed and prodded until they were back with their heads at the pillows. "I think we'll finish this conversation in the morning."

"Mmm."

CHAPTER NINE

Emma woke to the faint smell of coffee. Since she was wrapped solidly around Drew, she figured Toby must be an early riser. Though she couldn't see the clock without moving, she was pretty sure it was too early to be waking up, so she snuggled in closer and tried to go back to sleep. That plan died a quick death when Drew's hands began to knead her ass.

She gave his chest a light thump. "Don't get too eager down there. We should finish our conversation."

"The one about blow jobs?" he asked in a hopeful tone.

She laughed. "As if you don't get one any time you want. But hey, if you don't want to return to a discussion about Toby's sex life, I won't force it."

He gave her a little pinch, but it was fake and didn't even hurt a little bit, so she just laughed.

He sat up and leaned against the headboard, which forced her to sit up too. She propped her elbows on her knees, her chin on her arm, and waited.

"How are you feeling about taking this to the next level with Toby? I don't want any guessing games here. We're going to be very clear, one way or the other."

"I like him and I want to help him. I kind of want to cuddle him up and make him happy, but I don't really know how to do that. But I trust you to know what I'm comfortable with, and I trust you to know what he's comfortable with, so if he's okay with it, and you're okay with it, then, well, then I guess I'm looking forward to it. Though I'm kind of nervous, which seems strange."

Of course he wouldn't leave it at that.

"What part makes you nervous?"

"I guess—"She broke off when he frowned. "Okay, okay, no guessing. The biggest thing is the emotions. I don't want to mess up what we have, and I don't want to mess up your relationship with your best friend."

He nodded. "If we do this, my two main concerns are making sure that doesn't happen and making sure I don't make things harder for Toby, instead of better."

"That's a lot of responsibility for you."

"Your responsibility is to help me with that by making sure you let me know exactly what you're thinking and if you have any hesitations at any time."

"Still doesn't seem quite fair."

"Think about it this way. If you *don't* tell me when something becomes too much for you, you'll be punished."

It was her turn to frown, but she couldn't really argue. And she was finding the idea of seeing what Drew would do, how things might go, the feel of all those hands, the idea of the guys touching… She licked her lips.

"Are you…umm, are you going to touch him? Let him touch you?" she asked, having to clear her throat to get the words out clearly.

His lips twitched, but he showed no other reaction. "Would that bother you?"

"No," she said quickly. "Nope, wouldn't bother me at all."

He got off the bed without further comment. "Come on, let's not leave our poor guest for too long. There won't be any coffee left."

They pulled on clothes and made their way to the kitchen. She led the way, so she saw the sadness in Toby's eyes as he stared out the back window, his hands wrapped around the large mug that still looked pretty full. No steam rose from the coffee inside, and she wondered how long he'd sat there, not drinking. He jerked slightly when they entered, and offered a bright smile.

"It's a beautiful day."

"Looks like," she agreed. "We should go fishing."

Toby blinked and looked skeptical. "Fishing?"

Drew edged past her, brushing her ass with a caress as he made his way to the coffeepot. "Great idea.

Toby shrugged. "Okaaaay," he drawled, clearly not enthused but not exactly horrified. Emma opened the fridge and began tossing things to the guys, and with all of them working on chopping, toasting and cooking, they quickly had omelets on the table. They chatted about nothing and everything, politics and entertainment. They didn't talk about Emma, the nakedness from the previous day, or where the day was going to take them. Emma knew that she still shouldn't assume something would happen, but she was pretty sure it would. She'd wait for some sign from Drew that the time had come, and until then, she'd enjoy her day with two fun and interesting guys.

The weather was perfect for another day outside. Instead of the crisp, clear ocean air of the previous day, they made their way through the trees and sat by the river in the shaded tree line. The air was heavier, but not in an unpleasant way.

Arms full of supplies, they crossed Drew's land to a section of the river that he'd brought her to before. They'd needed a break after a particularly intense scene, and he'd suggested the walk. Used to cities, even small ones, it hadn't occurred to her that he could have his own bit of river.

The nice thick blanket she carried went down first, then they set up camp chairs and the fishing gear.

"So," Toby said as he watched Emma and Drew prepare their poles. "You've done this before."

She smiled. "Yeah. About a month after my brother died, my dad woke me up at five in the morning and dragged me out to the river. I had no idea what he was thinking. I still don't really know, I've never asked. It was a tough time for us. We were—are—a close family, but we still had a hard time talking about Michael."

"I'm sorry."

"It's okay." She gave him another smile. "It still hurts, it still sucks, but it's been a long time. Anyway, like I said, I'm not sure what my dad was thinking, but it worked. He and I sat out there for an hour, hardly said a word, but I felt so much better by the time we went home. We started going once a month or so. We talked more. Not about Michael, at least not for years. But we talked about other things, important and silly. And we were quiet."

Drew handed him his pole. "Actually, I've never gone fishing with anyone else. And never on this side of the country." Which was why she'd let Drew decide what bait they'd be using, taken what he'd selected.

Soon they had their lines in the water and were seated on the bank. "Do you mind talking about Michael now?" Toby asked.

"No. Now I like to. It makes him seem more real again, if that makes any sense. I know it's not the same with Caroline. And it won't be, not for a long time."

He nodded. "She's still almost too real. Still so here, and yet...not."

"I can't imagine how painful that must be. Do you want to talk about her?"

She flicked a glance at Drew, who was watching his friend intently. The pain she saw on his face as he clearly wished he could do something to help Toby nearly made her heart break. They loved each other so much. As she'd thought earlier, here was Drew's family. But how close had he been to Caroline? Was he still grieving the loss of a friend? Most likely, but he'd subvert that in the face of his friend's pain.

"I haven't wanted to. Not really. At the funeral I did, but it nearly broke me. After that it was too painful." He met Emma's eyes. "I was thinking about her a lot last night. About the time that we…" He glanced at Drew.

"I told her. It's cool." Drew's voice was soft, as if he was afraid to interrupt his friend.

"I know it would be different. Very different. It was a special thing for me, though, and last night was the first time I was able to remember something like that, think about one of our scenes, and be happy instead of sad, you know?"

Emma swallowed hard. "I'm glad."

Toby gave a small smile. "I thought about this." He twirled his finger around to indicate the three of them. "When Drew mentioned the possibility. I thought about it, of course. It was theoretical, since I hadn't met you, so I thought about all the different ways it might be. Of course, none of them are right, now that I've met you."

"It never really works out the way we think it might, does it?"

"I don't know. Drew, how did you think it would go, pulling a speeder out of her car and slapping her into handcuffs with the sole intention of getting her naked? That seems to have worked out well for you."

Emma put her face in her hands to hide her blush. Why she was embarrassed, she had no idea. The guys laughed and she stuck her tongue out at them.

"Yeah, that worked out really well, but I never in a million years imagined it would go as well as it did. But to be honest, it's not as if I was imagining what would happen. It was much too spur-of-the-moment. Hell, if I'd thought it through at all, it wouldn't have happened."

"That's because every scenario you imagined would have ended up with you being brought up on charges."

"Exactly. Never would have happened if I'd taken a minute to think about it."

Emma had known that in theory based on other conversations they'd had, but she'd never really thought about it, and it made her curious.

"So, why did you?"

He laughed. "Honestly, I have no idea. You looked so carefree and innocent. You actually smiled at me when I walked up and it wasn't the 'Gee, officer, what do I need to do to get out of this ticket' smile. And then, just as my brain starts to process the fact that you must be as sweet and innocent as you look, I see the necklace."

Shaking his head at the memory, he reeled his line in and checked that the bait was still there, then recast. "So the whole time I was running you and writing up the ticket, I'm picturing that necklace, wondering what your favorite activities were, making the huge assumption that you were a sub, wondering if you were collared and wearing the necklace as a public version."

That thought had never occurred to her. But then again, it wasn't as if she'd been wearing it as a lure for a potential Dom. It had just worked out that way. She laughed, checked her own bait, then Toby's. "And you weren't imagining me in your handcuffs during that time?" she asked.

"Nope. I walked back to you with every intention of handing you that ticket and walking away. At the most, maybe I'd have asked you where you were headed."

"But?" Toby asked. Setting his pole on the ground with no regard for its safety, he went to the cooler and pulled out a bottle of water. He offered it around and opened it when they declined.

"But. Fuck, Toby, she smiled at me again! As I handed her the ticket. And it wasn't fake, it was this amazing smile that said 'I'm having a fantastic day, and I hope you are too.' What the hell was I supposed to do?" He looked at them both as if they could tell him what his other options could have been.

Emma's chest warmed from the inside. Knowing she'd affected him like that made her so happy she was sure she was grinning like a damn fool, but she couldn't help herself. She watched Drew, who was watching her, and the heat flared brighter, moved lower. She licked her lips and Drew's gaze flicked down to watch. Hell, he was so gorgeous. Especially when he looked at her like this. As if she were the only thing in the world he could ever want.

She set her pole down without paying any attention to it and stood. He did the same. And then she was screeching, Drew shouting, as they were both splashed with cold water. They turned to Toby, who was waving the bottle back and forth, arcing the cold water between them, a maniacal grin on his face.

One more quick look at Drew was all it took. They both launched themselves at Toby, tackling him into the dirt, water splashing everywhere.

"I can't believe you did that!" she yelled, tickling his sides as Drew held him down, their legs entwined.

"You bastard," Drew huffed. He was bigger, but Toby's wiggles appeared to be hard for Drew to contain.

"What?" Toby gasped. "You wanted me to keep fishing while you two ravished each other in front of me? I don't think so." He was laughing and struggling and Emma leaned down and bit him on his side. His shirt had ridden up, exposing a vast expanse of flesh. Not nearly as much as she'd had her hands on the day before, but somehow this was different.

"Emma, back up," Drew ordered.

She did so immediately, clearing the space for Drew to seriously pin Toby. Once he had control of the other man, he maneuvered them so that they were both kneeling in the dirt, Drew holding Toby in front of him, legs secured beneath his, wrists held together at his back, one arm across his neck, gripping Toby's shoulder.

"I caught something for you, Emma."

"Oh, that is a fine catch, Sir." She stepped forward, ran her finger along Toby's jaw. So big and juicy."

Toby choked a laugh, but it didn't sound like one of amusement. He'd stilled in Drew's arms once it was clear he had no control, his body somewhat relaxed, but maintaining an awareness and tension that Drew found delicious.

"First you need to pull in our lines." Emma blinked at him before understanding what he meant. She nodded and moved to secure their poles.

When she'd stepped away, Drew dropped his lips next to Toby's ear. "Are you ready for this?"

"I told you I was."

"That was yesterday. We didn't really do anything, but you can't tell me it wasn't a step. How did you feel last night, once you were able to think about it?"

He felt Toby swallow against his arm. "I felt good. Wished we'd gone further, even though I knew we weren't really ready. Then."

"But you're ready now."

"I like her. A lot. She's great and after this is all over, when I'm safe at home and only talking to you on the phone, I'm going to be pushing you to figure out what the fuck you're doing, because it doesn't make any sense to me."

Drew huffed. "It doesn't have to make sense to you. Only to me and Emma."

"Uh huh. Whatever you say, Sir." It was said with more of a snort than an attitude of respect and Drew responded by lifting Toby's captured hands a little higher up his back. The gasp was loud enough to have Emma looking over at them. Whatever she thought she was seeing, she just smiled and hurried to finish her task.

"Anyway," Toby said when Drew had eased his hold. "She's yours, and you love me. I'm good." He laughed. "Besides, she's beautiful, sexy, funny."

"Yeah," Drew said, thinking about the simplicity of the statement. "She is." But was she his, as Toby had said? It was hard to convince himself she wasn't. Hard to imagine her with someone else. Well, with someone who wasn't his best friend, in a scene that he controlled.

He saw that Emma had finished but was waiting for his signal to return. "Anything you want to do? Or avoid doing?"

Toby didn't respond immediately, which Drew appreciated. "No. Nothing that you don't already know. I'll be fine, Drew. I know when to speak up if something's wrong."

Drew sighed. "I know you do, buddy, but it's been a while and things will have changed for you, whether you know it or not."

"You're probably right. But the only way I'm going to know that is to try, and it seems to me that the best time to try is with someone I trust completely hanging around to help out."

"Are you okay with Emma taking the lead with you?"

Toby barked out a laugh. "Really? Is that a question?"

Drew smiled. "Really. She's not a Domme. She's never topped anyone. But she wants to smack your ass."

"My ass is her ass, to do with as she pleases."

The tiny bit of sadism that lurked in his heart sparked to life. "Are you quite sure about that?"

Toby pulled in a sharp breath. "Are you—does she—I mean... Hell. Yes, I'm sure."

There weren't many people Drew would trust to do this with. Actually, there might not be anyone else he'd trust to do this with. But Toby was an experienced sub, one Drew trusted to know what he could handle, to know how to work with an inexperienced top without fucking with her. He grinned up at Emma, watched her eyes widen just a bit as she started forward. At least not to fuck with her in the wrong sort of way.

All grace, she came to a stop and knelt next to Toby, her face a perfect expression of submission and desire. Just the thing to light his blood on fire. His dick swelled into Toby's lower back. She lowered her eyes, placed her hands behind her back the way she knew now that he liked.

"You please me very much, Emma."

She actually blushed. His confident, bold Emma blushed, but didn't move.

"Tell me, Toby. Is your dick getting hard thinking about her?"

"Yes, Sir. But I'm not thinking of her being on her knees."

Drew laughed and he heard a muffled choking sound come from Emma.

"I don't know. I think she can make you pretty excited from her knees. What do you think, Emma?"

"I agree with you, Drew. I'd certainly like to try my best."

"You go ahead then. I'll just keep hold of our captive here."

"Thank you, Sir."

He figured she meant thank you for holding Toby just as she much as she meant thank you for giving her this opportunity. Adjusting himself so that his thighs bracketed Toby's tightly and he was more comfortable, Drew let go of the other man's wrists.

"Hold on to my shirt, Toby. You let go, we'll start Emma on practicing her spanking."

"Yes, Sir. That's not much of a deterrent, though." He grasped Drew's shirt in both hands and held on tight. Drew brought his freed hand around, pulling Toby more tightly into him, his arms crossed in front of the man, holding both shoulders. Drew knew that Toby liked bondage, wanted to make sure that he felt secured.

Emma stood and lowered herself in front of Toby, on her knees but not resting back as the men were. She leaned over Toby and offered her mouth to Drew. He accepted her offer, kissing her until she moaned and pulled back.

Her eyes were heavy lidded, her lips wet and puffy. Drew was certain that Toby was as captivated by the sight as he was. Emma reached down and squeezed the growing evidence of Toby's arousal. "Would you like my mouth here, Toby?" she asked, her voice barely above a whisper.

"Yes, please, Emma. If it pleases you." He gasped and Drew was sure she'd squeezed him.

"What will you do to earn that from me?"

"What do you want?" The words almost, but didn't quite, cover the sound of a zipper being pulled.

Drew could see her hand reach into the fly. Toby groaned. Hell, Drew damn near did as well.

"I want you to kiss me."

Drew blinked, returned his attention to Emma's face. She was watching Toby carefully. It hadn't occurred to Drew that she and Toby hadn't kissed yet. That Toby may not have actually kissed anyone since Caroline.

"I want to kiss you, Emma. You don't have to ask for that."

She smiled. "There are lots of places I want you to kiss me, though, Toby."

"Yes, Ma'am, I think I could handle that."

Emma put her hands on Drew's shoulders. The way she was leaning up, she was still taller than they were, so she used him to brace herself and met Toby's lips with her own.

Drew had known this was a completely different scenario than the previous threesome he'd had with Toby. He liked to think he'd thought it through, examined all angles. Except he'd honestly not considered what it would be like to see Emma kissing another man. But it wasn't just another man. It was his best friend. It didn't exactly turn him on, but it warmed him. Not what he'd really expected.

He studied the lashes lying against Emma's cheek, the sweep of hair falling across her ear. She was beautiful and he could happily stare at her for hours. She switched angles, Toby whining for the second it took him to understand she wasn't abandoning the kiss, giving Drew a glimpse of her mouth and tongue. Fuck, he was seriously lost if he was thinking about how beautiful her tongue was. Of course, that thought led to memories of her tongue on his dick. Toby rubbed back against the expanding swell of Drew's erection.

Emma broke the kiss, smiling slightly when Toby tried to lean forward and follow but was caught by Drew's arms. His friend blinked his eyes open, then licked his lips and ran his gaze over her body, clearly anticipating where else she'd like him to kiss her.

Squeezing Drew's shoulder, she leaned in and offered Toby her breast, still covered by t-shirt and bra. At least he assumed she was wearing a bra. Toby didn't seem ready to complain, but took what was offered. When Emma pulled back, the wet spot over her nipple jutted out from the rest of the shirt. She offered Toby the other side and he immediately accepted.

With her breast in Toby's mouth, Emma's face was just above Drew's. She curled enough that she could bring her lips to his. He suprised her by letting her kiss him, rather than the other way around, until she whimpered in frustration. Then he took over, pushing his tongue into her eager mouth, commanding her compliance, which she readily gave.

Before she could end the kiss, he did, earning a moan from her. He did so love to hear her moan. She blinked at him, then lowered her gaze before pulling back and releasing herself from Toby's attention.

She leaned in and gave the other man a brief kiss, then studied him. Drew angled so he could see Toby as well. His dick was hard, his skin tight, his eyes bright.

Emma pulled her t-shirt off and folded it into a strip. She glanced at both Toby and Drew and tied it around Toby's eyes when Drew gave her a brief nod.

Her instincts were good and he was fascinated by this side of her that she'd admitted even she'd never known was there. Toby was practically vibrating by the time the t-shirt was firmly in place.

Emma gave him a questioning look, pointing up. He understood what she wanted and rose up on his knees, pulling Toby with him. Emma moved quickly, easing Toby's jeans down to his knees before Drew resettled them. Toby's ass rested against his own jean-clad groin and Drew couldn't help but wish that the other man's was reddened from a spanking or flogging so that he'd really feel the jeans against his skin. Ah well, couldn't have everything.

Emma lowered herself to the ground, clearly trying to figure out the best arrangement for her task. She curved her fingers around Toby's length, lightly tapping along it like a very wide flute. Toby shivered.

Releasing him, she drew her nails down his thighs, sharply enough to leave four perfect red trails from upper thigh to where his jeans bunched around his knees. Toby arched slightly before catching himself, though he hadn't been able to move much because of Drew's hold.

Emma's face showed clear pleasure at the reaction and she did it again. Then, with no warning, she leaned down and engulfed his cock. Toby cried out, ground his head against Drew's shoulder.

Drew wished he'd thought to tell Emma to take her clothes off once Toby was blindfolded, but it was too late now. Still, her ass, straining against the material of her cargo pants as it wiggled and bounced was a hell of a sight. Knowing that Toby could feel his dick getting harder and harder was another bonus. He tightened his arms and his grip on the other man's shoulders, tightened his thighs against Toby's, gave him no room to squirm at all.

Toby's breathing had become gasps and stutters. Emma reached up to his ass, as far back as she could reach before encountering Drew, and raked her nails down his sides. She hummed loudly enough for Drew to hear it easily, and Toby shouted. She hummed again as Toby slumped back against Drew's chest.

Emma rose, wiping her mouth, which was lifted in a wicked grin. Oh yeah, she was pleased with herself. Since he was pleased with her as well, he waited to see what she wanted to do. She sat, carefully, legs to either side of Toby's, her ass firmly on Toby's lap. Drew let go of Toby and wrapped his arms around Emma to support her. She smiled her thanks, lifted her hands to Toby's face. She caressed his cheek and smoothed the sweat dampened hair from his forehead before slowly lifting the blindfold away.

Then she kissed the corners of his eyes, the bridge of his nose, each cheekbone, before meeting his lips. Her tenderness had Drew gripping her butt tighter and he saw her lips curl just before she joined them with Toby's. The other man hadn't moved, his head still resting against Drew's shoulder, so when she drew back, she didn't have far to go to meet his lips instead.

He kissed her gently, eased his tongue in to meet hers, caressed her, owned her. She melted against Toby, one hand curled around his nape, the other on Drew's. They stayed that way for a while before he finally had to admit to himself that he couldn't hold the position much longer.

Easing back, he boosted her butt up until she'd gained her feet.

"I don't think we're going to get any fish unless we go to the store." He decided that was exactly what they needed to do to give themselves a rest, time to process. "Let's get cleaned up and go into town." He'd be able to keep an eye on Toby while they got ready and drove to town. Make sure the little scene was settling well and Toby didn't have any bad reactions.

Emma looked surprised and he fought not to frown. He hadn't gone into town with her because it was too risky. He didn't need people asking questions about her. But three people who were clearly friends was a different situation. He didn't say anything, just put his hands on Toby's waist until the other man was standing steadily, then rose to his feet. His thighs burned, but he wasn't about to complain.

They packed their stuff away quickly and returned to the house. They didn't bother to shower, just brushed off as much of the dirt as they could and headed off to the store.

CHAPTER TEN

Emma trailed behind the men, pushing the cart but letting them figure out what they wanted to put into it. She just studied their butts and went along for the ride. A young woman coming the opposite direction turned to watch them as they passed then winked at Emma. She grinned and waggled her eyebrows. When she looked back, Drew was watching her, his face stern. Oh boy, she was in trouble now. She smiled unrepentantly and he went back to his task.

Soon they had enough food to last her for a week, though she suspected it was meant only for lunch and dinner. An older man and woman stopped to chat with Drew, but she hung back and they moved on quickly.

She knew it was hard for Drew to be out in public with her and she knew she shouldn't have a problem with that, honestly didn't think she *did* have a problem with that, except…well, suddenly it felt as if she had a fucking problem with that. A wave of sadness threatened to engulf her but she refused to let it. They were having a wonderful time and she wasn't going to let something so stupid screw it up.

She set her shoulders and concentrated on Toby's ass to cheer herself up. It was very inviting. Maybe she really would spank it. It had never been something she'd wanted to do before, but she could just imagine Toby trying to hold still while she peppered him with smacks. She supposed it wouldn't be as hard as when Drew spanked her, but he'd probably enjoy it.

That was what she needed to focus on. The fact that Drew was working hard to see that both she and Toby had a wonderful time, that they felt safe and secure. Though it had been only a few weeks, he cared about her, she was absolutely certain of that, just as she cared for him. And that was what she wanted. She couldn't imagine any other Dom she'd been with letting her explore as he was doing right now. He trusted her with his best friend.

The boys put the groceries in the car and she mentally smacked herself around. No way was she going to ruin this amazing experience by bogging down in shit that didn't even matter. Period. She almost threw herself into Drew's arms to cement the thought in her head, when she realized that would be exactly the opposite of helpful. Out here, they were just friends. If that. Shit. She pasted on a smile that she hoped neither of them could actually see as she ducked into the car. Toby had insisted it was her turn to ride shotgun. She put her feet on the dash and leaned back into the seat where her face wouldn't be in anyone's line of sight.

While they talked, she carefully reviewed their time at the river. Instead of skipping ahead to the more interesting portion, she thought through the conversation, remembered their sweet concern when she'd spoken about Michael, and the way she'd wanted to hug both of them extra tightly when Toby had talked about Caroline. Then she let herself remember everything that happened afterward.

By the time they'd reached the house, she was hot and bothered and in a much better frame of mind. Working together, it didn't take long to have everything ready. They set the food out on the table and Drew rubbed his hand over its surface and grinned at her.

"Wow, that's quite a blush," Toby said. "Care to explain?"

She shook her head, but of course, that didn't stop Drew.

"The only time Emma's ever said her safe word was at this table."

"Oh! Sorry, you don't have to tell me." He sounded sympathetic, which just made Drew laugh.

"I asked her to sit on the table and she said no."

"I was naked!"

Toby looked confused.

"Seriously, Toby, would you want to be eating at this table right now if you knew I'd sat up here naked and…you know, wet, and stuff?"

His eyes flashed, but it wasn't disgust she saw in them.

She balled up her napkin and threw it at him. "Pervert."

Both of the guys laughed. "Well, yeah, and proud of it," Drew finally said. He leaned over and kissed her cheek. "I'm sorry."

She rolled her eyes and took another bite of her fish.

"So, what you're saying," Toby teased, "is that you don't want to tie me to the table and spank me?"

"Sure, we can do that," she answered easily.

Drew raised his eyebrow at her.

"What, if he doesn't want to be naked for a spanking, I can respect that. Personally, I think he'd look a hell of a lot hotter tied to your footboard, bent over the bed with that naked ass begging for attention and completely available to whatever I want to do with it." She took a sip of water and shrugged. "But maybe that's just me."

Toby had stopped chewing and was staring at her, pupils gone wide. Drew was grinning at her over his glass. He winked and she smiled and turned her attention back to her plate. After a second she heard Toby gulping his drink and had to bite her lip to keep her smile from going supernova.

They finished the meal and Emma found herself rushing around the kitchen to get everything put away. She and Toby nearly tripped over each other in their haste, but Drew seemed to be taking his time, damn the man. Finally there was nothing left to do, and they both turned to Drew.

"Impatient, much?" he asked.

When neither of them responded, he just laughed. "You guys have one hour to bathe, groom, dress, whatever you need to do, and be in my bedroom. You can either be naked or in club clothes. There will be ankle and wrist cuffs on the bed. Be wearing them by the time I get there."

He turned and walked out of the room, heading into the den. Emma didn't waste any time, and decided she'd take Toby with her every step of the way. She grabbed his wrist and dashed up the stairs. He hesitated at the guest room, but she pulled him along to the master to grab her bag of club clothes.

She dropped it off in the guest room then led him to the bathroom. Never having used it, she took a look around. Nothing fancy, it had a shower tub and a single sink, with Toby's things scattered around the room. Taking a deep breath, she turned to him.

"Did you, um, already prep yourself?" she asked. She figured he had, since she'd found him to be fully shaved in the morning activities.

He nodded. "I'll just do a bit of touch up. You?"

"Want to help me?"

"Oh yeah."

She laughed and they quickly shed their clothing. Toby reached in to turn on the water and adjust the temperature, and she let her gaze roam his body. She'd pretty much seen everything by now, but not all at once. The long, lean line of him was very, very tempting. He had something of a farmer's tan, definitely more pronounced on his bottom half. She didn't suppose he had much time for sunbathing in New York.

He turned and caught her staring, but she didn't blush and neither did he. Instead, he took his time returning the favor, giving her a very thorough up and down that stirred her blood. She knew absolutely that they couldn't do anything now, and that there would be plenty of doing starting in an hour. It made it somehow nice and relaxing to take the slow journey into the lust.

Seemingly on the same wavelength, he winked at her and offered his hand, holding her securely as she stepped into the tub. It was ridiculous to find that charming, it wasn't as if she hadn't stepped into the shower a million times without the help of a man's hand, but she *was* charmed, damn it.

She wet her hair in the hot water, turned to find him with shampoo already in his hand. He looked a little sad all of a sudden and she knew they'd be having moments like these all night. It wasn't a bad thing, she reminded herself. She just needed to tread carefully.

Not saying anything, she waited.

"I always used to wash her hair," he finally said. He looked back down at his hands, carefully cupping the shampoo.

"You don't need to."

"Do you mind?"

"I don't mind either way. Whatever you like."

He nodded but didn't move. In no hurry, she waited, then moved aside when he reached his hands into the stream, rinsing them clean. She started to reach for the bottle herself, but he shook his head. He squeezed a fresh blob into his hand, then motioned for her to turn around. She did, tilting her head back, giving a slight moan as his hands massaged the soap into her hair.

It was obvious he'd had practice, his fingers firm against her scalp for a time before working his way down her hair. When his hands dropped to her hips, she turned in his sudsy grasp, letting the water sluice her hair clean. He reached over her shoulder to help, then repeated the whole process with the conditioner.

Again she reached for the shampoo bottle, and he seemed startled. He moved toward the bottle, then stopped, let his hands drop. When she had a good dollop in one hand, she set the bottle back in its rack and pulled the shower wand free of its stand.

"On your knees," she said, gesturing to her feet.

He blinked but said nothing, simply stepped back until he had enough room, then knelt at her feet. She enjoyed washing his hair, something she'd never done before. It seemed strange that when he'd washed hers, she hadn't felt either submissive or dominant. She'd simply enjoyed the experience. And she'd been perfectly passive, as he was being now. But the feelings she had now were definitely dominant. Almost possessive. As though he were hers to care for and they both knew it.

God, she really needed to be careful here. Rinsing his hair clear of the conditioner, she grabbed shaving cream and dropped to her knees in front of him. She handed him the wand, then wet her hands thoroughly in the steam before sitting all the way down, careful not to run into the faucet.

She spread her knees wide. "Can you wet me down, please." Not that she wasn't wet already from the shower, but better to be careful. He aimed the water at her center, moved it around until she told him it was enough. She smeared the cream everywhere, then looked at him expectantly.

"I didn't bring a razor."

He blinked, stood and took a razor from the ledge, then knelt in front of her again, bending low. With slow, careful moves, he shaved the little bit of stubble she had. When he was done, she took the razor and did her own armpits.

By the time they were finished, the bathroom was a steam bath. Figuring there was no harm in being seen mid prep, she opened the bathroom door, letting the cooler air from the hallway caress their still wet bodies. They dried themselves off, then Toby slathered her favorite lotion on her body. He refused any for himself, even when she pouted.

It hadn't occurred to her before, but this was one thing she missed in her encounters with Drew. Since she was usually coming from work or school, she didn't take much time getting ready for him. Couldn't get ready in the same types of outfits she would wear to Apex. Plus, she often stayed with Stephanie when in Boston, and they would get ready together, making the prep a whole event in and of itself.

Emma loved readying for her trips to the club. It made her feel feminine and beautiful and powerful when she prepped herself, slipped on her special outfits. This was similar, but also different. For one thing, she'd never gotten ready with a guy she planned on having sex with before. And yet, much of it was still the same. She found herself falling into the headspace that she usually did. Not subspace, but similar. After all, she usually had to drive to a club once she was ready. But the sense of excitement, anticipation, nervousness—all of it gelled into an expectation that she was familiar with, that she had come to love.

She could see the same happening to Toby, and it made them comrades. There was no chatter, only the necessary give and take of the preparations. He helped her blow her hair mostly dry, then nodded approvingly when she slicked it back into a tight ponytail. She pulled on a tight leather miniskirt and a small purple lace bustier. With ten minutes left in their allotted time, they headed to the master bedroom.

The room was empty, with the cuffs lying in two piles on the bed as promised. There was a table by the bed that wasn't normally there, a pillowcase covering whatever lay on top of it. Emma's heart rate picked up as she wondered what toys Drew might have picked out for them.

She held her hands out first, silently directing Toby to put the cuffs on her. When he was done, he immediately dropped to his knees and did first her ankles, then his own. When he stood, he offered his wrists to her. She secured the cuffs, then, without really thinking about it, guided his hands behind his back and secured the cuffs together. She put one hand on his shoulder and urged him down, brushing the hair away from his face when he'd complied.

Leaning down, she kissed his forehead. "So gorgeous," she murmured, then lowered herself beside him. She clasped her hands behind her back and settled herself. There was still an awareness of the man beside her, but her main focus was on Drew. Waiting for him. Being ready for him.

She knew the moment he started climbing the stairs, was able to trace his faint path to the room, knew he stood in the doorway, watching them. It was crazy how she could feel peaceful and anxious at the same time. Wondering what would happen, but not at all worried about it. Not anymore. Now, it was simply time to happen.

When his feet entered her viewing range, she smiled. Couldn't help herself. He was here. Bare feet had never been particularly sexy to her before. Had she even noticed Toby's? But these feet, brushed by faded and slightly straggly denim, were beautiful to her.

For the first time in her life, she sort of understood those with foot fetishes. Drew's hand came down in front of her face, palm up, in invitation. She took it and rose. He pulled her into him, joined his lips with hers. Oh yeah, she was really getting to be in trouble with this guy. A kiss and she was ready to do anything he asked of her. Hell, without the kiss, she was there.

He pulled back and she brushed the idea aside for later as he linked their fingers together.

"Let's take a look at what we have here, shall we?" he asked.

She smiled. "Oh yes, let's do that."

They turned to look at Toby. His head was slightly bent, his shoulders relaxed, hands resting on his ass. Drew didn't seem to mind that she'd attached the cuffs. He wrapped his hands around her waist and leaned to set his chin on her shoulder.

Toby's toes flexed and clenched and she was thrilled at that sign of his nervousness. He wore only a pair of boxer briefs and the cuffs. His longish hair, still damp, had fallen back over his forehead and again she reached out and brushed it back. She drew her hand down his cheek and along his jaw until she cupped his chin, raised his face up so they could see him.

Handsome, though she realized she hadn't necessarily thought that word in association with him before. He was a bit more tan than when they'd first met, his green eyes sparkled with desire, his lips, looking redder than they had when she'd looked at him only moments before, were parted just slightly, his breath brushing along her arm.

"You get me the best presents," she told Drew.

He chuckled. "Wait until you see what else I have for you."

"It can't be as perfect as him."

"Maybe not, but it will help you play with him, and I think you'll like it."

She turned her head so she could kiss him. "I'm sure I will."

"For now, what do you want him to do?"

So many thoughts ran through her head, but the one that stood out the most clearly was the one from lunch. And there was no reason to deny herself, was there? She licked her lips, delighted when Toby's eyes followed the movement.

"I want to put him at the foot of the bed, like I said earlier. Can I use your toys?"

"Of course." He stepped back, gestured to the small cabinet that she knew held his things. She strode to it and quickly located the tethers she needed. Her favorite flogger caught her attention and she stroked her hands over its suede lashes, but she resisted. There was already a lot of newness, a lot of learning. She didn't want to get crazy.

Moving back to the boys, she wasn't surprised to see that Toby hadn't moved, but was startled at how much it pleased her. He was staying still for her, though his toes were now digging into the carpet and his fingers had twined together.

"Toby, stand up and face the bed." She kept her voice quiet but firm. He didn't hesitate and she just stared for a moment, enthralled by his easy movements, his perfect willingness.

With a sigh of pleasure, she ran her palm down his back, snagged the waistband of his shorts and pulled them down to his ankles. He lifted one foot, then the other, at her direction. Using her nails but no pressure, she drew her fingers along the backs of his thighs and knees, then nudged his feet wide.

She secured each ankle cuff to a bedpost with the tethers, checking the fit of the restraints just as hers had been checked hundreds of times. She ran her hands back up his legs, using her whole hand this time, not just her fingernails. His muscles clenched and released under her touch.

She checked his face, found just what she was looking for. Desire, anticipation, the right kind of nervousness. At least she figured his expression was the mixture she was used to feeling, it sure looked like it to her. And she'd never realized how intoxicating the look was to the person watching for it.

She unhooked his wrists then attached them to the bedposts at shoulder height, letting Drew help her. Toby pulled against the straps reflexively, then relaxed.

Placing her hand on his bare ass, she caressed it for just a moment, then drew back and gave it a good smack. Yes, the setup would work just fine. She looked to Drew, who nodded his approval.

"What you make me want to do to you, Toby." She put every bit of the appreciation she felt for how he looked and the gift he was giving her into her voice. His head turned, trying to see her, and she moved to accommodate him, stepping to the side but keeping her hand steady on him.

"Stunning."

A quick flush rose up his neck and over his face, but he didn't look away. She pinched his side, then soothed the pain away.

"Please," he moaned.

She smiled and gave him what he wanted. The first spank stung her hand, but she was more focused on watching Toby than how it felt to her. The second blow jarred her shoulder, but she was pleased to see Toby's ass pushing out towards her. Drew had given her some pointers, let her know that Toby liked a spanking or a light flogging as a warm-up. He'd warned her that she'd be surprised how quickly her hand would grow tired and sore, and he'd been right. Of course. But she had a plan for that.

Glancing at Drew, she wasn't surprised when he held out his hand, offering his help. That was just like him, and she had no problem taking him up on the offer. She watched him give the first few spanks, watched Toby's head drop back at the pleasure from the harder smacks. Then she climbed up onto the bed, pleased when Toby's eyes snapped open and he watched her with eager anticipation.

She knelt in front of him and slowly removed the bustier to the music of Drew's hand striking Toby's flesh. Once free of the restrictive fabric, she palmed her breasts, tweaked her nipples. He moaned, though whether from a particularly hard smack or from what she was tempting him with, she wasn't sure. Until he licked his lips.

"Can you reach me, Toby?" she asked.

He immediately strained against his bonds, pushed his ass out as far as he could into Drew's striking hand in order to lower himself far enough to take one of her nipples into his mouth. He sucked hard, then twirled his tongue around the tight nub. She threaded her fingers through his hair, tugged him free despite his obvious desire to stay right where he was, then directed him to her other breast.

Humming his thanks, he gave that nipple equal attention, his body making little jerks against her each time Drew's hand landed on him. When she pulled him back again, he tried to turn his head to the other breast, but she held him firmly while she rose to stand on the bed, putting her pussy at his mouth level. With a bit of a shimmy, she pushed her skirt down and stepped in close to Toby.

Without hesitation, he dove in. She had to let go of his head with one hand to grab the bedpost tightly. Bracing herself, she smiled at Drew, enjoying the wicked grin he gave her in return.

"Toby, Drew will stop when I come."

Toby paused and she knew without a doubt that he was trying to decide which he wanted more, for Drew to continue or to make her come. It took him only a second and he was back in action, working fervently to bring her off. She didn't try to hold back, let the waves of pleasure run their natural course. Her head went back and she gave a long moan, locking her knees to keep from falling.

A final suckle and kiss, and Toby pulled back, his gaze meeting hers, full of pleasure at his accomplishment. She grinned in response and dropped down to her knees, kissed him hard, her hand gripping his hair, holding him still for her onslaught.

Finally, she needed to catch her breath. She pulled his head back, whispered in his ear, "How about Drew and I switch places?" she asked.

She felt him shudder, lifted her eyes to see what Drew was

doing. Her grin widened, threatening to jump off her face as she saw what he was holding. The black straps surrounding a deep blue dildo could only be a strap-on.

"Do you want to suck Drew off, Toby?" She licked his neck. "Would you like that?"

He drew in a stuttered breath. "Yes, Emma. I'd like that."

"Are you sure?" she teased. "I don't want to push you into anything you don't want to do."

He cleared his throat. "Please, Emma. The only thing I don't want to do is let you down."

She laughed. "Oh Toby, I don't see how that could possibly happen. My only other question is, what do you think I should be doing while your mouth is busy with Drew?"

He opened his mouth but she laid her finger on his lips. Instead of speaking, he touched his tongue to her finger. "How about a multiple choice option?" she asked, running her finger along his lips. She pushed her finger between his lips, not giving him a chance to speak, but his eyes were all expectation.

"Option one, I can sit where you can watch me and use the dildo Drew's holding right now to pleasure myself while you suck him off."

He sucked hard on her finger, used his teeth very gently to scrape her skin.

"Option two, I can return the favor. I enjoyed having you in my mouth this morning. I'd like to taste you again when you're naked. Let my fingers explore other parts of you. Would you like that, Toby? Do you think Drew could give me some pointers on how to bring you pleasure with my fingers as well as my mouth?"

He groaned his approval of the idea, but didn't try to speak.

"Last option." She pulled her finger free, ran her thumb along his bottom lip. "Are you ready?"

His eyes met hers and she loved the way that he checked to see what she wanted, correctly read the answer on her face.

"Yes, please, Emma. I want to know what you want."

She bent down and kissed his lips gently. "I'd be perfectly happy with any of the three options, Toby. I mean that."

He swallowed. "Will you tell me your last option?"

"All right. Option three is that I strap on the dildo that Drew is holding and I fuck you blind while you're sucking Drew's dick."

Toby stopped breathing.

"You know I've never done that before. I didn't even know that Drew had a strap-on."

He pulled in a shuddering breath.

"Do you think he bought it for us, Toby?"

"I—uh—I don't think he would have had one lying around. I can't imagine him inviting you to use it on him."

She laughed and so did Drew. "So, those are your options. I want you to think about them for a minute, decide what you want to do. Because once you decide, you get no more say in the matter."

"Yes, Ma'am."

He closed his eyes and pulled in a deep breath. She took the opportunity to glance at Drew. He smiled his approval and she relaxed. It helped so much to know that he was backing her up. It gave her the confidence she needed to keep going. Well, that and the look of utter desire and need that Toby still wore.

She wasn't sure how Domme-ly she was being, giving him the choices. She didn't care. It was working for her and she was pretty sure it was working for Toby. That was all that mattered. He opened his eyes and gave her everything in his look. Trust, want, need.

"Please, Emma. Fuck me hard."

CHAPTER ELEVEN

A shiver ran through her. She would have been perfectly happy with whatever answer he'd chosen. But this. This had her pussy clenching in expectation.

"Fuck, you two are hot," Drew said, coming to stand beside her. He took her hand in his, ran his thumb over her fingernails.

"Will you let me prep him for you?" he asked.

She glanced down at her nails. They weren't exactly long, but they weren't really short, either. She loved that Drew was watching out for both of them. And she absolutely loved the image in her head of Drew preparing Toby's ass for her entrance. Pulling their combined hands to her pussy, she rubbed her clit. Toby's eyes followed the movement and he licked his lips.

"That would be a treat to watch. Thank you, Drew."

She dropped her hand, though his stayed behind another few seconds to tease her. Remind her that she was his. As if she needed reminding. The worry that her concentration would be fractured had turned out to be ridiculous. She found she was fully capable of keeping her attention tuned to both of the guys. In the past weeks, her body had become used to watching Drew, looking for cues and following his lead without thought. There was no danger of her forgetting anytime soon.

Which was both wonderful and a worry for another day. For now, they would play.

She climbed up on the bed and brought her mouth to Toby's while she tracked the sounds of Drew retrieving the lube. Only her lips and tongue touched Toby's. She gave him no other contact, enjoying the way his whole body strained toward her, held back only by the restraints. Ending the kiss, she put her lips to his ear.

"He looks so fucking sexy coming for you, Toby. The look on his face...he's looking forward to touching you, opening you up for me."

Toby groaned and she smiled. His ass clenched and released as Drew approached. Shifting on the bed, she dropped her legs on either side of Toby and reached around to grip those luscious ass cheeks. She kneaded his muscles, then pulled, opening him up for Drew's slicked thumb.

Drew teased the puckered flesh until Toby pushed his ass out just a bit, then Drew slid the digit inside. Emma felt Toby's cock, trapped between their torsos, jerk at the entry. She cupped his butt, let her nails dig into the flesh where ass met thigh. Drew pulled back and added more lube, then came at Toby with two fingers.

She licked and nipped at Toby's side as Drew's fingers slid smoothly inside. Drew twisted his wrist and fucked his fingers in and out. He placed his other hand on Toby's neck, running his thumb over the other man's nape.

"It's been a while, Toby. I'm trusting you to tell us if anything isn't right," Drew reminded him.

"Ye—" Toby's whole body tightened on a gasp and Emma was left without a doubt that Drew had hit Toby's prostate. She let go of his ass and ran her hands up his back, holding him tight.

"Yes, Sir," he managed.

Emma pulled her heels along Toby's legs until she was able to put them on the mattress and push herself back. Toby watched her intently. She put one arm behind her to brace herself, and brought the other to her sex, twirling a finger through the moisture gathered there. His gaze was totally focused on her, though his body was moving slightly with Drew's intrusion.

She eased one finger inside, then brought it to her clit. Toby moaned and she smiled. Drew took a step back, then gave Toby a casual smack on the ass. She idly fingered her clit, occasionally pushing two fingers into herself as she watched Drew clean his fingers and retrieve the strap-on. Toby's focus was on her hands until Drew tossed the contraption onto the bed in front of him, between her legs.

Emma circled her finger through her cream, then rose to her knees, offered her finger to Toby. He sucked it into his mouth like a starving man, his tongue swirling to get every bit of her clean. She pulled free and looked to Drew.

"Get on your hands and knees and face Toby."

It took her only a moment to get into position and seemed all too convenient that Toby's cock was now at mouth level. But she waited to hear what Drew wanted from her before moving forward that last little inch. Instead, she blew a cool stream of air.

Lifting her gaze, she was pleased to find Toby biting his bottom lip. So fucking sexy. Drew's hand ran over her butt and she was surprised to feel the coolness of lube-slicked fingers at her anus. She clenched in automatic reaction, then pushed out, accepting him.

"Mmm, good girl."

He slid one finger in, then another. She stayed still, trying to keep as open as possible. Soon the smoothness of silicone replaced his fingers and a plug that felt awfully large pushed its way past her tight ring. She gasped when the whole thing was finally inside her, the flared base pressed tightly against her butt. And she knew she hadn't been wrong. This was definitely a bigger plug than the one they'd been using. Breathing through the fullness that wasn't quite pain, she worked to relax around the intrusion.

A shudder moved through her and she huffed out a breath, enjoying both the reaction of Toby's cock and the knowledge that even as she worked her way into Toby, she'd be filled by Drew. Even as he gave her this experience, encouraged her to explore this need she felt, he was with her, in her, surrounding her.

One last pat on the ass, and Drew's hands withdrew, only to return with soft leather straps. He pulled, buckled, smoothed and adjusted until he was satisfied. One strap ran between her butt cheeks, keeping the plug firmly in place. A wider strap around her waist supported the weight she could feel tugging from the front panel.

"You're all set," Drew said.

She stuck her tongue out, gave Toby a teasing lick as she rose to her knees. Then she looked down. The silicone cock jutted forward, bouncing a little as she steadied herself. It was…weird. Definitely weird. She'd certainly never considered men and their dicks as automatically superior, so why did wearing one make her feel…well, cocky?

The material felt silky under her questioning fingers. Warm. She wrapped her hand around it, enjoying the sounds of Toby's breathing hitching and then speeding up as she explored.

"What do you think, Toby?" She gave it an experimental tug. The straps held securely. Loosening her grip slightly, she used her hips to push the cock through the circle of her fingers, then pulled back and repeated.

"I—uh, I think you look incredible and I hope you're still planning on fucking me with that."

"I'd say that's a pretty safe bet." She looked to Drew. "Would you please unhook his wrists and give him the lube? I think he can probably do a better job with this than me." She continued to stroke the dildo idly.

Drew didn't seem bothered by her request. He stood behind Toby, leaned his body into the other man's as he stretched to release first one clasp, then the other. His lips lingered at Toby's ear as he released the second tether. She had no idea what he said but Toby gasped in a breath. Toby's gaze, however, never left her body. She knelt in front of him and grabbed one of the bedposts.

"Go ahead."

Toby's Adams apple bobbed as he squeezed slickness onto his fingers and brought it to the shaft she presented to him. She watched intently as his fingers worked to cover every inch. It was crazy how she could almost feel the sensation of his touch on her nonexistent appendage.

"Harder," she commanded, and wasn't surprised it came out sounding breathy and needy.

His grip tightened visibly, his movements, along with his own breathing, speeding up. God, she needed to get inside him.

"Stop." It was more of a gasp than a command, but his fingers clenched, then released. She looked to Drew. His gaze was hot on her, which almost kept her from noticing that he'd taken off his pants. His cock was erect, red and glistening. Inviting. He held a hand out to her and she took it, letting him help her move off the bed. He took her place, though farther back on the bed, his ass on his heels, hand stroking himself as he watched her move to stand behind Toby.

She put her hand on Toby's nape and urged him forward. He braced his hands on Drew's thighs, pausing to receive a nod of approval, then lowered his mouth to her lover's erection. Her lust somehow managed to ratchet up another notch. She ran her hand along Toby's back, his muscles stretched tight, ending in the glorious curves of his ass.

With one hand she brought the tip of the dildo to his hole, clutching his flank with the other. His whole body stilled and she glanced at Drew. He gave her an encouraging nod and she pushed forward. She could feel the hardness of the cock fighting against the pressure of Toby's muscles, eased by the slickness of the lube. Could practically feel the pop of the head as it breached the ring of his anus and settled inside. She didn't realize she was holding her breath until she had to gasp in air.

She released the dildo and grabbed tightly to Toby's hip, sure her fingers would leave impressions in his skin. Another flick of her gaze to Drew's for reassurance and she brought all of her attention to watching the blue cock slide slowly but surely into the eager hole.

Toby moaned and her fingers clenched even tighter. She moved her feet, bent her knees just slightly, and pushed forward with her pelvis until her thighs met his. A long sigh escaped her. The pleasure was so much more than the press of the strap-on against her clit, although that helped. It was the vision of Toby's body opening for her, straining for her. The sound of his mouth on Drew, the grunts and moans that both of them gave. It was the way he made tiny movements of his body, pushing back the little bit that he was able, reaching for her, needing her to move in him, to fuck him.

She pulled back, set up a careful, easy rhythm, letting him match her with his movements on Drew as the other man's breathing grew sharper. Confident now, she let go with one hand, managed to spank him in time with her thrusts a couple of times. His answering moans apparently had an effect on Drew, who gave a short shout as he released into Toby's mouth. She watched Drew's face. His hands were tangled in Toby's hair, his head dropped forward, hair matted along his forehead. He probably wouldn't appreciate hearing it, but she thought he truly looked beautiful. And sexy as hell. Even with her fake cock buried in another man's ass, she couldn't help but feel excitement knowing that he would turn his attentions to her soon enough.

In the meantime, she'd do her very best to bring herself and Toby as much pleasure as she was capable of. She waited until Drew gave her a tiny nod, then increased her tempo. Toby made needy sounds and she reached under him and grasped his cock.

Her coordination wasn't perfect and there was no way she was going to be able to make herself come as well, but that was the least of her concerns at the moment. She rubbed her thumb over the head of his penis and his whole body shuddered. She smiled and repeated the action, giving her hips an extra swirl.

He buried his face in Drew's lap and gave a soft moan as he came. She waited until his thighs began to relax their tightened muscles, then slowly pulled out. She leaned into him, pressing him harder into the mattress, raining kisses along his back, licking his shoulder blades until his breathing evened out.

Finally, despite wanting nothing more than to climb up on top of him and take a nap, she stood, her legs a bit shaky. The slight weight of the strap-on dangling in front of her made her clit throb but she turned to the master bathroom and went about the business of cleaning Toby up. When she finished, Drew settled himself onto the bed and Toby curled up around him, head on his thigh.

Emma grabbed a throw blanket and joined them, curling herself into Toby's back, her arm draped over him and onto Drew's thigh. Drew brought his hand to her head and stroked her hair until she fell asleep.

Drew wasn't at all surprised when Toby stretched a short while later. Emma was fast asleep, and together they were able to extricate themselves from the bed without disturbing her enough to wake up. They threw on clothes and headed down the stairs. Grabbing two bottles of beer and a half-empty bottle of tequila, he followed Toby to where he'd settled in the Adirondack chairs on the back porch.

His friend accepted the bottle without taking his eyes off the trees, though they were hard to see in the dim light of the moon. Drew set the tequila on the ground by his feet, not sure what was going to be needed for the conversation.

"You okay?" he asked after several minutes.

"Yeah. Mostly." Toby stretched his legs out, crossed his ankles and finally took a drink of his beer before turning to look at Drew. "Thanks. I needed that."

"I'm guessing you're not talking about the drink."

Toby smiled, took another pull from the bottle. "No, but thanks for that as well. And for having me here, for being there for me last summer and the summer before that. And…you know."

"I do know. You don't have to thank me for those things, Toby. You're my best friend. Of course I was there."

They sat in silence for a while, Drew trying to count how many different insect noises he could identify. He had no idea what Toby was thinking about. Caroline, Emma, Drew? Or maybe he was concentrating on the crickets. When Drew heard a wet sniffle, he put his beer on the ground and moved his chair close enough to put his hand on Toby's shoulder. They sat that way for a long time. It wasn't the first time since Caroline had died, but Drew had the sense that it was different. Still, it was painful as hell to know there was nothing he could do to help.

"Would another go with my girlfriend help?" he asked when Toby wiped his nose on his sleeve.

It earned him the laugh he'd hoped for, though he suspected he'd pay for using the term girlfriend once Toby decided to focus on him again. He picked up the bottle of tequila and offered it. Toby accepted and took a drink straight from the bottle.

Drew retrieved his beer and leaned back into the chair, waiting while Toby took another pull of liquor.

"It did help. Seriously, it probably sounds ridiculous, but that really did help, and I meant it when I said thank you. I know you don't want to talk about it, and that's fine, I won't, except to say that I think you guys have something pretty special going on, so it means a lot to me that you were both willing to share that with me."

"Hell, you know we both enjoyed it. And I don't think I ever would have gotten to see that side of Emma if it hadn't been for you."

"Does it bother you? That she has that side?"

"Are you kidding? It was hot as hell watching her order you around. Ream you out." He said the last part with a smirk and Toby punched him in the shoulder. Taking it as his due, Drew didn't respond other than to hold his hand out for the tequila. When Toby passed it over, he carefully poured a measure into his beer, then handed the bottle back.

"No, I'm not worried she's suddenly going to want to go Domme on me. Although it does make me curious to see her in action around other people. Maybe we'll head back up to Boston." He cocked his head, trying to decide if it would be more interesting to go to her club where she was presumably comfortable, in her element, or to take her to his, keep her slightly off base. So many possibilities.

"You look like you're thinking evil thoughts," Toby commented.

"Hmmm." He forced the thoughts away and returned his focus to Toby.

"Today helped, though, right? For real?"

"Yeah, it helped. I can't quite imagine being in a relationship, but at least I can imagine going to a club on my own again. Doing some scenes. It's not like I didn't play before Caroline, but we were so young when we met. It's been hard to separate any idea of sex from her. How it was with her. How I thought it would always be her."

Drew scowled. "The world is a fucked-up place."

Toby laughed. "Yeah, it can be that. But you can't experience a day like today, and not acknowledge the other side, can you? The world can be pretty fucking beautiful, Drew. Amazing. The world produced Caroline. I loved everything about her, even the things I didn't like all that much." He took a short drink of tequila, a long pull of beer, then shook his head. "You can't focus on the shit when you've got someone like Emma naked in your bed right now. She's a fucking treasure. To give of herself like that. For me, a total stranger."

Drew tried not to laugh as Toby's language took a turn for the drunk, but it came out as a cough that probably sounded pretty suspicious. Luckily Toby was too involved in what he was saying to notice.

"I thought she was beautiful yesterday, out on the water, naked breasts—what could be better?" He swung his arm out with the question, then back again for more tequila. "I'll tell you what was better. Naked except for a strap-on, that's what. Fucking gorgeous. Are you sure you don't want to give her a shot at your ass?"

The question was asked with the eager incredulousness of someone absolutely certain the pleasure he craved should be loved by all.

Drew couldn't hold in the laugh anymore. "I'm sure, buddy." Then he got serious. "So here's the thing. Emma has to leave for work early in the morning. We haven't had dinner, but we had a big lunch. So I'm thinking you can go ahead and get a serious drunk on. I'll join you, if you'd like. Or, you can stop drinking, spend some time sobering up, and we can wake Emma up to the pleasure of being the center of both of our undivided attentions."

Without hesitating, Toby leaned over and picked up the cap for the liquor bottle. He set the bottle down, put his hands behind his head and stared up at the sky. "Tell me again about how you two met. And this time, cough up some more details."

Drew just smirked.

Toby sighed. "Remember the day I met Caroline? That was a fucked-up day."

Drew nodded. "You had a flat tire, were late to a job interview."

"And I rush into the building and this lady knocks into me and spills coffee all over me. I wanted to strangle her."

"She told me you just stood there staring at her."

"I just could not believe it had happened, had no idea what to do next. Couldn't get my brain to engage."

"Because it was stuck on her boobs."

Toby laughed. "Nah, it took me a while to get that far. I wanted to scream at this lady, but she says sorry and smiles at me, and I can't get a word to come out of my mouth."

"So she took you in hand."

"Saw I was holding an application and CV, figured I was there for the interviews, took hold of my wrist and just led me to where I needed to be. By the time she'd introduced me to the principal and taken the blame for my being late, I was in serious lust. Damn, I loved the way she talked to that asshole."

Drew waived his beer bottle towards Toby in salute, then took the final drink. He took their empties and the rest of the tequila into the house, stood at the bottom of the stairs to listen for movement. There were no sounds, so he went back outside.

Toby rolled his head along the chairback and looked at him as he resumed his seat. "Maybe I'll hit a club when I'm in Atlanta. They must have something decent there."

"Call your club, see if they have a referral."

"Good idea."

"Be careful, though. It's been a long time since you were trolling a club for a hook up."

A disdainful snort was the only response he got to that, but Drew decided not to push.

"Emma's necklace sure made things easier, huh?" Toby asked. "You didn't have to tell her what you were into."

Drew laughed. "I remember the weeks of angst you went through before telling Caroline what you wanted."

"Yeah, that sucked. But she sure as hell took to the idea."

They both laughed, but Drew sobered quickly. "Tell me you're not thinking of getting a necklace like that for yourself, though. That is way too dangerous for you. Hell, it wasn't a good idea for her, either, and she doesn't wear it anymore."

"You're such a prude sometimes."

"I'm serious, Toby. You get fired for that shit and it will follow you everywhere. No getting away from it, no getting your life back."

"Yeah, yeah. I'm not getting the necklace Drew, I was just saying it's cool that it made your connection so easy."

Drew wasn't thrilled with Toby's lack of concern, but he let it go. It had been one thing for the married couple to hide their lifestyle together. Dating was a whole different story and Drew was worried for his friend.

"Don't be a stick in the mud, cop." Drew suddenly sat up straight. "Hey, I bet there are lady cop Dommes. With handcuffs. Oooohhh, that would be hot."

Drew chuckled. "It's not like you need to be a cop to get handcuffs."

"No, but it makes it extra cool. Come on, tell me you haven't used them on Emma."

Drew stayed quiet but Toby laughed. "Yeah, I knew it. Did you role-play? Did you play bad cop with her?"

"I'll play bad cop with you if you keep pushing."

Toby gave a mock shudder. "Is that supposed to stop me or encourage me?"

"You'll have to find your own bad cop. Tonight is going to be for Emma."

"I'm fully on board with that plan." Toby looked at his watch. "Is that long enough of a nap for her?"

Drew didn't have to check his watch. He stood up. He gave Toby a long look, determined the man was sober and no longer sad. He was excited and Drew was determined to thank Emma for bringing that spark back into Toby's eyes.

"All right. Let's do it."

The few times he'd seen Emma asleep in his bed without him, she'd amazed him with how she could share with him with no problems, but put her in the bed by herself and she would do her best to take up every inch of space. Limbs every which way. So he was surprised to find her still in the center of the bed, curled into a loose ball.

Her hands were tucked under her cheek, the blanket covering all but a bit of her shoulder. Her smiles were definitely one of his favorite features, but there was something so endearing about seeing her face completely relaxed in sleep. He almost didn't want to disturb her. Except he wanted to lick that tasty bit of shoulder. And there was no way he'd be stopping there.

Besides, he really wanted to give her this experience. How had she described her imaginings? Two tongues, four hands? Well, she was about to find out exactly what that could do to a woman.

He went to the toy drawer and selected what he wanted. They silently took their clothes off, then worked together to lift the blanket off without disturbing her. Toby watched him, waited for a signal. Drew watched Emma. After a minute or so, she felt the cold and her nose twitched. Damn, in the midst of a thousand lascivious thoughts about what he wanted to do to her body, suddenly he just thought she was damn cute and wanted to kiss her nose.

So he did. Then he took her mouth.

CHAPTER TWELVE

Emma gave a questioning little moan and opened up for him, accepting him without hesitation. He slid his tongue in, delighted with her response as always. Delighted with her.

He brought his hand up to her cheek, then slid it to her shoulder, gently urging her to her back while deepening the kiss. She threaded her fingers through his hair, though she didn't grip. It wasn't her strength that held him to her, but her sweetness. Not that he had plans to leave the warmth of her mouth right away.

He slid his hand down her body, urging her to stretch out. She did so eagerly and he knew she expected him to stretch out on top of her. Instead, he threaded his right hand through her hair and brought his left hand to her breast, watching out of the corner of his eye to make sure Toby was with him.

Toby followed his lead perfectly, their hands caressing her breasts in unison, Toby's long fingers moving to cradle her head as his did. He tightened his grip on her hair so she could be absolutely certain there were too many hands at play.

He couldn't help it, he smiled into their kiss as her tongue faltered. Her eyes flew open and she tried to turn her head to see what was happening. He tightened his grip, kept her gaze focused squarely on his as he broke the kiss.

"Tell me now. Yes or no?"

"I trust you. If this is what you want, then hell, yes."

He kissed the tip of her nose again. "Give him a kiss. Let him know he's welcome here."

Slowly, he slid his hand free of her hair and moved his mouth to her breast. Her nipple was already tight with her need. He pulled it between his lips, gentle at first, then rougher as he lifted as high above her breast as he could. She and Toby continued to kiss as she tried to arch her back off the bed. He put a hand on her chest and held her down, then let her nipple free.

She moaned, the sound muffled, and moved her legs restlessly. He smiled. This was going to be so much fun.

He nudged Toby until the other man broke their kiss and looked at him. He rolled his eyes at him and nodded at Emma's neglected breast. Toby got the hint and joined him. Watching carefully, Toby followed Drew's lead. Drew used his tongue to explore the tip of her breast, then blew on the hard nipple. Emma moaned, a beautiful sound that turned into a sharp cry when he opened his mouth wide and bit down on as much of her breast as he could manage.

At the same time, making sure that Toby was mirroring his actions, Drew ran his hand very lightly down her belly, toward her center. He lifted his mouth and lightly tongued her nipple as his fingers rested at the top of her mound.

She pulled her knees up, pushed her legs wider, but he didn't move his fingers.

"She's pretty, isn't she, Toby?"

"Beautiful."

Drew played with the flesh under his hands, now, squeezing and releasing her breast, thumbing the nipple. They'd lost their synchronization as Toby also worked her, so she wouldn't know what was coming, had opposing sensations at the same time. When she was squirming in earnest, Drew pulled back, slowed down, nodded approvingly as Toby adjusted as well.

"I love her skin. It's so responsive." Drew tickled his fingers along her side and watched goose bumps form, then pinched her stomach, enjoying her gasp. "Always a reaction of some sort." He leaned in and soothed the spot with his tongue.

Toby raked his fingers along her side, leaving fine red scratches in his wake. Then he repeated the process with the pads of his fingers barely skating along the path. Emma drummed her heels and tossed her head.

"Please," she moaned, and they both smiled.

"We are pleasing you, aren't we, Emma?" Drew asked.

"Drew, I need more, please. Let me suck one of you."

"Mmm, maybe later." He leaned in and stabbed his tongue into her belly button, then nipped the mound of her stomach. She went still and he knew she was afraid of discouraging his journey south.

He sat up. "Look at this, Toby." He slid a hand over her mound, his finger through her slit. "She's nice and wet for us."

He showed his finger to Toby, then wiped the slickness onto the nipple that was on Toby's side. His friend didn't hesitate, but leaned in and pulled her nipple into his mouth. Twin moans of appreciation made Drew smile.

Twirling a finger at her opening, he anchored her leg to the bed with his arm. Toby joined him again and trapped her other leg.

"Feel how soft she is, how warm."

Toby slid a finger next to his and together they pushed inside her. Her hips tried to thrust but they didn't allow her room to move. Drew used his thumb to tease around her clit, then nodded at Toby, who leaned in and flicked it with his tongue.

They had to work to keep her still, but Drew didn't mind. Didn't want to order her from moving. He liked feeling her buck against him, her unrestrained body unconsciously fighting for more of what he had to give her.

Her eyes were closed so he reached out and pinched her nipple. The unexpected jolt had her eyes shooting open and her channel clenching tight around their fingers. Clearly the little orgasm wasn't enough to satisfy her, though, as she tried hard again to push her hips up, begging them for more.

He pulled his hand free and gestured for Toby to continue. Toby moved so he was between her legs, his hands pushing her legs up so she was folded nearly in half. He buried his face in her pussy, his hair falling around them so that Drew couldn't see much, only hear the enthusiastic sucking and the hum of pleasure from his friend.

Drew reached for the butt plug and lube he'd gotten earlier, let her watch him prep the plug. Showing it to Toby, he wasn't at all surprised when his friend moved his attentions lower, though her squeak indicated she hadn't expected a tongue there. After a moment, he nudged Toby aside and worked the medium-sized plug into her ass.

She was watching. Her mouth was open on continued gasps, her face slick with sweat, but her eyes were watching him, naked with want and need and... He blinked, then kissed her. A hard, demanding kiss that brought her hands to his head. This time she did hold him tight, did clench his hair in her fists, but he didn't mind. She needed something to hold on to as Toby resumed his magic down below. She needed him.

He explored every bit of her mouth, then pulled back and dropped more kisses on her lips, her chin, her jaw. He moved to her earlobe and nibbled it before laving the sting away. His hands continued to caress and squeeze her breasts, tweak her nipples while her body rocked under Toby's attentions.

"Drew, ahh god." Her words were strained and he couldn't resist.

"Well, if you're going to call me a god, I guess you can get what you want."

He put on a condom while Toby entertained her, leaving a small bottle of lube handy. When he motioned, Toby moved to her side again, leaning in for a quick, wet kiss before putting on the condom Drew threw at him.

Drew sat up and offered her his hand, lifting her to her knees. He moved behind her, using his knees to nudge her legs wider apart. Wrapping one arm around her stomach, he used the other to guide himself to her slick opening. With one long push, he was all the way inside. He paused, needing to catch his breath, catch himself. He nuzzled her ear. "Fuck, baby, you feel so good. Look at Toby's face. He can't wait to get more of you to taste."

DREW'S WORDS nearly sent her into an orgasm, but it wasn't enough. Emma clenched her muscles around him, leaned her head back onto this shoulder.

"Please, Drew. Fuck me hard."

His arm around her waist tightened and she was afraid he would tease her more, but he did exactly as she asked. With Toby alternately sucking and biting, caressing and squeezing, his knees against hers keeping her from sliding forward, Drew fucked her hard. She could barely breathe, the pressure inside building to insane levels.

Drew whispered in her ear, causing her whole body to shudder. Following his suggestion, she filled her palm with the lube he handed her and reached for Toby's cock as if it were sitting there waiting for her. She squeezed, loving his answering moan.

She hoped like hell he was turned on enough to come quickly, because she wasn't sure how much longer she'd be able to last and she wanted him to enjoy himself. He was certainly hard enough. She tugged him closer without bothering to ask, until she could reach around him and finger his hole.

He leaned into her, Drew moving his arm from between them, wrapping around Toby instead. The feeling of being pressed between the two hard bodies was nearly too much. She had to concentrate to keep from coming, focusing on squeezing her pussy muscles around Drew, stroking Toby and sliding her finger into his ass.

He bucked into her at the same time Drew did. She was full, surrounded, needed, wanted. She was on fire and there was no more holding back. She bit Toby's shoulder as she came, trying to be careful not to hold him too tightly in her release. Drew slowed down but didn't stop, working her through the orgasm, prolonging it until all she could do was remain still and take what he gave her. He shouted as he came, her body quivering with another small orgasm, or maybe it was still the same one, she didn't know, didn't care, could barely think, certainly couldn't move.

Drew's hand slid down to join hers at Toby's rear, reminding her she was still supposed to be capable of movement. He wrapped his hand around hers, slid his finger in alongside hers. Toby bucked against them, against the hand she had sleeved around him. She took the hint, slid her hand up and down his length, faster and faster as Drew took charge of her other hand.

Toby threw his head back, his dick pulsing in her hand. Drew brought their fingers to a halt until Toby started to slump, then he pushed them back in and out and in. Toby cried out and went slack in her hand.

They all sort of tumbled to the side in a mad attempt to not crush each other. She felt oddly energized and made a playful attempt to assist them in removing their condoms as Drew slid her butt plug free. Her hands got slapped for her effort so she slapped their butts. Drew growled at her but when they both moved to the bathroom for disposal, she grabbed her robe and ran out of the room.

She supposed she should be exhausted, and she was tired in a just-finished-a-great-workout sort of way, but she wasn't sleepy. She made it to the kitchen and went about pulling together sandwiches. It made her happy that she knew what they liked, and she was just setting the creations on the table when the men walked in.

They'd both pulled on jeans only and she suspected Drew knew she loved that sight. He was so good to her, it made her want to do whatever he asked. They stood in the entryway glaring at her, but she saw the sparkle in both of their eyes. She held the food up in offering and Drew narrowed his eyes into a glare.

"You think that will make up for it?"

"Yes."

"You might be right. We'll reserve judgment until we've tasted."

"As is your right." She bit her lip and opened her eyes wide, hoping she managed to pull off contrite. Their expressions were amusingly stern, which made it impossible not to laugh so she turned around and went to get beers for everyone.

She'd noticed the empty beer bottles and mostly empty tequila bottle. Apparently the guys had been up while she'd taken her nap. She managed to get the necks of three bottles in one hand, the tequila bottle under one arm and three short glasses in the other hand. By the time she turned around, she had herself under control and delivered the items to the table, letting Drew pull the bottle out from her arm while Toby freed the beers. She set the glasses down and gave a squeak as Drew pulled her onto his lap. Okay, apparently she'd be eating from here. Not a bad thing in her opinion.

She leaned back and accepted the glass with a small shot from Toby, clinking glasses when the boys offered them up.

"To friends," Toby said with a wink. "Old and new."

"Who are you calling old?" Drew asked.

"To friends," Emma said, elbowing Drew. "Hot and hot."

"To friends," Drew said dryly. "Even when they're smart-asses."

She twisted around so she could stick her tongue out at them before they all did their shots. It was better tequila than she was used to and she was able to keep her gasp to a bare minimum. She snuggled down into Drew's lap, throwing her legs over the side of the chair, tucking her head into his shoulder. His arm wrapped around her shoulders, holding her securely, his other hand resting on her leg where he made idle strokes with his thumb. Perfect, so perfect just to snuggle in and listen to the boys, interjecting occasionally, but mostly just enjoying the rhythm of their conversation.

THE WEEKS after Toby's visit flew by as fall took hold. Emma had been quietly relieved that immediately after their weekend together, the guys were busy with their own plans and she was able to get a little bit of distance. Not that she hadn't loved everything they had done, she absolutely had. But it had been an intense weekend and the little bit of space had helped her find her equilibrium again.

She'd had to do some fancy footwork to keep Taryn from digging too deeply. The fact that she'd taken one look at her boss and blushed had clued the other woman into the fact that she'd had an exciting weekend. Still, she'd managed not to cross the line of giving too many details or try to imagine how the other woman's ménage situation compared to what she'd done. But she may have spent a little more time than necessary watching Taryn, Richard and Caleb when they were all in the shop together at one point. It was always ridiculously sweet to watch them, even if they were bickering, but she couldn't help but be thankful that Toby's visit was a limited time engagement. She had enough trouble keeping on her toes with one guy, let alone two.

Once Toby had left town, she and Drew had managed to get together a few times. He'd come up to her place once, when her time was eaten up by a project, but she much preferred seeing him at his house. No roommates, plenty of space, both inside the house and out. Her roommates had teased her about dating Drew. Even though he was only four years older, the fact that he was a cop and owned his own house was worth a lot of teasing, mostly because they were jealous. She'd had to assure Libby that she didn't need to worry about Drew going into her bedroom, that her girlfriend's pot stash was safe, as long as they continued their policy of not smoking in the apartment. And if they happened to be making their special brownies when he came over, they should just stay cool and not offer him any.

When the time had come to pay her speeding ticket, she'd not minded one little bit. In fact, she'd baked him a small cake, which he thought was ridiculous, she could tell, but he'd humored her and let her celebrate.

She'd asked him to take her back to the river once, and they'd made quiet love on the bank, wrapping up to watch the stars for quite some time. As much as she enjoyed their scenes together, the low-intensity moment had been very welcome. Except it had her stupid brain, and truth be told, her stupid heart, second-guessing their relationship. Which she was not supposed to be doing. She was supposed to be researching air fares and flight schedules for going home for winter break, not setting herself up for failure by intensifying a relationship that had no future.

She checked her watch. Her shift at the coffee shop would end in half an hour and she was supposed to head directly to Drew's. She had some homework to do but she would handle it at his house while waiting for him to get off shift because they were expecting a big storm and he'd suggested she make the drive before it got too bad. And he'd given her a key to his house.

The customers kept her hopping so the half hour flew by easily. She called her goodbyes to her coworkers and grabbed her bag. The clouds were dark and menacing when she walked out, making her glad that he'd made the offer. She was trying not to think too hard about the little glow of happiness that had infused her when he handed over the key. It wasn't that big of a deal. It didn't mean that their relationship was, or even should be, changing. It was a matter of practicality.

The miles flew by quickly as she tried not to think about the status of their relationship. It was exactly what she and Drew had agreed to. Exactly what she needed, really. They were having a fantastic time together, but there was no stress or worry about the future. Perfect, for both of them.

Still, walking up to his door and letting herself in felt…significant. She took her overnight bag up to the bedroom, then went back downstairs and set her books and laptop up on the dining room table. She buried herself in the work for over an hour before the gnawing in her stomach clued her in to the fact that her early lunch of a sandwich was but a distant memory.

The refrigerator wasn't even close to empty, but nothing seemed remotely interesting. She grabbed a piece of bread and munched on it absently while she finished up her work. There was more she could do but she wasn't really in the mood anymore and she'd done what was necessary. She sent her dad the information on the flights she thought would work best for Christmas, then put the trip out of her mind. She had a little over eight weeks to go before then. She'd focus her stress on finals instead of the fact that she'd be away from Drew for two weeks, and that she wouldn't get to see him at Christmas.

Restless, she wandered to the living room, looked out the window at the long dirt driveway. Had it only been two months since she'd first driven down its length? On the one hand that seemed crazy. But on the other, she felt so comfortable with Drew, it was practically a cliché. As she watched, the first few raindrops began to fall. Being a California girl, it didn't really matter how many rainstorms she'd gone through out here, she still loved it. Especially when she was warm and cozy inside with a big picture window to watch from.

She smiled at the sight, then felt the smile stretch even wider when she spotted the car coming down the lane. Since he didn't have the early morning shift, he was in his SUV, not the cruiser. Too bad, because she always loved seeing him in it, remembering. With her plans to go play in Boston that day, and Drew being so careful with his reputation, it really was a miracle that things had progressed as they had.

One she was determined to enjoy to its fullest.

Drew opened his door and got out, his gaze pinning her in place. She pivoted as he walked up and through the door. The casual saunter was all natural and she knew he'd just be confused if she told him how turned on she could get just by his walking toward her. But it was the truth. Without saying a word, he rested his hands on her hips and his lips on her mouth. Slowly, excruciatingly slowly, he opened his mouth and hers for a kiss.

Her body melted into his, her arms going naturally around his body, her feet sliding into place between his. She couldn't say how long they stayed like that, enjoying the kiss and the press of their bodies together, but when her stomach rumbled, she felt his lips smile against hers, and he eased her back.

"Hungry, I take it?" he asked.

"Apparently," she laughed.

He took her hand and led her to the kitchen.

"I guess I could have made something, had it ready for when you got home."

"Not if that meant you'd still have work you needed to get done after dinner," he teased. "I can make some sandwiches," he offered.

"Ugh. I want real food. Actually, I think I want Italian. Yeah, a big plate of pasta. Let's go to Mama's, the drive will be totally worth it."

She actually felt his body go still beside her. And realized her mistake. They didn't do "going out". They did staying in. Staying private. They did sex and play, not dating. Instead of feeling bad about her mistake, she felt irritated at his reaction.

"Look, Drew. You expect me to trust you in the bedroom, even when we're not actually in the bedroom. Can't you trust me not to start calling you Sir in public, or begging you to fuck me on the table?"

His eyes went frosty and he closed the fridge.

"Emma."

If he'd said it any other way, she might have laughed at herself and tried to have a reasonable conversation. Instead, he said it in his Dom voice. In his chiding, "you're being a brat, begging for attention" voice.

Anger erupted through her faster than she thought possible. "No, Drew. You don't get to pull that shit on me when we're like this. My walking through your door does not automatically mean we're in a scene and you can treat me like a sub. I know that's the only thing I'm here for, but there are still boundaries."

"That's not fair, and you know it."

"Really? Do I? Fine. You're right. We had an agreement and I'm being unfair. I'll go get dinner and when I come back, if I'm in the mood to fuck, I'll let you know. Otherwise, I'll head home and we can set up another play date."

She turned to walk away, but she didn't get far. Drew's hand on her arm wasn't painful, but it was insistent. "Jesus, Emma, you didn't even give me a chance to answer you."

"Oh please, your expression was answer enough, I promise you."

"You're not being—"

"Fair. Yeah, you said. I'm hungry, I'm sure I'll be much more reasonable after I eat.

"Dammit, we talked about this."

"I know, Drew. I know you don't want to date. That doesn't mean I don't need to eat. Like I said, I'll go out to dinner and come back. You can have a sandwich, like you said."

Her anger had already burned through, replaced by a vague nausea that she didn't want to examine too closely. "Look, I know you have an issue with going out in public with a play partner. I get it. But if you don't trust me well enough at this point to know that I can have dinner in public without embarrassing you, then I think we have a problem."

"I don't think you'll embarrass me." He shoved his fingers through his hair, gave a little tug. "But you have to admit, going out on dates will change things. Change this. Change what we both said we wanted."

She started to deny it, then clamped her mouth shut. He was right. Yes, they could go out and get a meal, like buddies. She could tell herself that was all it needed to be, but she'd be lying. She didn't just want a good meal, she wanted to spend time with Drew, sitting and talking. In public. She hadn't admitted it to herself, but she'd already started to see them as a pair. A couple.

Her legs felt weak as she moved to the table, pulled out a chair and plopped down. "You're right. I'm being unfair. I guess... I don't... Hell. I don't know."

He pulled out the chair next to her and sat, bracketing her legs with his, taking her hands in his. "I do trust you. I don't think you're going to out me in public and get me fired. But I do know that you're leaving the state in, what, seven months? Something like that? And I know that I don't want a long-term relationship."

"I think maybe we need to find a middle ground. I don't want to feel like your whore who's only good enough—"

She didn't get the rest of the sentence out before he dragged her off her chair and into his lap.

"Baby," he crooned carefully. "Tell me that's not really how you feel." He cupped her chin, met her gaze.

A lump had somehow lodged in her throat and she had to work to speak. "No, Drew, I'm sorry. I didn't mean that. I don't feel like that." A tear escaped and his eyes followed the path it trailed down her cheek. "I guess I just need more. I shouldn't have reacted like that, though. Honestly, I didn't realize what I was feeling."

He returned his gaze to hers and she felt as if he were seeing through her, seeing inside to every thought and feeling she was having. She hoped he understood the mass of confusion better than she did. He leaned in and kissed her forehead and the tight bundle of fear that had sprouted deep in her belly loosened.

"We'll find some middle ground. I don't want you to think I've been actively avoiding going out in public with you. I've just been having way too much fun with you in private to want to waste any time out and about."

He dropped his hands to her thighs, leaned back into the chair. "But, I have to be honest. Going to your friend's family restaurant seems like a whole lot more, not just a little bit."

She nodded. "You're right. And I don't want that. I'm not ready for that. I was totally overreacting."

CHAPTER THIRTEEN

Drew watched her face, trying to figure her out. Was she being honest? With herself, as well as him? Was it just an overreaction, or was she setting them both up for heartache? It shouldn't have come as a surprise. Everything had been going so well that he just hadn't considered the fact that the normal progression in that case was to move forward. To move into a real relationship, one with an expectation of a future.

There was no question that if he were even the slightest bit interested in such a future, Emma wouldn't have had to push. He'd already have nailed her down with a commitment and ensured that she was just as interested in a future as he was. But he wasn't. So he hadn't anticipated.

Looking at her closely, trying to fathom all that was going on inside her gorgeous head, he decided he believed her. She hadn't realized she'd been itching for more and had overreacted. The problem was, were they kidding themselves thinking that they weren't heading for disaster?

They could keep saying they didn't want anything complicated to develop all they wanted, that didn't mean that they weren't developing exactly that, just by being together. He was going to have to give it some thought, after his heart stopped racing. They'd fought, but it hadn't turned ugly. No name calling, no screaming. Nothing like he'd had to listen to constantly, growing up. He pushed the thought away. His parents' issues had no place here, nothing to do with his relationship with Emma.

He lifted her up. Right now, they both needed to eat. "Get your jacket. It might not be up to Mama's standards, but we have a pretty decent Italian restaurant not too far from here." He wrapped his arms tightly around her, one hand cupping her head, his nose buried in her hair.

"I'm sorry you were upset, baby."

She squeezed him tight. "It's okay. Not your fault. Thank you for listening and not overreacting. One of us in that state was enough." She pulled back and offered him a wobbly smile.

Dropping a quick kiss on her nose, he let her loose to get her jacket. He found an umbrella in the coat closet and led her to the passenger side door of his truck, then ran around to his side. He tossed the umbrella in the backseat and slid in.

It was a quick drive despite the weather, and while they were quiet, it wasn't uncomfortable. The parking lot was only half full, so he wasn't worried about their lack of a reservation.

"Wait for me," he ordered quietly, grabbing the umbrella. She did as he asked and he held the cover over her while she exited, then led her into the restaurant. It took only a few minutes to have them divested of their coats and seated in a warm booth.

He studied her while she read the menu. It hadn't been as hard as she might imagine not to get pissed off earlier. Yeah, his first reaction had been anger. But he'd quickly seen her pain, which had been like a punch to his gut. The anger had slid away to concern, a need to know why she was hurting and how he could fix it.

He held back a sigh. They'd only known each other two months and in that time he'd been telling himself they were just having fun. But the truth was, he'd never had fun with anyone like this before, hadn't realized how impossible it would be not to fall in deeper. How could he, when he'd never met anyone like her before? Her joy and enthusiasm, her sweetness with Toby, the way she responded to him, all of it was addictive, like a drug he hadn't realized he needed to be wary of.

Her hand came into his line of sight, rested on his clenched fist. He looked over, saw she was watching him, concern and worry easily read on her face.

He turned his hand, linked his fingers with her.

"Sorry, baby. It's nothing, I'm just realizing how much of an idiot I am."

Regret flashed through her eyes but he stopped her before she could speak, then was interrupted by the waiter. They ordered and when the man left, he lifted her hand to his lips, pressed a kiss to her knuckles.

"I'm not saying what we decided when we met was a mistake, because it made sense for us at the time. What I'm saying is, it was stupid of me not to realize pretty early on that it wasn't going to fly for very long."

"Well, if you're an idiot, so am I. I swear, I haven't been stewing about it or anything. As I said, it took me by surprise too."

"I guess neither of us is used to this kind of thing, which is sort of the point."

"You're right. We're just going to have to figure it out together as we go."

He looked away, swallowed hard. "I'm still not sure I can give you what you need." He wasn't used to being unsure, didn't like the feeling at all. Her gaze dropped to the table and he squeezed her hand. "The dating thing."

Her uncertainty was palpable. "Look. If your boss walked in right now and you introduced us, what do you think would happen?" she asked.

"I trust you. I don't think you'd try to hurt me, or even do so accidentally. But you told me you're trying to be free and open about who you are. I can't ask you to bottle that up inside like I do."

"I was trying something new, and here's the thing, it didn't really work. I mean, it did in that I met you, and that was amazing. But letting other people," she glanced around, made sure no one was anywhere near close enough to hear her low voice, "who are into kink know that I'm into kink didn't really do anything for me. It's really more about what I'm trying to figure out for myself, about myself. What I'm going to be able to live with when I move back to California, and what I won't be able to live without.

"Not wearing that necklace again isn't even about you. What I was looking for wasn't jewelry or even community. I already have that. I already knew where to go to be with people who were like me. Honestly, I think my tattoo serves as a better reminder to myself that just because I usually look and act one way doesn't mean I can't be smug about my naughty side. But I really don't want everyone to know I have the naughty side. I like being subtle."

"All right. You have class at one tomorrow?"

She sat back as the waiter brought them glasses of water and a basket of breadsticks. As soon as the man's hand was clear, she snatched one, quickly rattled her order off to the waiter then took a bite. Drew couldn't help but smile as he placed his own order, thankful that the mood had changed. He hated seeing her hurt, much preferred to see her enjoying her food. Although not as much as he liked seeing her enjoy him and what he did to her. But was that going to be enough? He clenched his jaw, forced the thought away.

Holding up a hand to indicate she would answer, eventually, she chewed her way through the bite, then took a sip of the water. "Yes, one o'clock. I should leave here by noon to be safe."

Now that he thought about it, he realized she liked to be early for things, hated to feel rushed. He wished he could change the fact that the burden of their meet-ups almost always fell to her.

"If it doesn't interest you in the least, tell me, but I thought in the morning you might enjoy a trip to the shooting range."

Her eyes got that satisfying look of anticipation he was used to seeing only in regards to sex, letting him know immediately that she liked the idea.

"Oh, that would be fun!"

"It might be a mistake on my part, introducing you to firearms," he said, giving her a wry grin.

She laughed and took his hand before giving him a mockingly serious expression. "I solemnly vow never to point a gun at you, no matter what you do."

He just couldn't resist her. He leaned in for a taste and she met him halfway. Her lips were buttery with a hint of garlic and he wanted to lick them, order her to stay perfectly still for him while he used one of the breadsticks to paint that buttery flavor all over her body. Her breath quickened, as if she could sense the direction of his thoughts, the heat of his desires. He knew the waiter was approaching so he forced himself to give her the small kiss that was appropriate to the environment, then leaned back.

He asked the waiter for more water, even though he didn't really need it, just to keep the man's attention on him while Emma sat back. The waiter didn't deserve to see the look of soft arousal on her face. She met his eyes as the plates were being set on the table, her attention focused solely on him.

Knowing he should do more, offer her more, give her more, he only gave her a cocky wink and looked down at his meal. The chicken looked delicious, but he found he didn't really care. Instead he cut himself a bite and ate it while mostly just watching Emma start in on her pasta. As he watched her lick her lips clean, he tried not to think that he was very much in trouble here.

THEY WERE both quiet on the drive home. He took her hand in his, rested them on her thigh. The rain had intensified but traffic was light, and he kept his speed nice and easy. He squeezed her hand and put the car in park. She didn't wait for him to open her door, but jumped out and twirled herself in the downpour. He could only shake his head and laugh at her obvious enjoyment as he followed her to the door.

Without saying a word they went upstairs and he undressed her. She remained still while he worked his way to having her naked.

Since she was sopping wet, he couldn't enjoy a slow reveal, but sent her to the bathroom to get a towel so he could pat her dry. She just smiled at him and let him do as he pleased. When she was dry, he cupped her jaw in his hands and licked her lips as he'd wanted to at the restaurant, worked his way along her jaw, down her neck to spend some time at the hollow of her collarbone.

Other than murmuring his name and bracing her hand lightly on his shoulder, she remained still. He enjoyed the ever-increasing tension as it worked its way through her body. Her nipples tightened hard under the barest brush of his lips, her chest flushed with her arousal, and her breathing accelerated.

He picked her up, eliciting a sweet little gasp, and laid her out on the bed. For a minute he just watched, her gorgeous body deeply aroused, her eyes heavy with need. He pulled his clothes off quickly and rolled on a condom without taking his eyes off her for more than a second. Stretching out on top of her, giving her some of his weight, wanting to feel the connection along their bodies as much as possible, he moved his fingers into her hair, his thumbs resting along her cheekbones. He met her eyes and slowly slid into her. Her hips tilted, easing the way while they watched each other. His rhythm slow and steady, he paused every few strokes to make sure her clit was getting the pressure she needed. When her gasps were coming steadily, her body arching up into him as much as possible, he caressed his thumbs along her cheek. "Let go for me, baby," he whispered. "I need you to come now."

She gave a small cry, her eyes closing, but only for a moment. They fluttered back open, watching him watch her come. So beautiful, his Emma. So perfect. He thrust into her squeezing channel, felt as if he was fusing their bodies together in a way that could only be described as amazing, and came. Only after he'd finished did he allow his eyes to close. He let more of his weight settle onto her welcoming body and he tried very hard not to worry about what the future held for them.

THE NEXT MORNING he dragged her out of bed without much more than a kiss and put her to work scrambling eggs while he made the coffee and toast. She wasn't exactly grouchy, but neither was she fully awake until they were finished eating, and he enjoyed the transition. They made quick work of the cleanup and he followed her back upstairs into the bathroom.

She watched him in the mirror, but when he didn't say anything, she went about her routine. He stood behind her, watching as she brushed her teeth and put lotion on her face, her expression questioning and expectant. When she reached one hand for her hairbrush and the other up to release her ponytail, he stopped her.

"Clasp your hands behind my back."

There was no hesitation as she complied, her gaze glued to his in the mirror. He let his expression show his appreciation for her quick obedience, then he broke the connection, needing to watch as his hands slipped inside the loose waistband of the yoga pants she wore. Within moments she was dripping wet, ready to accept the fingers he curled into her. Her head fell back to his shoulder, her hands pressing hard into his back. He worked her, the heel of his hand pressing into her clit, his fingers finding the spot inside that made her cry out.

He brought his free hand up to rest gently against her arched neck, his fingers loosely circling her. Her cunt clenched tightly around his fingers and she came with a sharp cry. Giving her only a few seconds to recover, he pulled his fingers free, brought them to her lips, a silent command. She opened her mouth, accepted his fingers into her mouth, cleaned them thoroughly.

He pulled free, met her eyes in the mirror once again. "On your knees."

A smile flashed across her face before the vision disappeared as she turned and dropped in front of him. She looked up for permission, received his nod, and quickly went to work pulling his pajama pants down to his ankles and wrapping her soft hands around his very hard shaft.

Her enthusiastic tongue, talented fingers and hums of appreciation made short work of the task he'd given her. When he was nearly ready, he grabbed her ponytail, wrapped the hair in a tight grip. She stilled immediately, her mouth going lax, tilting her chin to give him what he needed. He pushed in almost roughly, hitting the back of her throat before retreating, then again and again. He fucked her mouth, her hands braced on his thighs, her body open and willing to receive what he gave. When he gave one last thrust and paused, she sucked hard and he exploded into her.

She released her hold but he waited a moment before sliding clear, needing to catch his breath, loving the feel of her warm mouth around his sensitive flesh.

"So good, baby. Thank you."

Her eyes smiling up at him was her only response.

He found himself humming during his quick shower and she laughed at whatever look was on his face when he stepped out. He just smiled and brushed his teeth while she went in the bedroom to dress. They were ready at the same time and walked out of the house hand in hand. She paused near their cars but he tugged her along until they were walking down the driveway toward the barn.

"Aren't we going to need a car?" she asked.

"Nope."

He glanced at her as they walked. She looked a little unsure and he didn't like that she doubted his plans to take her out, but it was his own fault, so he just waited.

Inside the barn, he led her to a tarp in the far corner and pulled it free, revealing a motorcycle. She actually clapped her hands in excitement and he was glad the rain had moved on, leaving behind the gorgeous fall day so that he could give her this. He handed her two helmets and rolled the bike out into the sun.

"We'll go back up to the house, get better jackets," he told her as he helped her with her helmet. "I didn't want to give the surprise away."

She just grinned at him, waited until he'd straddled the bike, then climbed on. She tucked in close, wrapped her arms around his waist and he drove them slowly back to the house. They put heavier jackets on, remounted, and headed out.

It was a bit of a drive to the shooting range he'd selected but Emma was grinning hugely when they got off the bike. She handed him her helmet then threw her arms around him and smacked him with a kiss.

"That was awesome!"

He laughed. "I'm glad you liked it."

The place wasn't busy and it wasn't long before they had everything they needed and a lane assignment. He showed her how the gun worked, the bullets and magazine, then they both donned ear protectors and safety glasses. When he opened the heavy door, he watched her. Her nose wrinkled slightly at the sharp smells, but she grabbed his hand and tugged him to the number they'd been given.

There were partitions between the lanes and a small counter that he set the gun and ammunition onto. He hooked one of the paper targets he'd gotten into place, then pushed a button that moved the target back. He stopped it at twenty yards.

EMMA WAS SERIOUSLY BUZZING after the motorcycle ride and from excitement at being in the shooting range. It was an alien world—the sounds, the smells, even the fact that they'd gotten there on a motorcycle instead of in a car, served to make the whole adventure sort of surreal. She imagined that if she'd come with anyone else, she'd be nervous, but with Drew at her side, she was just excited and ready to try.

Together they loaded the gun as he'd shown her before they put on the ear protectors. She turned to the target and took her stance. He nudged the back of her thigh very gently, reminding her not to lock her knees. He put his hands on her shoulders until she remembered to pull them down away from her ears. She took a deep breath, relaxing and finding her stillness. When he rested his hands lightly on her hips, she knew he was ready for her to begin. Lining up the sights on the gun, she aimed at the target. The trigger was heavier than she'd expected and it felt as if she had to pull a long time, and yet somehow it was still sudden when the trigger snapped back and the gun kicked in her hand. The noise and recoil, though expected, still made her jump a tiny bit.

His fingers flexed reassuringly against her, but he didn't try to brace her. She looked at the target and saw a hole in the bottom corner. Careful to keep the gun pointed down the range, she turned and gave him a grin. His answering grin was beautiful and full of pride and it warmed her heart. Turning back, she took her time relaxing again and lining up the sights, then worked her way through the magazine, most of them hitting the target.

Then he moved the target back and took a turn, impressing the hell out of her with his speed and precision. He definitely wasn't using the sight on the barrel, like she was. She tried a final round, doing slightly better, even with the greater distance of the target. She was having such a great time, she actually gave a minute's thought to blowing off her class. But she couldn't do it and she wasn't about to suggest he call in sick, so she resolved to just enjoy the time they had left. And there was much to enjoy, the way he handled the powerful bike with ease, and, cliché or not, the feel of the thrumming machine between her legs as she was pressed up tight against him was certainly something she could enjoy. A lot.

They got back to the house just in time for him to give her a smoking-hot kiss that left her breathless and a little bit shaky as he eased her into her car. She blinked at the steering wheel for a minute before noticing his evil grin. Unable to do anything else, she laughed and started the car. And watched him in the rearview mirror until she had to turn onto the main road.

EMMA KNEW she was in a bit of a mood as she drove out to Drew's a week later. Her father had booked her ticket home for after finals and she was feeling a weird mix of happy to be going to see her parents and dreading how it was going to affect her relationship with Drew. The fact that her brother's birthday was three days after Christmas always made the holidays a mixed bag of emotions.

She'd considered cancelling on Drew, but she had only a couple of more weeks to see him before her trip and she didn't want to waste her chance. Determining to put her cranky pants firmly behind her, she turned up the music and spent the drive daydreaming what interesting things her man might have in store for her and reminding herself how much she liked it that he'd started calling her baby after her stupid little tantrum. She wasn't sure he'd even noticed, but she certainly had.

The smell of pizza was pungent as she walked to the door held open by a smiling Drew. He took her backpack from her and gave her a kiss before ushering her into the house and closing the door behind her. He gestured to his laptop, sitting on the dining room table.

"I got an email from Toby, if you want to see. He has some pictures from his trip, funny little stories. I called him after and we talked a while."

He moved into the kitchen and opened the oven to check the pizza. It was one of her favorite meals that he made. Using store-bought dough, he doctored up his own sauce and used plenty of cheese in addition to the sausage and mushroom toppings she favored. He swore it was the pizza stone that made the difference. She didn't care, she just liked that he made it often. Apparently deciding it could use some more time, he shut the door as she sat to look at the laptop.

"How did he sound?" she asked.

"Good. Really good. I was worried, since this was the first solo trip of the kind that they used to take together. But he said he was feeling better than he has since it happened. He credits a decent portion of that to you."

She blushed. "I think it was just the timing. Part of him was ready to start embracing life again. You helped him with that."

He took the seat next to her, reached his hand around her neck and brought her forward for a kiss. "Yes. And part of it was you, just being you."

Pleased that he thought so, she read the email, laughed with him over some of the stories and looked at the photos. By the time she was done, Drew had pulled the pizza from the oven and sliced it up. "How much work do you have, baby?"

She smiled as he handed her a plate. "Not much, maybe half an hour. How was work today?"

He told her about a domestic disturbance call that luckily had ended up more comedy than drama. She loaded the dishwasher and started it running while he went to take a shower. She was on the couch with her book and netbook, feet stretched out to rest on the coffee table, when he came down with his paperback. He sat at the other end of the couch, then leaned over, picked her feet up and swung them around so that her feet were in his lap instead.

She just rolled her eyes at him, but couldn't actually keep the smile off her face. He was careful not to distract her, as he always was when she was doing homework, but she was glad to reach the end of what she needed to do and shut the netbook down. She leaned over to put it and her textbook on the coffee table, then snuggled down a bit so she was reclining against the couch arm.

Setting his book aside, he picked up one foot and dug his thumb into her arch. Her eyes rolled up in her head and he laughed out loud. "Good?"

"Oh yeah."

"Tell me about your class."

No, she was done with schoolwork for today. She didn't want to think about it anymore. Didn't want to think about how close to being finished she was, how much work the next semester was going to be. And then it would be over. Done. Time to leave.

"Don't you have more important things to concentrate on right now?" she asked, pretending she didn't hear the note of belligerence in her own voice.

He raised his eyebrow at her, something that managed to look sexy but still come across as chiding. He switched feet and she tucked the toes of the finished foot under his thigh. "You're pretty good at that," she said when he didn't answer.

"Instinct."

"I do like your instincts." Well, mostly. Except when it had him giving her that penetrating look.

"I'm glad."

He moved his hand up to her ankle.

"Hey, you weren't done down there."

CHAPTER FOURTEEN

The look Drew gave Emma only caused her to pout. Interesting. Emma wasn't much of a pouter. Something was going on with her, but he had no idea what. He didn't think it was anything to do with Toby. Something with school? Should he steer the conversation back to that? She didn't seem inclined to talk about whatever the problem was, and he debated pushing it, or pushing her and letting the rest come out later.

She pulled her foot free of his grasp then set it in his lap. She wanted something more from him and it wasn't conversation.

He gave a light slap to her foot. "Behave, missy."

Her pout deepened, though he was sure at least some of it was put on.

"Maybe I don't want to."

Repositioning his hand on her ankle, he gave her a hard look. "Is that so?"

She tried to jerk her foot free again, twisted in his grasp. He watched her eyes fall partly shut at the sensation of being trapped. He didn't know why she was in brat mode, didn't know why she didn't want to talk anymore, but he knew the best way to find out.

Standing abruptly, he dropped her leg and pointed to the stairs. "Wait for me on the bed. No clothes."

She stared at him for a full minute, satisfaction, nervousness and arousal all clear on her face. Then she rolled off the couch and stomped into the bedroom. He heard her open the door harder than it needed as he walked into the kitchen and pulled a glass from the shelf. Taking deep breaths, he filled the glass with ice from the refrigerator dispenser, then water. The sound of the ice crackling under the flow of water always sounded sexual to him. He had no idea why, but it helped him center himself. He wasn't mad, knew she was testing him, testing herself in some way. But he needed to be focused, needed to figure out what it was that she was looking for, what she wanted, and most importantly, what she needed.

He drank the cold water slowly, until there was only ice left. Then he carefully placed the glass on the counter and walked to the bedroom. It didn't surprise him at all that she wasn't sitting in a submissive pose, calmly waiting for her master's orders. Still, he had to bite back a smile at what he found. While he was pretty sure she was naked, as ordered, she'd crawled under the covers, wrapped herself tightly within and was feigning sleep.

The covers moved too rapidly from her breathing for her to actually be asleep. Keeping as quiet as possible without actually sneaking, so that she'd have to struggle to track his movements, he walked to the dresser and selected an anal plug and lube from the drawer. When he moved to the side of the bed, her eyes were closed. He watched her for a moment, letting the anticipation build while he had the pleasure of studying her face. Her skin, that fascinating combination of brown with the hint of olive, looked striking against his sage-green sheets. He realized he'd started favoring the sheet set for exactly that reason. Her black hair spread out across the pillow, one skinny lock falling along her cheek, just in front of her ear. He'd never spent much time looking at a woman's nose, but he had to say hers was attractive. Not too big, not too small. Like everything else about her, it worked perfectly for her. Had he noticed that before?

She'd begun to make subtle movements under his scrutiny. A

hard swallow, a twitch of the eyelid, a crinkle along her forehead, quickly smoothed out. He reached out and grabbed the covers, flung them completely off the bed before she had a chance to react. Her eyes flew open but she made no further move.

"What?" she asked.

He held his hand out to her. "Put this in."

She sat up, looked at the lube and the plug. "Okay. Bend over. Don't worry, I'll use lots of lube."

It was a struggle not to laugh, to force his expression to remain stern.

"Emma."

She moved back, only an inch or two, but away from what he held, away from what he ordered. He dropped the items on the bed, grabbed her up and had her bent over his legs, ass in the air, before she had time to do anything more than squeak.

Three hard slaps had her breathing hard, her breasts pressing snugly against his leg, her body trembling ever so slightly against him. He opened the lube, squirted a large amount on her and worked it in easily. The plug was a small one, so he didn't need to do much prep. When she was wet, he picked the toy up and slid it neatly into her ass. She stiffened but said nothing.

He lifted his arm from her back and she rolled off, landing on the floor and scrambling away from him. But she made no move to touch her ass.

"Stand up."

She did so, but not with the graceful compliance she usually displayed. He took a step forward, knowing she'd take one in retreat. When she did, he crowded her, walking her backward until she was against the dresser with nowhere else to go. He spun her around, using his size and weight to hold her against the cool wood. His legs bracketed hers, his left arm going around her body and between her breasts until he rested his palm lightly against her throat. A full body shiver betrayed her and he let himself smile since she couldn't see.

With his free hand he opened a far drawer and pulled out

restraints. When he backed away from her body, he trailed his hand around until he gripped the back of her neck. Using only that touch he directed her back to the bed. He gave a small push, nudging her to bend over the bed, but she stood firm, locked her knees. In less than five seconds he'd kicked her feet apart, pulled her wrists behind her back, shoved his knee hard against the plug lodged in her ass and forced her cheek against the sheet. While his legs kept hers spread and his knee continued to manipulate the toy, he buckled the restraints around her wrists.

Her butt made tiny movements against his leg that he was sure she was completely unaware of. Sliding a hand under her torso, he cupped her breast, found her nipples hard. She breathed into him, but her eyes were shut, refusing to look at him. He pulled his hand free and spanked her again, once, twice. She made a needy sound in the back of her throat.

Keeping one hand firmly on her backside, he knelt next to the bed and wrapped her ankles in the cuffs. It wasn't the easiest thing to do one-handed, but it only took a couple of minutes. When he was done, he stood, leaned one arm next to her head, let most of his weight settle on her. Her mouth was open, her breath coming in little gasps. Sweat beaded along her hairline. She went limp under him, relaxing into the mattress. He fingered her hair back from her face, watched the tension instinctively fade from her features. Until she began to think again. Her eyelid twitched, her fingers curled against his stomach. He nuzzled her face, kissed her cheek. Then he moved.

Before she could react, he'd picked her up, turned her over and tossed her in the middle of the bed. He straddled her chest, sitting up high enough that she couldn't do anything with her legs but kick ineffectively. She pulled against his hands but he had the restraints attached to the clips in the headboard before she'd finished wailing "No." Within seconds he had her ankles similarly restrained to the footboard and simply watched as she tugged and pulled, jerking the heavy bed only slightly.

She stopped moving, only her heavy breathing indicating her

fight. Well, that and the glare she gave him as he stripped off his clothes and rolled on a condom. He went to the dresser and retrieved one more item.

"Let me go," she demanded when he moved up onto the bed, her eyes fixed on the small flogger he held.

"No."

He slapped her pussy with the flogger, letting the tails land with a sharp sting, then slide free with a heavy softness. She froze except for the rapid blinking of her yes. Stunned, she let the angry façade slip as her hips bucked up. It took her only a second to recover, however, and she screeched at him, "Let me go!"

"No." He flogged her breasts, first one, then the other.

She licked her lips and her nipples tightened even further. Twisting against the restraints, she managed to point most of her torso to the side, away from him. He took advantage and fingered the plug, twisting it, pulling it out a little, then pushing it back in. She turned her moan into a growl, which morphed into a gasp when he dropped the flogger and shoved two fingers into her slick pussy.

Her back dropped heavily to the bed, her hips pushing her pelvis up into his invading fingers. He pulled free and licked himself clean of her juices.

"Why do you need to be punished?" he asked, straddling her thighs.

She glared at him.

He slid his legs down along hers, propped himself up on his elbows so that their faces were lined up.

"Why do you need to be punished?" he asked again.

Her bravado slipped away, her body stilling as he brought the game to an end. She turned her head, looked away from him. He wrapped his fingers into her hair, pulled sharply until she was facing him again, barely loosened his grip.

"Why do you need to be punished?"

She swallowed hard enough that he heard it.

"I, um, didn't listen. Tried to get away."

He leaned in, bit her on the chin. The fact that he rubbed his chest against her nipples at the same time wasn't an accident.

"Why do you need to be punished?"

"You can be such an asshole!"

He reached one hand down, used it to once again move the plug out and back in. She tried to buck into him, but his hips held her steady. She tried to grind herself against his cock, but he didn't give her enough space.

"Drew!"

He tightened the fist holding her hair.

"Sir!"

Loosening his hold, he stared into her eyes.

"Why do you need to be punished?" His voice was calm and firm.

The fight drained out of her. Her eyes closed, but she forced them open before he could command her to.

"I was scared. And annoyed with myself."

His gut clenched but he allowed nothing to show. "Tell me."

"I— My Dad bought my tickets for Christmas. I'll be going out there for two weeks." She swallowed hard. "Michael...my brother, his birthday is...was, the twenty-eighth. So going home can be hard." Her gaze darted away. "And I know I'm going to miss you. A lot. But I don't know how you're going to react to that. So I got irritated. With myself, mostly." She forced her eyes back to his and he could clearly see the annoyance—mostly at herself, he thought, but some for him—as well as the hurt.

"I shouldn't have acted out like that, and I'm sorry."

As her lover who was trying to convince them both that they had no long-term future, he wanted to roll to her side, throw his arm over his eyes and retreat from the total intimacy of the position he'd put them in. It wasn't that he wanted to run, avoid the issue. Just lessen the intensity that the direct eye contact gave. Well, maybe it was all of the above.

As her Dom, there was no question of his doing that. To pull back so suddenly would harm her, and that wasn't an option.

He wasn't entirely sure of the motivations of his next move.

Reward for her honest answer, distraction from the question at hand, or just because it made him feel better. He slid into her in one long move, then held still. It sure as hell did make him feel better. Emma's eyes rolled back a bit before returning to meet his gaze. Some of the fear dissipated, the heat that was already there flaring up.

The links holding her cuffs to the bed rattled as she pulled against their restraint, but her hands were no longer fists fighting for freedom. Instead they were reaching, fighting to touch him, to pull him closer. He moved his hips, settled in a little deeper. She gasped and he drew in her breath. She moaned and he felt the vibration throughout his whole body.

"You know that it's your responsibility as much as it is mine to communicate when there's a problem."

Her eyes got wet and she blinked rapidly. "I know. I just reacted. I guess I wanted you to…I don't know, prove that you wanted me."

"Even if you were misbehaving."

"Yeah. I've never done that before."

"Neither of us has been in this situation before." He should have said relationship.

"Yeah," she repeated.

He kissed her and began to move.

EMMA MANAGED to hold back the tears until he kissed her. With the gentle invasion of his tongue, she felt the slow trickle escape from her eyes. She yanked her arms again, wanting to touch him. Stupid, she'd been so stupid to act out. She'd never considered herself a brat, but she'd sure proven otherwise tonight. Of course, now she could see why some subs liked to act that way. He'd reacted, just as she'd unconsciously hoped he would. By dominating her, proving he would fight her. Own her.

She was dangerously close to climaxing, but didn't want to break the kiss to ask for permission to come. Taking as deep a breath as she could, she forced her body to relax some, trying to stave off the inevitable. He rubbed against her clit and it was all she could do to hold on. Letting a whimper escape was the only plea she could make. It worked. He lifted his head and ordered her to come.

The shock wave blasted through her body, but it was as much emotional as it was physical. If her little fit of temper hadn't done the job, this did. She could no longer deny that she was falling totally and completely in love with this man. He commanded her body and was fast coming to own her heart. Later, she'd summon the energy to let that scare her.

When he rolled off her, she immediately missed the weight of him, though she was grateful that he quickly released her restraints. She wrapped her arms around him, kissed him hard. He let her, let her wrap her tongue around his, let her hold him so tightly she felt her fingernails dig into his skin. His hands ran lightly up and down her back. Soothingly. It took her a minute to realize she was still crying. When she did, she broke the kiss, leaned her forehead against his.

"I'm sorry. I don't know what's wrong with me."

"No need to be sorry for honest reactions." He slid one finger down the trail of moisture on her face. He returned his lips to hers, continued to soothe her with every part of himself. Finally she took a deep breath and pulled back again.

He smiled, cupped her face in his hands and kissed her nose. "Go take a shower."

She blinked. It was definitely an order, not a suggestion. Not sure what to think, she decided that actually she wasn't ready to think. Which he'd probably known. He eased the plug out of her ass and pushed her toward the bathroom.

The hot water pounded her shoulders, obliterating the slight ache. Part of her wanted to laze in there for an hour, but she allowed herself only a few minutes before beginning her normal bathing routine. It didn't take long before everything that needed to be washed was washed, and everything that needed to be shaved was shaved. When she got out, she found a glass of water waiting for her on the counter. No ice, just the way she liked it. Doms sure did hate it when you got dehydrated.

When she went downstairs, he'd turned on the football game. She sat next to him and didn't mind when he prodded her until she was lying along the couch, her head on his thigh.

His hand brushed her hair back from her face. He handed her netbook to her, knowing she liked to check her email while watching the game. Before she turned it on he squeezed her shoulder.

"When you get back from California, I'll take you to meet my parents."

Her breath stuttered to a stop.

"Then we'll talk about where our relationship is going."

She waited to see if he would say anything else, but he was quiet. "All right. I'm not sure what one has to do with the other."

"That's the way I need it to be."

That didn't exactly strike her as fair, but she figured she'd pushed him far enough tonight, and the fact that he'd agreed to have the conversation was a good thing. Probably. Besides, she was worn out and didn't think she could handle any more emotions right now, so she settled back against the couch and let her body relax.

"Okay, Drew."

His thigh relaxed under her head and they watched the game. Neither of their teams was playing, so she wasn't that into it, and found her eyes closing by the end of the first quarter. She only woke when he picked her up and carried her to bed.

THREE DAYS later Emma paced nervously in her apartment. Taryn had insisted they go play pool with her and her guys, something they used to do somewhat regularly, but hadn't had a chance to do since she'd hooked up with Drew. She'd told Drew she was going, then extended the invitation cautiously, making it clear, she hoped, that she wouldn't be upset if he declined.

However, he'd agreed to join them and even said he'd spend the night at her apartment if she wanted, or go home that night if she preferred. He knew having sex with her roommates at home sort of freaked her out, and she appreciated that he was considerate of that. She definitely wanted him to spend the night, because she hadn't seen him since her stupid bratty episode and she wanted to make sure he was okay. Plus, with finals about to start, she wasn't sure how much she'd be able to see him before she left for California.

So it had all seemed like a good plan, but now she was nervous with the thought of actually introducing him to Caleb, Richard and Taryn. Of behaving like a couple together in public. She didn't want to screw it up, do something to annoy him. She just had to be careful not to act annoyed with him instead of herself.

The distinctly male clomp of boots on the stairs outside her apartment had her opening the front door as Drew reached the top.

"Hey."

"Hey," he answered, moving directly into her with the kind of full-body kiss that always set her on fire.

"Mmmmm."

His lips smiled against hers and he pulled back, swiped her bottom lip with his thumb. "You look delicious."

He hadn't really seen her in a going out outfit since the night in her hotel. A disadvantage of not actually going out on dates that hadn't even occurred to her. He hadn't had many chances to see her at her best. Then again, he clearly liked what he had seen, which was her in every state other than her best, from bedhead to riverbank sex messy. Still, she'd enjoyed putting on her tightest jeans, her favorite boots and a sexy green top that clung to her curves and showed off more than a little bit of cleavage. Her usual pool hall outfit.

"Thanks, you look pretty hot yourself."

And he did. His jeans were a little bit nicer than she'd seen before and he had on a long-sleeve shirt in a burnt orange color. The shirt had three buttons at the top, all left undone, and molded itself faithfully to his torso.

She glanced at her watch, disappointed to see that an extra half hour of time hadn't magically appeared. The apartment was empty right now, and they could...no. She grabbed her jacket and walked out with him.

DREW ENJOYED WATCHING the interchanges between the married group. He didn't spend a lot of time with couples, let alone long-term committed couples. The genuine affection he found between them wasn't what he expected. He didn't know if that meant he had low expectations of relationships or if this group was happier than most.

Richard offered to sit the first game out, pitting Drew and Emma against Taryn and Caleb. Worrying he might embarrass himself and Emma, Drew was pleased to find that while the others were better, especially the girls, with a couple of lucky shots he was able to hold up his end of the team. And while Emma teased her friends and him good-naturedly, it was obvious she wasn't really all that competitive. If he'd sucked, he didn't think she would have minded much.

Richard appeared to have taken it upon himself to distract his spouses from the game. He casually bumped against them, palmed their butts, blew in their ears. When Drew was lining up a shot and saw Richard sidle closer, he braced himself to be included in the activities.

"Ricky," Caleb said sternly.

The other man stopped. Drew looked up to see Caleb pointing at a chair. Richard laughed and went to sit, though Drew was fairly sure that was because the waitress had just brought a tray of food and drinks to the table. Even without whatever distraction Richard had planned for him, Drew missed the shot. Emma popped a quick kiss on his cheek in sympathy, then focused her attention on Taryn's turn.

Drew moved to take a seat next to Richard.

"I'm going to need to practice," he said, dropping into the chair.

Richard slanted him a look, handed him a mug of beer. "I guess you will, if you're sticking around."

The affable flirt from before was gone.

Drew just raised his eyebrows at the doctor. "I'm here right now. She'll be leaving in six months. Who knows what will happen in that time?" It was what he'd been telling himself for the last few days, since Emma's confession about her fears.

Richard frowned at that. "That's pretty limiting, isn't it, to plan on an end from the beginning?"

Drew blinked. "How much have you had to drink?"

Richard scowled, then smiled when Taryn came by to do a little victory shimmy and grab a mug of beer.

Emma lined up a shot, conveniently aligning her cleavage with his gaze. He enjoyed the view while Richard sighed.

"I'm just saying. We love Emma, we don't want to see her hurt."

"Emma's perfectly capable of looking out for herself."

"That doesn't mean she doesn't deserve friends that are willing to do it for her."

"True enough." Drew held up his beer, saluting the other man.

Richard let loose an unexpected bark of laughter. Drew followed his gaze and could only see Taryn and Caleb standing closely together while Emma made another shot.

"What?"

"Taryn's annoyed at the idiots behind her. She's not much of a people person."

Drew watched, could see the college boys at the table behind her were a little bit rowdy, but nothing major.

Richard leaned in closer. "See how she's got her hand tucked into Caleb's pocket? That's to keep herself from turning around and saying something to them."

He looked and did see Taryn's fingers curled into Caleb's pocket, the knuckles visibly white even from this distance.

"How can she not be a people person? Doesn't she run a coffee shop?"

"Sure, but those people pay her for the privilege of coming into her shop. And she can kick them out whenever she wants."

Drew laughed, watched as Caleb slung an arm around his wife's shoulders and slowly worked her toward the other end of the table. Emma missed her shot and Caleb pushed Taryn toward the food before turning to examine the pool table.

When she reached them, Taryn took a long drink from her beer, Emma close on her heels for her own drink.

"Ugh, people are so annoying."

"Who? What?" Emma asked.

"Those Neanderthals over there." Taryn waived vaguely over her shoulder. "Bragging to each other about the chicks they've been nailing and whatnot. Reminds me why I hate people. Too many of them are idiots."

Emma laughed, picked up a nacho and shoved it in Taryn's face. "You like people, you're just cranky. Do you need food, or have these boys been failing in their duty to keep you satisfied?"

Drew choked on the beer he'd just swallowed. Richard kindly thumped his back.

"I'm just saying," Emma continued, "a happy boss makes for happy employees."

Caleb joined them, wrapping an arm around Taryn's waist. "What are you guys talking about?"

The girls burst into laughter. Drew rolled his eyes and went to take his turn. He made a ball in and Emma cheered for him. He just missed the next one and passed the table on to Taryn.

Taking back his seat and his beer, he kept his expression clear as Richard eyed him, waiting for a reaction. Drew just stretched his legs out, crossed his ankles, and watched the action. Caleb, he noticed, kept his body between Taryn and the college boys, and he wondered if that was to distract her or keep her from coming to the boys' attention. He supposed it was both.

"Anyway," Richard said. "She likes you."

Drew waited for more, but apparently that was all Richard had to say at the moment. "That's convenient, as I like her too." He took a drink.

Emma shot in the last of their balls and Drew got up to cheer her on for the eight before Richard had a chance to launch into another round. She sank it easily and leapt into his arms for a victory kiss he was more than happy to provide. When they broke free, Taryn was sitting in Richard's lap, a beer in one hand and a chicken wing in the other.

"Ricky, I think we should get drunk."

Emma looked surprised. "I don't think I've ever seen you drunk, Tare."

Caleb smiled. "She's flirty when she's drunk."

Taryn stuck her tongue out at him.

Caleb only stared at her, raised his eyebrow. She flushed and picked up her drink.

"Well, I have to be at work early tomorrow, and I don't think my boss would like it if I were nursing a hangover."

Taryn raised her mug in salute.

Drew pulled Emma in close, pleased when she leaned her weight back against him. Her hair brushed his cheek and her scent reminded him they had more plans for the evening. Not that he'd actually forgotten, but he'd managed to push it to the back of his mind so his cock didn't embarrass him. He felt like one of the college students at the next table—too many hormones, not enough brain cells.

After a few minutes of debating, Richard and Caleb took to the table, Drew pulling Emma onto his lap, Taryn taking Richard's seat. He let the conversation play out around him, interjecting here and there, while they watched Richard and Caleb play. All the while he kept his hands moving. First he rubbed Emma's knee, then lightly scratched her back. Nothing inappropriate, but constant. She began to squirm subtly in his lap, which was probably not his smartest maneuver, but he couldn't really complain. He pushed his fingers under her thigh, pressing hard into her leg. Her whole body reacted, though he wasn't touching anything that wouldn't have been bared by shorts.

When she squirmed again, he put his arm around her waist to hold her securely, letting his thumb inch up under her shirt and slide across her skin. Taryn gave a knowing grin and got up to cheer her men on, leaving them alone.

"Are you having fun?" Her question came out a bit breathy as he nuzzled her neck.

"I am."

"Do you want to play another game?"

He couldn't tell if she was hoping he'd answer with a yes or a no.

"Do you?"

Her hand gripped his thigh as he nibbled her earlobe.

"No, I think I'm good. Let's go."

He laughed. "You don't want to run out while they're in the middle of a game, do you?"

"Sure I do." But she didn't try to move from his lap.

"I like your friends," he said as he wiggled the fingers he'd trapped under her thigh.

"I-I'm glad."

"I have a question for you, though."

"Mmm, hmm?"

"At night, when you think about four hands roaming your body, two mouths licking you all over, are they ever *those* hands and mouths?" He pointed with his chin to the two men ragging on each other at the pool table.

"No." She turned to look into his eyes. "There weren't really faces before. And now, well, my memories are better than my imagination ever was."

He smiled, then urged her up off his lap. He could only tease her so far before he was just torturing himself. They went back to the game, cheering both men on until Caleb finally missed a shot and accidentally sent the eight ball into the corner pocket, giving Richard the game.

Emma doled out hugs and practically dragged him out to the parking lot. When they reached her apartment, he heard salsa music through the front door. Inside they found a woman in pajama bottoms and a tank top, her hair pulled up into a messy bun, dancing around with index cards in her hands. When she spotted them, she gave a small shriek and froze. A wry grin stretched across her face as she calmed.

"Sorry. I was trying to memorize my Spanish vocab. The music helps."

"I'm sorry we interrupted. Dana, this is Drew. Drew, one of my roommates, Dana. We'll just, uh, let you get back to it." She dragged him off to a small hallway, giving him no chance to do anything other than wave at Dana. "Feel free to keep the music loud," she tossed over her shoulder as they left the room.

The hallway had a door on each side and a bathroom at the end. She yanked open the door on the left and pulled him inside. He'd been there once before, though he hadn't met either of her roommates at the time. He found the small but neat room, the bed made up in a light green with lots of pillows, to be very, charmingly Emma. Her desk was overflowing with paperwork and an old computer, with textbooks lined up on small shelves dotting the wall, and he had no doubt she could find whatever she needed without hesitation.

He pretended great interest in the setup, ignoring Emma until she grew fed up enough to jump him from behind. Laughing, he secured her legs to his hips and spun her around until he faced the bed. She peppered his cheek with kisses as he walked the few steps, turned, and let her fall to the mattress. Then he was on her. No more teasing, he thrust his tongue to meet hers while his fingers worked on pulling her pants down. The bed springs gave off an awesome squeak and Emma froze, her fingers faltering in their duty to open his belt.

"She won't hear over the music," he assured her.

"You think?"

"You have any better options?"

She looked guilty, glanced at the floor. He dropped his head to her forehead, forced his brain to think.

"Seriously?" he asked, just in case he was wrong.

"Please?"

She sounded so hopeful and unsure, so unlike herself, he couldn't help himself. He grinned, then let her go, getting to his feet. She didn't move, just watched as he undressed himself, her gaze scanning over his whole body as if she hadn't seen it before. When she licked her lips, his cock gave a little twitch. He held out a hand, pulled her up off the bed, pointed to a clear space on the floor. She yanked off the comforter and spread it across the floor, as much of it as would fit, anyway. Then she waited.

She didn't have to wait long.

CHAPTER FIFTEEN

"Get naked," he whispered.

He could tell she wanted to tear her clothes off, but she slowed down, gave him a little bit of a show. When her bra finally fell from her hands, he moved right into her. Her full breasts pressed into him, her damp heat a tease against his thigh. He wrapped his arms around her so that his hands rested on her shoulders from behind and pressed down. Without breaking the kiss, they lowered to their knees.

He moved back a space, eliciting a moan of denial from her. He put his finger to her lips in reminder. "I want you to touch yourself. Your breasts, your nipples, your pussy."

He moved his hand to his cock, gave it a little tug.

She watched his hand, but she did what she'd been told. Both of her hands went to her breasts, plumping and messaging them, unconsciously matching the rhythm he set. He used his other hand to give his balls a tug. She freed one hand and moved it down, circling her opening, bringing the moisture up to her clit. Her other hand turned to pinching her nipples.

"Harder," he instructed in a low voice. Her answering moan was louder.

"Shhh."

She tugged her lip between her teeth and remained quiet.

Her breasts were flushed, her nipples hard and he wasn't sure how much longer he could wait to get inside her. Luckily, he didn't have to.

"Turn around, get down on all fours."

She did so, watching him from over her shoulder, watching as he stroked his cock, put on a condom. He put a hand on her butt, enjoying the contrast between their skin, the roundness of her ass, the hungry look in her eye. There was so much about his Emma to enjoy. He slid one finger, then two, easily into her. So ready for him.

He entered her, stopping when only the head had breached. She clamped down on him, hard, her body trembling under his hand as she fought the need to move, knowing he would tell her if she was allowed.

"Good girl, stay still for me. I know you can do it. Still and quiet."

At his words, her trembling lessened, her breathing deepened.

As he eased in farther, the loud music that he'd tuned out crashed to silence. They both froze.

A singsong voice called out. "Bye, Emma, I'll be back later!"

The front door slammed in a way he doubted was usual, and he choked back a laugh. Emma didn't bother.

"Well," she said breathlessly. "Better late than never, I guess!"

Without another word, he thrust in, hard and fast and complete. Taken by surprise, Emma cried out, but the cry turned into a wail as she came. He waited, but only for a few seconds. Then he moved, in and out, hard and fast, one hand holding her hip for what felt like dear life, the other moving to her front. He knew he found her clit when she cried out again and slammed back into him.

"Oh god, Drew, fuck, fuck, fuck," she muttered in time to his thrusts. He almost laughed, would have if he could've spared the breath. Instead he closed his eyes tight, holding back the groan even though they were in the clear, coming like he only seemed to with Emma.

He slid free of her, dropped down to his heels, tried to catch his breath.

She looked over her shoulder at him, her smug smile sexy as hell.

"Since you seem to be able to move, why don't you take care of this for me," he suggested with a nod to the condom.

As sinuously as possible, she turned around and slid a hand to his dick, slowly pulling the condom free. Then, in an abrupt change of mood, she darted a peck of a kiss onto his mouth, sprang to her feet and bounded out of the bedroom, leaving the door wide open. He stayed on his knees until she returned, warm washcloth in hand, and cleaned him with careful thoroughness.

She left with the washcloth and by the time she returned he'd manage to get up and put the blanket back on the bed. It groaned and squeaked as they climbed in and arranged themselves, and she laughed herself silly for a good couple of minutes.

He just held on, enjoying the beautiful sound before drifting off to sleep.

EMMA OPENED Drew's front door and turned to wave goodbye to her friend Cheryl, who had dropped her off on her way out of town. She'd taken her last final and had nearly twenty-four hours until she needed to leave for the airport. Drew had agreed to drive her into Boston and arranged his schedule to do so. He wouldn't be home for a couple of hours, which should work perfectly for her plans.

Finals had been tough, but now that they were over, she felt pretty confident in how she'd done. She was looking forward to seeing her parents, but still a little nervous about what two weeks away from Drew would do to their relationship. She hated that she wasn't confident enough in what they had to believe that there would be no issue. And she wasn't at all sure about the whole meeting his parents on her return thing. On the one hand, it seemed like a good step. But from his attitude, she didn't think it was all that simple.

Dumping her suitcase in the living room, she lugged the grocery bags into the kitchen, dropped them on the counter and turned Drew's radio on to her favorite rock station. She unpacked the bags and got to work. She'd decided to make him a romantic dinner, complete with candles and decorations. Well, she would be the decoration. To remind him of their first day together, but giving it a new spin, she'd gotten her own set of handcuffs with furry pink padding to make him smile. And to match the incredibly sexy lingerie she'd picked up. Pink wasn't usually her color, but she figured it made a statement in this case.

Hopefully that statement was something along of lines of *look what you'll be missing out on, bet you can't wait until I come back*. In the kitchen, she grabbed a beer and considered calling Taryn or Stephanie. She wasn't used to being this unsure about herself, and it was kind of pissing her off. But then again, she hadn't really been in any long-term relationships, so she couldn't be blamed for not knowing exactly what should be happening. What she knew was that Drew had said straight out he wasn't sure what they had could work, so she had reason to be scared. Which sucked.

Taking a pull on the beer, she went about getting the salmon marinating, then worked on dicing tomatoes, avocados and onions while the corn boiled for her fresh salad, in between a silly conversation with Toby by text message. When she was done, it was time to put the salmon in the oven and go take a shower. The fact that she had her favorite shampoo and conditioner here, that Drew had never given any indication that they, or the other small items she kept around the house, bothered him, gave her hope that even if he didn't realize it, they already were in a serious relationship, and doing just fine with it.

She shaved and lotioned and brushed until she felt pretty and sexy, then put on the pink scraps that were purported to be lingerie. Reenergized, she skipped down the stairs and rummaged in her bag until she found the sexy high-heeled sandals she'd borrowed from her roommate. She made a mental note to leave them at Drew's place rather than drag them to California with her, and brought the shoes to the dining room table. No need to put them on until she was ready.

The salmon smelled delicious as she took it out of the oven to rest. She spooned a heaping portion of salad onto one plate, opened a bottle of white wine and set the table with a placemat, napkin, fork, candles and one glass. She checked her watch and scurried over to the radio to change to a much more mellow station, smiling when she heard the car on the drive. Perfect timing. A quick transfer of both pieces of fish to the plate and she was all set. She turned out all of the lights except the one over the stove and one lamp in the living room, then did a quick check to make sure the car that was parking was Drew's and that he was alone.

Satisfied, she sat in the chair that she had used the first time she'd been in his house and put on the shoes. Placing her hands behind the chair back, she clicked the cuffs into place as she listened to the footsteps making their way up the steps and to the door. She'd left it locked, since she'd be in a somewhat precarious position, and she heard the knob rattle for a second, then a pause, then the key working the lock.

She took a deep breath and tried to find her center, but she was too excited, too nervous. It took tremendous control, but she managed to keep her eyes forward, head angled down slightly, rather than look to the door. There was a rattle and thump, and she knew he was putting his gun in the lock box in the closet.

His steps came closer and she had to grip the rail on the back of the chair to keep still. She held back a wince at the twinge of pain it caused, having already forgotten that she'd wrenched her wrist at work that day. If she let him know she had hurt it, she was afraid Drew would stop the scene and she was so not good with that idea. Tonight was about going full throttle and showing Drew everything he had with her, everything he would be missing while she was gone. Everything he would be missing if he decided not to take her back when she returned.

She clenched her jaw, pulling her thoughts back to the moment. Staying focused was key. At least until she could lose herself in subspace. But to do that, she would have to give up the very focus she was striving to maintain and she wasn't sure she could do that and keep her plan moving forward. Her thoughts stuttered to a halt when Drew's finger touched her chin, lifted her face to let her know she should meet his gaze.

Whatever he saw, he wasn't letting on what his thoughts were. She focused on his nose, on drawing in long, steady breaths, on the smell of dinner that was going to have her stomach growling soon if she wasn't able to dig in.

"You make a lovely surprise."

His voice sounded gruff, letting her know she'd probably achieved the reaction she was hoping for. She stopped looking at his nose and met his eyes.

"I wanted to give you a going away present."

"Thank you."

He leaned down and kissed her and she finally began to relax. When he broke the kiss, he leaned over to look behind her.

"Tell me those are the kind of cuffs you can open yourself," he said sternly.

"They are." She managed not to roll her eyes, even though he wasn't looking at her.

"Good." He sat in the chair next to her and brought the wineglass to her lips. The small taste was good, but she was looking forward to much better things. He took his own drink, then forked off a piece of the salmon. Scooping it up along with a portion of the salad, he gave himself the bite, his eyes steady on hers so that she was able to see the pleasure he took in the food she'd made.

"This is delicious."

"I'm glad you like it." He put together another forkful and fed it to her. The fish was cooked perfectly and was complemented by all of the flavors of the salad. Pleased that he was enjoying it, she relaxed. He asked her about her finals, told her about his day and worked their way through the whole meal and two glasses of the wine, until she was stuffed full. After the last bite, he kissed her.

Slow, lingering, devastatingly sexy, he told her without words how much he appreciated her efforts.

Long before she was ready, he pulled back and rose. "Did you plan anything for dessert?" he asked, picking up their dishes and carrying them to the kitchen.

She gave him a huge smile. "Only me."

"Mmm, my favorite." He cocked his head. "I just have to decide how best to prepare this evening's sweet thing."

She smiled until he told her to close her eyes. Her surprise at the direction had her taking too long to answer apparently, because he said, very quietly but in a tone that left her no doubt about his meaning, "Emma."

Annoyed with herself for missing the order, she closed her eyes. "I'm sorry, Sir."

He didn't respond and she was only able to catch small sounds that gave her no clues as to his actions. For a long stretch, there was nothing. Then, though there were no sounds, she was suddenly sure that he was standing directly in front of her. Somehow, just the knowledge of his presence, of his regard, made her less nervous but more anxious. She wanted him, as she always did. Wanted to please him, give him her body and her submission, as she always did. Wanted to experience the pleasure she knew he would give her, that he always gave.

Taking a deep breath, she reminded herself that their reality was awesome. She needed to focus on this, this moment, when she was away from him and not let her worries overwhelm her. If he didn't appreciate how great what they had was, there wasn't really anything she would be able to do to change that. In her heart, she couldn't believe he wouldn't realize that himself.

The light touch to her nose surprised her but she didn't react. He traced her lips, then pushed his way inside. She opened for him, accepted him, swirling her tongue around his finger, sucking, grateful for the point of contact that he was giving her. He pulled free, but she didn't want to let him go, following, pushing forward against the chair. Her sore wrist pulled against the cuffs uncomfortably and she forced her shoulders back to ease the tension. Drew's finger disappeared completely.

"Open your eyes, Emma."

His expression was stern. Was he annoyed she hadn't let his finger escape easily? She thought to apologize, but then wasn't sure she should speak.

"What's wrong?" he asked.

She blinked, not sure how to answer. "Nothing's wrong."

"You were in pain."

"I'm fine." She was not going to let tonight get derailed over a little sprain.

"If nothing was wrong, you wouldn't be in pain. Tell me what the problem is."

She shook her head, wanting to get past the interruption and back to what he'd started. "There's no problem, Drew, I'm fine."

The concern on his face morphed into the stern Dom look that told her she wasn't doing what she was supposed to be doing. She tried to think how she could assure him better that she was fine, but he didn't give her a chance.

"Emma. I didn't ask you if you wanted to tell me what was wrong, I told you to tell me. You still haven't done so. Do you think that is acceptable? You cuffed yourself to that chair, I was under the impression we were in an active scene, not just sharing a meal."

"Yes…I mean no…I mean, yes, we're in a scene and no, it wasn't acceptable. I'm sorry, Sir, I just…I'm fine. I strained my wrist at work, but Richard said it wasn't bad when he wrapped it up."

He didn't say anything and she thought it might be best to stay quiet. What he did do, which had her heart sinking, was go around the chair and open the cuffs.

"You went to a doctor, who wrapped your wrist, and not only did you not think it important to share that with me, you refused to tell me about it when I asked you straight out."

Oh shit. It hadn't really seemed like that as it was happening, but she supposed she could see his side of it. Again, he didn't give her a chance to respond.

"You've been in the lifestyle long enough to know that you should tell me if you have any changes in your physical condition. Am I wrong?"

"No, Sir." She just hadn't really thought about it like that.

"And you most certainly know better than to lie to me."

Her eyes went wide at that. "I didn't lie to you!" she cried out with a little too much vehemence, going by his reaction. His eyes went frosty.

"No?" he asked, his voice dangerously soft.

She pulled in a breath, tried to sound calm. "No. I am fine. I don't feel it at all right now."

"When did Richard wrap it?" he asked.

"Um, about four hours ago."

"It seems unlikely to me that he wrapped it and told you to only keep it on for a couple of hours."

Since he hadn't asked a question she figured it might be best to not respond.

"You took it off so that I wouldn't see it. You didn't tell me about it before starting a scene. And here's the kicker, Emma, and I hope you're listening closely because you seem to be having a hard time with this, you didn't tell me when I specifically asked you to."

Shit. Shit, shit, shit. She'd been so caught up in making tonight go perfectly, she'd paid no attention at all to the injury. Well, that wasn't even true. Obviously she'd thought about it enough to make the unconscious decision to keep it from Drew, or she wouldn't have taken off the bandage or tried to shrug him off when he was asking her about it. *Shit.*

She closed her eyes, the realization of what she was doing draining all the energy out of her. In addition to what he'd said, she'd been trying to control the scene. To control Drew and his reactions to her.

"I'm sorry, Drew. You're right. I screwed up. I was trying to control the scene. I promise you, though, I didn't realize I was doing it. It wasn't on purpose." She opened her eyes and gave him her, as real and honest as she could show.

He watched her for a moment, then pulled his chair back out, sat.

"Why?"

"I-I wanted tonight to be perfect. Amazing. Memorable."

His eyebrows went up. "Do you think I'll forget you in two weeks?" The pure incredulousness in his voice went a long way to making her feel better. And foolish.

"Not forget me. But maybe forget how good we can be together."

He sighed, scraped his hands over his face. "Emma, I don't think that would happen in two years, let alone two weeks."

She didn't say anything to that, just waited for him to decide what he wanted to do.

"Tell me honestly, do you think you should be punished?" he asked.

Her throat felt thick. "Yes, Sir."

"Obviously tonight is important to you. I'm not going to deny that you have the right to that. So you can decide, get the punishment over with tonight, or wait until you get back. Either way, I will be the one deciding how we proceed with your decision. Do you understand?"

"Yes, Sir."

"Good. Take a few minutes to think about it." He got up, went to the kitchen and poured a glass of water. She watched him, trying to figure out the best way to go. On the one hand, she didn't want to mar their memory of the night with a punishment. On the other hand, it would be hanging over her, over them, through any other scene they did. And throughout her trip. And on her arrival. Until it was done, she'd be in a weird limbo mode.

He sat back down, handed her the water. She took a drink, gave it back, stared at her knees.

"Do you need more time to decide?"

"No, Sir. I'd like to put the punishment behind us tonight."

"All right."

DREW SMILED, knowing Emma couldn't see as she'd dropped her head and couldn't be seeing much besides her knees, her posture dejected.

Teasing his thumb under her chin, he lifted slightly until she raised her eyes to his. "That's good. I'd say you just cut out half your punishment."

Tears filled her eyes. Because of her mistake? Or because she was being punished for it?

"Why the tears?" he asked gently.

"For disappointing you."

"No tears then. Show me you trust me to punish you fairly and be done with it."

She swallowed hard, straightened her shoulders. Offered him a tremulous smile.

"Yes, Sir."

"Good." He leaned in, kissed the corner of her mouth. She didn't move, didn't turn in for more. He pulled back. "Tell me what happened with your wrist."

She nodded. "I was at work and an elderly lady next to me started to slip. I caught her, but I jarred my wrist a bit. It was just an awkward angle. Richard said it would be tender for a few days."

"All right. Take off your clothes, then go into the living room and wait."

He picked up the chair that had arms and took it into the living room, then went upstairs and to his dresser, unbuttoned his shirt. He draped it over the top and opened the toy drawer. It had been fun shopping with someone specific in mind, and he'd assumed at some point he would need items specifically for punishment purposes. Including the ball gag he pulled out. Gags were on her club list as "maybe". He was quite sure she didn't like them. Next was the vibrator with a suction cup base and clit tickler, which could be used for pleasure, of course, but offered wonderful opportunities for punishment. It was hands-free, perfect for what he had in mind.

Butt plug next. The one he usually used, he passed over immediately. The one he'd used when Toby had visited was a maybe. But he did have a slightly larger one that she'd never experienced before. As his hand hovered between the two, he suddenly realized that he'd plugged her during their scenes with Toby, rather than giving her the double penetration he'd suggested early on. Surprise that he hadn't really thought about it, hadn't really realized it, but had unconsciously decided that no, his best friend wouldn't be fucking Emma, shook him.

Pushing the thought away, he selected the larger size and pocketed a bottle of lube. A handful of restraints and one of his ties, and he was ready. He grabbed the nipple clamps on his way out the door.

When he walked into the living room, she was standing next to the wooden chair, eyes on the floor. His anger was completely gone and he could see that while she was nervous, she was also a little excited. Her nipples had gone flat before, but were starting to bead up again. Her breathing was a little heavy and her thighs squirmed against each other before she realized he'd entered.

"Take a seat on the chair for a second, I want to see something."

She did so without hesitation. He visually marked where he needed to place the vibrator. Dropping most of the items he carried onto the couch, he turned to face her.

"Stand up."

When he moved closer, she didn't raise her head. "Emma, look at me."

He saw nervous fear mixed with uncertain excitement. Perfect. When he held up the ball gag, she grimaced, but quickly smoothed out her expression. Holding out his other hand, he offered her his tie, indicating that she should take it with her left, unhurt, hand.

"This will be your safe word. I'm not going to hurt you, but you should have it anyway. As long as you're holding it, I will continue as I see fit. Understand?"

"Yes, Sir."

She made no movement when he lifted the gag, but opened for

him easily. He buckled the strap in place and smoothed out her hair, making sure nothing was tangled up painfully.

"All good?" he asked.

She nodded.

"Good." He brushed her chin. "Don't move."

Going behind her, he pulled the chair over so that it faced the couch, then mounted the vibrator. He let the controller dangle to the side of the seat.

"Emma, come over here."

He positioned her in front of the chair and fingered her pussy. Wet, but not wet enough to take the dildo. Taking out the lube, he offered it to her and gestured to the chair. "You'll have to do it yourself."

A quick nod was her only response before she turned and squeezed a line of lube on the rubber-like shaft. He didn't think she'd put enough on when she turned to him, so he raised his eyebrows. She met his eyes steadily. Quickly, he fingered her, found her wetter than before. Holding back a smile, he nodded.

"Good. Use your good hand to brace yourself on the chair's arms, and sit."

She swallowed, and her cheek jerked, probably annoyed as well as tickled by the little bit of drool that escaped. Oh yeah, she'd hate that.

With one hand gripping the chair and the other steadying the toy, she slowly lowered herself. He listened to her breathing, judging her progress by that rather than trying to watch. He was already rock hard and needed to give himself some time to cool off, or he'd blow before he had a chance to finish what he wanted to start.

She raised up a bit, a slight slurping sound letting him know, then continued down. When she took a heavy breath through her nose, he checked. She was flush with the seat.

"Go ahead, move around a bit. Get comfortable."

After a minute she stopped adjusting her seat, nodded at him.

"Now stand up."

She blinked, but didn't hesitate. He handed her the lube again, along with the butt plug. "Can you do it yourself?"

Immediately she nodded, though she didn't look too happy about it. It could have been that she didn't want the plug, but he suspected it was that she wanted him involved, wanted him warming her up, easing the toy inside her as he'd done before. As he would do again. But not for punishment.

She put plenty of lube on the head and shaft and seemed to be unsure the best way to go about it. Amused but careful not to show it, he simply watched. Finally she squatted nearly to the floor, and reached around with her left hand to nudge the plug against her hole. It didn't go well, at first, but she took a deep breath and started to accept the toy into herself.

When the forward motion faltered, she tried again.

"No," he said. "Pull it out a bit, ease it back in. Tease yourself with it. I said I wouldn't be hurting you; you aren't allowed to, either."

She nodded her understanding, did as he'd instructed. Soon her asshole was stuffed full and she rose, turned back to face him. Her face was flushed and shiny with sweat, her eyes studying him. Looking for approval, he guessed. Keeping his face as expressionless as possible, he gestured behind her.

"Do you need more lube to sit down?" he asked.

She shook her head.

"Check."

Her eyes shuttered. He watched her face instead of her fingers. When she opened them again, nodded, he looked down. Her fingers were slick.

"All right. Sit."

She was slower now, her channel tighter. Her breathing increased and he listened carefully to ensure she was getting plenty of air. Once she was steady, he strapped her right arm to the chair, putting one cuff just below her elbow and the other halfway to her wrist. He wanted her to feel secure, controlled, and he wanted to make sure she couldn't move the wrist and accidentally cause herself pain. He strapped her other wrist and both ankles, making sure the tie was in her hand and that she had room to drop it. When he was done, he stepped back, examining her critically. Her face was still flushed, her nipples once again hard points. Which reminded him. He grabbed the nipple clamps and, without further preparation, put them on. A sharp inhale was her only response.

Her hands gripped the arms, but not too tightly and she wasn't pulling against the bonds. Her eyes were steady on his. Perfect. He grabbed the remote and took a seat on the couch. Their knees were almost touching and he could smell her arousal. So fucking perfect.

Leaning forward, he brushed through her curls and made sure the tickler part of the dildo was positioned correctly. "Tilt your hips toward me a little bit," he instructed. "There, stop. Is the plug secure?"

She nodded.

With no further warning, he thumbed the remote and turned on the vibrator. The remote was something he'd studied carefully on the web before making his purchase. With it, he could control all the parts of the vibrator separately, as well as turning on a preset program that would cycle through various settings. For now, he activated only the part that would torment her clit.

Her eyes closed against the sensations, but otherwise she remained still. Until she heard the snap of the lube lid as he opened it. Her gaze focused in on his hands, but he watched her face. Without needing to look, he poured a dollop onto his left hand, leaving the right clean to work the remote control. Her eyes widened when he stroked his cock, eased his hand over the shaft, then the head, spreading the lube. Slowly her forehead crinkled up.

Damn, the gag made it harder to read her expressions. No wonder he rarely used them. But he'd needed something she didn't particularly like without delving into anything she actively disliked. He wanted her uncomfortable, not unhappy. He figured she'd worried he might intend to replace the plug with himself, then realized he wouldn't have tied her to the chair for that. No matter, she'd figure things out soon enough.

He didn't usually masturbate in front of women. Generally he appreciated a much more hands-on approach. But there was something delectable about watching the cream trickle down Emma's thigh, her gaze riveted to his hand on his dick, her breasts heaving, setting the colorful little beads attached to the clamps into motion. Knowing that she wanted to touch, but couldn't. Her fingers clenched against the chair's arms, going white. Not because she wanted to get away, he knew. But because she wanted to touch. Wanted it to be her fingers wrapping around the base of his shaft, squeezing tightly, then loosening up to cup his balls.

"Emma, unclench your right hand."

She did so immediately, then blinked as she realized what she'd been doing. She gave him a look that he could interpret as apologetic, even through the gag.

"I wish they were your fingers."

CHAPTER SIXTEEN

Her eyes flashed. The heat he saw there, the want. Oh yeah, she'd think twice before disobeying him again.

"They're smaller, more delicate. But you always remember that and squeeze me hard when I need it. I like the contrast." He ran this thumb and forefinger from the base to the head, then circled the crown. "If you were touching me right now, my hands would be free to play with you. Fondle those breasts, tease those nipples." Needy sounds escaped from her throat.

His right hand fingered the remote next to his thigh where she couldn't see it. He pressed a button to make the dildo shaft rotate inside her. She moaned, closed her eyes, then immediately popped them open. Returned her gaze to his hand sliding languidly over his cock.

"You won't come, will you, Emma? Not without permission. My permission. Right?"

She shook her head slowly, without moving her eyes.

"If you did, I'd have to come up with a whole different punishment and that would annoy me." He added more lube, watching her carefully. When her breathing went choppy and her eyes a bit panicky, he turned off the vibrator completely. She moaned, but relaxed a tiny bit.

"If you were over here, instead of in that chair, you could put your sweet lips around me. I do love those lips. I'd much rather see them stretched over my dick than that gag. How about you? Would you rather have your face stuffed with that rubber ball or me?"

She shook her head. Nodded. Whimpered.

"Ah well. I guess you'll have to tell me some other time." He used a different button to turn the rotating beads embedded in the base of the dildo's shaft on. She jerked, huffed a breath out through her nose. Her fingers were now clenching and unclenching against the chairs arms, and he realized the rhythm matched that of his hand currently wrapped around his cock.

"And that tongue. It wasn't nice of you to tease me with your tongue earlier and then deny me the use of it now."

Her eyes were sorrowful as they met his.

"I love it when that sweet tongue tries to wrap itself all the way around me. Slides up and down…" He twisted his grip, brought his thumb over the head and teased the slit there. With his other hand, he reactivated the clit tickler. The whiny buzz almost drowned out the long whimper from Emma. He picked up the bottle of lube, leaned over and dropped a bit into her curls to slide down to where rubber met the bundle of nerves the vibe was torturing.

When a tear trickled out, he checked her over. "Are you going to come?" he asked.

She shook her head fiercely. Then waggled her head. He had to bite his tongue not to smile. He turned off the tickler, turned the rotating shaft back on and upped the speed on the beads. God, he loved this thing. When she didn't relax at all, he double-checked. "Are you all right?"

She nodded.

He lightened his grip on himself. He probably could have come just from looking at her, without touching himself at all. But that wouldn't have had quite the same impact. "I wish I could bury myself in your cunt. I wish it was my fingers stuffed up your ass. You look pretty with my toys filling you up, but you feel better wrapped around me."

Another couple of tears. He resisted the urge to lick them off her face.

"I'm going to have to come on my own now. Do you think that's fair?"

She shook her head.

His gaze roamed over her. The sweat at her hairline, the crinkles in her forehead, the slow stream of tears leaking from her eyes, her lips stretched wide over the gag. The pulse pounding in her throat, her nipples tight and dark and oh, so delicious looking. Her stomach muscles jerked and tightened, the blue vibrator working her relentlessly. Her arms and legs, muscles quivering. All of it for him.

He pumped his dick, watched her face, her eyes, used the remote to reengage the tickler. As she fought the sensations, fought the need to release, fought to obey him, he came. He pointed his cock at his own stomach so the fluid hit only him, and she fought. When she was as close to the edge as he judged she could take, he punched the remote, turned everything off.

In no hurry, he stayed slumped against the couch, semen drying against his skin. Emma's head hung down as she continued to struggle against her body's needs. Slowly, very slowly, her breathing evened out, her fingers loosened their grip and her shoulders relaxed. Damn, she was beautiful.

EMMA'S INSIDES still throbbed with the need to come, but it was manageable. Unhurried, Drew began to release her bonds. Her hands fell to her thighs and she waited patiently while he unbuckled the horrible gag. He smoothed her hair down and used his thumbs to massage the joints of her jaw. It felt wonderful.

After a minute, he gripped her elbows and helped her to stand up, free of the blasted vibrator. And to think she used to love the one she had that was similar. She clutched her hands to his sweaty chest as he reached behind her and eased the plug free. Dropping her head to his shoulder, she breathed through the riot of sensations. He didn't rush her, rubbed her back softly until she raised her head.

"Let's go get cleaned up."

Slowly, as the water sluiced over her, each of them cleaning themselves, though bumping often in the smallish shower, she came back to herself. She'd been punished before. Been "tortured" before. But nothing had ever felt like *that*. She'd never felt genuine sorrow for having failed her Dom before. It horrified her that she'd cried, though he hadn't seemed to mind. At least he'd known she wasn't in pain or trying to get him to free her. No, she'd just been so deep in the emotions, so sorry for not trusting him, for making him have to punish her. And afraid that she would fail him again by coming without his permission.

When they'd dried off, he took her hand and led her into the bedroom. She felt…subdued. Not in a negative way, but in the sense that she didn't really feel like engaging her brain. He handed her one of her ponytail holders.

"Okay, missy?"

"Yes, Sir."

He brushed a finger over her shoulder. "Still horny?"

"Yes, Sir."

He pulled on his jeans and her heart fell with the sudden realization that the punishment might not actually be over. She should just sit back and wait, but Drew usually didn't mind when she asked questions if she wasn't sure what he wanted.

"Drew, are you…is the punishment…umm, I guess, is the scene over?"

He pinched her chin between his thumb and fingers. "Yes, Emma, the punishment is over. No, Emma, we're not done playing." He leaned in, kissed her softly, then let go and stood back. "Go put your outfit back on."

DEPARTING THE PLANE, Emma was wiped. Drew had kept her up deliciously late, then woken her up with sweet caresses. And before he'd sent her off to security, he'd wrapped her in his arms and told her he would miss her. She'd almost cried, but managed not to. Thankfully. She knew a lot of it was emotion still running high from the night before. But she'd squeezed him tightly and simply said, "Me too."

Napping on airplanes wasn't in her skill set, so she read a book she'd been saving from her favorite romantic suspense author and tried not to let her thoughts run away from her. She mostly succeeded. Her father picked her up from the airport, giving her a big hug. She gave him an extra squeeze. Somehow it always surprised her how much she missed him, her mother, her home. She'd never really had a bout of homesickness, and figured that was because she had always known this would be temporary. Always known she'd be coming back, and was enjoying the time away more for the absolute certainty that home would be there waiting for her to return to.

When they drove up to the house she'd grown up in, her mother didn't wait for her to come in, but came out the door and was halfway to the car by the time Emma got out. Her mother's hug was even tighter than either her father or Drew's had been, and she suspected her mom might be letting a few tears loose while Emma couldn't see. By the time she stepped back, though, she was beaming.

"My beautiful girl, I'm glad you're home."

"I'm glad to be home, Mom. I missed you."

She settled in very quickly. It was after dinner while her parents were enjoying their coffees that her mother gave her a look. A very motherly, there's-something-going-on-here look.

"You've met a man."

Totally shocked, she just stared.

"Tell me."

"Well. I mean, yes, sort of, but, I've met men before. Why would you say that?"

"You look troubled, but you haven't told me about any problems. So it's a man."

"Huh."

She took a drink of her water. "Well, I have met someone, but I'm not really sure there's a future for us together, so I haven't mentioned him."

"He's not good enough for you."

Laughter bubbled out of her. "Thanks, Dad."

He winked at her, but continued. "Seriously, if he's known you for any length of time and doesn't know that you would be the best thing that ever happened to him, I'm not sure I like his intelligence."

"Well, he's established, back in Massachusetts. He's not a college kid, he's a cop, he owns a house. He knows that I'll be leaving this year."

"What's wrong with California?" her mother asked. "There are plenty of police stations here."

"There are other issues, but I don't want to get into it. We're exploring things and I've recently come to the realization that I do want there to be a future for us. So I'm going to work on that when I get back. I'm just not sure how it's going to go over, and I'm not used to being unsure."

Her mother nodded. "Like your father, I agree that he should already know if you're the perfect one for him. But, maybe it's not so bad for you to have to do a little work to show him that he's the one that you want. When it comes to boys, you have things too easy. Working for it will make it count for you."

Again, she gaped at her mother. "Too easy with the boys? I can't believe you would say that."

Her mother rolled her eyes. "Not that you are easy, *mija*, but the truth is, you're a beautiful woman who has confidence in herself. When you've been attracted to a boy and wanted to date, you've never had trouble making that happen."

Emma frowned. She supposed that was sort of true. Really, it was that she hadn't had many boyfriends, hadn't met many guys she wanted to go there with. She wasn't sure how accurate her mother's portrayal was, but it didn't really matter.

"Well. Maybe. I don't know, Mom, but I know that when I go back, I'm going to step things up and see what happens. If it fails, at least I'll know I've tried. And I'd really like it to work out. He's a great guy."

She managed to turn the conversation in other directions, though she knew her mom considered grilling her further. They talked about their plans for Christmas, and when she went up to bed, she went to send Drew a text, wanting to let him know that she was thinking of him. She realized she hadn't turned her phone back on after getting off the plane, and when she did, she found a message from Drew.

Hope your flight went well. Let me know you're home safe? Miss you already.

Filled with warm fuzzies, she texted him back that she was home, that she missed him and that he should stay out of trouble while she was away.

He answered almost immediately.

Hard to get into trouble without you around. More worried about what you might get up to out there without me to keep you safe. No speeding!!

She responded, *Yes, Sir!* before going to bed, a big smile on her face.

USUALLY HER TRIPS home seemed to fly by too quickly. Now she was in the very weird position of feeling as if it was going too fast, but also not fast enough. It didn't make any sense, but she supposed it didn't really have to. It was how she felt. She sent Drew a few texts throughout the day, and so did he. It was by no means the manic back and forth that she'd seen some of her college friends go through with their new boyfriends. But that didn't bother her. That just wasn't them. They talked at least every other day, depending on Drew's schedule and the time zones.

She spent time at the store and remembered how much she loved working there, seeing the families that she'd known her whole life, talking to strangers who were new in town, or just visiting. The general store was an important part of their town, a symbol of the way of life they were choosing to live. She looked around and felt a wrenching loss at the idea of leaving, though she tried to tell herself that there were other stores, other small towns, other ways of working and having the same love for her job. But she was afraid, really afraid, that she didn't believe herself.

On Christmas Eve, just as she and her parents were sitting down to dinner, the doorbell rang. Her father answered it but then called for her. When she saw the amazing bouquet the delivery woman had brought, she actually had to fight back tears. The explosion of color was in a long, slim vase. She snatched the card up and opened it while her father carried the flowers into the dining room, placing them in the center of the table.

Not as gorgeous as you, but they were the closest I could find. Merry Christmas, Drew.

She smiled and handed the card to her mother, who was about to break something, trying to read the card over Emma's shoulder. When she'd read it, she gave Emma a hug.

"This is a good start, *mija*."

"Yeah." Her smile was huge as she reached for the mashed sweet potatoes. "Yeah, it is."

The next morning she made breakfast for her parents and then they opened their gifts. They weren't extravagant, but a healthy mix of satisfying basic needs, thoughtfulness, and a touch of whimsy. When the last gift was opened and the last thank you said, she went upstairs and called Drew. He had agreed to work on Christmas day, so she knew if she managed to catch him, he wouldn't be able to talk for long.

"Good morning, baby," he said.

"Good morning, Drew. Thank you for the amazing flowers. I love them." She'd texted him, of course, but she still wanted to say it.

"I'm glad you liked them so much. Merry Christmas."

"Merry Christmas. I won't keep you long, I know you have to get going, but will you open your present from me?" She'd given him an envelope with instructions not to open it before Christmas.

She heard the tearing of paper, then his breath blowing out.

"Jesus, Emma, tell me you didn't spend this kind of money. These look like really good seats."

She smiled. "I didn't, I promise. Not like you think. And they are, lower level, courtside. I have a friend at school whose Dad has season tickets, and he sold them to me for a good price in return for giving his daughter some serious tutoring help."

"I've never been to a Celtics game, this is fantastic."

"I hope you can get the day off work, I figured February would be enough time to work the schedule."

"Baby, if I have to call in sick to go see a basketball game courtside, that's what I'll do. But yeah, February shouldn't be a problem."

"Good. I'm glad you like them."

"I love them. I will show you proper appreciation when you get home."

Home. She both loved and hated that he thought of her coming back as coming home.

She was thinking of that as she exited the plane in Boston. It did, in some ways, feel like coming home. Returning to school always had. A temporary home. She'd spent the last few days in California working in the store and seeing old friends. On Michael's birthday, she and her parents had gone to the cemetery and then to his favorite restaurant. It was sad, but they also had a good conversation, a good time together, and enjoyed telling stories about him, even though they all had heard or told them before. Still, her mom had cried at the gravesite and Emma had been pretty choked up herself. Her dad had wrapped his arms around both of them and they'd stood that way for some time.

She pulled her jacket out of her carry-on bag, shaking it hard to re-fluff some of the down that had been squished. Part of her, she supposed, would miss having real winters when she was back in California. But it wasn't a very big part of her. It didn't take long for her to get her bag and spot Caleb and Taryn, who had come to get her. Drew had told her on the phone the previous day that the department was having a very bad flu bug sweeping through, and there was no way he'd be able to get away to come get her. He'd sounded very sorry and worried about how she'd get home, but she'd assured him it wouldn't be a problem. Someone she knew was bound to be heading into the city. A fast-paced texting session with Taryn had resolved the issue quickly. Taryn had taken the question as a sign from God that it was time for her to take a day off from the coffee shop and force Caleb to take her into the city for a day of fun.

Taryn wrapped her in a big hug, then pulled her to the car, chattering the whole time, interrogating Emma on her trip and telling her about their day in town. They stopped for dinner at Mama's, where Richard joined them. She was exhausted and a little bit tipsy from only one glass of wine by the time she got to her apartment and called Drew. She got his voicemail, which most likely meant he was still working, poor guy.

She talked to him only once that day, and the phone call was quick. The next day she received a text and nothing else. Classes hadn't started yet, so she had a couple of full day shifts at Grounded and tried not to worry about him having to work so many hours.

When the phone finally rang that night with the song she'd assigned as Drew's, she tried not to snatch it up too quickly, but mostly failed.

"Hey, Emma." How those two words managed to convey such exhaustion and yet pleasure, she hadn't a clue.

"Hey, Drew. You okay?"

"Yeah. Thankfully, I'm not sick myself. Not so thankfully, half the department is or has been. I'm not even sure how many shifts I've worked this week."

"Oh, poor baby! I'm glad you're not sick, but that sounds pretty sucky."

"It's not the greatest thing ever. I've got the rest of the night and all the way until ten tomorrow morning before I have to go in. I miss you, baby, but I'm not sure when we'll be able to get together, there's still a shortage of able bodies at work."

"Would you like me to come out there and make you some dinner, tuck you into bed? I wouldn't mind."

"That's sweet, and part of me really wants to say yes, but honestly, I don't think I'd even be awake by the time you got here, so there's not much point. Get your own rest, because once I get a couple of days off in a row, I plan on doing whatever is necessary to fill up some of those hours with you. Even if that means driving out to your place and figuring out how to ravish you without your roommates catching us."

She laughed. "Okay, it's a plan. Get some rest and I'll see you soon."

After she'd hung up, she gave it some thought. He had sounded sincere when he'd said he'd like to see her. Maybe she should go ahead and drive up. If the lights were out when she got there, she'd turn around. The only thing she'd waste was a bit of time, and honestly she wasn't going to get much done lying here worrying about him anyway.

If he was awake, she'd cuddle with him until he fell asleep. Maybe do a load of laundry, pick up around the place a bit. Chances were good that he'd only had enough time to make a mess, not pick up. That kind of thing would annoy him once he got enough sleep to be thinking about anything other than sleep and work.

Decision made, she grabbed her purse and jumped in the car. The drive seemed almost short as she worked through one of her Spanish exercises. Less than an hour after hanging up, she pulled down his long driveway. It was a surprise to see another vehicle in front of the house, and she frowned at the sassy red Miata. Her plan to drag Drew to bed and ease him to sleep with some tender loving care looked to be in jeopardy. Shutting the car door with her hip, she slung her purse over her shoulder and started toward the house. Before she reached the porch, the front door opened.

Drew appeared, a big-breasted brunette in too tight jeans right behind him. He didn't react when he saw her approaching, but Emma still had the impression he wasn't pleased.

"Miranda, I really appreciate your bringing the soup by, but as I said, I'm expecting company. And I'm not sick."

The woman gave Emma a flick of a glance, not even bothering to assess her charms or lack thereof. Apparently Miranda had a healthy ego and wasn't worried about the competition. Emma almost smiled at the frustration that flashed across Drew's face.

Not sure if she was doing it to stake a claim or rescue her man, Emma pasted on a huge smile. "Oh good, I didn't really feel like cooking. Soup sounds wonderful." She moved to Drew's side and wrapped her left arm around his waist, thrusting her right hand in front of the other woman. "Hi, I'm Emma."

Miranda frowned and took Emma's hand, but her gaze never left Drew's. "You just let me know when you want to reschedule dinner, honey. I know you've been working yourself ragged. I want to do my part to keep our boys in blue happy and healthy."

"That's very kind of you, Miranda, but I'll be fine. I know your brother was starting to look a bit feverish at the end of his shift, though. You might want to go see how he's doing."

The woman waved that away. "Momma took Scottie some soup already. Don't worry, Drew," she threw over her shoulder as she made her way to her car. "I'll check up on you again later."

Drew opened his mouth but then sighed and turned Emma toward the door, not bothering to wait until Miranda's car began the journey down the driveway.

He pulled her in for a long kiss. "I should probably be mad you came, but I'm damn glad to see you."

She smiled. "I missed you. I figured if all I did was tuck you into bed, that was better than nothing." Lifting her chin in the general direction of the driveway, she asked, "Are you mad at me for that?"

Another sigh, and she wasn't pleased to be on the receiving end of it this time. "No. She broke up with a fireman a few weeks ago. She likes her men in uniform." His tone of voice said he was trying to joke, but she couldn't find it in herself to smile. *When she hears you've left the state, she's going to redouble her efforts, if she hasn't snared anyone else by then.*

"Drew, I think we owe it to ourselves to try to make this work. For real. No endgame in sight."

CHAPTER SEVENTEEN

Drew rubbed his eyes with the heels of his hands and she immediately felt bad. He was clearly exhausted. Before she had a chance to apologize, he wrapped his arms around her, nuzzled into her hair and breathed deeply. "I know, Emma. I don't want to put you off, and we will talk about it, I promise, but not tonight."

She ran her hands up his back. "You're right. I'm sorry, honey. Let's get you into bed. You need rest."

"Later," he growled, and walked her backwards toward the couch, until she hit it with the back of her legs and dropped down. He kept pushing until she was full out along its length.

That tone, that look on his face. Emma shivered.

His knee pushed between her legs, pressed lightly against her center. She fought not to press against him, let him give her what he would.

"I missed you," he repeated. "Missed your face." His finger traced her eyebrow. "Missed your conversation." He pressed his lips to hers, but didn't really kiss her. "Missed your body." His knee finally pressed in, gave her more of the contact she wanted. She held herself still, her heart beating wildly, her eyes fixed to his face. "Missed your submission."

She swallowed hard, wasn't sure if she was allowed to speak, to answer him. He didn't give her a chance. His hand had been caressing her jawbone, but he moved it down to slide underneath her shirt and cup her breast, while his mouth trailed kisses to her ear. He sucked her lobe between his lips at the same time he pinched her nipple lightly.

Her stomach muscles clenched tightly with the effort to keep the rest of her body from moving. To keep her back from arching into his hold, her thighs from bracketing his leg and forcing him closer, her head from turning to find his lips with hers.

"You are so beautiful," he murmured, sliding his tongue along the outside of her ear. "I've fallen asleep every night to thoughts of you in my bed, on my couch, on the floor." He lifted his head, met her eyes as he squeezed her breast. "On the kitchen table."

That startled a laugh from her, which turned into a gasp when he shoved her bra down and his hand met her hot flesh. His lips returned to her ear, but she could feel the curve of them as he smiled. "I love knowing that I can make most of those fantasies come true. And that I already had plenty of memories to draw from."

Her yoga pants were soaked now, the seam pressed tight into her core from the pressure of his knee. He pushed her breasts together and toyed with both nipples at the same time, still whispering into her ear.

"In my dreams I fucked you, again and again, loving every second of it." He bit not very gently on her neck, behind her ear. "But none of that, not one second, was as good as having you here, under me, for real." His knee took up a short, pulsing rhythm, his fingers pulled on her nipples, his breath washed over her neck, cool against the moisture he trailed behind his kisses. "Knowing you're here, to do with as I please. To pleasure all night long if I want to." His hand fell still, his knee pulled back. "Or to just hold in my arms."

She almost sobbed in frustration, her body needing him so badly, despite the way her heart and soul were rejoicing at his words. With him, it was all combined. The joys of the flesh inseparable from what her heart wanted, needed, no matter how much she'd tried to tell herself otherwise. If he'd wanted to just hold her, she would have been happy with that. Twenty minutes ago. Now, she needed him, needed his touch or she might just starve to death, right here, right now.

"Knowing," he said, slowly pressing his knee back into place, gripping her breast in a squeeze with just the right amount of pain, "that you're mine." He pressed hard against her clit, bit down on her neck, sucked hard. Her release rippled through her, arching her back, her heels digging into the couch, hands scrabbling against the soft material, unable to grip anything.

"Please," she moaned, her need still high.

"Please, what?"

"Please kiss me," she begged.

He drew his leg from between hers, slid it down her other side so that his thighs pressed tightly to hers, his hard length cradled in the vee. He braced both elbows beside her arms and threaded his fingers into her hair. And then he kissed her. Though the hunger inside her didn't diminish, she relaxed into the kiss, welcoming him with everything she had. His weight settled onto her, his scent filled her, and his taste. God, she'd missed his taste without quite realizing how much until she had him again. He moaned and she actually felt her eyes prickle at the unspoken acknowledgment that he wanted her as badly as she wanted him, despite the fact that he'd just told her so himself. Though the words meant everything to her, his unconscious actions thrilled her.

She ripped her lips free of his. "Drew, please."

He smiled, his heavy-lidded eyes focused on hers. "Please, what?" he asked again.

Licking her lips, she gave it some thought. "Please get naked," she demanded.

His lips quirked, but he said nothing about the fact that her begging no longer sounded like begging.

She was almost sorry for her decision when he rose, taking his warmth from her. But his hands went to the hem of his shirt and pulled it over his head in one smooth move, then immediately began to work on his jeans. Her throat went dry and she raised her hands slowly. "Please let me touch you."

He didn't answer, but he made no move to stop her as her hands came to rest on his chest, moving with him so that she didn't impede his progress of working his way out of his pants without actually getting up from the couch. His skin was warm, and she traced his tattoo, which she swore felt cooler than the rest of him. She wanted to trace it with her tongue, but she had to wait until he was finished undressing. By the time he'd managed to free himself of his jeans, she was torn with indecision. So much skin to touch, to taste.

"Please," she moaned in frustration.

"Please, what?" he asked with a knowing smile, resuming his place stretched out atop her.

"Oh god." She bit his shoulder and he gave a soft chuckle. She traced the dark lines as she'd wanted, but her attention was split as she moved her hands down to clutch his ass, squeezing tightly. "Please, please can we move to the bed?"

He rose, offered her a hand, which she needed. He pulled her into him and she tried to kiss him, but he shook his head and pushed her toward the bedroom. Which was what she wanted, she reminded herself with an internal growl. She started shedding clothes, though, so that by the time they stood next to the bed, she was as naked as he was.

She pressed one hand against his chest to push him onto the bed, but he remained unmoving. She blinked at the reminder that she was only sort of in charge of this little adventure, and that there were rules. Leaning in, she kissed his unopened lips, slid her hands around his shoulders and down his back, enjoying the different muscles she encountered along the way to his ass. God, that ass. Subverting the impatience that was trying to take hold, she turned her lips to his ear.

"Please, can you lie down on the bed and let me ride you?" This time, she really did beg. Let her want and need color every syllable she whispered.

He turned his head, offered her his lips, which she took without hesitation, patient now. When he finally broke free, she whimpered but stayed still, waited while he climbed onto the bed, bunched the pillows up under his head and held his hands out to her. She climbed up, straddled him and froze. She was skipping the part he usually took care of. He smiled when she reached into his bedside drawer and retrieved the condom.

Pulling his cock into her hands, she caressed it gently, then squeezed firmly. His hips arched up into her grip. She lowered her head but stopped when his hands gripped her hair, hard. Now she couldn't decide what she wanted. Beg for the taste of him, or go back to the original plan and ride him. She wanted both. She wanted everything.

"Please, may I taste you first?" Though she said the words out loud, she also begged with her eyes, getting into the spirit of the thing. She wanted his permission, wanted him to let her do this because she asked. His fingers relaxed and she slid her lips down over his shaft, her eyes still meeting his, full of the gratitude she now felt.

He smiled, but she saw his Adam's apple bob too. Again, she loved the sign that he was as affected by what they were doing as she was. His cock twitched between her lips, recalling her to her task. She swirled her tongue around as much as she could, then sucked in, hard. His hips lifted, but she moved with him, not taking any more than she already had. Bracing herself on her elbows, she wrapped one hand around his base and used the other to work his balls. Everything about his reactions turned her on. His tight muscles, his ragged breaths, the way his hips kept inching up, as if he had no control over them. No control because she'd stripped it from him.

She moaned and his thighs tightened around her, then released. When she found herself wanting to let him go with one hand so that she could reach down and touch herself, she forced herself to move back. With one final pull on his shaft with her mouth, she released him, rose over him.

"Please, Sir. Now?"

His hands came to her hips, helped lower her over him. She gasped when he breached her, held herself still to feel that gorgeous fullness lodged just inside her opening.

"Christ, Emma."

The words were harsh but sounded a whole lot like begging to her. Power and triumph slicked through her and she squeezed her pelvic muscles, then pushed down over him. He bucked up, filing her in two long thrusts. Oh yes, she had missed him. For the first time in her life, she had to bite back in the insane urge to tell someone she loved him. Now was so not the time and she wasn't even sure it was true, exactly. But she sure as hell loved this. Rotating her hips brought a gasp from both of them. She brought her hands to his shoulders, rested some of her weight there and began to move. Riding him as she's promised, as she'd begged for, she brought them both to the brink. When she wasn't sure she could last a moment longer, when she was pretty sure he wasn't thinking about anything other than finishing, she stopped.

"Please."

He blinked, seemed to have to force his brain to work. His gaze focused on her, and he remembered where they were, what they were about. Their bodies slick with sweat, his fingers tightened their grip on her hips and he took a breath.

"Please, what?"

"Please can I make you come?"

His lips twitched. "You were doing a damn fine job of it."

"Please can I come when you do?"

"You sure as hell better." He braced his heels, pushed back into her and came. She had absolutely no choice but to follow him over.

WHEN THE FLU had apparently swept its way clear of the police department and Drew had gotten some much-needed rest, he'd made his plans. He couldn't exactly say he was comfortable with his decision, but he couldn't come up with a better way to move forward. And it wasn't fair to keep trying to force their relationship to tread water until it was time for Emma to go home and they no longer had any options.

He made arrangements to take Emma into Boston for lunch, to a restaurant she had said she'd like to try, though he really had a destination just outside the city in mind. Of course, the traffic gods were laughing at him and they made amazingly quick time. When he bypassed the exits for the city, she looked at him, but didn't say anything.

He sighed. "I've asked my parents if we could drop by for a visit so I can introduce you."

"Shit, Drew, you don't think maybe I would have wanted to know that?"

"You would have just stressed about it the whole drive up."

She looked down at her snow boots, jeans and sweater. "Maybe, but I would be wearing something more appropriate. And I'd have something to bring them."

He laughed. "Baby, there is nothing you own that you couldn't wear to my parents' house, unless it's something you would wear to a club. You look beautiful. And there's absolutely no reason for you to ever give them anything."

She made a noise that he didn't bother responding to. And then she reached over and took his hand. There was no doubt in his mind that she was trying to give him support, rather than requesting it for herself. His Emma. He squeezed her hand, honestly not sure if he hoped that nothing would change after today, or if it would be the end that he had seen coming since he'd first walked into her hotel room in Boston. The end that had to come, because he couldn't see any other options.

He pulled up in front of a drive that could use some serious shoveling. The house could use a new coat of paint, but luckily the snow covered a lot of sins. He went around to Emma's side, but she was already stepping out. She held her hand out and he took it, hoping it wasn't sweaty. Charming.

When he rang the doorbell, she gave him a funny look. He suspected that at her parents' house, she would have just walked in, calling out a greeting. They waited long enough that he was debating a second push to the bell when he heard his mother's steps approaching.

The door opened to a woman who looked fifteen years older than her age, her expression not inviting or warm. It was mostly neutral, with a touch of annoyance. His mother didn't like her routine being disrupted, and her routine did not include visits from her children.

"Mom," he said, "this is Emma. Emma, my mother, Noreen."

Emma offered her hand. "It's nice to meet you, Mrs. Robinson."

"Noreen's fine," his mother said, then turned and walked into the house.

He didn't bother to check Emma's face to see her reaction. There would be plenty more in the next little while. His mother led them to the living room where his father sat in his lounge chair, beer in hand, gaze glued to the television. The gaze didn't move until Drew led Emma right up to the chair. "Dad, this is Emma. Emma, my father Ray."

"Meetcha," his father muttered, glancing up before swiftly returning his attention to the news.

Never a slow one, his Emma didn't bother to respond, just trailed along as he led her to the kitchen, where his mother had turned on the tea kettle. He held a seat out for Emma and took one for himself while his mother bustled around, putting cookies from a package onto a plate, pulling out mugs, milk and sugar and plopping them down onto the table, her whole demeanor screaming "put-upon".

Emma cleared her throat and gamely attempted conversation. "Is this the house you grew up in, Drew?"

"Yes, since before I was in school, anyway."

"It's a miracle we didn't lose the house, no thanks to our boys," his mother interjected.

"Ah," Emma said. "Did they nearly burn it down or something?"

His mother didn't sit, but stood next to the stove, arms crossed. "Didn't burn it down, did nothing to keep it over our heads when their father's job was ripped away from him."

"Ah," Emma repeated. "I'm afraid I still don't understand."

Drew smiled. "My father was laid off from his factory when he was sixty. He didn't find another job—"

"Nobody would hire a man that close to retirement."

"—mostly because he didn't look for another job. My brother had joined the Army and I was a senior in high school. Neither of us felt the need to supplement my father's early retirement with our own wages."

"Ungrateful of the roof we put over your heads your whole lives. Thinking it was easy, what we did. What we gave you."

Drew didn't bother to respond, just took a cookie and offered it to Emma. For her part, Emma remained quiet, an irritated look on her face that he couldn't interpret well enough to decide if it was with him or for him, though he strongly suspected the latter. She made no move to slow him down when he barely waited for their undrunk tea to cool before taking her hand and standing.

"Well, this was nice, Ma, we'll have to do it again sometime."

His mother didn't respond to his sarcasm. He walked back to the door by way of the living room, his short farewell to his father garnering a grunted goodbye. Without asking whether Emma still wanted to go or not, he drove them to the restaurant he'd promised to take her to for lunch. Neither said much on the drive, or as they were ushered to their seats.

"Well," Emma said at last. "That was hard to understand."

He shrugged. "That was reality."

She nodded and stuck her head in the menu.

Deciding not to push things if she didn't want to, he put his attention the menu as well, though he didn't think he could eat a single bite. Fuck, he was nervous, couldn't remember ever being nervous like this before. Maybe when he had his job interview for the department?

He'd fully intended to shock Emma with, as he'd said, the reality of his parents. He'd been somewhat prepared for her to admit to the defeat of their relationship, though he realized now that had been stupid. Emma wasn't that fickle or easily defeated, and he'd known that. He supposed it had been equal parts hope and fear, and all parts irrational. So be it. He'd move on from here. But, since she *was* still his, and she was distressed, he needed to make it better. Not the least because he'd been the one to bring about the situation.

Because he'd chosen the seat next to her, across the corner, rather than across the table, he was perfectly situated to rest his hand along the back of her neck, made enticingly convenient to him since she was tipped down, reading the menu. She stilled for a heartbeat, then resumed her reading without verbal comment. But her muscles relaxed under his motionless fingers. When she drew in a deep breath, he stroked his thumb idly along the strong column of her neck.

She relaxed even further, darting him a small smile before returning her attention to the menu. When she set it aside, she raised her head and moved back against the chair seat carefully, obviously not wanting to disturb his hand.

"What have you decided on?" he asked.

"Do you like artichokes? I would love to share the starter."

"Sure, I can do that."

"I've heard that the sauce on the pork tenderloin is amazing, so I'll try that. What are you getting?"

"Steak."

She laughed, leaned in and kissed his cheek.

And…it was all right. They were all right. Which made talking about it a lot less of a chore than he'd been expecting. But meant that everything he'd figured he'd need to say was out the window. He really had no idea what he needed to say. What she needed to hear.

"I have to tell you, baby, I have no idea what to do next."

"That's okay, honey. I'll walk you through it. First, the waiter should be coming by at any second to ask us our order. We'll go ahead and tell him what we want—mmmph."

She broke off when the hand he had on the back of her neck brought her to him and he covered her mouth with his, hard. He only stopped when he sensed a presence nearing the table, and he did so reluctantly. The dazed look on Emma's face and the lightening in his heart at her joke somehow made the previous hour just disappear. It no longer mattered to him at all.

When they'd eaten, and Emma was spooning ice cream to him even though he'd said he didn't want dessert, she paused, looked at him for a minute.

"It's hard for me to wrap my mind around what I just saw. Parents treating their child like that. Was that how it was when you were a kid?"

He resisted the instinct to evade the question or maneuver her into a different conversation. Thought back to his childhood. "It was different before my dad was laid off. We weren't exactly an ideal family, far from it. I guess they were always sort of indifferent to me and my brother."

"Not active in the PTA, I take it?"

He managed a choked laugh. "No, and they didn't sign us up for soccer or little league, either. When he was working there just wasn't a lot of interaction. We'd eat dinner together most nights, then everyone would go do their own thing. But once he was home all day, every day, with my mom, it just went to shit. I guess they finally realized they didn't much like each other. It started with small arguments and being snippy, until it was just like two roommates forced to live together, no love, no respect, but no intention of changing the situation."

"But how did they treat you guys?"

"There wasn't hitting, or even verbal abuse. Nothing like that. We mostly stayed out of their way."

She frowned, shook her head. "I think I get it now. You don't see a future for us because you just really can't imagine it, not in any way that is good. I don't see an end for us, because I just can't imagine it, I see so much good in what we have. If we both understand that, and we proceed on the assumption that for the foreseeable future, all is good, then let's just leave it at that for now."

He blinked at her, was pretty sure he'd followed along with her logic. "But you're leaving in less than six months."

"It's true that six months is foreseeable, but it's also a fair ways away. If you're willing to move forward for the now, I am too. Think of how much things have changed in the last six months. I don't think it's a good idea to make decisions right now about how we'll be feeling then."

It all seemed to make sense to him, but then so had their first relationship discussion, and look how that had turned out. Although, as she'd pointed out, it had changed, but not because either of them had done something wrong or bad. It had just changed because things, feelings, *they* had changed. So he took her hand, kissed her fingers and whispered okay into her ear. The soft look on her face was one he always liked to see.

"I was thinking I'd send my brother an email, tell him next time he's on leave he should be sure to come by for a visit."

Her whole face lit up.

"That doesn't mean he'll be interested," he cautioned.

She just rolled her eyes at him and took another bite of her ice cream.

He got her home and barely made it into the living room before his need for her overwhelmed him. He had her against the wall by the front door and then on the couch before hauling her upstairs and licking and sucking her until she came with an exhausted wail. As she slept in his arms, he couldn't help but wonder what the hell he'd gotten himself into. He tried to convince himself that the feeling of unease was natural for someone who hadn't been in this situation before. Perfectly natural. No problems. And there was no denying that it was less uncomfortable than the nerves he'd been feeling when he wasn't sure she'd want to move forward.

It was a long time before he joined her in sleep.

CHAPTER EIGHTEEN

Emma spent the next few weeks in a daze of happiness. She focused all of her attention and energies on enjoying the now. Any time her mind turned to the future, to graduation, she refused to allow it. In some respects, things hadn't really changed much between her and Drew. They spent the same type of time together, though he did go out with her and her roommates once. The girls had been a little intimidated at first, but he'd made an effort to charm them, which hadn't taken long to accomplish. He'd come by the coffee shop a couple of times as well, but it still made much more sense for them to get together at his house, rather than her apartment.

He was, however, more demonstrative, holding her hand or wrapping his arm around her shoulders. They still spent the majority of their time at his house, but he no longer seemed reticent about taking her out in Jackson.

The only slightly sour note was that he hadn't introduced her to any of his friends, other than Toby. As far as she could tell, however, he wasn't much in the habit of hanging out with guys from the department. He seemed to not care about hooking up with any of his friends from his club in Boston. When he finally made mention of going to a poker game on a night she'd told him she had to work on a group project, she asked him why he hadn't been going regularly. His answer that he would rather spend the time with her was sweet, but she couldn't shake the feeling that he was still shy about introducing her to his friends.

Since she was on closing shift with Taryn and the other workers had gone home, she gathered up her courage and brought it up.

Taryn rolled her eyes at Emma. "Oh please, I don't think that's a you thing, I think that's a guy thing. They just don't make the effort to get together, or think to make plans. And once they're married, they bitch about the plans you make for them, even though they enjoy doing whatever it is that you make them do."

"Huh."

"Seriously. I'm impressed he even has a poker night, though obviously he's cool with abandoning his guys in favor of nookie with you."

Emma laughed and felt relief. It was weird to her not to have that social connection, but it sort of made sense the way Taryn explained it. Now that she thought about it, she couldn't quite imagine Drew calling a buddy up to plan a bar excursion like she did with her girlfriends.

Letting her worry drop away, she focused on getting the shop closed out so she could go home to her man.

A week later, she realized she hadn't quite let it go all the way when she asked Drew about his birthday while they were getting into bed.

"Honey, do you want me to plan something for your birthday? You're working, right, but maybe we could do something the next night?"

"Sure, baby. Does it involve you wearing a special outfit?"

She laughed. "If you want that, I'm sure I can come up with something, but I meant outside the house, non-sex related."

"If you want to go out to dinner, we can do that."

Propping up on her elbow, she frowned at him.

"You don't want to do anything with your friends? Your poker buddies? Anyone?"

"If you want to go out to dinner, we can do that," he repeated.

It hit her then, as she watched him, her heart squeezing so tight she had to draw in a careful breath.

Slowly, carefully, she tried to make sense of her epiphany.

"You weren't lying when you told me it wasn't about me, about getting close to me, specifically. It *is* you. You won't let anyone in. You've let me in farther than you meant to, but even that's a minor miracle. You let Toby and his wife in a long time ago, so you're stuck with him, and the fact that you lost her just reinforces your decision not to form relationships. You don't want more. You're done."

He remained perfectly still as she spoke, still and quiet.

"You refuse to live with love because of the fear of loss. I don't know how much of that I'm going to be able to watch, Drew. I've had loss. I miss Michael every day. But that just makes it more important to love and be loved. I wish I could make you see that, because I love you."

His arms tightened around her, but it was a long while before he spoke.

"You're asking me to change who I am. I don't need a ton of friends. I'm just more choosy than you. I'm not closed-off."

She didn't answer and eventually they drifted off to sleep. She had no idea what he was thinking, but she was wondering how long she'd be able to sit around and watch him close himself off. And if there was any reason to keep fighting for their relationship when school would be over in two months and he was giving her no reason to think that she should stay.

DRIVING home from Drew's late at night because she had an early study date the next morning, she had a hard time stilling her mind. Drew had offered to come to her instead, but she'd said no. It had been a few weeks since their talk, if you could even call it a talk. When she was with him, she found it easy to be with him, in the now, loving their time together. Loving him. She hadn't told him again, but they both knew it.

When she was away from him, she threw herself wholeheartedly into her studies, because she didn't want to think about the reality that was bearing down on her. But on a quiet drive, her body happily sated but her mind a whirlwind, she had little choice. He was afraid to have a future with her. With anyone. Afraid of the loss, or that the relationship would become the travesty that was his parents'. She was certain that part of him knew that was his parents and didn't have to have anything to do with how he chose to live his life. But deep down, he was scarred. And scared. And she had no idea if he would be able to get past that enough to fight for them.

Her parents had booked their flights for her graduation ceremony. Taryn and Richard had said they would come. She hadn't even mentioned it to Drew. Didn't know what to say, what she could ask for. What she should ask for. Whenever she talked to her parents, she thought about asking how they felt about the idea of her not coming back to work the store. To eventually take over so that they could retire. But she never quite got the question out, partially because she was afraid of their answer, but mostly because she didn't think there was a future here worth changing her whole life plan for. Not if Drew didn't agree.

Graduation was supposed to be an exciting new beginning, the start of the rest of her life. And the idea of it made her nauseous. Something had to give and soon, and she was afraid she knew exactly what that something was. Pulling into the parking lot of her apartment building, she rested her forehead on the steering wheel. She needed to get inside, get some sleep. She picked up her phone, stared at it for a minute, then typed in *I love you* as a text to Drew. Then she deleted it, grabbed her purse and went into her apartment.

She wrote a long email to Toby, vomiting out her fears and worries, her opinion on Drew's emotional state and her concerns about his future. Then she deleted the message and sent him a joke instead.

DREW WAS at the end of what had felt like a very long shift when he checked his phone. He saw two missed calls from Emma and a voicemail. A stab of uneasiness hit him when he saw there were no texts from her. Since she'd told him she loved him, and he hadn't responded, he'd been anticipating…something. He didn't know what, exactly, but he knew that while she was happy they were together, she wasn't totally happy and it was his fault. He just didn't know what he could do about it.

Other than change who he was, which could only end up backfiring on both of them.

He called up the voicemail as he reached his car.

"Hi, Drew. I'm about to head out to the airport. They think maybe Dad's had a heart attack. I—my roommate is taking me. I don't know how long I'll be gone. I'll send you a message when I get there, but I don't think I'll be calling. Hospitals, and all that." Her voice was full of choked-back sobs and Drew's hand was clenching the phone so hard he had to force himself to pull back for fear of breaking it before he could hear the rest of her message.

"And I just—I don't know—I think maybe it would be best if we just end this now. Like I said, I don't know how long I'll be gone, then finals are in six weeks and I need to focus on that. I—you—well, anyway, I'm sure you've been waiting for the right time to tell me the same thing, so we might as well do this now. Thanks for everything, Drew. I have to go."

The last part was rushed, as if she could no longer expect to hold back the tears and felt she had to hang up before letting them free. He stood at his car door, so many emotions washing through him that he couldn't even name them all. Fear for what she was going through with her father. She was close to her parents, he didn't want her to suffer that loss. Despair that she hadn't thought she could ask him to go with her, to help her through this. Hadn't even asked him for a ride to the airport. He checked the message time. She'd left it fifteen minutes ago, known he was going off shift. But she hadn't asked. No, she'd actually broken up with him.

He tried her cell phone but she didn't answer. And what, exactly, was he going to say to her? She needed to focus on her father right now, not on him. Not on the pain that was making hard knots in his stomach. He got in the car and headed for home. Jesus, she was hurting, scared, and she'd broken up with him rather than reach out to him. And it was all his fault. There was no question of that. She'd told him she loved him and he hadn't even responded. She'd told him he needed to let love in and he'd said she shouldn't try to change him.

He was an idiot. A complete, fucking idiot. He hadn't told her he'd spent an hour at the jewelry store, trying to find her exactly the right graduation gift. Hadn't told her that on the nights she wasn't at his house, he found himself spending hours online looking at police openings in cities near her parents. Hell, he hadn't even admitted to himself what those things meant, pretended that he was just idly surfing the internet.

Complete.

Fucking.

Idiot.

Driving a little bit faster than he should, he made good time to his house and raced inside.

THERE HAD NEVER BEEN A LONGER flight home than the one Emma had just gotten off. She had managed not to spend the entire time in tears, but she was sure her seatmates were wary and they left her alone. Not having checked a bag, she was rolling her carry-on out the doors only minutes after they deplaned.

She spotted her mother at once, and was surprised, having expected another relative or friend.

"Mom!" she called, launching herself into her mother's arms. "What are you doing here? Why aren't you at the hospital? Is Dad—"

"He's fine, sweetheart. He's going to be fine. It wasn't a heart attack, it was pancreatitis."

That still sounded bad to her, but her mother had said he'd be fine. She burst into tears. The relief was just too immense to hold inside. Her mother wrapped her in her arms and gave her soft, soothing words until she got herself under control. Finally she realized that the longer they were there, the more time her father was in the hospital without them.

Pulling back, she started walking to the parking garage, holding her mom's hand. "Okay, I'm better now. Who's there with Dad?"

Tina laughed. "He's sent almost everyone home and he knew you would feel better if I picked you up, so he made me come and let your cousin Tony and his wife stay. Everyone else got kicked out. It will be fine, sweetheart, they're already treating it and expect he'll be going home tomorrow."

They reached the car and Emma had to stand at the door for a whole second letting that sink in before she could get in. When she did, her mom was watching her. "I was so scared."

"I know, *mija*. Me too."

They both took deep breaths, and then her mother drove them straight to the hospital. Within half an hour of landing, she was at her father's bedside, working hard not to lose it again, trying to channel her relief a different way. Her father made it easier by making her laugh. Even though they were there for him, he knew that she needed his help and didn't hesitate to give it to her.

By the time her father kicked them out of his room as well, it was late. They'd eaten at the hospital, but it wasn't exactly a lasting meal, so they set about making a snack. When her mother pulled down two wineglasses, Emma raised her eyebrows at her.

"Indulge me. I'm not going to be ready to go to sleep any time soon."

Nodding, Emma put the food on the table and opened the wine bottle that her mom handed her.

"Let's not talk about your father for a while," Tina said. "Tell me how things are with your man."

Emma could only imagine the look that came across her face since her mother's immediate reaction was to apologize.

"I'm sorry, sweetie, I didn't know that was the wrong thing to say."

With a sigh, Emma took a large drink from her wine.

"No, it's all right. The truth is, I broke up with him after I talked to you. Um, over voicemail. I haven't checked my phone since I turned it off on the plane to see if he's responded at all."

"Voicemail? Really?"

"I know, not very cool. I guess I was in shock after you called about Dad and while I was waiting for Dana to get home and take me to the airport, I realized that there was no reason to keep delaying the inevitable. We knew it wasn't going to last, but we were determined to enjoy it until the end. Well, finals are about to start, I didn't know how long I was going to be out here, it just seemed as if it was close enough to the end I might as well get it done. Then I could have one less thing to worry about while I was here and once I get home and focus on finishing up at school."

"I see. And why was it inevitable that you would break up?"

"For one thing, he lives there, I'll be living here."

"People do move, you know."

"He's never said he'd be willing to consider coming out here."

"And you're not willing to stay there?"

"The store is here. You guys are here."

"Isn't that pretty unfair, to want him to give up those things, but not be willing to do it yourself?"

Emma poured more wine. She was clearly going to need it. "It is. Which is why I wouldn't ask him to do it. But, you know, our store is our store. He could work at any police station. He's not very close with his coworkers. He's not at all close with his family. And that's actually the bigger problem. He has issues—"

Her mom's laughter interrupted her and she had to join in.

"I know, I know. We all have issues."

"I'm glad you know. But before you tell me about his, I'd like to point out that as much as we'd love you to take over the store, to stay here where we can see you all the time, it's a reality of life that people move on, move away. Families don't always stay in the same place. You never know, I may convince your father to retire to Florida."

Emma laughed at the idea. "Well, I guess I'm glad to hear you say that, though it's hard to imagine living with all that winter permanently. I do love our weather. And I love our store, but if I worked at it, I'm sure I could find or build something that I would love just as much out there."

"But there are issues."

She sighed, dipped an eggroll in sauce and bit in. God, she could never make them quite as good as her mother's. One of the things she looked forward to doing when she moved back was cooking more with both her parents. That hadn't been something she'd been very interested in when she'd lived at home, but now, after spending time with her extended families, and after living on her own, she really looked forward to it.

"I met his parents. And they were awful. They don't care a thing for Drew or his brother. It was just...bad. He grew up with that, and apparently it got worse and worse as he got older. I'm not sure he even realizes how much that affected him."

"That's hard to even understand."

"I know. Even after witnessing it, I have a hard time wrapping my brain around it. Then in college, he gets very close to his friend Toby, probably the first time he's had that close of a relationship with someone, which then extends to Toby's wife, Caroline."

"This doesn't sound as if it's going to end well," her mother commented.

Emma sighed. "Not so much. She was killed in a car crash. Toby was devastated and Drew spent a lot of time helping him get through that. But I think it reinforced his need to keep his distance from people. Not to form permanent relationships."

"So he doesn't do girlfriends?" Her mom's eyes narrowed at her.

"He doesn't, but he's not a player, either. He was very up-front with me about what we could have from the beginning. And since I knew I was leaving, I was okay with that."

She couldn't hold back the blush at her mother's knowing look, and tried desperately to keep her brain from remembering every kinky thing she'd ever done, knowing it would somehow show on her face.

Her mother laughed. "You've always been a good girl, Emma. Made your father and me very proud. I'm not going to give you a lecture on safety and responsibility because you *are* responsible, and we trust you. I'm glad to know you were able to let loose a bit in college."

Too many thoughts ran through her head so fast she thought it might spin. She focused on the conversation they'd been having, though she tucked that little speech away to take out later and think on.

"I told him I love him."

Now her mother showed surprise, poured more wine for herself.

"I know," Emma said. "I never thought it would be possible for me to fall in love with someone I hadn't even introduced you guys to. This whole thing has been…surreal, I guess you could say. Not what I imagined for the first time I said those words to someone."

"And can you imagine saying them to someone else?"

She swallowed, hard. "No. Tell me that will change. Tell me I'll get past this, and find something better, something more right for me, and be happy again."

Her mom covered her hand. "You will find happiness. That I can guarantee."

The implication that she might still find it with Drew had tears pricking behind her eyes.

"He can't—he won't let me in all the way. I think, after Caroline, he was so focused on helping Toby, he never really grieved her loss for himself. Just shut even more of himself off than already was, and decided it wasn't worth the risk to open himself up to that kind of pain."

The hand holding hers tightened in commiseration.

"We've known loss. We got past it, but it wasn't easy."

"I don't know how to help him. I don't think he realizes he needs help."

Her mother pulled back, took a drink, leveled her gaze on

Emma. "I almost slipped away. When we lost your brother. I look back now, and it scares me how close I was to slipping over the edge, giving into the grief. I didn't, but it was close. I missed him so much. Not just the him of right then, but who he was supposed to be. My little boy, becoming a man. The pain was so huge, I can't even…" She shook her head. "It's still there, of course. I think about him every day, my little Michael."

She fingered her glass, studied its contents.

"But we couldn't give into it, your father and I. We didn't talk about it, we didn't talk about much during that period. But luckily, we both came to it about the same time." She cleared her throat, but still, when she spoke, her voice was thick, bringing tears to Emma's eyes.

"He took you fishing. You were young, but not so young you didn't understand what was happening. Not so young you didn't hurt so big on your own, plus the pain and confusion of seeing your parents so devastated. We both saw it. So he took you fishing. And I forced myself to be alive, to be there, with you and him, every day, instead of in my head, in my grief. And we learned that we could live. Live with the pain, the loss, yes. But not in it."

Emma let the tears escape, "You're good parents." She sighed. "But he didn't have that kind of loss. Yes, he loved Toby's wife. But she wasn't his. Could it have been that huge for him? Like it was for you?"

Mom drank more wine, was quiet for a minute before she spoke. "You know how you hate to get a shot? At the doctor?"

Emma wrinkled her nose.

"Yes, you hate it. But you haven't had one for years. And if you did, you'd get over it in a minute. The shot is unpleasant, yes, but it's not that bad. But it becomes this huge thing as you build it up, the longer you wait. It's not the shot that's so terrible, it's the anticipation."

Emma made a face making it clear she wasn't sure she agreed, but neither was she going to argue.

"It's like that, I think. For him, maybe it's like that. What if you had a shot, at a young age. It wasn't so bad, but you hated it, detested it, so of course, the thought of another became this terrible anticipation and dread. But then, someone tells you, shows you, that no matter how bad you thought that first shot was, there was another one in store for you and it would be ten times worse. Maybe fifty times."

Emma let that sink in without comment for a few minutes. The she said quietly, "I gave up on him. Didn't fight for him."

"You told him you love him. You told me you love him."

"In some ways, I've shown him. But I need to do better. I need to not only show him that I love him, but that he loves me too, and that it's a good thing, for both of us."

"Yes, for both of you. You need to make sure he understands, really believes, that having him in your life is a good thing for you. Not just the other way around."

"He doesn't think he's good enough for me," she said, understanding dawning.

"He doesn't think he can give you what he's never had."

She nodded, and poured the last of the wine into their two glasses.

Her mother began to speak, but was interrupted by a quiet knock on the door. Checking her watch as she rose, Emma saw that it was just after eleven. Way too late for anyone to be at the door. In the old days, that wouldn't have made her hesitate to open the door, but since knowing Drew, she was more cautious of safety. She left the light in in the living room off, easily making her way through to the door. The porch light was always on, set to a sensor that turned it on at dusk and off at dawn, so when she looked through the peephole, she knew she'd be able to see. But she never would have expected to see Drew. Her shock was so complete that she just stood there staring for a whole minute, until Drew raised his hand and knocked again, this time a little louder.

She threw the door open and jumped into his arms without hesitation. He staggered back but caught her, his arms tight around her, his voice in her ear. "Oh baby, is it your dad?"

It felt like so much had happened since she'd left the voicemail for Drew, she forgot that he wasn't up-to-date. Without letting him go, she shook her head. "No. No, he's going to be fine. I was so scared, but by the time I landed, they knew he would be fine. It wasn't a heart attack, he's getting treatment and they should be releasing him tomorrow."

He squeezed her even more tightly. "I'm so glad to hear that, Emma. I'm sorry I wasn't there for you when you were scared."

She pulled back, just a little, so she could see his face. "That's my fault, not yours. I didn't ask you. I'm so sorry, Drew. I can't even believe I left that voicemail. I'd like to say I was out of my head, but the truth is I let my fears and doubts get the better of me, and I gave up on you, on us, when I shouldn't have."

"No, baby," he interrupted, causing her heart to seize. "It wasn't your fault. It was mine. You didn't ask me, because you didn't trust me to be there. And you didn't trust me to be there because I haven't given you reason to. All my fault."

The sound of her mother clearing her throat behind her finally had her pulling free of Drew's arms and stepping back. She blushed.

"Um. Mom, this is Drew. Drew, my mother Tina."

"Mrs. Lee, I'm sorry to intrude on your doorstep so late, but I'm glad to hear your husband is going to be all right."

"Thank you, Drew. Come inside. I hope you brought a bag? It's late, why don't you kids get settled into Emma's room and we'll talk in the morning."

Emma stood there speechless while Drew started to say that wasn't necessary, but her mother shooed him to his rental car to get his bag, ushered them inside and upstairs and assured Drew that Emma could point him to the clean towels in the morning. Her mother went into her bedroom and was closing the door when she stuck her head out.

"Don't worry, I'm getting old, my hearing isn't so good anymore."

"Mom!" Emma half gasped, half shouted, but the door was already closed.

She looked at Drew and he was blinking at her in either astonishment or confusion. Since she was experiencing both, she couldn't blame him. She just ushered him into her childhood bedroom, which, thankfully, was at the other end of the hall from her parents. He put his bag down next to the bed and stared at her. The confusion slowly drifted off his face, replaced by uncertainty.

"Emma, I don't have to stay. I don't expect you to trust me right away, after what I've put you through."

Her heart swelled and she launched herself at him.

CHAPTER NINETEEN

Drew caught Emma, again. And knew that nothing would ever feel as amazing as knowing that she loved him, despite the way he'd acted. He gently pushed her back, just enough that he could cup her face in his hands. What he saw there nearly knocked his legs out from under him. She loved him. And she wasn't afraid to show it. It was all there, written across her face. He worried that some of it was due to the emotional upheaval of her father's illness. That was okay. He'd be working hard, from now on, to show her that her love for him was deserved.

Taking a slow breath, he pulled back a little farther. Gave her the look. Her body stilled in that indefinable way and her attention on him intensified as she waited to see what he would do. What he would ask of her. He lifted a finger to her lips to indicate she should be silent. She kissed his finger and dropped her hands to her sides.

He picked them up, rubbing his thumb along her hand, speaking softly, knowing she would work to hear his words. "I love your hands. Your fingers. Not just when they're on me, which is always wonderful." He kicked his bag out of their way and moved them closer to the bed as he continued to speak. "But even when you're not naked, your hands are beautiful. Handing me a coffee cup, full of whatever fancy thing you've made for me, holding a menu. My favorite, though, is when you hold your hair back. Sliding your fingers in at your temple to rest your hand against the side of your face and keep your hair clear."

He reached behind her to pull back the covers on the bed, but kept his gaze on her face, her reaction. Oh yeah, that was the soft look, with an awful lot of wonder in it for someone with healthy self-esteem. A reminder that no matter how much a woman was confident in herself, she still liked to hear her man tell her she was beautiful. At least his woman did.

"That's another thing. I love your hair. So silky and shiny like one of those ridiculous shampoo commercials." He indulged himself by sliding a strand through his fingers, then stepped quickly away to turn on the bedside lamp and turn off the main light switch. From the corner of his eye he saw her mirroring his action as if she'd never felt her own hair before. She dropped her hand when he came back in front of her.

"Then there's your eyes. Amazing, your eyes. The color goes from dark gold to light brown, depending on the light, but also your mood. And your arousal. Oh yeah, I really, really like to watch your eyes get brighter and brighter, like they are right now. Your hair was the first thing I noticed about you, but your eyes, I think they were the thing that really made me want to take the risk of being with you."

She stared at him, didn't try to say anything, didn't try to move, completely in his thrall. Intoxicating. He put his fingers at the hem of her sweater, pushed it up by running his hands along her sides until the last possible moment before pulling it over her head. He tossed it aside, placed his hands on her shoulders, drew them down to cup her breasts.

"Your skin. I suppose someone could come up with the right color to describe it, but not me. I just know it makes me hungry. Ravenous." He leaned down to bite gently into her shoulder and she drew in her breath sharply but silently. "And what that skin covers," he said, giving her breasts a fairly hard squeeze. "That is something to give thanks for."

He unbuttoned her jeans, slid them down over her butt, giving the globes a long, firm squeeze as well. Urging her back to sit on the bed, he dropped to his knees and worked on her boots.

"So, thank you, Emma. For giving me you." He pulled her jeans off and looked up in time to see a tear spill from one eye, then the other. It took far less time to shuck his own clothes and slide them into bed, putting a condom on without seeming to rush. But he needed her. Needed her to know how much he needed her. "Because everything about you, everything that you are, is amazing to me."

He got on top of her, her body welcoming him, wrapping around him, accepting him. "I love all those parts of you and too many more to mention right now." He positioned himself, slid into her, knowing without having to check that she would be ready for him. His eyes were steady on hers, though hers were glassy with tears, when he was fully seated inside her. "I love you, Emma Lee. I love everything about you." Her whole body clenched around him, her fingers digging into his back, her ankles hooked around his.

"I love you, too," she gasped.

He smiled as she came around him. "I know."

She laughed and he came to the sound of that sweet music.

When they both had their breath back, he rested his forehead against hers. "I'm going to make it worth your while to keep on loving me, Emma."

She smiled up at him. "I know."

THEY STAYED in California for two more days. Her Dad was even able to take her and Drew fishing. She loved how accepting her parents were of Drew. They didn't hesitate to welcome him and begin to show him what it meant to be part of a loving family.

On the flight home, Drew told her that he'd looked at some postings for jobs in California. The fact that he was willing to do so, and that he had before her attempt at breaking up with him, had her crying into his shoulder on the flight. But only for a moment. She tried to tell him she was willing to move, too, but he insisted it was better the other way around.

By the time they got home, she was exhausted, so he took her to her apartment and they stayed the night there so she could get to class the next morning. It took a lot of work to catch up from her few days away, and then she launched into finals. The great thing about Drew's plan to look was that there was no hurry for her to get back. She could stay with him while he searched, and they could go out to California together. Taryn had said she could keep working at Grounded as long as she wanted to.

He went to her graduation and his pride was as strong, if not stronger than, that of her parents'. Taryn cried, knowing it meant Emma would be leaving soon, but her friend was so happy for her that she insisted it just meant she'd have to convince the guys to take vacations to California once in a while.

Emma agreed and said that she and Drew would have to come out for the occasional winter fix, as well. Drew said Toby was already making plans for places he wanted to visit in Northern California. Which got Emma thinking of some threesome plans of her own, which she described to Drew to very good effect one night.

A week after graduation, when her parents had left and she'd emptied her apartment out and moved into Drew's house, he told her he had a couple of solid leads on the job front. She knew he was anxious to get started in their new life, though she would miss the house where they'd fallen in love. And she still wasn't convinced it was fair that he was giving up everything and she was getting everything she wanted.

After dinner, he got the intense expression that she knew meant good things were in store for her. She got that little tingle and felt her body going still in anticipation of what he'd ask of her.

"Will you let me do something different? It might sound strange, but I want to push you, push your boundaries. Now that you really are mine."

She smiled. "You don't think what we've been doing has been pushing my boundaries?"

He cupped her face in his hands. "Not so much. And I'm not going to push hard. Just try something new. What I want to do, it's not meant to scare you. It's meant to show you how much you trust me, how much I trust you. It's not something I would ever do without being at this level of trust." He kissed her nose. "Does that make sense?"

She sighed. "I'm not really sure, to be honest. But it's obviously important to you, so, okay."

He gave her a soft kiss. "I want you to take a shower. Put your hair back, I don't want it in my way tonight. Make yourself ready for me. No clothes, though. Okay?"

"Yes, Sir."

One more kiss, and he stepped back.

She showered, brushed her teeth and braided her hair. It was easier now than it ever had been before, getting into the proper headspace for a scene. Before, she'd never played with one person long enough to reach this level of trust. She'd spend too much time during preparation wondering about the other player, or what they were going to do, to fully immerse herself.

She didn't need to do that now. She didn't need to give any thought to what was going to happen, other than a mild anxiousness about what he had in store for her. But that just made it easier, because even with the anticipation, there was the full knowledge that it would be okay, that it would be good, because it was Drew. She walked into the bedroom and found it empty so she pulled on a robe and headed into the living room.

For a change, he didn't seem to have heard her coming. From her angle she could see his face as he sat on the couch, reading something on his laptop. There was a gym bag on the floor next to him. The same one he'd brought to the hotel room in Boston. She eyed it, unsure of what it meant, then decided it didn't really matter. Instead she moved her attention to his face.

Had she ever noticed how long his nose was for his face? It had a little bump on the ridge and she wondered if it was natural, or if he'd broken it at some point. His ears were close to his head at the top, but the bottoms stuck out a bit and the lobes were detached. She remembered learning that was a genetic trait in high school biology. Her lobes were detached, too, so chances were good if they had children...

She watched his forehead crinkle as he reacted to something he was reading. Or maybe he was just wondering what was taking her so long. Still, she wasn't quite ready to give up her view, so she stayed quiet and kept watching him.

He had big cheekbones, which she would have thought should make a man look pretty, but instead gave him a commanding strength. His hair was getting a little long. He shifted in his seat. Okay, no more stalling. She took a deep breath and stepped into the room, dropping her robe onto the chair as she passed it to stand in front of him.

When he raised his head, he smiled at her. He set the computer down and rose.

"You look clean and fresh. How do you feel?"

"I feel good."

He studied her for a minute, then nodded. "Excellent. Tell me your safe words."

Her eyes widened at that, but he gave no reaction. She licked her suddenly dry lips before answering. "Red for stop. Yellow for slow down and discuss."

"Good." He pulled the throw blanket from the back of the couch and spread it out on the floor in front of the couch, folded in half so it was double thickness. He sat on the couch and indicated the blanket. "Sit there. You don't have to kneel. You can be comfortable, but I don't want you moving around a whole lot."

This was so not what she'd expected, but he'd warned her he wanted to try something new. She lowered herself to the floor and sat back against the couch, between his legs, close enough that she could feel the brush of his leg hairs against her arm. She was absurdly grateful that he'd only put on shorts, and realized he'd made sure the room would be plenty warm for her naked body.

There were movements behind her and she turned to look. He'd said she could move, but he stopped her with a gentle hand just before darkness settled over her. The blindfold was a proper one, not just a cloth folded up for the task. She strained to listen, to process as he adjusted the buckle against her hair, pulling the straps so that they were tight but not uncomfortable.

When he was finished, she straightened her head and faced forward again. Waited. The heat of his body disappeared. He was no longer sitting on the couch next to her, and she was blind. She tried to hear what he was up to, was certain he was close by, but she couldn't make out his movements.

Only her careful concentration kept her from jumping when his hands settled on her head, then drew down the sides of her face until they covered her ears. The underwater, ocean sound was strangely loud. The slide of his palms was thunderous. Then it was replaced by low thrumming as he pushed rubber earplugs into her ears. She heard herself swallow.

Sensory deprivation was something she'd marked as a maybe on her club sheet. Other than blindfolds and gags, it wasn't something she'd ever tried. She drew in a deep breath and waited.

Large thumbs brushed along her jawline, then pulled. She opened her mouth, fully expecting a gag to fill it, but the thumbs moved up, then along her cheekbones until they rested against her nostrils. She blinked behind the blindfold, confused, until the fingers pushed carefully, sealing off her nose. Breathing through her mouth, she felt his hands pull away but the pressure on her nostrils remained. Not tight enough to be a clothespin, she wasn't sure what it was, but it wasn't even uncomfortable, really, other than the fact that she had to breathe through her mouth.

He lifted her chin, used his thumbs to massage the joints of her jaw until she relaxed her gaping mouth to a comfortable position. A quick brush of his lips across her forehead reassured her and she felt her shoulders drop as she relaxed some.

Movement all around her had her holding her breath, trying to anticipate what was happening. Then everything stopped. She released her breath and took stock of what she could tell. His legs were touching her arms. He'd sat back down on the couch, right behind her so that his legs bracketed her body. She waited, but nothing else happened. Gradually, she relaxed back against the sofa, thrilled to feel his touch on either side of her. Eventually she remembered that she hadn't been ordered to stay still. Tentatively she inched her right hand out until she was touching his foot. When nothing happened, she relaxed again. Waited.

Time lost all meaning. She wasn't sure if it was minutes or an hour when one of his legs shifted slightly, a hand passed over her hair in a brief caress, and his leg resettled where it had been. Her thoughts were consumed with figuring out his movements. Had he reached out to get a drink, then replaced the glass and brushed her head in passing, in reassurance? Had he needed to scratch an itch between his shoulder blades? She chose to believe that whatever had precipitated the movement, the touch had been deliberate and thoughtful. A reassurance that he knew she was still there, that she was being good and obedient.

Her heart almost stopped when his hand, large and warm, settled on her shoulder, just for a few seconds. It traveled down her arm, then away again. More waiting. Gradually her thoughts stopped obsessing about what he was doing, what he was going to do next. Her mind drifted for a time, hardly registering the shift of his left leg so that it just barely made contact with the side of her breast. Part of her shivered in acknowledgement, but most of her was too far away to react.

The sounds in her ears seemed to change. No longer the thrum of a tunnel, it began to sound like her heartbeat. Like she was in a womb, hearing her own heartbeat. Or was it hers? Maybe it was his. Either way, she concentrated on the cadence until her mind drifted again.

She swallowed, and the feel of her lips pressing together brought her back to her physical self a little bit. It occurred to her that she could no longer feel the couch against her back, as if he'd denied her that sensation as well. She knew it was there, but the knowledge was meaningless. Only the warmth of his foot under her hand, the tickle of his legs against her arms, registered. They were her only points of contact with the world. He was her world.

There was enough of her left to realize that was the point. He'd done this to her on purpose, shown her that on purpose. A month ago she would have thought that was ridiculous. But now, she knew he would only do this because *she* was *his* world. And he wanted to make certain not only that she knew, but that he would make it good for her.

It clicked. Not that she'd really ever give her whole self over to someone's control and domination, but he knew that. Didn't want that, either. He would expect only her heart and her submission. In return, he was offering...himself. It didn't matter where they lived. As long as they were together, mentally as well as physically.

She took in a shuddering breath. They were in this together. She had to trust him. Trust him enough to talk to him, tell him what she wanted, and trust that he would do the same.

Her train of thought derailed when he took one of her earlobes between thumb and forefinger. Played with it. How the hell had her earlobe become so erotic? Sure, she loved it when he sucked on it, bit it, but this? He was just rubbing it between his fingers and she was breaking out in goose bumps. The hand she rested on his foot curled slightly, her fingernails scraping lightly over his skin. Somehow it translated into sensation all the way up her arm.

He kept his hand on her ear but she felt him rise behind her, almost cried out at the loss of his foot under her hand, his legs against her arms. He brushed a finger up her cheek, then disappeared.

She focused, not trying to hear or anticipate anything, but tried to regain that sense of release. Her body was his to do with as he pleased. What he gave her, she would take. One breath in, one breath out. She let the air cycle through her, settle her. She waited.

The touch of his finger against her lip brought her joy. She couldn't help the smile that stretched across her mouth. He traced the curve then replaced his finger with something else. Something plastic. She darted her tongue out, closed her top lip over it, and nearly shouted in triumph when she realized it was a straw.

Sucking carefully, she drank the water. When she was done, she simply opened her mouth again and the straw disappeared. The next touch was so light, she wasn't sure she was feeling anything at all, at first. The tickle in the crook of her elbow became stronger, then zigzagged its way down her arm. Her belly button was next and she tightened her abs in reaction. Was it a feather? Something soft and featherlike, at any rate. It touched her cheek, then jumped down between her breasts. Her nipples hardened in hope, but nothing else happened for a minute. Pinpricks raced suddenly across her thigh, then her stomach. Probably a pinwheel. She'd experienced one before, but it hadn't affected her like this. He got the back of her neck, next to her braid, and she couldn't stop a shiver.

There was another long pause and she took the opportunity to recenter. Now she could feel something he hadn't blocked from her. Moisture dripping from her pussy, signaling her readiness. Her need.

Something cold touched her lip. Liquid...but thick. She tested with her tongue, found it sweet. A firmer touch brought more of the sweet juice and she realized it tasted like peach. He eased a slice of the fruit between her lips and she accepted it, feasted on the delicious freshness. It was weird, eating with her nose plugged, like when she had a bad cold. Not uncomfortable exactly, but odd.

Expecting to eat another slice, instead she felt cool stickiness on the side of her neck, followed by the welcome heat of his tongue lapping it up. He repeated the action on her thigh, letting the juice get tantalizingly close to the crease of her pelvis, but not close enough. His nose brushed her stomach as he cleaned her, but her core was left untouched.

Again, he waited. No touch, no smell, no taste. Finally one thick, solid drip hit her nipple and she couldn't hold back the slight cry of thanks. More drips followed, then he painted her other breast with the peach slice, drawing it around her breast in circles before smacking her nipple with it. She wondered what it sounded like, what it looked like. Waited for him to taste it. When he used only the tip of his tongue to clean her, taking his time, she almost begged.

He abandoned her breast when it was still sticky, grabbed her shoulders and pulled her down to the floor. Whatever held her nose closed disappeared and she smelled him. Smelled sweet peaches and sweat and man. Smelled Drew. He fused his mouth with hers so that she could barely breathe, even with her nose clear. She tasted the fruit, cleaned him of the juices that were left on him as best she could.

When he pulled back she moaned, then again when he held more fruit to her lips. Wasn't he done with that? Wasn't he ready for more? She sucked the peach into her mouth and reminded herself that they were on his schedule, his timeline. They'd move forward when he was ready. She chewed slowly, carefully, as he ran his hands up her sides, pulled her arms up so that they were over her head, elbows bent wide, hands clasping.

He painted a path between her breasts with a fresh slice, dripping with juice. He circled her belly button, then stabbed her with an ice pick. That's what her brain told her, for a fraction of a second, before she realized he'd set an ice cube in the cavity of her belly button. Her chest heaved, but she fought not to dislodge the ice. A streak of heat started at her shoulder, lined its way across her collar bone and dipped into the hollow of her neck. Thicker than the juice, not really liquid, but hot. Honey? Was that sweet smell honey? It wasn't a flavor she'd ever much cared for, but as a body paint she'd give it full props.

The cold on her belly was almost forgotten as Drew again circled her breasts with his paint, delicious heat working its way slowly, *too slowly*, toward her nipples. At last, at last he was millimeters from her aching points. The heat enveloped her, much hotter than the streaks he'd painted. She lurched, the melted ice cube from below sliding down her side. Not hot, but cold. More ice cubes, held against her straining nipples, icy water dribbling down to mix with the thick warmth coating her breasts. Her gasps had a raw feel to them and she suddenly realized she had no idea if she was making sound or not.

The mix of hot and cold abruptly combusted with the heat of his tongue as he began to clean up his latest mess. He gripped her breasts, pushed them together and took both of her nipples into his mouth, sucking hard. She heard herself cry out, a dim sound from beyond the earplugs.

"God, Emma. What you do to me." The muffled words drove her higher, nearly pushed her over the edge of orgasm. He'd barely even touched her but she felt like he'd enveloped her in his warmth.

He released her breasts and she had a moment to fear he'd go away again, make her wait, but he found her lips with his, gave her the taste of honey and still that hint of peach. She was so focused on him, the taste and feel of him, she didn't know if she missed a sign, but suddenly he was there, his cock filling her up and there was no holding back. He could punish her later, she'd accept it without question, but there was no stopping the hard pounding release that tore through her. He moved against her, within her, until he broke free from her mouth and cried out. The muffled sound was music to her ears and she grinned.

Drew dropped a quick kiss on her cheek as he pulled the earplugs free. "I see that grin," he admonished. The fact that she could hear the answering grin in his voice only made her smile wider. The blindfold slid off and she blinked. And there he was. She brought her hands up to bracket his face, lifted up to kiss his lips. He slid his hand under her head to support her. Yes. There he was.

She pulled back, met his eyes. And burst into tears.

THE TEARS DIDN'T SURPRISE Drew. He scooped Emma and the blanket up and took her to the couch. She clung to him so sweetly, her sobs shaking her body. Her trust in him swelled his heart. As she had during the scene, she gave her body into his keeping, a gift he treasured. He held her close, occasionally dropping a kiss onto the top of her head, but made no attempt to quiet her down or hurry her through the process. It had been an intense scene and he would have been worried if she hadn't had an intense reaction.

Eventually, when the tears had stopped and the ragged breathing had smoothed out, he managed to reach for the glass of water without upending her, and held the straw to her lips. She lifted her head from his chest just slightly and drank her fill, then dropped heavily back into place. He slid a hand under the blanket to stroke her arm. After a long few minutes she sighed heavily and lifted her head up to meet his gaze.

He smiled at the exhausted pleasure on her face.

"You have my permission to test my boundaries occasionally," she told him, affecting the haughty tones of a queen.

"Yes, ma'am." He kissed her lips. "Thank you, ma'am."

Her joy shone brightly and he gave thanks that she was his and he was hers.

PERFECT STRANGER

PERFECT FIT BOOK 2.5

This book is dedicated to my readers. Thank you for every single one of your letters, reviews, likes, and best wishes. You make all of this craziness worth it!

PERFECT STRANGER

Dana only gave a brief glance to the poster declaring that there would be an auction that evening. She was at the BDSM club, but she wasn't even close to being ready to start playing with anyone. Not yet. Probably not for a while. Just getting herself into the club was a big enough step for now, and she'd promised herself she could work her way up into playing, take her time finding someone she'd be willing to take that step with.

She took a look around and spotted a few people she knew right away, though she'd never been there. Her former Dom had been a member before they'd connected and though she hadn't been interested in going to the club, she'd been willing to go to play parties with him and had met a lot of people in the lifestyle. Apparently she should have believed Harrison when he'd told her that the club he went to was nothing like the sleazy place she'd explored in college. Then again, he'd been happy enough to stick to playing with her at home or at play parties in private homes, so it hadn't been an issue.

Apex was attractive, though. Not too edgy or gaudy. There were comfortable looking seating areas, a bar that she'd been told didn't have alcohol but did have some snacks, water, soda and juice, and an area set up as a small store, with what looked like floggers, vibrators and various other toys. A man with a clipboard stood in front of a hallway that she suspected had the playrooms and she could hear music coming from behind a curtain, so she figured there was a public play area beyond.

A hand settled lightly on her shoulder and she only just managed not to jump. Vince met her gaze checking to see how she was holding up. He was one of the club's owners and a friend of Harrison's. She gave him a small smile. Though they'd been at the same parties a number of times, she'd never had much of a conversation with him. But when she'd gathered the courage to email him about visiting Apex, his response had been quick, courteous and welcoming.

She dipped her head politely.

"Thank you for arranging the guest pass."

"You're welcome. I'm glad you've made use of it." He gestured to the empty stage. "Perhaps you'd like a low-key start. One hundred percent of the auction proceeds go to a charity the members have voted on. The winners get two hours of the Dom's time. It might be a nice way for you to get to know someone without any pressure."

She looked at the stage, more as a way to avoid meeting Vince's eyes than because she thought anything had changed since her last look around. "I don't think so," she said softly. "Maybe next time. I'll just watch."

He carefully placed a finger under her chin, moving her gaze back to his with utter gentleness. "There's no pressure to move at a pace you're not comfortable with, Dana."

She swallowed around a lump that seemed ever present in her throat these days.

"Thank you, sir. I'm glad I'm here. It's good to see some familiar faces and your club is really very nice."

He smiled and it was beautiful enough to make her wish she was ready to think about exploring. "I'm glad you came. If you need anything, just look for one of the employees in the white shirts. They tend to stand out, and they can always get word to me."

She found a seat in a row of chairs filling up in front of the stage, figuring that watching the auction was a safer way to entertain herself for a while than heading to the public play area.

A man she didn't recognize, dressed in an elegant suit, emerged from behind the curtain. He moved to the microphone and gave it a little tap, then spoke.

"Ladies and gentlemen, we're about to start the auction. If you'd like to participate, please take a seat." Her attention shifted away from him as someone else stepped onto the stage. Though vaguely aware that the MC was still speaking and the crowd had begun murmuring over the arrival of a line of men, she didn't really hear anything past the pounding of her heart and the blood rushing in her ears. Her attention had focused completely on the man who had been at the front of the line, wearing a leather harness that screamed sub and an aura of power that shouted alpha male. He looked near her age, late thirties, with short, dark hair—but not too short. She could imagine him looking nearly as sexy as he did right now, completely covered in a suit and tie. His strong features and bright eyes called to her. Were they green? It was hard to tell from that distance.

He scanned the audience, his gaze dancing over her with no hesitation. Her throat went dry, an impossible feat as the rest of her felt sticky with heat despite the excellent air conditioning.

An idea began to form, one that she immediately dismissed as insane but still couldn't force out of her head. It took effort, but she managed to concentrate past her heartbeat, past the rumble of the crowd, to the man at the microphone and the instructions he was giving. Two hours, no sex allowed. She'd missed the name of the charity the money was going to, but it didn't matter, shouldn't matter, because there was no way she was going to participate. No way. *Bad idea.*

And yet, she still hadn't looked away from *him*. The first in the line of men very much *not* wearing suits. The man she could win tonight, claim two hours from…if she had totally lost her mind. And if she could focus well enough to figure out what she needed to do.

It had never occurred to her to consider a sub. There was no question that she was one herself; she'd never had the slightest desire to be a top. Now, a sub seemed like the perfect answer. She could do what she needed to do, without asking. She could take what she needed to take, give what she needed to give, and it would be his task to let her.

Her brain tried to convince her that she should look at the other men. Maybe find one that wasn't quite so attractive, or so…strong. She'd known of a couple alpha-male subs, mostly military men or high-powered executives. They wouldn't be looking for what she had in mind. Then again, the point here was that she would get to choose how they spent their two hours. Of course, being attracted to the man wasn't even a necessity and could actually be a distraction, so the smart thing to do would be to check out the other options. Her gaze never strayed while she considered that logic, and then ignored it.

"As you all know, these unattached Doms have agreed to be auctioned off tonight to support our charity drive." The MC's words finally managed to regain her attention.

She blinked. Doms? Flicking a glance at the rest of the lineup, she saw they were all similarly attired in basic sub fetish gear, hands cuffed together in front of them, so she felt excused in her assumption. And yet they still managed to pull off a Dominant vibe.

"What you may not know is that they lost a group bet, which is why they're up here dressed as you see, rather than as they'd prefer."

The audience laughed and offered appreciative catcalls. Dana briefly wondered what the bet must have been to have the stakes be so high. She couldn't imagine what would have a whole group of Doms agreeing to act as subs, but it must have been big. She wished they'd get on with things. Although, maybe now that she knew the men weren't really subs, she should reconsider. But they had agreed to play the part for this event, and now that she had the idea in her head, she didn't want to miss this opportunity. A stranger meant no expectations, no need to do the getting to know each other dance. Get in, get out, go home. Perfect.

A skinny guy on a couch against the wall called something out that Dana missed completely, but the man she was watching raised an eyebrow and gave him a very Domly look. The audience laughed. She shuddered. *Bad idea, this was definitely a bad idea.* Her gaze fixed on the simple leather collar he was wearing, leash attached but hanging freely down his chest, then travelled to the cuffs that held his wrists together.

Making herself look away, she scanned the area and spotted Vince. As if he felt her regard, he turned and met her eyes. There was no way to know what he saw in her, but he gave an encouraging nod and a little head tilt towards the stage.

"All right, enough of that now," the MC declared. "Let's get this thing started."

WHEN THE WOMAN now walking in front of Eric had grasped the leash hanging down his chest, turned on her heel, and begun leading him out of the room, the audience had given an audible gasp. He suspected she hadn't noticed. As she'd approached, he'd tried to get a read on her. Expecting flirtatiousness of either the shy or audacious variety, he'd instead found grim determination and a hint of sadness. All right, he could work with that. She'd just donated a nice sum of money to a worthy charity to get him alone for two hours. He supposed that earned anyone the right to be singularly focused.

They stopped at the door leading to a long hallway of playrooms. Marcos, one of the club managers, offered the list of available spaces. His nameless purchaser scanned the list and quickly pointed out her desired room before he could consider taking charge of the decision himself. Marcos shot him a look, but managed to keep any smirks to himself before turning to show them to their door.

She wore what could theoretically be called a plain black dress, but was in reality a sinful delight. It showed off her curves, stunningly long legs, and a whole lot of luscious, tan skin. What it didn't do was give a clue as to her kinky preferences. Top or bottom? Could go either way. And there were no accessories to make the proclamation. No wrist cuffs, no riding crop, not even plain jewelry.

Just the dress with the low back and high hem that made him want to get his hands busy exploring the landscape.

Marcos opened a door and she swept inside without a pause. He eyed the other man, hoping for some explanation, some clue, but received only an elegant shrug before the manager pulled the door closed behind him, leaving Eric alone with a woman who he had yet to exchange a word with. Not that that was a problem. He just wasn't used to being...unsure of what was happening. It left him unsettled and he pulled in a deep breath as unobtrusively as possible.

At the sound of the door closing, she pulled her shoulders back, dropped the leash, and finally spoke. Her murmured "stay here" wasn't exactly what he would have expected, had he gotten around to trying to anticipate what she was going to do rather than anticipating what her legs would look like wrapped around his ears. He curtailed his immediate impulse of responding with, well, anything, and managed to hold his tongue. He needed to figure out what was going on, what this woman was looking for, and, more importantly, what she needed, before he did or said something that would screw it up. It was pretty obvious that she wasn't just a sub looking to tease a Dom she'd never met before. Something was going on and her vulnerability called to his instincts, strongly. Of course, her beauty only intensified those instincts.

He considered himself a damn good Dom, which meant resisting the nearly overwhelming impulse to yank her to him, dropping them both to their knees so that he was surrounding her, letting her take comfort in his strength. No, unfortunately being strong for her right now was going to be a whole hell of a lot harder than that. It meant staying where he'd been when she'd issued her command and trying to figure out what this woman needed. Her tense shoulders, short breaths and the fact that she'd crossed the room, braced her hands against the bedpost and simply stared at the wall told him she for sure needed something. She hadn't just bid on him for a lark. The fact that she'd been allowed into the club, and more importantly, allowed to enter the bidding and walk off with him, told him she wasn't a clueless newbie. She had to have been vouched for by someone, though he was quite certain he'd never seen her before.

She turned, but didn't move back towards him. There was no mistaking the way her gaze met his for only a second before darting around the room, then settled on his chest; the way she nibbled nervously on her lip and twisted her fingers together before hiding her hands behind her back. That lasted only an instant before she jerked them back around and placed her palms defiantly on her hips, as if in challenge. Oh yeah, definitely a sub. He relaxed a bit.

He considered speaking. Taking control of the situation. But he couldn't yet predict her response, couldn't be sure he wasn't taking the wrong tack. So he waited. And was rewarded when she took a deep breath and walked towards him.

"My name is Dana." There was the tiniest hint of southern twang to her voice. It made him want to hear more.

"Eric."

"We have two hours and a 'no fucking' rule. I promise not to do anything that might push most peoples limits. But if you have any hard limits you'd like to give, to be safe, please feel free to do so. We can use yellow if I get close to anything you have issues or concerns with. And red, of course, if you need to stop." She looked past him, towards the bathroom. "If you have a problem with full nudity, I'll need to adjust my immediate plans."

So. She really was going to go through with it. He couldn't help but shake his head in denial, even though he'd suspected this was coming. She wrinkled her forehead and leaned back ever so slightly. He gave himself a mental slap at the involuntary response that had caused her to put more distance between them.

"I realize you're a Dom, but you signed up for this. You chose to do this. Right?"

Maybe he should come clean. Tell her that though the Doms had been dressed in sub gear, they hadn't been auctioned off as subs. The idea, other than raising money for charity, was to give subs the chance to choose who they would be able to scene with. Nobody from the club would ever have considered that the Doms on stage wouldn't be running the scene. He watched the tiny dots of sweat form above her lips. Watched her hold her breath, then force a jerky inhale. Her nervous determination called to his basic nature, enhanced the attraction that was already there. He'd taken on this task, so it was his job to give her what she needed, regardless of what she wanted, if he was able. And he suspected that in this case, giving her what she wanted might actually be what she needed. *Shit*.

He gave her a very brief, very tiny nod. He could do this. It wasn't as if he hadn't submitted before. Though it had been years ago, when he was new to the scene, he'd been encouraged by a mentor to experience both sides of the play. He'd agreed that it was the smart thing to do, but he hadn't had any intentions of repeating the experience after all this time. Still, he could man up if it was in the best interests of this woman who needed him. Maybe he was being egotistical to think that she needed him, that he had something he could help her with. But, well, he was a Dom after all. His ego was quite healthy.

"Yellow and red, then?" she asked, her eyebrows raised. He was impressed that she insisted on clarification. Holding her own in a role he was sure wasn't natural to her. Well, then, he could do the same.

"Yellow and red. Yes."

She licked her lips and darted a quick glance at his face. Slowly, and with only a barely discernible tremble, she reached a hand out to him. He managed to remain relaxed until she picked up the damn leash instead of touching him, and gave it a slight tug downward. His jaw locked and his fists clenched. But he forced his knees to bend and kept his mouth closed. She took a step closer. Then another, until she was close enough for him to smell the faint scent of her, feminine and enticing.

Though he still couldn't quite unclench his fists, he forced the rest of his body to relax. Even when she moved her hand up the leash and unclasped it from the damn collar. She stepped closer, her dress just brushing his nose. He resisted raising his cuffed hands and using them to yank her even closer. Or push the hem of her dress up higher. She slid her hands around his neck and unbuckled the collar. He felt a level of tension fall away along with the leather. Her fingers danced lightly along his throat, up his chin. She cupped his face, brushed gently along his cheekbones. It was...soothing. He didn't want to be soothed. It sort of made him wary.

For several minutes she simply stood there, stroking his face, brushing her fingers through his hair. It was something he could easily imagine doing to a skittish sub, someone who needed to be gentled to his touch and presence. It rankled. He didn't need to be gentled. He wasn't fighting her; he was giving her what she'd asked of him. Hell, he'd gone to his knees for her.

Her hands fell away and she stepped back. It was a strange relief, when before he'd just wanted her closer. She dropped down in front of him, her head bent so he was staring down at the crown of her auburn hair. Her fingers fumbled a bit but managed to remove both of the wrist cuffs. He let his arms fall to his sides, wondering what the hell she was planning. Maybe she trusted him to do what he was told without being tied into position. He honestly couldn't decide if that would be better or worse. There was still a little bit of hope that there would come a point when what she needed was for him to take over. Take control. Being untethered would definitely make that easier.

She rose, taking his elbow and urging him up as well. Then she kicked off her shoes and pulled her dress up over her head. It was interesting that she didn't order him to undress her. Wasn't taking her time or making a show of it. The black fabric was tossed to the side, leaving the smooth skin he'd already admired and now ached to touch. Preferably with his tongue. The small breasts that meant she didn't need a bra practically begged for his mouth. The scrap of black satin that was her panties disappeared quickly, and then she reached for him.

There were no orders given, but he knew she wanted him to remain still. He managed it by pretending he'd ordered her to undress him. She took more care with him than she had with herself, lending authenticity to his imagination. Of course, the fact that what she was removing was a leather harness that normally adorned a sub did the opposite. Still, her hands smoothed over his chest with care as she unsnapped this and peeled away that until he stood before her completely nude.

He expected her to take a step back, observe what she'd revealed. He should have remembered that nothing this woman had done tonight had been according to his expectations. Instead, she grabbed his wrist and led him past the bed and to the bathroom.

He managed to somewhat maintain the internal fiction that he'd told her to prepare them a shower as she turned on the water and patiently tested the stream until it was the temperature she preferred. He'd only used this room a couple of times, and never actually used the shower stall. It was huge, the stone tiles a warm, welcoming color that was only enhanced by the strategically placed, securely fastened bars that could be used for holding on or for attaching cuffs and chains. There was a long bench at one end, a rain showerhead on the ceiling, five showerheads arranged on two walls and a wand with a very long hose that would allow it to reach all corners of the stall.

It fully complemented the lush bathroom that was nearly as large as the attached bedroom. The jetted tub could seat four, if those four were willing to be very close to each other. He'd used it for just that purpose with a play partner who'd wanted to experience an orgy. He looked again at the plush rug, the fluffy white towels on the heated rack, the basket of every kind of toiletry you could imagine. There was a long, wide divan that was nearly the size of some beds and a toilet that looked like it had more computer components than his laptop. The bidet options could be adapted to some interesting play, so he supposed he was glad she seemed intent on the shower at the moment. He could only push his pretend scenario so far.

His mysterious beauty seemed satisfied with the temperature at last and stepped into the shower, reaching back for his wrist to lead him in behind her. The water wasn't quite as hot as the near boiling he usually set it to, but since the room itself was heated, he wasn't complaining. Water spattered against her back as she brought him to the center of the stall. He was tempted to watch the drops that hit her shoulders as they glided down towards her breasts, but he watched her face instead. He had to get a handle on her. Figure out what she needed from him. She looked determined, a little bit wary, and more than a bit sad. Her breathing was even and her nipples were starting to pebble, but he couldn't be sure if that was excitement or the environment. He suspected the latter. There was no telltale glint of moisture between her thighs. Was it time for him to take control? Lead her to pleasure? He'd been in scenes that were more about emotion than sex, understood sometimes that was what the sub, or even the Dom, needed. But even in those scenes, sex and pleasure, or sometimes pain, had been the path to emotional release.

Of course, in every one of those instances he'd known his sub, understood what it was that she needed and had a plan for how to satisfy her. To say he was flying blind right now was a massive understatement. As a Dom without a sub, he'd expected to be bid on by those who were too shy to approach him otherwise, or someone he'd played with in the past who wanted an encore. It hadn't occurred to him that someone would expect him to play the sub, nor had he imagined he'd be in any kind of emotional situation with the potential for serious consequences if he fucked things up.

Then again, maybe he was overthinking things. Assigning this neediness to her so that he could feel like he was playing the hero. He managed, just barely, to keep from rolling his eyes. Now she had him second guessing himself.

Dana took a deep breath and dropped his wrist. She examined the various shower heads and flipped switches until only one of the three behind her and both of those next to him were shooting water. One was above his head and she angled him until its stream hit his neck and shoulders with a pleasant massage. The other was lower, hitting his ribs, and he began to think of ways he'd like to direct all the streams on her.

"Are you all right?" she asked, her voice soft enough that he had to lean forward slightly to hear her over the water.

"Yes. Are you?"

Her lashes flew up as she met his gaze, and she blushed. Her swallow was almost audible, but she didn't answer him otherwise. He didn't really need her to. She wasn't all right, she was clearly going through something, and he was clueless as to how to help her.

Turning her back to him, she studied the bottles on a shelf in the wall before selecting one and pouring a large amount into her palm. She turned around and immediately placed her palms on his chest, the slightly cool gel warming quickly as she moved her hands over his flesh. Tentative at first, her touch firmed up quickly, intermingled with pauses while she squeezed his muscles in what he could only interpret as delight. Amused, he resisted the urge to flex.

Circling him, she washed his chest, back and arms before returning to his chest. When she darted a quick glance at his face and licked her lips, he mentally braced himself. Sure enough, her fingers lingered on the nipples she'd washed with a cursory once over. She flicked, then squeezed, though not hard enough to cause him any real discomfort. Laying her hands flat on his chest, she brushed her thumbs back and forth across his nipples. He wasn't particularly sensitive there, but he took pleasure in feeling her hands rest against him and in watching the delight dance across her face. He wanted very badly to thread his fingers through her wet hair and pull her mouth to his chest, then order her to finish cleaning him with her tongue.

He tensed with the effort and her hands tightened their grip against his slick skin. Too soon she leaned back, flicked her gaze to his face, then dropped her hands. She turned away to get more shower gel and he watched her pert ass while he fought for control. The view was counterproductive to his goal, but he was powerless to resist. She probably thought her butt was too big, but he had an urgent desire to fill his hands with the globes. She turned back to face him and he decided her breasts were an excellent alternative. Then she dropped to her knees and his mind went in a different direction entirely.

His partially erect cock hardened, though her hands had only gone to one ankle. She took her time working the soap up his leg, all the way to the crease of his thigh. His legs were spread wide enough that she was able to slide her hands the full length without brushing his balls. Damn it. She did the other leg then looked up at him as she put her palms on his ass. He almost laughed. He didn't manage to stay still. Her mouth was inches from his cock, her hands tight on his ass, one finger sliding between his crack for a thorough cleaning, and he broke. He gently cupped her head with one hand, the other going to her chin to pull her gaze up to his.

Her shoulders sagged a bit as she let his hand take her weight, turning her face just enough for him to feel relief that she was accepting his touch for the domination it was. But she closed her eyes. He brushed his thumb over her lips and watched her throat work around a hard swallow. Then she pulled in a deep breath and he knew she wasn't ready. Before she had to say anything, before she even opened her eyes, he dropped his hands back to his sides. He wouldn't make her give him unnecessary orders.

She blinked her eyes open and the gratitude and determination in them told him that at least he was now reading her correctly. She rose, her movements sure and practiced.

Lifting a hand to the back of his head, she gave the barest of tugs. "Tilt your head under the water." She ran her fingers through his hair. When she deemed it wet enough, she gently pushed him forward again. Moving to the bottles again, she made another selection.

"You can hold this handle if you need to," she said, gesturing to a bar on the wall next to her. "Close your eyes and bend over."

He did as she ordered, but placed his hands against the wall behind her instead of using the support bar she'd offered. She hesitated, and he knew he was pushing things by caging her between his arms, but he wouldn't hold the handle, and he sure as hell wouldn't clasp his hands behind his back, as he would expect his sub to. Not unless she specified. After a moment, she moved her hands to his head and he breathed a discreet sigh of relief. With his eyes closed and her fingers massaging shampoo through his hair, it took him a minute to realize that the tantalizing heat just in front of his mouth and nose was her breasts.

Defying her order, he opened his eyes. Probably a mistake, as his mouth began watering. A dozen options swam through his head before he made a decision on his next move.

"May I pleasure your breasts while you work?"

Her hands stilled on his head. If he wasn't concentrating so hard, he might have missed her whispered "you may". But he *was* concentrating, and he didn't hesitate. With slow, careful movements, he nudged his nose into the valley of her breasts. When he gave her a chaste kiss, her fingers began moving through his hair again. He turned to the side enough to explore the shape of one breast with his tongue. He wondered if she was aware that though her hands didn't try to direct his actions by moving his head, her body twisted slightly, giving him access to her nipple.

Taking the offering, he pulled the bud between his lips, giving gentle pulses in time with the fingers washing his hair. When she seemed to have moved the suds to her satisfaction and was about to pull free, he bit down gently. Her whole body shivered and her hands fell to her sides. His instincts fought between pushing her to take what he wanted to give, and letting her play out the she scenario she needed to explore. It wasn't just his ego that led him to believe he could take over the situation, it was the way her breath stuttered, her body leaned into his touch and her toes curled. With some regret, he decided he needed more information to best serve her as a Dom. He let her nipple pull free with a gentle plop, then brushed a kiss across her breast before closing his eyes and resuming his position.

DANA'S BRAIN took a minute to re-engage. The man in front of her had gone still after launching a burst of tingles through her body. She closed her eyes and took a slow breath, careful not to push her breasts into his face. His name was Eric, she reminded herself. She didn't know him. He didn't know her. He had nothing to do with the scene she was playing out, not really, but it was her responsibility to make sure she didn't harm him. It hadn't really seemed like an issue, since she wasn't going to be doing any play that could possibly seem boundary pushing, but she knew that any scene could be full of emotional landmines. Ones that could be triggered without the other party having the slightest awareness.

She wasn't really surprised he'd made a move. He was a Dom, after all, used to topping. The fact that she'd allowed it, hadn't even protested, and that he was the one who'd stopped it, showed her that though she was determined to play the scene out her way, she was still a sub more used to following orders than issuing them. Not that she'd had a doubt on that score. It wasn't like she was thinking of switching sides or anything. She just…needed to do this one thing. Needed him to let her do this one thing. After that, she figured she'd fly solo for a while.

"Stand up, tilt your head back." She didn't exactly sound commanding, but at least her voice didn't waver. She relaxed a little bit when she saw that his eyes were closed, as ordered. Resting one hand on his chest so he was grounded, she stepped to his side and reached up to help the water clear out the suds. It was better than staring at his face. Though not much. The feel of his warm skin and hard muscles beneath her hand and the silky strands of his short, almost black hair sliding through her fingers was a temptation nearly as strong as the smooth lips, strong jaw and piercing eyes. Of course, none of that compared to his strong presence, the one that had captivated her from the stage and nearly been her undoing on entering the room.

It had taken a numb determination to disregard all the doubts that began to clamber through her the minute the auctioneer declared her the winner, and make her way to the man waiting for her. She'd managed to grab the leash by doing her best to not look directly at him. The offer of available rooms had nearly overwhelmed her, but she'd seen the description of *decadent full-service bathroom* and taken it. Still, walking into the room with a giant bed had freaked her out. Her body started making assumptions about what she was there to do which were in complete contradiction with her intentions.

Her intentions. It wasn't like she'd had a real clear idea of what she wanted to do when she'd started bidding. Or when she'd raised the bid, again and again. Or when she'd taken possession of her winnings and selected the room. Wasting some of her precious time, she'd centered herself. Decided what she needed to do. Which she needed to get back to now before she ran out of time, or her Dom ran out of patience. Her heart stuttered a bit on thinking *her Dom*, but she pushed the thought back out and refocused her attentions.

"Okay," she murmured, her hand guiding his head back to upright. She regretted her completely unspecific order when he not only straightened his neck but opened his eyes. His calm, relaxed body and actions had led her to believe he was in a passive state. His intense, searching gaze proved her very wrong. If she'd had any doubts about his submission, they were quickly dashed away. Sure, he was doing everything she told him to do, but not for anything close to resembling the reasons she herself submitted. Since his submission hadn't been her goal or even her desire, it shouldn't scare her. As long as he continued to keep his toppy self in check, they would get through this just fine. And hopefully she'd find a bit of the peace that she was searching for.

Turning her back, she reached for the conditioner, letting her body's movement mask the deep breath she needed in order to continue. She kept her eyes level with his collarbone when she turned back. "Close your eyes, bend over," she repeated. He watched her for only a second before complying. This time, instead of holding the handle she'd suggested, or bracing himself against the wall behind her as he had before, he rested his hands on her hips. Her pussy gave a completely involuntary clench. It should have pleased her, to know that she could still be aroused. Instead, it made her feel traitorous. Her lover was recently dead and her body was ready to move on to the next commanding presence she found herself in? Closing her eyes, she brought Harrison's face to her mind. Let herself sink into the memories of the happy times, the love that she'd had for her Dom, the need that she'd come here to fulfill. One that had nothing to do with sex.

As she moved the cream through Eric's hair, she pictured Harrison in the hospital bed during that last week. His hair lank and dry, his skin thin and brittle. She moved her fingers through healthy hair and imagined a sick bed. Barely felt the tear slide down her cheek. It didn't matter though. She was finally getting to do what she'd needed to do. Serving her Master as she hadn't been able to do when it had mattered most.

Instead of speaking this time, she gave a gentle tug on hair that was dark instead of strawberry blond, guided him back into the stream until the water ran clean. The man in front of her wasn't bothering to hide the concern on his face, but that was okay. He wasn't stopping her, wasn't denying her what she needed.

Leaving him with the spray hitting his shoulders, she turned and made quick work of washing herself and her hair. She turned the water off and stepped out to grab a warm towel from the rack. Again, she started with his feet, taking gentle care with his sex but not lingering. Her mind tried to get distracted with his beauty, but she shoved it aside. He needed her to take care of him, and that was what she would do. The flesh she was drying was taut, not slack with sickness, but she took as much care with him as she would have her lover. If he had let her. She'd seen Harrison dry himself with a vigorous rub many times, and imagined this man did the same, but she patted him gently, blotting the moisture rather than abrading his skin, even though the towel was as soft as any she'd ever felt.

Moving behind him, she stood on the bench so that she could reach his hair without requiring him to bend over. She took her time, gently fisting the strands with the towel until there were no loose drops left to fall. A nudge on his shoulder had him turning towards her. With exquisite care, she used two fingers in the towel to pat his face dry, the concerned, healthy face flashing back and forth in her mind's eye with that of her dying Master, barely conscious most of the time, but still too commanding for her to defy by giving him the care she so desperately needed to when he'd forbidden it.

She dried Eric's ears, then behind them, noting the lack of any holes in either lobe. Wiped the towel across his eyebrows. Gently patted his lids and lashes dry when he lowered them closed. Finally she was done. She was careful to use one of the handles to ease her way off the bench rather than brace her hand on his firm shoulder, as she wanted to do. Not daring a look at his face, she took his wrist and led him out of the stall.

The bathroom was big enough that it was comfortably warm and not too humid from the shower. She knelt at his feet again and tapped one until he lifted it so that she could dry the bottoms as thoroughly as the rest of him. When she was done, she rose and stepped back, looked him over to make sure she hadn't missed anything.

What next? This was as far as she'd managed to plan. It felt... good, right, but not quite finished. Her look lingered on his cock, half erect as it had been through the whole process, and she knew. Though this hadn't been about sex, her Master's pleasure was an integral part of taking care of Harrison as she had so longed to do. She wasn't actually sure if the rules of the auction prohibited a blow job or not. Since she hadn't been thinking in that direction, she hadn't bothered to pay much attention, too busy staring at Eric on stage. Well, she'd have to ask permission even if it was allowed, since this was beyond the scope she'd promised him. If it was against the rules, he'd have to tell her so. And if he wasn't comfortable with it, she'd figure some other closure to the scene.

She made short work of drying herself, then bent over and towel dried her hair briskly. Finished, she tossed their used towels into the hamper and looked at Eric.

She met his eyes briefly, then dropped her gaze to his chin. "May I pleasure you with my hands or mouth?" If she'd tried to talk it out, tried to explain how giving this stranger the care that she hadn't been able to give her lover was bringing her the relief of closure, she was sure she'd talk herself out of the feeling. Eric was nothing like Harrison in looks, and she hadn't given him a chance to act like the Dom he was, so she had no idea if he was like her Master in that way. But already she felt better, like she could now imagine moving on, something that had seemed impossible only hours before. It made no more sense than the oppressive guilt she'd been feeling at not being there for Harrison, when he was the one who'd made that decision. Ordered her to let go and stay away.

When Eric didn't answer right away, she tried to think of what else she could do to end the scene and still fulfill the need she had to take care of him. She hadn't gotten very far when he interrupted her thoughts.

"You may."

Excellent. He hadn't specified one or the other. She could make this work. Finish this and be done. Move on with her life. A life without her Master, but without the ridiculous guilt that ate at her every day, even though she knew Harrison would be angry with her for feeling it. Well, she was doing what she could to assuage it, to stop feeling it, so he would have to get over himself. She nearly laughed at the idea of Harrison looking down on this scene and judging the success of her mission.

A tanned, vibrantly healthy hand started to reach for her, but she gave a sharp shake of her head and took a step back before she could stop herself. He hesitated, then dropped his arm back to his side. No, this needed to go her way. Sure, there was a part of her, a huge part of her, that wanted to place herself into his care, let him take over. But not only wasn't it what she needed, it would be unfair to him. To expect him to do it right, when she couldn't tell him what it was that she needed from him. From this.

Taking his wrist again, knowing full well he would prefer that she take his hand, she led him back to the bedroom and the elegant, high-backed wing chair next to the window. She had him sit down and hook his feet behind the chair legs. She lifted his hands over his head so that they lay along the back of the chair. Comfortable, she hoped, but out of her way, and a subtle reminder to him to let her control the action.

He actually gave a little grunt, but then seemed to settle back into the seat. It was cowardly, but she refused to look up at his face. Instead she pulled out the small pillow that was tucked under the side table and placed it between his feet. She checked the drawer, found an assortment of condoms and decided on cherry. Taking a breath, she dropped her knees to the pillow and focused on his cock. It had lengthened, hardened, since she'd asked for his permission to attend to it.

Leaning forward, she smelled the fresh, clean sent of male skin. The tingle of tears began deep behind her eyes, but she figured she had a little time before they came to the surface and escaped. She didn't want to traumatize the poor guy by crying on his erection, but it was so good to see a healthy man, reacting naturally, and know she was there to take care of it, of him. Making quick work of the condom, she tossed the wrapper on the table and let herself enjoy the treat.

She darted her tongue out teasingly, a lick here, a taste there, until she felt his thighs tighten around her as if he was going to make a move. Then she simply licked him from bottom to top, bringing one hand up to hold him steady and using the other to cup his balls. Another small grunt was the only reaction from him, but he didn't move. She repeated the action, her pointed tongue as stiff as she could make it until she reached the head, then she flattened her tongue, swirled it around, before dropping her mouth over him as far as she could reach. And she could reach far. She'd taken a deep breath and simply rested at the base of him, smiling as he twitched and lengthened further inside her unmoving mouth.

Finally, she hollowed her cheeks and slowly moved back up his shaft, her tongue gliding along until it teased the underside of his head. Playing there for a few minutes, she massaged his balls carefully at the same time. The tears were staying back, so she rolled her eyes up and risked a look at Eric. He was watching her attentively, his expression serious and not at all lost in the pleasure she was trying to give him. She couldn't quite decide if that was a good thing or not, so she moved her gaze down his perfect body.

With his arms up and back, his chest was thrust out, his abs pulled in, his body a display of muscles that she couldn't deny were achingly attractive. She'd never thought herself particularly superficial, had never dated a guy that she considered gorgeous, but *wow*. She clenched her thighs against the ache that was developing in her core just from looking at this amazing specimen of man. The truth was, she never in a million years would have had the nerve to approach a guy like this for a real scene, let alone a date.

Bringing her attention more fully back to her task, she figured she might as well get as much enjoyment out of it as she could. After today, she wasn't sure how long it would be before she'd be willing to risk a relationship with anyone, let alone a Dom. She promised herself a generous session with her credit card and her favorite online toy store when she got home.

She started moving on him rhythmically, her free hand coming to his thigh to brace herself and give her leverage to really move. The hand she used on his balls maintained its slow, steady motion, in contrast to the fast fucking she gave him with her mouth. Then she stopped, lodging him as deeply as she could, resting for just a second before rising slowly and allowing her teeth to graze him just slightly. When she reached the top she suckled hard, then resumed her previous pace. He only lasted another minute before his large hand came down to cup her head and hold her still while he released into the condom.

She was breathing hard, those damn tears sliding along her nose and onto his thigh, but she didn't mind his hold. It felt right. She'd given him what she could, served him as best she knew how, and it was almost over. She managed to stop the flow of tears and hoped he'd think the wetness was from her hair, strands of which draped across his thighs. She remained still, content to let him choose when to let her up.

It took a few minutes, but finally the hand holding her head slid off and she slowly released him from her mouth. She leaned back onto her heels and licked her lips before looking up at him. His face wasn't quite so serious now, she was pleased to see. Before that could change, she jumped up, slid the condom free and went into the bathroom. When she returned, he'd folded both arms across his chest and his feet were flat on the floor, the little pillow kicked to the side. But he was still sitting. She used a warm, wet wash cloth to clean him, then a hand towel to pat him dry.

She glanced at the clock on the wall. Fifteen minutes left of their two hours. Close enough. Since he didn't have any clothes other than the sub harness, as far as she knew, she didn't figure she needed to redress him. Keeping her head lowered, she quickly worked her dress over her head and adjusted it until it lay correctly. She picked up her shoes and gave him a deferential nod.

"Thank you, Sir."

She turned and crossed to the door, letting the tears free.

Eric waited until she had the door all the way open before he called out to her.

"Stop."

She did, one hand on the door, the other holding her shoes against the door jamb. She didn't turn around, but she didn't step forward either.

He moved up behind her, close enough for her to feel, but not quite touching her.

"We still have thirteen minutes."

Her head jerked to the side, an almost, but not quite, negative.

He closed the tiny distance between them, his arm going around her waist, pulling her back against him. He tried to see her face around the wet strands of her hair. Her eyes were closed but tears slid freely down her cheek. Fuck this. He picked her up, ignoring the little squeak she made, and returned to the chair. He much preferred a big lounge chair to this fancy one, but he'd make do. It took a little effort to tuck her up against him so that they were both comfortable within the leather embrace, but she didn't fight him.

She rested her head against his chest, and let loose. No longer silent tears, she sobbed against him wetly. He stroked her hair away from her face and leaned his head back to wait her out.

It didn't take long for her breathing to slow down and her sobs to ratchet down to sniffles. He snagged the hand towel she'd left on the side table and brought it to her face, growling at her when she moved to take the towel herself. She acquiesced and he blotted the tears from her face before putting the cloth to her nose.

"Blow."

She glared at him for all of half a second before giving in.

He debated his options, made his decision. Rising with her in his arms, he strode back to the bathroom and set her in front of the divan. "Dress off." This time she tried a scowl, but he turned away before seeing how long she'd last, worried he wouldn't be able to hold back his smile.

The jetted tub was easy to work and filled fast. By the time he'd selected an almond scented bubble bath and poured a liberal amount in, the tub was half filled. When he turned, the dress was off, her scowl had morphed to an uncertain frown, and her arms were crossed over her stomach. He knew modesty wasn't her issue, and actually would have been easier to deal with than whatever it was that she was still holding in.

He wasn't entirely sure she'd let him pick her back up and put her in the tub, so he held his hand out to her instead. She stared at it for a good minute before sighing and taking it. He helped her step in, then got in behind her and nudged her down between his legs until they were lying with her back resting against his front.

"Can you tell me what this was all about?" he asked gently.

"You agreed to let me be in charge," she reminded him.

"Your two hours are up now." His lips quirked, but he was pretty sure he managed to keep the amusement from his voice.

"We haven't negotiated a scene. I haven't agreed to obey you." She almost sounded belligerent, but it edged more towards tired and his smile faded away.

"True." The water was high enough, so he stretched for the

controls, turned the taps off and the jets on. Then he ran his hands through the hot water and up her uncovered arms. "Can you tell me what this was all about?" he repeated.

She sighed, let her head rest back against his shoulder. "I needed to say goodbye to someone. In a way I wasn't able to before he… died. I…I'm sorry if you feel used. That wasn't my intention."

"Not in a negative way," he assured her. He continued to move the hot water up her arms, pushed a small wave to where her breasts rose above the water.

"We're going to be very clean tonight," she observed.

He laughed. "I guess we are. There are worse things to be."

Her eyes had closed and her hands had floated to the top of the water, tangling slightly with his.

"Eric."

He waited patiently and was rewarded after three full minutes when she continued. "I was in love with my Master for a long time. Years. He died last month."

"I'm sorry to hear that."

She nodded her head. "It was…difficult. He was sick for a while."

Something in the way she said it let him know there was more. He stayed quiet, continued to move the water around them, let his arms tangle with hers, then separate.

Finally she sighed. "I was in love with him, for sure, about six months after he became my Master." Her voice was a little shaky and her arms moved back to wrap around her stomach. "At some point, I guess I wanted…needed more than he could give. But I loved him, so I didn't leave. And then, slowly, I stopped loving him. I'm not sure he ever loved me. No, that's not right. He loved me, in his way, but I don't think he was ever in love with me. It took me a while to decide it wasn't enough, and start to think about looking for more."

"Was it a club only relationship?"

"Basically, without the club, though. We played at his house or play parties. He didn't want a partner, a girlfriend. Only a sub."

"And you needed more."

"Yes. I came to. It wasn't his fault, I knew from the beginning what he was looking for. And it worked for me, for a long time. I didn't want a 24/7 Ds thing. He'd been in one and it had gone badly, so he was very wary of any kind of relationship outside of a scene."

"There's a lot of ground between scene-only and 24/7 slave."

She was quiet for a while before responding, "Yeah, there is."

"And that's what you started to want?"

"Yes, but I wasn't sure how I wanted to go about it. Everyone I knew in the scene, I knew through him. I didn't really want to start dating anyone else, or doing scenes with anyone else, but I realized I had to leave him so that I could get to the place where I'd be willing to look at someone else." She rolled her head against his shoulder. "I'm not sure any of that makes sense. I hadn't really sat down and figured it all out yet. Clarified it in my own head, you know? Because he got sick before I could decide what I wanted to do."

"And it was too late."

"Not just that, but he was sick, and his family came, and I…I wasn't needed. He didn't want me to help. Wouldn't let me take care of him. Which made sense for the relationship we had."

Ahh. "But not for the one you'd come to want." He crossed his arms over her torso and finally let his hands come to rest, one on each of her shoulders. Her breasts were squished underneath his arms, her arms trapped under his elbows.

The sniffles started again and she turned her head so she was facing away from him. "He was a good man, a good Dom. We had amazing scenes. He never shirked the after care, never pushed me too far, but never let me rest on my limits. He always took care of me. He…he was a good Dom."

"He didn't want a service sub."

"I didn't want to be a service sub." A hint of anger. "I just wanted to take care of him sometimes. See to his needs beyond a blow job. I know it's silly. I know I made him happy, gave him what he needed. That should have been enough for me."

"We all have different needs. It's unfair to expect one side's needs to be met and not the other."

"I loved him."

He squeezed her tight. "I know you did."

They sat there until the jets ran through their cycle and shut off. He helped her stand, and she stood quietly while he dried her off, then he returned the favor. This time, when she moved the cloth over him, his dick refused to listen to the message that now was not the time to get excited. When she was done, she looked at it, then up at him. The heat in her eyes was as unmistakable as the sorrow he'd seen earlier.

He led her into the bedroom, thinking.

"When did he get sick?" he asked, with a dawning realization.

"Almost a year ago."

When she'd said her lover had died a month ago he'd assumed… well, he shouldn't have assumed anything, but now he wondered if she was closer to letting go than he'd thought. Though she'd loved her Dom, she hadn't been *in* love with him for years and hadn't been sexually active with him for nearly a year.

"I'm honestly not sure what's best for you right now," he admitted.

Her eyes widened in astonishment and he laughed.

"You should probably go home. But I'd like to see you again. When you're ready. Both inside the club, and outside." He wanted to see where this might go.

She blushed, then nodded. "Okay." She looked down until he was pretty sure she was staring at his cock. Then she brought her right hand to her mound and slid a finger through her slit.

"Shit," he muttered. Then he cleared his throat. "Stop that."

A smile teased her lips. "We aren't doing a scene. We haven't negotiated anything, I haven't promised to obey you." Her finger moved up to tease her clit, then slid back into her wetness.

"You're staring at my naked dick."

"Well, you could put it away if you didn't want me to do that."

He crossed his arms over his chest and worked hard to glare at her. Which she didn't notice, since she wasn't looking anywhere near his face. "Bondage?" he asked.

Her finger stopped moving and she closed her eyes. "Yes, please." He had to strain to hear the whisper .

"Do you need pain play?" Somehow his hand had made its way to his cock and he was stroking it.

"No, Sir. I don't mind some, but I don't need it."

He swallowed, tried to keep focused. "Anal?"

She shivered. "That's fine."

"Anything you need from a scene?"

"No, sir. Just you. Just your orders. And your touch." Her hand stopped, then dropped to her side. She looked up at him, hesitated. Then gave in.

He could see it, though she didn't drop to her knees or offer her wrists or anything like that. But her body relaxed as she gave her submission to him. He was pretty sure she'd been near subspace a few times during their scene together as she'd sunk into the rhythm and routine of taking care of him. It was why he'd let her continue when he'd had to fight his other instincts, the ones that said take charge of the scene, demand information from her until he could give her what she'd needed. The fact that she'd clearly been getting something from the experience, something she'd seemed to need very badly, had stayed him. And made him intensely curious about what it would be like to play with her the way he normally would.

Now he was being rewarded for his patience. Handsomely.

"On your knees," he commanded, just so he could watch the graceful way she dropped to her knees and placed her hands at the small of her back, the controlled movement a testament to her desire to serve. He ran a hand over her head. The bottom half was wet from the bath but the top half was dry, though a bit frizzy from all the heat and the fact that the drying hair hadn't been brushed. It gave him an idea. He bent down to kiss the top of her head so that she would know she pleased him, then he turned away.

It only took a few minutes to gather his supplies, but he didn't hurry. When he passed by her, he wasn't surprised to see her in the same place, her face serene, her eyes downcast. He placed the items on the foot of the bed, then walked around the room, lighting the many candles with the fireplace lighter provided. He crossed to the door and flipped the light switch.

She was beautiful in the candlelight and he had to remind himself she wasn't his sub; this might only be for one night. Well, not if he could help it, but unfortunately he wasn't in charge of everything. Taking cuffs from the bed, he wrapped the padded wrist restraints securely around her, smoothing the Velcro down, checking the tightness carefully. He repeated his actions with her ankles, pleased that her breathing had deepened with only those actions. He resisted running his finger along her neck, not wanting to remind her that it was naked, that she didn't belong to him.

Giving a little shake of his head, he linked her wrist restraints, then lifted her to her feet with one hand under her arm. He led her to the foot of the bed.

"Lean over, cheek to the mattress, feet wide."

She did as instructed, choosing to turn her face towards the things he'd left on the bed, rather than towards the door. Letting her see, he picked up a small bottle of lube and squeezed a liberal amount onto a shiny silver butt plug. It wasn't a large one, and she didn't seem concerned, so he went ahead and moved his slick finger to her hole and rested lightly against the pucker. She shivered at the first contact, took a breath, let it out, and let him in. He teased the rim then pushed all the way in. It didn't take long before he added a second finger, scissoring them to open her up further.

She stayed perfectly still, her eyes turned towards him. He added more lube directly to her hole, then slid the plug in to the first knob. He played with it, teasing her with the fullness of the next bump before pushing it past her ring.

"Do you want more?" he asked.

"Please Sir, yes Sir, more."

He smiled at her breathy begging, rubbed his free hand over her ass. A little pinch brought a gasp and he slid the plug home. She wiggled for him and he gave her a light tap in appreciation. Sliding his hand under her arm, he helped her stand. Her face was flushed and her eyes had gone glassy. Perfect. He grabbed the hairbrush and brought her back to the chair, nudging the small pillow back into position. Taking a seat with his legs spread wide, he pointed at the floor.

"Turn around and sit back on your heels."

She settled quickly and he began to brush her hair, starting from the bottom and using his free hand to make sure he didn't pull unnecessarily. It wasn't exactly his usual style of play, but then again nothing about the night's activities had been the norm. When the auburn strands were silky smooth, he pulled off the band he'd wrapped around the brush's handle and secured her hair into a tail at the nape of her neck. It took a little more skill than he'd expected and wasn't quite an example of perfection, but it would do. He used the tail to gently pull her head back until it was resting on his thigh. Her color had faded but her eyes were still dreamy.

He ran a hand carefully down the column of her neck, ghosted it along the side of her breast, then traced a finger in circles around the tip, watching as her nipple began to pucker with no direct contact. When it was standing proud, he gave it an appreciative tweak. Her other nipple was half hard already when he repeated the process. Once it was tweaked to full firmness, he squeezed her pert breasts, one at a time, thumbing the nipples, until her breath was coming in sharp pants.

"If we play again, I'll have to put some pretty jewelry on these." He tried to keep his tone casual. "Would you like that?"

Her breathy "Yes, Sir" was gratifying, but he knew he couldn't actually hold her to anything she said in this state. Still, it made him smile.

"Good girl." He leaned down and teased her lips, upside down to his. She tried to take a kiss, but he refused, smiling against her as she mewled. He licked the corner of her mouth and stood, bringing her up as well. He turned her and slid his hands to her waist.

"Put your legs around me."

She blinked up at him in surprise then did as he'd ordered when he lifted her. "When I sit back down, I want you to drape your legs over the chair arms." She nodded her understanding and he carefully lowered them down, supporting her butt until she was fully settled. He debated unlinking her cuffs, the feel of her hands roaming his chest a strong temptation. But he wanted her unbalanced, dependent on him to hold her steady and safe for her ride.

He rummaged through the drawer of the side table and pulled out an unflavored condom, then danced the edge of the package along her breasts, her nipples, her collar bone. She pulled her shoulders back, displaying herself to him. He rolled the condom on, then put his hands at the small of her back, underneath her clenched fists. Holding her still, he leaned down to pull her nipple between his lips.

Dana cried out when the wet heat enveloped her nipple. Her fingers unclenched to reach for him, gripping his wrist, the only part of him she could reach. She was thankful for that bit of him to steady herself. She felt safe perched on the chair, wasn't worried she'd fall, but she'd felt untethered until she'd been able to grab onto him. It wasn't quite subspace, not like she was used to, but it was a similar floaty feeling that she wasn't sure if she should fight against, or give in to. She wasn't looking for a Dom, damn it. Or a relationship. Or—

He switched sides and she moaned, unable to stop herself. He didn't seem to mind her making noises though, had encouraged her to beg earlier. Of course, she wasn't at all sure she should be giving him what he wanted. He was already taking more than she'd meant to give. But how could she resist? He'd let her cry all over his amazing chest, then propositioned her. Even with her most-likely blotchy face and the disaster her hair must have been before he'd brushed it. And why had that felt so awesome? It hadn't been the least bit sexual, but she'd pretty much melted at his feet. Well, if she was going through with this, she might as well give it her all, which meant giving him what he wanted from her. Not that it was a hardship.

"Please, sir...I need you."

She felt his lips curl into a smile against her breast. He pulled free, just far enough to answer. "I'm right here, Dana." He kissed along the breast, then up her breast bone.

She'd meant to ask for his cock to fill her, but his mouth moving towards hers reminded her that he'd yet to actually kiss her.

"Ohhhh," she moaned as he nibbled along her chin. She tried desperately to remember what she'd been about to say. He bit her, then licked the sting away.

"Kiss me!" she shouted in triumph when her scattered brain seized the thought. "Please, please, Sir, I need you to kiss me."

"Mmm," he murmured, his mouth finding her ear and teasing her lobe. "Here?" he asked, the flesh caught between his teeth.

"Oh, yes...no! My mouth, Sir. Eric, please, kiss." His mouth covered hers, his tongue diving in and filling her just the way she'd wanted. Her fingers clenched on him. He pulled her up closer, his hands splaying across her lower back, the small adjustment making her feel the plug buried in her ass, which only served to remind her how empty she was elsewhere.

She opened her eyes and found him watching her. Hunger and pleasure were in his eyes and she gasped into his mouth. One of his wrists slid free of her grasp, but since he was reaching between them, she couldn't complain. He broke the kiss and they both looked down to where he grasped his erection and brought it to her sex. His other hand gripped her hip hard and helped her rise to join him. She would have plunged down, but he held her steady, the head of his cock lodging just inside her opening. He let go of himself and took complete control of her body, his hands guiding her down to envelop his hard length.

When he stopped her again she nearly sobbed. He pulled her up, teased her with the thought of pulling all the way free, then dropped her back down. His hips thrust up and he was buried fully inside her. She clenched her inner muscles, fell forward so that she could rest her head against his shoulder. Good, it felt so fucking good.

His fingers clenched, all the warning she had before he began to move her again, bouncing her gently, her legs waving wildly on either side of the chair. She used the leverage of the arms under her knees to help him, smiled when he cursed into her hair. Damn, she could get used to being with this man. She gave a little twist of her hips on the next drop and he growled. He turned his face to her, nipped at her until she turned to meet his mouth with hers. His tongue plunged into her and his rhythm got a little erratic. One hand deserted her back only to reappear between them. He pinched her clit and she screamed into his mouth, her orgasm taking her by surprise even though she felt like it had been building for ages.

His own release was immediate, his bellow next to her ear bringing a smile to her face. She collapsed against his chest, panting along with him. He tickled her waist but she only managed a slight shriek, and didn't even move. Her wrists popped free of each other and he gently massaged her shoulders, though they barely ached. She brought her freed arms around him and held on tightly as his fingers ran up and down her spine.

Only when he nuzzled her neck and made soothing sounds did she realize that she was crying again. Damn, hadn't she cried enough already? He was going to throw her out and never want to see her again.

The thought stopped her tears, not because it might be true, but because...did she want to see him again? It was too soon to start something with someone. *Right?*

"Okay?" he asked.

She forced herself to sit back up and look at him while wiping her face clean.

"Sorry."

"Don't be sorry. It's been an emotional night."

She nodded. "Thanks. For everything. I imagine my plans weren't quite in line with yours for the evening."

He shrugged. "Sometimes it's good to get thrown off course." He slapped her butt, then eased the plug free. "Come on, let's get you dressed and see if someone thought to bring me clothes."

With absurd regret, she let him lift her up and hold her until her wobbly legs figured themselves out. He took her hand and led the way to the bathroom, where he disposed of the condom while she washed her face. Then he lowered her dress over her head and smoothed it over her body until it lay just right.

When they went back into the room, she checked outside the door and found a small pile of clothing, which she handed over to him. She put on her shoes while he slipped on a faded pair of jeans and a black t-shirt. God, she could just stare at him for hours. His head popped free of the tee and he saw her staring, then grinned.

"Before we leave, I'm going to ask you for two things." He led her to the bed and stepped between her legs when she sat on the edge. His fingers roamed her thighs, flirting with the skirt's hem, then bypassing it altogether.

"First thing. I want a commitment to a date."

Her stomach muscles clenched. "A date?" The question came out as sort of a squeak, but at least it came out.

"A date. Dinner. Maybe some dancing, maybe a movie. Whatever you prefer."

She tried to reply but he put a finger against her lips.

"Second thing. I want a commitment to a play date. Here at the club."

She blinked, then frowned. "A...play date. And a date."

"That's right."

"You don't want to play at the end of the date? Or make the date part of the play?"

"No."

"Oh." Biting her lip, she forced her brain to think. She needed to be honest. With herself, and with him. "I'm, um, not sure I'm ready for ...dating."

He didn't answer for a minute.

"If you try it and find you're not ready, we'll figure out what to do next."

She frowned.

"Do you want to go on a date with me?" he asked, finally, his voice betraying no impatience.

His thumbs made little circles against her thigh and she wanted to kick him for distracting her. She managed to restrain herself. "Yes, I'd like that."

"And do you think you could handle one more session with me?"

His knowing smirk got the better of her. "Just like tonight? Me in charge to begin, then—"

She laughed as he assaulted her with tickles, growling into her throat as he knocked her back onto the bed.

"Okay!" she shrieked. "Okay!" He stopped the tickling immediately and propped himself up on his elbows.

"You'll give me those two things?" he asked.

She sighed. There was no possible way she could say no, so she didn't.

"Yes. I suppose I can agree to those terms." The grin trying to burst free on her face felt odd, but welcome.

His lips found hers and she truly relaxed for the first time in what felt like forever.

PERFECT ADDITION

PERFECT FIT BOOK 3

For Captain Richard, who was the first to dub me KB and has never wavered in his support and friendship. You brought sailing, Chris, Linda and that beautiful Hunter into my life, and I will be forever grateful.

CHAPTER ONE

The sights, sounds and smells of Apex were a familiar balm to Stephanie's mood. The BDSM club was her home away from home and she loved coming—seeing old friends, meeting new ones. Occasionally she wanted more, wanted a full-time relationship, someone she could take home to meet her parents, someone she could fall asleep with at night, and wake up to in the morning. It would happen, she was sure. For now, she would play.

She'd been thinking about that more and more, lately. Ever since her friend Emma had gotten serious with her guy. She'd teased Emma about not wanting to go to the club, about becoming stale, but the happiness on her friend's face and in her voice couldn't be denied. And the brat had been very clear that she and her guy didn't need a club to have all kinds of kinky fun.

Moving towards the small bar so she could grab a water and get a feel for the evening's activities, she tried to shake off her thoughts, put her mind in a more positive direction. She was here to play, not dwell on what she hadn't yet found.

Someone stepped in close behind her, butting into her personal space. She turned her head to meet the man's gaze as he settled a warm hand on her bare shoulder.

Trevor, a Dom who'd been coming to the club for a couple of months, raised his eyebrow at her.

"I believe we have a date." He sounded sure of himself, calm and cool. They hadn't actually set up a date, but they'd been eyeing each other for weeks, and last time they'd spied each other, they'd done a little dance of head motions that she was pretty sure had meant "next time". At least, that's what *she'd* meant and at the time, she'd been a little thrilled at the exchange.

This...invitation, for want of a better word, didn't exactly make her panties wet, but she was sure he could make it work for them, if she gave him a chance.

She lowered her gaze a bit and gave him a smile. "Yes, Sir."

He was older than those she was usually drawn to, but she thought maybe that was part of what was attractive about him. Over the last few weeks she'd found his maturity, his commanding presence and self-confidence very sexy. He held himself like a man who knew what he wanted and knew he was going to get it. It pleased her to know that he'd decided he wanted *her*, that he'd been thinking about her.

"Name?"

The brusque question had her blinking, but she didn't hesitate.

"Stephanie, Sir."

"Limits sheet?"

She pulled the sheet she'd reexamined and re-approved at the front desk, as required, out of her back waistband, where she'd stashed it. He plucked it from her fingers. Lifting her head enough to catch his frown, she wasn't quite sure what to make of the little *harrumph* he made under his breath. She didn't have long to consider as he folded the paper precisely in half and said, "Come along."

Turning on his heel, he marched to a whipping post and dropped the small duffel bag he'd been carrying.

Well. Okay then. Not exactly how negotiations usually went in her experience, but she'd wanted a man who knew what he wanted, right?

He looked her up and down.

"Top off, you can leave the skirt on."

She didn't bother replying, just unzipped the purple faux bustier and put it into a nearby cubby. She wasn't feeling super sexy at the moment, but she figured he'd get her heated up soon. Scenes she'd seen him involved in flashed through her memory. Definitely hot. She needed to be patient.

Grabbing her arm just above the elbow, he turned her roughly and put cuffs on her wrists. She swallowed back a comment and tried to think sexy thoughts as he linked the cuffs behind her back and attached them to the post.

On a deep inhale, she forced her shoulders to relax. The guy knew what he was doing. So did she; it wasn't like she was a beginner at this whole thing. She was in her favorite club, looking pretty damn hot, if she did say so herself, and about to get flogged, something that had brought her to climax when done correctly. Of course, the Dom who'd managed that had moved to Texas shortly after, damn it.

She flexed and tensed her muscles a bit, trying to get her blood flowing. Not something she normally needed to do. The flogger Trevor had pulled out looked like black suede. The fact that she'd seen him wield it to great effect before helped her relax. Until he whacked her breast with a not-at-all-gentle thwap.

She pulled in a sharp breath, her eyes actually watering a bit from the unexpected pain.

It wasn't as though she hadn't been expecting a flogging since he'd pulled the instrument from his bag. But she'd certainly expected some warm-up.

He swung again, this time the full brunt of the strands slapping across her belly. She bit her lip and tried to catch Trevor's gaze, let him know she was not feeling this at all. Try to give him a clue. His unblinking stare was unsettling.

He swung again and she unconsciously turned her body away from him, getting the hardest strike yet across the top of her breasts, one strand flying up to catch her chin.

That was it. She was done. "Red."

He checked himself mid-swing and stared at her.

"Excuse me?"

"I'm sorry, but this isn't working for me. We're done here."

"The hell we are, we were just getting started. You wanted this, you're getting this."

Her embarrassment at having to use her safe word transformed swiftly to anger, but she tried to be the bigger person. "Look, I'm sorry, I thought this was what I wanted, but apparently I'm not in the right mood. Just unhook me and we can go our separate ways."

The anger she saw on his face dispelled any lingering sense of attraction she might have had for him and had her scanning the room for one of the monitors. Marcos, in his bright white Apex shirt, was immediately visible to her and she was pleased that he noticed her right off. Clearly realizing she wanted him, he started over, arriving in time to hear Trevor's next words.

"You stupid little slut, you were begging for it. Begging for *me*. If you can't handle a little pain, you need to be taught. Otherwise, you're in the wrong place."

"Trevor. Stephanie." Marcos' warm, calm voice kept her from answering the idiot Dom the way she wanted to. Well, that and the firm grip her teeth had on her lower lip.

"Is there a problem?" Marcos asked, moving to unhook her cuffs from the post while he spoke. She loved him for not waiting to take action.

"This ridiculous excuse for a sub is safe-wording after three lousy strikes."

The monitor put his hand on her shoulder, checked her eyes. "Are you all right, darlin'?"

Taking a deep breath, she angled towards him so she could ignore the asshole in their midst. "I am now, thank you. This might be my fault, and for that, I'm sorry. I thought I was ready for a scene, but apparently I was wrong, at least for the kind of scene he wanted. But when I used my safe word, he got mean and rude."

She felt movement at her back and whipped her head around.

The two men who stood there brought a smile to her lips, even through her anger. Jesse, a friend she hadn't seen in way too long, and Grant, the reason Jesse hadn't been around the club. Seeing them now was a very welcome surprise.

As Marcos began unbuckling one of the cuffs from her wrists, Jesse moved in to work on the other.

"This is unbelievable," Trevor said, disgust clear in his voice. "You just let subs get away with teasing the Doms?"

"I'd be glad to have a conversation with you about that," Marcos said. "As soon as I take care of Stephanie. You can wait here, without saying anything more, or I can find you over near the bar when I'm done here."

Trevor shook his head as he put the cuffs into his bag. "This night is ruined. I'll be leaving now."

"Actually, if you want to come back to Apex, we need to have a talk," Marcos said as Jesse helped Stephanie back into her top. "I'll be with you in just a minute, over near the bar."

He led Stephanie a few steps away, looking at her inquiringly when Grant and Jesse joined them. She shrugged to show she didn't mind their presence, if he didn't.

"Are you all right?" Grant asked. *His* unblinking stare didn't bother her at all. She gave him a smile that wavered a bit. She wasn't hurt, but she was more unsettled than she'd realized.

"I'm fine, thanks for coming to check on me." She included Marcos and Jesse in her look. She held the bustier that Jesse handed her up to her chest and he worked the zipper in back. "I'd been looking forward to playing with him at some point, so it just really took me by surprise when he blew it so badly. I've never had anyone get mad at me for using a safe word before. I was stupid, should have talked to him more before starting." She hadn't noticed she was rubbing her arms until Jesse draped a blanket around her shoulders. "I think that's it for me tonight, I'm going to go home."

"You call yourself stupid again," Grant said as his hands moved to secure the blanket more firmly around her shoulders. "And you'll earn a punishment from *me*."

"And me," Marcos added, not trying to hide his grin.

She blinked at both of them. "Um. Okay."

"And you're not going home until I know you're good," Marcos continued. "I don't want you driving home and crashing suddenly."

She gave him a wry smile. "I'm not driving. And I didn't get anywhere near subspace, or anything good enough to risk a crash. Unfortunately."

Marcos narrowed his eyes at her.

"We'll take her out for dessert," Jesse said before either of the Doms could speak.

Her eyebrows shot up. "Don't you two have more exciting things to be doing together than taking me out? You haven't been to the club in ages, that I've seen." She pointed her chin at Jesse. "You should be tied to something."

He grinned. "Oh, honey, I was. But that was a while ago, and now I need something sweet with my sweet guy and you, who we haven't seen in forever. Come on, hot stuff, let's get this girl somewhere all to ourselves."

She managed to catch Grant and Marcos communicating in that nonverbal, masculine way that seemed especially inherent to Doms, before Jesse had her heading towards the front door.

"Thank you, Marcos!" she called over her shoulder, careful not to look where Trevor should be, in case she couldn't resist the urge to give him a smug look. Discretion being the better part of valor, and all that.

"I really am okay, guys."

"Good, then you can catch us up on all the new gossip," Jesse said, helping her exchange the blanket for her coat.

Somehow she found herself walking down the street sandwiched between the couple. Jesse had an arm around her waist and Grant had one around her shoulders. She should have felt smothered, but instead she felt safe and secure. She hadn't had a chance to get to know Grant well, but she really had missed Jesse.

The truth was, she'd spent a bit more time watching their scenes than might be considered polite. Had definitely spent way too many nights thinking about those scenes. There was just something so compelling about watching them together.

Worst of all, she'd actually maneuvered a young, newer Dom into ordering her to give him a blow job while she was able to watch Grant and Jesse play, so that she could fantasize about being a part of their action.

She'd been topping from the bottom, without question, and had been ashamed of herself for it. From that point on, she'd tried to avoid watching them together, but they'd stopped coming to Apex anyway. She'd talked to Jesse a few times, met up with him for lunch once, to hear how in love he was. There was no denying the happiness she felt for her friend's obvious exhilaration, but the break from seeing the two men together had probably been a good thing for her mental health.

"First you have to tell me where you've been and why you haven't been coming to Apex," she insisted as Grant angled them into a twenty-four hour diner. They moved to a four-top and Jesse slid in beside her, which gave her Grant as a view. It didn't suck. He wore his brown hair short, but long enough that she wanted to ruffle through it with her fingers. His blue eyes had seemed more gray in the club, but now, in the fluorescent light of the restaurant they were bright and piercing.

"We've been around, just not at the club."

"Oh crap, am I going to have to give the lecture about becoming old and stale again?" she asked as the waiter came by for their orders, offering a pot of coffee. She waved off coffee and ordered vanilla ice cream and fruit, Jesse asked for a brownie a la mode and Grant requested strawberry ice cream with chocolate sauce.

When the tired-looking waiter had left, Grant lifted a brow at her. "Do you think fun can only be had at Apex?"

"Wellllll," she drawled.

Jesse laughed and bumped her with his shoulder. "The club is about exploring yourself, trying new things, being around others like you, but for us it was mostly about trying new people. When you're with someone already, you don't need it."

"Exactly," Grant agreed. "Doesn't mean it's not fun to go once in a while, but you don't need it. Or at least, *we* don't. It's nice to shake things up a bit, see people you miss." He lifted his coffee to her, before bringing it to his lips.

She watched the action a bit more closely than she should. She'd been attracted to the man since the first time she'd seen him deliver a spanking that ended with him sucking the sub off to a howling orgasm. When he'd focused most of his attention on men, she'd been quietly envious. When he'd *really* focused his attention on her friend Jesse, she'd been thrilled for the other man.

Letting her head rest on Jesse's shoulder, she gave their words some thought. She supposed it was true that while it was amazing to go to the club and meet others like her, see the lifestyle in action, experiment and play, meeting people she could play *with* was sort of the true goal.

"When I was with Tony, we kept coming to the club. Nearly a year," she pointed out.

Jesse snorted before answering. "Tony liked to be seen working you. He liked people to see you, with *him*. You guys dated that long and never even moved in together. Sorry, honey, but you weren't that serious about him."

She supposed that was true, too. It hadn't bothered her, and she'd liked to be seen with him, hadn't she? Hell, she liked to be seen at all. They'd had a few scenes at home, but they'd never been half as hot as the ones they'd had together at the club. Both of them had gotten off on the exhibitionism, though maybe there'd been a bit of ego involved, on Tony's part, as Jesse intimated.

"Hmm. All right, I'll give you those points," she said as their food arrived. She picked up her spoon and waved it at them both. "But that doesn't mean you haven't made friends and that we haven't missed you while you've been off playing with each other and forgetting all about us."

Jesse slid his arm around her shoulders. "Honey, we could never forget you. Why do you think we came tonight?"

"Hmph," she mumbled around her bite of creamy goodness. Once she swallowed, she turned to give him a good study.

His hair was somewhere between her blonde and Grant's brown. She supposed it was the dirty blond that women seemed to hate, but looked great framing his hazel eyes. She'd seen them go from almost green to honey gold, something that fascinated her. He looked fantastic, somehow more healthy and vibrant than she'd ever seen.

"Have you been working out?" she asked.

He laughed. "He's been working me out." He pointed at Grant. "And I've been loving every minute of it."

"Well, love looks good on you. I'm happy for you."

His arm around her shoulder squeezed for a minute, and he offered her a bite of brownie. She accepted, wrapping her lips around his fork to take in the delicious morsel. Pulling back, she glanced over at Grant. His eyes were on her, them, she wasn't sure. But his look was pure heat.

A flush ran through her. Here was the nipple-tingling, skin-hopping anticipation she'd been waiting to feel all night. As much as she'd thought she'd been attracted to Trevor, he hadn't invoked this visceral reaction. She should have paid attention to her body. Of course, Trevor should have paid attention to her body, too.

She frowned at her ice cream before taking another bite. The boys were right. She'd been looking for a man, not just a play partner. She'd found Tony, and it had been good for a while, but they'd had different ideas about their futures and when he'd been offered a transfer to Ohio, neither of them had been too broken up about his decision to take it. Still, because they'd been together for a while, she'd been able to trust him more than her usual hook-ups, and that was a feeling she missed.

And looking for someone outside the club was so annoying. Trying to feel guys out for their willingness to tie a girl down and give a good spanking didn't usually end well, she'd found. Which left her the club, the same guys most of the time. It was enough to make her think she needed a break.

Maybe she should join one of the online kink sites, see if

meeting someone that way, getting to know them through emails before actually doing a scene, might make a difference. Something had to change. Tonight had been partially her fault. She'd gone to the club without really even thinking about if she wanted to. Just gone through the motions of getting ready, getting herself there, and immediately looking for someone to play with.

She dropped her head back against the seat. "Ugh. Tonight really was my fault, at least to start. I was going through the motions, not really even excited to play. Even with the new guy, who I'd been waiting to get my hands on."

Grant studied her. "In a bit of a slump?" he asked.

"I guess. I hadn't realized it."

"Still," Grant reached out and covered her hand with his. "He should have seen there was a problem, and even if he didn't, he shouldn't have disrespected your safe word, or *you* when you used it. You know that, right?"

She smiled at him. "Yes, I'm not so slumped I don't know that. *That* part pissed me off. But now that I'm over being angry, I'm annoyed with myself. I'm young and should be having fun!"

"Being kinky doesn't mean you get out of the usual ins and outs of dating," he pointed out.

"But it does mean you should have more fun during all those ins and outs," Jesse drawled.

They all laughed. Thank god they'd been there tonight, or she would have just gone home and slumped herself right into a fit of depression. Putting her spoon into the bowl and pushing it away, she snuggled into Jesse's side.

"I'm glad you guys were there. Did you have a good night, before I interrupted?"

"You didn't interrupt," Jesse assured her. "We were done. Just going through the main room to see if there was anyone, like you, that we wanted to catch up with."

"First, though, I put him into the webbing. We can't do that at home, and I do love seeing my Jesse strung up and helpless."

The heated look he directed at his lover made her happy and sad at the same time. She really hadn't understood how much she wanted that, until tonight. Hadn't realized how tired she was of looking, but not finding, the same thing for herself.

Jesse dipped his head, and murmured low enough that Grant *probably* couldn't hear, "Makes you all creamy, doesn't it? When he looks like that? Talks like that?"

"You are a lucky guy, Jesse Arnold."

The hand he had draped over her shoulder came up to play with her hair, teasing some of the loose strands. "This is very true."

"I bet you looked freaking hot up in the web."

"This is also true," Jesse drawled.

"What did he do to you?" she asked Jesse, though she was watching Grant.

Jesse gave a sharp tug, then soothed the spot with a little message. She shivered.

"Well, you would know if you hadn't gotten there so late," Grant said, eyeing the waiter coming to drop off their check. Stephanie went to reach for her purse, but Jesse restrained her as Grant took the bill.

"Let Grant get it, he loves rescuing damsels in distress and taking care of them."

She rolled her eyes. "That is so not necessary."

Grant pulled his wallet out of his back pocket, dropped several bills on the table and stood up. "But you'll let me do it anyway, because you understand my needs. Come on, let's walk and I'll tell you how amazing Jesse looked tonight."

Well, she couldn't really argue with that plan. She slid out behind Jesse, and he tucked her into his side. It was cold out, but they had their heavy jackets and didn't seem to mind strolling through the quiet streets. Grant took her other side, reaching an arm behind her to tuck his hand into the waistband of Jesse's leather pants. The heat of their arms shouldn't really have penetrated her heavy coat, but somehow it did. It was a good thing it was winter, keeping her cool. She had to remember that these two were a couple. Unavailable to anything but her occasional fantasies for being sandwiched between two gorgeous men.

She aimed a look up at Grant. "Tell me, tell me."

He smiled. "I faced him away from me, even though I knew he wanted to watch."

"I like to watch you working!" Jesse cried.

"Instead he had to watch the people who gathered to admire him."

"More like admire your handiwork," Jesse interjected.

Grant took his hand out from under Jesse's coat, slapped the man's ass, then returned to tuck into his waistband once again.

"I strapped him to the webbing at his wrists, elbows, upper arms, chest, hips, ankles, calves, thighs. I spent a good long time securing him to that thing."

"What was he wearing?" she asked.

"A harness to keep him plugged for me. A cock ring. A ball gag and a set of nipple clamps."

"Mmm. What color was the rope?"

"White, against the black webbing."

"Nice."

Picturing it, having seen Jesse naked or mostly so before, she wished she'd gotten to the club earlier. "What did you do then?"

Grant tugged and led them across the street at the crosswalk. Stephanie realized he was making a big square, leading them back to Apex, keeping them in the well-lit, somewhat populated streets. Keeping them safe.

"I spanked his ass until it was glowing for me. He has a great ass, as I'm sure you've noticed."

She murmured her agreement.

"Then I used the slapper. I wanted his whole body slick with sweat and aching with need."

"Oh, yeah," Jesse whispered.

"And finished off with a flogger, until he was making one long, begging moan behind that gag."

She'd stopped walking, so they both turned in slightly and she could see the memory in their faces, just as she could hear the lust in Grant's voice.

"And then?" She sounded breathy, but she didn't care. Both of their arms had tightened around her and she felt like she wasn't just a listener, but an active observer in the scene Grant was describing. Jesse's breath was warm against her hair, Grant's energy, his dominating presence, drawing both of them into his sphere, inviting them to be a part of his story, a part of his—

Stephanie blinked, gave a small jerk. Damn, he was a good storyteller. She was going to have some serious fantasy time with these boys once she was alone in bed. She cleared her throat, realized Grant was watching her instead of answering her.

"And then?" she repeated.

"And then I tucked up tight against his back, touching as much hot, slick flesh as I could with my body, and I reached around and took off the cock ring. Jacked him off in front of his audience. They loved what they were seeing. I could hear them watching, waiting, wanting to see him go off."

"I didn't hear them," Jesse said. "They didn't exist. I only heard you, whispering dirty things in my ear. Only felt your body covering mine, your hand on my dick. You told me to come. And you bit my shoulder."

"And you came."

Stephanie pulled in a huge breath. "I need to go home."

She stepped forward, breaking the intimate circle, and looked for a taxi.

Grant put one hand on her back and raised the other, and a cab appeared, as if by magic. Or maybe she wasn't paying attention because her brain was stuck in a sexual fog. She was totally turned on now, unlike when she'd been mostly naked and bound to a post for Trevor's attentions. That was a distant memory compared to the one she'd just heard which felt so much more real.

"Let me see your phone," Grant said, pulling her brain back to the present.

She dug it out of her coat pocket and handed it over.

"I'm texting myself. Use this number when you get home safe, let us know."

"I do have Jesse's number already in there," she pointed out.

"And now you have mine. You can text both of us, if it makes you feel better."

She tried to argue, but Jesse gave her a kiss on the cheek, Grant a smile full of heat that she assumed meant Jesse would be getting more attention when they got home, and she fumbled herself into the car. She managed to give the driver her address and spent the ten-minute drive trying to get herself under control. She mostly succeeded.

It only took a few minutes after getting through her front door to send the text, get naked, and climb into bed.

CHAPTER TWO

Though she'd been out late, Stephanie didn't sleep in much more than usual on Sunday. Her Pilates routine and breakfast of fresh fruit and oatmeal energized her and she did some work on one of her client's fitness plans, even though she'd promised herself the day off. Still, work when she didn't *have* to work was actually enjoyable, especially when she knew she could stop at any moment.

She'd just finished coming up with some new routines for a client she'd had for a couple of years, when her cell phone buzzed. The number came up as not being in her contacts, but looked familiar. As she was bringing the phone to her ear, she realized it was Grant. She could hear the smile in her voice as she answered.

"Hello?"

"Stephanie? It's Grant and Jesse." Grant's deep voice sounded warm and inviting.

"Good morning, sunshine!" Jesse's voice was enthusiastic and she guessed he was a morning person, like her.

"Hey guys, how nice to hear from you."

"We decided we didn't get enough of you last night, so you need to come over for dinner." Jesse said.

She laughed. "Is that right?"

"Definitely," Grant said. "Our place, six-thirty. I'll text you the address."

"I don't know about this," she teased. "Who's doing the cooking?"

"The Thai restaurant on the corner," Grant answered.

She laughed again. "Sounds good, then. I look forward to it."

"Not as much as we do," Jesse singsonged.

Hanging up, she was glad they'd called. She'd always enjoyed Jesse's friendship and had been pleased when he'd quickly snatched up Grant within months of the other man joining Apex. That had been, what? Seven months ago? Something like that.

Watching their scenes had been an exercise in pleasure and frustration. Pleasure because it made her hot and because she was happy to see Jesse match up with someone who complemented him so well. Frustration because though she'd known Jesse was gay and therefore off the table as far as potential play partner, she'd heard that Grant was bi and had been hoping to get a shot at him. Once she'd seen the two together, though, it had been obvious their relationship was special and she was content to watch and gain what pleasures she could from that.

Since she had the phone in her hand, she decided it was a good time to call her parents. They had a close relationship, though it had certainly gone through its ups and downs. Her friends had thought she was nuts for telling her parents about becoming active in the BDSM lifestyle, but she hadn't even considered not letting them in on such an integral part of her life. She'd waited six months or so, until she'd felt confident it was something that was always going to be part of who she was, rather than a phase or simple experimentation.

The fact that her dad was a cop made it both easier and harder. Easier because he wasn't an idiot, knew there were things out there that he didn't have to understand exactly in order to appreciate that they were right for an individual. Harder, because he was most familiar with the times the lifestyle could be dangerous. But that also meant that he forced himself to deal with it, become comfortable with it, because he preferred her telling him about it, to an extent, than keeping it hidden from him and not letting him advise her on safety issues.

So, even though she'd known Jesse for a while, and even though she was going to their house for dinner, not play, because she'd met them through the club, she would give her dad their names and address and let him know she was going to their house.

It was an extension of the request he'd made when she'd gone into business for herself as a personal trainer. Give him the names of clients she was meeting outside of gyms. Even as she knew it was unnecessary overkill, she appreciated that her dad wanted to see her safe. He didn't want to hear about what she got up to at the club, specifically, but he'd checked up on it, on the owners, and given his approval on its reputation.

Her mom answered the phone and they chatted about both of their work, as well as family gossip. When her mom passed the phone to her dad, they talked about his opinion on the mess that was Maine politics and the weather. Both of which he would never stop bitching about but also never consider moving to get away from. Eventually she told him about her dinner plans.

She always gave him the names of the people she played with outside of the club, though it was rare. She generally gave him the names of the people she played with inside the club, as well, though she felt a little weird about it. She knew that sometimes he ran their names, but she did trust him not to do anything bad with the information. Still, last night gave her pause but since she didn't ever intend to play with Trevor again, she didn't mention him.

The whole name thing was more to make him feel better about her safety than because she thought he would find anything to caution her about. Though he had twice asked her not to see someone because of the information he'd found, he hadn't told her what the information was and in both cases she'd already decided she didn't want to continue playing with those Doms. She couldn't deny that she was curious, but she didn't ask for details. She'd subtly given her opinion to a couple other subs who'd seemed interested and neither Dom had lasted long as members of the club.

By the time she'd hung up the phone, she was ready to get out of the house. The weather was cold but dry, so she decided to do her grocery run. When she got home, she took a long, hot soak. Her favorite waterproof toy and her imagination of how Grant and Jesse had looked last night made for a very pleasurable bath. She dried her hair, ate lunch, then lost herself in a romance novel until it was time to get ready for dinner.

She considered taking a cab but she had a client session early the next morning so she wouldn't be drinking much, even if that were an option. She decided to drive and made good time, getting to their apartment building with plenty of time to search out a parking space and still make it to their door five minutes early.

JESSE HOVERED near the front door, waiting for the buzzer to announce Stephanie's arrival. Grant wandered by and slapped his ass, but didn't stay to obsess like Jesse was.

He wanted tonight to go well. He wanted that very badly, since last night had gone so well. When they'd gone to Apex, they'd been hoping to see Stephanie, been disappointed when she hadn't been there. Seeing her at the last minute, as they were getting ready to leave, had been great. Seeing her in a not-so-wonderful situation, had sucked. It had worked out in the end and he was hopeful that it would work out even better tonight.

He'd thought about her a lot since things with Grant had calmed down from the initial all-consuming start of their relationship. When Grant had asked him if he'd ever consider adding a woman to their play, Steph had immediately sprung to mind.

He'd been attracted to her before he'd met Grant, but hadn't really known what to do with it. He was gay, after all. It had been silly, not knowing how to move forward, if she would welcome an advance from him, since they were friends. But he'd never been interested enough in a woman to have tried before, so he'd been sort of frozen. And then Grant had come into the club, and the attraction had been instant and overwhelming.

The buzzer sounded and he almost squeaked, but managed to hold back the embarrassing reaction. He looked over his shoulder and found Grant watching him with an amused smile. He hit the button that would open the lobby door for Stephanie, and unlocked and opened their front door. It would take her a minute to get up to the third floor.

He looked back at Grant. "We're set, right? We see if either of us has an opportunity to make a move on her, see if she's open to the idea, but you know it's most likely going to be you. She sees me as her gay friend, not someone she's interested in fucking."

"I told you, you didn't see her face last night when she was imagining you tied to the web," Grant reminded him.

"She snuggled up to me—"

"I noticed," Grant drawled.

"—because she thinks I'm safe. Gay. Non-sexual in her world."

"Mmm, hmm. I repeat, you didn't see her face when she was imagining you tied to the web."

"All right, all right, so we need to think positively and make this happen."

"It's going to happen," Grant said.

They shut up as the door to the stairwell opened. He had to smile. Stephanie was the only friend he knew who would have taken the stairs instead of the elevator. He certainly appreciated the athletic beauty of her body, but her soft brown girl-next-door eyes contrasted by her elegant blonde hair that was turned uber-sassy by the ever-colored streak she added to it was what really did it for him. Her current color was purple, though the last time he'd seen her it had been pink.

He pulled her into the apartment with a hug, then passed her off to Grant with a tiny shove. Grant rolled his eyes at him, but gave her a tight little hug.

"What would you like to drink?" Jesse asked. "Wine, beer?"

"I'll save the beer for when we're eating. Nothing right now, thanks." She smiled at him. "Are you going to show me around?"

He waved his arms to indicate the small space. "Nothing worth seeing, I promise. We've been looking for places to buy, actually." He led her to the couch and wasn't at all subtle about maneuvering her so she was sitting between them, though it meant they were all practically on top of each other.

"Oh, that's great! It's such a tough market though. Do you have a pretty good idea of what you want?"

He turned into her before answering, putting a hand on her knee. He felt like he was back in high school, but he was determined for her to see him as a possible sexual partner, not a buddy. Grant mirrored him on her other side, but without the hand on her knee.

"Yes, we think so. But it's so hard to know until you find the right thing," he said.

"Oh, sure. I keep thinking I should look for a place, too. Business is going really well. But I just have this nagging doubt, like what if I meet the man of my dreams and he already has a place, or together we'd want a completely different kind of place than I'll want on my own. Or, the fact is, right now I'm single, and since I work for myself I could decide to go anywhere, anytime. Nothing is keeping me here other than friends and being somewhat close to family. A mortgage would change that, tie me down."

"Do you want to go somewhere else?" Grant asked.

She shrugged. "Not so far. But the possibility, the option, is there."

"Where is your family?" Jesse asked.

"Maine. That's where I grew up. I like having some distance, but being close enough to go see them whenever I want. Not that I get up there all that often, but holidays, big birthdays, that kind of thing."

She'd left her hair down again, so Jesse reached up and tucked it behind her ear, then pulled a hank free and wound it around his finger. She blinked at him, but didn't say anything, or move away.

"That's nice. You're close with them?" he asked.

"Sure. I talk to my parents usually every weekend. My brother comes down to visit every so often. He's younger, just getting out of

PERFECT ADDITION

college, trying to decide where he wants to go. I think he'll probably stay in Maine, but he's exploring his options right now."

"That's great that you have that," Grant told her.

"You don't?" she asked.

"My family's okay. They try, but they're still waiting for me to grow out of the 'gay phase', and hoping it happens soon."

"Ouch." She turned to Jesse. "What about your parents?"

"It's only my mom, but she's pretty cool. We're not super close, but she doesn't have a problem with my being gay."

"No siblings?"

"Nope. I have some cousins that I see every few years. They invite me to weddings and whatnot. They're cool."

"That's good. My extended family is pretty big."

He gave a sharp tug on her hair and she retaliated by poking him in the stomach. He was very tempted to start a tickle fight. A classic hands-on maneuver for a reason. But he didn't think she was ready and thought Grant would be better off making the first move. Hopefully the first of many.

"Come on," he said, "let's go pick up dinner."

He gave her the menu and once they'd all decided, called the order in. By the time they walked down the stairs that he'd only used once or twice before, and down the block to the restaurant, the food was ready. It wasn't long before they were back, seated at the dining room table, and digging in.

"Oh, wow, this place is good," Stephanie said after a couple of bites.

"Would we steer you wrong?" Grant asked.

She laughed. "Of course not, I didn't doubt you, I promise. I just didn't expect it to be *this* good." She took another bite, then waved her fork at them. "So, I take it neither of you cooks?"

"We can make scrambled eggs and omelets as well as the next guy," Jesse defended.

"Steaks, burgers and baked potatoes too," Grant added.

"Please tell me you manage some vegetables in there somewhere," she demanded.

"Um. Sure. We eat out at least once a week, and there's almost always vegetables on the side," Jesse assured her.

She rolled her eyes at him. He suspected if they convinced her to come around more often, they were going to have to up their vegetable intake significantly. He could live with that.

"So, after dinner, movie or monopoly?" Jesse asked.

The look on her face was positively demonic. "Probably best that we watch a movie so that I don't make you cry in your own house."

Grant raised his beer towards her. "Oh, it's on now."

She shrugged. "If you're sure you can handle a beating."

"Oh, honey, I know which end of a beating I like to be on."

"Too bad we don't always get what we want, then, isn't it?"

"Don't I?" Grant asked.

"Bring it, mister tough guy."

"I'll clear the table, you guys set up the game," Jesse said, laughing. Grant was competitive, but not that much, not over a board game. He just liked firing her up, Jesse knew. And Jesse liked watching him do it.

He stacked their dishes and took them into the kitchen. He gave them a thorough rinse before slotting them into the dishwasher, then made coffee and pulled out cream and sugar.

It couldn't have been much more than five minutes before he walked into the dining room to ask how Stephanie liked her coffee, so he was shocked to see her pulling on her coat, heading to the front door, Grant staring after her, a look of uncertainty on his face.

"Hey!"

"Sorry, sorry, I forgot something." She was opening the door, not really looking at him. "I have to go now."

"But—" He looked to Grant, but the man was just standing there, scowling.

"Got to go! I'll talk to you later."

And she was gone.

Grant continued staring at the door until Jesse stepped right in front of him. "What the hell happened?"

"She freaked out."

"I see that. What did you do, command her to strip off all of her clothes or something?"

Grant gave him a look of disgust. "No, of course not." He shook his head, sighed. "I, well...like we talked about. Made a move. A small one."

He looked uncomfortable, not a state Jesse was used to seeing his partner in. As unhappy as he was with Stephanie's rapid exit, he couldn't help but see the amusement in the situation. Still, out of respect, he tried to keep it from showing.

"Okay, baby, but what did you do?" He put his hands on Grant's waist.

The aggrieved look was tempered by a blush. An actual *blush*. Grant wasn't used to being shot down and he certainly wasn't used to having to tell his lover about it.

Jesse bit down on the inside of his lip to keep from smiling.

"I uh, put my hand on the back of her neck, you know, rubbed my thumb up and down a bit. I said how glad we were to run into her last night, and I, you know, looked into her eyes." He ran a hand through his hair and Jesse squeezed his hands on Grants hips. "I swear there was attraction there, Jess. I'm not so out of it that I don't know when someone's attracted to me instead of repulsed by me. And she shivered. You *know* what kind of shiver. Then she just, gave a little jerk, ducked under my arm, and headed for her coat."

Jesse tried to imagine the scene, picture what could have gone wrong. He knew exactly how the move Grant had described would go over on someone who was attracted to him. The heat, the need, *oh yeah*, he knew the shiver that had worked its way through Stephanie. And he was positive Grant was right. She was attracted to him. Hadn't he been insisting on that very thing to Grant all day? So, she was attracted, and Grant gave her the sign that *he* was attracted. It should have been...*oh*.

"Oh."

"What."

"I think I know what happened."

"*What?*"

"She thinks you're bislutual."

Grant blinked at him. "She—I—*what?*"

Jesse started to answer but Grant interrupted him. "No, wait. I get it." He sighed again. "You think *she* thinks that I made a move on her behind your back."

"Right. She thinks that since you're bi, and you hit on her, you must be one of those sluts who thinks it's okay to cheat on his partner as long as it's with someone of the opposite sex."

"Great. Has a high opinion of me, doesn't she?" He pulled free of Jesse's hold and walked to the couch, dropped down into it.

"Well, from her perspective, you did wait until I was out of the room to make your move."

"You told me to!"

This time Jesse couldn't hold back the laugh. "I know baby. It's all my fault."

Grant's glare indicated he didn't appreciate the apology or the laughter.

"If you think about it, she was just being a good friend to me. I bet you money she contacts me to have a talk. Warn me about you."

Grant slouched back against the couch. "Great."

Jesse fell back next to him, but put a comforting hand on his man's thigh. "It's okay, baby, we can fix this."

"Yeah, yeah."

Grant shifted next to him, turning into him, but Jesse didn't open his eyes, afraid he'd laugh again.

"You laughed."

"Um."

A sudden sharp pain as his nipple was tweaked through his shirt. "Ouch!" he cried, opening his eyes. The amusement dancing in Grant's eyes took the last of the sting away. He couldn't help himself. He wrapped his arms around the other man and burst into laughter. Grant joined him and they ended up in each other's arms, lying across the couch. Of course, Grant managed to be on top.

Finally Grant rested his forearms next to Jesse's head and looked at him. "What should we do? Would it be too stalker-ish if we showed up at her place and tried to explain?"

"Do we know where she lives?"

"I think we could find out."

"Hmm. Maybe too far. But I don't know if she'd agree to meet up with us if we asked."

"And she might not even have gone straight home."

"Shit."

"Well, I guess we try her phone and see what happens."

Grant pulled out his phone and handed it to Jesse.

Jesse rolled his eyes at him and shoved him back so he could sit up.

He pulled out his own phone, scrolled to Stephanie's name and typed a message.

Hey sweetie, it's Jesse. Are you okay? I can explain, I promise, it's nothing bad. Can I call you?

They sat and stared at the phone for a minute. The perils of becoming used to instant gratification.

Jesse started to pick up the pieces of the Monopoly game laid out on the coffee table and return them to the box.

Grant stood up. "I'm getting a beer. You want one?"

"Yes, please."

The phone beeped just as Grant returned, setting both bottles onto the coffee table.

What did he tell you?

Jesse typed quickly. *Let me call you. Better, let us come talk to you.*

Her response this time was very quick. *What did he tell you?*

"Christ." Grant stopped watching him type and dropped back against the couch again.

"It's fine. It will be fine," Jesse assured him.

He told me he sort of hit on you. It's not what you think. Can we come explain?

This time there was a longer pause, but Jesse held tight.

When the phone beeped again, Grant gave up ignoring and read the screen too.

I'm still downstairs. In my car. I can come up, if you're sure it's a good idea.

Yes! I promise. It's all good. Please come back up.

Another pause.

Ok

"Woot!" Jesse leaned in and gave Grant a celebratory kiss.

Grant gave him a cautious smile. "Do we still want to do this? Or do we just apologize and move on."

Jesse gaped at him. This was so unlike his man. "Seriously? You're going to give up that easily?"

Grant gave him the look that said he'd underestimated his Dom. "Only if you want to. If you're uncomfortable."

Jesse retuned the look with two raised eyebrows. "Oh, please. We made a strategic error. Now it's time to fess up and put it all out on the table. Make this happen."

Grant's smile was wolfish. "Then let's do this thing."

CHAPTER THREE

Grant would admit, at least to himself, that the last few minutes had been a bit of a confidence shaker. He was not used to being rejected so quickly and thoroughly. Stephanie had practically run out of the apartment while he'd stood there gaping like an idiot.

It wasn't that he hadn't been turned down before. But never by someone he was that interested in or at least, not without a reasonable understanding of why. The person was already involved, or turned out they weren't a sub. *Something!*

Now that they'd realized what had happened, he felt back on even keel. Mostly.

The door to the stairway opened and he stepped back, letting Jesse go out into the hallway to encourage Stephanie inside. He only had a minute to decide how he should play it. Sheepish? Stern? Amused? It was a tricky situation, he didn't want to get her back up even more before they had a chance to explain.

He hadn't quite decided when they walked through the door, so he did what he almost always did. Went with instinct.

Jesse had barely closed the door and Steph was trying to avoid his eyes.

He took the two steps needed to move straight into her, one hand on her hip, one hand on Jesse's arm, and he kissed her.

He saw her eyes go huge as he came in. Her eyes remained open, darting to Jesse's face to judge his expression, Grant was sure. He felt Jesse move in closer, his arm going behind Grant's back in support, whether physical or psychological, Grant wasn't sure.

He teased her lips, kissed the corners, played with the full lower lip, flicked his tongue at the seam. Finally, she opened for him. Just a bit, a tiny gap.

All he needed.

He took full possession and she responded as he'd hoped she would. Her hands came up to his chest, gripping his shirt to pull him closer, her eyes drifting shut. He pushed back until she was against the door, Jesse's body a warm presence at his side, his voice a low murmur in Stephanie's ear.

Probably he should be trying to listen to whatever Jesse was telling her. Not possible. He was too consumed by the kiss, the sweet softness of her lips, the gentle torture of her tongue, the amazing relief of her surrender.

When the impulse to shove his knee between her legs surfaced, he let his brain regain control of his body. Easing back slowly, leaving his hands were they'd come to be, cupping her jaw, fingers in her hair, he stood up straight and looked at her.

Her eyes stayed closed for two seconds. Her lips were puffy and wet and red and only the fact that her lashes lifted distracted him enough to keep him from going back for more.

She stared at him wide-eyed, didn't say a word.

"How did she taste?" Jesse whispered.

His Jesse. How he loved the man. "Perfect," he answered, enjoying the shock that raced across her face.

Dropping his hands, he stepped back another full step and put his arm around Jesse so that they stood together, watching her. Her eyes darted left to right, taking them in as she tried to process what had just happened.

"Well," she finally said. "Damn."

He smiled. "Is that a good damn, or a bad damn?" he asked.

"That's a *hot* damn."

Slowly, he reached his free hand out, touched her arm in apology, let it show on his face. "I'm sorry about earlier. We fumbled that pretty badly. Can you come sit down? Talk about it?"

Her smile was rueful. "I'm not certain I'm capable of rational speech at the moment."

Jesse laughed. "I think that sentence proves otherwise."

She smiled. "Well, let's give it a shot, anyway."

He motioned for her to lead the way, taking the opportunity to look at Jesse. The man's grin was happiness, excitement and laughter all in one. He just shook his head and followed them into the living room.

Jesse was, of course, trying to get Stephanie to sit in the middle of the couch. Grant approved of this plan. Steph was balking. Then she looked up at him, her face still soft from his kiss, but her eyes a little bit pleading. "I can't think right, sandwiched between you guys."

Well, yeah, that was sort of the intention. But the fact that she turned to him, that it was obvious he could pretty easily talk her into sitting where they wanted her, but she was asking him to help her stay strong, was intoxicating. Either that, or she was playing him with those wide eyes. Not in a bad way, but, still, he wondered which was the case.

He held out his hand, and she placed hers in his with a little sigh. Pulling her forward, he turned and lowered her so that she was sitting on the coffee table. He let her go, took Jesse's arm and dragged him down so they were on the couch, across from her, Jesse's long legs making their knees bump a little.

It might make the conversation a lot longer than if they just overwhelmed her with sex, but then they'd just end up having the conversation over and over again. Hopefully, this way, once it was over, it would be over.

"I'm sorry," Grant started. "I didn't mean to distress you."

"I'll admit, I was really sad to think you were an asshole and that

Jesse was going to be upset. You guys make such a great couple, I've been so happy for you, seeing what you have together. Jealous, even. So, it sucks, thinking that might be over. Or, what? I don't know, I'm really confused."

"Jealous that we have something you want?" Jesse asked. "Or jealous that I have Grant, specifically."

"And that I have Jesse," Grant added.

"Um. Yeah, pretty much all of that. I don't want to see you fuck any of that up."

"Steph, we're very happy together. That's not a question. It also doesn't mean we don't think about making things even better."

She frowned. "I really don't understand." Turning to Jesse, she accused, "You want to share him? Let him have fun with other people?"

"Not exactly," Jesse said. "We both want to have fun. With you. Not other people. Just you."

"You're gay!"

He laughed and Grant smiled.

"What?" Jesse asked. "Are you telling me that if you met the right woman, someone you found attractive, enjoyed their company and wanted to get to know them better, you would turn your back because you're straight? You're more open than that, more aware."

She shook her head. "You've been looking for the right guy, the right *top*, since I've met you! And you didn't come onto me when you were single."

"You're right. That's what I was looking for. And I found him. So now, I can explore a little more." He leaned forward, his hand sliding on her knee, moving under to cup her leg, just above the knee. "I was attracted to you back then. Very much so. I just wasn't quite sure what to do with it. And like you said, I need a top, which you're not."

Stephanie stared at Jesse for a minute, then moved her look to Grant. He hated to see the confusion in her eyes, the uncertainty. He moved forward on the couch so that his leg was touching hers, thigh to thigh. He took her hand and gave her a reassuring squeeze.

"We're not trying to freak you out here. It's pretty simple really. We love each other. We like you, a lot, are attracted to you, a lot, and want to get to know you better. In a lot of ways."

"So, you guys talked about me?"

This time her confusion was adorable and he couldn't resist leaning forward and giving her a quick kiss on the lips. He was back in his seat before she could do anything other than blink at him.

"Yes, we talked about you. About a month ago, I guess, after we were, um, well satisfied I guess you could say, Jesse asked me about girls. I told him my most serious relationship before him had been a girl, but that mostly I'd dated guys."

"I admit it," Jesse said. "There was that tiny worry that he'd eventually want to quit playing around and settle down with a woman. He tied me up and had me begging for mercy until I promised that I understood that what we had together had nothing to do with gender and everything to do with who I was and who *he* was."

She smiled a sweet smile, then frowned. "So...I don't get it, what is *this*?"

Jesse waggled his eyebrows at her.

Grant laughed. "When he asked about women, I could tell that part of him was worried, like he said, but there was something in his voice that made me think he might be considering a specific woman. I may have tortured him for further information."

"And he mentioned me."

"He mentioned you. And he didn't need to tell me how much he wanted you. I could see it, easily. Besides, I remembered you, too. I knew exactly who he was talking about. Thinking about. Imagining."

Her eyes grew rounder as he spoke.

Jesse's voice softened. "We're not saying we expect anything from you. We just want to get to know you. Explore the possibilities."

"You would risk what you have, for that? For me?"

"We don't think it's a risk. We have a good, solid relationship. We're not worried about that."

Grant squeezed her hand again. "We're not trying to overwhelm you, or trick you, or talk you into something you don't want to do. I guess we did a pretty piss poor job of enticing you."

"If I weren't, uh, enticed, this wouldn't be so difficult."

"We can stop," Grant said, smiling when Jesse started to object. "For tonight. Let you go home and think about things. Nothing needs to happen right now. We didn't really mean for it to go very far tonight. Maybe just talk you into a play date at the club or something."

"I meant it to go far tonight," Jesse grumbled.

"You didn't make a move on me!" Stephanie said.

"That's because you had me in the gay-friend box and you refused to see me as something else. I told Grant he had to make the first move."

They both just looked at him until he dropped his eyes and mumbled, "Okay, that turned out to be a mistake."

Stephanie laughed and he joined her. It was a good sound. And a good look on her. He leaned forward more, very much into her personal space.

"We don't have to start anything tonight," he said, his voice low. "But we can give you something to think about."

She swallowed. "You've already done that. No question."

He smiled. "I think we can do better, don't you, Jess?"

"Oh yeah." He could hear the smile in Jesse's voice.

Grant brushed his fingers lightly across her cheek, tucked her hair behind her ear.

"How long has it been since you kissed a girl, baby?"

"Let's see, junior year in college. So, eleven years or so," Jesse answered.

She was watching him, reacting to their words, the color up in her cheeks, her eyes bright. He wanted to nibble on her freckles. He couldn't believe he'd never really noticed them before. They were light, probably covered easily with makeup.

"Kiss her, Jesse. I want to watch."

He didn't move back, didn't give her space. Jesse came up next to him, moving slowly, both of them watching her. Her breath was coming in quick pants now and she licked her lips. He managed not to smile.

"Do you want that, Steph? Do you want him to kiss you?"

Her "yes" was a puff of breath, nothing more.

Jesse didn't hesitate any more. He moved straight in, claiming her lips. Her hand came out, gripped Grant's knee tight, tighter. "Sweet, isn't she, Jess? I already want more."

Jesse didn't answer but Stephanie gave a tiny moan. Her other hand had moved up into Jesse's hair, pulling him in even as she moved closer.

"He's a great kisser, isn't he?" he murmured in her ear. "He's been wanting to do this for a while now. He told me how badly he wanted to taste you. Your lips. Your pussy. He's never tasted pussy." Her fingers dug into his knee and he decided it was time to stop them, as much as he hated to do it.

He put one hand on the back of each of their necks, and squeezed slightly. "Time to stop now. I think we've given Stephanie enough to think about."

When Jesse didn't immediately stop the kiss, he squeezed harder. One of them sighed, though he wasn't sure who, and they separated.

They both had that dazed look that he loved to see, though he usually liked to be responsible for it himself. He was rock hard from watching them, they were both so fucking sexy. He wanted to see them naked and entwined and at his mercy. He wanted that very badly.

"Jesse, why don't you go get Steph a glass of water?"

It took him a second, but Jesse nodded and went to the kitchen. Stephanie's fingers slowly released their hold on him and she leaned back. He let her, moved back a touch himself.

"I meant it when I said that we still want to be your friend, even if you don't want to take this to the bedroom or the club."

She swallowed and nodded. "All right. I'll, uh, think about all of this. You guys definitely took me by surprise."

He gave her the smile that Jesse swore made him lose IQ points.

"Tell me one thing. Have you ever had a fantasy that involved two men?"

She looked him up and down, then glanced over at Jesse as he walked back into the room. "Ohhh, yeah," she drawled.

He lifted his eyebrows. "Then why are you giving us such a hard time? Why aren't we taking this to the bedroom right now?"

She rolled her eyes at him. "Men. I fantasized about you guys because you were safe." She waved her hand between them. "Safe because you were a couple and I do not poach."

He dipped his head. "Fair enough." He snuck a look at Jesse, who was grinning widely at the news she'd fantasized about them. His own smug grin was fighting to get free, but he held back.

She accepted the glass from Jesse and took a long drink, her eyes on them the whole time. When she was done, she handed the glass back to Jesse and smiled. "Well, boys, you've definitely given me a lot to think about. I better get to that."

They walked her to the door and watched as she sauntered down the hall to the stairway. She looked over her shoulder before letting the door close, and called back, "Thanks for thinking about me."

STEPHANIE'S MIND was whirling as she left the guys' apartment. This was definitely *not* how she'd imagined their evening playing out.

When Grant had made a move on her, she'd been horrified. She hated cheaters. The betrayal of trust was just too much for her to deal with. She'd actually lost friendships over it, people who'd expected her to understand their situation and found her too judgmental when she told them she thought they were doing the wrong thing and couldn't support their decisions.

It had been a blow to think that Grant would cheat on Jesse. She'd rushed out in nearly a panic, not sure how she wanted to handle it, needing some time and space to figure out the best way to move forward. Right or wrong, she wouldn't have been able to keep it a secret from Jesse. Her heart had hurt for her friend and she'd sat in her car, unable to decide what step to take next.

When her phone had buzzed with his text, she hadn't known what to think. Certainly hadn't expected what happened next. Grant's kiss had been...well, she really couldn't think of any words to describe what that had been like. And when Jesse had started whispering in her ear, she'd gotten so turned on she hadn't known which way was up.

She sat in her car again, but this time she was trying to calm her thundering heart and raring libido before driving.

Opening the window a crack to get fresh, crisp air, she dropped her head back. *Holy hotness.* As she'd said, she'd considered threesomes in the past. Fantasized about them. Fantasized about them with Grant and Jesse. And yet, two kisses, two fully clothed kisses, blew those fantasies out of the water.

Smiling, she put the car in gear and drove home. There was no way she wasn't going to see the guys again. She just had to sort of wrap her brain around it. It wasn't like she didn't know about open relationships. She'd seen them in action and had no problem with them, since there was no lying, no betrayal. But she'd honestly never considered being involved with one herself, in any capacity.

They'd insisted that being with her was no danger to their relationship. She tried to decide if she should be insulted by that. It was good that they trusted their relationship, and it was intriguing that they wanted her, but wow, they weren't even a tiny bit worried they'd want to keep her around for more than play?

Well, what the hell was her problem with that? She *wanted* to play with them and they were handing the opportunity to her on a silver platter. If they had approached her in the club, invited her into a scene, she wouldn't have thought twice about it.

So, why was she now?

She was *so* going to play with them. The key would be to watch her heart. She already adored Jesse, was attracted to both of them. To play, have fun together, but not mix that up with a relationship, that was going to be the tough part.

Walking into her apartment, she dropped her keys on the little shelf by the door and slung her purse on its hook. It was a small space, but it was hers, and it was right in the city. She'd added touches of color in the pillows, a couple of pieces of artwork her mother had given her. The gray couch was a fold-out, where her brother stayed when he came to visit. The bedroom was barely big enough to hold a dresser in addition to the full bed, but it worked. She sat on the end of the bed and took off her boots, then shimmied out of her jeans.

Her sweater and bra quickly followed and she bundled up into her comfy sweats and slippers. She climbed onto her bed and opened her book. The book was good, but it was still a struggle to lose herself in it. She brushed her teeth, washed her face, and shrugged out of the sweats and climbed into bed, tried to make herself sleep. Eventually, she managed it.

FIVE CAME AWFULLY EARLY. Luckily, there wasn't much she needed to do to be ready for her five-thirty appointment besides brushing her hair and teeth. A very light touch of makeup and pulling on her workout gear was it, and she was out the door. The cold was a slap to her face when she exited the building, though somehow it didn't do much to wake her up. That was fine; her workout with one of her favorite clients would manage the task perfectly.

She was busy with clients and paperwork until well after lunch, but she had Grant and Jesse and their potential running through her mind most of that time. They figured the next move was hers, which was exhilarating and nerve-racking at the same time. At first she'd leaned towards asking them to meet her at Apex. It seemed the smartest plan and she did love playing at the club. In fact, she'd rarely had scenes *outside* of the club. Part of it was safety, part of it was the energy of the club, the equipment, the special rooms, the audience.

But maybe it would be hard for her, when they'd had enough fun experimenting with a woman in their play, to go back to the club without them. If she kept things outside of the club, it would be clean of memories of the three of them together.

She wasn't worried about playing at their apartment. After all, she'd already been there and not been hacked into small pieces. But not going to the club, choosing their home instead, that was...

Her brain shied away from it at first, but she had to be honest with herself. It added a level of intimacy, and she didn't want to go there unwittingly. If she opened herself up to that, it would be with full knowledge of what she was doing, what she was risking.

She would think of their home as a vacation island. A place apart from reality, so that when their adventure together came to an end, they could resume their friendship and seeing each other at Apex would be fun, not painful.

She parked in a space in front of her favorite adult toy store. Usually she preferred to buy her toys online, but she liked to see the sexy lingerie in person. If she was going to have a special night with Jesse and Grant, she felt it deserved a special outfit.

Though she was there for the clothes, she wandered down the toy aisles, looking for anything new and interesting to catch her attention. She was reaching for a vibrating butt plug when her phone rang. She pulled it free from her purse and checked the screen.

Grant.

Her heart rate picked up as she smiled and answered the call. She kind of liked the idea that he hadn't been able to wait a whole day to check in and see if she'd made up her mind.

"Hi, Grant."

"Steph. Are you ready for us?"

She blinked, then leaned against the shelves. His sexy, commanding voice left little doubt about what he'd meant, though her brain tried to pretend otherwise.

"Ready?"

"What's the next night you have free with no clients the following day?" he asked.

"Um. Friday my last client is at three and I don't have anyone else until Sunday afternoon."

"We'll pick you up Friday at seven-thirty."

She shook her head, even though he couldn't see her, feeling like she'd somehow fallen two steps behind. Wasn't she supposed to be making the next move?

"I thought you were giving me some time to think about this," she reminded him.

"I did."

"That wasn't even a whole day," she protested.

"Your point?"

"What if I hadn't decided to go forward?"

"You didn't decide that."

He was so damn cocky, she wanted to tell him he was wrong, but, damn it, she found his take-charge attitude as sexy as it was annoying. Which didn't make any sense, but whatever.

"I can just come to your place or the club, you don't have to pick me up."

"We're not going to either. We'll pick you up at seven-thirty. We'll get you home Sunday morning, in plenty of time for your appointment."

She straightened back up and moved towards the lingerie section, without saying anything.

"Say 'Yes, Sir.'"

Her sex clenched at his words, his tone.

"What if I don't know yet?" she asked, dismayed at how breathy the question sounded.

"You know you want to do this. You're just trying to take control of the situation, because you didn't expect it. Didn't plan it, or plan *for* it. You're used to making arrangements at the club, so the situation was in your control, even if the scene wasn't."

She'd come to a complete stop at his words, one hand raised to stroke the leather of a bustier on the rack in front of her, her other hand clutching the phone tightly. Was he right? She wanted to say no. She liked being a submissive, after all. Liked giving up control. But his words resonated deep within her.

Her hand dropped to her side and she stood there, waiting.

"Say 'Yes, Sir.'"

PERFECT ADDITION

She swallowed, hard. "Yes, Sir."

"Text me your address when you have a minute."

"Yes, Sir."

"You don't need to bring much, but pack something dressy, we'll take you out to dinner."

Her whole world had narrowed down to the phone in her hand, the voice in her ear. His voice had gotten lower, and she pressed the phone in hard to hear him clearly. "Yes, Sir."

"When you think about us tonight, this week, when you're trying to go to sleep but your body just won't stop imagining what it will be like…"

He paused, and she realized she'd whimpered out loud, but she couldn't care enough to lift her head and see if anyone was close enough to have heard.

"I want you to touch yourself," he continued. "When you pinch your nipples, think of Jesse's fingers doing the pinching. When you slide a finger through your slickness, it better be *my* finger you're imagining. No toys allowed. Just our fingers, working you, enjoying you, learning you. Do you understand?"

She tried to answer, had to clear her throat to manage it. "Yes, Sir."

"Good girl. Do you have any allergies I need to be aware of?"

She scrunched her forehead, trying to make sense of the change in topic. "No, no allergies."

"All right. I'll see you Friday night. I'll be thinking about you a lot this week, it's only fair you do the same."

She took a deep breath, pulling herself out of the hazy cloud of lust she'd fallen into. Mostly. "I think that's a pretty safe bet."

"Good. You okay to get back to what you were doing?"

"Yeah. I'm good."

"Yes, you are. " The smile in his voice was obvious and brought one to her own lips.

"Goodbye, Grant."

"Goodbye, Stephanie."

She hung up the phone and looked around. Nobody seemed to

be paying her too much attention. Quickly scanning the racks, she picked out a virginal, lacy white thong that was crotchless, and matching bra designed to just barely cover the nipples. The lacy cups would rub against her, keeping her hard and ready for the boys.

Making her purchases quickly, she went home and stressed about what she was going to pack, and tried to figure out how she was going to make it through the four days and three nights without losing her mind.

Tuesday morning, after her second client appointment, she saw that she had a voicemail from Jesse. Not sure what to expect, she rolled her eyes when the message simply asked her to call him, without giving any hints as to what was up. She selected the call-back button and had to smile when he answered cheerfully.

"Steph!"

"Hi, Jesse."

"I cannot believe I have to wait until Friday to see you. Don't you miss me?"

She laughed. "I do, yes, but I'm not sure I can handle too much of a good thing, you know?"

"Well, there is that. Are you busy?"

"Just walking home. My client appointment was at a gym only a few blocks away."

"Good. I want you to tell me about last night."

She frowned. "What about last night?"

"About however you imagined me touching you last night!" His tone clearly implied he shouldn't have to explain himself.

"Jesse!" She looked around, but of course nobody on the sidewalk was paying any attention to her or her conversation.

"Fine. You want me to tell you about how I imagined *you* touching *me*, last night?"

"Aren't you gay?" she asked. Sure, he'd indicated very clearly he

PERFECT ADDITION

wanted to get naked with her, but apparently she still had her doubts.

"So?"

She had to laugh. So Jesse. "Point taken." She'd reached her building and told him to hold on while she fished her keys out and opened the lobby door. She grabbed her mail and put the phone back to her ear as she ascended the stairs. "So, I thought you guys were letting me decide what I wanted to do. Then I get that phone call from Grant? He seems to have leapt over asking and into telling."

"You say that like it's a bad thing."

She had to laugh, again. "Yeah, at Apex, sure. But, out in the real world? I don't play that way. I may be submissive in the bedroom, but that's it. I guess I need to make sure he knows that."

Jesse was quiet for a second, and she appreciated that he wasn't going to just gloss over what she'd said. "Okay. It's like this. You said you're submissive in the bedroom only, but you don't mean that literally, because you mostly play at the club. Right?"

"Right," she agreed. "It's an expression. If we're in a scene, I guess I should say."

"Or negotiating a scene. And if you're at the club, even if you're not playing with a Dom, you'll generally give them a certain respect, behave a certain way."

She snorted. "Unless they're like that asshole Trevor, and I've lost all respect for them," she agreed.

"Exactly. 'In the bedroom' is more of a concept, and you're used to living that concept somewhat narrowly. When's the last time you had a relationship with a Dom outside of the club."

Opening her front door, she put her purse and keys away and moved to the couch, thinking. "Tony. Which is not a good example, I know."

"I think maybe," he said slowly, so she knew she might not like what came next. "You're a very independent woman who's worked hard to live the life you want to live without interference from anyone else. And therefore, even though you're a submissive, and you embrace that at the club, you're too wary of letting it spill over into your independent life out in the real world, so you keep a barrier up that prevents you from letting a Dom into your regular life."

She kicked off her gym shoes and propped her feet up on the coffee table, thinking through what he'd said.

"Maybe." It did make sense to her, though she'd have to give it some more consideration. She hadn't thought she was putting up any kind of barriers, but...

"Maybe," she said again. "But does that make it okay that he called me in the middle of the day and ordered me to go out with you guys?"

Jesse laughed. "Right, 'cause you were going to say no?"

She pouted, even though he wouldn't be able to see her.

"And I have no doubt that if you'd been with a client, or otherwise unavailable, you either wouldn't have answered the phone, or you would have told him so."

True. She supposed having a father who was a tough cop, who she'd fought hard to earn respect and gain her independence from, might have left some aftereffects.

"You're right—" She broke off when her phone beeped with another call.

"Hang on, Jesse, I have to see if this is a client."

She checked the screen and saw that the call was from one of the gyms that she sometimes saw clients at.

"Hi, this is Stephanie."

"Stephanie, hi, it's Cory at Fitness Express."

"Hi, Cory. Got a client for me?"

"No, actually, Tina wanted me to give you a call. She's not going to be allowing outside trainers anymore, and wanted to give you a heads up so you can redirect your clients."

Stephanie frowned. "Really, are you guys hiring some of your own trainers?"

"I'm not sure. She said something about the city cracking down on licensing, or something..." He trailed off.

"As far as I know, all the trainers you guys allow are certified. Including me," she countered.

"I don't know, I'm just making the call Tina asked me to make."

It really didn't matter, she only had one client left who liked that gym and their sessions were very sporadic. If the woman wanted to go with a gym-sponsored trainer, or pick a new place to work out, either would be fine with her.

"Okay, Cory, thanks for letting me know."

She hung up and switched back to Jesse, making a mental note to send her client an email after she got off the phone.

Jesse had to order dinner, so she let him go, but she was glad he'd called. The conversation had certainly given her something to think about.

Something else she needed to think about was what to tell her father. Normally she wouldn't even consider going away with a Dom without telling her dad. But she didn't know where she was going, and he wouldn't like that. It was too tempting to use it as an excuse to call Grant and ask him where he was taking her, and she suspected that what Jesse had implied was true. Although a sub, she was in the habit of taking too much control of her encounters.

She jotted a quick email to her client, then took a long, steamy shower. The imaginary fingers of Grant and Jesse played an important role and she was breathless when she stumbled out of the bathroom and collapsed on the bed.

CHAPTER FOUR

Jesse was trying very hard not to bounce around in his seat as they rolled up to Stephanie's apartment building, but it wasn't easy. Friday had taken forever to come along, and now that it was here he just couldn't wait to see her. See her, with Grant. Play together. He wiggled and could only give an apologetic shrug when Grant tossed a glance at him.

"You stay here, I'll go get her," Grant said, completely ignoring the frown Jesse tried to give him.

With a sigh, he fell back into the seat and jiggled his legs. With Grant gone, at least he could give his body the freedom of nervous energy. Not that he *was* nervous. Exactly. He just wanted everything to go perfectly. Wanted them all to have as amazing a time as he knew that they could.

He needed action, not this alone time to be thinking. Grant had told him not to be worried, but it wasn't that easy. He'd been mildly attracted to a few girls when he was younger, fooled around a bit when he was in high school, mostly just out of curiosity. But it had never gotten to the point of sex.

He thumped his head against the seat back. He was a nervous virgin. So embarrassing. Grant had assured him that once things got going hot and heavy he wouldn't even think about it. His lover had also whispered to him, while fucking him blind, about the slick heat that awaited him, how the heat of Stephanie's body would welcome him, how her flavor would enchant him.

He groaned at the remembered orgasm Grant had wrung from him, with his words as well as his actions. A noise outside gave him just enough time to scrub his hands over his face and pull himself together.

The car door opened and Stephanie climbed in, her eyebrows arched as she took in the interior of the limousine. He just smiled and grabbed her arm, pulling her into his lap. She laughed and slapped at him, but then settled into place when he didn't let her go, resting her head on his shoulder.

Grant came in behind her and took the seat across from them and rapped the window to the driver with his knuckles. The car pulled away smoothly and Jesse tightened his arms. It was time. They'd all waited long enough.

Grant stretched his legs out to either side of Jesse's, crossed his arms over his chest and eyed Stephanie. Jesse could feel her come to a kind of attention in his arms.

"Tough week?" Grant asked.

Stephanie kind of shrugged. "Not really. Just haven't been able to get to sleep as easily as I usually do." Her wry smile left them no doubt as to what had been keeping her up.

"You're not the only one," Jesse assured her, letting his hand roam from her hip to the hem of her shirt. He teased his thumb under it to find her bare skin.

"If you're going to touch her skin, Jesse, I get to watch. Help her undress. Stephanie, you can make noises, but no talking from you. You don't need to ask permission to come."

Her breathing stopped for a second, but she didn't move until Jesse gently pushed her forward. She cooperated as he eased her sweater off and tossed it on the seat, then pulled her shirt off herself. He stopped short at the sight of the lacy white bra that couldn't possibly be giving her any actual support. There was so little material that he could see the top of her areola peeking over the top edge.

His hands came to rest on her waist and he just stared for a moment, before twisting her around so Grant could enjoy the view.

His lover rose from his seat and kneeled in front of them, his hands twining with Jesse's. Her breathing grew heavier as they studied her, enjoyed her, their hands moving with the rise and fall, all of them able to measure the increase of her excitement with the movement of her body.

"Somehow I don't think you wear that on a normal occasion," Grant observed.

She shook her head slowly as he lifted his hand, ran his finger along the edge of the lace, dipped in, and nudged her very erect nipple so that it was sitting on top of the lace, instead of hidden behind. She opened her mouth on a tiny gasp.

Grant repeated the motion on her other breasts, so that her pink nipples were sitting proudly on display. "Did you do this for us, sweetheart?"

She nodded.

"Tell me."

Her ribs expanded on a deep breath and Jesse knew she was giving in, beginning the long slide of going under. "Yes, Sir."

"We appreciate it, don't we Jesse?"

"Yes, Sir."

"Let's see what else she brought us, shall we?"

"Yes, Sir!"

Jesse nudged Stephanie forward off his lap. Grant didn't move back, but guided Stephanie to kneel between his knees. His hands went to the button on her slacks, quickly freeing it and lowering the zipper. He slid the pants down over her hips, to her knees. Grant lifted her back to Jesse's lap and pulled the pants from around her ankles, tossing them aside.

Jesse watched Grant, instead of Stephanie. His man's eyes were hot with appreciation and desire, and Jesse knew the combination was a heady aphrodisiac to the recipient. Grant cocked his head and looked at the panties that seemed to match the bra. Virginal white lace that was all the sexier for the lie, since, from the view Jesse had received as she'd backed into him, they left her luscious ass fully exposed.

"Jesse, sit all the way back in the seat. Keep her nice and tight in your lap."

Wrapping his arm around her waist to support her, Jesse did as he was told, bracing his legs on either side of hers. Grant reached forward and took one of her ankles, brought it to the other side of Jesse's, then pushed Jesse's leg farther to the side. He did the same with their other leg, then sat back with a smile.

"Well. You've outdone yourself. Very, very lovely."

Jesse started to lean forward to see, but Grant stopped him with a look. "How about you touch, instead. Take your right hand and slide it down her stomach."

Surprised, Jesse did as he was told, taking his time, enjoying the warmth of her skin, the flush that rose up her neck as he made his way south. He hit the lace band and kept going at a nod from Grant.

And stopped when he hit the wetness of the open crotch. Realizing she was fully exposed to Grant's view, Jesse used one finger to tease through her slick opening, circling the sensitive flesh, then sliding up to give her clit a healthy pinch.

She jumped in his arms, but settled back down quickly. Another run through her slit verified that she was even wetter than before.

"How does she look?" Jesse asked.

"Pretty. Wet. Pink and puffy and needy."

"Mmmm."

"How does she feel?"

"Slick and hot."

"How does she taste?"

Stephanie's breath hitched. Jesse ran his finger along her seam, back into her core, hooking his finger and giving a little tug. He was rewarded with a full gasp. He retreated, bringing his finger to his lips and sucking it in noisily. He gave a vocal moan, letting them both in on his pleasure, his appreciation.

PERFECT ADDITION

"Delicious," he said. "Do you want some?"

"I think I do. But I'll take it straight from the source." He reached behind him to the bag he'd left on the seat, handed Jesse a roll of bondage tape and a pair of safety scissors. "Put her hands behind her back."

Stephanie cooperated by leaning forward and offering her wrists at the small of her back. Jesse wasn't used to being the one to use the tape, so there was little bit of fumbling, but he got her secured without too much effort. He started to hand the roll back to Grant, but received a head shake in response. "Blindfold her."

She gave a little whimper, which he suspected was from a desire to watch Grant in action. He smoothed her hair down, giving a tug to the bright purple section. It took him two tries, but he had a decent blindfold going without any twists or pulling that might hurt her. He looked to Grant and received a nod and a finger to the lips. Jesse smiled. No more talking to give her clues as to what they were doing.

It felt a little bit strange to be helping Grant do these things to another sub. Strange in a fun way, for sure.

"Stephanie, you doing okay?" Grant asked.

She wrinkled her forehead. "Yes, Sir?"

"You had a bad experience last time you played, and now you're tied up and blindfolded with two guys you've never scened with," he pointed out. "And you're not in a club, with monitors."

She opened her mouth, then closed it without responding. Her body tensed in his arms as she thought about it, then relaxed. "I'm fine, Sir. I trust you guys."

"Okay, just don't hesitate to say something if you start to feel anxious. I told you no talking, but you know I want to hear from you if you're unsure, right?"

She nodded. "Yes, Sir, I understand."

"Good girl."

Jesse leaned back, pulling her with him. When she was settled against him, he motioned with his hands towards her breasts, raising his eyebrows in question. Grant nodded and Jesse brought his hands to her still hard nipples, giving them little flicks, then a pinch.

Stephanie gave a low moan that turned into a shocked gasp as Grant put his head between her thighs.

Jesse tried to imagine what he was doing, exactly. He'd never gone down on a woman, hadn't given it much thought. Now he wanted to see what she felt like, feel her reacting to him. Her thighs tensed against his as she braced herself to hold steady. He tugged on her nipples, then caressed the tops of her breasts, moved his hand up her chest, tickling gently until he reached her throat. He cupped her carefully, never having been on this side of the touch, but knowing how much he loved to feel Grant hold him there, exert his power with the lightest of touches.

She swallowed and he felt the movement against his palm. It was fascinating, the feeling of power, of care and concentration, when usually he was just lost in the sensations. He ran his thumb up the side of her throat, watched goose bumps rise up in its wake. Her body was making tiny motions now, her butt wiggling into his lap, teasing his erection to full hardness. He should mind. He should be frustrated and feel left out. Instead he marveled at the softness in his hands, the weight of her pressed against him as she reacted to Grant's ministrations.

She arched her back, pressing harder into his groin. He squeezed her breasts and heard Grant growl down below. Her high, thin wail had his hands tightening even further. She slumped against him and Grant lifted his head, a huge, wet grin on his face.

"Enjoyed that, did you, Sir?"

"I did. Remind me to give you a chance at that later."

Jesse smiled. "Yes, Sir." He glanced out the window to try and figure out where they were and decided they still had quite a ways to go. He looked to Grant to see what he had planned next. The other man moved her ankles and grabbed her by the waist, pulling her into him so that Jesse was alone on the seat. Grant made a motion that Jesse interpreted as an order to strip. When he started unbuttoning his shirt, Grant nodded and returned his attention to Stephanie.

Making short work of his task, Jesse watched as Grant did nothing more than support Stephanie's weight so she wouldn't fall and run his finger up and down her spine. She dropped her head forward until it rested on his shoulder.

Finally Jesse was naked and Grant returned her to his lap. Then he reached into his bag and pulled out a condom.

He didn't make any effort to silence the tell-tale crinkling, so Stephanie's body went on the alert. Jesse swallowed hard as Grant rolled the condom down his shaft. The feel of Grant's fingers on him did what it always did, made him ready to burst. But he'd had plenty of experience holding back, fighting down the need. Those fingers gave his shaft a squeeze before letting go.

Grant picked up Stephanie's leg and this time he draped it over Jesse's thigh, then her other leg, so that she was spread out on top of his lap. Grant lifted her bottom a bit from where she rested against Jesse and grasped his cock. Grant stretched him forward and Jesse realize he meant to settle Stephanie down on top of his dick.

An excellent plan, Jesse heartily approved. He'd assumed Grant would want the first entrance into their beautiful girl, but he should have known. Grant was anything but selfish when it came to pleasing his lover.

Jesse helped steady her waist as Grant squeezed him tight, lining him up with her opening.

The first contact with her wet heat, combined with Grant's strong, sure fingers, was almost too much, but he bit his lip and concentrated on the sound of the car whooshing down the wet freeway, the slight vibration under his seat, anything but the exquisite pleasure of Stephanie's body enveloping him at Grant's hand, Grant's direction. He squeezed his eyes shut but her moan nearly undid him. Finally Grant let go of him, put his hands over Jesse's, guiding him as they lowered Stephanie all the way.

She was gasping, but so was he. It felt so good, he hoped like hell he'd be able to do whatever Grant was going to ask him to do, rather than embarrass himself. Grant sat back on his heels and studied them. Jesse wanted to ask him questions, or maybe just beg, but he stayed quiet. A finger to the lips wasn't how Grant usually ordered him to silence, but that was clearly what he'd meant, so Jesse bit his lip.

Grant picked up the bondage tape and with much more skill and finesse than Jesse had shown, wrapped it around their shins and thighs, so they were bound to each other. Jesse definitely approved, but was afraid he wouldn't be able to move inside Stephanie, and he was really, really wanting to move. Grant took his hand and placed it on her breast, half skin, half lace, then did the same with his other hand so that his arms were crossed over Stephanie's torso, his hands full of her luscious breasts. Then he wound the tape around their upper arms so that Stephanie was up tight against his chest, his hands able to squeeze her breasts but not move otherwise. Not that he was complaining.

Grant went back to the bag and pulled out Jesse's collar. It was a twisted steel, almost industrial looking, but also more delicate than a leather collar. He probably would never have thought to pick it out himself, but when Grant had first showed it to him, his knees had literally gone weak. He couldn't imagine wearing anything else, it was the perfect symbol of his relationship with Grant.

More bondage tape around their middle, and they were well and truly locked together.

His arms full of soft woman, for a second he had to wonder why he hadn't been interested in more women in his life. Then Grant begin to strip and Jesse could only feel sorry that Stephanie was missing out on the glorious sight. His lover enjoyed a good workout and it showed. And that cock. It hadn't taken Jesse long, after meeting Grant, to come to the conclusion that if his was the only other cock he saw again for the rest of his life, he was perfectly fine with that.

His mouth watered, especially when it occurred to him that Grant hadn't really left any other orifices for his own pleasure. He hoped Stephanie wouldn't be the only recipient, though he would be happy to share. To say that he loved sucking Grant's dick was a massive understatement.

Poor Stephanie, she was really missing out with that blindfold.

Grant had to bend over, his shoulders to the car roof, his hand braced along the seat back behind Jesse, but he managed it. He brought his penis to Stephanie's mouth, touched it to her lips, then slid it across her cheek to Jesse's open mouth. She turned her head, trying to capture the prize, but it was too late. Jesse sucked in with an enthusiastic moan that was sure to let her know where Grant had ended up.

Okay, so he could be mean too.

She whimpered in response and Grant, damn him, slowly pulled free. He brushed his now wet cock along her cheek again, letting her turn and suck him in. When she did, though, Grant paused, forcing her to stay where she'd captured him, rather than continuing to move forward. It was an awkward angle and she was clearly frustrated, trying to turn her head and encourage him around so she could get more of him. Jesse smiled and wasn't at all surprised when Grant gave her less time before moving back to his own eager mouth.

He moaned again, because it was good, but also because he was a teasing bastard, too. Couldn't help himself. He flicked his eyes up in time to see Grant's amusement, then focused his attention on his task. Stephanie had begun to move against him, tiny movements all that she could manage with how tightly they were bound. But it was enough to work him, to make him wish he could pound into her but he had to focus on Grant's—

He grunted his dismay when Grant pulled out again. Fuck.

Stephanie stilled her movements, making his torture even more complete. He managed a slight grind with his hips as he watched her fight not to turn in when Grant once again teased her with his wet cock against her cheek. She was a quick learner, though, and she waited to be fed her treat, even when he brushed the head against her lips. Her mouth was open, but she waited.

Grant rewarded her, pushing forward in one long slide, giving her the benefit of the doubt that she could and would take him all the way. Jesse licked his lips, savoring the subtle flavor of Grant as he watched her swallow him down. He squeezed her breasts and managed to buck his hips enough to make her moan around her prize and Grant grunted.

STEPHANIE'S BOUND hands scratched against Jesse's stomach, trying to find purchase, but she had nothing to hold onto. She was safe from falling, secured to Jesse, but it was hard to move, to accomplish anything, to do anything other than sit still, impaled on Jesse hard cock, mouth filled with the fleeting pleasure of Grant's, knowing he would pull out at any moment.

She gave him every bit of instinct and experience she could manage. Wrapping her tongue around him as he pushed in, stiffening the tip to glide against him as he pulled out, sucking hard when he was inside, swallowing when he was buried deep. When Jesse managed to move inside her, just a bit, she moaned and they were able to wring a grunt from Grant, but she wanted more. This time, as he pulled out, she somehow knew he was getting ready to move back to Jesse.

Very carefully, she let her teeth graze him, just a bit.

"Fuck."

She felt triumphant, even as he left her mouth completely and moved to Jesse. Against her back, Jesse rocked forward. They were nearly against her ear and she could hear every enthusiastic slurp and whimper. Now that she didn't have to concentrate on pleasing Grant, she resumed the small movements she'd managed to make against Jesse.

Her knees were hooked over Jesse's, so she could bounce, but only a tiny bit since they were wrapped together at the stomach and thighs. Grant gave another grunt and she wished she could see him, them, see anything.

She tensed her thigh muscles as hard as she could, and managed a shallow slide up and down Jesse's length. Normally it wouldn't be nearly enough, but in the position they were in, it felt like heaven. Jesse hummed, and she was sure it was as much in appreciation of her movements as in his task.

Jesse's hands began a rhythmic massage of her breasts. She wished he could play with her nipples, wished she could *move*. She timed her bouncing and squeezing with his hands, all the while listening to the sucking going on behind her, waiting for her turn.

Grant, who'd been very quiet, brought his hand up to her head, slid his fingers into her hair in a gentle caress. "Gorgeous," he murmured. "You both are so fucking gorgeous. How does she feel, wrapped around you, Jess? Is she tight and wet?"

Jesse gave a long moan, which she supposed was all the answer he could manage since his mouth was filled with Grant's cock. Grant's thumb caressed her cheek and she wanted to cry, wanted to move, wanted more of his cock, more of his voice, more of his hands, *more*. She whimpered, surprised at the sound. She'd never thought she was the whimpering type but if it was the only begging she was allowed, than she'd take it.

"So sweet," Grant said. "Aching for more, aren't you? Wishing Jesse could lay you down and pound into you?"

She wanted badly to say *yes, please* but managed to choke the words back, remain quiet as he'd ordered. His hand left her face and she dropped her head forward, missing the touch. She could feel his body next to her, though he didn't quite touch. Feel his heat, smell his sweat. She wanted to lick and suck anything she could touch. Instead, she concentrated on drawing in breath, moving her hips, waiting for her turn.

She was getting closer, closer to release. Grant had said she could come whenever, she just wasn't sure she'd be able to manage it this way. She used her Kegels, working Jesse as much as she could, giving him as much as she could manage.

Out of nowhere, fingers gripped her clit and pinched.

She wailed, her pussy spasming around Jesse. His hands stilled in a tight grip around her breasts and he came. She wished he wasn't wearing a condom, wished she could feel him splashing into her. Wished she could see Grant, damn it.

There was a moan and a groan and she was pretty sure Grant came when his hand in her hair fisted tightly. He turned her head, brought her mouth to his dick so that she could help Jesse clean him up. When he'd apparently decided that they'd done enough, he pressed back gently on her shoulder until Jesse was reclined against the seat. She felt him slide out of her, heard the condom being tied off and tossed, wished she could have seen Grant taking care of Jesse.

She turned her head so she could hear his heartbeat, complementing the whooshing of the car.

How far had they gone? How far were they going?

Grant's hands caressed her thighs and her sex quickly woke back up, wanting his touch. She felt him lean in, felt his presence and his heat, so she wasn't surprised when his lips claimed hers. Only grateful. He teased her with soft kisses, light brushes across her lips, a flick of the tongue here and there, until she wanted to cry in frustration. Jesse's hands were warm and firm on her breasts, her legs were spread wide, but empty and Grant was going to drive her insane if he didn't give her a real kiss soon.

"You beg so prettily, even when you're being good and not speaking," he said between too soft pecks. "Your lips open for me, your skin flushed for me." He squeezed her thighs, then began to draw circles on her skin with his thumbs, caressing the sensitive flesh near her core, but not getting nearly close enough. "Your muscles reaching for me, even though you can't move."

As soon as he said it she realized how much her body was straining forward, trying to get more of him. A whimper escaped and he rewarded her with a kiss, a real kiss, his lips hard against hers, his tongue exploring her mouth. He felt so good, tasted so good, she couldn't keep back a moan of approval. She felt his lips smile against hers but he didn't stop, didn't pull back, shared his taste, his passion and appreciation.

She wanted to move, bring her hands up, touch him all over.

How could she be so frustrated when she'd just been so satisfied? These guys were going to drive her insane before they even got to their destination, wherever that was.

As if the driver could hear her thoughts, the car made a sweeping turn off the highway and onto an obviously slower road. Grant ended the kiss, adding one to the tip of her nose before he pulled all the way back. His hands rubbed up and down her thighs a bit and she had to bite her lip not to speak, not to ask questions, not to beg for him to come back.

She heard the snip of scissors and felt the pressure holding her to Jesse ease off at her thigh. More snips and she was gradually freed, Jesse's hands going to her waist to hold her steady. He lifted her up so that she was kneeling on the floor.

She thought her hands would be next, but instead felt more tape being wrapped around her thighs. Again, she had to bite her lip to keep from saying anything, but it was a close call. More tape came around her arms and between her breasts, around and around until she felt almost like she was wearing a harness. It made the blood in her breasts rush, and her nipples tingle. She was lifted onto her side on the long seat, her ankles wrapped in tape, one hand coming to rest on her thigh, one gently caressing her hair.

"Tell me about your day, Jesse."

She was pretty sure she could hear Jesse getting dressed while he answered Grant's question with something about one of his usual passengers doing something funny. She couldn't really focus on the conversation because she was too busy trying to get her muddled brain to figure out what had just happened. Instead of releasing her, they'd bound her back up and were having a regular conversation? And just how far were they going to go, anyway? She managed to suppress a huff of annoyance, but just barely. Instead she let out a long, slow breath, to try and relax herself and still her mind.

With the sounds of their voices in the background, she focused on the heat of Jesse's hand on her thigh, Grant's sifting through her hair, below the tape, his fingers occasionally moving to dance across her shoulder or tease over her lips. He'd lifted her head to rest against his thigh, the muscles bunching and relaxing every so often. The leather was warm beneath her and she wondered idly who would have to clean the car or if it would smell like sex when the doors opened.

When Jesse said something that had Grant laughing out loud, her whole body shook with the motion. His hand cupped her shoulder to steady her. They'd begun making more turns and slowing for stops, then speeding back up again. She was safe and comfortable and no longer feeling quite so needy. She'd calmed down enough now to be interested in what they were saying.

They were talking about an upcoming birthday party for Grant's mom. Though she'd missed part of what was said, it sounded as though Jesse was saying he didn't need to go, since Grant's mom didn't particularly like him.

How could you not like Jesse? She rubbed her foot along his thigh in the only attempt at support she could manage.

"I want you by my side, like you're supposed to be. If she's not good with that, I don't need to be there. She's never said she doesn't want you there."

Jesse sighed. "She doesn't have to say it for me to know it. I'm not mad or anything. It's her day, she should be able to relax and feel comfortable."

"If that's the way you feel, we'll stay home. I don't want *you* to be uncomfortable, either."

"Don't be ridiculous, baby, you can't miss your mom's birthday party."

Grant tickled behind her ear. "If I miss some events, maybe she'll get the message of how important you are to me."

Stephanie had seen a fair number of good, healthy relationships, and she'd seen plenty of messed-up relationships where she couldn't fathom why the couples were together. It made her sad that Grant's family apparently wasn't very welcoming of Jesse, but she could hear the love they had for each other, the reluctance to allow the other to feel pain. Which sort of left the two in a stalemate.

"We don't have to decide right now," Jesse pointed out, squeezing her foot. "We have some time and something much more exciting to deal with."

Before she could really process that thought, she was distracted by the car coming to a stop. She heard, just barely, the sound of the driver's door closing. A door near her head opened and she caught the sound of a garage door coming to a close. Hands gripped her shoulders, then more hands and she found herself pulled out of the car and slung over someone's shoulder.

Grant told Jesse to lead the way, holding her upper thigh firmly. She'd never been carried this way. It wasn't very comfortable, but there was something primal about it. It spoke to a primitive part of her she would have hotly denied if she'd thought about it.

She considered the evening so far. Stripped naked, forbidden to speak, robbed of her sight, treated like a receptacle. Dismissed while the guys talked about mundane things.

She should be annoyed, pissed, bored or some combination of those things. *Why wasn't she?* Maybe because she hadn't, not for one second, felt ignored. Though she couldn't see, she knew without a doubt that they watched her. Though she couldn't speak, Grant had shown her that he was listening to what her body told him. Though she was being lugged around, she felt like a precious package, wrapped up in such a way to make them appreciate her assets.

There was no sense trying to guess why Grant had chosen to go about their first encounter this way, but she was positive it was for a reason. And what it came down to was that he was in charge and he was clearly determined to drive that point home. And the fact was she was turned on and that hadn't waned since she'd opened her door to Grant.

The space they'd entered felt like a home, though she supposed that was mostly based on her assumptions. It was a touch chilly and she heard Grant ask Jesse to go turn the heat up. They climbed some stairs and she realized she'd underestimated Grant's strength since he wasn't panting when they reached the top. By the time she was plopped onto the bed, carefully so as not to jar her bound arms, the heating system was humming.

"Stay there for a few minutes," Grant whispered into her ear. "I've got a present for you."

She thought she heard clothing being removed, but that might have just been wishful thinking. There was definitely some clinking that she hoped indicated restraints of some sort, but nothing touched her. Once or twice there was the low rumble of male voices, but she couldn't make out any words.

It felt like forever before a hand landed softly on her calf. She managed not to jump. The snip of scissors freed her ankles. The tape was quickly pulled free there, then her thighs. She was rolled so that she was fully on her stomach, and her hands were unbound. Strong hands she was pretty sure were Grant's rubbed at her shoulders until she'd fully relaxed them. Then the tape on her head was sliced and removed and she was able to blink her eyes open.

Grant crouched down beside the bed so that his face filled her vision. He smiled, traced his finger along her cheek.

"Okay?"

She nodded, not sure if she should speak yet.

"Sorry about the long drive," he said, then winked. Actually *winked*. "I hope you weren't too bored."

He didn't wait for an answer, but climbed onto the bed and hauled her up, turned her over and tucked her between his legs as he leaned against the headboard.

She didn't give much thought to her position, though, as her attention had been completely arrested by the sight in front of her.

Jesse stood just past the foot of the bed, hanging from a spreader bar that descended from chains in the ceiling. His wrists were in lovely black leather suspension cuffs, he wore a gorgeous silver collar and nothing else.

"Beautiful, isn't he?" Grant asked.

Jesse's eyes were aimed at them, waiting to see what would happen, she was sure. She snuggled back into Grant's embrace and studied the view.

"Oh, yes. Very. You're a lucky guy."

She still had the bondage tape around her breasts, making them extra sensitive, so she shivered when Grant brought a hand up to tweak her nipple. Jesse's hungry eyes watched them. She pushed up just a little, enough to see that there was a spreader bar at his feet, as well. Beautiful indeed.

"He could use some more decorations, though, don't you think?"

"Yes, Sir."

He pointed to a dresser. "Why don't you go pick out some nipple clamps for him?"

He didn't have to ask twice. She started to jump off the bed before remembering that she hadn't moved much for a couple of hours. Grant's hand had already latched onto her arm before she slowed down, slid her legs off the side of the bed and rose gracefully, and carefully, to her feet. He let her go and she walked to the dresser, going behind Jesse so that she could admire that view, too. Gorgeous. She had a thing for sexy male butts and his definitely qualified.

The top drawer seemed to be full of restraints. All types of restraints. She almost reached her hand in, just to touch, but decided she'd better do as she'd been told. The second drawer had nipple rings, cock rings, gags, plugs, hooks of some sort, pretty boxes she wanted to open up and explore and some things she couldn't immediately identify without pulling them out.

She picked two clover clamps that she thought would look nice with Jesse's collar and turned back towards the bed.

"I think a set for yourself, while you're there." Grant's voice managed to sound both commanding and amused.

Well, it wasn't like she was going to complain! She turned back and picked up some clamps of a style she'd never seen before. They were fashioned so that a screw could be turned to press two thin plates together, so theoretically they could be made as tight or as loose as the person turning the screw desired. They were attached together by a chain.

Walking directly to the bed, instead of going around to the other side, she knelt up onto it and crawled closer to Grant before presenting him with her choices. His face showed approval and she smiled. He looked down and nodded. "Would you like to put them on Jesse?" he asked, plucking the chained clamps out of her outstretched hands and setting them down on the bed.

"Yes, please, Sir."

"You'll need to get him nice and hard first."

"Yes, Sir."

She turned and crawled towards Jesse. His eyes followed her every movement. She slid off the bed and approached him slowly. "May I talk to him, Sir?"

"You may."

Glancing over her shoulder to smile her thanks she saw that he had moved to his side, resting his head on his hand so that he could watch them both. It was a sight worth seeing. His shirt was riding up, leaving a gap of tasty-looking flesh above his jeans. He'd taken his shoes off, and wore only white sports socks. There was really no reason that should be sexy, but it totally was. Whatever she'd planned on telling Jesse flew right out of her head.

Grant raised an eyebrow at her and she turned around to resume her task. Jesse's look told her he knew exactly what had stolen her attention. She stuck her tongue out at him and he had to bite his lip to keep from laughing.

But when she stepped in close and sucked his nipple into her mouth, she heard him draw in a sharp breath.

CHAPTER FIVE

Grant loved to hear Jesse gasping. It was one of his favorite things in the world. At one time he'd even considered figuring out how to make the sound his text alert for Jesse. But then he'd realized he didn't want to share that sound with the whole world. He found now, though, that he didn't mind sharing that sound with Steph. Not at all.

Her head bobbed over Jesse's chest for another moment before pulling back. He watched Jesse's face. He knew his lover's expressions, would know if she made the clamp too hard or not hard enough. She was almost there when she stepped back. He let her do the second clamp then moved to stand behind her.

He whispered into her ear. Not so that Jesse couldn't hear; he spoke loud enough for that. But so that she could feel his breath against her, hear the dark intent in his words. "A little bit tighter now." She rewarded him with a shiver. He watched carefully as she tweaked the devices.

When she was done, he reached out to the man he loved, flicked one tortured nipple. The little squeaky moan was exactly what he expected to hear. He looked at their visitor. She licked her lips and glanced down at his hand. He held the C clamps she'd selected. A very nice choice, but he'd only used them a couple of times so he'd have to pay close attention. Not that he had a problem with that particular chore.

"Already nice and plump," he observed. He brushed a finger softly over one of the pouty buds. He put one clamp on and began to tighten it. Her head was tilted down, watching, so he couldn't see her face very well. "Watch Jesse, not me."

Her head came up and the lust that came into her eyes when she saw Jesse made Grant's cock harder. There was no explaining it, really, but ever since they'd come up with the plan to approach her, he'd known it would be like this. That inviting her into their play would somehow make an already great situation even better. He'd learned to trust his instincts in certain areas. Business and kink being the two main ones.

Stephanie's expression went from lust to nervousness to pain as he tightened the screw. He stopped, cranked the screw back a turn, paused. She breathed in, blew the air out, and settled. So fucking hot.

He repeated the action on her other tit, found that one tolerated just a bit more pain than the other, wondered if she'd ever been told that before. But he didn't want to bring up other lovers, other Doms, so he didn't ask.

He gave the chain a gentle pull and she sucked in air. "Nice choice."

She swallowed. "Thank you, Sir."

He couldn't resist leaning down to give her a kiss. The chains above rattled as Jesse tried to move closer to them. Letting the teasing kiss linger a little longer, he twirled the tip of his finger around the chain between her breasts. When he finally pulled back, she tried to follow, only to be brought up short by the sharp tug on her nipples.

She gasped. "Sorry, Sir."

He nodded. "I think you're both feeling a bit empty right now. Go get a couple of plugs."

"Yes, Sir."

She went back to the drawer and picked up an anal hook. It was meant to be used with rope play, which wasn't the direction he was taking things, but he could make it work, if that was what she selected. He liked that she held it up to him for his approval. When he nodded, she went back to the drawer and selected a blue glass plug with a small base, for sitting comfortably but safely between the butt cheeks. She again checked for his approval, and when he nodded, picked up a bottle of lube and returned to him.

"Why don't you keep him entertained while I work on this?" He took the items from her, tossed the other plug on the bed and held up the hook for Jesse to see, loving the adorably confused expression on the other man's face. It was always good to keep 'em guessing. He moved far enough around that Steph could get to Jesse's front, but not so far that he couldn't lean over and watch what she was doing.

He pulled a doctor's glove out of his back pocket and slicked his fingers with lube. With Jesse, he usually only used the glove if they were edging into some medical play. It wasn't Jesse's favorite, but sometimes it was nice to switch up their activities. Back to that keeping-him-guessing bit. With extra bodies and holes, though, he figured it would be easier to keep things clean this way. He'd given the issue a lot of thought. He'd given everything about asking Steph to join them a lot of thought.

A little tease was all it took to have Jesse pushing back for more. Stephanie had gone straight in for a kiss and she seemed to be working it hard, up on her tiptoes, body pressed tightly against Jesse who had to brace against her weight while staying still for Grant. He didn't know if she did it on purpose or not, but it worked very well for all of them. He slid one finger in, then another as he watched her hand ease its way up Jesse's ribs and start playing with one of the nipple clamps.

He added another finger, but wasn't sure if Jesse's gasp was caused by his actions or Stephanie's. She was leaning her full weight against him now, and he strongly suspected that the hand he couldn't see was playing with Jesse's cock. Smiling, he braced his legs in case he had to support the pair, adding a third finger and hooking the middle finger just…so.

Jesse arched up onto his toes, his hands gripping the chains above his cuffs to support himself and Stephanie. Grant didn't wait, he pulled his fingers free and pushed the ball of the hook home. Jesse grunted in a deeply satisfying way. Quietly, Grant removed the glove so that it was inside out, dropped it where it would be out of the way. He wiggled the steel bar emerging from Jesse's hole as the man dropped back down to his feet. Stephanie took a step back and looked over to him.

He gestured for her to continue and she bent to place a kiss on Jesse's hipbone. Leaving them to it, he went to the drawer and selected a length of lightweight chain and two small carabiner-style clips, keeping them hidden from Jesse's distracted sight as he walked back behind him.

He used one clip to attach the chain to the loop at the end of the hook, usually used for rope. The other end he attached to Jesse's collar, then portioned out the length of chain, careful to get just the right amount of tension, depending on Jesse's movements. He gave a little tug so that his lover would understand what he'd done. The groan was exactly the answer he wanted.

Stepping back once again to survey his subs, he was pleased with what he saw. Stephanie had worked a wet trail of kisses up Jesses abdomen to the hollow at the base of his neck. One of his favorite spots as well, Grant watched as she nibbled on the collarbone.

"Tasty, isn't he?" he asked.

She hummed her agreement and started to step back. He put a hand on the nape of her neck to let her know she should continue with what she was doing. Then he quietly put on another glove and grabbed the other plug and the lube. He traced a non-gloved finger down her spine, slowly, enjoying the ripple of goose bumps that rose in his wake. Her kisses had made it to Jesse's chin as his finger reached the crack of her ass. He switched, sliding one slicked finger right into her.

He was watching their faces, so he saw her bite the jaw between her teeth, saw Jesse's knowing look as he gave a gasp of pleasure. Stephanie pushed back against him eager for more, so Grant complied, adding a second finger, screwing them into her until she was wiggling for more. The plug wasn't very wide so he slid it in quickly, giving her a sharp smack on the bottom when it was fully settled.

She jerked into Jesse who supported them. He leaned in behind her, bit her earlobe. "Keep playing," he told her as he reached around to check her wetness. Well, he hadn't really doubted she was enjoying herself, but he definitely didn't need to wonder now. He teased her, offering only light touches as she swiveled, trying to get more. She'd claimed Jesse's mouth, her hands wrapped around his collar, her thumbs teasing the flesh along its edges. It was something he liked to do as well, and he checked Jesse's face to make sure he was okay with it.

The closed eyes and blissful expression assured him that Jesse wasn't having a problem with anything that was happening to him right now.

Pulling his finger free, he raised it to their joined lips. Neither hesitated, opening for him instantly. He let them play for a minute, then backed away, returning to the dresser to grab a vibrating tongue ring that he slipped around one of his fingers instead. He put on a condom and opened another, before returning to them.

Without warning the pair, he reached between them and grasped Jesse's fully erect cock, giving it a little squeeze.

"Okay, Steph, step back now." She watched as he rolled the condom down Jesse's length. When he was done he reached up to free Jesse's wrists from the chains. "Take the bar off for me, sweetheart."

He met Jesse's gaze as he pressed up against him to reach the clips. They were full of anticipation. Definitely not the glazed subspace look he loved to see in Jesse's eyes, but that wasn't for tonight. Besides, he had a treat in store for his man, and it would be best accomplished with Jesse's full faculties present.

When Stephanie had released the ankle cuffs from the bar, he grabbed her wrist. "Jesse, grab the lube."

It had been a while since he'd fucked a woman up against the wall. It was a different maneuver than what he could do with Jesse and he looked forward to it enough that he'd already scoped out the best bit of wall for his purposes. He put his hands on her waist. "I want your right hand holding your left wrist, behind my neck. No letting go until after you come. And you'll wait until I give you permission this time."

"Yes Sir." She gave a little hop when he pressed on her waist, her legs coming around his middle perfectly. "Jesse, why don't you give us a hand here?" he asked, glancing over at the other man. The gleam in Jesse's eyes meant that he'd realized what Grant was going to offer him. It wasn't often he let Jesse fuck him, though they both always loved it.

"Yes, Sir!"

Grant smirked but said nothing as Jesse moved in. Of course, Jesse being Jesse, he didn't just do the task he'd been assigned. His left hand went to the top of Grant's ass, slid down to cup the cheek, while his right hand took a tight grasp on Grant's dick. He wished he wasn't wearing a condom, wanted to feel the full heat of Jesse's palm, the true slickness of Stephanie's welcoming cream as Jesse lined him up with her opening.

Working together, his arms bracing her, she used her thigh muscles to lower herself onto him. Her forearms pressed down into his shoulders, her eyes were at half-mast, her cunt gripping and releasing him, pulling him sweetly deeper and deeper. He surged up on his toes, slamming her into the wall, one hand behind her head, letting her feel the full impact of his dick and the wall. She cried out, breathing hard, her heels digging into his ass.

Jesse's hand was still gripping his ass, his body right up against theirs, his erection against Grant's hip. Grant turned, his unspoken request clearly understood since Jesse immediately leaned in for a kiss. Letting the wall help him support Stephanie, he kissed Jesse fiercely, his love for the man an always-burning

PERFECT ADDITION

fire in his heart that satisfied him like nothing in his life ever had before.

Though he knew Jesse was dying to get inside him, there was no sense of his pulling back from the kiss, only reluctance when Grant finally lifted his head. He smiled. "Fill me up, baby."

"Yes, Sir." The whisper was full of love and desire, need and appreciation.

The chill of lube hit him first, followed swiftly by the tease of Jesse's finger, circling his hole, reminding the nerves there of the pleasure that awaited them. He breathed out, pushed out, accepted the finger, swiveling his hips to encourage Jesse and pleasure Stephanie with a shallow thrust all in the same move. He flexed the arm under her butt, jiggling her some more as Jesse added another finger.

The chain running down Jesse's back jingled just a little and Grant smiled at the reminder. He might have to use that idea again. He imagined the same chain running up Stephanie's spine, ending at a collar he'd placed around her neck. Would she want a permanent collar from him? He wasn't sure, and it was way too early to tell. But he could picture it, picture her as part of them, with no trouble.

Intellectually, he'd wondered if adding a woman to their mix would unbalance them, but emotionally he'd been certain it would only add to their foundation, make them stronger. Not everyone would understand her addition to their partnership, but Jesse had been totally in sync with him. He could read the other man well enough to know if he was just agreeing with Grant to make him happy, and that was definitely not the case.

Jesse's dick breaching his hole pulled his thoughts back to the here and now quite effectively. Knowing what he liked, Jesse pushed in hard and fast, Grant working with him. They'd never done this with another person, so he was careful to take the brunt of the thrust and moderate what Stephanie received, until they all had the rhythm down. Her thighs wrapped tightly around him flexed as she rose when he backed up into Jesse's waiting embrace, then she dropped as he and Jesse surged forward.

Stephanie's head was pressed back into his palm, her eyes closed in concentration.

"Stephanie. Tell me how he looks. Is he enjoying himself?"

She blinked her eyes open, looked at him first, then behind him. She licked her lips as she studied Jesse, losing her concentration for a second which he used to his advantage, giving her another hard push into the wall. She wasn't really bound, but he was sure that she felt controlled, just the way he knew she liked. Her gasp was all pleasure and it took her a second to get her breath and wits gathered enough to answer his question.

"He looks very happy. Hot as hell. He's got those little lines in his forehead, like he's concentrating very hard." She laughed. "He winked at me." She turned her attention down to him. "You're hot as hell, too."

"Thanks, sweetheart." He grunted at a particularly enthusiastic thrust. "Tell me, Jess. Who do you think should get to come first?"

Jesse moaned in his ear. "You're just teasing me. You'll decide, it doesn't matter what I say."

"True enough. Do you have an opinion to offer, Steph?"

She was breathing hard, they all were. "Whatever Sir decides is what I want."

He laughed, enjoying her grin.

One of Jesse's hands was braced against the wall, the other hard on Grant's hip. "Jesse, give her chain a little tug for me."

The fingers on his hip tightened, Jesse's hard nipples pressing into his back as he reached around and jiggled the chain hanging between Stephanie's nipples.

"Oh, fuck," she gasped. "I don't know...Sir, please..."

"You can keep going," he answered. "I like being inside you. She feels good, doesn't she Jesse?"

"Yes Sir. So do you," came the pant from behind him.

He snorted a laugh, which for some reason brought him closer to the brink. He'd never done this before, never had anything inside him while he was inside another, never had his lover pounding him while he fucked the woman he'd been dreaming about. There was no way he was going to last much longer, as much as he wanted it to go on and on.

He clenched his ass, surprising a cry out of Jesse whose hand had gone back to the wall for support. Holding onto his control with all he had, Grant managed another few thrusts before he sensed both of them getting too close to the edge.

"No coming yet," he told them as he shoved into Stephanie one last time, coming hard. His forehead landed on her shoulder, her legs tight around him, her sheath clenching him as he spilled himself into the condom with a long groan. Jesse's fingers shook against him and he knew the other man was barely holding on.

Summoning what strength he could, he managed to move his arm from under Stephanie's butt until the finger with the mini-vibe was under her hole. He touched it on and told them they could come, just before setting the vibe to the base of the glass plug. Stephanie's scream drowned out any noises Jesse might be making, but his shuddering body, draped against Grant's, was telling enough.

He moved his arm so it was supporting Stephanie again as her weight settled more fully against the wall instead of relying on her legs wrapped around him. Jesse's legs trembled against his for a moment, but then he felt the other man gather himself and push from the wall. Steph's legs slowly dropped to the floor and they all stood in a shaky huddle for a minute.

"Help me out here, Jess." He put his hand on one of her nipple clamps, watched until Jesse had done the same. Stephanie braced her hands against the wall behind her. Without further warning, he said "Go," and unscrewed the clamp. He immediately dipped his head and sucked her nipple into his mouth, gently soothing it, enjoying the low whine coming from Stephanie. He bumped heads with Jesse and almost laughed, but managed to concentrate on the task at hand.

When he judged the job complete, he let her go with a little pop, then offered a final kiss to her abused flesh. Following his lead perfectly, Jesse did the same and they both stood. Then he smiled at

Stephanie, raised his eyebrows and jerked his head at Jesse. Her pout dropped away and turned into an evil grin.

"Hmph," was all Jesse said, but he put his hands behind him and squared his shoulders. Grant provided the same ministrations as he'd given Stephanie, though when he pulled back, he found Stephanie too involved in her task to notice he'd stopped. He had to clear his throat to get her to step away.

"Help each other with the plugs." He watched as they fought over who would help who first, grinned as they teased each other, and finally rolled his eyes as they collapsed onto the bed.

He stripped the condom from himself, then from Jesse, and retrieved the discarded gloves before accepting the plugs and heading into the bathroom. He snagged a bottle of water he'd left on the counter and returned to find they'd snuggled into each other.

They were wound together with a casual comfort that made him very happy. He shoved at Jesse until he could get to the release of his collar on the back of his neck. Jesse didn't cooperate much, because he liked wearing the collar, which didn't bother Grant at all. He gave him a slap on the butt before he could turn back over. "Why don't you guys start the shower, I'll be right there."

He went out the sliding glass doors and took the cover off the hot tub, turned the heat and jets on, and went to join them. Jesse was putting the much-depleted water bottle on the counter as Stephanie stepped into the thankfully huge shower. Grant finished off the water and stepped in behind Jesse who was already soaping Stephanie up. They were smiling and teasing each other and both immediately turned to include him in the play. He was a lucky son of a bitch.

JESSE KNEW Grant had gone to turn on the hot tub, so he was as eager as Grant to move things along, though Stephanie tried to linger in the shower. They rushed her out the door, not letting her stop to dry, dragging her into the cold air of the patio. When she caught sight of their destination, she gave a little squeal and bounded ahead. Grant laughed, reaching out to make sure she was steady as she climbed up and dipped her foot into the water. She shuddered, but didn't wait more than a few seconds before climbing all the way in. Jesse followed, loving the feeling of being enveloped by the heat.

He settled against the back, totally relaxed, but no longer as exhausted as he'd been before the shower. Now he was just pleasantly sated and very, very pleased with how things had gone. The chance to take Grant had been an awesome bonus, making what had already been a stellar evening absolutely perfect. Grant maneuvered Stephanie so that she was sitting on both of their laps, one leg draped over his, one over Grant's, her butt settled into their hips. She laughed and complained that her breasts were cold, so she scooted down farther until everyone was comfortable.

There was silence for a few minutes. Jesse tipped his head back, watching the stars. He loved coming to the beach house, and the hot tub was a big reason why, though the beach view edged it out as his favorite.

Tonight had been amazing and it wasn't even over yet. Being with Stephanie had been as wonderful as he'd dreamed. He'd known there was a risk, of course, but he just hadn't believed it could go badly. And it hadn't. Of course, there was still the chance it could, or that things would peter out without becoming anything long term. But he didn't believe it would.

There'd only been a few times in his life when he'd been certain a relationship was going to be permanent. The first had been his college sweetheart who had died of Leukemia their senior year. It had taken him years to get over that. He'd dated, even had a serious relationship, but it wasn't until he'd met Grant that he'd known he'd found something special again.

And now that his nerves about being with a woman were settled, he just knew this was going to work out. Did that make him bi now? Whatever, he didn't know or care, and he wasn't interested in any other woman. Just the one in his lap.

"Tell us your story," Grant said.

"My story? Hmm." She swirled the water in front of them. "Well, I grew up in Maine. Dad's a cop, Mom's a stay-at-home. Younger brother, Darren. He's still trying to decide what he wants to do and where he wants to do it."

"How did you decide to become a personal trainer?" Jesse asked, laying his arms along the back of the tub and twirling a piece of her purple hair.

"I considered being a physical therapist. But I fell into this while I was in school and I loved the challenge of helping people who were interested in getting healthy, showing them what would work for them, specifically, keeping them interested enough that they'd stick with it."

She dropped her head back to his arm. "What about you, how did you become a bus driver?"

He laughed. "Well, it wasn't something I grew up wanting to do, that's for sure. I actually had an uncle who was a supervisor and he had a ton of applicants, but he wasn't thrilled with what he was seeing, so he asked me to apply. He wasn't the one making the decision, so I still had to get accepted through the regular process. The pay was decent, so I figured I could do that while I was looking for a career. I majored in English, and funnily enough, that didn't exactly set me on an obvious path."

Laughing, she shook her head. "Yeah, I was majoring in philosophy before I switched to physical education." She turned to Grant. "And you? What's your story?"

"Parents, two sisters, one older, one younger. Family business, they basically raised me to take over. My dad is still president, but he's doing less and less. Luckily I enjoy it, though I won't be devastated if I ever have to walk away from it. One of my sisters is involved, the other couldn't care less. She's backpacking through Europe right now."

"And what is the business?" she asked. "I know you're a corporate guy, but not what kind of business."

"Glass."

She turned to look at him over her shoulder.

"Glass. Like, windows?"

"Windows, table tops, shower doors, all sorts of things."

"Huh. I have to say, I don't remember there being a lot of glass in your apartment."

"My hobbies dictate sturdier table choices."

She giggled and Jesse smiled, loving the sound.

"So, you're like, a vice president on his way to becoming president."

"Yep."

She turned her head back to look at Jesse. "Do you sing 'Happy Birthday Mister Vice President' to him?"

"Yep."

She laughed, hard, her whole body shaking against them. Her smile and laughter were infectious and he looked over her bowed head to share that appreciation with Grant. Yeah, it was for sure. He wanted to keep her.

Standing, she stepped away from them, then lowered herself completely under the water, coming up with her hands slicking her hair out of her face.

"How did a good girl from Maine become a naughty little sub with hair that changes more often than my car's oil?" Grant asked.

She put on an affronted look. "What makes you think I was a good girl?"

Grant simply raised an eyebrow in that way that he had.

"Okay, fine, I totally was. The hair is easy. Being that good girl, and a blonde, I guess I just like letting the color show that while I'm a fairly normal, responsible person, I have my bit of an edge, too. I change the color every time I get a trim, about six to eight weeks, so it's not *that* often. As for the other, I went to college, had a roommate who read erotic romances. She just liked them to read, but to me, they were like opening up a whole new world. At first it all just seemed so crazy. I had no idea, you know? And some of it was interesting, even hot, but it didn't speak to me, I guess you could say."

"What spoke to you the most?"

"Definitely the dominance and submission. I mean, the idea of a spanking seemed interesting, but it was hard to actually convince myself that could be sexy unless the book I was reading did a good job of submerging me in the characters wants and needs. But it was still hard to relate it to myself, the idea that getting hit, experiencing actual pain, not just a little pop, could be hot."

"What did you do to take it to real life?"

"Once I opened my eyes to it, I realized that stuff like this was going on around me, I just hadn't really recognized it before. Kind of like when someone you know gets a car you don't remember ever hearing of before, but then suddenly you see them all over the place and realize that they were there all along? After college I had a client who I realized was going to a club and I started asking him questions. His was a leather club, but the more I learned about things, the more people I met, and finally I went to a club with a group of friends, two who knew their way around and another two who were curious, like me."

"At least you went with a group," Grant grumbled, as if her safety were still in question after all these years.

She laughed. "I went to the club and it just felt so right. I started to play a bit. Very cautiously, at first. And when I knew it was something that was a part of me, not going away, I told my dad. He helped me look into the different clubs to decide which was safest and the best fit for me and that's how I found Apex."

"No shit?" Jesse blurted.

Her bubbling laughter was infectious, though he shuddered at the idea of having a conversation about clubs with his mom. She knew he was gay, was okay with it, but didn't want any more details than that.

"He's pretty cool. We had some battles when I started to fight for my independence, but we worked it out. I understand that he will never *not* have the need to protect me and he understands that I will ask his opinion on things but I get to make my own decisions."

"I understand the fighting-for-your-independence thing," Grant said. "I'm impressed you were able to make it work so well. My version of that is being willing to walk away at any time, but I can't imagine volunteering that kind of information about my personal life to my family."

"It's certainly not the only way to have a good relationship with your family. If your way works, then it's good. But, what do you mean by walk away? Just…stop being part of your family?"

"More the family business. They aren't so bad that I imagine it would get to the point of walking away from the family itself."

She looked confused and Jesse held his breath. Grant had really only started opening up more about his family in the last couple of months.

"They do things like, when I had my first boyfriend in college, they threatened to stop paying my tuition if I didn't end things and go back to dating the nice girls I'd been with before. I still don't know why they were shocked when I laughed and told them to go ahead. You would think at some point they would have noticed they'd been raising me to be an independent thinker, but somehow they never realized that would translate to them not being able to pressure me to do what they want. As it turned out, that relationship didn't last long, so somehow they convinced themselves they had won."

"Wow, those are not the kinds of games my family likes to play. We prefer board games and poker."

Grant laughed and Jesse had to lean in and kiss his smiling cheek.

"We love each other. We do. They were pretty good parents. After the boyfriend incident, as I was majoring in business, we had more conversations about me joining the company. They started using words like vice president. I knew they were angling for more control over me, but I didn't worry about it. As long as I'm willing to walk away, they don't have that power."

She blinked. "Wow. You come from a whole different world, I guess."

"Luckily for me, and not so much for them, they'd raised me to be strong-willed and cocky. While I love my family and like to see them happy, it's not my focus in life. They want to present a certain image, and they hate that I don't give a shit about that. They're still hoping I'll get over the gay thing, though."

"I'm sort of surprised they didn't raise you to be an asshole."

Jesse snorted but Grant ignored him, aside from sending a splash of water towards his face.

"*They* probably think I am, since I don't bow to their whims. But they're usually pretty good people, and my grandparents on both sides are fantastic. My grandfather on my dad's side, the company side, worked for what he built. I think he took extra pains when I was growing up to give me some sense of independence and self-motivation, so that I wouldn't be just another trust-fund brat."

"What about you, Jesse? Do you still have your grandparents?"

She hooked her arms on the ledge at the far side, letting her legs float towards them, her toes peeking out of the water.

"I have my mom's mom. My grandfather died of a heart attack a few years ago. We were close, so that sucked. I'm actually closer to my grandmother than my mother. My father ditched Mom when she turned up pregnant, but her parents took her in and helped raise me. She was more focused on getting to work and making a paycheck and paying her own way with them than she was on actually being around."

He shrugged when she gave him a sad look. "We love each other, I'm not suggesting it was bad. She worked hard for me, for us. We moved into our own place when I started middle school, but I still went over to my grandparents' house every day until she picked me up. We're good, we're just not as close as I am with Grandma."

"I'm glad you have her then, and had your grandpa."

"He was a good guy. Really didn't know what to do with the gay thing. Asked me if he should be marching in one of those parades." He laughed at the memory. "They didn't care much, as long as I was happy, same with my mom."

Grant rested his arm along the ledge next to Jesse's, brought his hand to Jesse's neck where the collar had been. He loved feeling Grant's hand there, and when he wore the collar it was like Grant never letting go.

"Jesse's grandma dotes on me," Grant said smugly.

Jesse laughed. "She totally does. My mom's more even handed, like she decided she would treat us the same, so that way she never has to wonder how to treat Grant."

"Aww," Stephanie said, then flicked her foot, shooting a small spray of water that fell just shy of his face.

Quick as a flash, he grabbed her ankle, giving it a little squeeze so she knew he could have tugged her to them. "Watch yourself, girlie."

She smiled and let him tow her back to them, settling with her kneeling, one leg on each of them.

Grant put a hand behind her neck, but didn't pull her closer. "Before we leave here, I'm going to fuck myself into you and I'm not going to move. Instead I'm going to hold you right in front of one of these jets until you scream and come around me."

Her breath was shaky but her smile was all invitation. "Sounds like an excellent plan."

Oh yes, Jesse really loved the hot tub here.

CHAPTER SIX

They dried off and gave Stephanie a tour of the little house. It was about a block away from the vacation house Grant's family had owned for years. At times it freaked him out that he had a partner who could buy a house in Cape Cod. The crazy thing was that Grant had discussed the whole plan with him first, laid out the options as he saw them, the upsides and downsides, how the market was doing at the time. Since they'd only moved in together a few weeks before, Jesse hadn't really thought it was any of his business but he'd been smart enough not to share that with Grant. He'd listened to what Grant had told him, asked a lot of questions, then offered his opinion, making it clear he would support whatever decision Grant made.

It was one of the reasons he'd really fallen in love with the man. Grant believed very strongly in their being partners, in every sense of the word. Well, except the BDSM sense. But really, they were then, too. The whole Dom/sub thing was a partnership, a symbiosis that didn't work without a complementary partner.

Stephanie seemed a little wide-eyed to realize they were in Cape Cod, especially when Grant pointed out the narrow trail that would take them down to the beach. He suspected she'd never really given much thought to what Grant did, any more than she'd thought about the fact that Jesse was a bus driver. He took her hand and smiled at her when she began to look a little nervous, then smacked Grant on the butt, just to remind her that Grant was still Grant.

Of course, Grant, being Grant, he turned around and gave a what-the-hell glare.

"I just wanted to show Steph how cute you are when you glower," he said, all innocence.

"Mmm, hmm. That's fine. I look forward to showing her how cute *you* are when you're begging for mercy."

He nodded. "Good plan. In the meantime, we should probably feed the poor girl."

They made grilled cheese sandwiches and debated what color she should add to her hair next, since she said it was almost time to change. Jesse wanted blue, but she said that's what she'd had before the purple.

"I'm thinking black. I've never done black before."

He cocked his head, trying to imagine stark black in the midst of her beautiful blonde. "It could work."

Grant didn't look so sure, but Jesse knew him well enough to know he was thinking that even if he hated it, it wouldn't last long, so why bother objecting?

By the time they finished eating it was late, so they climbed into the big bed, Grant in the center, Stephanie curled up into his side, and Jesse on his stomach, head on Grant's shoulder. He dropped into sleep, wondering what plans his man had for them for the next day.

IT FELT like no time had passed at all when Grant shook his shoulder. He grumbled. Grant was going to have to do a lot better than a shoulder nudge if he wanted to wake Jesse up with sex in the middle of the night.

"Come on, lazy. Stephanie's using the bathroom. Pull your warm clothes on and use the hall bathroom. Meet me at the front door."

He popped out of bed. Grant knew that Jesse loved a good sunrise at the beach and probably wanted to share the same with Stephanie. He hurried to the dresser for his warmest socks, jeans and a sweater, taking them with him to the hall bathroom. By the time he made it to the front door, Grant and Stephanie were pulling on their heavy jackets, Stephanie looking curious and awake.

"Good morning sunshine!" he said, giving her an enthusiastic kiss.

"Time for that later." Grant grabbed their arms and dragged them out of the house. He followed the beach path and brought them to Jesse's favorite little outcrop of rocks, where he laid down a blanket Jesse hadn't even noticed, and tugged them down beside him. Snuggled close to Grant, Stephanie pulled between Grant's legs, her hand wrapped securely around Jesse's thigh, Jesse was in heaven. Freezing, but happy.

The hopefully beautiful sunrise would be coming soon but even now it was soothing, watching the waves rolling in, listening to the sounds. He rested his head on Grant's shoulder and just watched. Leading a fairly stress-free life didn't mean he didn't appreciate moments of such beauty and peace. He wrapped his hand around Stephanie's to keep it warm and gave Grant a quick kiss of thanks for getting them out of bed. His man was not as much of a morning person as he was, and if the evidence suggesting Stephanie was a morning person as well was accurate…poor Grant.

They watched the light creep through the sky until the sun finally peeked over the horizon. None of them spoke until it made its full appearance and Jesse kind of wished he'd thought to grab his phone so he could take a picture, but he supposed it was better to just enjoy it for the moment it was.

It was still cold, of course, but he sort of felt like a warm glow surrounded them. He'd had a boyfriend who believed in auras, and Jesse had liked the concept a lot. He'd tried to convince himself he could sense them, even if he couldn't quite see them, but hadn't entirely managed it. At this moment in time, he almost got it. He felt like if he had an aura, it had learned Grant's ages ago and stretched to embrace the other man's whenever they were near. He was being silly, and he certainly needed more sleep, but it was as if he could *almost* feel his and Grant's auras stretching to encompass Stephanie's as well. To pull her into their fold.

He sighed at his fancifulness.

"Are you feeling neglected, my Jesse?" Grant asked, in response to his sigh.

Not sure what he was looking for, Jesse cocked his head in question. "No, Sir."

"I haven't beaten on you for days."

Jesse smiled. "You've managed to keep me entertained, and you've given me some lovely presents."

Stephanie had twisted to lean back against Grant's thigh, her feet under his other leg, so she could see them both.

"I'm glad you've appreciated them."

"Very much so, Sir."

Stephanie grinned at him.

"But of course, any time Sir wants to beat on me, I am of course his willing target."

Grant snorted at his overly solicitous tone and Stephanie giggled. He widened his eyes in affront and wasn't surprised when Grant grabbed his face hard enough to dent his cheeks as he pulled him in for a hard kiss, which succeeded in turning off his teasing expression and shutting him up from further comment.

Eventually he was shoved back, but by then he was breathless and had pretty much forgotten what they were talking about.

"Anyway," Grant said, tucking everyone back in nice and close. "Stephanie, it's been a while since we've seen you play. Anything new I should be aware of, anything that wasn't on your club list?"

She blinked at him. "You got the club to send you my list?"

"You would mind?" Jesse asked, surprised.

"Not that he got it, but I'm surprised they would send it outside the club without asking me."

"They didn't. I got it when we were there."

Now *she* looked surprised. "Oh, okay. I hadn't realized you guys had gone back there."

Grant smiled at her. "We didn't. I got the list when we went last weekend."

She blinked, and Jesse couldn't have said why he found it adorable.

"But I was with you the whole time after you saw me."

"Yes. I got it when I first got to the club. Did you think we were lying when we said it was *you* we wanted to see?"

"Well, no. I just…huh. Wow."

Grant raised an eyebrow at her.

"Um, the list is up-to-date."

Jesse wished he'd gotten to see the list, but it hadn't even occurred to him to ask for a peek until now. Too bad, it might have given him some insights into what Grant could be planning. Which, of course, meant Grant probably wouldn't have shared with him, even if he *had* thought to ask.

Grant ran a hand up through Jesse's hair. "Who's going to go fetch me a coffee?"

"We need Emma," Stephanie said. "She makes great coffees. I wish she wasn't so far out of the city."

"I haven't seen Emma in ages," Jesse remembered. "She must be almost done with school."

"Yep, her last semester. And she's met a man. Not sure how that's going to go, yet, but she was pretty head over heels last time I talked to her."

"Good for her," Grant said, his hand in Jesse's hair taking up a soothing massage.

"Some bossy alpha type, I suppose," Jesse teased.

Grant's hand fisted in his hair, the spark of pain almost better than the massage of a moment ago.

"A cop, apparently. He pulled her over for speeding."

"Ooh, official handcuffs. Why does that seem way hotter than when you buy them from the adult store?"

"Because they bring with them the vision of a hunky guy in uniform?" she asked.

"That must be it."

"Are you both going to sit here and daydream about cop Doms?"

"Well, in my imagination he had your face," Jesse said. "Does that help?"

Grant rolled his eyes.

Stephanie was enjoying relaxing in Grant's warm embrace, Jesse's leg tucked securely under her arm, the soft music of the waves, and the light banter from the guys. Last night, in the midst of the intensity, she wouldn't have been able to imagine a moment like this, and yet, it was perfect. Sweet and still sexy, full of satisfaction, as well as anticipation.

She was definitely starting to see danger in what she was doing. Danger of becoming addicted, wanting more. Their relationship was so compelling, so easy to fit into, it would be easy to forget that she was just a play partner.

They wandered back up to the house and made breakfast. She wondered how often they came out, since there was bacon and fresh orange juice in the fridge, but she didn't ask. It was too tempting to let things like Cape Cod houses and limo rides be part of the temptation, but that wasn't what mattered. Much better to focus on the way they made her laugh and the way they made her body sing.

While the guys showered, she did a quick fifteen-minute workout. Not her usual routine, for sure, but she'd told Grant she'd like to go for a run on the beach before they left, and he'd said he'd join her. Jesse had just laughed at her when she looked his way. Besides, she had the feeling she'd be doing a fair amount of stretching and sweating before they left the house again. She took a shower, did a fast blow dry on her hair, then pulled it into a ponytail. She found the guys in the living room, both of them reading books.

When she walked into the room Grant put his book down and

PERFECT ADDITION

studied her, then Jesse, making it clear he was ready to get started. Giving them a chance to object? Voice an opinion? She wasn't sure, but she was curious to see what he would do next. It felt a little naughty, decadent even, to be playing in the late morning. Sunlight streamed through the windows, though the blinds were angled up so no one could see, even if they walked close to the house.

Grant seemed to come to whatever decision he was considering. "I need to make some plans, decide on some scenarios. I need pretty scenery and inspiration, I think, while I make those plans. Get naked."

Well, that didn't sound like she was about to get some action, but Stephanie tried not to let her disappointment show. She took off the clothes she'd just put on, her yoga pants and tank top having been plenty in the nicely heated house. Her bra and panties followed, and she made a small neat pile that she set on the wide fireplace mantel, following Jesse's lead.

Grant picked up his duffel bag from beside the chair he was in. He pulled out what looked like leather with lots of buckles and chains. Once he'd sorted the two sets, she realized they were hog-tie restraints. She couldn't say she'd ever felt particularly sexy in them, but she could handle it.

He set the two devices down and reached for his bag, but then stopped and looked at her.

"Would you like to wear a collar today?"

Her eyes immediately darted to the bag wondering what he had in there. Probably a generic play collar, the kind people used in the club all the time to signify they were taken for the evening, even if it wasn't permanent. She didn't need one here, there was no one to signal off. But still, he'd offered.

And there was the part of her that glowed with joy, even though he'd been careful to limit the offer. He'd also, she noted, been careful not to indicate his preference one way or the other, by tone of voice.

She glanced at Jesse to see if there were any clues from that direction. He just gave her a soft smile that she couldn't really interpret. She went with instinct. "Yes, Sir, I would like that."

His smile was pleased, which made the glow she'd felt grow even brighter. She liked pleasing him. It was something that had taken a little bit of getting used to, when she'd begun exploring her submissive side. It seemed…not *wrong*, but sort of anti-feminist when she'd first realized how much pleasing someone else gave her pleasure. But she'd come to the realization that it was a natural thing for a lot of people, she just took it a couple of steps further than the average person.

He pulled out a purple collar that matched the stripe currently in her hair.

Stephanie blinked away the sting in her eyes at the realization that he'd bought it for her. This wasn't something they'd had sitting around, she was sure. The color could not be a coincidence.

He turned it over and held it stretched out so that she could see, and she realized it had been backwards. On the front, there was a strip of bright silver metal along it's length, the purple a narrow band above and below it. On the front was a small O-ring.

She swallowed hard, surprised at the emotion of the moment, turned and lifted her ponytail out of his way. He buckled it securely, but ran a finger underneath to check its tightness.

It had been a while since she'd worn one, and she hadn't remembered the impact it had on her, psychologically. Or maybe it had *never* really affected her like this before. She wasn't sure, but having Grant buckle his collar around her neck was not something she could take lightly, it turned out.

She lifted her head and met Jesse's eyes, saw total understanding. She had to blink hard again and take a deep breath, which of course gave her that little bit of pressure on her neck that she'd forgotten felt so powerful.

Grant turned her back around and reached behind him without looking, pulling out Jesse's collar. She watched Jesse's face as it was latched into place. His eyes closed for a second, and when they opened, they were softer than before, a little bit dreamy.

Since she was still watching Jesse, she missed Grant going back to his bag of tricks, but she did see him start to buckle more leather onto Jesse's biceps. It looked freaking hot, and when Grant connected the cuffs with a short strap, pulling Jesse's arms behind his back, it looked even more amazing.

Next, Grant attached the hog-tie cuffs to Jesse's wrists, but left the ankle portion dangling. She wasn't sure what he was holding when he came back from his bag, until he turned Jesse around. She sidestepped so she could watch as he buckled a cock ring around his partner. There was a leash attached to the little bit of leather that she found amusing, though she was careful not to show it.

Cocking his head, Grant studied Jesse, then took his own belt off. He wrapped it around the other man's legs, just above the knees, cinching it tightly. Then he picked up the leash and strode to the couch, leaving Jesse to hobble after him as quickly as possible, though Stephanie definitely saw the leash straining a bit.

"On the couch," Grant said. Jesse didn't hesitate, but fell forward, even with his arms behind his back and his legs strapped together. Grant held the leash to the side, then tucked it along Jesse's torso before picking up Jesse's legs and helping him lift them onto the couch. Jesse bent his knees, lifting his ankles into the air. She wasn't sure if that was because he knew the hog-tie was coming, or because his legs wouldn't fit all the way down the couch. Either way, Grant quickly buckled the remaining straps.

How had she thought it wouldn't look good? If she looked half as sexy as Jesse did right now, she'd never doubt the effectiveness of the hog-tie position again. He looked gorgeous, with his arms pulled back, wrists resting alongside his ass, framing the cheeks. She'd never had a thing for feet, but suddenly his looked masculine and elegant, and she badly wanted to run her hands along the muscles of his back.

Her hand twitched in jealousy when Grant did exactly that. Then she gasped when he bent down and locked his teeth onto Jesse's scrumptious ass. Whatever tension Jesse had been holding seemed to melt out of him. His body settled fully into the couch. At least, the parts of him that weren't being held in the air.

Grant stood up and studied Jesse for a moment. Then he turned to her. She remained still under his penetrating gaze. He couldn't really see inside her head, no matter how much it seemed like it as he watched her. Hell, *she* didn't even know what she was thinking right now, no way *he* could make more sense of the jumble of thoughts running through her brain.

Gripping her upper arms, he maneuvered her into the position he wanted her in before stepping behind her. She realized she was directly in Jesse's line of sight and didn't think that was an accident. Watching his knowing gaze as she felt the thick leather being buckled onto first one wrist, then the other, she felt tension she hadn't known she'd been holding, leaking out of her muscles. This was such a new thing, sharing an experience so specifically with another submissive.

The restraint wasn't as narrow as what she was used to, leaving her arms to fall almost to her sides, only a little bit behind her, so that they were resting against the side of her butt. She could feel the coolness of the metal links against the bottom of her ass and looked at Jesse again, imagining the leather and hardware framing her ass as it did his.

Grant ran his hands up her arms, massaged her shoulders a bit, teased the line where the collar met her neck. She hadn't realized she'd swayed back into his touch until he settled her back firmly upright.

"Sorry, Sir," she whispered, not sure if he wanted her to talk, though he hadn't said not to. He kissed her head, so she figured she was okay on both counts, though she shouldn't start up a dialogue right now.

Grant stepped away and she immediately missed his body heat. He went to the large ottoman and shoved it to where he wanted it, giving her a giant clue where he was going to put her, since Jesse was on the couch. She eyed it, trying to figure out if it was really long enough for her body, even with her legs bent at the knees. She wasn't so sure, but figured he'd deal with whatever needed to be dealt with.

She wished he'd let her lay down before securing her hands. He held her upper arm and wordlessly encouraged her to go down. Bending forward until she was able to rest the side of her face and her shoulders, she slowly let the rest of her body descend. Now her face was level with Jesse's and they were looking right at each other. His eyes were alive with interest, letting her know he was as fascinated watching her as she had been watching him.

Grant tapped her left thigh and she raised her leg. He grasped her ankle and had it cuffed and secured within seconds. Her right leg soon followed and he stepped back, letting her feel the tension of the restraints pulling against all four limbs. It was much more comfortable than she'd imagined, the balance between her wrists and ankles equalized so it felt like they were supporting—rather than pulling against—each other.

Her head just barely fit on the ottoman, her cheek resting against it, but her forehead actually hanging over the edge. Most of her thighs were in contact with it, so she felt fully supported. With her head twisted to the side, she was very conscious of the collar wrapped around her neck, a pleasant sensation.

Without warning, the whole ottoman moved slightly and her heart lurched for a second, though her brain knew Grant would make sure she didn't fall. When he had her where he wanted her, she once again had a perfect view of Jesse, and he the same of her.

Grant's fingers danced lightly up her back, then brushed across her cheek. He resumed his seat on the end of the couch, his hand automatically going to Jesse's head, brushing through his hair. Stephanie felt a clutch of jealousy, which she pushed aside. They couldn't both be on the couch and this way Grant was able to touch Jesse but watch her. Was Jesse jealous that his Dom was watching her, instead of him?

Even as she wondered, his hand left Jesse to pick up his book and his gaze moved to its pages.

Well. Okay. This was definitely a new experience for her. When she met with Doms at Apex, they had a limited amount of time. They didn't waste it by reading books. She might spend some time in bondage waiting for the top to get everything together, or even have a conversation with someone else. Jesse's relaxed, almost sleepy pose convinced her that she was in for a much longer wait than those experiences, however.

She knew subs who liked to be in cages, and Doms who liked to put their subs in them whether they liked it or not. But she'd always been more into active play than... Well, truthfully, she wasn't sure of the purpose of sitting in a cage. Or, for that matter, lying on an ottoman while her Dom read a book.

Which didn't mean she didn't try to follow his spoken and unspoken orders. She remained quiet rather than asking him what they were going to have for dinner. She curbed her fidgeting as much as possible, though she was certain she didn't remain nearly as still as Jesse.

Keeping her eyes trained on him, she tried to emulate his calm quiet. Actually, the fact that he seemed pretty good at this worried her. Did that mean this was a favorite activity of Grant's? Leaving his sub bound to lie around doing nothing? She was an active woman and not at all sure that was something she could handle, let alone learn to enjoy.

Jesse's eyes were open, so she knew he hadn't fallen asleep, but though they remained pointed in her general direction, she got the sense that he wasn't really seeing her anymore. She didn't think he was in subspace, though. Maybe she was wrong. Or maybe it was more like meditation.

She barely managed to suppress a huff and flicked her gaze back to Grant. He may not be turning her submissive crank at the moment, but he sure did hit all the right buttons for her. Hot without being too pretty, alpha without being an asshole, sweet without being annoyingly mushy. She felt her body move against the fabric and realized she'd kept her laugh silent but not still. Grant didn't appear to be watching, though, so she didn't stress about it and went back to her musings.

She had no idea how long she'd been lying there thinking not-very-submissive thoughts when she realized Grant had put his book down and was watching her. Stilling, it was only then that she realized she'd been using her legs to pull her arms into a nice stretch, releasing, then repeating for, well, who knew how long?

He didn't seem mad and he hadn't actually told her not to move around, but she watched him warily to see what he would do next. When he saw that he had her attention, he smiled. It was not the masochistic smile of a Dom about to dole out punishment. It was the genuine smile of a man about to offer a woman a present. His hand moved to Jesse's back, but he kept his gaze on her.

"Would you like to help me play with Jesse?"

CHAPTER SEVEN

She felt her eyes go wide but she immediately answered, "Yes, Sir." Her gaze moved to find Jesse watching her, his lips edged up into a small, eager smile.

Grant rose and came to her, crouched down so she could see his face. "You're not done. You'll be back here when we're finished with Jesse. All right?"

"Yes, Sir."

He put his hands under her armpits and hauled her up so that she was kneeling, making sure she was steady before letting her go. She used her core muscles so she didn't need to brace her hands against her legs while she felt him unhooking the clasps holding her ankles to the center O-ring. He left the leather cuffs where they were, simply disconnecting all the clasps until she was free.

She thought he would let her up then, but he brought two of the clasps around to her front and used them to hook her wrists back together, though with a little play between them since he used two, instead of one.

She gave them a little pull, then waited. He stood and offered her a hand, helped her off the seat. His hands came to her upper arms, holding her still for a minute while he kissed her deeply. She would have melted into him if he hadn't been holding her. However long she'd been lying on the ottoman had been too long to not be touched by him. She shivered a little, though she knew it wasn't from cold, or even from anything sexual. It was the knowledge that she wanted his touch, more of his body than his two hands holding her.

"Jesse's turn," he reminded her when he broke the kiss.

He was going to let her play with his Jesse. She could totally live with that. His hand came up to her nape and they turned to look at the man lying on the couch. They were standing too close for Jesse to see their faces, and for them to see his eyes, but she was pretty sure he was breathing more heavily than he had been when she'd been lying across from him.

"Makes you want to touch every inch of him, doesn't it?" Grant asked conversationally.

"Oh, yes, Sir."

"Kneel down next to him while I get the bag. You can give me a hand." His smirk told her he hadn't forgotten that he'd restricted her hands, but at least they were in front of her and he'd indicated she'd be able to touch.

She knelt near Jesse's hip. His luscious ass was right in front of her but she forced herself to wait for Grant's direction and kept her hands to herself. If she leaned in, she could bite his big toe. The thought reminded her that she'd actually heard Jesse use his safe word once, at the club. It was long before Grant had become a member, but it turned out that Jesse's feet were very ticklish and he'd had to call a halt to the play because his top at the time hadn't quite realized how serious Jesse was when he said he didn't want them played with. It was too bad, because they really did look elegantly masculine in their cuffs.

Grant knelt beside her, his bag to his left so she still couldn't see into it. He showed her his hand though, and the half dozen clothespins that he held.

Oh. She managed not to say it out loud but she formed the word with her lips. He darted in and kissed her, causing her to smile.

PERFECT ADDITION

"I think she's looking forward to this, Jesse. Think she has a little sadism in her, after all?"

"I think all women do, Sir."

That got a laugh out of her, but didn't distract her from the task at hand. She looked at Grant expectantly, wanting to know what he would have her do next.

"I'd be careful there, baby, she's looking quite eager."

"Bring it, Sir."

She laughed again. Grant reached between Jesse's upper arms and pinched a fold of skin, then handed her a pin.

"Make sure you put the handle with the hole in it facing us."

Each pin had a small hole at the end of the handle. It was awkward, with her wrists bound together, the space between Jesse's upper arms narrow since he was bound there as well as his wrists, but she maneuvered around Grant's hand and put the clothespin in place, so that the hole was towards them. Grant let go and she watched the long pin bounce in place for a moment before stilling. Repeating the maneuver, they made a line of five down the far side of his back, and then another line on the side closest to them. The twin trails narrowed to his waist, just above the swell of his ass.

Usually she was on the receiving end of the pinches, or viewing a scene from much farther away. She'd never actually seen it so up close and personal. She would have expected the skin to be much redder. The light sheen of sweat that was beginning to dot his back and the fact that Jesse's breathing had become faster but shallower were the only signs that he was in pain.

"Can I lick him, Sir? Please?"

Grant chuckled. "He does look tasty, doesn't he? Go ahead, right between the trails."

She half stood, leaning over to get her face between his arms and the two lines, then licked a long, slow path up his spine.

He shuddered under her tongue and she smiled. He tasted clean and good and hot. Sitting back on her heels, she looked to Grant. He handed her another clothespin and made a pinch of skin on the center of Jesse's far thigh, very close to where his calf pressed in.

She did her part and watched in fascination as their new strip marched up the firm ass cheek to meet the old strip.

Grant handed her a ball of twine. "Feed that through the holes."

She tried to be careful, but as she pushed the twine through each small hole, the pins jostled. By the time she finished the second row, Jesse was breathing very quickly, though she wasn't sure if that was from the current pain, or because he knew what was coming. She'd never experienced a zipper pull and knew for a fact that she didn't want to. A couple of clothespins here and there were one thing, but this level of pain was definitely beyond her.

Grant offered her one of the string ends, a question on his face.

Oh, hell no! She didn't think she was capable of causing that kind of pain any more than she was of receiving it. He smiled reassuringly at her, so she knew he wasn't disappointed.

"Are you ready, Jesse?"

"Yes, Sir," Jesse answered, though it sounded like he did it through gritted teeth.

"You can touch him, Steph, however you like, just keep your hands clear of the pins."

She stood, then knelt on the couch, her knees between his, her hands on his calves. One look at Grant assured her that he approved of the move.

"Just be careful in case he kicks a little by accident."

"I won't, Sir."

"Good boy. Okay, here goes."

Grant stood and pulled the far string in one long, clean move, the pins popping clear of Jesse's skin with a sound that had Stephanie cringing.

Jesse cried out, but didn't move his legs in her grip. He was panting hard by the time Grant finished, but Grant gave him no rest, no warning before he began on the second pull.

As soon as he was done, he shoved his cock into Jesse's open mouth, in a move that Stephanie assumed they'd done before.

Leaving her position, she moved back to his side and began to kiss the angry red spots one at a time, sometimes licking, sometimes giving a light suck. Jesse moaned around Grant's dick and Grant's hand came to her head, guiding her up and down Jesse's back and buttocks for a while. The little moans and grunts they both gave was a symphony she enjoyed as she did her part to soothe and pleasure Jesse.

When Grant's grip tightened on her, she stilled, her face pointed towards Jesse's feet so she couldn't see, only hear as Grant found his release.

Since it was there, she rested one palm on Jesse's ass cheek, letting the other rest against his side as she waited for Grant to recover. He let go of her hair and she sat back on her heels. Grant's hand was clenched firmly in Jesse's hair and Jesse was no longer exhibiting any signs of pain that she could see. No, he was licking his lips.

Grant had dropped back to his heels as well and he looked at her.

"Want to give it a go?" he asked.

"Hell, no."

He laughed. "I didn't think so." He let go his grip, stood and moved around her. Lifting Jesse's hips until the other man got his knees under him and his arms down behind his butt so the chain rested on the backs of his knees, he gestured her towards Jesse's head. "Why don't you give him something else to suck on, get your nipples nice and hard for me for when it's your turn."

She wasn't going to argue with that. Scooting over until she was even with his face, she found Jesse seemed just as eager as she was to follow the order. He latched on with a strong suction that pulled a gasp from her. She rested her hands on his back, enjoying the feel of his muscles bunching under her fingers as he worked her breast and reacted to the slicked-up thumb Grant was teasing his asshole with.

Pulling back, enjoying the small pain as Jesse resisted, holding onto her nipple as long as he could, she moved enough to offer him her other breast, but her gaze remained on Grant's ministrations. He replaced his thumb with a dildo and worked it like it was his own cock, in and out, peppering Jesse's ass with smacks every few thrusts. He slid it all the way in and motioned for her to join him. He took one of her hands and led her to Jesse's balls, then ducked himself down and engulfed Jesse's dick in one motion.

Jesse cried out. Stephanie cocked her head so she could watch Grant for a minute, fondling Jesse balls the whole time. Grant had one hand still holding the dildo in place, the other gripping the base of Jesse's cock as he worked his head up and down the shaft furiously. It was a beautiful sight, but she needed to stop enjoying the show and start helping out more. It was awkward to maneuver to the correct angle to get between Jesse's thighs and reach him, but she managed it. She pulled his balls into her mouth and rolled her tongue around them, enjoying the occasional contact with Grant's hand.

She could feel the balls tightening in his sac, feel the urgency in Grant's motions, his hand going faster. The hand above her, resting on Jesse's butt moved with a sharp crack, and Jesse started to beg.

"Please, Sir, can I come?"

She heard Grant hum against his mouthful and Jesse's thighs tensed even more.

"Please, Sir, please, let me…come for you."

She scraped the nails of her free hand down his upper thigh halfway through his begging so it ended on a more urgent and slightly higher tone than it began. Grant laughed; Jesse squeaked and appeared to be beyond forming sentences.

"Sir, please, Sir. I need…Sir. Please."

"Now," was all Grant said before covering Jesse's penis again. Stephanie felt the movement in is balls, the rigidity of his thighs. She took her mouth off him, replacing it with gentle fingers, sat back and watched Jesse's face as he opened his mouth in a silent scream. She raked his thighs again, though not very hard, and his legs shuddered, then went limp.

Grant didn't come up immediately and Jesse pulled against his restraints a bit. She wondered what he was doing down there, but simply flattened her hands and offered Jesse what comfort she could. When Grant did finally duck out from under Jesse, he had a full grin on that she couldn't help but respond to.

He reached under her arm and unlatched the two clasps holding Jesse's feet to the O-ring, then the wrists. He maneuvered and shuffled until he was sitting on the far end of the couch once again, this time with Jesse's head in his lap, his arm wrapped securely around Grant's legs. Grant patted Jesse's rump, inviting Stephanie to rest against it. She cocooned herself behind Jesse's drawn-up legs, resting against his butt. She wasn't even sure when Grant had pulled out the dildo, but it was nowhere she could see without bothering to look around.

Grant produced a sports bottle and held it to Jesse's lips. He drank deeply for half a minute then relaxed. From his bag of tricks, Grant pulled out a wet wipe. He started to reach over, then seemed to realize Stephanie was in an even better position to help, so he handed it to her. She held up her still-attached wrists in question, but he just smiled and started petting Jesse's hair.

Managing not to harrumph out loud, Stephanie wiped Jesse's cock clean, folded the wipe in half and used the fresh edge to the get lube from around his asshole. Folded it in half again and handed it back to Grant. She moved her wrists forward so they were on Jesse's rib cage and rested her cheek against his hip.

That had been quite a show and she was glad to have participated in it. It was kind of weird to be the Dom's assistant. She wondered if she could have a t-shirt made. Or maybe an apron she could wear with nothing else. She sort of doubted Grant would let her wear anything when they were in play mode, but the vision made her smile.

It wasn't actually the first time she'd assisted in aftercare. She'd sat with subs while their Doms had to clean up their play area, as well as offering to clean up the space so the Dom could stay with their sub. It was different, though, doing that favor for a friend and being an active participant in the cuddling as well as the playing.

Jesse tucked his legs more tightly against her, and she knew he was squeezing Grant, too.

She closed her eyes and wondered if they were done for now. At that moment, she couldn't quite imagine going in for a round herself. Though she hadn't come, she was pretty well relaxed now. She breathed in deeply, inhaling the smell of Jesse, and dropping a kiss on his skin.

Grant moved and she started to look up, but his fingers cupped her head, held her still. He pulled her ponytail holder loose and threaded his fingers into her strands, tightened his grip deliciously. There was just something about a man holding her still by the hair, grip unforgiving and commanding that brought moisture to her pussy.

The sound of more water being drunk made her wonder if Jesse was starting to come back to reality, but she didn't try to move. Instead, she reached her tongue out as far as she could and drew a lazy zigzag on Jesse, then blew cool air onto the spot, fascinated by the little goose bumps that popped up.

"That was very nice, Jesse."

"Yes, Sir. Thank you, Sir."

Jesse moved, giving her time to sit up so that he could do the same. He looked at her and she gave him a grin which slowly melted away as the heat in his eyes intensified. Her eyes widened. Shouldn't he be feeling satisfied? Not quite so hungry? She glanced at Grant and found he was watching her too.

She blinked and sat back against the arm of the couch. Not retreating exactly, just surprised. Surely what they'd just done was enough for now. Especially if there was going to be more tonight.

The tingle starting in her sex assured her that her body was on board with the looks in the guys' eyes. She licked her lips, watched both of their gazes drop to her mouth. And she smiled.

"My turn?"

"Oh, yeah," Grant drawled. "Get on the ottoman, on your knees."

Wow, what that tone could do to her.

She slid of the couch and gave her walk a bit of a wiggle, though she only needed three short steps to get to the end of the ottoman. She kneeled up onto it, as tall and straight as she could manage, her

PERFECT ADDITION

bound wrists hanging in front of her, face forward, eyes directed at the floor about four feet in front of her. Movement from the couch told her one or both of them had stood, but she remained still.

Hands—she was pretty sure they were Jesse's—pulled at her hair, re-affixing the ponytail holder. He reached around her, unclipped her wrists.

"Put your hands behind your back." Grant's voice didn't sound very close. Was he still sitting on the couch?

Her wrists were quickly reattached, the chain resting on the swell of her butt.

"Move forward more," Grant directed. "So your legs are completely on the seat." She shuffled until the tops of her feet were flat against the cushion. Jesse made clinking noises and tugs against her bonds but he must have added more clips to the restraint because while her arms were pulled away from her body, her back remained upright.

"That's lovely," Grant said.

He moved into her line of sight now, but too close for her to see anything other than his shirt. He brushed his fingers softly around her breasts, drawing squiggly circles and making light scratches with his nails, but avoiding her nipples.

"They look eager for attention, don't they, my Jesse?"

"Yes, Sir. And decoration."

"True. Do you want to share yours?"

Her stomach clenched at the memory of the clothespins. She was sure that Grant knew she wasn't interested in the kind of pain the zipper had caused Jesse. Almost completely sure. The edge of fear brought her heart rate up and she felt the sweat start to prickle at her hairline. It was fine, she knew that if he misjudged her, she could use her safe word. He wouldn't be upset with her. But she didn't want that to happen.

His fingers had been soft, but he suddenly pinched the side of her breast. Jesse's hand came from behind her and placed a clothespin on the spot Grant offered. She breathed through the pain, pulling it in, letting it spread through her. It wasn't even as painful as the little nipple press from last night, it was just in a different spot than she was used to.

Without warning, of course, he pinched a spot on the far side of her other breast. Jesse's breath was warm against her skin as he angled around to add the pin.

Grant's hands left her breasts and he tilted her chin up to look at him. He studied her as she breathed, focused on his face instead of the sharp bites of pain that were slowly fading to dull throbs. "Very pretty."

She blushed. It was silly. It wasn't like she hadn't been naked in front of him for an hour now. But his compliment as he watched her deal with the pain he caused pulled a flush to her skin.

He smiled, leaned down for a very welcome kiss. As his tongue explored her mouth, Jesse's hands massaged her shoulders. All of which completely distracted her until Grant's fingers suddenly pinched her nipples. Hard.

She squealed, not a sound she enjoyed making. Grant stepped back and she worked hard not to glare at him, even when he chuckled softly.

When Grant began to lightly tickle her ribs, she grew nervous. She wasn't particularly ticklish, so she managed not to squirm much, but she wasn't in love with the idea of clothespins there either.

Sure enough, there soon came a pinch, followed by the bite of the damn wooden pin. More deep breathing, she remained tense until he did one more on her left side, then two on her right. When he stepped back and looked at her, she wasn't sure what look she should go for. Calm? Pained? Nervous? Hell, she didn't know *what* she looked like, she just concentrated on breathing.

He moved to his bag and didn't attempt to hide the small flogger he pulled free. She tried to get a good look without moving her head. It looked like suede. He gave a light swing and it brushed softly across her thighs. Definitely suede. Although, she hoped it was a synthetic version.

Despite the small pinches of pain and the impending flogging, she relaxed a little. He knew she wasn't Jesse, didn't want the same levels of pain as his sub. Which she'd known, of course, but…well, he'd played on her fears on purpose, she supposed. Damn Dom.

Her thighs were warm now, the blood flowing under her skin. A couple of the strands had danced enticingly close to her clit, but nothing had actually landed. He aimed at her sides, her stomach. One strand nicked one of the clothespins on her rib, and she gasped sharply, but the pain had receded again by the time her breath left her.

He moved around behind her, careful of how her arms were stretched, but warming her up very nicely. The stings were harder now, the bites deeper, and she thrust her breasts out in invitation. One he immediately took her up on. The pins jerked and she gasped again, but she wanted it now, the little bits of pain somehow sensual gifts rather than torments.

"Close your eyes," he whispered.

His voice alone brought fresh cream to her thighs. With her eyes closed, she almost got dizzy as he circled her. She tightened her core, concentrated on her center of balance. At least until Jesse's fingers began to tickle their way along her thigh. It was hard to reconcile the whisper-like caress with the intense pulse of the flogger.

Those searching fingers made their way to her pussy and. Jesse suddenly abandoned light and gave her clit a pinch. At the same time, one of the strikes managed to catch a clothespin and her nipple. Her breath caught in her throat, and it wasn't until another strike landed on her flank and Jesse's finger circled her vagina that she was able to breathe again, although at a much faster pace than before.

Jesse eased one finger into her, then another. She was impressed with how they were able to work seamlessly together. Were any of the blows landing on Jesse as he worked her? His touch never faltered, his exploration of her core very thorough as Grant rained down blows, heavier and faster.

Her legs wanted to collapse and she wished her arms were

secured above her head, giving her something to pull against, to hold herself up. Instead she had only her quivering thighs and straining core.

A solid hit to her back was followed by Grant's voice. "Jesse."

She cried out in denial when Jesse stopped touching her. Clinking behind her gave warning that she was about to move again.

Someone grabbed her calves and jerked.

Strong hands caught her upper arms and lowered her down safely, but her heart was in her throat. She turned her head to the side so she could rest her cheek on the cushion, but they'd left her too far forward and she could only drop her chin down to rest on the side of the ottoman.

Her breasts were smushed into the cushion, but it didn't seem to really affect the pins. Her legs were spread the width of the seat and reattached to the O-ring with the short length, giving her the subtle pull from earlier. Her whole body was alive, feeling the softness of the fabric, the air against her sweaty skin, eager for more contact from the guys. But nothing happened for what seemed like whole minutes. Small sounds gave her no real clues as to what they were up to.

Finally, a brief brush of stiff leather against her butt warned her what was next. A crop. She would rather have continued with Jesse's fingers in and around her pussy, but okay, she was warmed up enough to welcome the crop.

Except, she never would have expected the slap to land on her upturned foot.

The shock of it tore a scream from her, though it wasn't really that painful. She barely had time to react before her other foot received the same treatment. She'd never had her feet played with before, wasn't really sure she wanted to. Another hit came at the same time lubed fingers eased straight into her hole. Blows to her arches, soles and the pads of her feet continued as fingers moved in and out of her ass only to be replaced by something hard. It took her longer than normal to recognize anal beads, because her head was much more focused on the strange sensations on her feet. Sensations that had actually started to feel kind of good, like a massage.

The beads stopped moving, a large warm hand caressed her ass, and then everything stopped.

Her body was alive, tingling, aching, but nothing was happening. She wanted to wave her feet in invitation. More crop, more flogger, more something, she wasn't even sure what she wanted at this point, but she wanted more.

It seemed as though an hour had passed and she realized she was crying, though she wasn't sure if it was frustration or pain.

Her mouth was open and the words were spilling out before she made a conscious decision to speak. "Sir, please."

A flick to her butt.

"Please," she tried again.

Nothing happened.

"Sir!" She wailed. An open-handed smack to her foot.

"Please, Sir, please, Sir, please, Sir."

She continued chanting as hands grabbed her hips, pulled them up through the chain between her wrists and someone began to enter her. Her legs could only open so wide with the restraints, but he pushed forward.

"Sir, Sir, please." Her voice was more of a gasp now and it was cut off when his hand gripped her hair, lifted her head by the ponytail. She hadn't been sure if it was still Jesse down below, but she was absolutely certain it was Grant's hand lifting her head so that she could see the cock straining for her mouth. She would have lunged for it, but she couldn't move. Jesse's grip on her hips and Grant's hold on her hair, her empty hands clasping and unclasping, unable to move, she was totally at their mercy.

Grant teased her, rubbing the head of his penis along her lips. She gasped against it when Jesse entered her fully, but he still held just shy of letting her taste.

"Sir," she moaned. "Please."

He gave her just the tip and she

out, slammed back in with force, but with their hands holding her steady, her head didn't move. She took the drop of pre-cum Grant had produced, rolled it around his head with her tongue, brought her lips together to give it a kiss.

His free hand moved down and he pulled one clothespin free. She gasped and he lowered her head down, giving her more. He didn't give her a break, but reached over her and pulled the pins from her ribs as Jesse changed the angle of her hips and had her crying out. When Grant switched the hand holding her hair, she knew what was coming. She concentrated all her thoughts on the taste and feel of him on her tongue as he removed the pins from that side.

He pulled her up slowly, letting her swirl her tongue around him as much as she could, then fucked up into her mouth, hitting the back of her throat. She swallowed, won a grunt from him, and hummed. He must have signaled Jesse because they began to work in sync, one going in as the other pulled mostly out, they moved faster and faster until Grant pulled all the way free and Jesse slammed home, stilled as he came.

She waited for Grant to return, but he lifted her by her shoulders as Jesse pulled free and helped move her so she was sitting on her calves. Jesse's fingers curved into her cunt, his other hand pinching her clit as Grant stood in front of her, fisting his dick, her saliva still making it slick.

"Are you ready to come for me?"

His voice was hoarse and she clenched hard around Jesse's fingers.

"Yes, Sir, please, Sir. I want to come for you."

His hand moved quickly, up and down his shaft twice more, then he pointed it at her chest, let loose.

"Now, come now," he said, when the soft, warm liquid hit her breasts. Jesse pinched her clit again and began to pull the anal beads f........ .w her head back and screamed.

                    ke j.... to the couch. She wasn't even exactly
                         ded up un-cuffed and on the floor,

in Grant's lap with Jesse running a fantastically cool wipe over her sticky chest. Probably it was going to be a while before she felt like taking that jog.

She snuggled her head into Grant's shoulder and shut her eyes, leaving them closed even when he nudged her lips with a water bottle. She'd taken a few healthy sips before it occurred to her that the water was cold and she heard the rattle of ice, the way she preferred it. Unlike what he'd given Jesse earlier.

Her brain was fuzzy, but not so much she didn't realize that he'd made the effort to learn her preference and provide it. She needed to give Jesse a big ol' kiss of thanks for being willing to share such a talented and thoughtful Dom. If she'd had him first, she wasn't so sure she'd have been able to do the same. As it was, she was definitely pleased the two had decided to invite her into their games.

THREE SHOWERS and two frozen pizzas later, she and Grant tried to convince Jesse to join them for their jog. His laughter at the very idea chased them down the street as they started off. It was cold out, but they quickly settled into a fast pace that warmed them up and seemed to be a good compromise of their natural strides. She didn't usually jog with anyone else. She cherished the time as her own, since a lot of her working out was done with clients. This, though, was very nice.

"Jesse mentioned your family has a house nearby, too. Did you spend a lot of time out here, growing up?" she asked.

It had never occurred to her that Grant was rich, before the conversation in the hot tub. She'd really never given any thought or attention to his financial stability at all, though she supposed she'd assumed he and Jesse together made a decent living, since they had the nice apartment. Even hearing that he was the heir to the throne of the family business, she hadn't really considered that meant the kind of money she guessed a house on Cape Cod represented.

"When I was a kid, we always came up for a good portion of the summer. The occasional weekend in other seasons, but not often.

Later, I'd meet them here a few times in the summer, or come out during the off-season with whoever I was seeing at the time. Now that my father's working less, they come a bit more often. When Jesse and I got serious I decided it made more sense to have our own place. Privacy for when the whole family is in town, and not having to ask permission to use the place otherwise."

He pointed to a path coming up on her left and she took his direction, seeing that it would allow them to have a nice view of the water, but stay off the sand.

"It reminds my parents that they don't get to decide how I live my life, and they better not try to play games with me. Plus, I really love the beach when it's quiet like this. And I don't mind the cold."

"It's beautiful," she agreed. "I'm sorry your family situation isn't what you'd like it to be."

He shrugged. "It's not bad. Now that it's become clear Jesse's going to be a permanent part of my life, they need to pull their heads out of their asses, or they'll find I just won't be around to be bothered by their attitudes. They're used to family that needs their validation and approval, because that's tied in with their money. They sometimes forget that I don't give a shit for any of those things."

He gave her a little hip-check when she frowned. "It's good, sweetheart. I'm pretty sure they'll come around, but if they don't, I promise, it will work out. It's not something I'm very worried about, and you shouldn't worry about it at all."

"If you say so." She didn't think she could one-hundred-percent follow the order, but she'd let it rest for now. She looked up at the darkening sky. "I think we might be in for some major weather soon."

"Yeah, we do get a lot of it here. It's nice to get out of the city occasionally, though we don't usually hire a car. That was more so that we could pack in plenty of playtime with you." He glanced over at her. "And maybe to give you an experience I was guessing you'd never had."

She laughed. "You guessed correctly. I don't have a lot of experience playing outside of clubs at all, and none inside a moving vehicle."

"How come you kept to the club scene so much?"

"I guess part of it is that's where I felt comfortable doing it. Meeting new people, giving them a chance in a safe environment. And I love the atmosphere, the camaraderie, the energy. I like knowing people are watching and getting excited by what I'm doing, how the scene I'm in is playing out."

It had only been a few months ago that she'd teased her friend Emma for saying she was having as much, if not more, fun playing with her new guy at home than she had at the club. Stephanie had accused her of becoming a fuddy-duddy, honestly having a hard time imagining not wanting to go to the club. Now, here she was, perfectly happy to keep playing as they were. She sort of liked that it was private. Just between them. No one gossiping about them, wondering how long she was going to last as their play partner, if anyone was going to get upset or hurt by the time they were done.

"We had fun going back the other day. I admit, the main reason we did was to see if you would be there, but when you weren't we enjoyed ourselves. But once we started playing at home, we just never really had any reason to leave. We could do most everything from the club, and then some. Actually, that does bring up something I wanted to talk to you about."

Her breathing had gotten fairly heavy by now and she was gratified that his had as well. It would suck to have to hate him for being in better shape than she was. He took a long drink from his water bottle and she did the same.

"Jesse doesn't always want or need heavy play, but he does like it once in a while and he's not a big fan of doing it at the club, in front of the group. He doesn't like people assuming he's a big pain slut and thinking that's all that he's good for."

She frowned, hating the idea that anyone would feel inhibited in any way at Apex, since the whole point was to be able to get what you wanted, what you needed, in a safe and comfortable environment. But she sort of understood his point. People formed impressions about you and it could be hard to change their minds sometimes.

"Okay," she said before taking another drink of water.

"I'd like to give him a real flogging tonight. If it makes you uncomfortable, we can wait until we get home. If you don't mind but don't want to be there, that's fine. If you want to watch, that's cool, too. If you want to participate a bit, I can make that work too. Your choice."

She didn't bother to ask if Jesse was good with all of those options, because she trusted that he wouldn't have offered anything his boyfriend wasn't okay with. She certainly would have understood if they'd asked her to steer clear of a scene they wanted to play, though she had to be honest enough with herself to admit she would have felt a bit jealous and maybe even a little hurt. And though she wasn't into the level of pain she was assuming Grant was referring to, she generally had no problem observing. She even found it hot. She just didn't want to experience it.

"I'm okay just watching if that's easiest, but if you have a role in mind for me that doesn't involve me getting hit any harder than you did today, I'm up for that."

"Just so we're clear, you would be up for a round of flogging, even after the session you had this morning, this soon?" Grant asked.

His question made her pause. She was a little bit sore, and now that she thought about it, she would normally never have considered another session so soon. It just wasn't normally a question because she always had at least a day between club visits, and even that was rare.

"Hmm, good point. I hadn't really thought about it, but I think you're right. It probably would be too soon for me to go again tonight."

"I thought so, but it never hurts to check."

They were breathing heavily now and Grant motioned that they were going to make another turn, taking them away from the beach.

She gave the crashing waves one more appreciative look before turning her attention back to Grant.

"So, what did you have in mind for tonight?"

"I was thinking I'd tie you up in rope and give him something to watch while I'm working on him."

She shivered, despite having worked up a nice sweat.

They turned another corner and Grant pointed out one of the larger houses they'd seen. "That's my parents' house."

"It's lovely. I think—"

She forgot what she was going to say when the rain started. Only a couple of drops at first, then more, until it was a heavy sprinkle. She looked at Grant and he grinned, picked up the pace. They began to run flat out, the water a cool relief to her hot body.

She looked over at Grant again and almost tripped. Hair wet, t-shirt wet, huge grin, he was gorgeous.

He turned one more corner and she saw his house. The door was open and Jesse was standing there, watching for them, giving them something to run home to. She put on a last burst of speed, unsurprised when Grant matched her pace, and threw her arms around Jesse, knocking him back into the house. He laughed, wrapping his arms around her to keep them both standing.

"You bitch, you did that just to get me wet!"

"Pretty much. Now you should get in the hot shower with us."

"I can get on board with that plan."

She turned towards the hallway and was very pleased to see that Grant had already taken off his shirt. Jesse seemed to think that was a good idea, because she felt his hands at her waist and her shirt rising. Laughing, she tried to bat him away but Grant moved to help him and she was soon naked.

CHAPTER EIGHT

Jesse knew that Grant had told Stephanie to pack clothes for a nice dinner out, and made reservations at their favorite fancy restaurant, but once he'd seen the reports on the storm, he'd decided to change things up. They'd all showered, then separated to get dressed, lest they get more distracted and end up in bed. He quickly pulled on his slacks and shirt, but didn't bother with a tie or shoes and socks, and darted down the hall while Grant was brushing his teeth.

He finished the preparations he'd begun while they were out jogging and made it back to the master bedroom in time to stop Grant from putting on his socks.

"You can stop there, I've cancelled our reservations."

Grant looked up in surprise. He was sitting on the end of the bed, socks in hand, tie draped around his neck but not yet knotted. "You did?"

"Yeah, the news says the storm is going to be pretty big."

Grant cocked his head and they both listened to the heavy beat.

"Okay. We can scrounge something up here." He stood and started to unbuckle his belt.

"Don't change. You look hot just like that."

Grant paused, gave Jesse a long look. "You didn't cancel the reservation just now."

"Nope. I decided that staying in was no reason to deprive us of seeing Stephanie all dressed up."

After a moment, Grant shrugged. "I can't argue with you there." He tossed his socks on the bed and stood. "Did you make dinner while you were at it?"

"No, but I promised Henry loads of cash if he'd send dinner over from the inn."

The restaurant they'd made reservations for was in one of the hotels and Grant and Jesse had become friends with the concierge.

Grant put his hand on Jesse's shoulder and squeezed. "Excellent plan."

Jesse led the way down the hall to the room that Stephanie had appropriated for her preparations. The room was more neutral than the somewhat masculine master bedroom. The maple bed and dresser set were accented by the slate-blue duvet. The pillows were a darker blue, the curtains cream. It gave a somewhat beachy feel without going so far as to invite seashell decorations or nautical accents. Not that there was anything particularly wrong with those things, Jesse thought, but Grant's parents' house abounded with them, so they'd shied away from that look when decorating.

Stephanie stood in front of the long dresser, using the mirror. She was reaching behind her neck to clasp a necklace, and Jesse moved in to help. She smiled her thanks at him in the mirror and he had to force himself to look away long enough to work the clasp. Then he was able to stand back and admire the view.

She wore a dress of some sort of muted purple. *Eggplant?* He didn't know and he didn't much care, he just enjoyed the way it complemented the blonde hair as well as the brighter purple that streaked through it. Instead of sleeves it had wide lacy straps that seemed to cup her shoulders. They led to a neckline that plunged quite invitingly between her breasts, though it somehow managed to tease without actually showing more than a hint of the flesh he'd come to enjoy so much. Still, the naked expanse of her chest was lovely, set off perfectly by the chunky gold necklace he'd helped her secure. Its long, thick links made him think of chains, an association he was certain she'd encourage.

The dress flirted with her knees and she'd already donned strappy heels which did sinful things to her legs.

"You look stunning," Grant said.

"Thank you," Jesse answered without taking his eyes off Stephanie.

Stephanie threw her head back and laughed, full bodied, her arm coming up to her stomach. She really was beautiful.

Grant moved up next to him and they both just watched her laugh until she finally stopped, leaned in to give Grant a kiss on his cheek, said "thanks" and brushed between them to leave the room. Or she would have, if Grant hadn't stopped her with a hand on her arm.

"Not so fast, beautiful."

She blinked at him, then at Jesse, then looked down at their feet, apparently realizing she was taller than she normally would be next to them. She looked back up and probably would have said something, but Grant stopped her with a kiss. He cupped her head in his hand and fused his mouth with hers. His fingers pushed up into her hair and Jesse had to take a moment to appreciate her short hairstyle that he hoped meant she wouldn't mind if it got a little mussed. Because he liked seeing Grant holding her so securely, working her so surely, enjoying her so thoroughly.

Stephanie's hands came up to Grant's chest, one slipping through his open collar to his chest, the other sliding up to his shoulder. She bent one knee and leaned her whole body into him and Jesse wished he had a camera. They were beautiful together, and it was a very good thing he was fully secure in how fantastic a couple he and Grant made, as well.

But the three of them together? Now *that* was the best sight of all. He stepped in.

The minute his hands touched each of their sides, they both moved. They didn't break their kiss, but neither hesitated in putting an arm around him and drawing him closer. Perfect proof that when he'd suggested adding Stephanie to their play, he'd had one of the more brilliant moments of his life.

Grant's hand moved down to his ass and Stephanie's moved under his arm to the small of his back, urging him closer. He leaned in, and only stopped when the damn doorbell rang.

Grant groaned but didn't end the kiss. Jesse put a hand on both of their chests and pushed.

"I'm not leaving you two in here alone while I go rescue our food from the rain. I'll come back and you'll both be naked and our fantastic meal will get very, very cold."

Grant pulled back an inch. "And your point is?"

"That I slaved away on this meal and you will come eat it and appreciate it."

"You phoned in an order."

"Which is a whole lot more than you did for it." He gave them another shove, though the one he gave Stephanie was mostly pretend, given the needle-thin heels she was wearing. "Come on kids, the poor delivery person is waiting in the rain."

The second ring of the doorbell aided him in his cause and Grant finally dropped his hands and took a full step back. He turned and headed for the front door without another word.

Jesse took Stephanie's hand and pulled her from the room.

"Wait, I thought we were going out to a restaurant," she said.

"We were. But the storm is supposed to be pretty bad, so I ordered it brought to us, instead." He led them to the living room. At first he'd started to set the dining room table, but that hadn't seemed quite right. Instead, he'd laid the tablecloth out in the living room in front of the bay window. He'd moved a couple of side tables around so each person had somewhere to put their glasses of wine and water. He'd put candles throughout the room, on pretty much every flat surface available. Instead of turning on the stereo he'd cracked one of the windows so the sound of the rain seemed to fill the room.

Grant was handing money over with one hand and accepting

bags with the other. Jesse moved to help him. When he turned around, Stephanie was where he'd left her, staring into the living room, her eyes looking shiny in the candlelight.

His heart stuttered. *Was she crying?*

"Honey?" he asked. "You okay?"

"This is so pretty, Jesse. And so sweet."

"He just didn't want to get wet," Grant teased, bringing another sack into the room.

Stephanie just smiled and finally moved to join them.

"I like it, and I appreciate it, and I'm going to tell him so," she said, walking straight up to Jesse. She put her hands on his chest and leaned up for a kiss, not having to go as far as normal since she was wearing her heels and he was barefoot. He accepted her kiss, closing his eyes and relaxing into the sensations.

"Yeah, yeah, come on before the food gets cold."

She pulled back and he opened his eyes to meet her gaze, full of sweetness and laughter. Reaching down, she took the bag from his hand and set it on the ottoman, opened it up and began pulling out containers. He stared at her a moment, then moved to help while Grant poured wine for them.

He'd ordered a mix of everything so they all took what they wanted, family style. Once they were settled, he was glad to see Stephanie dig into her food with enthusiasm. They all perked up when the rain suddenly turned into hail, sharing smiles but keeping quiet to enjoy the sound while they were safely tucked away inside.

Eventually they began talking, keeping their voices to low murmurs, and he was very glad he'd decided on this intimate scene, rather than the public restaurant. Especially when Stephanie pushed herself away from her plate and came to his side, curling up into him. He wrapped his free arm around her shoulders and they continued talking about a movie that she had seen but they hadn't made it to yet.

He probably would have kept eating more of the delicious food, but the call to explore more of her body was too much. Putting his fork down he shoved away the ottoman he'd been using as a table and leaned back against the front of the couch, taking her with him. She adjusted, re-snuggled, humming in her content. She still wore her shoes, her feet curled up near her butt, her long legs smooth and glowing in the candlelight.

Grant moved from his position in front of the lounge chair and joined them, resting his head in Jesse's lap. Stephanie immediately moved to tease her fingers through his hair, pulling lightly at the strands, then smoothing them back.

"You guys didn't tell me how you got into the lifestyle," Stephanie murmured.

Grant's eyes rolled up so he could meet Jesse's, his look clearly telling Jesse he should go first. Jesse smirked, but he didn't mind.

"I had a boyfriend who was a hardcore masochist. Much harder than I am. He didn't care about bondage, domination, any fetishes. He needed pain. I found out he'd been seeing someone for that area of his needs while we were getting to know each other. Not knowing anything about BDSM, I accused him of cheating on me and we broke up. He begged me to see it from his perspective, to understand why he hadn't told me about his needs. I was twenty-two and thought I knew everything about everything, but I did like him quite a bit, so I went with him to a club."

Stephanie gave a chuckle. "I'm guessing that was a bit more eye-opening than you had anticipated."

He laughed. "Yeah, a bit, you could definitely say that. It was a gay club, lots of leather men and boys. Let's just say, it wasn't long before I figured out that I was destined to be much closer to his end of things than the sadist end of things. Still, we tried to give it a go, him seeing a sadist on the side, but it didn't work out. I'm not sure how much of that was because of him, because I was starting to explore my desires as a submissive, or just because we weren't meant to be."

"Do you ever talk to him?" Grant asked.

It occurred to Jesse that they'd never had this conversation together. "No, he moved to San Francisco years ago and we lost touch." He nudged Grant's shoulder. "What about you?"

Grant propped his feet up on the lounge chair and yawned. "I had a college professor who thought I would make a great top. She invited me to a club. I wasn't interested in her, but I was intrigued, so I went. She was pissed that I was so obviously into what I was seeing, but not enamored of *her*. I dared her to give me a bad grade and never spoke to her again. I explored other clubs and tried some out, but I did stay away from hers out of a sense of fair play."

Jesse snorted. "And what grade did you get?"

"An A. One that I earned."

Stephanie's fingers left Grant's hair and began to explore his face, tracing his eyebrows, drawing a line from his forehead to the tip of his nose, scratching her nail lightly along his lips. Grant did nothing to stop her, other than to give her fingertip a small nip when it got too close to his teeth.

Jesse traced the strap of her dress, then began to draw random patterns on her upper arm. She shivered under his touch, but didn't move. The rain intensified and a gust of cold air hit them. He reached for the tie still lying loose along Grant's collar, picking it up and then smoothing it down his chest.

"Don't give me ideas about that unused tie," Grant murmured, his eyes closed.

Jesse just smiled. He never regretted giving Grant ideas. He guessed they were still going to do some playing later, but he liked seeing his lover relaxed and at peace. Watching Steph explore the faint lines of Grant's forehead was somehow entertaining. They had plenty of time.

He was glad Grant had arranged this time away from their normal lives. Truthfully, he'd been a little bit skeptical about the plan, because he was worried that it would seem too much like a vacation fling to Stephanie. A time apart, away from her real life. He wanted her to see what they could have, that they could be a part of each other's lives, not encourage her to think of them as momentary.

Now, though, he had to admit, they were having a good time, even when they weren't in an active scene. Showing her that they could be like this, maybe it would bleed over to real life, too. He hoped so, because he wanted her to be a regular part of their lives.

They talked for a while longer, letting the food settle, before Stephanie made them get up and put the leftovers away. For some reason he found it amusing that she was a little bit OCD about getting the dishes into the washer, the food put away, the living room set back to rights. She'd always struck him as so free spirited, and it made him smile to see this side of her.

When he teased her, she gave him a wry smile. "I lived in a very small apartment with a roommate for years. I became a bit anal about putting everything away."

"Have you ever lived with a boyfriend?" Grant asked, taking the question right out of Jesse's mouth.

"No," she said, putting the last of the food into the fridge. "How long were you two together before you moved in?"

"Two months," Jesse answered.

She shot him a wide-eyed look. "Seriously?"

Grant hooked his arm around Jesse shoulders, gave him a kiss on the temple. "It's different when it's right. You just know."

She smiled at them. "I'm so glad you guys found that."

Jesse met Grant's eyes. He knew they were thinking the same thing, but there was no need to voice the thought. She didn't get it yet, but that was okay. There was no rush. She was in a different situation than they were, it was going to take some time to get her on the same page.

Stephanie had finally taken her shoes off, so she had to get up on tiptoes to give him a kiss, then Grant. "Grant promised something fun for tonight's entertainment. Is it that time?"

Jesse turned to look at Grant.

"Yeah, honey, it's about that time." Grant met his gaze. "I talked to Stephanie about giving you more than she's used to seeing."

Jesse didn't give him a chance to ask a question. "Yes, please."

Grant rolled his eyes. "Why don't you to go to the room and get naked. I'm going to close up the house and I'll be right there."

Jesse didn't wait for further instruction. He grabbed Stephanie's hand and pulled her to the master bedroom. Not that she was lagging behind. He loved that she was excited. He'd been a bit nervous that the level of pain he occasionally liked from Grant would be too much for her, so he'd asked Grant if they could give her a sampling, see how she reacted. If she didn't like it, that would be fine, they could work around it, he was sure. They didn't all three need to be together every time there was a scene. But he would much prefer it if she found all of their time together sexy.

She presented him with her back and he lowered the zipper, teasing the exposed flesh with light brushes of his fingertips. After a moment, she twirled around, her eyes dancing.

"Don't go getting us into trouble, Jesse."

"No? What's he going to do, beat me?" he joked.

"Or not, if you don't behave."

He gave a mock full-body shudder and she laughed as she began to unbutton his shirt. By the time he heard Grant coming down the hall, they were down to their underwear. He stepped back from the temptation that she presented just by being herself, and dealt with his briefs while watching her unclasp her bra. She was sliding the garment off when Grant spoke.

"Lift your hair up."

She paused for a beat, then did as he'd instructed. Her breath hitched when he buckled the collar around her throat. Jesse watched her swallow hard, then she finished her task, adding the bra and panties to her dress which she'd set on top of the dresser.

Jesse pulled in a deep breath, tried to settle himself. Usually when Grant promised him a heavy session, the only thing on his mind was the release that the pain gave him and the visual he always enjoyed of Grant raising a sweat working him. Now there was that little bit of nervousness about what Stephanie would think, as well as the concern that she would be bored or feel left out of the play. It was like when he'd first started seeing Grant outside of the club.

It wasn't a bad thing, just different. He had no doubt that Grant would get him in the proper headspace in due course. And he was sure Grant had a plan for Stephanie, as well.

In his typical way of casual overachieving, Grant proved him very right. He used his best, softest rope to secure Stephanie. She was on the bed, propped up against the pillows so she could enjoy the view, her knees bent to her chest, hands secured to her feet, legs wide open. Grant had put a small vibrator into her, as well as a butt plug. Jesse wished they had a purple one to match the color of her collar. He'd helped Grant pick the collar out, and had promised to be the one to switch the ribbon whenever she changed her hair color. He suspected Grant would balk at getting plugs in all the bright colors Stephanie favored.

Grant adjusted his last knot and stood back, looking Stephanie over. He nodded his satisfaction then pulled a small jar from his pocket. Jesse wasn't sure what it was until Grant began to dab it onto her clit and nipples. Some sort of heating cream, he guessed. Grant didn't go back for more, but he wiped the excess ointment on her lip. Stephanie swallowed hard but didn't try to move out of his way. Jesse itched to join them, to touch and tease her, but he'd been told to stand at the foot of the bed, so he could only watch as Grant readied Stephanie.

Again, Grant stood back, studied the results of his work. "Are you comfortable?"

"Yes, Sir."

"I'm going to be paying a lot of attention to Jesse, I want you to promise to let me know if you become uncomfortable or start to get numb or anything."

"Yes, Sir. I promise."

Grant nodded, turned to Jesse. Jesse's heart rate immediately accelerated. He loved the look on Grant's face, the casual sternness that meant he was working hard to give Jesse nothing. No clues or hints as to what was in store for him. Which was, of course, the only clue Jesse needed.

Grant moved behind him, soon followed by the amazing feeling of his collar settling around his throat.

"Hands at the back of your neck."

The words were clipped but they sent a thrill straight up Jesse's

PERFECT ADDITION

spine. As Grant moved to the dresser with their toys, Jesse laced his fingers behind his neck and kept his gaze trained straight ahead. Directly on Stephanie. *Her* face wasn't expressionless it all. It was full of lust and heat and he felt his already growing erection surge.

Grant kept out of view as he returned, so Jesse didn't get to see what he held. Instead, he could only feel as Grant stood directly behind him, close enough for his heat to penetrate Jesse's skin, and to force Jesse to concentrate to keep his body still, rather than sway back into this lover's warmth.

Strong hands gripped his ass and he drew in a careful breath, which he then found himself holding as those hands slid over his hips and towards his dick. Grant's body pressed into him as he buckled on a cock ring, then cupped and fondled Jesse's balls. His fingers tightened against each other, but otherwise he managed to remain still. Grant stepped back, running his hands along Jesse's flank, then giving him a light slap on the ass before moving far enough away that Jesse could no longer feel him.

When Stephanie smiled, he guessed Grant was showing something to her. He wasn't sure what to make of that smile until the first touch.

Oh, crap. Vampire glove. He hated the things, which was somewhat well known to members of Apex after a particularly memorable night, early on in his and Grant's relationship. To him, the sensation wasn't painful, it was an odd mix of itch and tickle that drove him crazy. His toes tried to curl into the floor and his biceps bunched with the effort of keeping his arms where they were.

"Does he look like he's enjoying himself, Steph?"

"Not particularly, Sir."

"That's too bad, isn't it?"

"I guess that depends on your definition of bad."

Grant laughed and Jesse bit his lip to keep his own laugh in. He was rewarded with a light slap from Grant's gloved hand. The zing of pain shot through him and he nearly moaned. So much better than the scratchy annoyance of what Grant had been giving him. And continued to give him. After the slap, Grant went back to running the prickly glove over his back, his shoulders. Thank god his fingers were covering his neck, Jesse wasn't sure what he would have done with that sensation there.

Stepping to his side, Grant curved the glove over his shoulder and down his chest, not hesitating to run the spikes over his nipples. Jesse held on to the slight burn of that, trying desperately to ignore the rest.

"You look so incredible, being all stoic for me," Grant murmured into his ear. "Taking it, even when you wish I'd just get on with the rest." He pressed his hand deeply into Jesse's sternum, then ran it lightly down his stomach. "But I like to see you like this, flushed as your blood starts to flow under my hands, tense as you work not to wiggle and jerk. Very nice, my Jesse."

Jesse swallowed, the words working, as they always did, to help him focus, relax into the sensations. He loved hearing Grant talk to him like this, low and intense, their version of sweet nothings.

"Do you want me to keep going, Jesse?"

It was too open of a question of course. Keep going with the glove, keep going with the words, keep going with anything at all?

"Whatever you want, Grant. I'm yours."

"Yes, you are," Grant agreed, his gloved hand moving to wrap around Jesse's cock.

That was definitely *not* an itchy feeling. Jesse pulled in a sharp gasp, every muscle in his body tensing for a brief second before he made them relax. He forced himself to breathe, concentrating on different muscles until he'd released them all.

"Do you know what you do to me?" Grant asked, breaking his concentration.

He almost turned to meet Grant's eyes, but managed to resist.

"Sometimes, Sir."

The low chuckle in his ear was like music. "I'm going to start working you now. I'm not going to tie you to anything. I'm not going to restrain you. I'm not going to use a spreader bar. But you're going to stand still for me, stay open for me, take it for me."

It wasn't a question, but he couldn't keep himself from answering. "Yes, Sir." He wasn't surprised that it sounded like begging.

He met Stephanie's eyes. Her expression was pure lust, desire and need. He didn't know if it was fair to keep her lying there, watching them, unable to do anything *but* watch them. But he couldn't deny that knowing she was watching, that she was getting pleasure from that, made it all that much better.

He watched as her pussy clenched and unclenched, moisture glistening on her grasping lips. He met her eyes just as the first thud of the flogger hit. It was the deerskin flogger. With lots of tails, it gave a deep, heavy blow that rocked him onto his toes and nearly made him take a step forward. Grant had never used it on him when he wasn't restrained and his hands started to come loose to balance himself, but he settled just in time for the next blow, and the next.

He felt the blows deep in his body, the exact opposite of the niggling sensation from the vampire glove. The strikes rained on his back, butt and thighs and he was breathing hard, working to stay as still as possible, though there was no way to remain motionless.

"Put your hands at the small of your back."

Relief for his aching shoulders was immediate though his cock gave a nervous twitch when Grant walked around to his side, clearly preparing to focus his attentions on Grant's front. He bent his knees slightly and was prepared for the heavy slap to his chest and stomach. Having his elbows out to the side within striking range somehow made him feel more vulnerable than before, though he had total confidence in Grant's aim with the familiar flogger.

He concentrated on watching Stephanie's fingers where they gripped her ankles, kept there by the black ropes that wound around her. Her knuckles had gone white where she squeezed herself.

Grant passed in front of him, breaking his stare and he let his eyes follow the man he loved. The flogger went up, came down, settling into a rhythm that Jesse's body craved. It wasn't pain, not really. That part was coming, he knew. These heavy blows were more like a massage, just one he had trouble standing against. He wanted them to go on forever as much as he wanted them to end, so that they could move on to the next stage. It was a good thing he didn't have any choice in the decision.

A hearty blow to his thigh had him almost gasping. A soft caress from Grant only a second later succeeded in pulling a moan from him. Light fingers trailed the paths the flogger had made, brushed over his pecs, stomach and thighs, a sensation too light and yet just right, because they were Grant's fingers. His breathing had grown harsh and he checked to make sure Stephanie was no longer matching his rhythm. Her eyes were half lidded and her fingers had unclenched as she watched Grant stroke him, pet him.

"Is she watching us?" Grant asked, his hands gliding up Jesse's rib cage.

"Yes, Sir."

Grant leaned in, flicked his tongue into Jesse's ear, making him want to rub it madly to free himself of the sensation. Grant knew—Grant always knew—and made him suffer a minute before he used his thumb to soothe the spot.

"Are you ready for more?"

"Yes, Sir."

"What should I give you next?"

"Whatever you want."

Grant had removed his shirt before starting. He stood near enough for the slacks of his pants to brush Jesse's leg, but his bare torso remained close without making contact. Only his hand, constantly moving, teasingly soft against the flesh he'd just walloped, gave Jesse the touch he craved.

"You know how much I love it when you tell me that."

"I hope so, Sir."

Grant kissed his chin and Jesse had no complaints about the softness of the contact. He knew Grant's lips weren't really hot but the simple touch seemed to sear itself into his skin in a way that was only good.

"Please, Grant."

"Please what? Are you ready for what you asked for?"

"Please kiss me."

The lips against his skin curved up. "I am kissing you."

"My lips, Grant, I need your mouth. Please!"

Tiny kisses as Grant worked his way towards Jesse's lips had him breathing as hard as the flogging had. When Grant finally made it to Jesse's lips he hovered there and it took all of Jesse's will not to lean forward and take the kiss he so desperately wanted.

"So good, my Jesse."

Then he leaned in and he gave. Jesse moaned. He loved Grant's kisses, especially in moments like this where every sensation was magnified, every want and need somehow more intense. The feel, the taste, the pleasure, all worked to drive him nearly mad before Grant pulled back. But it was a good kind of mad, the best kind, and only the promise of what was to come kept him from begging for more.

From behind his back Grant produced the flogger Jesse had asked for. No more waiting. Jesse moaned. The rubber tails, all eighteen of them, provided both thud and sting in a way he didn't want every time, not even most times, but every once in a while, it was perfect.

Grant moved away from him, reaching over to the bed where Stephanie lay. A second later, Jesse heard the unmistakable whine of a vibrator. He'd finally turned on the one he'd placed inside Stephanie. Jesse watched her try to keep her wiggles to a minimum. He kept watching as Grant moved behind him.

"Hands at your neck."

He moved his arms back to their original position, his gaze trained on Stephanie's. She licked her lips and he mirrored her. He knew by the widening of her eyes that Grant was taking a swing.

The sweet lick of fire shot across his back and he gasped, even though he'd been expecting it, aching for it. He smiled and Stephanie laughed soundlessly, shaking her head at him.

He watched her watching him as Grant continued, lash after lash, down his back, butt and thighs, left and right, creating a rhythm that Jesse began to sink into. His eyes were still on

Stephanie, but he couldn't really focus, as the pain moved through him, consumed him, transported him. Part of him had to stay aware to a degree he didn't normally need to be, since he wasn't bound, had nothing to hold on to, nothing to brace against. But the rest of him floated on a sea of endorphins, the smell of Grant surrounding him, the sound of Grant's instrument as it connected, the feel of Grant's will as he took the strikes, made them a part of himself. Thighs, stomach, chest, all of them were just extensions of the gift he offered Grant.

His cock throbbed and he wondered if their usual routine would change, just as Grant took the back of his neck in one large palm and bent him over the bed, ass in the air. The sounds of condom package and lube bottle assured him their routine was still good, though he angled his chin up so he could see Stephanie, rather than his usual attempt to see Grant coming at him from behind.

Grant's familiar hands grabbed his hips and he eased his cock in past the head, then slammed in all the way. Jesse cried out once, then again as Grant lay across his stinging back, putting his mouth to Jesse's ear.

"I'm going to jerk you off, then I'm going to fuck you blind. Do you think you might manage to put your mouth to good use with our girl while I'm doing all that?"

"Yes, Sir!"

"I'll even let you use your hands," Grant offered.

Jesse didn't hesitate a heartbeat. Grant let him up enough to reach out to Stephanie's bound body and pull her to him. He dived in just as Grant's hand grasped his cock.

Before they'd even approached Steph at the club, he'd asked Grant to tell him all about eating pussy, in case he wanted to try it. He hadn't been sure he'd want to, but once they'd started to play with her, he'd let Grant know that he was definitely curious.

He gave a lick, just to experience his first taste.

Mmm, somehow it was pure Stephanie.

It was so different than tasting Grant. She was so soft and wet and...puffy. He'd enjoyed touching her earlier, playing with her folds and that tantalizing little bundle of nerves. He'd had fun exploring and teasing and watching her reactions. But he'd resisted the urge to taste. Until now. He touched his tongue to her clit, smiling when she jerked beneath him and moaned.

"I think she's earned the right to come first, for being patient while we played in front of her, don't you?"

"Yes, Sir." Jesse could feel the buzz of the egg in her channel as he took her clit into his mouth. He sucked hard, knowing she was already primed from the show, the cream and the vibrator. She tilted her hips into him, giving him more, a silent request for harder that he had no problem answering. He sucked her against his teeth for a moment as Grant squeezed him before starting a fast-paced hand job. Jesse let go of her clit and worked his tongue around and into her pussy, listening to her little moans and sighs, all the while reveling in the slow, steady fucking Grant was giving.

"If you want me to go faster, you're going to have to get her off," Grant said, reading his mind as usual.

"Yes, Sir," he said into her flesh. Then he remembered Grant had said he could use his hands. He was braced on his elbows but he moved one arm up her side and palmed her breast, giving it a good squeeze. He yanked the little vibe out with his other hand, and thrust first two, then three fingers into her. She clasped him hard, and he curled his fingers up to the wall of her channel as he settled his mouth back over the bundle of nerves that he was learning to love to torture.

She cried out, then again when he tweaked her nipple hard. Her neck arched back and she came around his fingers. He left his mouth on her but switched to a light caress as he eased his fingers from her.

"I don't know," Grant said. "That looked like it only took the edge off."

Jesse lifted his head and agreed with Grant's assessment. Grant ran a hand lightly up his hot, stinging back, cupped his head until he turned to look over his shoulder at the other man. He met Grant's gaze.

Grant smiled, reached somewhere behind him and came up with another condom.

Oh yeah. Jesse straightened with a wince, took the condom and sheathed himself, then pulled Stephanie closer to the edge of the bed. He fit his body between her bound legs and pushed himself inside her. She made a low keening noise as she accepted him, her eyes on his. He braced his arms on either side of her head and kissed her. Grant's hands on his hips urged him back, and together they set up a new rhythm, Jesse working in and out of Stephanie as Grant did the same to him, every motion causing a twinge of pain as his sweaty skin slid along their bodies.

The pain helped him hold himself together against the dual pleasures of fucking and being fucked. He brought a finger lightly to Stephanie's clit, then harder when she only gave a begging moan. Grant's hand landed on his shoulder, curved over his collar, bracing himself against Jesse as he orchestrated their movements. His balls were pulled in tight and he wasn't sure how long he could hold on.

Grant paused them and whispered in his ear. "Kiss her."

Jesse leaned down, captured her mouth with his, sucked her tongue in hard, barely heard Grant over the roaring in his ears.

"Stephanie, come for us now."

Her cry was captured by his mouth, her squeezing muscles making it nearly impossible for him to not follow her over into orgasm. He closed his eyes tightly, held his body as still as possible as Grant began to move again.

Tearing his mouth free, he could only beg. "Please, Grant, please let me come."

Grant ran his fingers hard over the welts on Jesse's back. "Come for me then."

The words hadn't fully left his mouth before Jesse did just that, feeling like his balls were shooting out through his dick. He braced his forehead on Stephanie's, as Grant continued to fuck him, his shaking hands barely keeping him from collapsing on the trapped woman. He clenched tightly around Grant and was rewarded with a long groan as the other man found his release.

After a moment, Grant removed his condom then helped him up onto the bed at Stephanie's side. He could only lie there and watch as Grant quickly released the knots holding her in place, freeing her within minutes. They snuggled together as Grant got rid of the condoms and came back to the bed with ointment for Jesse.

Usually Jesse just stretched out on the bed while Grant applied the cream, but this time he got to cuddle the very pliant and warm woman in his arms. At least until it was time to do his front. He didn't want to move, but Grant ordered him onto his back and Stephanie snuggled into his side, her head on his shoulder.

When Grant had deemed him sufficiently tended to, he made them both drink some water and climbed on the bed, propped up on pillows and pulled them both in close. Jesse drifted into sleep, his head on Grant's chest, his arm wrapped around Stephanie's arm, totally content.

CHAPTER NINE

The drive back to town was lazy, Jesse taking advantage of the limo to nap with his head in Grant's lap, Stephanie doing some work on her phone. Grant was checking his emails as well, but happened to be looking at her when she frowned.

"What's wrong?" he asked quietly.

"One of the studios I do Pilates work at sent me an email that they no longer have room on their calendar for me."

"Do you have a contract?"

"Yes, but they're allowed to cancel with two weeks' notice. It's just...their email doesn't really give an explanation, and I've been using their space for three of my clients who live nearby, for like two years. It's weird because it's the second time this has happened in the last week."

He put his phone down. "Second time you've been booted from a contract?"

"Basically, yes. Usually *I* leave a space because it's no longer convenient to my clients. It's happened this way before, a couple of times, but I knew it was coming. A gym beefing up their own trainer program, that kind of thing."

He started to offer his help in some way, but she looked back at her phone. "I'll call Jink tomorrow, get the word from the studio. It's not a big deal, just weird."

Biting his tongue and feeling proud of himself for doing so, he went back to his own emails. He figured he knew her well enough to think she'd be annoyed by unsolicited advice. Especially when the only thing he could think to offer was to look at her contract or contact the management at the two facilities. He would definitely be annoyed if anyone not in his business made those suggestion to *him*, so shutting up was a good plan. Just…difficult.

He thought about how he should try to move them forward. She'd enjoyed the weekend, that was a certainty. So had he and Jesse, obviously. He was pretty sure she was thinking of things as a play scenario, just a very extended one. Like they were club buddies who just happened to be scene-ing somewhere other than the club. He wanted her to understand it was more than that to him, to Jesse, but he didn't want to scare her away before she had a chance to see how good it could be.

So, how to get her out on some non-play dates without freaking her out?

Using his phone, he checked on what events were happening that she might be interested in. If he wanted to convince her that they should be in a real relationship, it was time to pull out the old-school dating methods. Just because there would be three of them on the date, didn't mean the tools for seducing a partner had changed.

He found something he thought would be suitable, bumped his thigh to nudge Jesse awake. "Hey, we still haven't managed to go see the most recent Cirque du Soleil yet. I can get tickets for this week."

"Oh, yeah, cool. I've totally been meaning to look into that, but I've been distracted." He sat up and smiled at Stephanie. "Have you seen it?"

She hit a button on her phone and set it aside. "No, I've always wanted to go to one, but never made it. You like them?"

"Wait," Jesse exclaimed. "You've never seen *any* of them? We get to be your first?"

Her frown was adorable. "My first? I don't—"

"I'm ordering three tickets," Grant interrupted. "Which night is best for you?"

"We'll go to dinner, first," Jesse added. "I think it's Grant's turn to pick a restaurant." He looked at Grant. "I'm going to insist that Stephanie wear an awesome dress, because I've never gone on a date with a woman in an awesome dress, and last night convinced me that it's something I need to do. So, make sure you pick a place that complements an awesome dress."

Grant blinked at him, then nodded solemnly. Jesse turned back to Stephanie. "The one you wore last night would be fine, but if you have another feel free to show it off instead."

"We still need to pick a night," Grant said.

They both looked to Stephanie who was just staring at them, dazedly.

"Um. Thursday?"

"Perfect," Jesse said, and dropped back down to his nap.

"Wait, how much are the tickets? Especially so last minute?"

"Our treat. And done," Grant said, clicking the needed options on his phone. He managed to keep his smile to himself.

"Okay. Well, thanks, it sounds like fun." She looked like she was trying to decide between being annoyed and being pleased.

He toed off his shoes and propped his feet up on the seat across from him, next to her hip. Stephanie tweaked his big toe through the sock, then rested her hand on his ankle. He didn't think she was even aware of the unconscious contact.

"So, I'm curious about telling your parents you were in the lifestyle. How did that go?"

She shrugged. "It wasn't the easiest thing in the world, but it was okay. It's like you were saying before, they raised me to be smart, strong and think for myself, they can't be too surprised when I turn out to be independent and determined to do my thing."

"Yeah, that contradiction bit my parents in the ass, for sure. They somehow thought they could raise me that way, but that I would be on board with whatever plans they had."

"And there's definitely a bit of a bias because I'm a girl. It's old fashioned, for sure, and I had to point that out to my parents, but the fact that sex and clubs were involved made them super nervous, because I'm a girl."

"What did you tell them? That you were a submissive and you were going to the clubs to find a Dom?"

"Basically. I pointed out that it was safer than randomly trying it outside of a club."

He cocked his head in thought. "I wonder how differently they would have reacted if you'd said you were a Domme."

She blinked at him. "That's an interesting question. On the one hand, like I said..." she pointed to herself. "Independent. But on the other hand, they weren't surprised by the sub announcement. It's part of who I am. They just weren't real comfortable with the whole sex aspect of it. But if I had Domme tendencies?" She smiled ruefully. "I think you're right, they would have been less worried. I guess that means they weren't being sexist exactly. I'm not sure what they were being, now."

"They just perceive the sub as being more vulnerable, which means they worry. And they weren't wrong, exactly. The sub has the ultimate power, but the vulnerability is there."

"We found our balance, pretty quickly. I don't talk about it with my mom unless it's time to tell her about a particular relationship. Which is normal, I think, it's not like most people are running to Mom with stories about their sexual hookups."

"And your dad?"

"I give him the names of people I'm playing with or considering playing with. He doesn't know which names I actually have sex with. If I see the person outside of the club, I let him know. That's it. He doesn't come back to me often, but a couple of times he's asked me not to see someone again without talking to him first. Each time it's been someone I've already written off."

"That's good. You sound like you have a great relationship."

"And you?"

"They're annoyingly not on board with Jesse, or any guy, actually. They know they have to be polite and deal with it, but I wish they were actually okay with it. I don't let it stop me from being me and living my life, but it keeps us from being as close as we could be. I just can't fully respect people who choose to completely discount a part of who I am, let alone a person I'm introducing to them as being important to me."

"That sucks. It's great that they're not outright hostile, like people can be, but terrible that they're not actually supportive and welcoming."

"Yes. I've given them a while to get used to it, but pretty soon we're going to have a talk. They need to do better now that they've seen he's a great guy and a permanent part of my life."

"They'll come around," Jesse murmured, sleepily.

He gave little tug on the other man's hair. "They better."

The car gave a long, sweeping turn and Stephanie tightened her hold on his calf. "They'd have to be idiots not to warm up to Jesse, and considering they raised you to be you, that's hard to imagine."

He grinned at her. "You've only seen the sweet side of him. And the sexy side of him. Maybe the smart side of him. He has a couple of other sides as well, you know."

"Hey!" Jesse slapped his thigh.

"I've seen his naked sides. All of them. They were pretty good."

"There's the jealous side," he teased, but Jesse cut him off.

"What? I'm not jealous!"

"You tried to give that San Genaro's waitress a voodoo curse because she rubbed her boobs on my arm while putting our plates down."

Stephanie laughed, while Jesse spluttered.

"That skank deserved it! She wasn't even subtle and she knew we were together-together. That wasn't jealousy, that was just straight up the proper reaction." He sat up, putting his legs on the opposite seat as well, so that Steph was caged in.

She leaned forward, her eyes sparkling. "You know voodoo curses?"

Grant rolled his eyes. What had he started?

"Well, not exactly," Jesse hedged.

"Only from Saturday morning cartoons," Grant explained.

Stephanie laughed and leaned back again, putting one hand on each of their legs.

"Clearly I gave up on cartoons too early in my life. Do you think your curse was successful?"

"Well—" Jesse started, but Grant interrupted him. "He successfully convinced her he had something in his eye. She offered to get him some saline solution."

She couldn't quite keep the laugh inside and Jesse retaliated by poking her with his toes until she smacked his feet and threatened to tickle him.

When they got to Stephanie's, they all exited the car, Jesse grabbing her bag, Grant taking her hand and leading the way to her building. He pulled her to him when they reached the main door. "Thanks for an amazing weekend," he said.

"I think that's my line," she whispered.

"It was equally amazing for all of us," he agreed. "We'll pick you up on Thursday, I'll text the time."

"Okay."

He cupped her cheeks and laid a soft, gentle kiss on her, enjoying the way her hands clutched at his shoulders. After a moment he pulled free, dropped another quick kiss on her lips, and turned her towards Jesse.

Jesse tossed her bag at him, wrapped his arms around Stephanie and dropped her over his arm in a dramatic dip. She squealed and laughed as Jesse tried to kiss her, batting at his arms. Jesse raised her up, kissed her for real, and let her go.

"Thanks guys. It really was the best weekend."

"For us, too," Jesse assured her.

When she turned to put her key in the door, Jesse's hand snuck into Grant's. He knew exactly what his partner was thinking.

PERFECT ADDITION

Grant arrived at his office in a good mood. He took a call from his mother, and managed to keep the good mood, partially because he listened with only one ear while he ordered flowers to be delivered to Stephanie's apartment.

Two meetings and a conference call later, he looked up to find Jesse in his doorway with a sack that likely contained lunch.

"You take good care of me," he said, going to give the other man a big kiss.

"It's not hard, and you do the same for me. I don't have long, though, so we have to eat fast."

Jesse took containers out of the bag, revealing burritos, chips and salsa.

"What's going on at work lately, anything new and interesting?" he asked.

"All the usual drama. Scotty in maintenance broke up with his girlfriend and is an absolute mess.

Grant checked his memory. "The biker dude that only wears denim?"

"Yeah, that's Scotty. And Mara's mother-in-law is driving her crazy, to the point she's about to give her husband an ultimatum."

"That can't be good."

"Not even a little bit. Jerome, the guy who started last year, hit a parked car on Friday."

"Oops."

"Big time."

"I'm a bit behind. Have I been too focused on getting Stephanie to join us?"

His serious tone had Jesse looking up from the salsa he was scooping with a chip, meeting his eyes. "Baby, I've been right there with you. She's a bit of an obsession with us right now, but once we get her on board, we can find a new one. Like restarting *Game of Thrones* from scratch. Even better, we'll have three opinions on who to love and who to hate each episode, and one more memory bank to use to try to figure out who everyone is again."

Grant laughed. "Sounds about right."

Jesse leaned over their burritos and gave him a salsa-flavored kiss. "Don't stress about us. We've been good and we'll stay good."

"Yeah, okay. Thanks, babe."

"The flowers get delivered tomorrow?"

"Three at the latest."

"Too bad we don't really know her schedule. I guess it would be a bit stalker-ish if we tried to pin that down this early?"

"Considering we haven't even taken her out on a date yet, probably. Might end up getting a visit from her dad."

"He sounds cool. For some reason I'm not actually worried about the whole meet-the-parents thing. Is that weird? Maybe I'm just being naive, and when the time comes I'll be freaked."

"Have you ever had a bad meet-the-parents? Worse than my family, I guess I mean."

"You know your family wasn't bad. Some were good, and some were meh, but no one yelled at me. My second boyfriend in high school did *not* go well. I think the screaming coming from his mom was an attempt to cast the devil out, but I'm not certain, since it wasn't in English."

Grant laughed.

"Anyway, I have to get back to work." He shoved his box and napkin back into the sack and held the sack out to Grant, who did the same. Then winked.

"I adore you," Grant said. He gave his man a gentle kiss. "Thanks for coming by."

"You can pay me back later by making me come."

Grant smacked his ass and shoved him towards the door.

CHAPTER TEN

Stephanie's day had been very full for her, and active. She was exhausted and ready to give herself the night off. Tomorrow she'd be able to fit in the computer work she needed to do around her two clients, easily.

She'd gone ahead and rescheduled her Thursday afternoon client to earlier in the day, something she very rarely did. But it would give her the time to get ready without stressing about the clock. And that particular client didn't work and was flexible, so she shouldn't feel guilty at all. But she did, a tiny bit. It was a one-time thing, though, and she trudged up the stairs determined not to let it become a habit no matter how full her social life might become because two sexy men suddenly wanted her in their lives.

This date thing had her a bit confused. It sure didn't seem like they wanted to keep her in the play department. But maybe they were just showing her that they could be friends, do friend things, and then also get together for play? Maybe.

She started down the hall to her apartment and came to a halt.

In front of her door was a beautiful bouquet of flowers. Bright and sunny, it held several kinds of cheery flowers she couldn't actually name.

She dropped her gym bag and pulled the little card out of its holder. Then she stopped herself, used her key on the door, picked up the vase and shoved her bag in with her foot. Only once the door was closed and she'd set the vase down on the little bar counter in her kitchen, did she pull the card out of its tiny envelope.

It was from them. Of course it was from them, there hadn't really been a question. But she was still stunned. They'd sent her flowers. *Flowers*! And they were taking her on a date. Dinner at a nice restaurant, and a show.

She was going to need to talk to them. Or, she should see how Thursday went. Get a gauge for what they were trying to do. Then, if she was unsure, or felt things were moving in the wrong direction, she would be an adult and talk to them about it.

But what was the wrong direction? What did *she* want from *them*?

She had to be honest with herself. If it was up to her, she wanted to try a relationship with them. If there were no risk to what the two of them had together, and no risk to her heart, that was what she wanted. Of course, there *were* risks, there were always risks, so she was going to have to decide if they were worth taking.

And, now she knew it was time to call her dad. She picked up the phone.

"Yeah."

She had to smile at her dad's brusque phone technique.

"Hey, Pops."

"My girl, how are you?" The pleasure in his voice made her smile grow bigger.

"I'm awesome, actually, how are you?"

"Be better if my girl came to visit."

"Then I'll make that happen."

"You setting up a new client?" he asked.

"No, actually, it's a new relationship. Kind of."

"That's an interesting way of putting it. Have you gone gay on me, then?"

She laughed. "Would you mind?"

PERFECT ADDITION

"Heck no. Boys are trouble. Find yourself a girl, settle down."

"Sorry, Pop, it's not a girl. It's a guy. Well, that's the thing. It's *two* guys. We're kind of dating. Well, not dating really. We're just seeing each other. Outside of the club. And we're friends, so we're going to see Cirque du Soleil on Thursday."

Silence.

"I've been friends with Jesse for a while. I was attracted to him, but he was a sub, and gay, and then he met this other guy and they hooked up, so, you know, I just lusted from afar. For both of them."

She heard some shuffling around, but nothing else, so she went on.

"They've got themselves settled in together and decided to look me up. See how I felt about, well, joining them."

"Uh, huh."

"Like I said, we're mostly just friends who are having fun together. Because they're a couple."

"I'm not sure I understand the difference between dating and being friends who go out on dates that end in…sex."

Well, she'd never accused her father of being an idiot.

"Yeah, well, I'm not entirely sure I understand anymore, either. I'm just trying not to hurt their relationship, or get hurt myself."

"My girl doesn't make decisions out of fear," he reminded her.

And it was true. She wouldn't be in the scene, wouldn't live in the city on her own, or have a job that required her to meet up with strangers on a regular basis if she let fear rule her. She worked smart, but she did what she wanted to do. That was the deal she'd made with her dad a long time ago.

"Yeah. I'm going to work on that."

"I'm going to assume that you know what you're doing, unless you need some help or advice."

"I have absolutely no idea what I'm doing."

This time she let the silence last a minute. She smiled, imagining him rolling his eyes.

"Dinner. Soon. Pick a date and let your mother know."

"All right, Pops. Will do."

"You coming alone?"

"I've only been seeing them for like a week. Kind of early to drag family into it, don't you think?"

"I think you're a good girl. But boys are a hell of a lot of trouble. You sure you don't want to find yourself a pretty lesbian? You can adopt some babies, make your mother happy."

She smiled. "We'll see if I can't make her happy some other way."

"You need to, because your brother's not doing the job."

They talked for another few minutes, her dad giving her the lowdown on her brother's inadequate job prospects. She heard her mother calling for him in the background. Time for dinner.

"I love you, girl."

"I know Pop. I love you too. I'll see you in a couple of days. Give Mom a hug for me."

She hung up and stared at the flowers. It was time to make a real choice. Walk down to the juice bar, or do some meditative yoga and see if she could come to some decision about what the heck she was doing with her love life.

The decision was pretty simple. She grabbed her keys and slung her little pouch purse over her head.

As she walked, she couldn't help but think about the incredible weekend she'd had. The fact the guys had steamrolled her into this thing on Thursday. It occurred to her that they hadn't been very vocal about what they wanted from her. They'd really only discussed it that one time, when Grant had made his move on her. She'd been so thrown off, the discussion probably hadn't been as comprehensive as it could have been.

What had they said? They'd wanted to explore the possibility of being with her. All three of them, together.

In the state she was in at the time, she'd taken that to mean they wanted to scene together, add her to their play, but that it wasn't really a relationship thing.

Where had she gotten that idea? She wasn't sure anymore. To be honest, she'd been so lustful at the idea of playing with them, she probably would have agreed to anything, as long as it was consensual on all sides. And hot damn, but she'd been proven right with that decision.

But where did that leave them, now? They sure weren't acting like it was a club kind of deal. Or was she getting ahead of herself? They hadn't actually gone out in public together. Even at the Cape Cod house they'd ended up burrowing inside. Maybe when they went to this show, it really would be as friends. It was stupid to get too far ahead of herself.

She opened the door to the juice bar and had to face the facts. It may be stupid, but she was already sensing the grave danger to her heart. She was going to have to seriously evaluate the situation after Thursday and see if the amazing sex was worth the risk of falling for two guys who were already in love, but not with her.

She ordered her drink and tried to focus on the people around her, rather than her inner monologue. One of her neighbors was at a table by the window, so she waved. A guy she'd never seen before tried to give her the eye, so she turned back to the counter. The girl working the machine recognized her and handed over her smoothie. With a hearty thanks, she walked out, taking a small drink so as not to go into instant brain freeze.

By the time she made it back to her apartment, she knew only one thing. No meditation was going to solve her problem. Instead, she took a bath with her trusty waterproof vibe.

INSTEAD OF DRAGGING BY, Thursday appeared before she knew it. She'd tried to get Emma up to visit the city and go to the salon with her, but her friend was out in California, with her family. She'd sounded happy, but rushed, and hadn't been able to chat.

Steph had gone with a sort of pastel green for her hair, and tied a cute matching ribbon around her neck. Then she'd taken it off. Too close to the collar Grant had used. Instead she'd curled her hair and pulled it back from her face, doing her eyes with a more dramatic look than normal. She pulled out a dress she'd worn to a friend's wedding a couple of years ago, and never had occasion to wear again. She thought it did an excellent job of pulling off the line between sexy and classy.

She'd texted the guys a thank you for the flowers, and the three of them had maintained a steady stream of texts throughout the week. Enough that she knew they were thinking of her, but not so much as to be annoying. She received texts from them individually, and together. They made her laugh and she enjoyed the banter she had with both of them.

There was no reason to be nervous about tonight. She put a hand against her stomach and pulled in a deep breath through her nose, and exhaled through her mouth.

A glance at the clock had her cursing. She touched up her lipstick then pawed through her purse trying to decide what to transfer into the tiny little bag she'd bought to go with the dress. The lipstick, credit card, a bit of cash, ID, house key. Anything else? She glanced around for inspiration, but couldn't think of anything. Then she glanced around again, to make sure everything was picked up. It was. Of course it was. *Why was she nervous?* She was making herself crazy.

She wanted them to like her.

Damn it, she already knew they liked her!

She did the deep breathing thing, then almost choked when the doorbell sounded in the middle of an inhale. There had been no call from the security box downstairs, but it wasn't that unusual for someone exiting the building to hold the door open for people coming in. Idiots.

Walking to the door, she grabbed the coat she'd left on a chair. "Who is it?"

"It's us!" Jesse sang out.

She couldn't help but smile. Which stretched into a full-on grin when she saw the guys. They were always good-looking, but dressed up in their suits, they were scrumptious. Grant's hair was a little unruly like maybe Jesse had goaded him into raking his fingers through it, a fun contrast with the elegant suit. It fit superbly and made her want to run her hands up and down the crisp white shirt. Jesse was a little more casual, and a bit more adventurous with a dark purple shirt, and she mostly just wanted to jump on top of him and see if he would catch her.

Jesse pursed his lips and whistled, then twirled a finger, indicating she should turn around. She rolled her eyes, but complied.

"Ooh, baby! You look fantastic. Well done on the awesome-dress front, my sincere thanks for that."

She laughed, and kissed him. "You're welcome."

Grant took her arm and gently pulled her in for a kiss. It was long and deep and when he let her go she swayed a bit. "You look amazing." He touched the tip of a finger to her streaked hair.

She had to blink a bit before she could respond. "Thanks. You too." She looked at Jesse as she pulled on her coat. "Both of you look fantastic. I'm going to be the envy of everyone there."

"That's what you think," Grant murmured as he ushered them through the door.

Jesse grabbed her hand, and Grant put his lightly at the small of her back. A gesture she could be annoyed at, or charmed by, based solely on the person pulling it. Tonight she was charmed. Jesse led them to the elevator and pushed the down button. He turned, and he and Grant both rested a hand at her hips.

She almost burned at the twin points of contact, but it wasn't enough. Her breathing picked up, and then the elevator gave a ding that seemed incredibly loud in the charged silence.

Jesse grinned hugely and stepped back, pulled her into the elevator. Her legs were a little shaky as she moved inside, where an older woman already waited. Stephanie smiled and turned to the door, taking in an unsteady breathe.

"You lot must be going somewhere nice," the woman said.

Jesse told her about the show but Stephanie barely listened. Grant slid his hand inside her coat and played his fingers along her lower back, his heat easily penetrating the thin material of her dress. Jesse had draped an arm across her shoulders. His thumb teased the curve of her neck, and she just stood still, trying not to appear as though her panties were soaking through. And the date had only been going for five minutes.

It was going to be a long night.

The elevator discharged them and they exited the building. It was cold, but she could tell winter was on its way out and was looking forward to spring. She wondered what the beach at Cape Cod would be like in a couple of months. Good for a stroll with her guys?

A butterfly flew a quick little dance in her belly. Shit, she was already getting in deep.

A nice car with a discreet Uber sign was waiting at the curb and Jesse held the back door open for her, then went around to get in on the other side while Grant got into the front passenger side.

It was only a few minutes to the restaurant and they were quickly seated. Stephanie decided the occasion definitely called for wine and agreed when Grant suggested they get a bottle.

She picked up her menu. There was a linguini dish that looked delicious, but she never ordered long pastas when out on a date. Except, this wasn't really a date, was it? But it sort of was. *Argh.* Well, regardless of who she was with, it was probably best to stick with her ordering philosophy as it had more to do with managing to eat with elegance and dignity than it did with who she was sharing the meal with.

"Oh my god," Jesse exclaimed when the waiter left with their orders. "I can't believe I forgot to ask you if you went to the auction at Apex."

Stephanie burst out laughing. "It. Was. Awesome. I can't believe you missed it." She gave a quick side-eye to Grant before returning her attention to Jesse. "You know about the bet, right?"

"I don't know why there was a bet or what the bet was about, but I do know that the Doms lost and therefore had to dress up in sub gear. I wanted to go but Grant insisted that it wasn't a good enough reason to miss my grandma's birthday party. I swear he maneuvered her into planning it for that night on purpose, once he found out about the lost bet."

She grinned over at Grant, who rolled his eyes. "Right, I don't remember what the bet was about and I don't care. The only reason it matters is that the Doms were so sure they'd win whatever it was, they were willing to agree to the switch in clothes. And it was awesome. But that's not even the best part. Did you hear about Eric?"

"Only that he got bought up by someone nobody knew, and she led him out of the room by a leash!"

"You could sound a little less giddy by the idea," Grant observed.

Jesse slapped his arm, lightly. "Aw, come on, Eric's a good guy, but that shit is funny."

Grant's lips twitched.

"It was. I think it was partly that it was Eric that made it so funny. If it had been someone super intense, I probably would have been too worried about the girl to enjoy the moment, but he's a good guy. Have you heard anything about what happened? I haven't gotten any good updates."

"Not a damn thing," Jesse answered. "I was hoping you would know more."

Stephanie started to answer, but gave Grant a second look. "Is that a twinkle in your eye? Oh my god, you know something you're not telling us!"

He just looked at her, face expressionless. When she and Jesse both pouted, he raised his eyebrows in that uniquely Dom way.

"What I heard was that the auction was a success and the club was able to make a very nice donation to the charity we voted on."

She sighed, Jesse huffed, and they both reached for the brown bread that was in the middle of the table.

"Anyway," Jesse finally said after he'd buttered his piece and shot his boyfriend a dirty look. "I can't wait for you to see the show tonight. I've been to all of them. There is pretty much always an abundance of naked male chest to keep you entertained. And the acrobatics are pretty cool, too."

She laughed. "I'm looking forward to it." She leaned back as the waiter brought their salads.

"Did you talk to the studio that had to cancel on you?" Grant asked as they tucked into their food.

"No, I haven't heard back. I need to leave another message. It's not a big deal, I was able to find a place that opened up nearby. One of my client's switched with me, and one decided she wanted to move to private workouts in her home."

Jesse lifted his glass to her in cheers and she smiled.

"You like working for yourself?" Grant asked. "Or is there some other long-term plan?"

"I absolutely love working for myself. And not just that, but the flexibility I can build in to the job itself. I mean, I work hard to meet my clients' needs and be accommodating, but the more successful I am, the pickier and choosier I can be, if I need to. I can choose to only work certain days or certain hours or with certain types of clients. And I can change and adapt as needed."

"What do you mean by types of clients?" Grant asked.

"Pilates, yoga, strength training, weight loss, boot camp, that kind of thing."

"That's great you're able to be picky," Jesse said, pushing his salad plate aside. "Are you starting to narrow down the types of clients you take?"

"Right now I actually like the variety. I still do a couple of classes, but I'm mostly doing one-on-ones. I could get rid of the classes altogether, but I like them as a change of pace, and they're a great way to meet new potential clients."

"So this is what you want to do long term?"

"Definitely. I have a business plan and everything. I've set up my own retirement account and insurance. Unless business suddenly goes sideways, I don't see any reason I'd ever want to change. But never say never, right?"

She hummed in appreciation as the waiter set down her entree. Scallops in a sauce that looked delectable and asparagus cooked just the way she liked. Maybe she'd bring Emma here for dinner to celebrate her friend's college graduation. Assuming the food was as delicious as it looked. Which she quickly discovered it was. She offered a bit of scallop to Grant who leaned forward to accept the piece directly from her fork, his eyes focused on hers.

"Mmm," was his only comment.

She licked her lips. Jesse put a finger to the sauce on her plate and sucked on it, giving her a leer. She laughed and Grant smacked him upside the head.

"Hey!" All wounded dignity, Jesse managed to hold his look of outrage for a whole eight seconds before he joined her in laughing.

Without asking, she stuck her fork in Jesse's penne and pulled a cheesy tube free, shaking it a bit to make sure the sauce was secure. "What about you, Jesse? Long-term plans?"

"Well, I like my job well enough. But I'm also thinking it would be cool to be a stay-at-home Dad. Maybe. I've never actually watched a kid by myself for more than a few hours, so maybe I'd hate it."

"Hmm, maybe, but maybe not. I don't think you can know for sure until you give it a shot, but it's not like you're making a lifetime commitment, you can always change your mind one way or the other."

"True. What do you think about kids? Would you want to stay at home?"

She swallowed her food and took a sip of wine. "Honestly I haven't given it a lot of thought, since I've never been in a situation where I'd actually consider having a child. I know for sure I don't want to do it on my own. Way too much work, stress and responsibility for me, even though I know my parents would help. My first instinct is that I would prefer to keep working, but I suppose once you're faced with the idea of dropping them off with someone else, things might change. I guess since I have such flexibility in my schedule, I could maybe fit all my client's into a few days and do sort of a part-time thing with the daycare," she mused.

"It's hard to know what you would need or want to do until you know what kind of situation you would actually be in," Grant agreed, pouring more wine into all of their glasses. "But you do want kids?"

"I always assumed I would have them, if I met the right guy. But I don't think I would be devastated if it didn't happen." She laughed. "Although my mom might be."

"I would be," Jesse said. "I've always wanted kids."

"Were you thinking adoption, surrogate, or what?"

"At first I assumed adoption, but I don't really care. Maybe a combination. There are plenty of kids out there that need homes."

Jesse offered her his last bite of penne and she shook her head. She was completely full. Grant took the forkful instead and drank the last of his wine.

"That was delicious," she said.

"I love this place," Jesse said.

"Thank you for including me."

"Our pleasure," Grant said, running his hand along the back of her shoulder.

"We enjoy spending time with you, and not just when the restraints are out," Jesse added.

"Although we enjoy the hell out of those times, as well," Grant said.

She smiled. "You guys give good date. Both play and otherwise."

Their smiles were sexy as hell, but the waiter chose that moment to bring the check and clear their plates, so they didn't have a chance to say anything else. Grant looked at his watch and immediately handed his credit card to the waiter. "We're doing well on timing," he told her.

"Grant likes to get situated before all the seats fill up," Jesse told her.

She just shrugged her shoulders. "You guys are the experts." She stood and accepted Jesse's offered hand as they headed for their coats.

CHAPTER ELEVEN

"That was amazing!" Stephanie said, twirling in a small circle in front of them as they stood outside of the theater. "The skill and athleticism and artistry. Truly spectacular."

Jesse grinned at her. "Right? I'm so glad you loved it like we do."

Grant enjoyed the glowing smiles on both of their faces. He'd had to resist the urge to tease them during the show, to use the cover of darkness to get away with driving them crazy, but he hadn't wanted to distract Stephanie from the full experience of the show, so he'd behaved himself. Barely.

"Thanks so much for bringing me." Stephanie wrapped her arms around Jesse's neck and give him a light kiss on the lips.

Grant reached over and rescued her coat as it was about to fall to the ground. She turned to him and treated him to the same gesture before letting him help her into the coat.

"How early do you have to work tomorrow?" he asked, shrugging into his own coat. "Can we interest you in a nightcap?"

She gave him a considering look. "Not too early, but can I be selfish and suggest we get the nightcap at my place?"

He drew a finger from her collarbone to the neckline of her dress, keeping his gaze straight on hers. "Lady's choice."

"But not, like, every time," Jesse laughed, putting his arms around Grant and resting his head against Grant's shoulder.

Stephanie laughed, too. "No, not every time."

He pulled out his phone and ordered the car, using her address as their destination.

When Stephanie pulled her coat tightly closed and shoved her hands in her pockets, he and Jesse stepped in so that they were tight against her.

"No gloves or scarf?" he asked.

"Not worth it when the car will be here in a minute."

Grant put his hand on the back of her neck, under her hair. She moaned and leaned into it.

"The downside to a beautiful dress and fantastic shoes, I guess," Jesse said. "At least it's not snowing or raining."

"I don't know, the rain worked out pretty nicely for us, last time," Stephanie said in a seductive whisper. "Although Grant owes me a trip to the hot tub."

"Any time," Grant assured her.

Jesse stepped in even closer.

Grant smiled as he spotted the car pulling up to the curb. One of the benefits of being at a popular location, there wasn't much of a wait on the car service.

Nudging the others, he pointed at the car. Stephanie blinked at him, then headed for the car. Jesse gave him the bedroom eyes that had first made Grant want to eat the man all up.

"Tell me we're spending the night at her place."

"If I have anything to say about it, we sure as hell are."

"That's my man," Jesse approved, leaning in for a quick kiss before he followed Stephanie to the car.

By the time Grant got in, Stephanie was already giving their driver a passionate review of the show, which carried them through the short drive back to her apartment.

A woman and young boy were exiting the building as they walked up and Stephanie greeted them by name, squatting down to give the boy a hug. They made it to the elevator, and this time, when

PERFECT ADDITION

the doors opened, it was empty. He glanced at Jesse who had a very discernible gleam in his eyes as they backed a laughing Stephanie into the corner.

"Oh, no you don't, there are cameras in here!"

"Do you think anyone's actually watching them?" Grant asked, reasonably.

"If there is, don't you think they deserve a show?" Jesse asked, not so reasonably.

Stephanie put her hands on her hips and pretended to glare. "Keep your hands to yourselves or you don't get a drink."

Jesse looked at Grant, who shrugged. "It's not alcohol I'm thirsty for."

She dissolved into giggles as they put their hands on her shoulders and hips. When the elevator bell rang their arrival, Grant plucked the keys she'd pulled out of her purse and tossed them to Jesse, then swept her up into his arms. Her laugh turned into a squeal.

Jesse had the door open by the time they got there and Grant considered taking Stephanie all the way to her bed and bouncing her onto it, but that was probably a bit much. When the door was closed and locked behind him, he wrapped an arm securely around her waist and let her legs drop slowly to the floor, her middle pressed tightly against his. Jesse stepped in behind her and breathed in her scent again.

"Mmm, a Stephanie sandwich." Jesse took a nibble of the top of her ear as he eased her coat off.

She gasped softly. "I didn't think you guys wanted to play tonight."

"Because we asked you out for a drink, and we don't drink when we play?" Grant guessed.

"Y-yes." She stuttered as Jesse's hand rested on the zipper at her back.

"You were right. We don't want to play."

Her eyes had fluttered shut be she opened them again. "Oh."

He kissed her softly, just a light brush of his lips against hers.

663

"No playing. Are you okay with that?"

Jesse ran his tongue along her ear. "Say you're okay with that."

"Oh yes, definitely okay with that," she breathed.

Grant met Jesse's pleased eyes. Gave a slight nod. Jesse slowly began to pull the zipper down on her dress.

"We can wait, though, if you wanted that drink," Grant murmured, his hands coming up to shape her breasts.

"Not thirsty," she managed as his thumbs played over her hardening nipples.

"Good," Jesse answered, the zipper opened nearly to her butt. "Then as much as I like this pretty dress, I think we're ready to lose it for the night, don't you?"

"Mm," Grant answered. "I do like the way it feels under my hands here. But then again, Steph's sweet flesh feels even better, as I recall."

"It feels like it's been forever since we had our hands on you," Jesse said. His hands moved inside the dress, sliding up her stomach until he was stopped by Grants hands outside the dress. Grant let go, moving up to her shoulders to ease the dress down. Jesse's hands immediately replaced his, cupping her breasts from behind.

Stephanie's head fell back to rest against Jesse's shoulder. Her dress fell to her feet. Grant took a step back, so he could take in the beautiful sight. His lover, his Jesse, still completely dressed in his suit, arms wrapped around their Steph, wearing only her bra, panties and heels.

"I wish I had a camera," he said.

Stephanie's eyes opened, took in his look. She blushed, but reached for him. "I think you guys need to lose some clothing.

"You work on that," Jesse encouraged. "I'll work on this." His hands squeezed her breasts until she gasped.

"No fair," she moaned.

"Come on, my hands are full, you need to do your part and get our Grant naked."

Grant did his part by stepping closer. He stood still, watching their faces while her hands began to unknot is tie. Jesse's face showed total absorption in his task. He'd admitted to Grant that he'd never been much for boobs, but he found Stephanie's to be captivating. He certainly looked captivated *now*.

Grant watched as the other man slid his hands into Steph's bra and tweaked her nipples. Her hands clenched on his tie, jerking him a little bit closer to her. He didn't mind, but she smoothed her hand against his chest in apology.

She pulled the tie free and tossed it over her shoulder. She moved to his belt and he watched her delicate fingers work the clasp. Not so different from Jesse's, and yet, totally different. He needed to make sure at some point soon he'd have both their hands on his cock at the same time.

Said cock jumped a bit in anticipation and Stephanie picked up her pace. She whipped the belt out of the loops and tossed it to the side.

He liked that she was all in on this, totally down with the difference between what they were doing and the playing they'd done before. If they were in scene, she never would have treated his belongings that way. He loved dominating these two, but right now, he was looking forward to making love with them.

Which didn't mean he wasn't willing to take charge. When she started to push his pants down, he stopped her with his hands on her wrists. "No, shirt first."

She pouted a little, but did as she was told. In the meantime, Jesse had unhooked her bra and was sliding it down her arms so that she had to shake it free. Grant went back to watching Jesse's hands on her now naked breasts. His mouth watered. Deciding there was no reason to deny himself, he ignored her hands on his shirt and leaned down to pull the nipple that was between Jesse's fingers, into his mouth.

"Not fair," Stephanie whispered. He smiled but didn't bother to answer as he felt her still working on the buttons despite the awkward position. He lifted his eyes to see Jesse watching him from above Steph's shoulder. The happy and lustful smile made him grin around his treat.

"I'll leave these to you for a bit," Jesse said and moved his hands down to Stephanie's hips. He kissed her shoulder, than between her shoulder blades, and Grant lost sight of him as he made his way down to her underwear.

"Grant, you have to help me," Stephanie complained.

He pulled free of her nipple and stood up straight to give her better access, though his arms were unapologetically in her way as he continued to play with her plump breasts. She worked around him and managed to get the shirt off his shoulders before she got stuck. She growled.

Smiling he let her go long enough to shrug the shirt off then whip his undershirt over his head. He only saw her happy smile for a second before she stepped into him and latched on to *his* nipple. Damn, she was fast. He sucked in a breath at the sensation of her lips on his skin, though his nipple wasn't very sensitive. Her hands went around his back, pulling him closer to her, fingers digging in.

A squeak from Stephanie had him looking over her shoulder, down the length of her body. Jesse was on his knees, his hands pushing her underpants down to her ankles, his mouth on her ass. He chuckled and reached around, pulling her cheeks apart for his lover.

Her teeth bit into his pec in response.

"I guess we're all a little bit hungry. Let's take this to the bedroom, shall we?" he asked.

Stephanie kissed the spot she'd bitten and Jesse rose to his feet. Grant held Stephanie's hand while she kicked off her shoes and stepped out of her underwear. Jesse took the opportunity to get his shoulder into her stomach and tossed her over his shoulder. She slapped at his ass but he just laughed.

"If you want down, you better tell me where your bed is," Jesse said.

"It's a one-bedroom apartment, I think you can manage to find it on your own," she answered.

"Well, okay then." Jesse headed down the hall and Grant followed, enjoying the way Stephanie braced her hands on Jesse's

PERFECT ADDITION

ass and tossed her hair back so she could look at Grant. Her grin was huge and he couldn't help but laugh. He wasn't sure he'd every laughed as much with previous lovers as he did when the three of them were together. Even he and Jesse tended to be more serious in bed. Something about adding Stephanie to the mix just brought an extra level of joy to the situation. Not just the sex, although that part was fun, too.

Jesse nudged a partially open door farther open and Grant followed them in. The space was a little bit girlie, but definitely inviting. She had a bright green bedspread with a smattering of colorful flowers that made him glad Jesse had suggested they send a bouquet earlier in the week. He made a mental note to do that again.

Speaking of which, he spotted the flowers on her dresser, right across from her bed. He liked that she'd chosen to put the flowers in her bedroom, rather than the living room. Jesse tossed her onto the bed and leapt on top, bouncing over her on all fours. She laughed and pulled him down to her, rolling so that she was on top. Her naked, straddling Jesse who was still fully clothed, was another picture-worthy moment.

"We need to get our boy naked," she said as she began to work on his tie.

"Can't argue with that," Grant agreed, and moved to take off Jesse's shoes. He toed off his own, while he was at it. Jesse took the opportunity to play with her breasts from the front. He bobbled them around and she stopped what she was doing to laugh at him.

"What are you doing?"

"They're kind of fun to play with, I'm just experimenting a bit."

"Haven't played with many, I take it?"

"Nope. Never really wanted to before."

"Gee, I'm so honored," she giggled.

"You should be!"

"Fine, but I want you naked. Both of you."

"That's *your* problem, I'm busy here."

"Ha, that's what you think." She rose up off him and gave him her back as she began to work on his belt.

"Hmm," was his answer. Grant watched his hands begin to caress her ass, and smirked. Stephanie gave him a saucy little wiggle and Jesse responded with a light slap.

"Careful now, you'll get me all hot and bothered," she teased, pushing at his pants until Jesse cooperated by lifting his hips.

"Isn't that the idea?" Jesse asked.

"Sure, but look what I have in front of me to relieve my ache," she answered, pulling him free from his boxers. Her hand wrapped around his length, giving it a little tug.

Jesse moaned and Grant sat next to Stephanie, cupped the other man's balls.

"No fair," Jesse panted.

"Mmm," Stephanie hummed. She slid her hand up and down his length while Grant gently massaged his balls. Jesse did an impressive ab crunch and sat most of the way up, tugging his shirt off and tossing it to the side. He reached around and slid his finger into Stephanie's pussy, coming up nice and slick.

Grant grabbed his hand and moved it to his mouth, sliding Jesse's finger between his lips. He twirled his tongue around it, sucking Stephanie's flavor right off, but adding his own slickness. Jesse hummed his approval and when Grant released his finger, he moved it to her rear. They both gave little moans as Jesse teased Steph's hole and Grant gave a light squeeze to Jesse's balls.

Stephanie curled down, sticking her butt closer to Jesse's face, but making it so she could put her mouth over his cock. From Grant's perspective it appeared that she'd sucked him in deep. Considering Jesse's moan, he figured that was pretty accurate. Grant let Jesse go and watched as the other man pulled Steph's hips into position so that he could reach her pussy. He pushed his face up into her and earned a moan as well.

Grant pulled his pants off quickly and climbed onto the bed, straddling Jesse legs and facing Stephanie. He fisted a hand in her hair and gently pulled her free from Jesse's cock. She fought him, but only a little bit. He moved forward so that he could fist both himself and Jesse, at the same time, something he knew from experience that Jesse loved. The slide of their shafts together always set his lover on fire.

"Oh, yeah," Stephanie murmured. She braced her hands on Grant's legs and let him guide her by her hair until she was once again positioned with her mouth over their erections. She licked at the head of Jesse's cock while Grant slid his down, then switched as Grant slid back up. He paused, then reversed course, allowing her to switch again. Up, pause, down, pause, as her breaths became more unsteady from Jesse's actions.

Her nails dug into Grant's thighs, her little moans humming down the length of him when it was his turn for her mouth. She was going to come. He reached under her arm and tweaked her nipple. "Come for us."

She tore her mouth free of Jesse and gasped her release.

Grant's cock leaked pre-come. He grabbed the condoms he'd pulled from his pants and sheathed himself and Jesse while they watched.

He tossed Jesse the little bottle of lube he'd also brought. Jesse opened it without question and slicked two fingers, began to work them into Stephanie's back hole. Grant took her hand and eased her up into a kneeling position, moving off of Jesse's legs. Jesse followed along, his fingers never stopping, as he pulled his legs up and kneeled behind her.

"Anyone have any objections to this arrangement of tab As and slot Bs?"

They both blinked at him and he had to laugh. Okay, so they were both more used to orders than questions. He waited.

"I'm good," Stephanie said finally.

"Me, too."

"All right, just checking," he said with a grin. He leaned over Stephanie's shoulder and took Jesse's mouth in a kiss.

Jesse loved Grant's kisses, but right now it seemed like a special kind of torture. He had Stephanie in his arms, warm and willing and soft after her orgasm, his dick was hard and leaking and ready but Grant's kiss was slow and teasing and Jesse wanted it to last forever at the same time he wanted to pull free and pound into Steph. He growled his frustration and felt Grant's lips smile against him. Teasing bastard. No wonder Jesse loved the hell out of him.

Grant jerked against him and Jesse suspected that the lovely Stephanie had done something to distract him. Guessing the most likely source, he traced a hand down her arm and indeed, found her hand wrapped securely around Grant's cock. Damn, she had good ideas. He threaded his fingers through hers and encouraged her to hold their prize a bit tighter.

He left her to it and moved his hand around to squeeze Grant's butt. It was a mighty fine butt and he didn't often get the chance to play with it. They had a bottle of lube around here somewhere.

Grant broke the kiss, which immediately made Jesse wish he hadn't and want more. But then he remembered he had an armful of woman to deal with. He pressed in tight to Stephanie's back, which pushed her breasts against Grant, who braced his knees and supported them all.

Jesse leaned back and fisted himself. "Who first?" he asked, and wasn't even embarrassed at how breathless he sounded.

"Lady's choice," Grant offered.

"Oh god, I don't know, I don't care, just want you both."

"Baby, you won't get a choice very often," Grant reminded her.

"Okay, Jesse. Jesse first," she said as she continued to fondle Grant's length.

"Yee haw!"

Grant and Stephanie both managed a chuckle, but Stephanie's turned into a gasp as Jesse immediately set to his task. Her passage was tight, despite all the lube he'd used, so he went slowly, easing in and out, smiling as she began to move with him, backing into him for more.

She squeezed him unexpectedly, and he looked over her

shoulder to see Grant teasing her clit. She was so fucking responsive. He loved that about her, had been so certain she would bring more to his and Grant's relationship, was so fucking thrilled with how right he'd been.

He may not be an expert on many things, but he was damn sure an expert on what worked for him, and as soon as he'd met Grant, he'd known. And once their relationship had solidified, he'd known what he wanted, what he needed, to take that relationship all the way to perfect. It had taken a minute to convince Grant she was worth the risk, but he'd never believed it was a risk at all.

Stephanie pushed back, he surged in and just like that they were fully together. He nuzzled her ear, his new favorite spot.

"You good?" he asked.

"Yeah. So good."

He met Grant's eyes. "Bring it, big boy."

Stephanie laughed which did interesting things to his cock, buried deep inside of her. He wrapped his arms around her and cupped her breasts as Grant moved in closer and began to work his way in.

Jesse closed his eyes. God, it was so fucking amazing. As Grant pushed in, he could feel their cocks rubbing together, through Stephanie. He had to concentrate not to lose it too soon. Grant's hand landed on his hip and Jesse tightened his hold on Stephanie with one hand, and slid his other to her clit. She jumped a little in his arms when he rubbed his thumb gently over the little button. He was having so much fun learning the things that made her jump and quiver, moan and beg. Setting his teeth on her shoulder, he bit carefully as he played with her, and Grant continued to work his way in.

"Fuuuuuck," she moaned.

"Is it too much?" Grant asked, though Jesse noticed he didn't pause.

"No!"

Jesse opened his eyes and licked and nibbled the bite mark he'd left. He lifted his gaze to Grant and once again had to work very hard not to come immediately. Grant was always hot but now he was fucking gorgeous as he reveled in what they were doing. He gave one final shove and seated himself fully inside Stephanie, his length pressed tightly against Jesse's dick.

"How does that feel, Steph?" he asked, trying to distract himself from the need to explode.

"Full. So full," she panted. "Amazing."

Okay, that didn't help at all. Her sexy voice and Grant's hand squeezing his hip and her tight grip and oh god he was going to die. "I have to move," he gasped.

"Go," Grant urged.

He pulled out slowly, felt Grant do the same.

"No!" Stephanie cried.

He watched Grant's eyes and they easily found their rhythm, as if they'd done this a hundred times. Pushing in, pulling out, feeling Grant along the way. He closed his eyes tight again, memorizing the feeling of all this perfection.

They weren't going to last long. Stephanie's body was quivering constantly, her breaths coming hard and fast. He held her hips, but she didn't remain still, working with them in small movements as they climbed higher and higher. He tapped lightly on her clit, a move Grant had suggested he try, and was rewarded by a thin scream as she came.

Grant's fingers dug into him and they both came, Grant with a shout and Jesse gasping out Stephanie's name, then Grant's, and who knew what other babble as he lost his concentration and his mind.

Awareness came back to him and he realized Grant was supporting them both and watching Jesse with an amused smile. Jesse gave him a wink and slowly pulled free of Stephanie's hold. She gave a long "mmmm" and turned to look at him over her shoulder. Perfect satisfaction and a little twinkle in her eye.

Damn, he loved this woman.

He collapsed back onto the bed and held his arms open in invitation. She gave Grant a quick kiss, then dropped down to snuggle into Jesse's arms.

Grant huffed out a laugh, then staggered off the bed. Jesse heard him turn on a light and run some water, so he wasn't surprised when his tough master came back and removed the condom from Jesse, then gently cleaned Stephanie. He disappeared again only for a moment before climbing into the bed and wrapping his arms around both of them.

"Better get some rest," Grant advised them. "You're going to need your energy."

Stephanie gave a happy little laugh and Jesse just sighed. Everything was going to plan.

CHAPTER TWELVE

By Sunday, Stephanie was tired, but not in a bad way. They'd spent a good portion of Thursday night wrestling in bed, and Friday morning Jesse had nonchalantly handed her a key "to make things easier when you want to come over." Her pleasure had carried her through the workouts of the day, and she'd headed to their house Friday for an energetic play date that had involved more exploration of the toys that Grant seemed to have in abundance.

They'd kept things relatively early since she had clients on Saturday, and the guys had an event that they had to attend for Grant's work on Saturday night, so she'd snuggled in on her couch to catch up on some shows and eat a large bowl of ice cream. With all the exercising she'd been doing, she didn't even feel a tiny bit guilty about buying the carton of deliciousness.

Things had changed between them, and she had no complaints. Or, actually, it wasn't so much that things had changed, but her understanding of them had. With Jesse's handing over of the key, and the way they'd made love after the show, she realized that she'd been forcing their relationship into the play category as a safety measure. For her heart. But now it was clear that what was happening between the three of them was the real deal, not just them bringing her in to add some fun to their relationship.

Which made her nervous, but excited. Okay, maybe even scared, but excited. Sure, she'd known them for a while, but on the one hand everything seemed to be moving so fast! On the other hand, she felt like she wanted more time with them, even if it was just their company as she watched her shows and ate her ice cream.

She wondered what kind of ice cream they preferred and if they took the time to doctor it up with chocolate sauce and nuts like she did.

She got off the train and made her way to her dad who stood watching the crowd until she was close, then turned his full attention on her. She gave him a hug. His strong arms reminded her that it was okay to be scared, she came from tough stock and would make damn sure her life was awesome no matter who was in it. But it would be *most* awesome if things worked out the way she was starting to hope they would.

He shook his head at her, but didn't comment on the green in her hair, long since used to the fact that she refused to just let the blonde be blonde. They drove to the house she had been raised in, the sight of it always a happy thing for her. She knew they wanted to downsize, but were waiting until her brother established himself somewhere, like she had. She would miss it, but she figured they were right to start the next phase of their lives.

Her mom was in the kitchen and Stephanie moved to her immediately to offer a kiss and then start helping. Greek lasagne, her favorite. Damn, her parents were awesome.

She accepted the glass of wine her dad offered while following her mom's directions. The music played and her dad made helpful and not-so-helpful interjections and she wondered what it would be like to bring her guys to visit. Would they feel comfortable? Enjoy her parents as much as she did?

She stirred the white sauce and accepted the bit of lamb meat her mom offered. So good. It didn't take long before they had all of the components ready and began to layer the lasagna.

Once it was in the oven, they worked quickly to clean the kitchen and then moved to the living room. Her mom had already prepared the salad.

She wondered what Grant and Jesse were doing. Jesse had said they were going to have a quiet evening, but she didn't really know what that meant, because for the most part when the three of them had been together, they had been *doing things*. Maybe they would get to the point where she was included in the actual day-to-day of being together.

"You keep going somewhere else," her mom remarked.

She blushed. "Sorry."

"Things are getting serious," her dad said.

"Yeah, I guess they are. They took me to the Cirque Du Soleil show on Thursday. We had such a nice evening, dinner and the show. I really enjoy spending time with them."

He studied her face. "You look happy. I don't think I've ever seen you this wrapped up in a guy before."

Her stomach jumped. "I know, right? It's too early. I mean, I've known them for a while, but we've only been hanging out for a couple of weeks. When I think about that, I know it's too fast, too much. But when I think about *them*, and when I'm with them, everything just feels so right. It's crazy."

Her mom laughed. "You know better than that. You're just so used to knowing what you don't want that you're not prepared to find what you *do* want."

She blinked at that. "I'm not sure what you mean."

Her dad took over. "You've not had many relationships, because you knew right away that they weren't who you wanted. You've pushed a couple of them longer, I think just to see if you were right, and probably to see what a relationship was like, but you never really invested your heart. Ever."

"That's true. I was never really tempted. But this isn't what I thought I wanted. To come into an existing relationship and have to worry that I'm going to screw them up somehow, as well as get my heart broken."

"There's always a risk. You could have fallen for a guy with kids, then you'd be worrying about messing *them* up."

"I guess my brain is telling me it's all too fast, but really I want to wake up with them in the morning and do the simple things together, like grocery shopping. That's what I was just thinking about. Normal life instead of dating."

"It's okay to look forward to the things you'll do as a permanent relationship and start dreaming about living together, marriage, kids. People do that with someone they just met all the time. And," he added, "the way you are together, you have to give your trust so early, it's only natural that those feelings will push through faster. Which doesn't mean you should run out and get married tomorrow, or even in a month, just be aware of it and not afraid to move forward even if it's not logical."

"You know your father and I were married six months after we met," her mom said.

"I know. I guess I never thought to ask when you knew that would happen."

"I told your uncle I'd found my wife, the day after our first date."

"I told my mom to start thinking about wedding plans the day after our second date."

She blinked at them. She'd always known their relationship had been quick, she just figured she wasn't the same, since no guy she'd ever met had inspired anything close to those kinds of feelings so quickly. It had seemed so old fashioned, to be honest.

"That helps. I mean, I don't want to start planning a wedding, and I'm not really sure where *they're* at with the whole thing, but now I don't feel so silly about actually giving my heart to them, really treating this like it's a long-term relationship, not just having some fun together."

"You'll bring them here. Soon." Her dad's voice was gruff.

"You're not going to, like, interrogate them or anything, are you?" she teased.

"No promises."

She got up and went to sit beside him on the couch, wrapping her arms around him.

"You look happy," he said. "Really happy. And that's good. But if they make you *not* happy..." he glowered.

She laughed. "I know, Pop."

The meal was delicious and they had a good time together. When she was back on the train, she texted the guys to see what they were up to. Jesse immediately asked if she was coming over and Grant asked if she was home safe yet.

She laughed silently as she let them know she was still on the train. They kept her entertained while she rode, asking about her dinner, telling her about theirs, Jesse demanding that she make the Greek Lasagna for them, once she'd described its yumminess.

It seemed like the fastest train ride ever when she pulled up to her stop. She gathered her things and walked off the train, stepping to the side to send them a quick message when some instinct had her looking up.

There they stood, smiling at her.

Talk about yumminess. Her heart melted and she felt her smile stretching across her face. She stuck her phone in her back pocket and walked up to them.

"This is a treat," she said.

"We missed you," Grant said. He leaned down and accepted the quick kiss she offered.

"Are you going to come home with us?" Jesse asked, swooping in for his own kiss.

She checked her watch though she knew it was nearly ten. "I shouldn't. I have an early morning client." She frowned. It was worth getting up a little early to spend some more time with them. She was trying to figure logistics as Grant led them to his car.

"We'll take you home and give you good night kisses, then leave so we're not tempted to keep you up half the night.

She pouted.

He laughed and opened the door for her.

"If you're working early tomorrow, does that mean you have the evening off?" Jesse asked?

She turned in her seat to look at him, sitting behind Grant. "I'll have a bit of computer work to do, but not a lot. What are you thinking?"

"Grant has a meeting. You and I can go to dinner. I know this great place where lots of people go either on first dates, or to break up. I don't think it's on purpose, but I swear there is *always* some fun drama to watch, it's better than television."

She laughed. "I'm in." She looked at Grant. "That sucks you have to work late."

He frowned. "It's not something I allow to happen too often."

"Well, that's good at least."

He flashed her a smile. "You guys can get me some dessert from the restaurant. Will you be able to bring it by yourself?"

She did a mental check of her schedule. "I would need to be out of your place by ten on Tuesday."

"Works for me," Jesse said. "I don't have to be out until about ten-thirty, so we can have breakfast together."

They pulled up to her street and Grant began looking for a parking space.

"Don't bother coming up, guys, it's silly to try and find a spot, only to turn back around and leave. I wish you could stay, but I really do have an early start tomorrow."

Grant didn't look convinced, but he stopped in front of her building and double-parked. She leaned in and gave him a long, slow kiss. She'd meant it to be reassuring, but she sort of lost herself in the moment and forgot that there was any message involved other than how much she wanted him. His hands pulled her closer but the center console brought her back to herself enough to pull away.

The fire in his eyes matched the one in her gut. "Maybe you guys could come up, you know, for a few minutes after all," she whispered.

He smiled a slow smile, but then looked at the clock. "You know we want to, sweetheart, but it's already late. You come back to our place after dinner tomorrow and we'll finish what you've started here."

She scoffed. "Me? That was all you, buster." A deep breath, and she thought maybe she could manage to get out of the car without falling over on shaky legs. She turned to Jesse. Oh no. Maybe a peck on the cheek would suffice?

As if. He swooped in and claimed her, his tongue doing delicious things that made her body quiver in need.

He was the one who broke the kiss, his expression one of sly satisfaction.

"You're a turd," she said, trying to get her breathing back under control.

"I can't help it that you're hot for me," he countered smugly.

"Oh please, you actively work to make me hot for you."

"Well, yeah, but it's your fault it's successful."

She stared at him. "That doesn't even make sense!"

He just laughed, putting his arm around Grant's shoulder and leaning his head against the back of the seat. "Let's drive somewhere private and make out like teenagers."

Looking pointedly around the interior of the car, she raised an eyebrow.

"Hmm, good point. Maybe we should buy a minivan."

She burst out laughing. "We had a limo! Did you already forget?"

"Another good point. We should do that again."

Leaning in, she gave him a quick peck, pulling back before he could get grabby, then did the same with Grant. "Thanks for picking me up, guys, I really appreciate it. I'll see you tomorrow."

She jumped out of the car, humming to herself as she made her way inside. She turned and waved before shutting the door. Skipping the elevator, she jogged up the stairs on a burst of happy energy.

There was a note taped to her door, from the building's management company, so she pulled it free and went inside. She put her things away, put the letter with her laptop to handle the next day, grabbed a glass of water, turned off the lights, and went to her bedroom.

Her nightly routine didn't take long, and as soon as she slid into bed she wished she'd asked the guys to stay. Her bed had never seemed so big and empty before. She thought about grabbing her cell phone and calling or texting them, but then she'd never get to sleep. Wrapping her arms around a pillow, she took long, even breaths, and willed herself to sleep.

JESSE CLOCKED out and checked his phone. He and Stephanie were on schedule to meet up at the restaurant he'd told her about. He sent a quick text to Grant asking how his day was going, and letting him know that he wished the other man were joining them instead of going to some boring meeting, but he hoped that it wouldn't be too excruciating, for Grant's sake. The reply was an emoji sticking its tongue out at him.

Satisfied, he jumped onto the bus going the right direction, standing next to the driver so they could have a little chat while they made their way down the block. When they reached the correct cross street, Jesse bid his coworker goodbye and hopped off. It was only a couple more blocks to his destination so he walked, taking in the active scene around him. He loved living in the city, loved people watching. Loved people. It was one of the reasons he liked his job, interacting with so many different people every day, but also getting to know his regulars.

He walked inside and scanned to make sure Steph hadn't already been seated, then greeted one of his favorite waitresses. "Hey, Sandra, I'm meeting my girlfriend and we want some drama, so if you've got it, sit us by it."

She laughed. "Oh, you know we've always got some drama going on. Let's see." She scanned around the room. "That couple in the corner, I heard her say something like, 'what do you mean you have a son?', and I'm pretty sure they've been together a while." She turned a little and did a chin lift. "That young couple over there, definitely a first date. They just sat down, though, so I don't know if it will be sweet or awful."

He rubbed his hands together. "Let's go with the first date. I hate to see kids dragged into a mess. If you'll put the menus down, I'll wait for Stephanie outside. Thanks Sandra, you're the best."

She gave him a hug and did as he asked while he turned back to the front door. He stepped outside and checked the direction he expected Stephanie to be coming from. She'd let him know that she'd gotten all of her computer work done and was free for the rest of the night. All his, until Grant came home. Then, all theirs.

He spotted her from several stores down. She was looking up, her face to the setting sun. An outdoors girl, but happy in his city. Maybe they should take her fishing or something. Was that a thing? His only real outdoor activity was the beach house and that had only been for the last few months.

She stopped to give something to a guy sitting against the side of a building, playing his guitar. He could see her smile from here. But when she resumed her walk and caught sight of him, the smile grew so perfectly, he felt it in his heart. He couldn't move, just stood still while she bounced up to him and wrapped him in a hug. She put her lips next to his ear.

"Can I kiss you?" she asked softly.

He didn't bother to answer, just took her face in his hands and brought their lips together. She opened for him immediately. He kept it short and sweet since they were out in public, but he was very glad she'd be coming home with him.

"Let's eat," he said, tugging her to the door.

"Good plan. Then we can get dessert." She waggled her eyebrows at him and he laughed. When they were seated he leaned in close and whispered in her ear.

"The young couple over there is purportedly on their first date, so we might get some fun entertainment in that direction. But the food is excellent, so the entertainment is only a bonus."

"Good to know. Any recommendations?" She picked up her menu.

"I know it's kind of a joke for millennials and all, but the avocado toast is really yummy."

She laughed. "I'm not an amazing cook or anything, but I *will* make you avocado toast. You don't need to pay restaurant prices for it."

He beamed at her. "Okay, that works. Then I can also recommend the three-cheese ravioli, the penne with pesto and any of the calzones. There's a salmon dish on there that Grant likes. In fact, remind me and I'll order one for him to go."

He let her read while he tuned into the couple at the next table.

"You mentioned you've played Skyrim," the woman said.

"I'm surprised you want to talk about games," the man, whose tone of voice made Jesse immediately label him as Loser, said. "You appear to be very intelligent and should know that I usually date women who are more on the athletic side."

Jesse kicked Steph's foot and made big eyes at her, indicating the table.

The woman, who was wearing a very pretty pink dress, so he decided to call her Pinky, blinked at Loser. "You mentioned the game in your message to me, so I'm surprised that *you're* surprised I would consider it a topic of conversation. Since the only conversation you've started so far was about the food and an unfair and unnecessary critique of a random woman's body shape, I thought maybe I should give it a go in another direction."

"Calm down, I can see we're going to need a drink here." Loser looked around and waived down a waiter. "Two glasses of Pinot."

"I'll have an iced tea," Pinky added quickly.

Loser frowned at her. "You said you like wine."

"I do." Jesse could see her mentally taking a breath. She offered a game smile. "Have you done any of the wine tastings around here? I haven't had a chance, but I've heard it can be a nice outing."

The waiter had left and Jesse met Steph's eyes.

"Oh my," she said. "This is amazing. You see this kind of thing all the time?"

"All the time. Once you know what you're looking for, you'd be astonished how often you can pick out the first or second dates when you're at the right restaurants."

"I wonder what kind of men she's been dating that she's still sitting there. I think I would have left already."

"Right? Loser is good entertainment. Plus, if you pay attention, sometimes you can play white knight and rescue a woman who clearly needs to be extricated from a horrible date. I've played the dashing hero once, and the gay best friend twice."

"Wow, that's crazy."

She paused when Jake came to their table for their orders. She asked for the salmon for her and one to go for Grant. He asked for the ravioli and handed his menu to Jake, giving him a great view of Loser reaching out to rest his hand on the back of Pinky's. She jolted, then moved her hand to pick up her water glass, taking a healthy drink from it.

"Does he really think she'd be receptive to that?"

"I think there's a class of men who've been told you can't fail unless you try, or something like that."

"I mean, her body language is not inviting. She's as far back in her seat as she can get, he can't be that clueless."

"Oh, I think he can."

Loser had apparently steered the conversation back to exercise and was telling Pinky how often he went to the gym. She seemed to be surprised, though she didn't comment on its apparent lack of success in keeping him in shape, as Jesse wished *he* could.

"I walk my dog every day, it's a great way to get out and see my neighbors at the park, get some fresh air, and keep my dog from going stir crazy," Pinky said.

"It's good you keep somewhat in shape," Loser said. "I hear it makes it easier when you have kids, too. Helps you bounce back faster. Plus, you have a good body for having kids. My poor sister is thin as a rail and had a tough time with labor."

Pinky just stared at him. Jesse had to fight not to do the same and Steph put her hand over her mouth to stifle her gasp.

Finally Pinky nodded and seemed to settle into her seat, getting more comfortable. "I'm not sure I want kids, actually."

Jesse leaned across the table. "I think she's decided to see how bad he can get. She's just gone from maybe this will work somehow to how great of a story will this be to tell later."

"I hope she has a good memory, there's going to be a lot to recount."

"So, what? You're just going to get married and get old and die? Not do anything to help make the world a better place?"

Pinky choked a bit on her iced tea. "Are you saying that the only purpose your parents had in life was to make you and your sister? That's their great accomplishment?"

"My dad is a well-respected doctor, but my mom, yeah. We were her thing."

"And how has that worked out for her?" Pinky asked, and Jesse was sure Loser would hear the mocking in her tone.

"Obviously she's very proud of me," Loser said, oblivious.

"What's the worst date you've ever been on," Jesse asked Stephanie.

"Paul. Totally Paul. He was a manager at one of the gyms I worked with. He told me about how his family had this restaurant, and it was the best food in the city and I was missing out since I hadn't been. I said okay, I'll try it, give me the details, and somehow he managed to turn that into a date. I wasn't really excited, but I figured what the hell."

Their food arrived and she paused to sample it, giving a long hum of appreciation. "So we get there and he's rude to the staff, ordering them around unnecessarily. Then he tells me how this place is his legacy, and they wanted him to come and run it, but he just wasn't ready to settle into that life yet. He made it sound like he was enjoying himself slumming with the rest of us until he was ready to settle down and be an actual adult."

She rolled her eyes and took a drink of her soda.

"The food looked pretty good, but when he berated the waitress for bringing a basket of bread to the table when she knew he was gluten intolerant, I noped out of there."

"Oh my god, what did you do? And did it not occur to him that the bread was for you?"

"Clearly not. I took a piece of bread from the basket and began to butter it while he was chastising her, and when he paused to take a breath I asked for the bill for my drink."

Jesse laughed. "That's awesome, how did he react?"

"He looked all shocked, and asked me what I was doing. I said that I had just remembered that I had an appointment with my hairdresser in a few minutes and I needed to run. I drank my wine in like two swallows and the waitress brought my check almost immediately. I handed her a twenty and walked out."

She grinned at him as she reached over and speared a piece of ravioli, swiping it through the cheesy, creamy sauce before bringing it to her mouth. "What about you?" she asked.

Before answering, he checked on Pinky. Loser had reached out and toward her arm, but she moved it before he made contact, not even pretending to go for her drink this time.

"I've always found shorter men to be…preoccupied with themselves and their place in the world," Pinky was saying.

Stephanie laughed and clutched at Jesse's arm. "I'm glad we don't have to worry about her. It would be awful if someone was being a terrible date but the other person was just taking it."

Jake swung by and asked if they wanted dessert, so they looked at the menus again, but ordered them to go.

Jesse resumed their conversation when Jake left. "Yeah, I've seen that a couple of times. I swear this one woman got this poor guy to take her out just so she could get a free meal in this restaurant. She was ordering expensive drinks before she'd even finished the last, texting on her phone the whole time, and being obnoxious as hell, but he was just quiet and not saying much."

Stephanie shook her head in disgust.

"So, my worst was Greg. I met him on a BDSM website and he was a Dom, obviously."

She clinked his glass with hers in salute. "Obviously."

"We'd been chatting online for a couple of weeks and decided to meet at a bar, see how we got on in person before trying anything."

"Sensible." She forked up her last bite of salmon and offered it to him.

Declining with a shake of his head, he finished off his water. He looked to the side to see Pinky motioning to the waiter for a check. "Anyway, we meet outside and he goes for a handshake, which I thought was a little odd, but whatever. We manage to find a small table, but the place is crowded so there's not a lot of room. I think I put a hand on his shoulder or something, and he totally overreacted, and that's when I realized he was in the closet."

"Oh, shit. I'd think a guy would mention that before going out in public, on a date, with another guy."

"I certainly thought so. I finally asked him, and he admitted it. Acted all affronted that I was mad. I mean, I try to be sympathetic to guys who feel the need to stay in the closet, but come on. He had a pretty good sense of me from our chatting, knew I was totally out and never thought to bring it up? Lame."

He leaned back in his chair. "I gave him a blow job in the alley and never talked to him again."

She stared at him. Waited a beat. Then finally threw her head back and roared with laughter.

Loser looked over with a frown. Pinky stood up and walked out of the restaurant. The older couple on his other side smiled at him. He waited until she had quieted. "Well, I thought about it, because he was really hot, but I told him if he wanted help and support with coming out, to get in touch with me, but otherwise I wasn't comfortable with the level of deception he seemed okay with, and I paid for both our drinks and left."

She leaned across the table and kissed him quickly.

"You're a good guy, Jesse Arnold."

He was distracted enough by that to not grab the check first as it was set on the table. She just laughed at his disgruntled look. Damn, he loved to hear her laugh. He rolled his eyes at her as she danced the check close to him, teasing him to try and grab it.

"Brat."

Loser stood up, looking down his nose at them as he passed by, and this time they both erupted in laughter.

They left soon after. He carried Grant's food and the desserts in one hand and swung her hand with the other, as they walked down the street. He offered to take her backpack, but she said she was good. He agreed, with a leer.

It was dark now, though being in the city it never quite reached full dark, not like at the beach house. They window shopped a bit as they strolled, and she asked him how to get back to his place by bus, so they decided to do that. They chatted with the driver, then bounced off the bus a few blocks from the house.

He texted Grant to see how their timing was, and found that he'd just arrived home not long before. Jesse let him know that they were close and that they came bearing food.

CHAPTER THIRTEEN

Grant put his phone down and looked at the glass of whiskey he'd just poured. It had seemed just the thing he needed when he walked into an empty house after a ridiculous excuse for a meeting.

Now, he reconsidered. Would they be in the mood to play? Was he? Not at the moment, but he couldn't discount the fact that when they were all together, the mood had a way of finding him.

He took two more glasses down, and split the drink into thirds. It didn't amount to much, so he added a splash to each glass as he heard the door open.

"Honey, we're home," Jesse sang out.

"I'm in the kitchen," he called out, just the sound of his man's voice finally bringing a smile to his face. He pulled a plate down, grabbed a fork and napkin. He flipped the coffee maker on, as well as the electric kettle he'd picked up the other day after noticing that Steph had one in her kitchen that seemed well used.

By the time he'd poured himself an ice water, they were walking into the kitchen, all smiles and clearly having had a better couple of hours than he had. He *could* find that annoying. Instead, he was charmed by the way they both immediately walked to him and wrapped their arms around him. He held the glass away so it wouldn't spill, and just soaked in their happy affection.

"Hello," Jesse said, before moving in for a kiss. Grant could feel his tense muscles relaxing as he let the other man have his way with his mouth. Jesse pulled back and Steph went up on her tiptoes to offer him the same welcome.

"I take it your meeting wasn't the greatest," Jesse asked. Grant looked to see him picking up the glasses of whiskey and taking them over to the table, where he'd set the restaurant bag.

"You could say that, but my evening's looking up." He gave Steph a squeeze, then motioned to the kettle as it began to boil.

"Want some tea?" He showed her the variety box of tea bags Jesse had bought.

"Awesome. You sit down, I'll get this. Do you want one, Jesse?" She pulled a mug out of the cupboard.

"I'll have some of that coffee I smell." Jesse was busy putting the food they'd brought on the plate Grant had taken to the table. He hip checked Grant on his way past. "Sit, relax. I'll heat this up and we'll join you with the drinks."

In a better mood already, he sat and sipped his whiskey, watching the two as they worked around each other. Stephanie pulled the cream out of the fridge and added just the right amount to Jesse's coffee. Jesse stuck his finger in the fish, frowned, and added more time to the microwave.

He liked what he saw. He knew it was too early to push Stephanie, but he hoped it wouldn't be long before they could talk her into moving in. At the rate they were going, they'd be spending most nights together anyway, so how hard of a sell could it be?

From there, they'd start checking out houses. He and Jesse had done some looking, but they hadn't been ready to move forward, and he knew they wouldn't until Stephanie was a confirmed permanent member of their household, and part of the real estate shopping herself.

Maybe he was moving too fast, but he was used to going with his instincts, and they rarely failed him. If this was the exception, he'd deal with it, but for now, he was determined to keep moving forward.

Jesse brought the plate of food and set it in front of him. Stephanie set both mugs down, then poured her glass of whiskey into her tea. She gave it a little stir with her finger, and offered the wet appendage to Jesse to suck clean. Jesse obliged, his eyes twinkling.

Grant threw his drink back in one swallow, mentally abolishing his bad mood with it. He went to work on his delicious salmon and listened as the two recounted their adventures at the restaurant. By the time he'd finished, he was in a good enough mood to recount the story of his own evening.

"So," he began. "Apparently someone got hold of my cousin Sharon and gave her an earful about me."

Jesse frowned. "What kind of earful?"

"About my membership in a sex club," Grant said, finally seeing the humor in the situation.

"Oh *shit*," Stephanie said.

"Something like that," Grant confirmed. "Now my family is trying to figure out what is worse, my being gay or my being a member of a sex club. They at least seemed mollified when I mentioned that I was a Dom, not a sub, as if that somehow made a difference in anything."

"Wow," Stephanie said, putting her hand on his shoulder.

"You, of course, offered to quit," Jesse assumed, pointing at him with his glass of whiskey.

"Of course."

"Oh shit," Stephanie repeated.

"It's not as bad as it sounds," Jesse reassured her. "And anyway, they won't actually let him."

"He's right," Grant told her. "Part of me wants to leave, to strike out and do my own thing, rather than taking care of the business being handed down, and they know that. So they can't push me too hard."

She frowned. "I'm sure you're great at your job and all, but why do they worry so much about it? Nobody should be irreplaceable in their job, surely they can find someone else to take your place if you quit."

"True, but they only want family in my position. My father is president in name only, at this point. He's not been interested in keeping up with the advances in the last few years, so he's all but retired, he just isn't ready to spend all day at home with my mother, so he still goes into the office every day."

"He needs to take up golf," Jesse said.

Grant laughed. "Maybe. At any rate, the only other family members that could, in theory, take my place, let alone my father's, are not people my parents actually trust to do the job."

"Ah," Stephanie said, putting down her cup.

"The problem *there*," Jesse added, "is that two cousins *think* they're good enough to take over and only Grant is stopping them, and don't actually realize that they do not, in fact, have the confidence of Charlotte and Steven, and it's ultimately their decision who will be in charge when Steven does retire."

"So," Stephanie said, "they don't want you to quit, because of business, but they think they have some right to judge your personal life."

"I think the information was presented to Sharon in such a way as to suggest that it could be a terrible scandal to the company."

She frowned. "How?"

"Apparently this unknown person who gave Sharon an earful embellished his news of my membership with the assertion that I have a terrible reputation at the club for mistreating subs, breaking rules right and left, and in general, being an asshole."

"Who the hell *is* this person?" Jesse asked.

Grant drank some of his water, pleased that he was maintaining his good mood, despite recounting the annoying story.

"She wouldn't say. Obviously she was trying to convince my mother and my aunt—*her* mother—that it was in the company's best interest to quietly remove me, and she was willing to make the sacrifice to slide into my place, but they pretty much just laughed at her." That part, at least, had been nice. "I have to admit, I was a little bit tempted to use this as an excuse to walk away."

Jesse reached out and held his hand, an expression of concern marring his handsome face.

"But I remembered that I'm proud of what I've done there and when I'm ready to leave, it will be because I've decided to, not because someone else made a foolish move. Plus, I must admit, though they were definitely scandalized, and weren't pleased, my parents stood by me and did not entertain any talk about getting rid of me."

"If you like your job, why would you want to leave?" Stephanie asked.

"The family politics can get irritating," he told her. "But they're mostly manageable."

"Yeah, because you've made it clear you're not going to play those games," Jesse said.

"Basically."

"Well, then, as long as you're enjoying it. Still, that's weird that someone would just approach your cousin like that."

"It is, yes. I'll be looking into that part of it further. That they would know about my activities, but then lie about them so boldly. I'm definitely not happy about that."

"So," Jesse summarized. "Now your parents know you're gay and you're a Dom. Did you tell them about Stephanie, get it all out there?" He was grinning as he said it, but Grant knew it was actually a serious question.

"No, I didn't want to dignify the meeting with actual important stuff."

He finished his water and looked at the pair. Although he was definitely in a better mood, he wasn't exactly in a romantic one. Or a sexy one. Let alone a Dom one. Of course, his Jesse read him in an instant.

"Let's watch a movie," Jesse suggested. "We'll get in our pajamas, get comfy on the couch. I vote *Buffy the Vampire Slayer*."

"I vote *The Boondock Saints*," Stephanie said immediately.

Jesse frowned. "Is it on Netflix? We don't have it."

She pouted. "No, I don't think so."

"How about we get changed and go see what's available?" Grant asked.

They grabbed his dishes from him and their glasses, and had the dishwasher loaded in seconds. When they made it to the bedroom to change, he reconsidered. Stephanie just laughed and threw her jeans at him, changing into a pair of yoga pants and borrowing a sweatshirt from Jesse.

They settled onto the couch with him sitting at one end, Jesse laying along the back, his head on Grant's thigh, Stephanie tucked in close to his front, her head propped up on a toss pillow. They argued about the movies a bit until they found something none of them had even heard of, but looked sexy.

"This is kind of terrible," Stephanie commented, about fifteen minutes into the movie.

"Whoa," Grant said with a wince, forty minutes into the movie.

"Oh, no, that's not good," Jesse said during the supposedly climactic love scene.

"Damn," Grant said when the moaning and groaning that wasn't the least bit sexy got to be a bit too much.

"Well," Stephanie said when the heroine tried to emote upset at the dramatic moment.

"Yikes," Jesse added, when the hero's look of pained torment wasn't quite what it was meant to be.

When the credits rolled, they stayed silent for a whole minute.

"I may never have sex again," Stephanie finally said.

"Or a boyfriend. Or a friend of any kind. Or a life," Jesse agreed.

"Why didn't we turn it off?" Grant asked.

"I think I need a shower," Stephanie said. She rolled off the couch and turned to look down at them.

"That is the only plan that makes any sense right now," Grant agreed.

Jesse pushed up and they all trooped to the master bathroom.

It was a much less excited trio entering the shower together than the last time, Grant noted with a wry grin. But seeing his lovers naked was starting to bring him around.

"My dream home has a big tub with jets," Stephanie said as she stepped into the stream.

"Not a hot tub?" Jesse asked, stepping in close to share the water.

"Well, I guess I never dreamed big enough for a house with a yard," she laughed. "I always assumed a condo."

Grant pulled down the bottle of shampoo, poured a bit into his hand and waited for her to step back a bit. He motioned with his hands and her eyes lit up. Closing them, she tipped her head back slightly to give him access.

He rubbed the shampoo between his palms then slowly worked them down her hair, from top to tip. Then he scrunched it all up to her scalp and smooshed it all around. He'd never done this before, and found it strangely intimate. He let the hair fall down, then worked his fingers into her scalp. He knew the massage was successful when she offered a little moan.

Jesse reached past him for the body washed and positioned himself in front of Steph.

Since her eyes were closed, she gave a little start when he cupped her shoulders with soapy hands. He caressed her collarbone with his thumbs, then moved his hands down her arms, lacing her fingers with his.

He looked over her shoulder at Grant, who knew that look perfectly. Grant nodded and Jesse smiled.

Jesse brought their hands to the small of Stephanie's back while Grant pulled his fingers free of her hair. He gathered the length up into his fist, and slowly tightened it. He knew when she opened her eyes, and used her hair to move her head so that she could meet his gaze.

"Do you want to play?" he asked, very softly.

She swallowed and licked her lips. "Yes, Sir."

"Keep your hands where they are."

"Yes, Sir."

He moved her head back so she was facing forward. "Let's rinse out the shampoo." She waited, not moving, until he guided her around and back under the spray. He lifted his chin at Jesse, who immediately went to work, pulling her into the spray and massaging her hair until it was clean.

Her eyes stayed open, her focus on him as he slicked his hands up and down her body, cleaning all the spots Jesse hadn't gotten to, except her breasts, her pussy and her ass. He lingered on the back of her knee, felt her shiver. He moved her back out of the spray when Jesse indicated he was done, and handed the other man the conditioner. Then he re-soaped his hands and reached around to her rear. He pulled her cheeks apart, slid a finger down to tease her hole.

He only teased her for a minute, before going back for more soap. He let Jesse rinse her hair again as he massaged and 'cleaned' her breasts. When her nipples were well and truly clean, he sucked one into his mouth, bit gently. Then not so gently. She gasped.

He moved to the side of her breast and sucked hard, knowing he was marking her. He glanced up when he sensed Jesse stepping back. Jesse held his hands out to indicate he was finished. Grant stepped back. "Close your eyes, Stephanie. Keep them closed until I tell you otherwise. Your mouth, too."

She complied immediately. He knew that being naked and wet in a slippery shower, with her eyes closed and her hands restricted would make her feel vulnerable. He put his hands on her hips and moved her back, adjusting the spray so that it landed on top of her head, rushing all round her, down her face and back, clouding her hearing.

He motioned Jesse to his side and pointed. Jesse's eager anticipation didn't disappoint. He dropped to his knees and carefully nudged her legs apart. Then he leaned in and licked.

STEPHANIE ALMOST GASPED when a tongue found her clit. It wasn't like it was unexpected, exactly, not when hands hand just positioned her legs. But somehow the water flowing down her head, over her face, messed with all of her senses. She normally wasn't a huge fan of water on her face, but this was different. It didn't bother her, it somehow...sensitized her.

She didn't know whose hands and mouth were down below, an enthusiastic exploration that felt more like Jesse than Grant, but she wouldn't swear to it. But that left the other person's hands tormenting her up above. A whisper of touch on her lips, which trembled as she fought to keep them closed. A tickle along her shoulder blade, a poke in her butt cheek. The sudden pinch of her nipple. She moaned, but she did it with her mouth closed.

Her fingers clenched together tightly as a finger entered her pussy. Slowly, but firmly, her body not as slick as normal due to the hot water, she accepted the intrusion. She tightened her muscles as if she could pull that finger in faster.

Up above, fingers danced along her rib cage and hands pressed into her hips. She squeaked when a finger poked at her ear, and couldn't stop herself from rubbing it against her shoulder. Careful fingers pushed her hair back from her face, rubbed at the offended ear, traced along her eyebrows. All while the tongue and finger, *gah*, make that two fingers now, worked her higher and higher.

She whimpered, unable to stop herself, and needing to let Grant know she was close. The tongue at her clit disappeared and she almost whimpered again, but at least it kept her from hurtling over the edge without permission.

Suddenly her body was pressed between both men, one on either side of her, holding her up, two hands at her sex, one pushing into her, the other pressing against her clit. Grant's voice was in her ear, low and growly, telling her to come. Telling her to scream. The water over her head disappeared, the finger at her clit pinched, and the one inside her hooked around to that magical spot.

Scream. She was pretty sure she did, although she may have blacked out. She actually felt light-headed now that the water was gone, which seemed strange, but she was too busy trying to regain some sense of self to understand it. Her knees trembled, but she felt secure, no matter the fact that she was nearly boneless, standing on slick tile.

Flashes of light sparked behind her eyelids and she realized they weren't just closed, but squeezed tight. She relaxed them, fought to breathe normally. The water still pounded behind her and she wasn't sure her ears were working correctly. She felt like she was deprived of her senses, which was crazy since the only one blocked was her sight. She was certainly feeling touch, as the men held her tightly between them.

Slowly, she regained her faculties. Her panting gave way to normal breathing and she was able to pick up the sounds of the guys harsh breathing. They were obviously a little affected, too. She smiled and Grant nosed her hair aside and kissed her temple.

"Open your eyes, sweetheart," he said.

She blinked them open slowly, adjusting to the brightness. She looked up at him and her smile increased.

He laughed, nudged her into the corner where there was a little bench built in, probably for women to use when they shaved their legs. At least, that's what she would use it for.

"Sit down for a minute while we wash up."

She complied and watched as they hurriedly handled their own shampoo and conditioner. When they turned off the water, she stood, feeling much steadier. Grant held a hand out to her and led her out of the shower. He handed her a towel and she wrapped her hair. They all dried themselves off quickly, towel dried their hair, and went into the bedroom. She grabbed a hair tie on her way and pulled the wet mess into a tail. It would probably be a nightmare in the morning, but she'd worry about that later.

Grant slapped the end of the bed as he walked past it, on his way to the toy dresser. "Kneel here."

She followed Jesse, who climbed up on the bed and positioned himself at the end, butt on his heels, hands at the small of his back. When she'd done the same, he gave her a little shoulder bump. She looked at him and he grinned and winked. She managed not to laugh. Barely. She faced forward and waited.

It seemed to take a while and she wondered what Grant was doing, Probably mostly stalling, to up their anticipation levels. Well, it was working. Her lethargic body was re-energizing bit by bit. Jesse smelled clean and fresh beside her and she wanted to lick him all up.

She heard the familiar clinking sound of restraints and still nothing happened. He was probably watching them, seeing how long they would hold the position.

She reminded herself it had only been about five minutes. Actually, probably less. It suddenly occurred to her that she hadn't gone to the club this weekend or the last. Weird. Emma was so going to tease her about this.

Another clink and a slide of the drawer brought her attention back to the room. She'd been pleasantly surprised by the amount of equipment they had split between the beach house and their apartment.

Grant turned and walked to the side of the bed, dropping an armload off behind them. He came around to the foot of the bed and moved directly to Jesse, holding up his collar. Jesse gave a happy little sigh and Stephanie saw a small smile tugging at Grant's lips as he buckled the color onto his sub. When it was in place, Grant kissed Jesse for a good minute, before moving over to Stephanie.

He held out her collar so she could see the strip of green ribbon. It wasn't quite the same shade as her hair, but it was the right color and she felt a warm fluttery feeling in her belly. He buckled the collar into place and she felt herself shifting fully into that mental space she thought she'd already found in the shower.

When he stepped back, she had that inexplicable mix of the delicious buzz of anticipation, yet calm surrender. Grant walked away, his hand trailing along her arm, then Jesse's chest as he made his way back to the side of the bed. She felt him get up on the bed behind them and heard again the clink of metal. The bed depressed as he moved closer, but she kept her head and gaze forward. She wanted to watch what he was doing to Jesse, as she had last time, but had faith she would get to see and enjoy the final product. Unless he blindfolded her, or had her close her eyes again. As much as she'd enjoyed that in the shower, she really loved seeing the guys together, so she hoped not.

The bed moved again as he came closer to her. Cool leather caressed then enveloped one arm, then the other. She let go of her wrist as he manipulated her arms into an armbinder. Her shoulders were pulled back as he tightened the laces that attached the devices together, from her wrists to her elbows. She'd worn them before, but not often, and it was a different sensation, a different feeling of restriction, than just having her wrists cuffed.

Grant got off the bed. "Up you go."

She lifted up and he kept a hand on her to be sure she was steady, but she had no trouble getting off the bed and standing next to it. He positioned her close to the bedpost, attached a cuff to it, and clipped her collar to the ring in the cuff, keeping her head only a couple of inches from the post.

She was angled towards the bed a bit, so was able to watch as Grant moved to help Jesse from the bed and to a similar position at the opposite post. She saw that Jesse was wearing a tan leather harness, a long strip of leather that ran down his spine to a belt at his waist, and the belt had cuffs attached at the small of his back. She had to grin at the clear evidence that he was excited.

Grant stepped up close to Jesse, teased his lips without giving a real kiss, nipped his jaw, scratched at his pecs. He reached behind Jesse to the bed and came back with a cock ring. Stephanie couldn't quite make out the words Grant said as he worked the ring onto Jesse, but she definitely heard the low moan of need Jesse gave.

Another reach to the bed and Grant stepped back between them holding a light suede flogger. He draped it over Stephanie's shoulder, then down, letting it fall over her breast in a soft, promising caress. He swished it lightly over her hips, then gave a light backhanded slap to her pussy.

"I'm not going to flog you. Not tonight," he said, giving light slaps to her sides and thighs that seemed to contradict his statement.

She wasn't even disappointed, that's how sure that whatever he had in mind, she would be well and thoroughly satisfied.

"I'm going to work Jesse for a while. He deserves a bit of attention, don't you think?"

She dipped her head a bit, not enough to pull against the restraint or lose eye contact, but enough to show her agreement.

He returned the flogger to the bed and she bit back any sound of displeasure. This time he held a gag, the kind that looked like a penis.

He held it to her mouth and she opened obediently, though it wasn't her favorite thing. He buckled the straps around her head securely, testing it with his fingers. She immediately wished she could lick her lips. Her tongue explored the shape, getting used to the taste and texture of the rubber-like plastic. It wasn't unpleasant. She kept her gaze on Grant's, waiting for his instructions.

"I'm going to work Jesse for a while. He deserves a bit of attention, don't you think?"

She dipped her head a bit, not enough to pull against the restraint or lose eye contact, but enough to show her agreement.

"I want to hear you working that cock in your mouth as if it were one of ours. I want to know you're watching us, even when I'm not looking at you, and I'm going to know that because you're going to make sounds even though you're wearing that gag. *Because* you're wearing that gag. I want to hear sounds so wet, I feel like your mouth is on me. Do you understand?"

Already the association of the gag with either of the guys' appendages was building in her mind, his words making her wet and eager. She showed him her agreement with her eyes and he smiled, kissed her cheek where the strap rested.

"Good girl."

She started slowly, again exploring the shape of the small shaft as she watched Grant grab the flogger and move back in front of Jesse. As he'd done with her, Grant started by giving Jesse just the feel of it, sliding it around his body more than hitting. She sucked on her gag and gave a little moan of pleasure as the strands of the flogger swirled around Jesse's hard dick. She imagined her tongue working him as Grant moved back up Jesse's chest, the light sounds becoming harder, thicker.

She always hated the moment with a gag when the saliva escaped her control, but it also never failed to remind her that loss of control was the point. Now the saliva gave her what she needed to follow Grant's orders. She sucked hard on the gag, letting it slurp, trying to make sure that the sound was as loud as the thwaps and thuds of the flogger.

Grant leaned into Jesse, swinging the flogger around to the backs of Jesse's legs. "Do you hear her? That's our cock she's sucking on so enthusiastically. If her jaw gets tired, do you think she'll still want the real thing when we're done here?"

Jesse gasped at the hardest hit yet. "Yes, Sir, I do."

Grant glanced over, meeting her eyes, his look full of appreciation and approval. "Yeah, I think she will, too."

He tossed the flogger onto the bed and reached for another, coming back with a leather one with knots on the end. He didn't pause, just went right to work on Jesse's torso and legs, occasionally stroking the tails over Jesse's straining dick. She gave another enthusiastic suck, moaning as she imagined it was his hot flesh in her mouth instead of the slick rubber.

Grant picked up his pace and every stoke sent a shiver along Stephanie's skin, as if she felt a fraction of what Jesse felt. She fought not to rub her thighs together, to stay in the position Grant had placed her in. She clenched her fingers, her shoulders flexing against their restraint. She felt safe with her arms encased in the leather sleeves, as though it were Grant's hands keeping her steady as she took in the erotic sight before her and swirled her tongue around the gag.

"Doesn't he look good?" Grant asked softly. He didn't look at her but she felt his attention.

She moaned in agreement.

"All flushed and straining and sweaty for us. He can hear his cock in your mouth, even if he can't quite feel it. He can feel my touch every time the flogger connects, can't you my Jesse?"

"Oh, god, yes Sir."

Grant switched floggers again, with barely a break in strikes. The new flogger had short tails and he worked Jesse's shoulders and upper arms without fear of hitting the other man's face.

"It's a pretty music to work to," Grant said as Stephanie made more eager noises. "Maybe I should have left her hands free so we could hear her work herself, too. But I think we'll save all that nice juiciness for us."

Jesse and Stephanie moaned together.

"Yeah, that's nice." He put a hand to Jesse's chest. "So nice and warm for me." He tweaked a nipple. "Always so good for me."

Stephanie felt the drool drip down her chin and didn't even care, she just sucked harder, her gaze glued to the scene. Grant pinched Jesse again, but she was the one who whined at the ghostly sensation on her own skin.

More flogging, more sucking, she fell into the rhythm, the mindless pleasure and sensation so she almost started when the next hit didn't come and Grant stepped back. But her eyes lit up when he snatched lube from the bed and stepped in close to Jesse. She'd swear she could feel the heat as their bodies came together, skin to skin.

"No coming," Grant said sharply as he reached around and pushed a lubed finger into Jesse.

"Fuck. Sir." Jesse's chest was heaving against Grant as the other man worked him.

"You don't want to leave Steph hanging, do you?" he asked, amusement clear in his voice at Jesse's predicament.

Stephanie gave a loud moan in agreement.

Jesse gave a little shake of his head.

Grant kicked Jesse's legs farther apart, putting a slight strain on Jesse's collar, since it was attached to the post. He tilted his head back, teeth clenched as Grant started to enter him. Stephanie watched his face, then Grant's, the concentration and pleasure on both simply mesmerizing. Jesse grunted and she returned her attention to him The cords of his neck were standing out, his thigh muscles straining. She wanted to—

"Stephanie," Grant said between thrusts.

She blinked, looked back to Grant's face. He was intent on Jesse.

"Why can't I hear you?" he asked.

Oh shit. She whined in apology for forgetting her task and worked the gag like mad, watching Grant's hips flex and bunch. She groaned, wishing she could touch herself, her breasts, her pussy, anything, but the only thing she had was the little rubber cock, so she suckled and clenched her vaginal muscles and watched as Grant pounded into Jesse, who could only strain to stand still and receive his fucking.

Grant stilled, dropping his forehead to Jesse's shoulder as he came. Jesse was panting but he turned to kiss Grant's hair. Stephanie continued to suck and work the gag, her moans almost continuous now as she watched Grant pull free from Jesse.

He reached around and released the attachment holding Jesse's collar to the bed, then unclipped his cuffs from the belt.

"Take the cock ring off, my Jesse," he said as he moved to Stephanie.

JESSE MANAGED to do as he'd been told without coming and tossed the cock ring onto the bed, then waited. Grant stepped up to Stephanie and unbuckled the gag. He cleaned her lips and chin with this fingers, then massaged the joints of her jaw for a moment.

"You did well," he said before giving her a quick kiss and moving behind her.

Jesse remained still, watching as Grant twined his legs with hers until he was holding her open and she was actually standing on his feet. He wrapped his arms around her, holding her tightly to him, though she was still attached to the bed at her collar. She was flushed and looked oh so needy, but she wasn't moving in inch, held securely by Grant's whole body.

"Jesse, get a condom from the bed," Grant said.

Moving quickly, Jesse did as he was told, then carefully eased the condom on when Grant gave him the nod. Maybe it was time for them to have the condom talk with Stephanie…

Later. Right now he just needed to be inside her. Her breasts rested along one of Grant's arms and she was panting hard. Hell, so was he. He explored with one finger and found her dripping wet. God, she was so made for them. Watching them together had done this to her. He slipped two fingers inside, twisted and spread. She was so ready for him and he was past ready for her.

One hand on her hip and one guiding his cock, he pushed in. Slick heat had him biting back a curse to keep from coming too soon. He kept going as Grant moved one hand from her shoulder to her breasts, tugging and tweaking.

"Please, please, please," she chanted, but he wanted to give her more.

He pulled out, pushed in, a rhythm as slow as he could stand, watching her eyes, glazed with passion and need, then Grant's, not glazed at all, but full of fire and love. He couldn't help himself at that, he jerked into a faster tempo, wrapping one arm around Grant's waist and the other to hold onto the bedpost.

He tried to slow back down again but she began to use his name and he was lost.

"Please, Jesse, please, Jesse."

Faster and harder, he gave her everything he had. He squeezed his eyes shut, bent his knees slightly to change the angle and nearly shouted when she seized around him, her orgasm seeming to last for ages as she cried out.

When she'd stilled, he took a breath, gave himself two strokes, and let go. His knees went weak with his release, but he held on, dropping his head back.

When he could breathe without gasping, he opened his eyes and found Stephanie's heavy-lidded and half closed, and Grant's fully open and on him with an amused expression. He offered a cheeky grin and stepped back. Grant unhooked Stephanie's collar from the post before easing away and steadying her.

They lay on the bed for a while until Jesse decided they should have dessert. He bullied them into getting up. Stephanie accepted a sweatshirt from Grant, who pulled on his jeans while Jesse grabbed his favorite robe and they trooped out to the kitchen.

"Feeling better?" he asked Grant when they'd dug into their desserts.

Grant looked at him with heavy eyes. "Maybe."

Jesse laughed. "If you need more cheering up, you just let us know."

"I'll do that."

He put in his *Buffy the Vampire Slayer* movie but his silly lovers opted out.

"I'm going to bed," Grant said, laying a long kiss on him.

"Me too. I think I'll read, but I probably won't last fifteen minutes." Stephanie gave him a kiss and followed Grant into the bedroom.

Jesse snuggled down into the couch and tried to focus on the movie, rather than think about buying a house, seeing Stephanie pregnant with their child and getting enthusiastic hugs from a little boy who looked just like Grant.

He wasn't very successful.

CHAPTER FOURTEEN

Stephanie wasn't being particularly quiet when she opened the guys' apartment door, but she stopped when she heard a loud moan. Quickly realizing it was sex noises, she smiled to herself.

She'd had a last-minute cancellation from a client, so was surprising the guys with an unexpected visit for the first time. She closed the door quietly now. Maybe she'd get naked out here and jump them on the bed. If they were on the bed. She'd have to sneak a peek and see what, exactly, was up.

Setting her coat and purse on a chair, she toed off her shoes.

She heard Grant's laughter. "No, fuck Jesse, don't do that. You have to hurry, she could be here at any time."

"No, no, we still have time, I promise," Jesse said, his words coming out in choppy pants.

The words gave her pause. How did they know she was coming? She hadn't texted them. She started to unbutton her shirt.

"Yeah, but not time for *that*." More laughter rang from the room. "I can't believe we have to sneak this time together like horny teenagers, this is ridiculous."

Grant's words, said with clear annoyance, had a lump forming in her throat. She backed up to the door, re-buttoning her shirt.

"I know, I know it sucks sometimes, but it's totally worth it most of the time. Just another minute, I'm almost there," Jesse said. "Oh, *fuck yeah*."

Grant's moan, usually music to her ears, had tears coming to her eyes. The lump in her throat turned acidic.

She tugged her shoes on, picked up her coat and purse and worked the door closed as quietly as she possibly could.

Trying to take deep breaths, but finding it impossible, she nearly ran to the staircase. She made herself slow down as she descended, but still found herself gasping as she exited the building. She'd parked a block away and she managed to get back to her car without really paying much attention to anything around her. She bumped into someone and mumbled an apology, but she made it to her car and safely inside before tears started to fall.

This was all her fault. In the last two weeks, since the night she'd had dinner at her parents' house, she'd begun to think and act like this was a real relationship, but she hadn't had the common sense to actually ask them about that. To confirm. She'd just assumed they were all on the same page.

So stupid. At first she'd assumed it was just play, then she'd assumed it was a real relationship, but she hadn't been adult enough to actually have a damn conversation about it!

They'd given her that key, but really it had been so that they didn't have to let her into the building, and then into the apartment, when they were home. And once, when they'd all been meeting up at their place, she'd gotten there first, so it made sense to have the key. But she'd only used it when they'd specifically invited her, she realized now. Belatedly.

Gah, how could she be so dense?

She swiped angrily at her tears. They hadn't promised her anything, but she had to admit, it hurt to hear them laughing and complaining about trying to get alone time. It wasn't as if she spent every night with them, although it was most nights. And they were usually the ones pushing her to come over, or staying with her. Not that she minded, but she knew—*knew damn it*—that it wasn't all her.

Okay. She took a breath. Okay. So, they wanted her. That was clear. They just also needed some time together. Hadn't she been happy to spend some time with just Grant, the other day, when he'd gotten tickets to a Celtics game and Jesse had zero interest in going? Just like she'd enjoyed having dinner with Jesse that night Grant had the late meeting. They'd not spent a great deal of time that wasn't all three of them, but they'd had their moments and she'd enjoyed it as much as she'd enjoyed being all together. So, surely it made sense that they'd want that time together, too.

Except, they *did* have that time, and usually teased her for abandoning them.

Gah, this made no sense. Unless the newness, the fun of her being added to the mix, was starting to wear off? Maybe they were ready to go back to their full-time relationship and remind themselves that they were just having some fun with her. She herself had hit that point with the few relationships she'd tried, hadn't she? It was pretty normal. Of course, it didn't feel, to her, like they were at a point like that, but then again, the guys she'd dumped hadn't always felt the same as her, either.

And they weren't dumping her, they'd just wanted a little time to themselves. Totally fair. She shouldn't be so upset. It wasn't their fault she was falling for them. Had fallen? Okay, it was totally their fault she'd fallen for them. Theirs, and her parents'.

Yeah, she should totally blame her parents for this.

She banged her head on the steering wheel a couple of times, but somehow it didn't knock any sanity back into her.

She needed to go home. Maybe meditate for a bit, find her center, her calm. But she shouldn't drive in this state. Grabbing her phone, she called Emma.

When her friend answered, she barely let her say hello before launching into it.

"Oh my god, I've screwed up so badly."

"What happened?"

"I fell in love."

"And that's bad? Who are we talking about, last I heard you were seeing Jesse and Grant, and you sounded pretty happy. Are you in love with one or both of them, or someone else?"

"Both of them. And they don't love me."

"Well, okay. I mean, first of all, you sound pretty sure about that. And second of all, it's still pretty early days."

"Says you, how long did you wait before falling in love with Drew?"

"We're not talking about me and Drew, we're talking about you and Grant and Jesse. So maybe they're in love with you, or maybe they're in the process of falling in love with you, or maybe not. Tell me what's happened."

"I thought they were falling in love with me, but now I think they're just having fun, playing, not in a mean way, just, you know, like I first said when it first started, having some fun, seeing how things go, trying things out, adding to the mix—"

"Oh my god, girl, take a breath, you're not even speaking English."

Stephanie took a breath. Then another. "Okay. Right. It's cool, I just needed to talk it out a bit. See, at first I assumed they had a great relationship and just wanted to have a threesome thing for a bit, like adding a new toy. Until you get tired of it." She ignored Emma's little growl and hurried on. "Not in a mean way, right, just having fun, on all sides. But then I started to think they wanted a relationship. To see if it would work for longterm."

She grabbed a tissue from the center console and wiped her nose. "But here's the thing, Emma. We didn't actually talk about it. I made assumptions, both times. It was just so clear to me, I didn't think we needed to talk about it. And obviously I was wrong one of the times. I was just wrong about *which* time I was wrong. You see?"

Emma was silent for a minute. "Sort of…" she drawled.

"It's obvious to me now. I mean, we go on dates, both play and just, you know, dates, but we don't plan future dates. I mean, a few weeks ago they were talking about Grant's mom's birthday party, and they didn't invite me. Like that. So now I get it. Not mean, just not on the path I thought I was on."

"Um, wasn't 'a few weeks ago', like, right when you first started seeing them?"

"Yeah, but they haven't even brought it up again. Right? I'm not saying they should have, I'm just using that as an example of where we're at, in their minds. Instead of in my mind, which was clearly on another planet."

"Uh huh." Emma didn't sound convinced. "Didn't you say there was some strain between them and Grant's family? Isn't it likely that's why they haven't said anything about the party?"

"That's what I thought before, but now I realize it's the other thing."

"Right. So, listen. Why don't you ask them about where they're at with this, instead of making another assumption and risking being wrong. Again."

"Hmm. Yeah, I should do that. I just have to get my head back to being okay with it not being real, first. Or my heart, I guess. And decide if I'm willing to keep doing this, if it's not moving forward, like I thought it was. I mean, I love the time I spend with them, should I just give that up if they're not looking for a future with me?"

"No, not necessarily. Maybe they'll realize that's what they want, even if they weren't looking for it. But you can't know until you have *the talk*."

"Yeah. But it might break my heart."

"True, but it will break your heart if you don't talk to them, too."

"Damn."

"I'm sorry, sweetie. I know you really like being with them. I think there's still hope that will work out."

"I don't know. I'm going to go home and do some yoga, see if I can clear my mind a bit. Thank you for talking it out with me. I love you."

"I love you too, get your ass down here for a visit."

"Yeah, right, you get your ass up to the city where normal people live."

She hung up and leaned her head back against the seat. She had to remember that they weren't responsible for her feelings. She was. The fact that she was falling for them was her problem, not theirs.

Oh, bullshit, this was totally their fault for being so awesome. She was either going to have to enjoy the ride, make them fall in love with her, or walk away. But she didn't have to decide that in her car, a block from their apartment.

She started the car and drove home, but stopped at the juice bar first. If ever she needed a smoothie, now was the moment.

By the time she'd gotten home, finished her smoothie and done an hour of yoga with her phone turned off, she felt better. Centered. She concluded that there was no reason to stop doing something she found so much joy and pleasure in. No reason to stop seeing them, to bring herself that pain, when they were happy to keep things the way they were.

She turned her phone on and saw a text from Grant, asking when she was coming over. As she stared at the message, one popped in from Jesse, asking her if she wanted popcorn or ice cream with their movie tonight.

She sighed. Was it any wonder she was misunderstanding their relationship? She needed to be a damn adult and just talk to them.

She answered back to say she was on her way, resisting the silly urge to let them know that they needed to talk. That would just be unnecessary drama, when she could just tell them when she got there.

When she got to their door, she almost knocked, instead of using the key. She closed her eyes and took two deep breaths. She was really letting this get to her, which indicated how shocking the whole thing had been. And really drove home that despite her earlier thinking, she was probably going to need to break up with them. She wasn't going to be capable of just continuing on how they'd been and pretending they didn't matter to her as more than just friends with benefits.

Damn.

She worked up a smile, used the key and walked in. Jesse was walking through the living room but he immediately turned and bounded to her, pulling her into a little twirling dance. She couldn't help but laugh, though part of her wanted to cry instead.

Grant's arms were suddenly there, pulling her from Jesse's embrace.

"If you're not going to kiss her, I sure the hell am," he said before laying one on her.

She melted into it, determined to get these last pleasures before *the talk*. Before the probable end.

"Hey, no fair, I had her first," Jesse exclaimed, trying to pull her back.

Grant pulled his lips free. "Finders keepers."

Shit, she didn't think she could do this.

Why couldn't she do this? Things had been going so well and *nothing had changed!* She had to keep reminding herself of that. Only her perceptions had changed. She just needed to roll with it until she decided it wasn't working for her. Or they decided the same.

Jesse pulled her out of Grant's arms while she was distracted, and kissed her softly.

"I missed you," he said.

"Missed me? I just saw you Friday night." It came out sharper than she'd meant it to, but how the hell was she supposed to keep up?

He blinked at her.

"I assume you guys had a good day yesterday? Anything interesting?" she asked. Small talk. That's what they needed to bring things to some kind of normal.

Now Grant was frowning at her. "Actually, I talked to Marcos yesterday," he said.

Well, they'd gone to the club. Without her. Now it was so obvious, she couldn't even understand why she hadn't seen it. She was *so stupid.*

"That reminds me," she interrupted him, trying to keep her voice even when it wanted to edge into hysteria. "I need to update my limits sheet. I think it's safe to say I can add menage to it now." She laughed, but they just stared at her.

"Are you all right?" Jesse asked.

"Sure, I'm fine, I was just thinking, earlier, about when I get back to the club. It's been weeks since I've been there, which is crazy. Longest I've gone since I first joined, they're all probably wondering if I died. Or got married." She tried another laugh but quickly gave it up.

"Maybe we should sit down," Grant suggested. "You look a little bit like you're getting sick."

She put a hand to her stomach. Well, that seemed accurate enough.

"No, I'm fine. I was just talking to Emma earlier and it got me thinking about the club and when I'll be going back on a regular basis. You know, whenever we decide this isn't…" She couldn't bring herself to say it, so she just sort of waved her hand vaguely towards the door.

"I see," Grant said.

"I didn't realize this was still so casual for you," Jesse said, his voice tight as he moved in closer to Grant.

Stephanie's stomach clenched but she managed not to choke up. "I'm not sure what you mean. You guys are a couple. You wanted to have some fun and I'm totally on board with that. I'm not going to get ideas about what that means for me."

"I thought we were building something here," Jesse said.

Grant's arm went around Jesse.

Oh god, she was going to lose her mind. Again. Still? She couldn't do this, not like she'd thought. She needed to get out of there. But she needed to let them know she understood.

"You're talking crazy. You guys are in love. Don't make out like you want me to be a part of that."

"Have we been acting like you're *not* a part of that? You're the one talking crazy."

She was starting to feel dizzy with all the crazy, that was for sure. "I don't want to screw up what you guys have, and I don't know why you're saying these things. I know you don't want me as a permanent addition. You love each other, you're great together. Don't confuse having some fun with me as part of that."

"We do love each other," Grant said. "We have a very good thing together. And we both agreed that we wanted to search you out, find you, see if being with you as well would work in real life. Maybe we're being unfair, expecting the real life you to be as interested in us as the fantasy you was. The problem is that we like the real life you even more than the fantasy you, so it's difficult. But if you're not interested in being with us, why are you here?"

She stared at him. "What? But—? No. I don't understand what's happening here. You just asked me to come play with you. That's a very different thing than being with you, like for real. You know that! Don't make me out to be the crazy one here. I heard you guys. Not three hours ago you were thrilled to have some time without me. I get it. I'm not mad. I'm being very careful not to step outside the play boundaries, *you're* the ones pushing the line all over the place so I can't keep up."

"What are you talking about? Every time you're not here we wish you were. We're fucking good together, how can you not see that?" Jesse reached a hand towards her, but let it drop before he connected.

She turned from them, walked several steps away, trying to find reason. "I came here, earlier. My client cancelled. I used the key you gave me, came in and was going to surprise you. But you guys were in bed, enjoying some time together. You didn't want me there. You were laughing about it."

"Stephanie," Grant started.

"Oh, honey," Jesse said at the same time. "That's not what we were talking about. At all. Reggie was coming to clean today. We're always trying to schedule her for when we're not home, but it's sort of become a joke with us that it always works out to be when we *are* home. This afternoon, you and I were talking, teasing, and I got all hot and bothered but then you had a client. But Grant was here and Reggie was actually coming in later for a change, so I attacked Grant. We were laughing because it's so rare."

"Sweetheart, haven't you figured out how much we need you? Want you? Crave you?" Grant took a step towards her, but stopped.

"I—I was being so careful. I was so afraid to screw up your relationship. I really, really don't want to do that. I loved you guys, I couldn't have that on my conscience."

"Loved? Past tense?"

"Well, that was before. When you were my friends that I cared about. But then you kept at me and kept being so awesome and then today I couldn't understand why you were being that way with me when you only wanted it to be play, to not be a real relationship. It didn't make sense and it was tearing me apart."

"Oh, sweetheart." He took another step towards her, but stopped, obviously afraid of upsetting her again. "I understand why you thought what you did, but I'm telling you now, straight out, that we want you. To be with us. As lover and partner. You bring so much happiness to us, you *must* know we wouldn't just throw that away."

Jesse moved up beside him. "Surely we've shown you that?"

She couldn't answer, her throat was too choked up. So she took a running leap, straight at her men, assuming that between the two of them they could keep her from falling on her face.

They caught her, pushed and pulled at her until she was wrapped arms and legs around Grant, with Jesse at their side, hugging her tightly.

"That's better, then," Grant said, his hand cradling her head to his shoulder. "So, to be clear, you'd like to stay with us?"

She managed a half sob, half laugh.

"Okay. I'm trying to decide on a suitable punishment."

She cleared her throat for that one. "Hey, you said you understood why I thought that."

"I understand why hearing that might lead a person to the conclusion you reached. Except for three things. Me. Jesse. And you. You know what we have together. So, in that context, your reaction was wrong. You should have just talked to us."

"Well, I mean, that's what I came here to do tonight."

"Well, you're not very good at it."

"Hey! I almost texted you that we needed to talk. That would have been worse."

Jesse laughed. "Yeah, that would have been worse."

"But, seriously guys, it's been like…" she thought back. "A month. We've been seeing each other for a month."

"And?" Grant asked. "Isn't that long enough to know this is really fucking good?"

She stared at him. At them. She swallowed hard. And then she nodded. "Yeah, it is. Because it is. Really fucking good. And since it's impossible to deny that, then I guess it's silly to pretend it doesn't make all the difference in the world."

"Yep," Jesse said, leaning in to kiss her cheek. "It's okay, we're used to the amazingness of feeling this way. You're not. It takes a little getting used to."

Yeah. She smiled. And then she burst into tears, because her heart had been broken but she'd refused to admit how much that had hurt, but now it was fixed, so she could admit it had sucked. Big time.

GRANT CARRIED Stephanie to the couch and sat down with her in his lap. Jesse ran to get a box of tissues and held one out to her. He hated seeing her like this. One look at Grant's face told him he wasn't alone in that.

She gave a couple of big sniffles and wiped her face. "Thanks, Jess. I'm sorry, guys."

"Well, it's good to know you were upset by the idea of not being with us," Jesse pointed out.

"Yeah," she said, trying to sit up but not succeeding because Grant's arms didn't loosen. She huffed out a breath but put her head back on his shoulder.

Suddenly she blinked, and frowned. "Did you guys go to the club? Is that what you said earlier?"

Jesse was confused, but then he remembered Grant saying something about Marcos. He looked at Grant, who hadn't answered. If he read his man right, the poor guy was afraid of restarting the floodgates.

"I'm not mad," she said. "I swear."

"No, it's not that," Grant answered.

He sighed and stood, depositing Stephanie back on the couch, next to Jesse, then sitting on the coffee table facing them both. Uh oh.

"Marcos called yesterday," he began.

"You didn't tell me that," Jesse interrupted.

Grant heaved a breath. "I was trying to. *Am* trying to."

Jesse rolled his eyes nodded for Grant to continue. Never mind that they'd spent most of the day together yesterday.

"Marcos said someone was spreading rumors about us at the club. He called to let us know, and also to reassure us that they were tracking the rumors back, they were pretty sure of the source, and that management and our friends were already moving to nip it all in the bud."

"What? That's crazy. What kind of rumors?" Jesse asked.

"That we were playing mind games with unsuspecting Doms."

"Oh my god," Stephanie breathed.

"Surely nobody believed such bullshit," Jesse demanded.

"Oh my god," Stephanie said louder.

"Don't worry, sweets, we'll get it all sorted out easily enough. The core group there is solid, the management is supportive, we won't have any—"

Stephanie interrupted Grant's reassurance. "No, seriously! Don't you see? Someone's trying to trash our reputations at the club. Someone contacted your cousin and tried to get you in trouble. A couple of my gyms have cancelled on me."

"Oh shit," Jesse said.

"Fucking bastard," Grant said.

"Trevor," Stephanie said.

"That stupid prick," Grant added.

"I totally forgot to tell you guys that someone called the office and told Wanda that I had made insulting and racist comments to a passenger last week."

"Oh no," Stephanie said, her eyes wide.

He waved her worry away. "It's no big deal, she totally laughed at him. She knows me, knew it was bullshit. We laughed and I forgot all about it. But still. Trevor."

"And *I* forgot to tell you that someone made a noise complaint to my building manager about me. I was able to convince her I wasn't even home that night, so it didn't come to anything, but still. I assumed someone wrote down the wrong apartment number and forgot all about it."

Grant got to his feet.

Jesse stood up and put a hand on his shoulder. "Now, Grant. Let Marcos and the others at Apex handle this. And Stephanie's Dad."

"Fuck that. It's gone beyond the club."

Stephanie rose to join them.

"Actually, we can do better than that." She pulled out her phone, hit a couple of buttons.

"No, Steph, stay out of it. I'll talk to Marcos, get this dick's info, and handle it."

She rolled her eyes at him and put the phone to her ear.

"Hey Pop."

"Oh shit," Jesse and Grant said at the same time.

The conversation didn't last long. At one point Stephanie held the phone away from her ear and Jesse heard some colorful swear words. She just smiled and continued on. Jesse gave Grant a questioning look, but Grant just shrugged.

When she hung up, she flopped back down on the couch. "So, he and his partner will go visit Asshole Trevor, in uniform, tomorrow. He's checking the guy out to see if it would be better to go to his home or his work, see what the best play is. He said most of the time, that's sufficient, but with some assholes, that actually ramps them up, so be aware, be careful, and let him know if anything else happens."

Grant paced on the other side of the coffee table. "Fine. For the next few days, until we know how it's going to play out, you—we—text each other when we're leaving somewhere and when we're arriving."

Jesse narrowed his eyes. "Nice save. I know you were going to say we should text *you*."

"I will mostly be in a secured office building. You guys are the ones running around town all day."

Jesse inclined his head. "Fair point."

"And assholes tend to think subs are fair game, more than Doms," Stephanie pointed out.

Jesse glared at her. "You're not helping."

"I try to be realistic about danger. I don't have the safest job, or hobby for that matter, so I deal with reality, not how I wish things would be."

"Don't try and use logic on me, that's just not cool."

She laughed patted his butt. "We just need to be careful and aware of what's going on around us. He was kind of a tool, anyway, I'm sure you could take him if you had to."

Slightly mollified, he leaned back on the sofa. At least she'd managed to defuse Grant. "If he's such a tool, how is it that he's managed to convince all these people that we suck. I mean, sure, Wanda ignored his ass, but Grant's cousin, and those managers at your gyms totally fell for his bullshit.

She blushed. "I have to admit, I did too, at first. That's why I played with him that night we met up. He really did put on a good game for long enough that I was looking forward to doing a scene with him. And then it just turned to shit. But he's persuasive and charismatic, at least to an extent."

Jesse gave her a quick kiss. "You figured his shit out quickly enough, don't let that get to you."

"Thanks. And I'm definitely going to go see those managers, who've been dodging my calls. It's not cool that they took some stranger's word over mine."

Jesse nodded. "And we should still call the club, let them know what's up."

"And, we should go Saturday night," Grant said.

"I'm always up for that, but you sound like you have a specific reason," Jesse said.

Grant was looking at Stephanie, who didn't say anything. "For one, I'd like to confront any rumors or attitudes straight away," he said. "For another, it's been a month since Stephanie's been there, and that's not like her."

"Well, yeah, but she's had us to play with." He turned to her. "You've been having fun with that, right? Are you missing the club."

She smiled at him. "I've definitely been having fun with that. I wasn't angling for a trip to the club."

"No," Grant agreed. "But it's surprising that you haven't brought it up. You've always been a bit of an exhibitionist, and that's one thing we can't give you with home play." He paused. "Well, I suppose we could invite people over, but that's probably not going to happen."

"I'm fine, I don't need that. What we have is awesome."

Jesse cocked his head, studying her. Grant was right, they were missing something.

"You don't want to play with us. In public." He frowned, trying not to be hurt, trying to understand.

"No, it's not that," she said quickly. "It's just…if we did scenes at Apex, I was worried that when we stopped playing together, it would be too painful to go back there."

"And you still feel that way?" Grant asked.

She nibbled on her lip. He hated that she was still uncertain. What did they have to do to show her that they were fully invested in this relationship? He wanted her to be on the same page with them, but it was unfair to expect her to be.

"So, look," he said, not waiting for her to come up with an answer. He figured just jumping in was the best plan, since trying to be subtle had only caused miscommunication from the very beginning. "We're all-in on this relationship thing. With you. I don't know how clear we've made that, so I just want to be one-hundred-percent. We want you. With us. All the time."

"Right. Okay." She took a deep breath. "So, you want to come meet my parents?"

He wasn't sure if she said it with hope, or in challenge, but it didn't matter to him. "Yes."

She blinked. "Really?"

"Yes," both he and Grant answered at the same time.

"And Grant's mom's birthday party at his parents' house is next Sunday. We expect you to come."

Jesse gave a side-eye to Grant, who looked pained.

Stephanie raised her eyebrows. "Is that right?" She looked pointedly at Grant.

Grant sighed. "It's not a you thing. I'm not sure yet that I want to go at all. I'm happy to tell my family about you if we're all in agreement we're at that stage. But I'm not happy to subject either of you to an uncomfortable situation. So, I'll tell them what's up, and if I get the feeling they're going to be nasty about it, then none of us are going to the party."

"They'll probably be thrilled that you're seeing a woman, even when you say that you're still seeing me," Jesse pointed out.

"We'll see. But I'm at the stage where I'm going to stop choosing to give them more chances to be decent to you. To either of you. So, I'll tell them, and maybe we'll go to the party and maybe we won't, but the decision will have to do with them and how they're acting, and has nothing to do with my commitment to you." He looked pointedly at Stephanie. "And my commitment to you includes giving you everything you need as a sub, which means public scenes. So, unless you can give me a good reason that shouldn't happen, we'll be going on Saturday."

She shivered and Jesse realized Grant was right. She'd missed being on display.

"I think it's hilarious that you would rather introduce us to your parents than go to the club with us."

She gave him a sheepish smile. "Well, it's not like you would keep showing up at my parents' house if we broke up," she pointed out.

PERFECT ADDITION

"I don't know, it sounds like your mom is an awesome cook, so I wouldn't bet on it."

"Yeah, but her father is armed," Grant reminded him.

"Damn. Another fair point."

Grant sat back down on the coffee table and took Stephanie's hand in his. "We all agree we've got a good thing going on here. I expect it to work out. I'll work *hard* to make it work out and I expect the two of you to do the same. But if for some reason it doesn't, and it makes you uncomfortable to have us at Apex, we'll give you that. We'll go somewhere else."

"We'll probably be too devastated to be out in public anyway," Jesse agreed.

She laughed and hugged them both. "You guys are awesome. How did I get so amazingly lucky?"

"Just by being you," Grant said, leaning in to kiss her.

"Aww," Jesse said. "So, anyway, does that mean we're going to the club and showing you off? Can we wear matching sub gear? Let's go shopping tomorrow."

Grant rolled his eyes. "I'm hungry." He looked at Stephanie hopefully. "Jesse said you were going to make avocado toast."

She laughed. "Fine. Should I assume you have avocados?"

"Welllll," Jesse drawled. He'd meant to pick some up, but grocery shopping was *not* the kind of shopping he liked to do.

"You doing okay?" Grant asked Stephanie as they walked out of the grocery store. Somehow Jesse had been left behind to hold down the fort while he and Stephanie made the avocado run. And somehow the avocado run had turned into two bags of groceries.

She looked up at him and smiled. Tucking a hand around his arm, she leaned into him as they walked down the block. "Yeah, I'm okay. I'm sorry about the freak-out."

"I'm not. Well, I'm sorry you were upset, but I'm glad that it got things out in the open. I *am* sorry that we weren't better at communicating how we felt things were going. We were afraid to push you."

"I understand that. I mean, I did the same thing. I didn't think we needed to talk about it, because I thought we were on the same page. And we were. But when I heard what I thought I heard, I started to doubt everything. And it hurt, because everything was so great."

"Yeah, we're pretty great."

She laughed and slapped his chest with the back of her hand.

"No, really. And by 'we're' I mean the three of us."

"Okay, good save."

They turned the corner for his building and he felt Stephanie tense up a bit, just as he noticed a guy Trevor's build walking up to the door. But then the guy smiled at a woman and child as they exited the building and gave him a hug. He was very glad to realize that Stephanie was doing as promised, staying aware of her surroundings. Jesse was a people watcher, so he hadn't been too worried about him, but he was glad to know that Stephanie paid attention.

"I should give a disclaimer," she said as they approached the door. "I don't know what the restaurants do for avocado toast, this is just how Emma always makes it. She's from California, she said she grew up eating it like this."

He held the door open for her and followed her in. "I feel I can say with confidence that if it involves both avocado and toast, I will be happy with the results."

She laughed and headed for the stairs, not even looking at the elevator. Fuck he was seriously falling in love with this woman, since he found that adorable.

He admired the view as they climbed the stairs. Her jacket didn't hide her butt and it was a very, very nice butt. She glanced over her shoulder at him and smirked.

"What?" he asked, all innocence.

"I can feel you watching me."

"And that's bad?"

"Did I say it was bad?"

They arrived at his floor and she held the door open for him. When they made it into the apartment, they found Jesse snoring on the couch. He smiled and shook his head, but they headed into the kitchen as quietly as possible.

He helped pull the items out of the bags, then hopped up on the counter to watch her work. She started by pulling out the bread which was much browner and oatier than he was used to, but he decided not to say anything.

"You know," she said as she grabbed the olive oil from the pantry. One of the few items she hadn't needed to get at the store. "I was being honest when I said I haven't been missing going to the club. We've been having a hell of a lot of fun here."

"I know. But I also know you *do* want to go. And be seen. With us."

"True." She'd drizzled the oil on six slices of bread and set them on a cookie sheet. Also something she hadn't needed to buy, as Jesse was in the habit of buying squares of cookie dough that magically transformed into cookies when placed in the oven for a few minutes.

"But we have plenty of time to do all the things. I'm not in any rush." She glanced over as she pulled out a knife and grabbed one of the avocados. "I'm happy to go on Saturday if that works out, but I can be patient, too. I know we'll get there."

She'd sliced it in two and used the knife to flick the seed into the trash can as she talked. She scooped the meat out into a bowl and grabbed the second avocado.

"My point is, I'm not shy about letting you know what I want, as far as scenes go. I haven't said anything, because it's been fun seeing what you come up with and everything has been fully to my satisfaction."

She peeked into the oven at the bread and then used a fork to mash up the avocado.

"Okay."

Narrowing her eyes at him, she kept mashing. "Okay? That's all you have to say?"

"Nothing you're saying is a surprise to me, but I appreciate your saying it."

"Hmph." She sprinkled salt and pepper into the bowl, then garlic powder. Which was most of the contents of their spice rack. "But you still want to go on Saturday."

"No reason not to, that I'm aware of. We've solved your concern. We'll all enjoy ourselves. And we can get a feel for what's happening down there, as far as these rumors go."

She nodded absently as she stirred her concoction, then set it aside. She used one of their two potholders—but hey, at least they matched— and pulled the tray out of the oven. Setting two pieces of toast on each of the three plates she'd set on the counter, she began to scoop the avocado onto each slice.

"That's true. Do you think I should call some of my friends?"

"No, let's see what we find when we go. I doubt he'd be so stupid as to talk directly to a friend of yours. Besides, they would have called you already."

When she'd spread her mixture out on all the pieces of toast, she licked the fork clean and set it aside in the now empty bowl. She opened the cheese they'd bought and picked up a little grater she'd also insisted on. He'd told her they did have a grater, but she'd said it was the wrong size.

She deftly grated tiny bits of parmesan cheese over each slice, allowing the white stuff to fully top the green stuff. He was surprised, he'd figured she'd just give them a tiny sprinkling. He liked that she was healthy but not fanatical. She eyed the six slices critically, added another dash of cheese over one of them, then put the grater in the bowl and wrapped up the cheese.

He hopped off the counter and moved the dirty dishes to the dishwasher as she put the rest of the items away. He carried two plates to the living room and she carried one.

"Wake up, sleeping beauty," she called as they walked in.

Jesse's eyes opened to mere slits. "Come kiss me awake," he invited.

She laughed, but obliged. "Do you want your avocado toast, or not?"

"Want."

"Then you better move your ass," Grant said, setting the plates down on the coffee table and shoving Jesse's legs off the couch.

Stephanie plopped her butt down on Jesse's lap, earning a grunt.

They all grabbed a slice of toast and bit in.

Grant liked avocado as much as the next person, but he had to admit, the toast was delicious.

"Oh my god," Jesse exclaimed.

"Like I said, I've never ordered it from a restaurant. How does it differ?" Stephanie asked.

"We need never speak of restaurant avocado toast again," Jesse said solemnly. "There is no comparison."

Stephanie rolled her eyes. "That's just because *this* avocado toast was hand delivered to you on the couch."

"That part doesn't suck." Jesse took a huge bite, then spoke around it. "But this is fantastic."

They ate in silence for a while, then snuggled up on the couch, Jesse and Grant reading, Stephanie working on a client's fitness plan on her laptop.

The book he was reading was good, but Grant was having a hard time not being distracted. It had been an intense evening. He hated that they'd accidentally hurt Stephanie, but as he'd told her, he was glad they'd finally talked about it. He blamed himself for not having brought it up earlier, but he'd truly thought it was too soon to push her for a verbal commitment. He knew that in their hearts, he and Jesse had been committed pretty much from the beginning, but it wouldn't have been fair to expect the same from her.

The next challenge was family. He wasn't as sure of their welcome from her parents as Jesse seemed to be. But really, it was *his* family he was worried about. With Jesse, they'd shown that they could be bitingly polite, instead of welcoming. He didn't want that for either Jesse or Stephanie. He was kind of pissed at himself for not addressing their treatment of Jesse before now, actually. He'd considered it, but was honestly afraid that if they didn't step up and do the right thing, he would be too tempted to just write them off and walk away.

It wasn't that he didn't love them. He did. Especially individually. But as a group they had a tendency to revert to some kind of ridiculous Lord of the Manor attitude that was just not his style. He wasn't even sure when they'd started with it. Sometime while he was in elementary school, he supposed. They'd moved to the large house his parents and one sister still lived in, when she was in the country. They'd joined the country club. Yeah, that was probably when it began. For whatever reason, the pretentious nonsense had never stuck with him. And he sort of felt like they only approved of him as long as he came close to toeing their line.

The temptation to throw himself well over the line had been nagging at him since college. He'd considered majoring in something Liberal Arts to really freak them out, but the thing was, he loved business. Loved the challenge of it, the potential and the recognizable success when you did your job well. And he liked their family business, so it made sense to stick with it and see what he could accomplish there. But he was one hundred percent willing to walk away, if they ever forced the issue in any way.

And they just might. He was not willing to let the cold-shoulder treatment of Jesse continue. And how would they react to a personal trainer as a girlfriend? He was impressed by her plans for the future, her business acumen and her success, as well as the fact that she was one of the very few people he knew who actually seemed to love their jobs. But would they see that, or would they see the yoga-pant-wearing daughter of a beat cop and assume she had no ambition and no future? He would be disappointed in them if that was the case, but unfortunately he wouldn't be surprised.

Stephanie closed her laptop and nudged him. "You're either very, very into that book, or thinking very hard."

"Families are annoying," he told her.

She laughed. "True enough."

He poked Jesse. "I should have done something about mine in the last couple of months, but I've been feeling very all-or-nothing, and I wanted to give them another chance before I chose nothing."

"That's a bit drastic, isn't it?" Jesse asked.

"Is it? They know me well enough not to think I'm just randomly bringing a guy home as some sort of act of defiance or crazy phase, or whatever excuse they might dream up. Or at least they should."

"I had a good time when we took your sister and her husband out for dinner," Jesse reminded him.

"True. I guess it's mostly my mom and my cousins who piss me off."

"Your cousins are hoping your mom will finally side against you on something. Anything."

"Maybe she will."

"Even if she does—which I don't think is the case, she just needs time to adjust to the new reality, but even if—it doesn't mean you need to write off the whole group."

"No, but I can decline invitations to group activities, and just deal with the people I give a shit about."

"You could."

"You don't think I should."

"I think family deserves a few chances. You're taking a pretty hard line with them. You've spent the last several years preparing yourself for the day when you have to walk away. Probably since that moment they threatened your college tuition. But you don't want to, because you do really love them. All of them."

"I think I've been pretty patient. Too patient. I've let them be rude to you and I shouldn't have."

"More scarily polite than rude." Jesse sat up and took Grant's face in his hands and kissed him, hard. "I appreciate that you're mad on my behalf. But I don't want to be responsible for a rift in your family. They aren't awful to me. And it's only been seven months."

Grant wrapped his arms around the other man. "We knew right away. So it's not okay."

"We can't expect them to understand that."

"I can."

Jesse laughed, and so did Stephanie. He glared at them both.

"This is a Dom thing, isn't it?" Stephanie asked. "Yes, you're pissed they're not treating Jesse as well as they should, but you're also pissed that they aren't just believing you when you say he's an awesome guy who's in your life now and they need to adjust."

"Well. Yeah."

They both laughed again.

"Why don't you wait and see how they take it when you tell them about Stephanie, and then we'll see how the birthday lunch goes. Then you can reevaluate," Jesse suggested.

Grant could feel himself frowning but he supposed that was the best plan. "Fine."

"Hey," Jesse said. "I just realized tomorrow is our one-month anniversary. We should have a nice dinner followed by a really nice dessert. And by dessert I mean raunchy sex. Are you working in the evening, Steph?"

"I can make sure I have the evening free. But why don't I make us dinner, since you've been going on about it?"

"Not that I want to discourage you because I can't wait to eat a meal you make, but you shouldn't have to cook when the celebration is for you, too," Jesse said.

She laughed. "I like to cook. And then the bedroom will be very close when we've finished, and we can move on to the the 'dessert' portion of the evening."

"That is an excellent point," Jesse agreed. "And we can help."

"We'll do it at my place, so we don't have to buy up the whole staples section of the grocery store."

"That's fine, but if you make a list, we'll pick up anything you want stocked in the kitchen," Grant said.

"I noticed somebody put a chunky peanut butter next to the already opened smooth peanut butter. Thank you."

Grant pointed his chin at Jesse. "I noticed you bought coffee and creamer for your place."

She smiled. "You guys bought a tea kettle."

"We're awesome like that," Jesse said. "You keep showing up without sweatshirts. I think you just like to wear ours."

"You're not wrong. I think I've shown great restraint in returning them all. So far."

Jesse laughed and Grant grinned. "We appreciate that."

She pointed a finger at Grant. "You've shown great restraint, and don't think I haven't noticed."

He didn't know what she was referring to, but he aimed a look of pure innocence at her anyway.

"You've held back from asking me any real questions about my business plan, business practices, retirement plan. You've stuck to generalities, and I think it's probably driving you crazy."

"Totally and completely. But I figured that could wait until month two."

She laughed. "Well, I appreciate it. I wouldn't mind some conversations about those things though. In month two."

"Tomorrow," Jesse sang out. "We'll bring a bottle of wine."

"Works for me," Stephanie agreed.

CHAPTER FIFTEEN

Stephanie looked at her watch and then picked up her pace. It was Saturday and she was heading to the guys' to meet up for the evening. Unfortunately, they were *not* heading to Apex, as originally planned. Instead, they were driving to Maine to have dinner with her parents. While she had definitely wanted to go to the club, she wasn't hating the fact that when her mom had said Saturday was the best night for them to come have dinner and meet the family, her guys hadn't hesitated to agree.

They were taking the whole full-time relationship thing seriously, and making an effort to both show and tell her so. They'd had their anniversary dinner on Monday which had gone very well. Grant had given her some very pretty silver stud earrings that went with everything but didn't get in her way when she was working out and Jesse had brought her a beautiful bouquet of flowers. She's been completely embarrassed that she hadn't gotten them gifts, but they'd been insistent that her making them a meal was her gift, and she'd believed their sincerity. If some of her previous attempts at relationships had bought her jewelry for a one-month anniversary, she probably would have freaked out. Which just went to show how differently this relationship was from any of the others.

Now they had dinner with her parents, followed by Grant's mom's birthday brunch on Sunday. What a weekend.

She let herself into their building and started to head up the stairs, but heard their voices coming down. She checked her watch again. She was on time, but just. They were nervous, she knew, and didn't want to be late and make a bad impression.

She understood the feeling. They'd taken Jesse's grandmother out to dinner on Thursday. It had been a long time since she'd been that anxious about meeting someone, but the wonderful woman had immediately put her at ease. There had been no discomfort at all. Of course, the fact that they'd been in a restaurant meant that there wasn't much in the way of public displays of affection, but she was pretty sure that Sheila would have been okay with it. At the end of the evening, when they'd dropped her off at her home, the sweet woman had given Stephanie a big hug, before admonishing both of the guys to get 'their girl' home safely.

Smiling at the memory, she watched as the guys reached the lobby and spotted her. The fact that their happiness at seeing her was instantaneous and obvious made her heart do a little jump. She was totally gone for them, there was no denying it. Nor did she want to.

She stood still to see who would reach her first, but they managed to reach her at the same time and wrap her up in their arms without her feeling like a tug toy. Impressive. Jesse claimed her lips first, and Grant took the opportunity to nuzzle her ear. She shivered and Jesse laughed as he pulled back.

"Somehow I don't think the shiver was mine," he said.

Stephanie couldn't answer since her mouth was now full of Grant.

Grant cut things a little shorter than usual, though, and nearly dragged her to the door to the garage. She laughed. "We're okay on time. And they'll understand if there's traffic or anything that delays us."

"Uh huh," Grant acknowledged, without slowing down.

She rolled her eyes at Jesse who just grinned in response.

"You take the passenger seat and be the navigator," Jesse said, opening the door for her.

"I could just drive," she pointed out.

He gave her a look that asked *really?* without actually pointing at Grant.

"Yes, Sir," she said, smartly, moving to take her seat.

He slapped her butt in response.

As soon as they'd hit the road, Steph turned to look behind her. "So, what did Grandma Sheila have to say about us? I meant to ask on Friday and *someone*," she jerked her head at Grant, "made me forget all about it when they dragged me into the apartment the second I opened the door and attacked me."

"Are you complaining?" Grant asked, dryly.

"Not even a little bit. But I still want to know the answer."

"We haven't talked, but she texted me. She likes the emojis. Let's see," Jesse said, pulling out his phone. "She sent a thumbs up, a face with two hearts for eyes, a pink heart, a purple heart, a face with two stars for eyes, and a kissy face." He put his phone back in his pocket as Stephanie burst out laughing.

"I love her, she's great."

Jesse smiled his huge smile. "I know, right? We'll make sure she's at dinner when we meet Mom, too, but I wanted her to have her own special night first."

Stephanie beamed at him. "So, how was work this morning?"

They chatted about their day. She'd spent the night with them but had to leave early for a client session. She'd actually spent every night with them, since her freak-out. Of course, she'd been spending most nights with them before that. She was beginning to see why they'd moved in with each other so quickly in their relationship. If you were going to be there every night anyway, you might as well get comfortable.

They hit only the expected amount of traffic and were pulling up to her parents' little house before she knew it. Her brother's car was already there and she wondered if he'd brought a girl. She hadn't thought to ask, but he hadn't been seeing anyone special, as far as she knew.

By the time she got her purse and coat in hand, Jesse had opened the door for her and Grant was at the trunk. Curious, she went to him and found him pulling a bottle of wine and a bouquet of flowers out of a cooler. Grant definitely hadn't had them when he'd come downstairs to meet her, so he must have already stashed them in the trunk before she'd arrived. She closed the trunk for him while he handed Jesse the wine.

"You guys are awesome, they'll love you, I promise."

She kissed both of their cheeks then led the way to the door, which was already open. Her mom was smiling at them, her dad had his eyes narrowed.

She just laughed and gave her mom a hug. "Mom, Dad, this is Grant Sumner and Jesse Arnold. Jesse, Grant, my parents, Joan and Hank Walsh. And that's my brother Darren," she added as he walked up.

Grant handed her mom the flowers and Jesse offered the wine to her dad.

"It's a pleasure to meet you both," Grant said.

"Thank you for inviting us," Jesse added.

"We're very glad to meet you," her mom said, taking the flowers, clearly delighted. "Come in, come in. These are beautiful, I'm going to put them in water." She led them to the living room and Stephanie nudged the guys to the couch. She chose the middle and they sat on either side of her. Jesse's leg started to bounce a bit, and she put a hand on his knee to help him relax.

Her father took his normal chair and her brother stood beside him, glowering.

Stephanie tried not to laugh, she really did, but she just couldn't help it. "Darren, what's wrong with you?"

"What? We're here to make sure these 'guys,'" he said, complete with finger quotes, "are good enough for you. That's what I'm doing."

PERFECT ADDITION

She laughed again while her father just shook his head in exasperation.

"No, that's not why you're here. You're here so they can see what they have to saddle themselves with if they choose to stick with me," she teased.

Jesse snorted and Grant coughed into his hand, then patted her knee.

"I'm a brother, too, I know what it's like. Feel free to go about your plan of making sure we're good enough for Stephanie, it won't bother us."

She wrinkled her nose at him. "It'll bother *me*."

"But you'll put up with it, just like you do all the inane guy things you have to put up with. Like letting me drive tonight and letting me pay for meals when we go out and letting me open the door for you when you're perfectly capable of opening it yourself."

"I put up with a lot of guy stuff for you guys. Double the normal amount. It's a damn good thing you're so handsome or you might not be worth it." She winked at him.

"I know, it's your burden to bare, but we try to make it worth your while."

"Mostly you succeed."

Her mom came in with the flowers in a cut crystal vase that she set on the fireplace mantel. Stephanie glanced at her brother who seemed to be trying to figure out what to say after that little scene. She managed not to laugh again.

Jesse put his hand on top of hers, resting on his leg. "You have a lovely home, Mrs. Walsh. I really like the way you've pulled that shade of blue-gray from the dining room walls there, to the accent colors here in the living room."

Her mom's face lit up with pleasure. "Why thank you, Jesse. I had a lot of fun redecorating last year, since we decided to wait a bit before selling. We're thinking of downsizing, but want to wait until Darren's sure he's found his own situation."

Darren blushed and Stephanie had to *really* bite her lip.

"Mom," he said, sounding like the immature young man her comment had painted him to be.

Her mom just turned to him. "Yes?"

Darren shook his head and Grant spoke up. "Something smells delicious, Mrs. Walsh. We've heard glowing reports about your cooking skills and are very appreciative that you've shared those skills with Stephanie. She made your Greek lasagna the other day and it was one of the best things I've ever eaten."

More mom smiles. "Please, call me Joan. We do love that recipe. It takes a bit of work, to be sure, but it's worth it."

Stephanie groaned and Jesse snickered.

"Is that right?" Grant asked. "I believe Stephanie's words were 'it's a super simple recipe, no need for you guys to help, just bring the wine.'"

"Umm," her mom said, biting her lip.

"Were you showing off, or afraid that their version of help would just mess you up?" Darren asked, laughing now.

"I've never known Stephanie to be a showoff," Jesse said, looking at her accusingly.

"So it was the latter," Grant confirmed, also looking at her.

She pursed her lips and looked up to the ceiling, as if there might be help from that direction.

"Are you guys that terrible in the kitchen?" her dad asked.

"Yes," they both answered at the same time.

She couldn't help it. She burst out laughing. "Oh my god, they totally are. I mean, they can make pancakes, but the kitchen is a complete disaster by the time they've finished. I didn't even know it was possible to dirty up that many dishes to make pancakes." She turned to Grant, then Jesse. "I'll make you help with some stuff, but for that recipe, you would have just been in my way and I wanted our anniversary dinner to be perfect."

"Anniversary?" Darren asked, suspiciously.

"Yes," she answered. "One month."

"And they couldn't afford to take you out?" he asked.

PERFECT ADDITION

"Oh my god, stop. You're being ridiculous. Do you want them to show you their tax forms from last year?"

Darren opened his mouth to respond but her father beat him to it.

"Steph tells me you're a bus driver, Jesse. How's city work going for you?"

"It has its ups and downs. I have some seniority now, so I'm starting to have more say in what routes I get, which is great. The pension if I keep with it is terrific. But the politics can be a bit annoying. I like working with the public, though."

"Yeah, that's about what I deal with," her father said.

"We won't bring up the getting shot at aspect," Darren said, earning a backhand to the gut from her father.

Stephanie's mom pretended not to hear.

"Darren, why don't you go help your mother finish dinner? I'll give our guests a tour of the house."

Darren opened his mouth with the clear intent to argue, but one look from her father shut him up.

JESSE DIDN'T THINK Hank was all that interested in showing them the house, since he led them directly to his office, vaguely gesturing towards the bathroom and guest room as they passed. When they'd all filed in, Hank closed the door and leaned up against it. Grant put his hip to the desk and Jesse sat with Stephanie on the small sofa.

"What's up, Dad?"

"I wanted to fill you in on my conversation with that Trevor."

Jesse hadn't been sure when the right time to bring the subject up was, so he was very glad Hank had done it himself.

"How has he even managed to pull all of this off? He figured out where we all work, where I live, how to contact family and employers. It's crazy," Stephanie said.

"Turns out he works in research. He works with private investigators, people who do background checks, that kind of thing. My partner and I went to see him, and I feel confident in saying that he's not a physical danger. He's a fuckwit, but I'm certain he's not *that* kind of dangerous. He has a bit of a history of trying to ruin the businesses of someone he's crossed paths with, though. We've made it clear that if it happens again, we'll be conducting interviews with his clients and they probably won't like being questioned."

Jesse frowned, not sure that was enough of a threat to satisfy him, but he didn't want to interrupt.

"I've spoken to people at Apex, and they feel they have that side of it under control. That leaves your professional lives as the main way he can mess with you."

Grant nodded. "That's good to know. We'll still be careful, of course, but it relieves my mind quite a bit to know it likely won't go to a physical level."

"Unless you punch him in the face," Jesse added, perfectly happy to let Grant take on that task should it become necessary. Bruised knuckles would make Grant happy, but they would irritate Jesse.

"Unless I punch him in the face," Grant agreed.

Stephanie rolled her eyes when her father just nodded.

"He was not happy to see us and definitely intimidated. I'm fairly certain that we impressed upon him that fucking with a police officer's daughter was not a particularly healthy action on his part. But I don't know that he's smart enough to have put this behind him completely, I'm sorry to say."

"The good news is that our jobs are pretty secure. Stephanie was the most vulnerable in that regard."

Hank nodded. "That's good. If anything else happens and you'd like us to have another word with him, believe me, it won't be a hardship. Just let me know."

"Thanks, Dad. We appreciate what you did."

Hank looked at Jesse, then Grant. "How did she manage to keep you from doing anything and letting me have *my* chance, first?"

Jesse just smiled and looked at Grant.

Grant pursed his lips. "There may have been a steamroller involved. It's hard to remember, for sure, once I regained consciousness."

PERFECT ADDITION

Hank laughed. "That's my girl."

He stepped away from the door and opened it, just in time to hear Joan call out that dinner was ready.

"It smells delicious," Jesse said as they entered the dining room. "I'm sorry we didn't help any."

"Nonsense, Darren and I had it under control. Are you boys okay with this wine you brought, or would you like something else? I've already opened it and poured myself a glass, it's wonderful. But there's also beer, soda, water?"

"The wine would be great, Joan, thank you," Jesse assured her.

"I'll get some waters for everyone, too, mom," Stephanie said, kissing her mom on the cheek as she passed her.

They were soon settled and digging into the roast. It had been years since he'd had Yorkshire Pudding, but Jesse managed not to moan out loud when he bit into it. They all complimented the chef extravagantly. Stephanie's mom filled her in on some family gossip about cousins. Stephanie grilled Darren about his job and lack of girlfriend. Joan asked about his and Grant's families, so Stephanie shared about the dinner they'd had with his grandmother.

He was pretty sure that their simply being polite guests as well as being attentive to the needs of Stephanie and Joan were enough to win Joan and Hank's approval. He figured they had enough respect for Stephanie that unless he and Grant had come in and acted like outright assholes, they would have been pretty good.

And he couldn't exactly blame Darren for being overly cautious, since it was the guy's sister they were talking about. He hadn't asked Stephanie how much Darren knew about her lifestyle. Just because she'd discussed it with her parents didn't mean her younger brother was in on the info.

He sort of suspected that if Darren had been in the know, it would have come up during dinner, which would have pissed off his family. The guy definitely needed to do some growing up. Still Jesse liked him, and Hank and Joan, and he enjoyed dinner immensely. It was great knowing that of their three families, there was only one potential dud. And he fervently hoped that Grant's family would pull their heads out of their asses and come around. Because he believed that Grant truly was willing to walk away if he thought it was necessary, and Jesse would hate that for him.

They carried the conversation through dessert and coffee, and by the time they left he was certain they had parental approval. There had been some questions during dinner that could be interpreted as polite interest, or as subtle interrogations, depending on one's mood, but Jesse was sure that their answers were well received.

He offered to drive home, and so did Stephanie, but Grant declined. Stephanie insisted on letting him have the front seat this time, and then promptly fell asleep when they hit the freeway. He gestured to her and Grant took a peek in his mirror, then grinned at him. Grant pulled Jesse's hand into his and rested them on his leg. They made the journey home mostly silently, feeling sated and talked out.

When they got off the freeway, Stephanie stirred. He turned to watch her as she checked her phone. Her low hum of approval intrigued him.

"What? Tell me. I want to know."

She laughed. "Well, I have a message from my Sunday morning client letting me know she has to cancel."

"That's good you won't have to rush for that before brunch," Grant said.

"Does that mean we can stay up late tonight, and play?" Jesse asked.

Grant scowled. "It's not like either of you two will sleep in no matter that she doesn't have to run out for a client."

"But you'll be doing most of the work, and we'll be quiet and let *you* sleep in."

"I'll be doing the work, huh?" Grant pulled into the garage and parked, then raised an eyebrow at Jesse.

"Sure, 'cause you like to be in charge and all." Jesse got out and threw a teasing grin over his shoulder. He was hoping a little reverse psychology would work and he and Stephanie could get their hands on Grant for a while. Of course, if his hopes were dashed, he'd still be pretty happy at the end of the night, so it was win-win for him. And them.

They made it up to the apartment with Grant giving him fake glowering looks and Stephanie trying not to giggle. Jesse knew it was too late for them to have a full scene, but he figured some good, sweaty orgasms would help them break up the stress of meeting families all weekend.

Dinner at Stephanie's parents had gone great, but it had still been stressful beforehand. And brunch at Grant's parents' wasn't going to be terrible, he knew, but all that frigid politeness could be draining and he wasn't sure how much longer Grant would tolerate it before he had harsh words with his parents. And it was impossible to predict how they were going to react to Stephanie. He suspected they would embrace her and hope she replaced Jesse, but there was always the chance that they would be disdainful of her job and consider her a slut for hooking up with two guys.

He was going to need to be on his toes to make sure neither of his partners did or said anything they would regret. So, they needed some stress relief for tonight.

He helped Stephanie off with her coat and gave her a wink as he moved to hang it in the closet. She just shook her head and smiled. Game for whatever was coming, he knew. Damn, he loved her.

When he closed the closet door and turned, Grant was right there, in his space. Jesse shivered. Grant moved closer, using his body to back Jesse against the door. His breathing stuttered. He wanted to look up at Grant's face, but kept his eyes lowered, his body loose. Ready for whatever his Dom wanted to give him. Or take.

GRANT KNEW JESSE. He had no doubt his lover was angling for himself and Stephanie to have some playtime with Grant's body. Not something Grant was opposed to. But he'd kept an eye on both Jesse and Stephanie throughout the evening, and he'd noticed that though Jesse claimed to not be worried about meeting the family, his shoulders had been tight and he'd rubbed at his neck a couple of times.

And knowing what was coming up for them the next day, Grant was more interested in making sure his Jesse knew how important a place he held in Grant's life than having two sets of loving hands all over his own body. As nice as that would be, he'd save it for another time.

He backed Jesse up against the closet door, absolutely loving the way the other man's body immediately went motionless. His breathing picked up and that calmness that only saturated Jesse's body during scenes settled over him. Jesse was a mover. He had a tendency to tap a finger or shake a leg or bounce on his toes. Not to an annoying or obnoxious degree, but enough that when he switched to this stillness, Grant felt satisfaction all the way to his bones.

Brushing his lips along the line of Jesse's jaw, he put his hand out towards Stephanie. She took it immediately and he drew her close. He teased Jesse's nose with his own, kissed his cheekbone, murmured low into his ear where Stephanie could also hear.

"Were you hoping to get your hands on me tonight, Jesse? Feeling the need to take care of me a bit?"

He let his mouth hover over Jesse's, waiting for an answer. It took a minute for the other man to blink and focus his efforts on speech.

"I thought that might be nice."

Grant smiled, but didn't close the distance between their lips.

"It certainly would be nice. But I'm afraid I have some needs of my own, so you're out of luck in that regard."

"Okay," Jesse breathed. "Sir. I mean, yes, Sir."

"Turn around and face the wall. Hands behind your back." He only stepped back a small amount, leaving Jesse struggling to carefully turn without bumping into him.

"Don't move."

He stepped back, bringing Stephanie with him, and drew her

down the hall. Her eyes were bright and curious, anticipation written all over her face.

"In the linen closet is a thick bath sheet. It's green. Grab that and spread it over the bed, then get the massage oil from underneath the bathroom sink. I think our Jesse needs some help loosening up."

"Yes, Sir."

She moved to do as he'd instructed while he retrieved both of their collars, two sets of restraints, and the four straps he'd need. When he turned around, the towel was in place, the bottle on the bedside table and she was on her knees next to the bed. So perfect. He ran his hand over her head in appreciation, giving the green section an extra little tug. Her sigh was silent, but he saw it.

"Good girl. Stand up for me."

She rose gracefully, her head up, but her eyes lowered.

He set everything else on the bed and wrapped the collar around her neck, watching her face while he buckled it into place. She licked her lips, which did an excellent job of giving him ideas.

"Kiss me."

Her eyes darted up to meet his gaze, even as she moved up on tiptoes to do as he'd commanded. He held her shoulders to support her, but let her bring her lips to his. She teased his mouth with her tongue, slipped inside when he opened his lips in invitation. He indulged himself for several sweet moments before forcing himself to move on. They didn't have all night, unfortunately, though he was very thankful her morning client had cancelled.

He eased back and drew her hands in his, then attached the wrist restraints.

"Sit on the foot of the bed."

When she'd complied, he held out a hand, gesturing with the additional cuffs.

She raised one foot without difficulty, allowing him to buckle the cuff on, then switched legs.

"Kneel here and wait for me. When I bring Jesse in, you can undress him for me. No talking."

"Yes Sir." She sank to her knees and resumed her position at the foot of the bed.

He grabbed a blindfold and Jesse's collar, and left everything else on the bed.

He found Jesse exactly as he'd left him, standing in position. He knew the other man was aware he'd entered the room, but he made no move. Grant walked up behind him and kissed the back of his neck before latching the collar into place. Jesse drew in a breath, but made no other response.

When the blindfold was on and secure, Grant took Jesse's hand and led him slowly down the hall, to the bedroom. He positioned him in front of Stephanie and nodded at her. She rose to her feet and immediately began her task. He watched as she deftly worked the buttons on Jesse's shirt, then pushed the shirt off his shoulders and down his arms.

Jesse cooperated, raising his arms so she could tug off his undershirt, raising his feet when she tapped on his legs to remove his shoes, socks and pants. He was soon naked and evidently happy to be with them.

Grant smiled at Stephanie when she stepped back, her job complete.

"Jesse, turn around and get up on the bed. Crawl forward until I tell you to stop, then lie down on your stomach."

He held the towel down as Jesse shuffled toward the headboard.

"There."

Jesse stopped moving forward and lowered himself to the bed, his face turned in Grant's direction, his arms down by his sides.

He handed Stephanie a wrist and ankle cuff, and they both worked quickly to attach them.

He used the short straps to attach the ankle cuffs to the footboard, and the longer straps to do the same with the wrist cuffs, so that Jesse arms rested beside his body, with enough space that he or Stephanie could kneel over his legs and butt.

When he was done, he held his hand out to Stephanie, who came to his side of the bed. He pulled her into his front and wrapped his arms around her.

"Pretty, isn't he?"

"Stunning."

"I suspect there are a lot of knots in that fine body right now. Want to help me work that out?"

"Yes, Sir."

"Get the lotion."

He let her go and climbed up onto the bed, straddled Jesse's ass. He held out his hand and Stephanie squeezed out a generous portion of oil.

"You work on his legs, but be careful with his feet," he told her, rubbing the oil between his hands.

"Yes, Sir."

"I wanted to do this for *you*, Sir," Jesse said before a quiet moan when Grant began to work his shoulders.

"So I figured. Maybe if you're good, we'll have time for that, too."

"Mmmm."

Grant chuckled. "Now be quiet and let me and Stephanie concentrate."

Jesse wrinkled his nose but kept his mouth shut.

Grant glided his oiled hands over Jesse's shoulders, getting the lay of the land. Definitely some knots, but nothing too terrible. He used his thumb and started digging in, keeping his ears trained on Stephanie's actions behind him.

Jesse's muscles melted beneath his hands. When he'd finished with the shoulders, he moved off the bed and he and Stephanie worked together to massage Jesse's back and arms until every inch of him was relaxed and supple. At least from the back, Grant thought, with an inner snicker.

He released the straps and told Jesse to roll over before hooking them back up. He poured oil directly onto Jesse chest and he and Stephanie dived in, more like they were playing with finger paints than giving a proper massage. He winked at her, letting her know it was okay to start playing. They tugged on Jesse's nipples, came teasingly close to his hard erection, but slicked up every part of him except that long length.

Jesse's head started to thrash about before Grant finally gave in. He reached for Steph's hand and placed it around Jesse's cock. Jesse's hips immediately pushed up and Grant flicked his ribs in reprimand.

The hips dropped and Jesse bit his lip. Hard.

Grant joined Stephanie, four hands working Jesse's cock and balls with the slick oil until Jesse's moans were continuous and his heels were digging into the bed with his effort to stay still.

Giving him a tight squeeze with one hand, Grant fished a tissue from the nightstand with the other and positioned it. "Come for us, Jesse, but don't move."

Jesse grunted, those heels digging in even more, and came hard. He exhaled loudly and slowly relaxed his body.

Grant grabbed a towel from the bathroom and wiped his hands before handing the towel to Stephanie. He eased the blindfold up and off, enjoying the way Jesse's eyes blinked open sleepily and immediately moved to meet Grant's gaze.

"Better?" Grant asked quietly.

"Awesome."

Grant chuckled and released the straps on the wrist and ankle cuffs on his side, while Stephanie moved to do the same on the other side. Giving Jesse a hand off the bed, he motioned toward Stephanie with a grin.

"I think we're going to need another towel."

Jesse nodded enthusiastically and Stephanie shivered. She was naked within two minutes.

CHAPTER SIXTEEN

Stephanie woke up feeling too amazing to be worried about brunch. She propped her head up and watched her guys sleeping. If she'd thought about it, she would have supposed that sharing a bed with two large men would be super annoying. She would have been wrong. She loved snuggling up with the guys. Jesse was spooning Grant, who had his arm wrapped around her waist.

As if he felt her watching, Jesse opened one eye and blinked. Smiling, she slid off the bed and cocked her head in question at Jesse. He rolled free and pulled the blankets back up to cover Grant, then left the bedroom with her.

"Want to do some Pilates with me?" she asked.

"How about I watch? I can even make up score cards for you, like a judge."

"Only if you're not worried about waking up missing vital body parts someday," she said lightly.

"Let's avoid that."

"Think about how flexible you could be if you joined me a few times a week," she said, rolling out her yoga mat.

"All right, all right," he grumbled. "I'll give it a try."

She grabbed her extra mat and took him through some slow and easy Pilates moves, working them both up to a sweat, though it wasn't quite her usual workout. She'd see if Grant wanted to go for a jog after the party.

When they went to the bedroom to shower Grant rolled over and stretched. Her mouth watered. She checked her watch. Damn, probably not enough time to get anything started. Resisting temptation, she pushed Jesse into the bathroom and laughed when a pillow hit her in the back.

They showered without getting into too much trouble, even when Grant joined them. She dried her hair while they made omelettes. When she joined them, Jesse handed her a mimosa. She looked from her glass to his.

"Why is mine more pale than yours?"

"Because I'm a lightweight?"

She snorted, but accepted the glass. She wasn't going to say no to a little champagne courage.

"You look very pretty," Grant said, stealing a kiss as he brought their plates to the table.

She'd selected a long-sleeved dress and boots since the weather was mostly cooperating, but it was still a bit chilly.

"Thanks, babe. You look pretty great, too."

Both the guys were wearing slacks and cashmere sweaters that looked soft and inviting. Grant's was dark blue and Jesse's pale green with a V neck. She wondered what it would be like to be naked and pressed between them. She took a long drink of her mimosa and sat down.

Grant's eyes twinkled and she wondered how he'd come to be so good at reading her mind.

"So, what did you tell your parents about me?" she asked when they tucked into their food.

"I told them that Jesse and I have become involved with a woman named Stephanie. That you were very important to us and that I was certain they would like you. And that they needed to be very careful how they treat the people that are important to me, if they want me to keep coming to family events, since I will not be coming alone and leaving those people behind."

Stephanie raised her brows, but nodded. Seemed fair enough.

When breakfast was over they piled into the car. It wasn't a long drive, but Grant had wanted enough time to stop and pick up flowers for his mom. She'd quizzed him about getting a gift for his mom, but he'd insisted that flowers in the fancy vase he'd bought and the bottle of champagne he'd picked up, would be appropriate for all of them.

They had fun working with the florist to pick out flowers for the arrangement, but it wasn't long before they were entering a gated community and pulling up to a large estate. Grant parked next to a Maserati and she felt her stomach dance. She glanced back at Jesse who gave her an amused look of understanding but didn't say anything.

She had several clients who were much better off than she was, as far as salaries, but nothing at this level. Mostly because she kept close to home, not attempting to expand her client base outside of the city proper, though maybe she needed to reconsider that business plan.

"How many people are going to be at this family brunch?" she asked, eyeing the large amount of cars.

Jesse chuckled softly and she watched Grant give him a quelling look. A look, she couldn't help but notice, that had no effect on Jesse.

"Probably around thirty."

"Huh. Okay."

She supposed it didn't really matter. Actually, bigger was better, right? More people to mingle with if she found anyone she didn't want to talk to.

She waited by her door to see how Grant wanted to play their entry. He grabbed Jesse's hand and wrapped his other arm around her waist, then tugged them towards the front door. Which, she saw now, was already opening.

A striking woman stood at the door, her hair nearly identical to

Grant's. She wasn't smiling, but she wasn't frowning either. Stephanie had the immediate and uncharitable thought that Botox might be preventing her from either. She dashed it aside and pasted on her own small smile.

A little girl, around seven, Stephanie figured, brushed past the woman and dashed down the two steps to hurl herself at Jesse and Grant, flinging skinny little arms around one of each of their legs.

"Uncle Grant, Uncle Jesse, you're here!"

Grant let her go to reach down and pick the girl up, swinging her easily into his arms.

"Maddie-bug," Grant said, giving her a tight squeeze before passing her off to Jesse who swung her around so she was riding piggyback. They reached the steps and the woman proved her Botox supposition false by frowning. "Madeline, you're wearing a dress."

"I know Grandma, isn't it the prettiest dress ever?" she cried out in a high-pitched squeal. Stephanie didn't try to hold back her smile.

"It's a very pretty dress, but I don't think it's appropriate for you to sit on Jesse's back when you're wearing it."

By this time a swarm of other kids had made it past Grandma and were crowded around the guys, waiting for hugs and kisses. Maddie kept her perch through it all, and Stephanie secretly cheered her on. She appreciated the reprieve the kids had given her, because she didn't think Grant's mom was going to be her biggest fan.

Some of the kids were shy with her, but most said a quick hi while trying to lure Grant and Jesse off to join in whatever fun they were having, but eventually they scattered.

"Mom, I'd like you to meet Stephanie Walsh. Steph, my mother Charlotte Sumner."

"It's nice to meet you, Mrs. Sumner." Stephanie put on her most polite smile and held out a hand.

"My dear, it is so nice to meet you!" The warm greeting was followed by a hug and Stephanie gave bug eyes to Jesse over the woman's shoulder. He looked amused but only shrugged his shoulders in response.

Pulling back, Charlotte put her hands on Stephanie's shoulders and studied her. "Please, you must call me Charlotte. Aren't you just so lovely?"

Figuring that was rhetorical, Stephanie didn't bother to respond. She edged back, out of the embrace, and took Grant's hand. He smiled at her, and seemed genuinely pleased by his mother's welcoming behavior.

"You have a lovely home."

Charlotte beamed. "Thank you, we've been here since Grant was a boy and we're very happy with it. Let me show you around."

She led the way inside and Stephanie held a hand out for Jesse, encouraging him to come around to her other side. He gave her hand a squeeze and held it throughout the unbearably long tour. When Charlotte turned around and caught sight of the hand-holding, her mouth pinched in and she turned away quickly.

Halfway through the tour, they met Steven, Grant's dad. He was pleasant, but slightly reserved, which she sort of appreciated after his wife's enthusiasm.

They settled in the family room, though she could hear the kids playing upstairs, and she met Grant's sister Diana. Tara was the sister backpacking through Europe, and Stephanie had seen a lovely portrait of her in the formal living room, as well as Diana and Grant's. She'd admired Grant's portrait in a clinical sense, but had been unmoved by it. The photographer had completely failed to capture his spark, in her opinion. One she'd kept to herself.

As they'd moved down the hall, Grant had leaned into her and whispered, "I hate that picture."

Jesse had leaned in as well. "Not as much as I hate it."

They'd shared knowing looks and she gave them a wink before catching up with Charlotte.

Diana seemed a little wary, but not necessarily negative. She was the mother of three of the kids, the rest belonging to two of Grant's cousins, Travis, and Frank and their spouses. The room was large and there were aunts and uncles and spouses.

Grant led them to a couch and just let people come by to be introduced, rather than dragging her around to everyone else. Some of them were friendly and welcoming to Jesse, and curious and kind to Stephanie. Some of them barely stuck around for introductions after greeting Grant. She genuinely liked a couple and decided to follow Jesse's example of not being bothered by those who had no interest in her.

It was the ones who wanted to talk to her and Grant, but exclude Jesse, that got her back up. His mother managed to ride the edge very closely, including Jesse just enough to not be rude. Stephanie was not impressed.

She kept waiting to be introduced to Sharon, the cousin who had designs on Grant's job, but it didn't happen. She ended up in a conversation with Grant's father about the benefits of exercising first thing in the morning, versus later in the day. She refrained from sharing anecdotes about her experiences of Grant and Jesse's morning energy levels.

When it was time to eat, they moved to the dining room and another room that had been set up with additional tables. She had no idea what the room's usual purpose was, but then again, in this house, maybe it was always used as a second dining room. Grant was ushered to the middle seat on one side, and Jesse pushed her into the seat next to him, taking her other side. She smiled her appreciation that he would take on whichever family member sat next to him, leaving her safely cocooned between her two guys.

Diana sat across from her, jiggling a baby on her knee. They talked about fitting in exercise routines around busy life schedules, and the fact that they'd gone to the same college, though Diana was eight years older than Stephanie. She enjoyed chatting with the woman, and when she was done eating, she offered to hold the baby so Diana could use both hands to eat for a change. Her husband pretended to be insulted, as he'd already offered to take the baby, but they just waved his protestations away.

She walked around the table, collected the tiny bundle, and returned to her seat, cuddling the three-month-old boy.

"Isn't that sweet," Charlotte called from her end of the table. "Do you plan to have children, Stephanie?"

Slightly unnerved to be speaking down the length of the long table, past the now staring others who'd stopped their conversations, she shrugged. "There are really too many variables to say for certain. It's a possibility, but I don't think I'll be devastated if it doesn't work out that way."

"My greatest achievement in life was being a mother," Charlotte said, a beaming smile stretched across her face.

"Well, you certainly seem to have done a fine job of it, judging by Grant and Diana," was the only reply Stephanie could come up with.

That seemed to satisfy Charlotte who went back to her meal.

Jesse gave a very low snort and put his arm along the back of her chair. She leaned back so she could feel the heat of him, even as she smiled to hear the slight scratching sounds of Jesse's fingers playing with Grant's shoulder. She offered the baby her finger and he grabbed on with a strong grip.

Grant leaned in and ran a finger along the tiny little knuckles. "Amazing, isn't he?"

"Totally. But I'm not going to lie, it will be nice to pass him off when the time comes."

Grant laughed. "I love being an uncle and getting to have the fun, but also enjoy the pass off, like you said. Although I think I'll enjoy keeping them around, when the time comes and they're my own."

"No doubt," she agreed. She'd never pictured any of her partners with babies before, but she did so now. Jesse, wearing no shirt, holding a tiny baby in his arms, Grant, also shirtless wrapped around him, the baby holding his finger. Oh, yeah, she could see it. And she could feel little tingles in her girly parts that assured her she had those female instincts she'd read about.

Jesse leaned into her more, and with Grant leaning in from his side, they made a tight little group, hovering over the wide-eyed baby, Jesse's arm resting on Grant's shoulder. The baby blew a spit bubble and they laughed.

She glanced up and found most of the table watching them. *Yikes.* Charlotte looked a mix between confused and thoughtful, Diana was smiling though it looked a touch uncertain, and her husband looked like a proud peacock.

Charlotte stood up. "Time for cake, I think!" The servers began picking up the lunch plates and the baby didn't like the noise. He started to look a bit cross, his forehead wrinkling up adorably.

"And time to give this guy back to his parents, I'm thinking," Jesse said. Stephanie nodded and handed the baby to Jesse when he rose and held out his arms. He looked a natural, though Stephanie wished he wasn't wearing a shirt, so she could judge the full affect. She tried to hold back the naughty smile that wanted to break free, and managed until she caught sight of Grant wearing the same grin. She laughed with him, silently, as they watched Jesse deliver the now whining kid to his father.

Diana's smile had grown more genuine and Stephanie held out hope that at least part of the immediate family was coming around.

The singing was mostly done by the kids and Charlotte let them help her blow out the candles. Immediately one of the servers scooped the cake back up again and carted it off to the kitchen.

Grant's hand landed on her knee.

"You doing okay?"

"Yeah, I'm fine. It's a nice celebration. Most everyone is pretty cool. A few, well, it seems pretty likely I don't have to worry about them being nasty to me, I just have to watch out for them being rude to Jesse."

He nodded, a little frown on his face. "I don't feel like anyone's crossed the line enough for me to call them out on it."

She agreed.

"They haven't," Jesse promised.

"You'll tell us if they do when we aren't there to see it, though, right?" Stephanie pushed.

Jesse's eyes slid away and she figured he hadn't done that in the past.

"Yes, you will," Grant said firmly.

Jesse sighed. "Yes, I will."

Stephanie kissed his cheek, then leaned back as plates of cake were set in front of her and Grant. Grant's cousin, sitting on his other side, asked him something about the business, so she turned her attention to Jesse.

"Seriously, you're okay?" she asked.

He smiled. "I like a decent portion of these people, so yeah. And it makes Grant happy, so it's all good. I can handle being snubbed by the few idiots who haven't quite figured out that I'm here to stay."

"I wish you didn't have to handle it. And I hope they figure out that I'm on your side, not theirs, or they're not going to like hearing what I have to say."

"Grrr, my attack tiger. But seriously, don't feel like you need to protect me. I'm good."

She leaned and bumped his shoulder. "No promises." Sitting back, she tried not to notice the people watching them. "The food was definitely good. I'm not used to catered events, but then again I'm not used to family events with more than ten people, unless it's a wedding or something."

"Yeah, it can take a little getting used to."

"I'm glad my birthday is in spring, so I can actually do things outside."

"My birthday is in July, which is too hot sometimes. Although last year we had just gotten the Cape Cod house, which was nice. But full-on tourist season. Grant's is in November, which is back to cold. We should ditch Grant's family and take him to the Bahamas."

"That is an excellent plan, my friend."

The cake looked delicious but Jesse still hadn't received a piece. She looked up and saw that most of the table had been served, but there were still a few waiting. She saw that Grant was still involved with his conversation, so she slid her plate to Jesse and Grant's plate in front of herself. Hopefully someone would notice the heir apparent was without and rectify that situation.

He glanced over, then down at the plates, and back at her. His smile was so warm and indulgent that her stomach gave a little lurch.

"Make sure our Jesse eats his cake all gone. He doesn't indulge in sweets often enough."

"That's because I don't indulge in exercise often enough," Jesse said, just before he forked a large piece of cake into his mouth.

Grant reached past her to wipe a tiny smear of whipped cream off the corner of his lips, then offered it to Stephanie, who glared at him. "We're at your parents' house!" she hissed.

He just laughed, licked his finger and turned back to his conversation.

She dared a glance at his mom, but she must not have noticed their little scene, as she didn't look constipated, but almost pleasant.

Stephanie blew out a breath and forked up a piece of cake.

GRANT RESISTED CHECKING his watch when he finished the conversation with his cousin. He turned back to Steph and Jesse to see that they'd finished their cake and there was a fresh piece in front of him. They still had present opening to get through, though thankfully his mother traditionally kept that to a minimum and only opened the presents from the little kids.

He took a bite of cake and tuned into the conversation his partners were having with his sister. She'd brought a chair and the baby around to their side of the table and was bouncing him on one knee while Jesse made him giggle by poking at his belly.

He had never given serious thought to children until this little guy had been born a few months before. And then, it was only seeing Jesse's pure joy and enthusiasm with the baby that had made him start to see a future with kids. Not that he'd ever been against it, he'd just never actually seen it in his head until he saw how easy Jesse was with them.

PERFECT ADDITION

"Where's Sharon?" Grant asked.

Diana shrugged. "She told Mom she'd be a little late and that she was bringing a date."

"Fantastic," Grant said, dryly.

"Yeah, Dad told me what she tried to pull. What a little shit. She seriously has no clue that Mom and Dad would never hand the company over to her, no matter if you were there or not?"

"No clue at all."

"Is she not good at her job?" Stephanie asked.

"She's okay at her job. Not excellent. But through trial and error we've determined it's best to keep her scope limited in order to make sure she *stays* okay at her job. She is not good at big picture."

"As I recall," Diana added. "It took a while to find a job she could do decently at the company." She looked at Stephanie. "Mom and Dad do try to make sure that any family who wants to work in the business can, but they certainly don't promise that anyone can be executive level."

"That makes sense, but in my experience it's the people who are too stupid to know that they're stupid that cause the most trouble."

"Truer words," Grant grumbled.

Diana laughed, then turned to Jesse. "When are you going to quit your job and open a daycare?"

He smiled. "I think I'll wait and fill up my house with my own kids."

Grant really liked the sound of that.

"Hey, I never considered how much easier it would be to be a parent if there are three of you instead of two," Diana said.

Grant was about to respond when there was a small commotion. He sensed Stephanie go rigid beside him.

He looked up and couldn't believe what he saw. "Oh, fuck that."

He stood, as did the others.

When he passed a wide-eyed Jesse, the other man put a hand on his arm but Grant was not stopping. He marched up to his late-arrival cousin Sharon and her date, and, without pausing, grabbed Trevor's arm and pulled him out of the room and into the foyer.

"Get your hands off of me," Trevor demanded.

Grant ignored him. Daniel, their longtime butler, opened the door as Grant approached. He inclined his head to the other man in thanks and didn't stop moving until he and Trevor were at the foot of the steps. The idiot sputtered all the way, but couldn't pull free of Grant's grip.

"Grant! Let him go, how dare you! This is unconscionable. I know you can be a bully, but this is abuse!" Sharon kept up her litany as they exited the house.

"What the hell is going on?" his father demanded.

Stephanie had her phone in her hand, but he shook his head. He wanted to see if they could handle this before she called her father.

"See?" Sharon demanded. "I *told* you he was abusive and out of control."

His mother stepped up beside him. "Explain yourself, Sharon."

"What is there to explain? You saw it. We never even said a word and he just attacked Trevor."

Grant turned to find half the family, including some of the kids, spread out on the steps. "Everyone back inside."

They didn't move at first, but he glared at a couple people until they flushed and started moving the crowd into the house.

"I *did* see that. And I know my son. So, I'll give you one more chance. Explain yourself or leave."

"I've already explained what he's like. What kinds of things he does with these people." She gestured to Stephanie and Jesse and Grant had to hold himself back from going to her. She was going to sink herself, she didn't need any help from him, as tempting as it might be.

Jesse reached for his hand, behind his mother's back, and he accepted it gratefully. Stephanie moved up behind him on this other side and put her hand on his shoulder.

"Now you can see for yourself what a bully he is." Indignation rang in Sharon's voice.

Grant took in a deep breath, gave Jesse's hand a squeeze. "Stephanie had to put this asshole in his place a while back," he said.

"Jesse and I were happy to help with that, but it wasn't necessary. He tried to trash our reputations at the club, but he wasn't successful. So he took things *outside* of the club. He tried to hurt Stephanie's business, though, again, he wasn't successful. He tried to get Jesse in trouble at work. Again, he wasn't successful. He took it to Sharon. And I'm ashamed to say he apparently found some success there."

Sharon turned beet red at that. Trevor said nothing, his jaw clenched tight.

"What have you to say for yourself, Sharon?" Charlotte asked.

"You're just going to believe these...*degenerates* over me?" she asked, again gesturing towards the group.

"Of course I am. I've only known Stephanie for a couple of hours, so I suppose I can't speak to her actions. But I've known Jesse for months now, and Grant for his entire life. And I've never known either of them to be rude, petty or unnecessarily vindictive. You, on the other hand, have shown yourself to be all three over the years."

Sharon gasped and he was pretty sure Stephanie did as well. Her forehead rested against his shoulder and he thought she might be laughing.

Trevor finally spoke up. "I've come here to *help* your family, save you from the embarrassment that your son and his activities are going to bring you—"

"Nobody is speaking to you and nobody is interested in anything you have to say," Grant's father said.

Charlotte put her arms around Jesse's and Grant's waists.

"Sharon, I'm very disappointed in you. You knew that this man considered Grant an enemy and you entertained his stories and brought him to my house."

"Aunt Char—"

"We will *not* be discussing this while that man is here. When you've gotten rid of him you may make an appointment with your uncle and me to apologize and explain your actions, if possible. If Grant is willing to hear from you, I will so inform you."

Steven stepped forward and pointed behind Sharon in a wordless command that she leave. She gaped at him, at all of them, then turned on her heel and left, Trevor following in her wake.

Charlotte stepped clear and turned to face him. Jesse and Stephanie moved in to claim their places at his side.

"Stephanie, Jesse, I'm very sorry you experienced such rudeness in our home."

Neither responded for a moment and Grant could only assume the shock of the apology had rendered them speechless.

"No need to apologize, Charlotte," Jesse said. "It's clear that Trevor approached Sharon because he saw her vulnerabilities."

His mother came as close to snorting as her manners would allow, which was a small huff. "That is a very nice way of describing her stupidity, Jesse."

AFTER THEY WENT BACK INSIDE, the party was drama free. Jesse found Charlotte to be attentive in a way she'd never before been with him, while also treating Stephanie with less suffocating politeness than she had at the start of the afternoon. Jesse gave a questioning glance to Steph, but she just shook her head.

When they had said their goodbyes, which included tossing Maddie into the air a couple of times, despite the fact she was wearing a pretty dress, they climbed into the car. Jesse took shotgun this time, but turned to Stephanie as soon as he'd buckled in.

She beat him to it. "'That is a very nice way of describing her stupidity, Jesse,'" she nearly shouted. They burst out laughing as Grant reversed the car and drove them away from the house. When they hadn't managed to stop laughing by the time he exited the gated community, he pulled into a gas station parking lot and just stared at them.

Jesse tried to rein it in, but every time he looked at Stephanie, she tried to look serious and he lost it again. Luckily Grant was smiling at them, but still, Jesse worked to bring it to an end. He cleared his throat and looked at his boyfriend.

"That went well."

This time both Grant and Stephanie burst into laughter.

When they finally calmed down and got back on the road, Jesse had to ask.

"How is it that being nice and polite to your mother all these months earns me nothing. Bring one psycho into the mix, and suddenly she's my biggest fan?"

Grant reached over and took his hand.

"Not exactly accurate. Your nice and polite all these months set the foundation. But bringing the family under attack by an outside force brought out the mama bear."

"I guess." He wasn't sure what to think of that, exactly, but he should relax and take the change of pace as a good thing. To be fair to Charlotte, he hadn't even been around a year and she'd never been outright rude to him.

"I really can't think how Sharon thought there would be any good outcome though. That's what has me puzzled. I know she's not the most strategic thinker, but there was no possible way for that to end in her favor." Grant shook his head, frowning.

"You forget that he really can be charming. He was at the club for a couple of months, and as far as I know, nobody had anything but good things to say about him. I think he had her seduced by the possibility of proving you weren't the perfect heir-apparent, so she was sure that if your mom and dad heard his version, which she fully believed, they would finally give her the chance she thinks she deserves."

Grant grunted, and Stephanie laughed.

"You met him with no chance of liking him, so you have an unfair advantage. Think of the way he was able to convince the managers I worked with for years to let me go. He obviously has some skills."

"I guess," Grant said.

"I think you're giving her a bit more credit than she's due," Jesse said. "But the outcome was to our advantage and hopefully he'll see now that he's been blocked at every avenue. The club, you," he nodded at Stephanie. "Because of your dad. This will certainly all make for a good story to tell our kids someday."

Since Stephanie just smiled her agreement, Jesse winked at Grant and didn't push the conversation. He looked at the clock as they approached their building. Stephanie had a client appointment at four, but they were doing okay on timing. When they got inside, Grant took Stephanie's hands in his and looked into her eyes.

"You okay with what happened?"

She blinked at him. Jesse knew what it was like, being trapped in the tractor-beam gaze. She nodded, but Grant just waited.

"I'm fine. Really. I didn't even have a chance to get bothered, to be honest."

Grant studied her for a second, then nodded. He kissed her. "All right, sweets. You need anything from us before your appointment? Need a ride?"

She smiled. "No, I'm good, thanks. I just need to change."

When she left, Jesse waited. He knew that look.

Grant turned to him. "I have an idea for tonight."

Oh yeah, he knew that look.

When Stephanie left, they made their plans. Which included Jesse handling dinner so Stephanie wouldn't have to cook and they could have something other than steak. By the time he came back with the take-out bags, she'd returned. He shoved the bags in the fridge and they lazed on the couch watching home improvement shows until they were hungry.

When he brought out the salads he'd picked up, she dropped her mouth in shock.

"What?" he asked innocently. "Now that you've shown me where some good salad places are, I like them. I never realized how many salads came with chicken and steak." He passed them out and handed over the dressing containers. They all doctored their salads and dug in as another episode started up.

"If you could have any kind of house you wanted, would you like a workout studio to bring clients to?" Grant asked Stephanie.

She thought about it while she chewed, shook her head. "No, I

PERFECT ADDITION

think I prefer working out of the gym, or the occasional park, when I don't go to the client's house. I don't think I'd like bringing clients into my own home."

"Especially once you have kids," Jesse said.

She frowned. "Yeah, even more then."

"What about an office space," Jesse asked, as the actors on the show added some hideous accessories to the office area.

"It would be nice to have a walk-in closet kind of thing where I can keep all my files and paperwork, but I don't see myself sitting at a desk. I like using my laptop wherever I want, be it the couch or the kitchen table or whatever."

"If we got a house together, I would let you have the master closet, and I could use the guest-room closet for my clothes," Jesse told her, watching her reaction out of the corner of his eye.

But she didn't really react. "Aww, that's sweet, thank you. But I think that would be annoying. I don't have a ton of clothes, we might be able to do something to make a biggish closet work for three people. Have a couple of dressers, that kind of thing. And some places have little dressing room type closets. Something like that would probably work perfectly."

She took another bite of her salad and Jesse winked at Grant, who just smiled and shook his head. They finished their dinner and watched one more episode, then Grant grabbed the remote and turned off the television.

Stephanie turned to look at him and Jesse was pretty sure that was hope on her face. Especially when she waggled her eyebrows at Grant with a big grin.

He shook his head and huffed out a laugh. "I'm sorry we didn't make it to Apex this weekend. Do you want to try and go during the week, or plan on Saturday?"

"Don't be sorry, everything about this weekend was important to me, too. And I'm totally good with Saturday."

Jesse leaned over and gave her a noisy kiss on the cheek. "Good answer."

"Are you up for something tonight?" Grant asked. "What time is your first client tomorrow?"

"Not until nine, so I'm definitely up for something tonight if you guys are."

"Excellent. I want you both to be naked and kneeling for me in the bedroom in five minutes."

They didn't hesitate, but immediately rose. They grabbed the take-out cartons and silverware, rushed into the kitchen to deal with them, then split up, Jesse waving Steph on to the master bathroom while he took the guest bathroom. They reconvened at the bed, tore off their clothes, tossed them in the hamper and were on their knees before they heard Grant start walking down the hall.

Jesse leaned over and kissed Stephanie. He timed it so that they had just enough time to straighten up and lower their eyes before Grant walked through the door.

CHAPTER SEVENTEEN

This was a sight that would never get old to Grant. His lovers, naked for him, patient for him, giving themselves to him. Putting their wants, needs and desires in his hands and trusting that he would not only take care of them, but give them ultimate pleasure, time after time. He was truly humbled by the responsibility of it. And so thankful.

He got their collars first. Crouching in front of Stephanie, he watched her face, as he liked to do, when he placed the beribboned metal around her neck. Her eyes closed and her lips parted. He brushed a feather-light kiss across them, then moved to Jesse.

Though it had been more than six months now since he'd first done this, it never failed to impact his heart to place the collar around that strong neck. Those trusting eyes held his gaze for just a moment, before dipping down in submission. He teased Jesse's lips with his thumb, pushed it into the eager mouth. Jesse sucked deep and hard on the digit, whimpering when Grant withdrew.

"Jesse, would you get a blindfold for our Stephanie?"

"Yes, Sir." Jesse rose to his feet and quickly returned with the blindfold.

"May I put it on her, Sir?"

"You may."

He watched as Jesse placed a soft kiss on her forehead, then slipped the blindfold over her head. He smoothed her hair down and secured the cloth. He looked to Grant who nodded his approval and held out his hand. Jesse gave Steph a quick kiss on her lips then joined Grant.

Grant jerked his head towards the door and Jesse moved off, per the plan they'd discussed while Steph had been out. He watched Stephanie control her breathing and her body as nothing happened and no sounds occurred to give her clues. He was impressed with her skills, but then again, she was no novice. He supposed her yoga practice helped as well. When he judged enough time had passed for Jesse to be ready, he spoke.

"Come to me, sweetheart."

She rose and followed the sound of his voice, only slightly hesitant as she neared. She stopped a little too far back.

"Closer."

She took two large steps and made it to within a couple of inches of him.

"Do you know what you do to me? To us?" he asked, softly. "So beautiful. I want to show you off to the whole world, declare you as mine, as ours, and then whip them for daring to look at what's mine. I want them to talk about what a lucky son of a bitch I am and then I want to punch them for daring to speak of you. I want to bring you to orgasm in front of them so that they can all know what they're missing out on."

She shivered at his words, her breath hitching at each new statement. Her body jerked when they heard the front door open and close with a heavy thunk.

"It doesn't matter who looks at you, does it Steph? As long as they all know that you belong to me, along with Jesse. You are mine and nobody gets to touch you and enjoy you but me and my Jesse. Is that right?"

"Yes Sir. Nobody but you and our Jesse."

He smiled at her immediate and claiming response. He brushed a kiss over her shoulder, teased a finger through the fine hair covering her pussy.

"They can watch," he said, timing it perfectly as a low murmur of sound came from the living room. "They can fantasize. But they can't touch, taste or experience." He floated a finger along her hip, barely touching, then her breast.

"Tell me again," he ordered.

"All yours, Sir. Only you and Jesse."

"Good girl." He rewarded her with a kiss, deep and hard, his hand at the back of her head, digging into her hair, careful not to disturb the blindfold. The sounds from the living room got louder, including the distinctive sound of ice clinking in glass, then faded again.

He pulled free, not wanting her to get lost in sensation. He wanted her brain to work again, her nerves to rise a bit.

"Go get your wrist cuffs from the top of the dresser," he told her. He took her by the shoulders and pointed her in the right direction.

She hesitated only a heartbeat, then cautiously stepped forward. She held an arm out in front of her, though she knew it was several feet to the dresser. Since she stayed mostly on course, he didn't need to direct her. She slowed to shuffling steps as she neared the drawers and found the dresser. She picked up the cuffs from where he'd left them on top and turned back to him.

"Put them on and clip them together behind your back."

She swallowed, tucked one under her arm while she fastened the other. He was pretty sure she'd never put them on blindfolded, but she'd used them hundreds of times and was able to accomplish it without much difficulty. She had a little more trouble with the right wrist, but not much. He'd left a clip on one cuff and she was able to reach behind herself and attach the clip to the ring on the opposite cuff. She looked towards him and smiled her pleased triumph.

"Well done. Now come back to me."

She was a little more sure this time until she realized she couldn't put her arm out to gauge her distance to him. He waited until she was several steps away before aiding her.

"Almost there."

Her look of relief and happy appreciation was beautiful.

"Thank you, Sir," she whispered.

She didn't stop until her toe found his shoe.

A somewhat loud thump came from the living room, followed by a change in the sounds, softer, then louder again, just barely discernible as voices. Jesse was outdoing himself.

A little furrow appeared between her brows and she pulled her lip between her teeth.

He pulled a delicate chain from his pocket. It was meant to be the shoulder strap on a woman's handbag, so it had a small clip on each end. He used one end to clip to her collar, making it obvious what he was doing, then giving it a little tug to drive the point home.

Her breath left her in a whoosh.

"You're going to come with me down the hall. No speaking. You will listen carefully to what I tell you, as you always do. Don't get distracted. Do you understand?"

Her "Yes, Sir," was immediate, but he heard her uncertainty for the first time since they'd begun playing together.

He moved forward with a small pull on the leash, letting her get close enough to the doorjamb to feel when they passed out of the bedroom and into the hallway. The scrape of a chair and the sound of the water dispenser on the refrigerator filling a glass were nearly simultaneous. He'd have to give Jesse props for really setting the auditory scene.

Watching her carefully as he kept a light tension on the leash, he saw her swallow hard, her mouth twitching. Her shoulders had climbed up near her ears. He'd meant this to be a fun play on his promise to take her to the club, since he hadn't been able to follow through on that yet. But she wasn't excited. Not in the right way.

Was it from seeing Trevor that afternoon? Being reminded that her last public scene had not gone well? But she'd been able to put a stop to it right away, and she'd claimed to not be upset by it when they started playing together. He knew she liked to be seen, it hadn't just been a fantasy of hers, but a lived reality.

But this wasn't right. And now he needed something from her. Her trust.

STEPHANIE'S HEART WAS POUNDING, but not in the good way she usually experienced. She'd never, not for one second, doubted her time with Grant, but now…she was unsure. Could he really have invited people over to the apartment? And if he had, would it be a bad thing? She liked to scene in public. That was a fact both she and Grant were aware of. So if he'd done this, he'd done it for her, so why the fuck was it freaking her out?

She felt it as they moved out of the bedroom and into the hallway. More sounds came at her, confirming her suspicions. That wasn't just the television, which would be crazy anyway as Jesse wouldn't have started watching TV while they were playing. Something was definitely happening.

The question was, why was it upsetting her? And if it was upsetting her, she needed to let Grant know, but since she didn't understand why, she didn't want to halt the scene. God, if he'd gone to all this trouble for her, she'd hate to ruin it.

Calling out her safe word with him would be nothing like it had been with Trevor. She knew that, down to the bones. He would stop and help her in whatever way she needed. She just felt sick at the idea of disappointing him.

The loud pop of a champagne cork startled her into a jerk, which she felt especially in her collar. *His* collar. Liquid pouring into several glasses, she wasn't even sure how she understood what that sound was, but it was clear as day to her.

Her feet stopped moving and her mouth opened. She couldn't hold it back any longer. She needed Grant, and there was one way to let him know.

"Yellow." It came out as more of a croak than a whisper, but he was instantly there, his hands a comforting presence at her waist.

"What's wrong, sweetheart?" he asked, his voice calm and sure.

"I'm sorry, Sir. I don't know. I—Are there people out there?"

"Does it make a difference if there are?" he asked.

He didn't sound mad. Not at all. His thumbs took up a gentle sweep, somehow grounding her.

"I think so. I don't know. I'm sorry."

"There's nothing to be sorry for." He kissed her cheek. "You please me very much, as you always do."

"I don't understand."

"I don't know why you wanted to stop, but I knew you did from the minute you walked out of the bedroom. I was trying to decide if I should let you push through, if you wanted to, or stop you. Thank you for saying your safe word so that I would know. I'm proud of you."

"Oh." She swallowed hard. He'd already known something was wrong. Too bad she didn't really understand what that something was.

"Jesse," he called out, using hardly more than his normal speaking voice.

She didn't hear anything but Grant continued almost immediately.

"Stand behind our girl. You can put your hands here."

Jesse's presence warmed her back and she suddenly realized she'd started to feel cold, something she never felt when naked in their apartment. His hands replaced Grants, who slid his up her arms to cup her shoulders.

She felt surrounded. Enveloped. Loved.

"I'm sorry," she said again, not knowing quite why she said it.

"Uh oh, now you're angling for a punishment," Grant admonished.

She blushed and ducked her head, then forced it back up.

"Tell me what you were thinking, coming down the hall," Grant ordered.

Sighing, she tried to bring her scattered thoughts back into focus. "I thought it sounded like there were people in the apartment.

I wondered if you would invite people in for this scene, as a treat for me, since we weren't able to go to the club. And I wondered why I didn't like the sound of that."

"Go on."

"It's not like I don't trust you to invite only appropriate people. So it should have been fine. I told myself that. It should have been fine. Fun even. A sweet gesture from you."

"But?"

"I don't know. I just don't like it."

"Okay. Good job." He kissed her cheek again. "Jesse, take off the blindfold."

"Did I ruin the scene?" she asked, trying not to cry. Everything he'd done indicated he wasn't mad, wasn't disappointed. There was no reason to cry.

"I can't imagine how it would be possible for you to ruin *any* scene unless it was to not say your safe word when you needed to. So, no," he said as the blindfold slid free. "You absolutely did not ruin anything."

She blinked at him and a couple of tears escaped, despite her strict orders to the contrary. Her damn brain was *not* cooperating. She almost apologized, but bit it back in time and settled for "oops".

He smiled and wiped the tears away. "Do you trust me?"

"Yes Sir," she said without pausing.

He nodded and turned, and headed down the hallway, giving her leash a tiny tug. She moved forward, no longer worried about what she would find. Jesse let his hands fall free of her hips, but stayed close behind her.

When they entered the living room, the lighting was dim, but there were several candles. For some reason the ceiling fan was going, which swirled the candle smoke around. She drew in a deep breath. There was the faintest hint of perfume here, a touch of cologne there. Three glasses of champagne, a glass of ice water, and another glass of water, no ice, sat on the table.

There were no people.

She swallowed hard. "You tried to give this to me." Her voice broke on the last word.

Grant turned back, took her into his arms. "We did. Not everything we do is always going to work one hundred percent, Steph. You know that. It's different, when you're in a relationship. It's not like when you're at the club and you're negotiating every scene. Sometimes maybe you and I will plan something for Jesse, and when he walks through the door he'll have had a shit day, and the last thing he'll want to do is whatever we planned. But as long as he tells us, we're okay. As long as we're honest, we're okay."

She felt Jesse nod above her head, and then he spoke. "We thought you would get a kick out of this, but we don't give a shit that you don't. Honestly. The sucky thing would be if you'd let us keep going. You know that."

She nodded. She did know that. "The thing is, it was a really good idea. And you did it so awesomely. I was completely sucked in. Grant's words in the bedroom, everything you did out here, Jesse. I honestly don't know why it didn't work for me."

"That's totally fine," Grant insisted. "You don't ask Jesse why we can't play with his feet. I don't ask you why you don't like to be hung upside down. Although, I have to say, I was surprised to see that spelled out so clearly on your limit sheet."

She laughed. "Well, I didn't know until I tried it."

"Kind of like this?" Grant asked.

"I guess so." She pulled her head out of his chest and looked around the room again.

"You guys are pretty clever. I'm bummed it didn't work out."

"Knowing that I don't always ask you how you want something to go, think carefully now. If you could have any outcome you wanted right now, what would it be? Continue on? Take a break? Pop some popcorn and snuggle on the couch with a movie?"

She thought about it. She was not feeling sexy at all anymore, but she had zero doubt that her guys could get her there in seconds. If she put the blindfold back on, could she lose herself in the scene? Maybe.

Looking at Grant, she saw patient understanding, but also her Dom. He was going to give her what he thought she needed, regardless of what she said she wanted. It sort of freed her. "I wouldn't mind continuing the scene, but I guess if I had the choice, I would end the scene and ask you to fuck me brainless."

Grant nodded thoughtfully. "What about you, Jesse? If you could have the next hour go anyway you wanted, how would it go?"

Jesse put an arm around both of them. He looked at Grant, then at her. "Any way I wanted? That would be to have Stephanie agree to move in with us, and then to fuck her brainless."

She pulled in a sharp breath. *What the hell?*

"What about you, Grant? What would you want, if you could have anything right now?"

"Easy. For Stephanie to agree to move in with us and then to fuck her brainless."

She had to laugh. And cry. Which was especially messy because her fucking hands were still clipped behind her back and she couldn't even wipe her face.

"You guys are nuts, you totally planned that!"

"Well, yeah," Jesse said. "What's nuts about that? I think that shows we're pretty damned smart."

"You need to unhook my arms," she said, angling her back towards Jesse.

"I don't know," he said to Grant. "Do you think she's trying to run away?"

But he deftly unhooked her.

As soon as she was free, she threw her arms around them, with enough enthusiasm that Jesse grunted. She was still crying, and still laughing a bit, and she was happier than she'd ever been in her life. She and Jesse were naked except for their collars, Grant was fully clothed, she was a teary mess, and she felt totally and completely loved.

She sniffed and rubbed her nose on Grant's sleeve. "I love you guys."

"Well thank fuck, because if you didn't Grant would have to tan your ass for that nose wipe."

"You say that like it's a bad thing," she teased.

"Oh, right, good point."

She rested her head over Jesse's heart, Grant's finger's threading through her hair. And she felt at home. The building didn't matter. As long as she was with her guys.

"I love you," Grant said.

She met his eyes. "I know. That's so crazy, but so awesome."

He leaned down and kissed her, drawing her away from Jesse's chest until she had to break away, breathless.

"My turn," Jesse said. And leaned past her to kiss Grant.

She laughed, feeling the happiness all the way to her soul.

Jesse let Grant go and turned to her. "I love you, too."

"Yeah," she whispered, and kissed him.

When she pulled free, she looked at them both. "Now, let's move on to the fucking-each-other-brainless portion of the evening."

"Not so fast," Grant reminded her.

"Tell us you're moving in," Jesse said.

"Okay, I'm moving in," she said. "Now get to it." She pulled free and ran down the hall, the little chain leash bouncing against her back. She didn't get very far before hands grabbed her, mouths claimed her and she was completely, awesomely, fucked.

- To be notified of new releases, sign up for KB Alan's newsletter here.

EXCERPT

Alpha Turned
  (Wolf Appeal Book 1)
  By KB Alan
  (Available Now)

Not all men are bad...

Strong, independent, and happy on her own, Hillary has grown from the naïve person she was four years ago after a brutal rape turned her into a werewolf. The normal life she's made for herself is only upset once a month when the moon calls to her and she has an uncontrollable urge to turn furry and chase small creatures. And she doesn't need a man for that. Until she finally meets another werewolf, this one a gorgeous, sexy guy who is determined to change her mind about one furry man in particular–him.

No, some men are very, very good...

The minute Zach scents Hillary he knows she's the mate he's been searching for. Though both the wolf and the man are itching to claim her, first he has to convince her that he's one of the good guys, and that there are certain benefits to being an alpha werewolf. And there's no better way of making Hillary see that, than giving her himself—body, mind, and soul.

Alpha Turned

Chapter One

Hillary was not a happy camper.

Meeting new people always made her nervous, but here she was on her way to meet her boyfriend's family. Being in a relationship with Jeff for the past four months had helped her get over her aversion to strangers, somewhat. He not only boosted her confidence but occasionally managed to drag her out to parties and other social occasions that she otherwise would have ignored. And sometimes, she had fun. If she didn't, chances were he didn't either, and they could leave to do something else. Somehow she didn't think that would work quite so well when it came to a three-day spring break visit with his family.

Her lapse into silence must have signaled her worry to Jeff because he reached over and took her hand. "Don't be nervous, hon. They'll love you."

She flashed him a smile, appreciating that he'd known what was wrong.

"I'm sure they're great, I'm just not used to big families." Massive understatement.

"I know when your parents died, you lived with guardians. Didn't you have any other family to go to?" Sympathy and understanding didn't quite drown out his obvious disbelief that such a thing was possible.

She shifted in her seat. It wasn't something she liked to think about often, let alone talk about. But one of the reasons—actually, the main reason—that she'd agreed to the road trip was so that they could get to know each other better. The six hours of driving time

EXCERPT

between their college in Los Angeles and his family in Phoenix had seemed perfect.

"Well, my mom's grandparents were in a nursing facility. My dad has a brother on the East Coast somewhere, but they weren't in touch."

He gave her hand a squeeze and changed the subject to tell her a funny story about the song playing on the radio. That was one of the things she liked about him. He was careful not to push her too much. She'd taken things very slowly, reluctant to let a relationship distract her from her studies. While she had some money from her parents' estate, her scholarship was very important to her and she had made school her number one priority. She'd been very clear about that to Jeff when he'd first started asking her out.

Only once had he pushed for more than she was ready to give. When she'd suggested that they break up he'd immediately backed down, never again pushing when she said she didn't have time for what he was suggesting. In return, she'd tried to be careful not to use that as an excuse to put off going out, when she really only wanted to stay in. She'd come to recognize that isolating herself from other people was a defense mechanism that she needed to get over.

When he'd asked her to join him for this trip, she'd known he was hoping that by its end she would feel comfortable enough to finally sleep with him. A big part of her hoped that he was right. She was nervous about it. He would be her first and she really hadn't been ready to take that step before. But things had been getting hot and heavy between them and she was at the point that she wanted more.

"So your parents will be there, and your uncle, you said. Any cousins?"

"No cousins yet. Uncle Ken is single." He sounded pleased that she was asking. "But there's other extended family and they have kids, so there are always some rug rats running around." He slanted her a quick look that she couldn't read.

"Do you ever think about having kids?" he asked carefully.

EXCERPT

Had she made it so hard for him to talk to her about real issues that he was afraid to ask her questions?

"Sure, in an indefinite, theoretical, far-in-the-future sort of way. I guess I just always assumed that I would, when the time was right. You're an only child too. Would you want to have more than one?"

The fact that she answered and didn't snap at him seemed to relax him. Wow, maybe she really had been way too hesitant to discuss personal matters. Sometimes she wondered why he'd put up with her for this long.

"I think I'd like a large family. You're right, though, it seems so far in the future. Right now it's hard to imagine what will happen after I graduate next year."

They pulled off the freeway and headed away from the city. Jeff got her talking about a class she was looking forward to taking next semester with her favorite professor, distracting her enough that she was only a little bit nervous as they made their way down a long driveway.

She took a deep breath and looked around. Ahead of them and to the right was a large ranch-style house. There was a cluster of smaller homes past Jeff's window. People began walking toward the main house as they drove past, seeming to have headed over at the arrival of their car.

"Oh good, looks like everyone is coming over, probably for a barbecue," Jeff said, opening his door.

"Great," Hillary muttered softly, plastering a smile on her face. She wouldn't even get to meet the parents first before the rest of the family. She got out and moved to the back to get her things. Glancing over her shoulder, she saw three people rounding the corner of the house, Jeff heading toward them. She shouldered her backpack and made her way toward the group, pleased when Jeff stopped to take her hand before leading her to the others.

"Mom, Dad, Uncle Ken, this is Hillary Abbott. Honey, these are my parents John and Shannon Cage, and my uncle Ken Cage." He smiled proudly and she blushed.

EXCERPT

Hillary put her hand out but Shannon Cage grabbed her up in a hug.

"We are so glad to meet you! Jeff has told us how special you are and we can't wait to get to know you," the woman squealed.

Hillary glanced up at John and Ken Cage. John was smiling as broadly as his wife, and sending a satisfied look toward his son. Ken looked...condescending? Hillary wondered. Maybe calculating? Whatever was going on there, she didn't care for it. She backed out of Shannon's embrace and shrugged the backpack higher up on her shoulder. Shannon took the hint.

"Let's get you and your things to your room. You'll want to freshen up after that long drive. Dinner will be ready soon and then we'll have the bonfire."

Jeff seemed a little surprised by that. "We're having a bonfire tonight, Mom? Shouldn't we wait a couple of days?"

They began moving toward the front door.

"Nonsense. We want to be able to enjoy as many days as possible with both you kids before you have to drive back to school."

Hillary didn't really see what that had to do with anything, but decided she didn't particularly care, either. She wasn't too surprised that she didn't immediately like Jeff's family. Quite frankly she didn't immediately like anyone, but she was a little bit worried about how uneasy she felt. Unlike the parties they attended together at school, she couldn't expect Jeff to agree with her that it would be more fun to leave early and go off to do their own thing. This time she was just going to have to suck it up.

Besides, two minutes with three people didn't mean that she couldn't have a good time. There must be twenty people milling around, so chances were she'd like at least some of them. Jeff stopped in front of a door and opened it for her. She gave him a kiss and a smile.

"I'll just freshen up a bit. Fifteen minutes?"

"I'm glad you came. I think, after the bonfire, we'll be closer than ever." He leaned in and gave her a soft kiss.

She willed her tension to drain away. "I'll be right out."

EXCERPT

The look of excitement on his face made her smile as she closed the door. Making him happy would make her happy. She'd been awfully selfish in their relationship. It was time to make a little bit of effort for him.

It took only a few minutes to wash her face, brush her hair back into a neat ponytail and reapply a bit of makeup. She stared at her reflection and tried out a welcoming smile. Not exactly Miss Mary Sunshine, but not terrible, either. It wasn't as though she had to become best friends with these people. The three days would fly by and then they would be home.

The sun was going down but it was still warm outside so she changed into a clean pair of shorts and a tank top. Practicing the smile once more, she headed for the door.

The next few hours were unsettling. She met many people and most of them were nice to her. A few were even too nice. She wasn't sure what it was about them as a group that was making her so uncomfortable. Some of the family treated her as if she were Jeff's fiancée, rather than a relatively new girlfriend. She'd swear many of them had been sniffing her, which made her especially uncomfortable since she'd been sitting in a car for six hours before meeting them.

There seemed to be a larger percentage of creepy guys and bitchy girls than she thought was normal for a group this size. Jeff's mom insisted on dragging her around and cheerfully introducing her until she'd officially met every single person present.

It just couldn't be normal to be that cheerful all the time, Hillary thought as she finally managed to escape the slightly mad woman. Jeff was sitting on a log near the fire pit. She sat down beside him and put her head on his shoulder, needing to feel as if someone there liked her for herself. She would sit with him for a few minutes, then tell him she was tired and excuse herself to bed.

Jeff put his arm around her and she closed her eyes, enjoying the familiar comfort. After a while she realized it had gone quiet. She opened her eyes and lifted her head. People were quietly coming to the fire pit area and sitting down, ending their conversations.

Hillary realized the children were all gone now and figured that was a good sign that it was late enough for her to excuse herself. Ken, Jeff's uncle, was the only one left standing, and everyone was looking at him expectantly.

"As you all know, Jeff has brought a guest today, his girlfriend Hillary, to introduce her to us. You've all had a chance to meet her, talk to her and form your own opinions. Jeff has asked permission to mate, and I've decided that the female is acceptable."

There was a low murmur of approval, some sniffs of disapproval. Hillary wondered if she had fallen asleep. Otherwise this group was even more insane than she'd first thought. She tensed, and Jeff's arm around her waist tightened. He straightened his spine, and she waited to hear what he had to say to this ridiculousness.

"Thank you, Alpha. I am honored that you have approved my first choice." He bowed his head for a moment. Hillary, looking at him as if he were crazy, realized that the odd gleam in his eye might in fact mean that he *was* crazy. She rose, but he rose with her, squeezing her to his side.

Ken spoke again. "It will remain to be seen if she is your mate, as you believe. Once she's taken the bite, you and I will know for sure. If so, we will all be pleased for you."

Hillary looked around, expecting to see at least some of the people laughing at the show, but everyone was looking very seriously at either her or the freak speaking.

"However," Ken continued, "as you know, if she is not your mate after all, you will allow the hierarchy their chance to discover if she is one of theirs before you marry, if that is still your wish."

Jeff bowed his head again, "Of course, Alpha."

The conversation was so bizarre that Hillary wasn't sure how to react. She *was* sure that she didn't want Jeff holding her anymore. She elbowed him in the ribs and stepped back when his arm jerked free. Some of the men laughed, and she distinctly heard "feisty", "bitch" and "uppity" from the crowd. Hillary decided enough was enough and turned to leave.

Deep growls stopped her midstride. She turned back around just in time to see three of the men turn into wolves. *Holy shit.* Anger turned to terror in a heartbeat. Ken, who was staring right at her, held up his hand. All eyes were on him as Hillary began backing away. Ken's arm dropped, the wolves howled and all hell broke loose. She turned and ran toward the house, knowing she had to get behind a locked door before the pack of wolves got to her.

She didn't make it. What felt like a ton of bricks landed on her back. She hit the ground hard, barely getting her hands up in time to save her face from hitting first. There were growls and snarls, teeth and nails and slobber, as she fought, screamed, kicked and cursed. Finally, she found herself on her back, being held down, a man at her wrists, above her head, a woman on one leg, a wolf on the other. But it was the thing on top of her, clearly Jeff but part wolf, his face distorted into a muzzle baring sharp teeth, his very hairy arms ending in clawed hands, that convinced her that she was living a true nightmare.

"She's all yours, Jeff," the man holding her arms said to the creature snarling in her face. "At least for now."

Hillary looked into the beast's eyes and the fact that they were Jeff's was almost more than she could comprehend. She didn't believe in witches or fairies, vampires or werewolves. While her mind prayed that this was the most bizarre and vivid nightmare she'd ever had, her body struggled for freedom. Her eyes flicked right and left and she realized that she was surrounded by at least a dozen wolves. She bucked upward, trying desperately to free some part of her body, just as Jeff's jaws opened and descended on her neck.

The pain was incredible for a long time as she swam in and out of consciousness. Her whole body was screaming. She tried to concentrate but it was too much and she was swallowed back down into the darkness. At some point she became aware of being on a bed and realized that Jeff had woken her up. He was trying to thrust his fingers into her dry passage as he began to kiss her.

Was it better, or worse, that he was back to his old self, the Jeff who she'd thought she was coming to love instead of the monster

EXCERPT

that had attacked her? She turned her head but the pain from her neck wound was incredible. She tried to hit him, but her arms were tied down. He bit her neck, hard, on the side that wasn't already wounded. He grabbed her hair and forced her lips to his. She kept her mouth closed and he yanked until she gasped then plunged his tongue in deep. She bit him and he jerked back and slapped her face. She nearly passed out again, and wished that she had when he forced his cock into her.

It felt as if she was being ripped apart and she tried to struggle, but her legs were tied down as well as her arms. She didn't cry until she realized what he was saying, over and over, as he thrust into her passage, now slick with blood. "I love you, I love you, I love you..." She gave up, letting the darkness take her.

Hillary woke up feeling as if she were dying of thirst. Instead of being tied to a bed, she was on a mattress lying on a concrete floor, in a windowless room. It smelled damp and contained the mattress, a toilet and a sink. There was a rough bandage taped to her neck.

Crawling to the sink, she hoisted herself up far enough to drink some water. She used the toilet then tested the door. Locked and probably even sturdier than it looked. She sat down on the floor next to the door, her back to the wall. The mattress smelled of her rape and she was dimly aware that she'd been in this room for a couple of days, long enough for at least three men that she could remember to come in and take their turn. She also remembered Jeff raping her again, enraged, screaming, "You were supposed to be my mate. Why aren't you my mate?" She barely made it back to the toilet before she vomited.

On the fourth day, when they came to get her, she was so weak she could barely even think about escaping, let alone act on it. She hadn't eaten since the barbecue, had only water from the sink. Two men, possibly Jeff and his father—she was simply too weak to notice —came to drag her from the room. She cried out faintly as the wound in her neck throbbed at the movement.

They brought her outside and dumped her on the ground.

Hillary was vaguely aware that she was surrounded by many people. The moon was shining brightly enough for her to see that they weren't really paying much attention to her. Everyone was stripping out of their clothes and holding their faces up to the moon. Her body began to tingle and her battered mind wondered if what had already happened wasn't the worst to come.

It took only a moment before she was once again surrounded by wolves. Some of them came to her where she was lying on the ground trying desperately to figure out what she should be doing, how she could escape these monsters. They began to nip at her and nudge her—and not in a playful way. She ignored them and concentrated on the feeling that was filling her up inside. Somehow she knew it was the moonlight, that it was warming her up when she hadn't even realized she was cold.

Part of her recognized that it felt good and powerful, but the other part of her was so exhausted and terrified and *angry* that she resisted its pull for as long as she could. The wolves grew tired of watching her and took off, yipping and howling.

In and out of consciousness, Hillary heard them, running and playing, grunting and fucking. The warmth and tingling were nearly overpowering her, making her body tremble. The wolves became human again, going past her into the house in small groups. Some of them stopped to kick at her.

"What a waste. Too weak to be one of the chosen," a male voice said.

"She didn't even turn. She won't make it through the night." The woman sounded young and pleased.

"Damn, I wish I could have had her again before we have to bury her."

She was sweating with the effort of holding back whatever it was that was happening to her when she heard Jeff's voice.

"I guess all that toughness was just an act. Stupid bitch."

Hillary used the disgust and anger his words caused to hold on, to be stronger. Finally, when she hadn't heard anyone for more than an hour, Hillary at last gave in to the feeling, let the power of the

EXCERPT

moon wash through her. She realized that she hurt less at about the same time she realized she was seeing in black and white. She stumbled to her feet—all four of them.

To Join KB Alan's newsletter and be informed of new releases, sign up at kbalan.com/newsletter!

For links to purchase Alpha Turned go to kbalan.com/books/alpha-turned

ALSO BY KB ALAN

Perfect Formation (Perfect Fit Book 1)
Alpha Turned (Wolf Appeal Book 1)
Bound by Sunlight
Keeping Claire
Sweetest Seduction
Perfect Alignment (Perfect Fit Book 2)
Perfect Stranger (Perfect Fit Book 2.5)
Challenge Accepted (Wolf Appeal Book 2)
Perfect Addition (Perfect Fit Book 3)

kbalan.com

ABOUT THE AUTHOR

KB Alan lives the single life in Southern California. She acknowledges that she should probably turn off the computer and leave the house once in a while in order to find her own happily ever after, but for now she's content to delude herself with the theory that Mr. Right is bound to come knocking at her door through no real effort of her own. Please refrain from pointing out the many flaws in this system. Other comments, however, are happily received.

Visit her website at www.kbalan.com.

To be join her newsletter and be informed of new releases, sign up here.

facebook.com/kbalan

twitter.com/KB_Alan

instagram.com/authorkbalan

Made in the USA
Monee, IL
28 January 2024